'Throughout my life my greatest benefactors have been my dreams and my travels; very few men, living or dead, have helped me in my struggle…'
Prologue to the Greek edition of *Zorba the Greek*

Nikos Kazantzakis was born in 1883 in Herakleion on Crete, then part of the Ottoman Empire. His father, idealised as Captain Michales in *Freedom and Death,* was a farm trader. During the Cretan revolt of 1897 the family was sent to the island of Naxos, where he attended the French School of the Holy Cross, run by the Franciscans. From 1902 to 1906 he studied law at Athens University. He also worked as a journalist. His first book, *The Serpent and the Lily,* was a lyric narrative influenced by D'Annunzio. He wrote several plays. His remarkable travels began in 1907 and there were few countries in Europe or Asia that he didn't visit in the course of his life He made four journeys to the USSR. He attended Bergson's lectures in Paris and in 1908 wrote his doctoral dissertation on Nietzsche, as well as his first novel, *Broken Souls.* He worked for Venizelos during the first Balkan War and subsequently made a pilgrimage to the ancient sites of Greece with the poet Sikelianos. They spent forty days on Mount Athos. Two years later he unsuccessfully ran a lignite mine in the Peloponnesus with George Zorbas, immortalised in *Zorba the Greek.* He studied Buddhism in Vienna and later belonged to a group of radical intellectuals in Berlin, and began his great epic *The Odyssey* (33,333 lines, completed in 1938). He wrote more novels, plays, travel journal, articles and translations. He visited England in 1940 and spent the war years on the island of Aegina under German occupation. He was minister without Portfolio in the Sofoulis coalition government and worked briefly for Unesco. In 1954 the Vatican placed *The Last Temptation* on the Index. He finally settled in Antibes with his second wife. He died of leukaemia in October 1957, shortly after his return from a journey to China and Japan. He is buried at Herakleion, where the epitaph on his tomb reads: 'I hope for nothing. I fear nothing. I am free.'

by Nikos Kazantzakis

CHRIST RECRUCIFIED
FREEDOM AND DEATH
REPORT TO GRECO
THE FRATRICIDES
GOD'S PAUPER
THE LAST TEMPTATION
ZORBA THE GREEK

THE LAST TEMPTATION

Nikos Kazantzakis

Translated by
P. A. BIEN

faber and faber

First published in English in 1961
by Bruno Cassirer, Oxford
This paperback edition first published in 1975
by Faber and Faber Limited
3 Queen Square, London WC1N 3AU

Printed and bound in Great Britain by
Mackays of Chatham plc, Chatham, Kent

Translated from the Greek
with a note on the Author and his Language
by
P. A. Bien

A CIP record for this book is
available from the British Library

ISBN 0-571-17856-1

6 8 10 9 7

CONTENTS

PROLOGUE

THE dual substance of Christ—the yearning, so human, so superhuman, of man to attain to God, or more exactly, to return to God and identify himself with him—has always been a deep inscrutable mystery to me. This nostalgia for God, at once so mysterious and so real, has opened in me large wounds and also large flowing springs.

My principal anguish and the source of all my joys and sorrows from my youth onward has been the incessant, merciless battle between the spirit and the flesh.

Within me are the dark immemorial forces of the Evil One, human and pre-human; within me too are the luminous forces, human and pre-human, of God—and my soul is the arena where these two armies have clashed and met.

The anguish has been intense. I loved my body and did not want it to perish; I loved my soul and did not want it to decay. I have fought to reconcile these two primordial forces which are so contrary to one another, to make them realize that they are not enemies but rather fellow-workers, so that they might rejoice in their harmony—and so that I might rejoice with them.

Every man partakes of the divine nature in both his spirit and his flesh. That is why the mystery of Christ is not simply a mystery for a particular creed: it is universal. The struggle between God and man breaks out in everyone, together with the longing for reconciliation. Most often this struggle is unconscious and short-lived. A weak soul does not have the endurance to resist the flesh for very long. It grows heavy, becomes flesh itself, and the contest ends. But among responsible men, men who keep their eyes riveted day and night upon the Supreme Duty, the conflict between flesh and spirit breaks out mercilessly and may last until death.

The stronger the soul and the flesh, the more fruitful the struggle

7

and the richer the final harmony. God does not love weak souls and flabby flesh. The Spirit wants to have to wrestle with flesh which is strong and full of resistance. It is a carnivorous bird which is incessantly hungry; it eats flesh and by assimilating it, makes it disappear.

Struggle between the flesh and the spirit, rebellion and resistance, reconciliation and submission, and finally—the supreme purpose of the struggle—union with God: this was the ascent taken by Christ, the ascent which he invites us to take as well, following in his bloody tracks.

This is the Supreme Duty of the man who struggles—to set out for the lofty peak which Christ, the first-born son of salvation, attained. How can we begin?

If we are to be able to follow him we must have a profound knowledge of his conflict, we must relive his anguish: his victory over the blossoming snares of the earth, his sacrifice of the great and small joys of men and his ascent from sacrifice to sacrifice, exploit to exploit, to martyrdom's summit, the Cross.

I never followed Christ's bloody journey to Golgotha with such terror, I never relived his Life and Passion with such intensity, such understanding and love, as during the days and nights when I wrote *The Last Temptation*. While setting down this confession of the anguish and the great hope of mankind I was so moved that my eyes filled with tears. I had never felt the blood of Christ fall drop by drop into my heart with so much sweetness, so much pain.

In order to mount to the Cross, the summit of sacrifice, and to God, the summit of immateriality, Christ passed through all the stages which the man who struggles passes through. That is why his suffering is so familiar to us; that is why we share it, and why his final victory seems to us so much our own future victory. That part of Christ's nature which was profoundly human helps us to understand him and love him and to pursue his Passion as though it were our own. If he had not within him this warm human element, he would never be able to touch our hearts with such assurance and tenderness; he would not be able to become a model for our lives. We struggle, we see him struggle also, and we find strength. We see that we are not all alone in the world: he is fighting at our side.

Every moment of Christ's life is a conflict and a victory. He conquered the invincible enchantment of simple human pleasures; he conquered temptations, continually transubstantiated flesh into spirit, and ascended. Reaching the summit of Golgotha, he mounted the Cross.

But even there his struggle did not end. Temptation—the Last Temptation—was waiting for him upon the Cross. Before the fainted eyes of the Crucified the spirit of the Evil One, in an instantaneous flash, unfolded the deceptive vision of a calm and happy life. It seemed to Christ that he had taken the smooth, easy road of men. He had married and fathered children. People loved and respected him. Now, an old man, he sat on the threshold of his house and smiled with satisfaction as he recalled the longings of his youth. How splendidly, how sensibly he had acted in choosing the road of men! What insanity to have wanted to save the world! What joy to have escaped the privations, the tortures, and the Cross!

This was the *Last Temptation* which came in the space of a lightning flash to trouble the Saviour's final moments.

But all at once Christ shook his head violently, opened his eyes, and saw. No, he was not a traitor, glory be to God! He was not a deserter. He had accomplished the mission which the Lord had entrusted to him. He had not married, had not lived a happy life. He had reached the summit of sacrifice: he was nailed upon the Cross.

Content, he closed his eyes. And then there was a great triumphant cry: It is accomplished!

In other words: I have accomplished my duty, I am being crucified, I did not fall into temptation. . . .

This book was written because I wanted to offer a supreme model to the man who struggles; I wanted to show him that he must not fear pain, temptation or death—because all three can be conquered, all three have already been conquered. Christ suffered pain, and since then pain has been sanctified. Temptation fought until the very last moment to lead him astray, and Temptation

9

was defeated. Christ died on the Cross, and at that instant death was vanquished for ever.

Every obstacle in his journey became a milestone, an occasion for further triumph. We have a model in front of us now, a model who blazes our trail and gives us strength.

This book is not a biography, it is the confession of every man who struggles. In publishing it I have fulfilled my duty, the duty of a person who struggled much, was much embittered in his life, and had many hopes. I am certain that every free man who reads this book, so filled as it is with love, will more than ever before, better than ever before, love Christ.

NIKOS KAZANTZAKIS

I

A COOL heavenly breeze took possession of him.

Above, the blossoming skies had opened into a thick tangle of stars; below, on the ground, the stones were steaming, still afire from the great heat of the day. Heaven and earth were peaceful and sweet, filled with the deep silence of ageless night-voices, more silent than silence itself. It was dark, probably midnight. God's eyes, the sun and the moon, were closed and sleeping, and the young man, his mind carried away by the gentle breeze, meditated happily. But as he thought: What solitude! What Paradise! suddenly the wind changed, thickened; it was no longer a heavenly breeze, but the reek of heavy greasy breaths, as though in some overgrown thicket or damp luxuriant orchard below him a gasping animal, or a village, was struggling in vain to sleep. The air had become dense, restless. The tepid breaths of men, animals and elves rose and mixed with a sharp odour from sour human sweat, bread freshly removed from the oven, and the laurel oil used by the women to anoint their hair.

You sniffed, you sensed, you divined—but saw nothing. Little by little your eyes became accustomed to the darkness and you were able to distinguish a stern straight-trunked cypress darker than night itself, a clump of date palms grouped like a fountain, and rustling in the wind, sparsely-leafed olive trees which shone silver in the blackness. And there on a green spot of land you saw wretched cottages thrown down now in groups, now singly, constructed of night, mud and brick, and smeared all over with whitewash. You realized from the smell and filth that human forms, some covered with white sheets, others uncovered, were sleeping on the rooftops.

The silence had fled. The blissful uninhabited night filled with anguish. Human hands and feet twisted and turned, unable to find repose. Human hearts sighed. Despairing, obstinate cries from hundreds of mouths fought in this mute God-trodden chaos to unite, toiled to find expression for what they longed to say. But they could not, and the cries scattered and were lost in disjointed ravings.

But suddenly there was a shrill heart-rending scream from the highest rooftop, right in the centre of the village. A human breast was tearing itself in two: "God of Israel, God of Israel, Adonai, how long?" It was not a man—it was the whole village dreaming and shouting together, the whole soil of Israel with the bones of its dead and the roots of its trees, the soil of Israel in labour, unable to give birth, and screaming.

After a long silence the cry suddenly tore the air again from earth to heaven, but now with even more anger and grievance: "How long? How long?" The village dogs awoke and began to bark, and on the flat mud roofs the frightened women thrust their heads under the armpits of their husbands.

The youth was dreaming. He heard the shout in his sleep and stirred; the dream took fright, began to flee. The mountain rarefied and its insides appeared. It was not made of rock, but of sleep and dizziness. The group of huge wild men who were stamping furiously up it with giant strides—all moustaches, beards, eyebrows and great long hands—they rarefied also, lengthened, widened, were completely transformed and then plucked into tiny threads like clouds scattered by a strong wind. A little more and they would have disappeared from the sleeper's mind.

But before this could happen his head grew heavy and he fell once more into a deep sleep. The mountain thickened again into rock, the clouds solidified into flesh and bone. He heard someone panting, then hurried steps, and the redbeard reappeared at the mountain's peak. His shirt was open, he was barefooted, red-faced, sweating. His numerous gasping followers were behind him, still hidden among the rough stones of the mountain. Above, the dome of heaven once again formed a well-built roof, but now there was only a single star, large like a mouthful of fire, hanging in the east. Day was breaking.

The young man lay stretched on his bed of wood-shavings, breathing deeply, resting after the hard work of the day. His eyelids flew up for an instant as though struck by the Morning Star, but he did not awake: the dream had again skilfully wrapped itself around him. He dreamt that the redbeard stopped. Sweat streamed from his armpits, legs and narrow deeply-wrinkled forehead. Steaming at the mouth from exertion and anger, he started to swear, but restrained himself, swallowed the curse and merely grumbled dejectedly, "How long, Adonai, how long?" But his rage did not abate. He turned around. Fast as lightning, the long march unrolled itself within him.

Mountains sank away, men vanished, the dream was wrenched into a new locale and the sleeper saw the Land of Canaan unfold above him on the low cane-lathed ceiling of his house—the Land of Canaan, like embroidered air, many-coloured, richly ornamented, and trembling. To the south, the quivering desert of Idumea shifted like the back of a leopard. Further on, the Dead Sea, thick and poisonous, drowned and drank the light. Beyond this stood inhuman Jerusalem, moated on every side by the commandments of Jehovah. Blood from God's victims, from lambs and prophets, ran down its cobbled streets. Next came Samaria, dirty, trodden by idolators, with a well in the centre and a rouged and powdered woman drawing water; and finally, at the extreme north: Galilee—sunny, modest, verdant. And flowing from one end of the dream to the other was the river Jordan, God's royal artery, which passes by sandy wastes and rich orchards, John the Baptist and Samaritan heretics, prostitutes and the fishermen of Gennesaret, watering them all—indifferently.

The young man exulted in his sleep to see the holy water and soil. He stretched forth his hand to touch them, but the Promised Land, made up of dew, wind and age-old human desires, and illuminated like a rose by the dawn, suddenly flickered in the fluffy darkness and was snuffed out. And as it vanished he heard curses and bellowing voices and saw the numerous band of men reappear from behind the sharp rocks and the prickly-pears, but completely changed now and unrecognizable. How crumpled and shrivelled the giants had become, how stunted! They were panting dwarfs, imps gasping for breath, and their beards dragged along the ground. Each carried a strange implement of torture. Some held bloody leather belts studded with iron, some clasp-knives and ox-goads, some thick wide-headed nails. Three midgets whose behinds nearly scraped the ground carried a massive unwieldy cross; and last of all came the vilest of the lot, a cross-eyed pygmy holding a crown of thorns.

The redbeard leaned over, gazed at them and shook his large-boned head with disdain. The sleeper heard his thoughts: They don't believe. That's why they degenerated, that's why I am being tormented: they don't believe.

He extended his immense hairy hand:

"Look!" he said, pointing to the plain below, which was drowned in morning hoar-frost.

"We don't see anything, captain. It's dark."

"You don't see anything? Why then, don't you believe?"

"We do, captain, we do. That's why we follow you. But we don't see anything."

"Look again!"

Lowering his hand like a sword, he pierced the hoar-frost and uncovered the plain beneath. A blue lake was awakening. It smiled and glittered as it pushed aside its blanket of frost. Great nests-full of eggs—villages and hamlets—gleamed brilliantly white under the date palms all around its pebbly shores, and in the middle of the fields of grain.

"He's there," said the leader, pointing to a large village surrounded by green meadows. The three windmills which overlooked it had opened their wings in the early dawn and were turning.

Terror suddenly poured over the sleeper's dark wheat-complexioned face. The dream had settled on his eyelids and was brooding there. Brushing his hand over his eyes to be rid of it, he tried as hard as he could to wake up. It's a dream, he thought, I must awake and save myself. But the tiny men revolved about him obstinately and did not wish to leave. The savage-faced redbeard was now speaking to them, shaking his finger menacingly at the large village in the plain below:

"He's there! He lives there in hiding, barefooted, dressed in rags, playing the carpenter, pretending he is not the One. He wants to save himself—but how can he escape us: God's eyes have seen him! After him, lads!"

He raised his foot and got on his mark, but the dwarfs clung to his arms and legs. He lowered his foot again.

"There are many people dressed in rags, captain, many who go barefooted, many carpenters. Give us a clue who he is, what he looks like and where he lives, so that we'll be able to recognize him. Otherwise we're not budging. You'd better know that, captain—we're not budging, we're tired out."

"I shall hug him to my bosom and kiss him. That will be your clue. Forward now, run! But quiet, don't shout. Right now he's sleeping. Take care he doesn't wake up and escape us. In God's name, lads, after him!"

"After him, captain!" shouted the dwarfs in unison, and they raised their big feet, ready to start.

But one of them, the skinny cross-eyed hunchback who held the crown of thorns, clutched a prickly shrub and resisted.

"I'm not going anywhere," he screamed. "I'm fed up! How many nights have we been hunting him? How many countries and villages have we tramped through? Count: in the desert of Idumea we searched the monasteries of the Essenes one after the other; we went through Bethany, where we practically murdered poor Lazarus to no avail; we reached the Jordan, but the Baptist sent us away, saying: 'I'm not the One you seek, so be off with you!' We left and entered Jerusalem, searched the Temple, the palaces of Annas and Caiaphas, the cottages of the Scribes and Pharisees: no one! No one but scoundrels, liars, robbers, prostitutes, murderers! We left again. We raced through Samaria the excommunicate and reached Galilee. In one lump we took in Magdala, Cana, Capernaum, Bethsaida. From hut to hut, caique to caique, we searched for the most virtuous, the most God-fearing. Every time we found him we cried: 'You're the One—why are you hiding? Arise and save Israel!' But as soon as he saw the tools we carried, his blood ran cold. He kicked, stamped, shrieked: 'It's not me, not me!' and threw himself into a life of wine, gambling and women in order to save himself. He became drunk, he blasphemed, he whored—just to make us see he was a sinner and not the One we sought. . . . I'm sorry, captain, but we'll meet up with the same thing here. We're chasing him in vain. We won't find him: he still has not been born."

The redbeard grabbed him by the nape of the neck and held him dangling in the air for a long moment. "Doubting Thomas," he said, laughing, "doubting Thomas, I like you!"

He turned to the others:

"He is the ox-goad, we the labouring beasts. Let him prick us, let him prick us so that we may never find peace."

Hairless Thomas screeched with pain; the redbeard set him down on the ground. Laughing again, he swept his eyes over the heterogeneous company.

"How many are we?" he asked. "Twelve—one from each of the tribes of Israel. Devils, angels, imps, dwarfs: all the births and abortions of God. Take your pick!"

He was in a good mood; his round hawk-like eyes flashed. Stretching out his great hand, he began to grip the companions angrily, tenderly, by the shoulder. One by one, he held them dangling in the air while he examined them from top to bottom, laughing. As soon as he released one, he grabbed another.

"Hello, skinflint, venom-nose, profit-mad immortal son of Abraham. . . . And you, dare-devil, chatterbox, gobble-jaws. . . . And you, pious milktoast: you don't murder, steal or commit adultery—because you are afraid. All your virtues are daughters of fear. . . . And you, simple donkey that they break with beating: you carry on, you carry on despite hunger, thirst, cold, and the whip. Laborious, careless of your self-respect, you lick the bottom of the saucepan. All your virtues are daughters of poverty. . . . And you, sly fox: you stand outside the den of the lion, the den of Jehovah, and do not go in. . . . And you, naive sheep: you bleat and follow a God who is going to eat you. . . . And you, son of Levi: quack, God-pedlar who sells the Lord by the ounce, inn-keeper who stands men God as a drink so that they will become tipsy and open their purses to you and their hearts—you rascal of rascals! . . . And you, malicious fanatical headstrong ascetic: you look at your own face and manufacture a God who is malicious, fanatical and headstrong. Then you prostrate yourself and worship him because he resembles you. . . . And you whose immortal soul opened a money-changing shop: you sit on the threshold, plunge your hand into the sack, give alms to the poor, lend to God. You keep a ledger and write: I gave so many florins

16

for charity to so and so on such and such a day, at such and such an hour. You leave instructions for the ledger to be put in your coffin so that you will be able to open it in front of God, present your bill and collect the immortal millions. . . . And you, liar, teller of tall tales: you trample all the Lord's commandments underfoot, you murder, steal, commit adultery, and afterwards break into tears, beat your breast, take down your guitar and turn the sin into a song. Shrewd devil, you know very well that God pardons singers no matter what they do, because he can simply die for a song. . . . And you, Thomas, sharp ox-goad in our rumps. . . . And me, me: crazy irresponsible fool, I got a bee in my bonnet and left my wife and children in order to search for the Messiah! All of us together—devils, angels, imps, dwarfs—we're all needed in our great cause! . . . After him, lads!"

He laughed, spit into his palms and moved his big feet.

"After him, lads!" he shouted again, and he started at a run down the slope leading to Nazareth.

Mountains and men became smoke and disappeared. The sleeper's eyes filled with dreamless murk. Now, at last, he heard nothing in his endless sleep but huge heavy feet, stamping on the mountain and descending.

His heart pounded wildly. He heard a piercing cry deep within his bowels: They're coming! They're coming! Jumping up with a start (so it seemed to him in his sleep), he blockaded the door with his workbench and piled all his tools on top—his saws, jack- and block-planes, adzes, hammers, screwdrivers—and also a massive cross which he was working on at the time. Then he sheathed himself again in his wood-shavings and chips, to wait.

There was a strange disquieting calm—thick, suffocating. He heard nothing, not even the villagers' breathing, much less God's. Everything, even the vigilant devil, had sunk into a dark fathomless dried-up well. Was this sleep? or death, immortality, God? The young man became terrified, saw the danger, tried with all his might to reach his drowning mind to save himself—and woke up.

He was soaked in sweat. He remembered nothing from the dream. Only this: someone was hunting him. Who? . . . One?

Many? Men? Devils? He could not recall. He cocked his ear and listened. The village's respiration could be heard now in the quiet of the night: the breathing of many breasts, many souls. A dog barked mournfully; from time to time a tree rustled in the wind. A mother at the edge of the village lulled her child to sleep, slowly, movingly. . . . The night filled with murmurs and sighs which he knew and loved. The earth was speaking, God was speaking, and the young man grew calm. For a moment he had feared he remained all alone in the world.

He heard his old father's gasps from the room where his parents slept, which was next to his own. The unfortunate man could not sleep. He was contorting his mouth and laboriously opening and closing his lips in an effort to speak. For years he had been tormenting himself in this way, struggling to emit a human sound, but he sat paralysed on his bed, unable to control his tongue. He toiled, sweated, drivelled at the mouth and now and then after a terrible contest he managed to put together one word by voicing each syllable separately, desperately—one word, one only, always the same: A-do-na-i, Adonai. Nothing else, only Adonai. . . . And when he finished this entire word he would remain tranquil for an hour or two until the struggle again gripped him and he began once more to open and close his mouth.

"It's my fault . . . , my fault . . . ," murmured the young man, his eyes filling with tears.

In the silence of the night the son heard his father's anguish and he too, overcome with anguish, began involuntarily to sweat and open and close his lips. Shutting his eyes, he listened to what his father did so that he could do the same. Together with the old man he sighed, uttered desperate inarticulate cries—and while doing this, slept once more.

But as soon as sleep came over him again the house shook violently, the workbench toppled over, tools and cross rolled to the floor, the door opened and the redbeard towered on the threshold, immense, laughing wildly, his arms spread wide.

The young man cried out, and awoke.

18

II

HE sat up on the wood-shavings and propped his back
against the wall. A strap studded with two rows of sharp
nails was hanging above his head. Every evening before
he went to sleep he lashed and bled his body so that he would
remain tranquil during the night and not act insolently. A light
tremor had seized him. He could not remember what temptations
had come again in his sleep, but he felt that he had escaped a great
danger. "I cannot bear any more, I've had enough . . . ," he murmured, raising his eyes to heaven and sighing. The newborn light,
uncertain and pale, slid through the cracks of the door and gave
the soft yellow cane-work of the ceiling a strange glazed sweetness, precious, like ivory. "I cannot bear any more, I've had
enough . . . ,' he murmured again, clenching his teeth with indignation. He riveted his eyes upon the air, and suddenly his whole
life passed before him: his father's staff which had blossomed on
the day of his engagement, then the lightning flash which struck
the engaged man and paralysed him; afterwards how his mother
stared at him, her own son, stared at him, saying nothing. But
he heard her mute complaint—she was right! Night and day his
sins were knives in his heart. He had fought in vain those last few
years to vanquish Fear, the only one of the devils which remained.
The others he had conquered: poverty, desire for women, the
joys of youth, the happiness of the hearth. He had conquered
them all—all except Fear. If only this might be conquered too, if
only he were able. He was a man now: the hour had come.

"My father's paralysis is my fault," he murmured. "It's my fault
that Magdalene descended to prostitution; it's my fault if Israel
still groans under the yoke. . . ."

A cock—it must have been from the adjoining house where his
uncle the rabbi lived—beat its wings upon the roof and crowed
repeatedly, angrily. It had obviously grown weary of the night,
which had lasted far too long, and was calling the sun to appear
at last.

The young man leaned against the wall and listened. The light struck the houses, doors opened, the streets came to life. Little by little the morning murmur rose from earth and trees, and slid out through the cracks in the houses: Nazareth was awakening. Suddenly there was a deep groan from the adjacent house, followed immediately by the rabbi's savage yell. He was rousing God, reminding him of the promise he had made to Israel. "God of Israel, God of Israel, how long?" cried the rabbi, and the youth heard his knees strike crisply, hurriedly, against the floor-boards.

He shook his head. "He's praying," he murmured, "he's prostrating himself and calling on God. Now he will bang on the wall for me to start my prostrations." He frowned angrily. "It's bad enough I have to deal with God without also having to put up with men!" He knocked hard on the dividing wall with his fist to show the fierce rabbi that he was awake and praying.

He jumped to his feet. His patched and repatched tunic rolled off his shoulder and revealed his body—thin, sunburnt, covered with red and black welts. Ashamed, he hastily gathered up the garment and wrapped it around his naked flesh.

The pale morning light came through the skylight and fell upon him, softly illuminating his face. All obstinacy, pride and affliction. . . . The fluff about his chin and cheeks had become a curly coal-black beard. His nose was hooked, his lips thick—and since they were slightly parted, his teeth gleamed brilliantly white in the light. It was not a beautiful face, but it had a hidden disquieting charm. Were his eyelashes to blame? Thick and exceedingly long, they threw a strange blue shadow over the entire face. Or were his eyes responsible? They were large and black, full of light, full of darkness—all intimidation and sweetness. Flickering like those of a snake, they stared at you from between the long lashes, and your head reeled.

He shook out the shavings which had become tangled in his armpits and beard. His ear had caught the sound of heavy footsteps. They were approaching, and he recognized them. "It's him, he's coming again," he groaned in disgust. "What does he want with me?" He crept towards the door to listen, but suddenly he stopped, terrified. Who had put the workbench behind the door and piled the cross and tools on it? Who? When? The night was full of evil spirits, full of dreams. We sleep, and they find the doors open, pass in and out at will and turn our houses and our brains upside-down.

"Someone came last night in my sleep," he murmured under his breath, as though he feared the visitor were still there and might overhear him. "Someone came. Surely it was God, God . . . , or was it the devil? Who can tell them apart? They exchange faces, God sometimes becomes all darkness, the devil all light— and the mind of man is left in a muddle." He shuddered. There were two paths. Which way should he go, which path should he choose?

The heavy steps continued to draw nearer. The young man looked around him anxiously. He seemed to be searching for a place to hide, to escape. He feared this man and did not want him to come, for deep within him was an old wound which would not close. Once when they were playing together as children the other, who was three years older, had thrown him down and thrashed him. He picked himself up and did not speak, but he never went after that to play with the other children. He was ashamed, afraid. Curled up all alone in the yard of his house, he spun in his mind how one day he would wash away his shame, prove he was better than they were, surpass them all. And after so many years, the wound had never closed, had never ceased to run.

"Is he still pursuing me," he murmured, "still? What does he want with me? I won't let him in!"

A kick jarred the door. The young man darted forward. Summoning up all his strength, he removed the bench and opened the door. Standing on the threshold was a colossus with a curly red beard, open-shirted, barefooted, red-faced, sweating. Chewing an ear of grilled maize which he held in his hand, he swept his glance around the workshop, saw the cross leaning against the wall, and scowled. Then he extended his foot and entered.

Without saying a word he curled up in a corner, biting madly into the maize. The youth, still standing, kept his face averted from the other and looked outside through the open door at the narrow untimely-awakened street. Dust had not yet been stirred; the soil was damp and fragrant. The night-dew and the light of the dawn dangled from the leaves of the olive tree opposite; the

21

whole tree laughed. Enraptured, the young man breathed in the morning world.

But the redbeard turned.

"Shut the door," he growled. "I have something to say to you."

The youth quivered when he heard the savage voice. He closed the door, sat down on the edge of the bench, and waited.

"I've come," said the redbeard. "Everything is ready."

He threw away the ear of maize. Raising his hard blue eyes, he pinned them on the youth and stretched forth his fat much-wrinkled neck:

"And what about you—are you ready too?"

The light had increased. The young man could now see the redbeard's coarse, unstable face more clearly. It was not one, but two. When one half laughed the other threatened, when one half was in pain the other remained stiff and immobile; and even when both halves became reconciled for an instant, beneath the reconciliation you still felt that God and the devil were wrestling, irreconcilable.

The young man did not reply. The redbeard glanced at him furiously.

"Are you ready?" he asked again. He had already begun to get up in order to grab him by the arm and shake him awake so that he would give an answer, but before he could do so a trumpet blared and cavalry rushed into the narrow street, followed by the heavy rhythmic march of Roman soldiers. The redbeard clenched his fist and raised it towards the ceiling.

"God of Israel," he bellowed, "the time has come. Today! Not tomorrow, today!"

He turned again to the young man.

"Are you ready?" he asked once more, but then, without waiting for a reply:

"No, no, you won't bring the cross—that's what I say! The people are assembled. Barabbas has come down from the mountains with his men. We'll break into the prison and snatch away the Zealot. Then it will happen—don't shake your head!—then the miracle will happen. Ask your uncle the rabbi. Yesterday he gathered all of us together in the synagogue—why didn't Your Highness come too? He stood up and spoke to us. 'The Messiah

22

won't come,' he said, 'as long as we remain standing with crossed hands. God and men must fight together if the Messiah is to come.' That's what he told us, for your information. God isn't enough, man isn't enough. Both have to fight—together! Do you hear?"

He grasped the young man by the arm and shook him.

"Do you hear? Where is your mind? You should have been there to listen to your uncle—maybe you would have come to your senses, poor devil! He said the Zealot—yes, the very Zealot the Roman infidels are going to crucify to-day—might be the One we've waited for over so many generations. If we leave him unaided, if we fail to rush out and save him, he will die without revealing who he is. But if we run and save him, the miracle will happen. What miracle? He will throw off his rags and the royal crown of David will shine on his head! That's what he told us, for your information. When we heard him we all shed tears. The old rabbi lifted his hands to heaven and shouted: 'Lord of Israel, today, not tomorrow, today!' and we, everyone of us, raised our hands, looked up at heaven and yelled, threatened, wept: 'Today! Not tomorrow, today!' Do you hear, son of the Carpenter, or am I talking to a blank wall?"

The young man, his half-closed eyes pinned on the strap with the sharp nails which hung on the wall opposite, was listening to something intently. Audible beneath the redbeard's harsh and menacing voice were the hoarse, muffled struggles of his old father in the next room as he vainly opened and closed his lips, trying to speak. The two voices joined in the young man's heart, and suddenly he felt that all the struggle of mankind was a mockery.

The redbeard gripped him on the shoulder now and gave him a push.

"Where is your mind, clairvoyant? Didn't you hear what your uncle Simeon told us?"

"The Messiah will not come in this way," murmured the young man. His eyes were pinned now on the newly-constructed cross, which was bathed in the soft rosy light of the dawn. "No, the Messiah will not come in this way. He will never renounce his rags or wear a royal crown. Neither men nor God will ever rush to save him, because he cannot be saved. He will die, die wearing his rags; and everyone—even the most faithful—will abandon him. He will die all alone at the top of a barren mountain, wearing on his head a crown of thorns."

The redbeard turned and gazed at him with astonishment. Half his face glittered, the other half remained completely dark.

"How do you know?" he asked. "Who told you?"

But the young man did not answer. It was fully light out now. He jumped off the bench, seized a handful of nails and a hammer, and approached the cross. But the redbeard anticipated him. Reaching the cross with one great stride, he began to punch it rabidly and to spit on it as though it were a man. He turned. His beard, moustache and eyebrows pricked the young man's face.

"Aren't you ashamed?" he shouted. "All the carpenters in Nazareth, Cana and Capernaum refused to make a cross for the Zealot, and you. . . . You're not ashamed, not afraid? Suppose the Messiah comes and finds you building his cross; suppose this Zealot, the one who's being crucified today, is the Messiah. . . . Why didn't you have the courage like the others to answer the centurion: 'I don't build crosses for Israel's heroes'?"

He seized the absent-minded carpenter by the shoulder:

"Why don't you answer? What are you staring at?"

Lashing out, he glued him to the wall. "You're a coward," he flung at him with scorn, "a coward, a coward—that's what I say! Your whole life will add up to nothing!"

A shrill voice tore through the air. Abandoning the youth, the redbeard turned his face towards the door and listened. There was a great uproar outside: men and women, an immense crowd, cries of: Town crier! Town crier! and then once more the shrill voice invaded the air:

"Sons and daughters of Abraham, Isaac and Jacob—by imperial command: attention! Close your workshops and taverns, do not go to your fields. Mothers, take your babies, old men, take your staffs—and come! Come, you who are lame, deaf, paralysed—come to see, to see how those who lift their hands against our master the Emperor—long may he live!—are punished; to see how this villanous rebel, the Zealot, will die!"

The redbeard opened the door, saw the agitated crowd which was now silent and listening, saw the town crier upon a rock—

skinny, hatless, with his long neck and long spindly legs—and spat. "Damn you to hell, traitor!" he bellowed. Slamming the door furiously, he turned to the young man. His choler had risen clear to his eyes.

"You can be proud of your brother Simon the traitor!" he growled.

"It's not his fault," said the youth contritely, "it's mine, mine . . ."

He paused a moment, and then:

"It was because of me that my mother banished him from the house, because of me—and now he . . ."

Half the redbeard's face sweetened and was illuminated for an instant as though it sympathized with the youth.

"How will you ever pay for all those sins, poor devil?" he asked.

The young man remained silent for a long time. His lips moved, but he was tongue-tied.

"With my life, Judas, my brother," he finally managed to say. "I have nothing else."

The redbeard gave a start. The light had now entered the workshop through the skylight and the slits of the door. The youth's large pitch-black eyes gleamed; his voice was full of bitterness and fear.

"With your life?" said the redbeard, taking hold of the other's chin. "Don't turn your head away from me. You're a man now, look into my eyes. . . . With your life? What do you mean?"

"Nothing."

He lowered his head and was silent. But suddenly:

"Don't ask me, don't ask me, Judas, my brother!"

Judas clasped the young man's face between his palms. He raised it and looked at it for a long time without speaking. Then, tranquilly, he let it go and moved towards the door. His heart had suddenly been roused.

The din outside was growing stronger and stronger. The rustle of naked feet and the flapping of sandals rose into the air, which jingled with the bronze bracelets and thick ankle rings of the women. Standing erect on the threshold the redbeard watched the crowds that continually poured out of the alleyways. Everyone was mounting towards the opposite end of the village, towards the accursed hill where the crucifixion was to take place. The men did not speak; they cursed between their teeth and beat their staffs against the cobbles. Some of them secretly held knives in their fists beneath their shirts. The women were screeching. Many had thrown back their kerchiefs, undone their hair and begun to chant the dirge.

The head-ram of this flock was Simeon the old rabbi of Nazareth—shrunken, bent over with the years, warped and contorted by the evil disease, tuberculosis: a scaffolding of dry bones which his indestructible soul held together and kept from collapsing. The two skeleton-hands with their monstrous bird-like talons squeezed the sacerdotal crosier with the pair of entwined snakes at its top and banged it down on the stones. This living corpse smelt like a burning city. Seeing the flames within his eyes, you felt that flesh, bones and hair—the whole ramshackle body— were afire; and when he opened his mouth and shouted: God of Israel! smoke rose from the top of his head. . . . Behind him filed the stooping large-boned elders with their staffs, bushy eyebrows and forked beards; behind them the able-bodied men, then the women. Bringing up the rear were the children, each with a stone in hand, and some with slings over their shoulders. They all advanced together, rumbling softly, mutely, like the sea.

As Judas leaned against the doorpost and watched the men and women, his heart swelled. They are the ones, he reflected, the blood rushing to his head, they are the ones who together with God will perform the miracle. Today! Not tomorrow, today!

An immense high-rumped man-like woman broke away from the crowd. She was fierce and maniacal, and the clothes were falling off her shoulders. Bending down, she grabbed a stone and slung it forcefully at the carpenter's door.

"Damn you to hell, cross-maker!" she cried.

All at once shouts and curses rang out from one end of the street to the other and the children took the slings from their shoulders. The redbeard shut the door with a bang.

"Cross-maker! Cross-maker!" was hooted on all sides, and the door rumbled under a barrage of stones.

The young man, kneeling before the cross, swung the hammer

up and down and nailed, banging hard, as though he wished to drown out the hoots and curses of the street. His breast was boiling; sparks jumped across the bridge of his nose. He banged frantically, and the sweat ran down his forehead.

The redbeard knelt, seized his arm and snatched the hammer violently out of his grasp. He gave the cross a blow which knocked it to the floor.

"Are you going to bring it?"

"Yes."

"You're not ashamed?"

"No."

"I won't let you. I'll smash it to smithereens."

He looked around and put out his arm to find an adze.

"Judas, Judas, my brother," said the young man slowly, beseechingly, "do not step in my way." His voice had suddenly deepened; it was dark, unrecognizable. The redbeard was troubled.

"What way?" he asked quietly. He waited, gazing anxiously at the young man. The light now fell directly on the carpenter's face and on his bare small-boned torso. His lips were twisted, clenched tight as though struggling to restrain a great cry. The redbeard saw how emaciated he was, how pale, and his misanthropic heart felt pity for him. He was melting away; each day his cheeks sank more. How long was it since he had last seen him? Only a few days. He had left to make his rounds of the villages near Gennesaret. A blacksmith, he beat and fashioned the iron, shod horses, made pickaxes, ploughshares and sickles, but then hurried back to Nazareth because he had received a message that the Zealot was to be crucified. He recalled how he had left his old friend, and now—look how he had found him! How swollen the eyes had become, how sunken the temples! And what was that bitterness all around his mouth?

"What happened to you? he asked. "Why have you melted away? Who is tormenting you?"

The young man laughed feebly. He was about to reply that it was God, but he restrained himself. This was the great cry within him, and he did not want to let it escape his lips.

"I am wrestling," he answered.

"With whom?"

27

"I don't know. . . . I'm wrestling."

The redbeard plunged his eyes into those of the youth. He questioned them, implored them, threatened—but the pitch-black inconsolable eyes, full of fear, did not answer.

Suddenly Judas's mind reeled. As he bent over the dark unspeaking eyes it seemed to him that he saw trees in bloom, blue water, crowds of men; and inside, deep down in the gleaming pupil, behind the flowering trees and the water and the men, and occupying the entire iris—a large black cross.

He jumped erect, his eyes popping out of his head. He wanted to speak, to ask: Can you be. . . , you. . . ? but his lips had frozen. He wanted to clasp the young man to his breast to kiss him, but his arms, stretched in the air, had suddenly stiffened, like wood.

And then, as the youth saw him with his arms spread wide, his eyes protruding, his hair standing on end, he uttered a cry. The terrifying nightmare bounded out of the trapdoor of his mind—the entire rout of dwarfs with their implements of crucifixion, and the cries: After him, lads! and now too he recognized their captain, the redbeard: it was Judas, Judas the blacksmith, who had rushed in the lead, laughing wildly.

The redbeard's lips moved.

"Can you be. . . , you. . . ?" he stammered.

"I . . . ? Who?"

The other did not answer. Chewing his moustache, he looked at him, half of his face again brilliantly illuminated, the other half plunged in darkness. Jostling in his mind were the signs and prodigies which had surrounded this youth from his birth, and even before: how, when the marriage-candidates were assembled, the staff of Joseph—among so many others—was the only one to blossom. Because of this the rabbi awarded him Mary, exquisite Mary, who was consecrated to God. And then how a thunderbolt struck and paralysed the bridegroom on his marriage day, before he could touch his bride. And how later, it was said, the bride smelt a white lily and conceived a son in her womb. And how the night before his birth she dreamt that the heavens opened, angels descended, lined up like birds on the humble roof of her house, built nests and began to sing; and some guarded her threshold, some entered her room, lit a fire and heated water to bathe the expected infant, and some boiled broth for the confined woman to drink. . . .

The redbeard approached slowly, hesitantly, and bent over the young man. His voice was now full of longing, entreaty, and fear:

"Can you be. . . , you. . . ?" he asked once more, but again he dared not complete the question.

The youth quivered with fright.

"Me?" he said, sniggering sarcastically. "But don't you see me? I'm not capable of speaking. I haven't the courage to go to the synagogue. As soon as I see men I run away. I shamelessly disobey God's commandments. I work on the Sabbath. . . ."

He picked up the cross, stood it straight again and seized his hammer.

"And now, look! I construct crosses and crucify!" Once more he struggled to laugh.

The redbeard was vexed and did not speak. He opened the door. A new swarm of tumultuous villagers appeared at the end of the street—old ladies with dishevelled hair, sickly old men; the lame, the blind, the leprous—all the dregs of Nazareth. They too were mounting, short of breath; they too were crawling towards the hill of crucifixion. . . . The appointed hour drew near. It's time for me to leave and join the people, the redbeard reflected, time for us to rush forward all together and snatch away the Zealot. Then it will become clear whether or not he is the Saviour. . . . But he hesitated. Suddenly a cool breeze passed over him. No, he thought, this man who is to be crucified today will not be the One the Hebrew race has awaited for so many centuries. Tomorrow! Tomorrow! Tomorrow! How many years, God of Abraham, have you kept pounding us with this tomorrow! tomorrow! tomorrow! All right—when? We're human, we've stood enough!

He had become ferocious. Throwing a wrathful glance at the young man who lay prone on the cross, nailing, he asked himself with a shudder: Can he be the One, can he be the One—the cross-maker? God's ways are obscure and indirect. . . . Can he be the One?

Behind the old women and the cripples, the soldiers of the Roman patrol now appeared with their shields, spears, and helmets of bronze. Indifferent and silent, they herded the flock of men, looking down on the Hebrews with disdain.

The redbeard eyed them savagely, his blood boiling. He turned to the youth. He did not want to see him any more: everything seemed to be his fault.

"I'm leaving!" he cried, clenching his fist. "You—you do what you like, cross-maker! You're a coward, a good-for-nothing traitor like your brother the town crier! But God will throw fire on you just as he threw it on your father, and burn you up. That's what I say—and let it be something for you to remember me by!"

III

THE young man remained all alone. He leaned against the cross and sponged the sweat from his forehead. The breath had caught in his throat; he was gasping. For an instant the world revolved about him, but then it stood still once more. He heard his mother light the fire so that she could put the meal on bright and early and be in time to run like the others to see the crucifixion. All her neighbours had left already. Her husband still groaned, fighting to move his tongue; but only his larynx was alive, and he made nothing but clucking sounds. Outside, the street was again deserted.

But while the youth leaned on the cross, his eyes shut, thinking nothing and hearing nothing except the beating of his own heart, suddenly he jolted with pain. Once more he felt the invisible vulture claw deeply into his scalp. "He's come again, he's come again. . . ," he murmured, and he began to tremble. He felt the claws bore far down, crack open his skull, touch his brain. He clenched his teeth so that he would not cry out: he did not want his mother to become frightened again and start screaming. Clasping his head between his palms, he held it tightly, as though he feared it would run away. "He's come again, he's come again. . . ," he murmured, trembling.

The first, very first time—he was already twelve years old and sitting with the sighing, sweating elders in the synagogue listening to them elucidate God's word—he had felt a light, prolonged tingling on the top of his head, very tender, like a caress. He had closed his eyes. What bliss when those fluffy wings grasped him and carried him to the seventh heaven! This must be Paradise! he thought, and a deep, endless smile flowed out from under his lowered eyelids and from his happy half-opened mouth, a smile which licked his flesh with ardent desire until his entire face disappeared. The old men saw this mysterious man-eating smile and conjectured that God had snatched the boy up in his talons. Putting their fingers to their lips, they remained silent.

The years went by, He waited and waited, but the caress did

31

not return; and then, one day—Passover, springtime, glorious weather—he went to Cana, his mother's village, to choose a wife. His mother had forced him, she wanted to see him married. He was twenty years old, his cheeks were covered with thick curly fuzz and his blood boiled so furiously, he could no longer sleep at night. His mother had taken advantage of this, the acme of his youth, and prevailed upon him to go to Cana, her own village, to select a bride.

So there he stood, a red rose in his hand, gazing at the village girls as they danced under a large newly-foliaged poplar. And while he looked and weighed one against the other—he wanted them all, but did not have the courage to choose—suddenly he heard cackling laughter behind him: a cool fountain rising from the bowels of the earth. He turned. Descending upon him with her red sandals, unplaited hair and complete armour of ankle bands, bracelets and ear-rings was Magdalene, the only daughter of his uncle the rabbi, decorated bow to stern like a frigate sailing with the wind. The young man's mind shook violently. "It's her I want, her I want!" he cried, and he held out his hand to give her the rose. But as he did so, ten claws nailed themselves into his head and two frenzied wings beat above him, tightly covering his temples. He shrieked and fell down on his face, frothing. His unfortunate mother, writhing with shame, had to throw her kerchief over his head, lift him up in her arms and depart.

From that time on he was completely lost. It came when the moon was full and he roamed the fields, or during his sleep, in the silence of the night; and most often in springtime, when the whole world was in bloom and fragrant. At every opportunity he had to be happy, to taste the simplest human joys—to eat, sleep, to mix with his friends and laugh, to encounter a girl in the street and think: I like her—the ten claws immediately nailed themselves down into him, and his desire vanished.

But never before this daybreak had they fallen on him with such ferocity. He rolled himself up under his workbench and buried his head in his breast, remaining this way for a long time. The world sank away. He heard nothing but a hum inside him, and above, the furious beating of wings.

Little by little the claws relaxed, unhooked themselves and freed

—slowly, one by one—first his mind, then the bone and finally the skin of his head. Suddenly he felt great relief, and great fatigue. Emerging from under the workbench, he put his hand to his head and hurriedly ran his fingers through his hair to investigate his scalp. It seemed to him that it had been pierced, but his searching fingers found not a single wound, and he grew calm. But when he drew out his hand and looked at it in the light, he shuddered. His fingers were dripping with blood.

"God is angry," he murmured, "angry. . . . The blood has begun to flow."

He raised his eyes and looked: no one. But he smelt the bitter stench of a wild beast in the air. He has come again. . . , he thought with terror, he is all around me and beneath my feet and above my head. . . .

Bowing his head, he waited. The air was mute, immobile; the light—apparently naive and harmless—played on the wall opposite him, and on the cane-lathed ceiling. I won't open my mouth, he decided within himself, I won't breathe a word. Perhaps he will take pity on me and leave.

But as he made this decision, his lips parted and he spoke. His voice was full of grievance:

"Why do you draw my blood? Why are you angry? How long are you going to pursue me?"

He stopped. Bent over, his mouth open, the hairs of his head standing on end and his eyes full of fear, he listened. . . .

At first there was nothing; the air was motionless, silent. But then, suddenly, someone above was speaking to him. He cocked his ear and heard—heard, and shook his head violently, continually, as though saying: No! No! No!

Finally he too opened his mouth. His voice no longer trembled:

"I can't! I'm illiterate, an idler, afraid of everything. I love good food, wine, laughter. I want to marry, to have children. . . . Leave me alone!"

He remained still again and listened.

"What do you say? I can't hear?"

Suddenly he had to put his hands over his ears to soften the savage voice above him. With his whole face squeezed together, holding his breath, he heard now—and answered: "Yes, yes, I'm

33

afraid. . . . You want me to stand up and speak, do you? What can I say, how can I say it? I can't, I tell you! I'm illiterate! . . . What did you say? . . . The kingdom of heaven? . . . I don't care about the kingdom of heaven. I like the earth. I want to marry, I tell you; I want Magdalene, even if she's a prostitute. It's my fault she became one, my fault, and I shall save her. Her! Not the earth, not the kingdom of this world—it's Magdalene I want to save. That's enough for me! . . . Speak lower, I can't understand you."

He shaded his eyes with his palm: the soft light which entered through the skylight was dazzling him. He had riveted his eyes upon the ceiling above him, and was waiting. He listened, holding his breath, and the more he heard, the more his face glowed mischievously, contentedly. His thick fresh lips tingled with numbness, and suddenly he burst out laughing.

"Yes, yes," he murmured, "you understand perfectly. Yes, on purpose, I do it on purpose. I want you to detest me, to go and find someone else; I want to be rid of you! . . .

"Yes, yes, on purpose," he continued, finding the courage to speak out, "and I shall make crosses all my life, so that the Messiahs you choose can be crucified!"

This said, he unhooked the nail-studded strap from its place on the wall and belted it around him. He looked at the skylight. The sun had at last risen high. The sky above was hard and blue, like steel. He had to hurry. The crucifixion was to take place at noon, under the full fury of the sun.

Kneeling, he placed his shoulder under the cross and clasped it in his arms. He raised one knee, braced himself—it seemed incredibly heavy to him, impossible to lift—and staggered slowly towards the door. Gasping, he took two steps, then a third and reached the door at last, but suddenly his knees gave way, his head swam and he fell face down over the threshold, crushed under the cross.

The small house vibrated. A shrill female cry was heard from within; a door opened, his mother appeared. She was tall, with large eyes and dark wheat-coloured skin. She had already passed the first stage of youth and entered the uneasy honeyed bitterness of autumn. Blue rings encircled her eyes, her mouth was firm and frizzly like her son's, but her chin stronger than his and more

34

wilful. She wore a violet linen kerchief, and two elongated silver rings, her only jewellery, tinkled on her ears.

As soon as she opened the door the old father became visible behind her. He was seated on his mattress, his upper body unclothed, his flabby skin pale yellow, his eyes glassy and motionless. She had just fed him and he was still laboriously chewing his meal of bread, olives and onions. The curly white hairs of his chest were full of drivel and crumbs. Next to his bed was the celebrated staff which had been predestined to blossom on the day of his engagement. It was dry now and withered.

When the mother entered and saw her son fallen and palpitating under the cross she dug her nails into her cheeks and stared at him without running to lift him up. She had grown weary of having him brought to her unconscious every two minutes in someone's arms, of seeing him depart to wander through the fields or in deserted places, to remain day and night without food, refuse to work, do nothing but sit for hours with his eyes pinned on the air, a day-dreamer and night-walker whose life was bare of accomplishment. It was only when a cross was ordered for a crucifixion that he threw himself body and soul into his work and laboured day and night like a madman. He went no longer to the synagogue; he did not want to set foot in Cana again, or to go to any of the festivals. And when the moon was full his mind reeled, and the unfortunate mother heard him rave and shout in a delirium as though he were quarrelling with some devil.

How many times had she prostrated herself before her brother-in-law, the old rabbi, who was versed in exorcizing devils. The afflicted came to him from the ends of the earth and he cured them. Just the other day she had fallen at his feet and complained: 'You heal strangers but you do not want to heal my son.' The rabbi shook his head:

"Mary, your boy isn't being tormented by a devil; it's not a devil, it's God—so what can I do?"

"Is there no cure?" the wretched mother asked.

"It's God, I tell you. No, there is no cure."

"Why does he torment him?"

The old exorcist sighed, but did not answer.

"Why does he torment him?" the mother asked again.

"Because he loves him," the old rabbi finally replied.

Mary looked at him, startled. She opened her mouth to question him further, but the rabbi closed her lips.

"Do not ask," he said to her. "Such is the law of God." Knitting his brows, he nodded for her to leave.

The malady had lasted for years. Mary, even though she was his mother, had grown weary at last, and now that she saw her son fallen face down over the threshold with the blood oozing from his forehead, she did not budge. She only sighed from the bottom of her heart, sighed however not for her son, but for her own fate. She had been so unfortunate in her life, unfortunate in her husband, unfortunate in her son. She had been widowed before she married, was a mother without possessing a child; and now she was growing older—the white hairs multiplied every day—and yet she had never known what it was to be young, had never felt the warmth of her husband, the sweetness and pride of being a wife and mother. Her eyes had finally been drained dry. Whatever tears God apportioned her she had already spilt, and she looked at her son and her husband dry-eyed. If she still sometimes wept, it was in the spring when she sat all by herself and gazed out at the green fields and smelt the perfumes which came from the blossoming trees. At these times she cried not for her husband or her son, but for her own wasted life.

The young man had risen and was sponging up the blood with the edge of his garment. He turned, saw his mother regarding him severely, and became angry. He knew that look which forgave him nothing, knew those compressed embittered lips. He could stand it no longer. He too had become weary in this house with its decrepit paralytics, inconsolable mothers and the daily servile admonitions: eat! work! get married! Eat! work! get married!

His mother parted her compressed lips:

"Jesus," she said reprovingly, "who were you quarrelling with again early this morning?"

The son bit his lips so that an unkind word would not escape them. He opened the door. The sun entered, and also a scorching dust-laden wind from the desert. Without speaking, he brushed the sweat and blood from his forehead, put his shoulder in place once more, and lifted the cross.

His mother's hair poured out down to her shoulder-blades. She ran her hands over it, gathered it together under her kerchief, and took a step towards her son. But as soon as she saw him clearly in the light, she quivered with astonishment. How incessantly his face changed! How it flowed—like water! Each day she saw him for the first time, found an unknown light on his forehead, in his eyes and mouth; a smile, sometimes happy, sometimes full of affliction, a gluttonous lustre which licked his forehead, chin, neck—and devoured him.

Today, large black flames were blazing in his eyes. Frightened, she wanted for a moment to ask him: Who are you? but she restrained herself. "My boy!" she said with trembling lips. She remained quiet, waiting to see if this grown man was truly her son. Would he turn to look at her, to speak to her? He did not turn. Giving a heave, he adjusted the cross on his back and, walking steadily now, strode out of the house.

His mother leaned against the doorpost and watched him step lightly from cobble to cobble as he mounted the slope. The Lord only knew where he found such strength! It was not a cross on his back, but two wings, and they propelled him!

"Lord, my God," the confused mother whispered, "who is he? Whose son is he? He doesn't resemble his father, he doesn't resemble anyone. Every day he changes. He isn't one person, he's many. . . . Oh! my mind is upside-down."

She remembered one afternoon when she was in the small courtyard next to the well, holding him to her breast. It was summer, and the vine arbour above her was heavy with grapes. While the newborn nursed she fell into a deep sleep, but not before she was able to see—in the space of an instant—a limitless dream. It seemed to her that there was an angel in heaven who held a star dangling from his hand, a star like a lantern, and he advanced and illuminated the earth below. And there was a road in the darkness, with many zigzags, and glowing brightly, like a flash of lightning. It crept towards her and began to extinguish itself at her feet. And while she gazed in fascination and asked herself where this road could have begun and why it ended at the soles of her feet, she raised her eyes—and what did she see: the star had stopped above her head, three horsemen had appeared at the end

37

of the star-illuminated road, and three golden crowns sparkled on their heads. They stopped for an instant, looked at the sky, saw the star halt, then spurred their horses and galloped towards her. The mother could now make out their faces clearly. The middle one was like a white rose, a beautiful fair-haired youth with cheeks still covered with fuzz. To his right stood a yellow man with a pointed black beard and slanting eyes. A negro was at the left. He had curly white hair, golden rings in his ears, and dazzling teeth. But before the mother could sort them out any better or cover her son's eyes so that he would not be dazzled by the intense light, the three horsemen had arrived, dismounted and knelt before her.

The white prince was the first to advance. The infant had left the breast and was standing erect now on his mother's knees. The prince took off his crown and laid it humbly at the baby's feet. Next, the negro slid forward on his knees, removed a fistful of emeralds and rubies from beneath his shirt and spread them with great tenderness over the tiny head. Lastly, the yellow man held out his hand and placed an armful of long peacock feathers at the child's feet for him to play with. . . . The baby looked at all three of the men and smiled at them, but did not put out his tiny hands to touch the presents.

Suddenly the three kings vanished and a young shepherd appeared, dressed in sheepskins and holding a tureen of warm milk between his hands. As soon as the infant saw the milk he danced upon his mother's knees, bent his little face down into the tureen and began to drink the milk, insatiably, happily. . . .

Leaning against the doorpost, the mother recalled the limitless dream, and sighed. What hopes this only son had given her, what wonders the sorcerers had prophesied for him! Had not the old rabbi himself gazed at him, opened the Scriptures, read the prophets over the tiny head and searched the infant's chest, eyes, even the soles of his feet, to find a sign? But alas! as time went on her hopes withered and fell. Her son had chosen an evil road, a road which led him further and further from the ways of men. . . .

She secured her kerchief tightly and bolted the door. Then she too began to mount the hill. She was going to see the crucifixion —to make the time go by.

IV

THE mother marched and marched, hurrying to slide in among the crowd and disappear. She heard the screeching of the women in front; behind them were the panting exasperated men, barefooted, with uncombed hair and unwashed bodies, their daggers thrust deep down under their shirts. The old men followed, and still further back came the lame, the blind and the maimed. The earth crumbled under the people's feet, the dust flew up in clouds, the air reeked. Above, the sun had already begun to burn furiously.

An old woman looked around, saw Mary, and cursed. Two neighbours turned away their faces and spat in order to exorcize the ill omen; shuddering, a newly-married girl gathered together her skirts lest the mother of the cross-maker touch them as she passed. Mary sighed and enclosed herself securely in her violet kerchief, leaving visible only her reproachful almond-shaped eyes and her closed, bitter mouth. Stumbling over the rocks, she proceeded all alone, hurrying to hide, to disappear within the crowd. Whispers broke forth all around her, but she fortified her heart and proceeded. What has my son descended to, she was thinking, my son, my son, my darling! . . . She proceeded, biting the edge of her kerchief to keep herself from bursting into tears.

She reached the mass of people, left the men behind her, slid in among the women and hid herself. She had placed her palm over her mouth—only her eyes were visible now. None of my neighbours will recognize me, she said to herself, and she grew calm.

Suddenly there was a great din behind her. The men had gathered momentum; they were pushing their way through the mass of women in order to take the lead. The barracks where the Zealot was imprisoned were close-by now, and they were impatient to smash down the door and free the captive. Mary stepped to one side, concealed herself in a well-hidden doorway, and looked:

long greasy beards, long greasy hair, frothing mouths; and the rabbi, mounted on the shoulders of a giant with a savage expression, waving his arms towards heaven and shouting. Shouting what? Mary cocked her ear, and heard:

"My children, have faith in the people of Israel. Forward—all together. Do not be afraid. Rome is smoke. God will puff and blow her away! Remember the Maccabees, remember how they expelled the Greeks, the rulers of the whole world, how they put them to shame! In the same way we shall expel the Romans, we shall put them to shame. There is only one Lord of Hosts, and he is our God!"

Swept away in a divine ecstasy, the old rabbi jumped and danced upon the giant's broad shoulders. He had grown old, devoured by fasts, prostrations and great hopes, and had no strength to run. The huge-bodied mountaineer had grabbed him and was running with him now in front of the people, waving him back and forth like a banner.

"Hey, you'll drop him, Barabbas," the people shouted.

But Barabbas advanced without the slightest worry, tossing and dandling the old man on his shoulders.

The people were crying for God. The air above their heads caught fire, flames bounded forth and joined heaven to earth. Their minds reeled: this world of stones, grass and flesh thinned out, became transparent, and the next world appeared behind it, composed of flames and angels.

Judas caught fire. Thrusting forward his arms, he snatched the old rabbi from Barabbas's shoulders, threw him astride his own and began to bellow: "Today! Not tomorrow, today!" The rabbi ignited in his turn and began to sing the psalm of victory in his high voice, the voice of a man with one foot in the grave. In a moment, the entire people intoned:

> *The nations compassed me about; in the name of my*
> *   God I disperse them!*
> *The nations girded me round; in the name of my*
> *   God I disperse them!*
> *They encircled me like wasps; in the name of my*
> *   God I disperse them!*

But while they sang, scattering the nations in their minds, the enemy fortress suddenly loomed before them in the heart of Nazareth: square, stoutly-built, with four corners, four towers, four enormous bronze eagles. The devil inhabited every inch of these barracks. At the very top, above the towers, were the yellow and black eagle-bearing Roman standards; below these, Rufus, the bloodthirsty centurion of Nazareth, with his army; still lower, the horses, dogs, camels and slaves; and lower yet, thrust in a deep dried-out well, his hair untouched by shears, his lips by wine, his body by women—the Zealot. This rebel would but toss his head, and men, slaves, horses, towers—all the accursed levels above him —would come tumbling down. God always works in this way. Deep in the foundations of wrong he buries the small despised cry of justice.

This Zealot was the last of the long lineage of the Maccabees. The God of Israel had held his hand over his head and kept the sacred seed from perishing. One night Herod the aged king of Judea—a wicked damnable traitor!—had smeared forty adolescents with tar and ignited them as torches because they pulled down the golden eagle he had fastened to the previously-unsoiled lintel of the Temple. Of the forty-one conspirators, forty were caught, but the leader escaped. The God of Israel had seized him by the hair of his head and saved him—and this was this Zealot, the great-great-grandson of the Maccabees, a handsome adolescent at the time, with cheeks still covered with fuzz.

For years after that he roamed the mountains, fighting to liberate the holy soil which God had presented to Israel. "We have only one master—Adonai," he used to proclaim. "Do not pay poll-tax to the earthly magistrates, do not suffer their eagle-shaped idols to soil God's Temple, do not slaughter oxen and sheep as sacrifices for the tyrant emperor! There is one God, our God; there is one people, the people of Israel; there is but one fruit on the entire tree of the earth—the Messiah."

But suddenly the God of Israel drew his hand away from him and he was captured by Rufus, the centurion of Nazareth. Peasants, workers and proprietors had set out *en masse* from all the nearby villages; fishermen had come from the lake of Gennesaret. For days and days now an obscure cross-eyed doubled-sensed message had been leaping from house to house, fishing boat to fishing boat, and also catching passers-by on the road: "They're crucifying the Zealot, he's done for too—finished!" But at other times the message was: "Greetings, brothers, the Saviour has come! Take large date-branches and forward, all together—march to Nazareth to welcome him!". . .

The old rabbi stood on his knees atop the redbeard's shoulders, pointed to the barracks and began once more to shout:

"He's come! He's come! Standing in that dried-out well is the Messiah—erect and waiting. Waiting for whom? For us, the people of Israel! Onward, smash down the door, deliver the Deliverer, that he may deliver us!"

"In the name of the God of Israel!" Barabbas cried in a wild voice, and he raised the hatchet he held in his hand.

The people bellowed, daggers stirred under their shirts, the children loaded their slings and everyone—Barabbas in the lead—charged the iron door. But all eyes had been blinded by the great light of God, and no one saw a tiny squat door in the barracks which opened just a crack, revealing Magdalene, pale as death and wiping her tear-filled eyes. Her soul had pitied the condemned man and she had gone down to the pit during the night to give him the ultimate joy, the sweetest which this world can offer. But he was of the wild battalion of the Zealots and had sworn that until the deliverance of Israel he would neither cut his hair, put wine to his lips, nor sleep with a woman. Magdalene sat opposite him the whole night and looked at him; but his eyes were on Jerusalem, far, far in the distance behind the woman's black hair, not the subjected and prostituted Jerusalem of that day, but the holy Jerusalem of the future, with its seven truimphant fortress-gates, its seven guardian angels and the seventy-seven peoples of the earth prostrate at its feet. As the condemned man touched the cool breast of the future Jerusalem, death vanished and the world about him sweetened, grew circular, filled his grasp. He closed his eyes, held the breast of Jerusalem in his palm and thought of one thing only—of the God of Israel, the God whose hair had never been touched by shears, whose lips had never been touched by wine, whose body had never been touched by woman. The Zealot held Jerusalem on his knees all night long and constructed the kingdom of heaven deep down in his bowels, not out of angels and clouds, but as he wanted it, warm in winter, cool in summer, and made of men and soil.

The old rabbi saw his disreputable daughter emerge from the barracks. He turned his face the other way. This was the one great humiliation of his life. How had this prostitute issued from his chaste god-fearing bowels? What devil or what incurable pangs had hit her to make her go the way of shame? One day, after she returned from a festival in Cana, she wept and declared she wished to kill herself, and afterwards she burst into fits of laughter, painted her cheeks, donned all her jewellery and began to walk the streets. Then she left the paternal roof and set up shop in Magdala—at the crossroads, where all the caravans passed by. . . .

With her bodice still undone, she advanced fearlessly towards the crowd. The make-up on her lips and cheeks had been washed away; her eyes were cloudy and dull from having watched the man all night long and wept. When she saw her mortified father look the other way she smiled bitterly. She had already left shame far behind her, as well as fear of God, love of her father and care about the opinions of men. Scandal had it that she was possessed with seven devils, but her heart did not contain seven devils, it contained seven knives.

The old rabbi began to shout again. He wanted the people to turn and look directly at him so that they would fail to see his daughter. God saw her, and that was enough—he would judge.

"Open the eyes of the soul and regard the heavens," he cried, pivoting on the redbeard's shoulders. "God stands above us. The heavens have opened, the armies of angels have come forth, the air has filled with red and blue wings!"

The sky turned to flame. The people raised their eyes, looked above them and saw God—armed and descending. Barabbas lifted his hatchet. "Today! Not tomorrow, today!" he screamed, and the mob charged the barracks. They fell upon the iron door, applied crow-bars, put ladders against the walls, brought flaming brands to set the place afire. But suddenly the iron door opened and two bronze cavalrymen appeared. They were armed to the teeth, sunburnt, well-nourished, sure of themselves. With fixed expressions they spurred their horses, lifted their lances—and all at

43

once the streets filled with howling feet and backs which began to flee towards the hill of crucifixion.

This accursed hill was bare: nothing but flint and thorns. You found dried drops of blood under whatever stone you happened to lift. Every time the Hebrews raised their hands against the Romans in order to seek freedom this hill filled with crosses, and upon them the rebels writhed and groaned. At night the jackals came and ate their feet, and the next morning the crows flew down and ate their eyes.

The people halted at the foot of the hill, gasping for breath. More bronze cavalrymen overwhelmed them, rode up and down, crowded the mass of Hebrews together into one area, then formed a cordon around them. It was almost noon now and the cross had still not come. At the top of the hill two gipsies waited, holding the hammers and nails in their hands. The village dogs arrived, anxious to eat. The faces of the people were on fire, turned up towards the hill, under the torrid sky. Pitch-black eyes, hooked noses, sunken sun-baked cheeks, greasy sideburns. . . . The fat women, their armpits drenched, their hair splattered with drippings, melted away under the sun, and reeked.

From the lake of Gennesaret a group of fishermen, their child-like eyes wide with wonder, had come like the others to see the miracle: as the unlawful pagans led the Zealot to be crucified, he was going to throw off his rags, and an angel would then bound forth from underneath, scimitar in hand. . . . Their faces, chests and arms corroded by sun and wind, they had arrived the night before with their baskets chock-full of fish. After selling these for their full value and then some they settled down in a tavern where they got drunk, forgot why they had brought themselves to Nazareth, remembered Woman and sang her glory, then began fighting among themselves, became friends again—and at daybreak suddenly recalled the God of Israel, washed and set out, half-awake, half-asleep, to see the miracle.

They had waited and waited, and soon grown weary. A lance-blow on the back was all that was needed to make them strongly regret they had come.

"I say we should return to our boats, lads," said one with a curly grey beard. He was well-preserved and vigorous for his age, and had a forehead like an oyster-shell. "The Zealot will be crucified like the rest, and mark my words, the heavens won't open. There's no end to God's anger, or to the injustice of men. . . . What do you say, son of Zebedee?"

"I say there's no end to Peter's foolishness," laughed his companion, a wild-eyed fisherman with a thorny beard. "Forgive me, Peter, but you haven't developed good sense to match your white hairs. You flare up in a flash and burn out just as quickly, like kindling. Wasn't it you who roused us to come here in the first place? You ran like a madman from boat to boat and shouted, 'Drop everything, brothers, a man sees a miracle only once in his life. Come on, let's go to Nazareth to see the miracle!' And now you're smacked once or twice on the back with a lance, and right away your mind turns upside-down, you change your tune and shout, 'Drop everything, brothers, let's go home!' You're not called 'Weathercock' for nothing!"

Two or three fishermen heard this conversation and laughed; a shepherd who smelt of billy-goats lifted his staff:

"Don't scold him, Jacob, even if he is a weathercock. He's the best of all of us, and has a heart of gold."

"You're right, Philip—a heart of gold," they all agreed, and they extended their hands to caress and pacify Peter, who was puffing with rage. They can say what they like, he was thinking, whatever they like—short of calling me Weathercock. Maybe I am one, maybe I'm prey to every breeze that blows—but it s not out of fear, no, it's because of my good heart. . . .

Jacob saw Peter's sullen expression and felt distressed. He regretted having spoken so hastily to the older man and asked, in order to change the subject:

"Say, Peter, how's your brother Andrew? Still in the Jordan desert?"

"Yes, still there," Peter answered with a sigh. "They say he's been baptized already and eats locusts and wild honey, the same as his teacher. May God prove me a liar, but I wager we'll soon see him making the rounds of the villages and screaming 'Repent, Repent! The Kingdom of Heaven has come!' like all the rest. What kingdom of heaven—this around us? Have we no shame, I ask you!"

Jacob shook his head and knit his thick brows.

"I've seen the same thing happen to that know-all brother of mine John," he said. "He went to become a monk at the monastery in the desert of Gennesaret. It seems he wasn't made out to be a fisherman, so he left me all alone with two old greybeards and five boats, to bang my head against the wall."

"But what did the blessed fellow lack?" asked Philip, the shepherd. "He had every gift God could give! What came over him just at the flower of his youth?" He asked, but inside him he rejoiced secretly that rich men also had a worm which devoured them.

"He grew uneasy all of sudden," Jacob answered, "and he began to toss and turn all night long on his bed like a teen-ager in need of a woman."

"So, why didn't he get married. There were brides for the asking."

"He said he didn't want to marry a woman."

"What, then?"

"The kingdom of heaven for him—just like Andrew."

The men burst out laughing.

"And may they live happily ever after!" shouted an old fisherman, rubbing his calloused hands together mischievously.

Peter opened his mouth but before he could utter a word, hoarse cries filled the air:

"Look! The cross-maker, the cross-maker!"

Simultaneously, they turned their bewildered heads. Down the road the son of the Carpenter could be seen mounting on unsteady feet, panting under the weight of the cross.

"The cross-maker! The cross-maker!" roared the crowd. "The traitor!"

The two gipsies looked down from the top of the hill. When they saw the cross approaching they jumped with joy: the sun had been roasting them. Spitting into their palms, they took their pick-axes and began to dig a pit. The thick flat-headed nails they placed on a nearby stone. Three had been ordered; they had forged five.

Men and women had joined hands and formed a chain in order to block the cross-maker's passage. Magdalene broke away from the crowd and pinned her eyes on the son of Mary, who was mounting. Her heart swelled with distress as she recalled the games they used to play together when they were still small children, he three years old, she four. What deep unrevealable joy they had experienced, what unspeakable sweetness! For the first time they had both sensed the deep dark fact that one was a man and the other a woman: two bodies which seemed once upon a time to have been one; but some merciless God separated them and now the pieces had found each other again and were trying to join, to reunite. The older they grew, the more clearly they felt what a miracle it was that one should be a man and the other a woman, and they looked at each other in mute terror, waiting like two wild beasts for the hunger to increase and the hour to come when they would flow one into the other and rejoin that which God had sundered. But then, one evening at a festival in Cana when her beloved held out his hand to give her the rose and seal their engagement, merciless God had rushed down upon them and separated them once more. And ever since then . . .

Magdalene's eyes filled with tears. She stepped forward. The cross-bearer was passing directly before her.

She leaned over him. Her scented hair touched his naked, bloody shoulders.

"Cross-maker!" she growled in a hoarse, strangulated voice. She was trembling.

The youth turned and riveted his large afflicted eyes upon her for a split-second. Convulsive spasms played about his lips. His mouth was contorted, but he lowered his head immediately and Magdalene did not have time to distinguish whether the contortion was from pain, fear, or a smile. Still leaning over him, she spoke, gasping for breath:

"Have you no pride? Don't you remember? How can you lower yourself to this!"

And after a moment, as though she had heard his voice give her an answer, she shouted:

"No, no, poor wretch, it isn't God, it's the devil!"

The crowd meanwhile had darted forward to block his path. An old man lifted his stick and struck him; two cowherds who had dashed down from Mount Tabor to join the others at the miracle nailed him in place with their goads. Barabbas felt the hatchet go

47

up and down in his fist. But as soon as the old rabbi saw the danger, he slid off the redbeard's neck and ran to his nephew's defence.

"Stop, my children," he screamed, "It's a great sin to block God's path—do not do it. What is ordained must come to pass. Do not step in the way. Let the cross through—it is sent by God; let the gipsies make ready their nails, let Adonai's apostle mount the cross. Do not be afraid; have faith! God's law is such that the knife must reach clear to the bone. Otherwise no miracle will take place! Listen to your old rabbi, my children. I'm telling you the truth. Man cannot sprout wings unless he has first reached the brink of the abyss!"

The cowherds withdrew their goads, stones fell from clenched fists, the people stepped aside to clear God's path, and the son of Mary stumbled onward, the cross upon his back. The grasshoppers could be heard sawing the air in the olive grove beyond; a hungry butcher's dog barked happily on top of the hill. Further on, within the mass of people, a woman wrapped in a violet kerchief cried out and fainted.

Peter now stood with gaping mouth and protruding eyes. He was watching the son of Mary. He knew him. Mary's family home in Cana was opposite his own, and her aged parents Joachim and Anne were old bosom-friends of Peter's parents. They were saintly people. The angels went regularly in and out of their simple cottage, and one night the neighbours saw God Himself stride across their threshold, disguised as a beggar. They knew it was God, because the house shook as though invaded by an earthquake, and nine months later the miracle happened: Anne, an old woman in her sixties, gave birth to Mary. Peter must have been less than five years old at the time, but he remembered well all the celebrations which followed, how the whole village was set in motion, how men and women ran to offer their congratulations, some carrying flour and milk, others dates and honey, others tiny infant's-clothing: presents for the confined woman and her child. Peter's mother had been the midwife. She had heated water, thrown in salt, and bathed the wailing newborn. . . . And now, here was Mary's son passing in front of him loaded down with the cross, while everyone spat on him and pelted him with stones. . . . As Peter looked and looked, he felt his heart become roused.

His was an unlucky fate. The God of Israel had mercilessly chosen him, the son of Mary, to build crosses so that the prophets could be crucified. He is omnipotent, Peter reflected with a shudder. He might have picked me to do the same, but he chose the son of Mary instead and I escaped. . . . Suddenly Peter's roused heart grew calm, and all at once he felt deeply grateful to the son of Mary, who had taken the sin and lifted it to his shoulders.

Just as all this was jostling in his mind, the cross-bearer halted, out of breath.

"I'm tired, tired," he murmured. He looked around him to find a stone or a man he could lean against, but saw nothing except lifted fists and thousands of eyes staring at him with hatred. Then he heard what seemed to him wings in the sky, and his heart leapt up. Perhaps God had taken pity on him at the very last moment and dispatched his angels. He raised his eyes. Yes, there were wings above him: crows! He grew angry. Obstinacy took possession of him and he resolutely lifted his foot in order to continue walking and mount the hill. But the stones sank away from under his sole. He tripped, began to fall forward. Peter rushed out in time to hold him up. Taking the cross from him, he lifted it to his own shoulder.

"Let me help you," he said. "You're tired."

The son of Mary turned and gazed at the fisherman, but did not recognize him. This entire journey seemed to him a dream. His shoulders had suddenly been unburdened and now he was flying in the air, just as one flies in one's dreams. It couldn't have been a cross, he thought, it must have been a pair of wings! . . . Wiping the sweat and blood from his face, he followed behind Peter with sure steps.

The air was a fire which licked the stones. The sheep-dogs which the gipsies had brought to lap up the blood stretched their well-fed bodies out at the foot of a rock, by the edge of the pit their masters had dug. They were panting, and sweat poured from their dangling tongues. You could hear the drumming of the people's heads in this blast-furnace, the bubbling of their brains. In such heat all frontiers shifted—good sense and foolishness, cross and wings, God and man: all were transposed.

Several tender-hearted women revived Mary. She opened her

eyes and saw her barefooted emaciated son. He was at last about to reach the summit, and in front of him was another man carrying the cross. Sighing, she turned around as though seeking help. When she saw her fellow-villagers and the fisherman she started to go near in order to lean against them—but too late! The trumpet blared at the barracks, new cavalrymen emerged, clouds of dust flew up, the people crowded together again, and before Mary had time to step up onto a rock in order to see, the cavalrymen were on top of them, with their bronze helmets, their red cloaks, and the proud well-nourished horses which trampled the Jewry underfoot.

The rebel Zealot came forward, his arms tied behind his back at the elbows, his clothes torn and bloody, his long hair pasted to his shoulders by blood and sweat, his grey thorny beard immense, his motionless eyes staring directly in front of him.

The people were terrified at the sight. Was this a man, or hidden deep within his rags was there an angel or a devil whose compressed lips guarded a terrible and unconfessable secret? The old rabbi and the people had agreed that in order to give the Zealot courage, as soon as he appeared they would join all together singing at the top of their voices the psalm of war: "Let my enemies be scattered". But now the words stuck in their throats. Everyone felt that this man had no need of courage. He was above courage: unconquerable, insuppressible—and freedom was enclosed in those hands fettered behind his back. They all looked at him in terror and remained silent.

Riding in front of the rebel and pulling him along with a cord attached to the rear of his saddle was the centurion, his skin baked hard by the oriental sun. He had long ago begun to detest the Jews. For ten years he had put up crosses and crucified them, for ten years he had stuffed their mouths with stones and dirt to silence them—but in vain! As soon as one was crucified a thousand more queued up and anxiously awaited their turns, chanting the brazen psalms of one of their ancient kings. They had no fear of death. They had their own bloodthirsty God who lapped up the blood of the first-born male children; they had their own law, a man-eating beast with ten horns. Where could he catch hold of them? How could he subjugate them? They had no fear of death, and whoever has no fear of death—the centurion had often meditated on this here in the east—whoever has no fear of death, is immortal.

He drew back on the reins, stopped his horse and swept his eyes over the Jewry: eroded faces, inflamed eyes, soiled beards, greasy mops of hair. . . . He spat with disgust. If he could only leave, leave! If he could only return once more to Rome with its many baths, its theatres, amphitheatres and well-washed women! He detested the east—its smells, its filth, its Jews!

The gipsies were shaking their sweat onto the stones. They had set the cross into its hole at the top of the hill. The son of Mary sat on a rock and looked at them, looked at the cross, the people, at the centurion who dismounted in front of the crowd; looked and looked, but saw nothing except an ocean of skulls beneath a fiery sky. Peter approached and leaned over to speak to him. He spoke, but a stormy white-capped sea was beating against the youth's ears, and he did not hear.

At a nod from the centurion the Zealot was released. He drew tranquilly to one side in order to recover from his numbness, and then began to undress. Magdalene slid between the legs of the horses and started to approach him, her arms spread wide, but he repulsed her with a wave of his hand. An old woman with a stiff aristocratic air pushed her way through the crowd without a word and took him in her arms. He lowered his head, kissed both her hands for a long time, clasped her tightly to his breast and then turned away his face. Mute and dry-eyed, the old woman remained where she was a few moments longer and looked at him.

"You have my blessing," she murmured finally, and she went and leaned against the rock opposite, together with the gipsy sheep-dogs that were stretched out panting in the scanty shade.

Stamping his foot on the ground, the centurion leapt back into the saddle so that everyone could see and hear him. Brandishing his whip over the multitude to command silence, he spoke:

"Listen to my words, Hebrews. Rome speaks. Quiet!"

He pointed with his thumb to the Zealot, who had already removed his rags and was standing under the sun, waiting.

"This man who now stands naked before the Roman Empire lifted his hand against Rome. While still a youth he pulled down the imperial eagles; then he took to the mountains and besought all of you to join him there and to raise the banner, telling you that the day had come when the Messiah would issue from your bowels and destroy Rome! . . . Quiet out there, stop your shouting! . . . Rebellion, murder, betrayal: those are his crimes. And now listen, Hebrews, listen to what I ask—I want you to be the ones to pass sentence. What punishment does he deserve?"

He swept his eyes over the crowd below him and waited. The people were in an uproar. They bellowed, pushed one another, left the area assigned to them and rushed up to the centurion, right to the feet of his horse, but then immediately recoiled in terror and flowed back in the opposite direction, like a wave.

The centurion grew furious. Spurring his horse, he advanced towards the multitude.

"I ask you," he roared, "what punishment for the rebel, the murderer, the traitor—what punishment?"

The redbeard bolted forward in a frenzy, no longer able to control his heart. He wanted to shout Long live freedom! and had already parted his lips, but his companion Barabbas seized him and placed his hand over his mouth.

For a long moment there was no sound except a rumble like that of the sea. No one dared speak, but everyone groaned quietly, sighing and gasping for breath. Suddenly a shrill voice was heard above this unsettled din. Everyone turned, both out of joy and fear. The old rabbi had climbed once more onto the redbeard's shoulders. Lifting both his skeleton-like hands as though he wished to pray or bring down a curse, he boldly cried:

"What punishment? The royal crown!"

Feeling sorry for him, the people bellowed in an effort to drown out his voice. The centurion did not hear.

"What did you say, rabbi?" he called, cupping his hand over his ear and spurring his horse.

"The royal crown!" the rabbi repeated with all his might. His face gleamed, his whole body was on fire; he shook, jumped, danced upon the blacksmith's shoulders: it seemed he wanted to take to the air and fly.

"The royal crown!" he shouted again, delighted that he had become the mouth of his people and of his God, and he stretched forth his arms to either side as though he were being crucified in the air.

The centurion went wild. Jumping off his horse and unhooking the whip from its place on the saddle-horn, he advanced towards the crowd with heavy steps. Shifting the stones, he advanced silently, like some heavy beast, a buffalo or a wild boar. The crowd stood motionless, holding its breath. Once more nothing could be heard except the grasshoppers in the olive grove, and the impatient crows.

He took two steps, then one more, and stopped. The stench from the open mouths and sweaty unwashed bodies had hit him. The Jewry! He advanced further and arrived in front of the rabbi. The old man was looking down on him from his place atop the blacksmith's shoulders, a smile of beatitude spread over his entire face. All his life he had longed for this moment, and now it had come: the moment when he too would be killed, just like the prophets.

The centurion half-closed his eyes and glanced at him. It was with a great effort that he controlled his arm, which had already risen to smash the old rebellious head with a single punch. But he checked his fury, for it was not in Rome's interests to kill the old man. This accursed unyielding people would rise to its feet again and start a guerilla war, and it was not in Rome's interests to have to thrust its hand once more into this wasps' nest of Jews. Governing his strength therefore, he wrapped the whip around his arm and turned to the rabbi. His voice had grown hoarse:

"Rabbi, your face is deemed worthy of reverence only because I revere it, only because I, Rome, want to give it value—of itself it has none. That is why I'm not going to lift my whip. I heard you, you passed sentence. Now I shall do the same."

He turned to the two gipsies, who stood on either side of the cross, waiting:

"Crucify him!" he howled.

"I passed sentence," the rabbi said in a tranquil voice, "and so did you, centurion. But there remains one, the most important of all, who must also pass sentence."

"The emperor?"

"No. . . . God."

53

The centurion laughed. "I am the mouth of the emperor in Nazareth; the emperor is the mouth of God in the world. God, emperor and Rufus have passed sentence."

This said, he unwound the whip from around his arm and started towards the top of the hill, maniacally lashing the stones and thorns below him.

An old man lifted his arms to heaven:

"May God heap the sin upon your head, Satan, and upon the heads of your children and your children's children!"

The bronze cavalrymen meanwhile had formed a circle around the cross. Below, snorting with wrath, the people stretched on tip-toe in order to see. They were trembling with anguish: would the miracle happen, or not? Many searched the sky to see when the heavens would open. The women had already discerned multi-coloured wings in the air. The rabbi, kneeling on the blacksmith's broad shoulders, struggled to see between the horses' hoofs and the cavalrymen's red cloaks. He wanted to discover what was happening above, around the cross. He looked, looked at the summit of Hope, at the summit of despair—looked, and did not speak. He was waiting. The old rabbi knew him, knew him well, this God of Israel. He was merciless and had his own laws, his own decalogue. Yes, he gave his word and kept it, but he was in no hurry: he measured time with his own measure. For generations and generations his Word would remain inoperative in the air and not come down to earth. And when it did come down at last, woe and three-times woe to the man to whom he decided to entrust it! How often, from one end of Holy Scripture to the other, had God's elect been killed—but had God ever lifted a finger to save them! Why? Why? Didn't they follow his will? Or was it perhaps his will that all the elect should be killed? The rabbi asked himself these questions but dared not push his thoughts any further. God is an abyss, he reflected, an abyss. I'd better not go near!

The son of Mary still sat off to one side on his stone. He held his trembling knees tightly with both his hands, and watched. The two gipsies had seized the Zealot; Roman guards came forward too, and they all pushed and pulled amidst cursing and laughter, struggling to raise the rebel up onto the cross. When the sheep-dogs saw the struggle they understood and jumped to their feet.

The noble old mother drew away from the rock she had been leaning against, and advanced.

"Courage, my son," she cried. "Do not groan, do not make us ashamed of you!"

"It's the Zealot's mother," murmured the old rabbi, "his noble mother, descended from the Maccabees!"

Two thick ropes had now been passed under the rebel's armpits. The gipsies hooked ladders over the arms of the cross and began to lift him up, slowly. He had a huge heavy body, and suddenly the cross tilted and was about to topple over. The centurion kicked the son of Mary, who rose on unsure feet, took the pickaxe and went to steady the cross with stones and wedges so that it would not fall.

This was too much for Mary, his mother. Ashamed to see her darling boy one with the crucifiers, she fortified her heart and elbowed her way through the crowd. The fishermen of Gennesaret felt sorry for her and pretended they did not see her. She started to rush in among the horses in order to grasp her son and take him away, but an elderly neighbour took pity on her and seized her by the arm. "Mary," she said, "don't do that. Where are you going? They'll kill you!"

"I want to bring my son out of there," Mary replied, and she burst into tears.

"Don't cry, Mary, said the old woman. "Look at the other mother. She stands without moving and watches them crucify her son. Look at her and take heart."

"I don't weep for my son alone, neighbour, I weep also for that mother."

The old woman, who had doubtlessly suffered much in her life, shook her balding head.

"It's better to be the mother of the crucifier," she murmured, "than of the crucified."

But Mary was in a hurry and did not hear. She started up the hill, her tear-filled eyes searching everywhere for her son. The whole world began to weep. It grew dim, and within the deep mist the mother discerned horses and bronze armour and an immense newly-hewn cross which stretched from earth to sky.

A cavalryman turned and saw her. Lifting his lance, he nodded for her to go back. The mother stopped. Stooping down, she looked under the horses' bellies and saw her son. He was on his knees, wielding the pick-axe and making the cross fast in the stones.

"My child," she cried. "Jesus!"

So heart-rending was the mother's cry, it rose above the entire tumult of men, horses and famished, barking dogs. The son turned and saw his mother. His face darkened and he resumed his strokes more furiously than before.

The gipsies, mounted on the rope-ladders, had stretched the Zealot on the cross, keeping him tied with ropes so that he would not slip down. Now they took up their nails and began to nail his hands. Heavy drops of hot blood splashed Jesus' face. Abandoning his pick-axe, he stepped back in terror, retreated behind the horses and found himself next to the mother of the man who was so soon to die. Trembling, he waited to hear the sound of ripping flesh. All his blood massed in the very centre of each of his hands; the veins swelled and throbbed violently—they seemed about to burst. In each of his palms he felt a painful spot, round like the head of a nail.

His mother's voice rang out once again:

"Jesus, my child!"

A deep bellow rumbled down from the cross, a wild cry from the bowels not of the man, but from the very bowels of the earth:

"Adonai!"

The people heard it—it tore into their entrails. Was it themselves, the people, who had shouted? or the earth? or the man on the cross as the first nail was driven in? All were one, all were being crucified. People, earth and Zealot: all were bellowing. The blood spurted out and splashed the horses; a large drop fell on Jesus' lips. It was hot, salty. . . . The cross-maker staggered, but his mother rushed forward in time to catch him in her arms, and he did not fall.

"My boy," she murmured again. "Jesus . . ."

But his eyes were closed. He felt unbearable pain in his hands, feet and heart.

The aristocratic old lady stood motionless and watched her son's spasms on the two crossed boards. She bit her lips and was silent. But then behind her she heard the son of the Carpenter and his mother. The anger rose up in her and she turned. This was the apostate Jew who constructed her son's cross, this the mother who bore him. Why should a son like this, a traitor, why should he live while her son writhed and bellowed upon the cross! Driven on by her grievance, she stretched forth both her hands towards the son of the Carpenter. She drew near and stood directly before him. He lifted his eyes and saw her. She was pale, wild, merciless. He saw her, and lowered his head. Her lips moved:

"My curse upon you," she said wildly, hoarsely, "my curse upon you, Son of the Carpenter. As you crucified another, may you be crucified yourself!"

She turned to the mother:

"And you, Mary, may you feel the pain that I have felt!"

As soon as she had spoken, she turned her head and riveted her eyes once more upon her son. Magdalene was now embracing the foot of the cross and singing the dirge for the Zealot, her hands touching his feet, her hair and arms covered with blood.

The gipsies took their knives and began to slash the crucified man's clothing in order to portion out the pieces. Throwing lots, they divided his rags. Nothing remained but his white head-cloth, splotched with large drops of blood.

"Let's give it to the son of the Carpenter," they said. "Poor fellow, he did a good job too."

They found him sitting in the sun, curled up and shivering.

"That's your share, carpenter," one of them called, tossing him the bloody kerchief. "Best wishes for many more crucifixions to come!"

"And here's to your own, carpenter!" laughed the other gipsy, and he patted him lovingly on the back.

V

"LET us go, my children," cried the old rabbi, opening wide his arms to collect the bewildered mass of despairing men and women. "Let us go! I have a great secret to reveal to you. Courage!"

They began to run through the narrow lanes. Behind them raced the cavalry, herding them on. The housewives shrieked and closed their doors—more blood was going to be spilt. The old rabbi fell twice while running and started to cough again and spit up blood. Judas and Barabbas took him in their arms. The people arrived in flocks and burrowed into the synagogue, panting. They stuffed themselves in, filled the courtyard too, and bolted the street-door.

They waited, hanging upon the rabbi's lips. Amid so much bitterness, what secret could the old man divulge to them to gladden their hearts? For years now they had suffered misfortune after misfortune, crucifixion after crucifixion. God's apostles continually sprouted out of Jerusalem, the Jordan, the desert, or rushed down from the mountains dressed in rags and chains and frothing at the mouth—and every one of them was crucified.

An angry murmur arose. The branches and palm-trees which decorated the walls, the pentagrams, the sacred scrolls on the lectern with their pompous words: chosen people, promised land, kingdom of heaven, Messiah—none of these could comfort them any longer. Hope, lasting too long, had begun to turn to despair. God is not in a hurry, but man is, and they could wait no longer. Not even the painted hopes which took up both walls of the synagogue could deceive them now. Once while reading the prophet Ezekiel the rabbi had been swept away by God. He jumped up, shouted, wept and danced, but still did not find relief. The prophet's words had become part of his flesh. In order to relieve himself he took brushes and paint, locked himself in the synagogue and began in a divine frenzy to cover the wall with the prophet's visions: endless desert, skulls and bones, mountains of human skeletons, and above, a heaven brilliantly red, like red-hot iron. A gigantic hand shot out from the centre of the heavens, seized Ezekiel by the scruff of the neck and held him suspended in the air. . . . But the vision overflowed onto the other wall as well. Here Ezekiel stood plunged up to his knees in bones. His mouth was bright green and open, and coming from inside was a ribbon with red letters: "People of Israel, people of Israel, the Messiah has come!" The bones strung themselves together, the skulls rose up full of teeth and mud, and the terrible hand emerged from heaven holding the New Jerusalem in its palm—the New Jerusalem, freshly-built, brilliantly illuminated, all emeralds and rubies!

The people looked at these paintings and shook their heads, murmuring. This angered the old rabbi.

"Why do you murmur?" he shouted at them. "Don't you believe in the God of our fathers? One more has been crucified: the Saviour has come one step closer. That, you men of little faith, is what crucifixion means!"

He seized a scroll from the lectern and unrolled it with a violent movement. The sun entered through the open window; a stork descended from the sky and alighted on the roof of the house opposite, as though it too wanted to hear. Out of the devastated chest bounded the happy triumphant cry: " 'Sound in Zion the trumpet of victory! Proclaim in Jerusalem the joyous news! Shout! Jehovah has come to his people. Rise up, Jerusalem, lift high your hearts! Look! From east and west the Lord herds your sons. The mountains have been levelled, the hills have fled, all the trees have poured forth their perfume. Put on the trappings of your glory, Jerusalem. Happiness has come to the people of Israel for ever and ever.' "

"When, when?" was heard from the crowd. Everyone turned. A tiny old man, slim, and wrinkled like a raisin, had stood up on tip-toe. "When, Father, when?" he was shouting.

The rabbi angrily rolled up the prophecies.

"Are you in a hurry, Manases?" he asked.

"Yes!" answered the tiny old man. Tears were running down his face. "I have no time, I'm going to die."

The rabbi stretched forth his arm and pointed to Ezekiel buried in the bones.

"Look, Manases! You'll be resurrected!"

"I'm old, I tell you, and blind: I cannot see."

Peter intervened. The day was nearing its end. At night he fished the lake of Gennesaret, and he was pressed. "Father," he said, "you promised us a secret to comfort our hearts. What is that secret?"

Holding their breath, they all crowded around the old rabbi. As many as could fit came in from the courtyard. The heat was intense and there was a heavy smell of human sweat. The sexton threw tear-shaped pellets of cedar sap into the censer to deodorize the air.

The old rabbi climbed up onto a stall to avoid suffocating.

"My children," he said, wiping away his sweat, "our hearts have filled with crosses. My black beard long ago turned grey, my grey beard turned white, my teeth fell to the ground. What old Manases cried I've been crying for years: 'How long, Lord, how long? Shall I die without seeing the Messiah?' I asked this over and over again, and one night the miracle happened: God answered. No, that was not the miracle. God replies every time we question him, but our flesh is bemired and almost deaf: we do not hear. That night, however, I heard—and that was the miracle."

"What did you hear? Tell us everything, father," Peter called. He elbowed his way through the crowd and stood in front of the rabbi. The old man bent over, looked at Peter, and smiled:

"God, Peter, is a fisherman like yourself. He too goes out to fish at night when the moon is full or nearly full; and that night it was full—it sailed in the sky white as milk, so exceedingly merciful and benevolent that I could not close my eyes. The house constricted me, I marched through the narrow lanes and left Nazareth, climbed up high, perched on a rock and stared towards the south —towards holy Jerusalem. The moon leaned over and looked at me like a human being, smiling; I looked at it—at its mouth, its cheeks, at the corners of its eyes—and sighed. I felt it was speaking to me. speaking to me out of the silence of the night: yet I could not hear. . . . Not a leaf stirred on the earth, the unmown plain smelt just like bread, milk cascaded down the mountains around me, down Tabor, Gilboa and Carmel. . . . This is God's night, I thought. This full moon must be the nocturnal face of the Lord. Nights in the future Jerusalem will be such as this. . . .

"No sooner had this thought come to me than my eyes filled with tears. Grievance and fear took hold of me. 'I've grown old,' I shouted. 'Am I going to die without the Messiah first having gladdened my sight?'

"I jumped to my feet. The sacred fury had seized me again. Removing my belt and all my clothes, I stood before God's eyes just as I was when my mother begot me. I wanted him to see how I had aged, how I'd withered and shrivelled up like a fig leaf in autumn, like the bare dangling stem of a cluster of grapes which has been plundered by birds. I wanted him to see me, pity me, and move quickly!

"And as I stood there stark naked before the Lord, I felt the moonlight penetrate my flesh. I had become wholly spirit: one with God. I heard his voice, not from outside or above, but from within me. Within me! God's true voice always comes to us from within. 'Simeon, Simeon,' I heard, 'I shall not let you die before you have seen the Messiah, heard him, and grasped him with your hands!'

"'Lord, say that again!' I cried.

"'Simeon, Simeon, I shall not let you die before you have seen the Messiah, heard him, and grasped him with your hands!'

"I was so happy, I went out of my mind. Stark naked, I began to dance under the moon, clapping my hands and stamping my feet on the ground. I don't know if this dance lasted a split-second or a thousand years, but in any case I had enough finally—I found relief. Putting on my clothes and buckling my belt, I went down to Nazareth. The moment the cocks saw me from their perches high up on the rooftops they began to crow. The sky laughed, the birds awoke, doors opened and bade me good morning. My shabby house glittered from top to bottom—doors, windows, everything: all rubies. Wood, rocks, men, birds: all smelt the presence of God around me. The centurion himself, bloodsucker that he is, halted with astonishment. 'What's the matter with you, rabbi?' he asked me. 'You're a lighted torch. Watch out, don't set Nazareth on fire!' But I said nothing: I did not want him to soil my breath.

"I've kept this secret hidden close to my skin for years and years. I've enjoyed it all by myself, jealously and proudly—and I've waited. But today, this black day that has seen a new cross nailed into our hearts, I am unable to guard it any longer. I pity the people of Israel. Therefore I unveil to you the joyous news: He is coming, he is no longer far away. He has probably stopped for a drink of water at some near-by well, or for a slice of bread at some oven where the loaves have just been removed. But no matter where he is, he will appear—because God said so, and what he says, he does not unsay. 'Simeon, you will not die before you have seen the Messiah, heard him, and grasped him with your hands!' . . . I feel my strength leaving me day by day, but to the degree it departs, by so much does the Saviour approach. I am eighty-five years old. He cannot delay any more!"

A hairless cross-eyed man with a sharp skinny snout jumped up. He looked as though someone had forgotten to add the yeast when he was kneaded.

"But what if you live a thousand years, father?" he interrupted. "What if you never die? We've seen that happen. Enoch and Elijah are still alive!" His tiny wry eyes flitted slyly from side to side.

The rabbi pretended that he had not heard, but the cross-eyed man's hissed words were knives in his heart. He lifted his hand commandingly:

"I want to be alone with God. Leave—all of you!"

The place emptied out, the crowd dispersed, the old rabbi remained all by himself. He locked the street-door and fell deep into thought, leaning against the wall where the prophet Ezekiel hovered in the air. He is God, he reflected, and omnipotent: he does what he likes. Can that rascal Thomas be right? Woe is me if God decides I should live a thousand years! And if he decides I should never die—then the Messiah. . . ? Are the great hopes of the race of Israel all in vain? It has held the Word of God in its womb for thousands of years, nourishing it like a mother nourishes her seed. Our flesh and bone have been devoured: we have melted away, living only for this Son. But now the race has gone into labour, Abraham's seed cries out. Release it, Lord, release it at last! You are God, you can endure—we cannot. Mercy!

He paced up and down the synagogue. The day had finally waned. The shadows snuffed out the painting and swallowed Ezekiel. The old rabbi looked at the penumbra which descended about him, and suddenly all that he had seen and suffered in his life rushed into his mind. How many times and with what longing he had run from Galilee to Jerusalem, then from Jerusalem to the desert in pursuit of the Messiah! But without fail a cross had put an end to his hopes and he had returned to Nazareth ashamed. Today, however. . .

He squeezed his head between his hands.

"No, no," he murmured in terror, "no, no, it's impossible!"

For days and nights now his mind had been drumming, ready to split. A new hope had come to him, a hope too large for his mind—a madness, a demon which was devouring him. But this was not the first time. This madness had been digging its claws into his mind for years. He would banish it, and it would come again. But it had never dared appear during the day, it had always come in the darkness of night, or in his dreams. Today, however, today—at noon, in broad daylight! . . . Was he the one?

He leaned against the wall and closed his eyes. There he was, passing once more in front of him, gasping, with the cross on his back; and all about him the air trembled, just as it must tremble around the archangels. . . . Look! he raised his eyes. Never had the old rabbi seen so much of heaven in the eyes of man! Was he the one? "Lord, Lord," the rabbi murmured, "why do you torment me? Why don't you answer?"

The prophecies tore like lightning-flashes through his mind. At one moment his aged head filled with light, at the next it sank without hope into the darkness. His bowels opened and the patriarchs came forth. Within him, his hard-necked persevering race, covered with wounds and led by Moses, the head-ram with the twisted horns, started again on its endless journey from the Land of Slavery to the Land of Canaan; then the journey continued from the Land of Canaan to the future Jerusalem. In this new march, however, it was not the patriarch Moses who blazed the trail, but another—the rabbi's mind throbbed—another, bearing a cross upon his shoulder. . . .

He reached the street-door with one bound and opened it. The wind hit his face; he inhaled deeply. The sun had set, the birds were going home to sleep. The narrow streets filled with shadows; the earth grew cool. He locked the door and slipped the heavy key under his belt. For an instant he lost courage, but then all at once he made his decision. Head bowed, he set out towards Mary's house.

Mary sat on a high stool in the tiny yard of her house. She was spinning. It was still bright outside: the summer light drew slowly away from the face of the earth and did not wish to leave. Men and oxen were returning from their work in the fields. Housewives lit fires for the evening cooking; the fragrance of burning wood invaded the afternoon air. Mary spun, and her mind twirled now this way, now that—together with the spindle. Memory and imagination joined: her life seemed half truth, half fable. The petty round of daily tasks had lasted for years and then suddenly the stunning uninvited peacock—the miracle—had come and covered her tormented existence with its long golden wings.

"Take me where you want, Lord; do with me what you will. You chose my husband, you presented me with my son, you gave me my suffering. You tell me to cry out and I cry out; you tell me to keep still and I keep still. What am I, Lord? A handful of mud in your hands, and you knead me as you please. Do what you want. There is only one thing I beg of you: Lord, pity my son!"

A brilliantly white dove flew down from the roof opposite, beat its wings for a moment over her head and then alighted with dignity on the pebbles of the yard and began to walk methodically round and round Mary's feet. It spread its tail-feathers, bent its neck, turned its head and looked at Mary, its round eye flashing in the evening light like a ruby. It looked at her—spoke to her. It must want to inform me of some secret, she said to herself. Oh, if the old rabbi would only come. He knows all about the language of the birds and could interpret for me. . . . She looked at the dove and felt sorry for it. Leaving her spindle, she called the bird in a very tender voice, and the delighted dove took a hop and landed on her joined knees. And there, as though its whole secret was that it had been longing to reach those knees—it squatted, drew in its wings, and remained motionless.

Mary felt the sweet weight and smiled. Ah, if it were possible for God always to come down so sweetly over men! As she thought this, she recalled the morning she and her fiancé Joseph had

64

climbed to the prophet Elijah's summit, to heaven-kissed Carmel. They wanted to beg the fiery prophet to mediate with God so that they might have a son, whom they would then dedicate to the prophet's grace. They were to marry that same evening and had departed before dawn to receive the blessing of this flaming prophet whose great joy was the thunderbolt. Not a cloud in the sky; it was a lovely autumn, the human ants had gathered in their crops, the must was boiling in the jars, the figs drying, strung up on the rafters . . . Mary was fifteen at the time, her groom an old man with grey hair, but in his firm hand he held as a support the staff which had been ordained to blossom.

They reached the holy summit at exactly noon. They knelt and touched the sharp blood-stained granite with their fingertips, trembling. A spark flew out of the rock and cut Mary's hand. Joseph opened his mouth to call the summit's wild inhabitant, but before he could utter a sound the bellowing hail-laden clouds bounded angrily down from the foundations of heaven and formed a swirling funnel over the sharp granite. As Joseph darted forward to clasp his fiancée and take her to the shelter of some cave, God slung a terrifying flash of lightning, heaven and earth joined and Mary fell over backward in a swoon. When she came to and opened her eyes and looked around her, she saw Joseph lying face-down on the black granite—paralysed. . . .

Mary placed her hand on the dove which sat upon her knees. She caressed it, lightly, so that she would not frighten it. "God descended in a savage form on top of the mountain and spoke to me in a savage way," she murmured. "What did he say to me?"

She had often been questioned on this by the rabbi, who was bewildered by the repeated miracles which surrounded her.

"Try to remember, Mary," he would say. "This is the way God sometimes speaks to men—by means of the thunderbolt. Fight hard to remember, so that we may discover your son's fate."

"There was thunder, Father. It rolled down from heaven like a creaking ox-cart."

"And behind the thunder, Mary?"

"Yes, you're right, Father—God spoke behind the thunder, but I wasn't able to discover the actual words. Forgive me.". . .

Caressing the dove, she struggled to bring the lightning back to mind after thirty years and to untangle its hidden meaning. . . .

She closed her eyes. In her palm she felt the dove's tiny warm body and beating heart. . . . Suddenly—she did not realize how, she did not know why—dove and lightning were one; she was sure of it: these heartbeats and the thunder—all were God! She uttered a cry and jumped up in terror. Now, for the first time, she was able to make out the words hidden in the thunder, hidden in the dove's cooing: "Hail, Mary. . . , Hail, Mary. . ." Without a doubt, this was what God had cried: "Hail, Mary. . ."

Turning, she saw her husband propped up against the wall, still opening and closing his mouth. It was dark now, yet he still toiled and sweated. . . . She went to the doorway, passing in front of him but not speaking to him. She wanted to see if by any chance her son was coming. She had watched him twist the crucified man's bloody kerchief over his hair and start down the road towards the plain. . . . Where had he gone? Why was he late? Was he going to stay out in the fields again until daybreak?

As she stood on the threshold she saw the old rabbi approaching. He was puffing, leaning heavily on his crosier. The tufts of white hair at each of his temples waved in the evening breeze which had begun to come down from Mount Carmel.

Mary stepped to one side with respect, and the rabbi entered. He took his brother's hand, patted it, but did not speak to him—what could he say? His mind submerged in dark waters, he turned to Mary.

"Your eyes are shining, Mary," he said. "What's the matter? Did God come again?"

"Father, I've found it!" said Mary, unable to restrain herself.

"You've found it? Found what, in God's name?"

"The words behind the lightning."

The rabbi gave a start. "Great is the God of Israel," he cried, lifting high his arms. "This was precisely why I came, Mary—to ask you once more. . . . Today, as you know, one of our hopes was crucified, and my heart. . ."

"I've found it, Father," Mary repeated. "While I was sitting this evening and spinning and thinking again about the lightning, I felt the thunder grow quiet within me for the first time, and behind it I heard a serene clear voice, the voice of God: 'Hail, Mary!' "

The rabbi collapsed onto a stool. Squeezing his temples between his hands, he plunged deep into thought. After a considerable interval he lifted his head.

"Nothing else, Mary? Bend far down within yourself so that you'll be sure to hear. The fate of Israel may depend on what you say."

When Mary heard the rabbi's words she became terrified. Her breast began to tremble, and once more her mind strained to discover what was behind the thunder.

"No," she murmured finally, exhausted, "no, Father. . . . He said more, much more, but I can't hear it. I'm trying as hard as I can, but I cannot hear what he said."

The rabbi placed his hand on top of her head, above her large eyes.

"Fast, Mary, and pray; do not dissipate your mind on daily tasks. There are times when a glowing halo as bright as lightning moves all around your face. Is it truly light, I wonder? I can't tell. . . . Fast, pray, and you will hear. 'Hail, Mary. . .': God's message begins with kindness. Try hard to hear what follows."

In order to hide her agitation Mary went to the shelf where she kept the jugs. She unhooked a brass cup, filled it with cool water, got a handful of dates also, and bent over to hand them to the old man.

"I'm not hungry or thirsty, Mary," he said, "thank you. Sit down; I have something to say to you."

Mary took the lowest stool and sat at the rabbi's feet. Tipping up her head, she waited.

The old man tested the words one by one in his mind. What he wanted to say was difficult: it was a hope so spidery-fine and slippery that he was unable to find words spidery and slippery enough to avoid giving the hope too much weight and turning it into a certainty. He did not want to terrify the mother.

"Mary," he said finally, "a mystery roams outside this house, like a desert lion. . . . You are not the same as other women, Mary. Don't you feel that?"

"No, I don't, Father," she murmured. "I am like all women. I love all the cares and joys of women. I like to wash, to cook, to go to the fountain for water, to chat merrily with the neighbours; and in the evening, to sit in my doorway and watch the passers-by. And my heart, Father, like the hearts of all women, is full of pain."

"You're not the same as other women, Mary," the rabbi repeated in a solemn tone, raising his hand as though he wished to prevent all objections. "And your son. . ."

The rabbi stopped. How could he find words to express this, the most difficult part of all. He looked up at the heavens and listened. Some of the birds in the trees were preparing to go to sleep, others to wake up. The wheel turned; the day sank below men's feet.

The rabbi sighed. How the days rushed by, how rabidly one pursued the next! Dawn, dusk, the passage of the sun, the passage of moon after moon. . . ; children became men, black hairs whitened, the sea ate into the land, mountains were stripped bare —and still the One they awaited did not come!

"My son. . . ?" said Mary, her voice trembling. "My son, Father?"

"He is not like other sons, Mary," the rabbi boldly replied.

He weighed his words once more, and continued after a moment:

"Sometimes when he is alone during the night and thinks no one is watching him, the whole circumference of his face gleams in the darkness. May God forgive me, Mary, but I've made a small hole high in the wall. I climb up and watch him from there; I spy on what he does. Why? Because—I confess it—I'm completely confused, my knowledge is of no help whatsoever: I unroll the Scriptures tirelessly but I cannot comprehend what or who he is. . . . I spy on him in secret therefore, and in the darkness I discern this light which licks him and devours his face. That is why he's been growing paler day by day and melting away. It's not because of sickness, fasting or prayer; no, he is being devoured by this light."

Mary sighed. Woe betide the mother who bears a son unlike all the rest, she thought. But she did not speak.

The old man bent over her now and lowered his voice. His lips were on fire.

"Hail, Mary," he said. "God is all-powerful; his designs are inscrutable. . . . Your son might be. . ."

But the unfortunate mother uttered a cry:

"Have pity on me, Father! A prophet? No, no! And if God has it so written, let him rub it out! I want my son a man like everyone else, nothing more, nothing less. Like everyone else . . . Let him build troughs, cradles, ploughs and household utensils as his father used to do, and not, as just now, crosses to crucify human beings. Let him marry a nice young girl from a respectable home—with a dowry; let him be a liberal provider, have children. . . , and then we'll all go out together every Saturday to the promenade—grandma, children and grandchildren—so that everyone can admire us."

The rabbi leaned heavily on his crosier and got up.

"Mary," he said severely, "if God listened to mothers we would all rot away in a bog of security and easy living. . . . When you're alone, think over everything we have said.

He turned to his brother in order to bid him good-night. Joseph, his glassy eyes misty and his tongue hanging out, stared into the air, struggling to speak. Mary shook her head.

"He's been fighting since morning and still hasn't freed himself." She went up to him and sponged the contorted drooling mouth.

But the moment the rabbi held out his hand to say good-night to Mary also, the door opened furtively and the son appeared on the threshold, his face gleaming in the darkness. The gory kerchief was pasted to his hair, but the night obscured the large tears which still furrowed his cheeks, as well as the dust and blood which coated his feet.

He strode over the threshold, looked hastily about him, discovered his mother and the rabbi, and in the darkness near the wall, his father's glassy eyes.

Mary started to light the lamp, but the rabbi held her back.

"Wait," he murmured, "I'll talk to him." Emboldening his heart, he approached.

"Jesus," he said tenderly, lowering his voice so that the mother would not hear, "Jesus, my child, how long are you going to resist him?"

69

And then the entire cottage shook with the savage shout: "Until I die!"

All at once, as though every ounce of strength had flowed out of him, the son of Mary collapsed to the ground and leaned against the wall, gasping for breath. The rabbi wanted to speak to him again. He leaned over him, but immediately drew back with a jolt. He felt as though he had approached a great fire and burnt his face. God is all around him, he reflected, yes, it's God who is around him, and he lets no one come near. I'd better leave!

He departed, plunged in thought. The door closed, but Mary did not dare light the lamp: a wild beast lay in wait for her in the darkness. Standing in the middle of the house, she listened to her husband's hopeless clucking and to her son who, fallen in a heap on the ground, gasped in terror as though being strangled. Someone was choking him—who? The unfortunate mother dug her nails into her cheeks and asked God, asked him again, complained, shouted: "I'm a mother, don't you pity me?"—but no one answered.

And while she stood there, fixed and speechless, hearing every vein in her body tremble, there was a wild triumphant cry. The tongue of the paralysed man had been loosed and the entire word had issued at last from his contorted mouth, syllable by syllable, and reverberated throughout the house: A-DO-NA-I! But as the old man unmouthed this word, he sank instantaneously into the depths of sleep, like lead.

Mary nerved herself and lit the lamp. The food was boiling. Going to the hearth, she knelt and removed the lid of the earthenware pot to see if any water was needed, or perhaps a pinch of salt. . . .

VI

THE sky shone bluish-white. Nazareth was asleep and dreaming, the Morning Star tolled the hours over its pillows, the lemon and date trees were still wrapped in a rosy-blue veil. Deep silence. . . . Not even the black cock had crowed. The son of Mary opened the door. Dark blue rings circled his eyes, but his hand did not tremble. He opened the door, and without closing it again, without looking back to see either his mother or his father, he abandoned the paternal roof for ever. He took two steps, three, and stopped. He thought he heard two heavy feet moving along with him. He looked behind him: no one. He tightened the leather nail-studded belt, tied the red-spotted kerchief over his hair and went down the narrow twisting lanes. A dog barked at him mournfully; an owl sensed the approach of day, took fright and flew silently away over his head. He hurriedly left the bolted doors behind him and came out into the gardens and orchards. The first song-birds had already begun to twitter. In a kitchen garden an old man was in harness, turning the winch over an irrigation-well. The day had begun.

He had neither wallet, staff nor sandals, and the road was long. He would have to go past Cana, Tiberias, Magdala and Capernaum, then circle the lake of Gennesaret and enter the desert. . . . He had heard of a monastery there for simple, virtuous men: they dressed all in white, ate no meat, drank no wine, never touched a woman—did nothing but pray to God. They were versed in herbs and healed the diseases of the body; they were versed also in secret charms, and cured the soul of devils. How many times had his uncle the rabbi spoken to him, sighing continually, about this holy monastery! He had spent eleven years there as a monk, praising God and healing men. But alas! one day he was mounted by the Tempter (he too, of course, is almighty): he saw a woman, abandoned the holy life, stripped off his white cassock, married—and fathered Magdalene. Served him right! God gave the apostate his just reward. . . .

"That's where I'll go," murmured the son of Mary, quickening his pace. "There, inside the monastery, I shall hide under his wings. . . ."

What a joy this was! What a long time—ever since his twelfth birthday—he had longed to abandon house and parents, to forget the past, escape his mother's admonitions, his father's bellowing and the petty workaday cares which devour the soul; had longed to shake man from his feet like so much dust and to flee and take refuge in the desert! Today—finally—he had thrown everything behind him with one toss, had extricated himself from man's wheel and taken hold, body and soul, of God's. He was saved!

His pale embittered face suddenly gleamed. Perhaps God's claws had clutched him all those years precisely in order to bring him where he was now going of his own volition, free of the claws. Did this mean that his desires were beginning to join with those of God? Wasn't this the greatest and most difficult of man's duties? Wasn't this the meaning of happiness?

His heart felt relieved. No more claws, no more wrestling and screaming. . . . This morning at daybreak God had come filled with compassion, had come like a cool gentle breeze and said to him: "Let us go!". . . He had opened the door; and now—what a delicious feeling of reconciliation! what happiness! "It is too much for me," he murmured. "I shall lift high my head and sing the psalm of salvation: 'You are my shelter and my refuge, Lord. . .' "

His joy could not be contained in his heart; it overflowed. He proceeded in the sweet light of the dawn, surrounded by God's great wealth—olive trees, vineyards, wheatfields; and the psalm of joy bounded out of his loins, trying to reach the sky. He lifted high his head and opened his mouth, but suddenly his heart skipped a beat: he had just clearly heard two bare feet running behind him. He shortened his stride and listened carefully. The two feet checked their pace. His knees gave way and he stopped. The two feet stopped also.

"I know who it is," he whispered, trembling. "I know. . ."

But he emboldened his heart and whirled abruptly in order to catch sight of her before she vanished. . . . No one!

The eastern sky had turned dark cherry. The ears of grain were fully ripe; the stalks inclined their heads in the windless air and

72

awaited the sickle. Not a single object was on the plain—not a beast, not a man. Only in Nazareth, behind him, was there any sign of life. Smoke had already begun to rise from one or two houses. The women were awakening.

He felt somewhat reassured. Better not lose time, he reflected. Let's run for all I'm worth and get around to the other side of that hill, to lose her. He started to run.

On either side of him the wheat towered to the height of a man. It was here in this plain of Galilee that wheat had originated, as had the vine, and wild vines still crept up the mountainsides. An ox-cart creaked in the distance. Donkeys shook themselves up off the ground, sniffed the air, lifted their tails and brayed. He heard laughter and chattering. Honed sickles flashed; the first mowers appeared. The sun saw them and fell on their lovely arms, necks and shins.

When they glimpsed the son of Mary running in the distance they burst out laughing.

"Hey there, who are you chasing," they called to him, "or who's chasing you?"

But when he came closer and they were able to get a better view of him, they knew who he was. They all stopped their chatter and huddled one next to the other.

"The cross-maker!" they murmured. "A curse on him! Yesterday I saw him crucify. . ."

"Look at the gory kerchief he's wearing!"

"It was his share of the clothes of the Crucified. May the blood of the innocent fall upon his head!"

They continued hurriedly on their way, but now the laughter stuck in their throats and they were silent.

The son of Mary went past them, left them behind him, crossed the wheatfields and reached the vineyards which covered the gentle slopes of the mountain. Seeing a fig tree, he started to slow down in order to pick a leaf and smell it. He liked the smell of fig leaves very much: they reminded him of human armpits. When he was little he used to close his eyes and smell the leaves, and he imagined he was snuggled again at his mother's breast, sucking. . . . But the moment he stopped and put out his hand to pick the leaf, cold sweat poured over his body. The two feet—which had

73

been running behind him—suddenly stopped too. His hair stood on end. His arm still in the air, he looked all around him. Solitude. No one but God. . . . The soil was wet, the leaves dripping; in the hollow of a tree a butterfly struggled to open its dewy wings and fly.

I'll scream, he decided. I'll scream to find relief.

Whenever he remained alone on the mountain or on the deserted plain at the hour of noon, what was it that he felt so abundantly— joy? bitterness? or was it, above everything else, fear? He always sensed God girding him about on all sides, and he would utter a wild cry, as though he wanted to make a desperate attempt to escape. Sometimes he crowed like a cock, sometimes he howled like a hungry jackal, sometimes like a dog being whipped. . . . But as he opened his mouth now to cry out, his eye caught sight of the butterfly that was struggling to unfold its wings. He bent over, lifted it up gently and placed it high above the ground on a leaf of the fig tree, where the sun began to beat down upon it.

"My sister, my sister," he murmured, and he looked at it with compassion.

Leaving the butterfly behind him to become warm, he set out once more and immediately heard the muffled tread of the two bare feet over the moist soil, a few paces to the rear of him. In the beginning, when he first left Nazareth, her sound was very faint: it seemed to come from far away. Little by little the feet had gained courage and drawn closer. Soon, the son of Mary thought with a shudder, they would catch him up. "Lord, O Lord," he murmured, "grant that I may reach the monastery quickly, before she pounces on me."

The sun now invaded the plain, beating down upon birds, beasts and men. A heterogeneous rumble mounted from the soil; on the mountainsides goats and sheep began to stir and shepherds to sound their pipes: the world grew tame and civilized. In a few moments, as soon as he reached that tall poplar ahead of him on his left, he would see Cana, the merry village he loved so much. While he was still a beardless stripling—before God dug his claws into him—how many times he and his mother had come here to the boisterous festivals! How many times he had joined the others in admiring the girls from all the surrounding villages as they

74

danced beneath this tall thickly-foliaged poplar and the happy earth trembled under their stamping feet. But once, when he was twenty years old and stood gasping for breath under this poplar, holding a rose in his hand. . .

He shuddered. Suddenly he saw *her* of the thousand secret kisses standing once more before him. Hidden in her bosom were the sun and the moon, one to the right, the other to the left; and day and night rose and fell behind the transparent bodice of her dress. . . .

"Leave me alone, leave me alone!" he cried. "I've been dedicated to God; I'm on my way to meet him in the desert!" Hurrying along, he passed the poplar. Suddenly Cana unfolded before him: the squat houses all anointed with whitewash, the square drying-platforms, brilliantly gilded with the maize and huge gourds which had been spread out under the sun. The young girls, their bare feet dangling over the edges, were stringing red peppers along cotton thread, to decorate their homes.

Lowering his eyes, he rushed by this trap of Satan's as fast as he could. He did not want to see anyone or to be seen by anyone. Behind him the two bare feet now stamped loudly over the cobbles: they were rushing too.

The sun had mounted; it now covered the earth. Singing merrily, the reapers swung their sickles and mowed. The handfuls quickly became armfuls, bundles, then stacks which towered above the threshing floors. As he proceeded, the son of Mary hastily wished the landowners a good harvest: 'Each ear big enough to fill a sack!"

Cana had vanished behind the olive groves. The shadows snuggled close to the roots of the trees; it was almost noon. And as the son of Mary rejoiced in everything around him, keeping his mind fixed on God, the sweet smell of newly-baked bread suddenly hit his nostrils. All at once he felt hungry, and the moment he did so, his entire body jumped for joy. How many years he had felt hunger and yet never experienced this holy yearning for bread! But now. . .

His nostrils sniffed the air. Following the aroma, he strode across a ditch, climbed a fence, entered a vineyard and discovered a squat hut beneath a hollow olive tree. Smoke ascended, untwisting as it passed the thatched roof. An old lady was bent over, wrestling with a small brick oven which stood in the hut's entranceway. She was quick-moving, had a nose like a skewer and eyes without eyelashes. At her side was a dog, black with yellow spots. He had placed his front paws on the oven and opened wide a deep famished mouth filled with teeth. As soon as he heard footsteps in the vineyard he barked and charged the intruder. Surprised, the old woman turned. When she saw the youth her tiny eyes gleamed. Delighted to see a man enter her solitude, she stopped work, the wooden shovel in her hand.

"Welcome," she said. "Hungry? Where have you come from, with God's grace?"

"From Nazareth."

"Hungry?" the old woman asked again, laughing. "Your nostrils are twitching like a greyhound's."

"Yes, ma'am, I'm hungry. Forgive me."

But the old lady was deaf and did not hear.

"What?" she said. "Speak louder."

"I'm hungry, ma'am. Forgive me."

"Forgive you—why? Hunger isn't anything to be ashamed of, my fine lad, nor is thirst, nor love. They're all God's—so come closer and don't be ashamed."

She laughed again, revealing her one precious tooth.

"Here you'll find bread and water. Love—further on, in Magdala."

She grasped a loaf which she had placed with the others on the stone bench next to the oven. "Look, this is the loaf we reserve for passers-by each time we empty the oven. We call it the grasshopper's bread. It's not mine, it's yours. Cut a slice and eat."

The son of Mary felt calmed. He sat down on the root of the ancient olive tree and began to eat. How tasty this bread was, how refreshing the water, how sweet the two olives which the old lady gave him to accompany his bread. They had slender pits and were as fat and fleshy as apples! He chewed tranquilly and ate, feeling that his body and soul had joined and become one now, that they were receiving the bread, olives and water with one mouth, rejoicing, the both of them, and being nourished.

The old lady leaned against the oven and admired him.

"You certainly were hungry," she said with a laugh. "Eat. You're young, you've got a long road ahead of you still, and no end of troubles. Eat, make yourself strong so that you'll be able to endure."

She broke off the corner of another loaf and gave him two more olives. Her kerchief slipped from her head, revealing her balding scalp. She hastily tied it up again.

"Where are you headed, with the grace of God?" she asked.

"To the desert."

"Where? Speak louder!"

"To the desert."

The old woman contorted her toothless mouth; her eyes grew fierce.

"To the monastery?" she screamed with unexpected anger. "Why? What business do you have there? Don't you pity your youth?"

He did not speak. The old woman shook her bald head and hissed like a snake: "You want to find God, do you?" she asked sarcastically.

"Yes," said the youth, his voice extremely thin.

The old lady kicked the dog, which was tangled up in her reed-like legs, and approached the youth.

"Ooo, unlucky devil," she shouted, "don't you know that God is found not in monasteries but in the homes of men! Wherever you find husband and wife, that's where you find God; wherever children and petty cares and cooking and arguments and reconciliations, that's where God is too. Don't listen to those eunuchs. Sour grapes! Sour grapes! The God I'm telling you about, the domestic one, not the monastic: that's the true God. He's the one you should adore. Leave the other to those lazy sterile idiots in the desert!"

The more the old lady spoke the more enflamed she became. She talked and screeched, had her fling of revenge, grew calm.

"Excuse me, my brave lad," she said, touching the young man's shoulder, "but once I had a son, a fine one like yourself. He went out of his mind one morning, opened the door and left to go to the monastery in the desert, to the Healers—a plague on them and may they never heal anyone as long as they live! Well, I lost him and now I fill the oven and empty it—to feed whom? My children? my grandchildren? I'm a withered, fruitless tree."

She stopped for a moment to wipe her eyes, then began again: "For years I lifted my hands to God. 'Why was I born?' I shouted. 'I had one son, why did you take him from me?' I shouted and shouted, but who could expect him to hear! Only once did I see the heavens open. It was at midnight, on the top of the prophet Elijah's mountain. I heard a thunderous voice: 'Shout yourself hoarse for all I care'. Then the heavens closed again; and that was the last I ever called to God."

The son of Mary got up. He held out his hand to say good-bye to the old woman, but she drew hers back. Once more she began to hiss like a snake:

"So it's the desert, is it! You too have an appetite for sand, eh? But where are your eyes, my fine lad? Don't you see vineyards, the sun, women? Go on, I tell you, go to Madgala—that's where you belong! Haven't you ever read the Scriptures? God says: 'I don't want fasting and prayer, I want meat!' In other words, he wants you to produce him children!"

"Farewell, ma'am," the young man said. "May God repay you for the bread you've fed me."

"May God repay you too," said the old lady, mollified; "may he repay you for the good you have done me. It's been years since a man stopped at my broken-down hovel, and if anyone did pass by, he was always old. . . ."

He strode back again through the vineyard, jumped over the fence and came out onto the main road.

"I can't stand the sight of men," he murmured. "I don't want to see them, even the bread they give you is poison. Only one road leads to God: the one I chose today. It passes amidst men without touching them, and comes out in the desert. Oh, when will I arrive!"

His words had still not faded away when laughter broke out behind him. He turned, startled. A mouthless laugh convulsed the air, a hissing, rancorous, malevolent laugh.

"Adonai! Adonai!" was the shout which escaped his constricted larynx. His hair standing on end, he gazed at the guffawing air; then, in a raving frenzy, he started to run—and immediately

78

heard the sound of the two bare feet which were running behind him.

"No matter where they are, they will catch me soon; no matter where they are, they will catch me soon," he murmured, and ran.

The women were still mowing. The men carried the bundles to the threshing floors; others, further on, had started to winnow. A warm breeze caught the chaff and sprinkled the earth with golden powder, leaving the heavy grain to pile up on the threshing floor. Passers-by took a fistful of wheat, kissed it and wished the land-owners a similar harvest the following year.

Sitting between two hills in the distance, imposing, newly-built, full of statues, theatres and painted women, was Tiberias, the idolatress. The sight of it filled the son of Mary with fright. Once, when he was still a child, he had come here with his uncle the rabbi, who had been called to rid a well-born Roman lady of her devils. It was obviously the devil of the bath which had mounted her, for she used to go out into the streets stark naked and waylay the passers-by. The rabbi and his nephew entered her palace at a time when the noble lady was again governed by her demon. She was running towards the street-door in the buff, the slaves hot in her pursuit. The rabbi put out his staff and stopped her—but the moment she saw the boy, she pounced on him. The son of Mary screamed and fainted; and ever since then, whenever he recalled this shameless place, he trembled.

"This city is damned by God," the rabbi used to tell him. "When you pass this way, go quickly, keep your eyes on the ground and your mind on death; or look up at the sky and keep your mind on God. If you want my blessing, whenever you travel to Capernaum, take another route."

The hussy laughed now in the sunlight, people poured in and out of her gates, both on foot and on horseback; flags with the two-headed eagle waved over her towers, bronze arms flashed. . . . Once the son of Mary had seen a mare's carcass stretched out in a green bog outside Nazareth. It was puffed up with the skin stretched tight, like a drum. Armies of crabs and dung-beetles paraded in and out of its open belly, which was full of guts and filth; a cloud of immense gold-green horseflies buzzed in the air above, and two crows sucked away, their sharp bills thrust into

79

the large eyes, just below the long lashes. The carcass was resplendent. Thickly-inhabited, it seemed to have come back to life: you thought it was rolling delightedly in the springtime grass, completely content, with its four shod hoofs stretched out towards the sky.

"Such—like the mare's carcass—such is Tiberias," murmured the son of Mary, unable to remove his eyes from the glittering city. "Such, also, are Sodom and Gomorrah; such the sinful soul of man. . ."

A vigorous still-juicy old man went by astride his donkey. He saw Jesus and stopped.

"What are you gaping at, lad?" he asked. "Don't you know her? She's our new princess: Tiberias the whore. Greeks, Romans, Bedouins, Chaldeans, Gipsies and Jews mount her, and she's always ready for more. She's always ready for more—do you hear what I say? Two and two make four!"

He removed a handful of walnuts from his saddle bag and treated Jesus, "You look like a fine upstanding fellow," he said, "and a poor one. Take these to munch along the road and don't forget to say: God bless old Zebedee of Capernaum!"

His forked beard was fully white, his lips thick and gluttonous; he had a short bull-neck and black quick-moving rapacious eyes. This squat fat body must have eaten, drunk and kissed amply in its time—and it was still far from satisfied!

A great hairy colossus came along. His shirt was open down the front, his knees bare; in his hand he held a hooked shepherd's staff. He halted, all wrought up, and without greeting the old man, turned to the son of Mary:

"Your Honour mightn't be the son of the Carpenter, from Nazareth? You mightn't be the one who builds crosses and crucifies us?"

Two old women who were mowing in the field opposite heard the conversation and approached.

"I. . . ," said the son of Mary, "I. . . ," and he started to leave.

"Where do you think you're going?" shouted the colossus, seizing him by the arm. "You don't get away so easily! Crossmaker, traitor—I'll murder you!"

But the juicy old man grabbed the crook and snatched it out of the shepherd's hand.

"Wait a minute, Philip," he said. "Listen to what an old man has to say. Now will you please answer me this: Everything that happens in this world is willed by God, isn't it?"

"Yes, Zebedee, everything."

"All right then: it's God's will that this fellow build crosses. Leave him alone. And a word to the wise: it's best not to meddle in the Lord's affairs. Two and two make four."

The son of Mary, meanwhile, had extricated himself from the bumpkin's pincers and gone off at a run. The two old reapers screeched after him, shaking their sickles maniacally.

"Zebedee," said the colossus, "let's both go and wash our hands because we touched the cross-maker; let's go wash our mouths too, because we spoke to him."

"Don't worry about it," said the old man. "Well, let's not stand here. Come on, keep me company—I'm in a hurry, My sons are away. One went to Nazareth to see the crucifixion, or so he said, and it seems the other has gone to the desert to become a saint. So here I am all alone with my fishing boats! Come on, help me pull in the nets—they're probably loaded with fish by now. I'll give you a skillet-full."

They set out. The old man was in a merry mood.

"Good Lord, just think what poor old God must go through also," he said with a laugh. "He certainly got himself in hot water when he created the world. The fish screams: Don't blind me, Lord, don't let me enter the nets! The fisherman screams: Blind the fish, Lord, make him enter the nets! Which one is God supposed to listen to? Sometimes he listens to the fish, sometimes to the fisherman—and that's the way the world goes round!"

The son of Mary, meanwhile, had gone along the steep goat's path in order to avoid Madgala. He did not want to be soiled by this charming, open-hearted, but wicked hamlet which lay amid date-palms at the rich crossroads where caravans passed day and night, some from the Euphrates or the Arabian desert, headed for the Great Sea, others from Damascus or Phoenicia, headed for the tender green bed of the Nile. At the village's entrance was a well of cool water, and on its brim sat a painted woman with naked breasts, smiling at the merchants. . . . Oh, to flee, to change route, to cut straight for the lake and reach the desert! There, in a dried-up well, God was sitting, expecting him.

His heart swelled as he recalled God, and he quickened his pace. The sun finally took pity on the girls who were reaping: it began to set. The air grew cool. The mowers stretched out on their backs on the hay-ricks in order to catch their breath and tell an off-colour joke or two to relieve their minds. They had caught fire, working and sweating as they had all day long in the sun with exposed bosoms, next to the men who were sweating too. They had caught fire, and now, by means of jokes and laughter, they were cooling off.

The son of Mary overheard their laughter and teasing. He blushed. Impatient for the time when he would no longer hear human beings, he forced his thoughts elsewhere and began to turn over in his mind the words of Philip, the loud-mouthed shepherd.

"No one realizes how much I suffer," he murmured with a sigh; "no one understands why I make crosses or with whom I am wrestling. . . ."

In front of a cottage, two farmers were shaking the fine layer of chaff from their beards and hair, and washing themselves. They must have been brothers. Their old mother was laying out their poor-man's dinner on the stone shelf beside the oven. Maize was roasting on the hot coals. The aroma filled the air.

The two farmers saw the son of Mary. He was exhausted and covered with dust, and they felt sorry for him.

"Hey you, where are you running to?" they shouted. "It looks like you've come quite a way, but you have no sack. Stop awhile and join us for a mouthful of bread."

"And eat some maize too," said the mother.

"And drink a bit of wine to put the colour back in your cheeks."

"I'm not hungry, I don't want anything, thank you," the son of Mary answered, continuing past them. Once they find out who I am, he was thinking, they'll feel ashamed that they touched me and spoke to me.

"Three cheers for your pig-headedness," one of the brothers called to him. "We aren't good enough for you, eh?"

I'm the cross-maker, Jesus was about to reply, but he turned coward, bowed his head, and went on his way.

The evening descended like a sword. Before the hills had time to glow rosy-red the soil turned purple and then straightway black, and the light, which had climbed to the tops of the trees, jumped into the sky and was lost. The darkness found the son of Mary at the summit of a hill. An aged cedar had taken root there. Though lashed by the winds and continually tormented, it held on strongly: its roots had eaten into the rock. The aroma of wheat and burnt wood ascended from the plain, and from the scattered cottages rose the smoke of the evening meal.

The son of Mary was hungry and thirsty. For a split-second he envied these labourers who finished their day's work, returned dead-tired and famished to their hovels, and saw from afar the lighted fire, the smoke rising and their wives preparing the dinner.

He suddenly felt more completely alone than even the foxes and owls, for they at least had a nest or lair and warm beloved creatures awaiting them. He had no one, not even his mother. He squatted at the foot of the cedar and huddled up into a ball. He was shivering.

"Lord," he murmured, "I thank you for everything: for the loneliness, the hunger, the cold. I lack nothing."

As he said this, however, he seemed to sense the injustice which was being done him. He swept his eyes around him like a trapped beast, and his temples drummed with anger and fear. Getting up onto his knees, he riveted his eyes upon the dark path. The naked feet could still be heard. They were dislodging the stones and mounting. They reached the summit finally and then, involuntarily—he himself was startled to hear his own voice—the son of Mary cried out:

"Come closer, my Lady. Do not hide—it's night now, no one sees you. . . . Reveal yourself!"

He held his breath and waited.

Not a soul replied. Nothing but the eternal sounds of the night rising sweetly, peacefully into the air: crickets and grasshoppers, goatsuckers sighing; and far in the distance, dogs that discovered in the darkness things invisible to men, and barked. . . . He stretched his head forward. He was positive that someone stood under the cedar, directly before him.

"My Lady. . . , my Lady," he whispered now in a hushed beseeching tone, trying to entice the invisible. He waited. He had stopped shivering. Sweat poured from his armpits and brow.

He stared, listening intently. At one moment he imagined he heard the laugh again, coming softly out of the darkness, at another that he saw the air whirl, congeal and become a body which was no sooner formed than unformed and lost.

Melting away with the effort, the son of Mary fought to tether the dark air. He did not cry out now, did not beseech; he simply knelt with outstretched head under the cedar and waited, melting away. . . .

The rocks bruised his knees. He changed his position, leaning against the trunk of the cedar and closing his eyes. And then, without losing his tranquillity or uttering a cry, he saw her—inside his eyes. But she had not come in the way he expected. He expected to see his bereaved mother with both her hands on his head, calling down her curse upon him. But now what was this! Trembling, he gradually opened his eyes. Flashing before him was the savage body of a woman covered head to foot with interlocking scales of thick bronze armour. But the head was not a human head, it was an eagle's, with yellow eyes and a crooked beak which grasped a mouthful of flesh. She looked tranquilly, mercilessly at the son of Mary.

"You did not come as I expected you," he murmured. "You are not the Mother. . . . Have pity and speak to me. Who are you?"

He asked, waited, asked again. Nothing. . . Nothing but the yellow glitter of the round eyes in the darkness.

But suddenly the son of Mary understood.

"The Curse!" he cried, and he fell face downward onto the ground.

VII

THE heavens sparkled above him while below, the earth wounded him with its stones and thorns. He had stretched out his arms; he struggled convulsively and moaned as though the whole earth was a cross on which he was being crucified.

The darkness passed over him with its large and small attendants—the stars and the birds of the night. On every side the dogs, submissive to man, barked on the threshing floors and guarded the wealth of their masters. It was cold; Jesus shivered. Sleep overcame him for a moment and led him on an airy promenade to warm far-away lands, but straightway threw him back down again to earth, onto the stones.

Towards midnight he heard merry bells passing at the foot of the hill, and behind the bells, the melancholy song of a camel driver. There was the sound of conversation, someone sighed, the clear fresh voice of a woman spouted out of the night, but the road quickly grew silent once more. . . . Mounted on a golden-saddled camel, her face grooved from weeping, the make-up on her cheeks turned to mud, Magdalene was passing by—in the middle of the night. Wealthy merchants from the four corners of the earth had arrived. Finding her neither at the well nor in her house, they chose the camel with the richest, the most golden harness, and sent their driver to bring her to them post-haste. Their route had been extremely long and dangerous, but they kept constantly in mind a body they would find at Magdala, and this gave them strength. They had not found it, however, so they dispatched the driver and queued up in Magdalene's yard, where they now sat with closed eyes, waiting.

Little by little the bells in the night grew dimmer, sweeter. They now seemed to the son of Mary like tender laughter, like purring jets of water which gushed into a deep orchard and called him caressingly by name; and in this way, gently, following the seductive ring of the camel's bells, he slid back again into sleep.

He had a dream. The world seemed to be a green meadow, all

in bloom, and God an olive-skinned shepherd boy with two twisted horns, newly-grown and still tender, who sat next to a cistern of water and played his pipe. Never in his life had the son of Mary heard such a sweet, bewitching sound. While God the shepherd boy played on, the soil, fistful by fistful, quivered and stirred, grew spherical, came to life—and graceful deer with wreath-like antlers suddenly filled the meadow. God leaned over and looked at the water: the cistern filled with fish; he lifted his eyes to the trees: their leaves changed colour, became twittering birds. He had gathered momentum; the piper's music grew furious, and two insects as large as men emerged from the ground and at once began to embrace on the springtime grass. They rolled from one end of the meadow to the other, coupled, separated, coupled again, laughed indecently, scoffed at the shepherd boy, and hissed. The boy lowered his pipe and regarded the audacious and obscene pair. Suddenly his patience gave out. With one blow he crushed his pipe under his heel and all at once deer, birds, trees, water and the glued man-woman vanished. . . .

The son of Mary uttered a cry and awoke, but not before his eye was caught, just at the moment of awakening, by the pasted bodies of a man and a woman hurling down into the dark trap-door of his bowels. Terrified, he jumped to his feet.

"So, such is the mud within me, such the filth!"

He unbelted the nail-studded leather strap, trampled the clothes he was wearing underfoot and, without speaking, began pitilessly to scourge his thighs, back and face. The blood spurted out and splashed him. He felt it and was relieved.

Dawn. . . . The stars grew dim; the frosty wind pricked his bones. The cedar above him filled with wings and song. He turned around. The air was empty; in the light of the day the bronze eagle-headed Curse had become invisible again.

I must go away, must escape, he thought, must not set foot in Magdala—curse the place! I won't stop till I reach the desert and bury myself in the monastery. There I shall kill the flesh and turn it into spirit.

He placed his palm on the ancient trunk of the cypress and stroked it. He felt the tree's soul rise from the roots and branch out to the highest, tenderest twig.

"Farewell, my sister," he murmured. "Last night under your shelter I brought shame upon myself. Forgive me."

He spoke and then, exhausted and with dismal forebodings, started down the hill.

He reached the main road. The plain was awakening, the first rays of the sun fell and filled the loaded threshing floors with gold. "I must not go through Magdala," he murmured again. "I'm afraid. . ." He stopped to decide which way to turn in order to reach the lake. He took the first narrow road he found on his right. He knew that Magdala sat to the left, the lake to the right, and he proceeded with confidence.

He marched and marched, and his mind wandered. He was running from Magdalene, the whore, to God; from the cross to Paradise, from his mother and father to distant lands and seas, to myriad-faced men, white, yellow and black. Although he had never crossed the boundaries of Israel, ever since his early childhood he had shut his eyes within his father's humble cottage and his mind, like a trained hawk with golden hawk-bells, had darted from land to land, ocean to ocean, screeching with joy. It was not hunting anything, this hawk-mind of his; he had become oblivious of the body, he was escaping the flesh, ascending to heaven—and this was all he could possibly desire.

He marched and marched. The twisting path wound in and out through the vineyards, rose once more, reached the olive groves. The son of Mary followed it as one follows running water or the sad monotonous chant of a camel driver. This whole journey seemed a dream to him. He scarcely touched the earth; his feet trod his human seal, the heel and five toes, lightly into the soil. The olive trees waved their laden branches and welcomed him. The grapes had begun to shine; the heavy clusters hung down until they touched the ground. The girls who went by with their white kerchiefs and firm sunburned calves greeted him sweetly: Shalom! Peace!

Sometimes, when not a soul was visible on the path, he heard the heavy footsteps behind him again; a bronze splendour flared up in the air and was then snuffed out, and the evil laughter exploded once more over his head. But the son of Mary forced himself to be patient. He was approaching deliverance; soon he would see the lake opposite him, and behind the blue waters, hanging like a falcon's nest between the red rocks—the monastery. . . .

He followed the path and his mind ran on, but suddenly he stopped, startled. There before him in a sheltered hollow, spread out beneath the date-palms, was Magdala. His mind turned back, turned back, but his feet, against his will, began to lead him with sure steps to the perfumed hermitage of his cousin Magdalene, to the house which was condemned to the fires of hell.

"No, I don't want to go, I don't want to go!" he murmured in terror. He tried to reverse his course, but his body refused. It stood its ground like a greyhound and smelt the air.

I'll go away! he decided once more within himself, but he did not budge. He could see the clean whitewashed houses and the ancient well with its marble brim. Dogs were barking, hens cackling, women laughing. Loaded camels knelt about the well, ruminating. . . . I must see her, must see her, he heard a sweet voice within him say. It's necessary. God has guided my feet— God, not my own mind—because I must see her, fall at her feet and beg her forgiveness. . . . It's my fault, mine! Before I enter the monastery and put on the white gown I must beg her forgiveness. Otherwise it will not be possible for me to be saved. . . . Thank you, Lord, for bringing me where I did not want to come!

He felt happy. Tightening his belt, he began the descent to Magdala.

A herd of camels lay on their bellies around the well. They had finished eating and now, still laden, were slowly, patiently chewing their cud. They must have come from fragrant far-away lands, for the whole area smelt of spices.

Jesus halted at the well. An old woman who was drawing water tipped her jug for him, and he drank. He wanted to ask if Mary was at home, but he was too ashamed. God has pushed me to her house, he reflected. I have faith: she will most certainly be there.

He started down a well-shaded lane. There were many strangers in town, some dressed in the long white jellab of the Bedouins, others with expensive Indian cashmere shawls. A small door opened; a fat-bottomed matron with a black moustache emerged and burst into laughter as soon as she saw him.

"Well, well!" she shouted, "Greetings, carpenter. So you too are going to worship at the shrine, eh?" She closed the door amid peals of laughter.

The son of Mary blushed scarlet, but gathered up strength. I must, I must. . . . , he thought; I must fall at her feet and beg her forgiveness.

He quickened his pace. Her house was at the other end of the village, surrounded by a small orchard of pomegranates. He remembered it well: a green single-leafed door decorated with a painting of two intertwined snakes, one black and one white, the work of one of her lovers, a Bedouin; and above the lintel, a large yellow lizard, its legs stretched out on both sides as though it was being crucified.

He got lost, retraced his steps, returned to where he had been—ashamed to ask his way. It was almost noon. He stopped under the shade of an olive tree to catch his breath. A rich merchant passed by. He had a short black curly beard, black almond-shaped eyes, many rings, and an aristocratic air. The son of Mary followed him.

He must be one of God's angels, he thought as he walked behind him and admired the noble stature of his young body and the expensive cashmere shawl, embroidered with stunning birds and flowers, which covered his shoulders. He must be one of God's angels, and he came down to show me the way.

The foreign nobleman strode unerringly through the winding alleys. Soon the green door with the two intertwined snakes came into view. An old crone sat outside on a stool. She had a grate filled with burning coals and was broiling crabs. Next to this were roasted pumpkin-seeds and in two deep wooden plates, chick-pea meatballs which she sold smothered in pepper.

The young nobleman bent over, gave a silver coin to the old lady, and entered. The son of Mary entered behind him.

Four merchants, lined up one behind the other, sat cross-legged on the ground of the courtyard: two old men with painted eye-lashes and nails, two young men with black beards and moustaches. They all had their eyes riveted on the tiny squat door of Mary's chamber. It was closed. Now and then a shout issued from inside, or laughter, or the sound of someone being tickled, or the creaking of the bed—and the worshippers immediately broke off the chattering they had begun and, gasping for breath, shifted their positions. The Bedouin who had entered such a long time ago was late in coming out, and all the others in the courtyard, young and old alike, were in a hurry. The young Indian nobleman sat down in his place in the queue, and behind him sat the son of Mary.

An immense pomegranate tree laden with fruit was in the middle of the court and two imposing cypresses stood on either side of the street-door, one male with a trunk as straight as a sword, the other female with wide open spreading branches. Suspended from the pomegranate was a wicker cage containing a richly-decorated partridge which hopped up and down, nipped, kicked her rails and cackled.

The worshippers were munching dates which they took from their girdles, or biting nutmeg seeds to sweeten their breath. They had engaged each other in conversation in order to pass the time. Turning, they greeted the young nobleman, and looked with disdain at the poorly-dressed son of Mary behind him. The old man who was first in line sighed.

"There's no martyrdom greater than mine," he said. "Here I am in front of Paradise, and the door is closed."

A youth with golden bands around his ankles laughed:

"I transport spices from the Euphrates to the Great Sea. Do you see this partridge with the red claws here in front of us? I'm going to buy Mary with a shipment of cinnamon and pepper, put her in a gold cage and take her away. So, my lusty friends—what you have to do, do it quickly: it's the last kiss you'll get."

"Thanks, my good-looking stalwart," the second old man interrupted at this point. He had a snowy-white scented beard and slim-boned aristocratic hands, the palms of which were dyed with cinchona. "Thanks, what you've just said will season today's kiss that much more."

The young nobleman had lowered his heavy eyelids. His upper body swayed slowly back and forth and his lips stirred as though he was saying his prayers. Already, before entering Paradise, he had plunged into everlasting beatitude. He heard the cackling of the partridge, the tickling and the creaking inside the bolted chamber, heard the old woman at the door load her grate with live crabs, which then hopped onto the coals. . .

This is Paradise, he meditated, overcome with a great lassitude, this, the deep sleep we call life, the sleep in which we dream of Paradise. There is no other Paradise. I can get up now and go, for I require no further joy. . . .

A huge green-turbaned man in front of him pushed him with his knee and laughed. "Prince of India, what does your God have to say about all this?"

The youth opened his eyes. "All what?" he asked.

"Here, in front of you: men, women, crabs, love. . ."

"That everything is a dream.

"Well then, my brave lads—take care," interrupted the old man with the snowy beard, who was telling his beads on a long amber chaplet, "take care not to wake up!"

The small door opened and the Bedouin emerged. Swollen-eyed, he came forward slowly, licking his chops. The old man whose turn was next jumped up at once, as nimble as a strapping twenty-year-old boy.

"Bye-bye, grandpa. Pity us and do it fast!" yelled the three whose turns followed.

But the old man was already removing his belt and advancing towards the chamber. This was no time for chatter! He entered and slammed the door behind him.

They all eyed the Bedouin with envy, no one daring to speak. They sensed that he was cruising over deep waters far far away, and indeed he did not so much as turn to look at them. He staggered through the courtyard, reached the street-door, missed knocking over the old crone's grate by a fraction of an inch, and disappeared finally into the crooked lanes. At that point, in order to redirect their thoughts, the huge fat man with the green turban started out of a clear sky to talk about lions, seas and far-away coral isles. . . .

The time went by. Now and then the slow gentle clicking of the amber beads could be heard. All eyes were pinned once more on the squat doorway. The old man was late, very late, in coming out.

The young Indian nobleman got up. The others turned with astonishment. Why had he got up? Wasn't he going to enjoy his kisses? Was he about to leave? . . . He was happy. His face was

91

resplendent; a gentle glow patched his cheeks. He wrapped the cashmere shawl tightly around him, put his hand to his heart and lips, and took his leave. His shadow passed tranquilly over the threshold.

"He woke up. . . ," said the youth with the golden rings about his ankles. He tried to laugh, but a strange fear had suddenly overcome them all and they began with anxious haste to discuss profit and loss, and the prices current in the slave markets of Alexandria and Damascus. . . . Soon, however, they reverted to their barefaced talk of women and boys, and they stuck out their tongues and licked their chops.

"Lord, O Lord," the son of Mary murmured, "where have you thrown me? Into what kind of yard? To queue up with what kind of men! This, Lord, is the greatest degradation of all. Give me strength to endure it!"

The pilgrims were hungry. One of them shouted and the old crone entered, portioned out bread, crabs and meatballs to the four men, and brought them a jug of date-wine. They crossed their legs, placed the meal in their laps and began to clap their jaws. One of them, feeling in a good mood, threw a large crab-shell at the door and shouted, "Hey, grandpa, do it quick, don't take all day!" They all burst into peals of laughter.

"Lord, O Lord," the son of Mary murmured again, "give me the strength to stay until my turn comes."

The old man with the scented beard felt sorry for him.

"Hey you, my fine lad," he said, turning, "aren't you hungry or thirsty? Come here and have a bite—it will give you strength."

"Yes, poor fellow, you'd better eat," the colossus with the green turban added, laughing. "When your turn comes and you go inside, we don't want you to put us men to shame."

The son of Mary blushed scarlet, lowered his head and did not speak.

"This one's dreaming too," said the old man, shaking out the crumbs and bits of crab which had filled his beard. "Yes, by Saint Beelzebub, he's dreaming. He'll get up now like the other and leave, mark my words."

The son of Mary looked around him, terrified. Could the Indian nobleman really be right? Could all this—yard, pomegranate, grate, partridge, men—be a dream? Perhaps he was still under the cedar, dreaming.

He turned towards the street-door as though seeking help, and saw his eagle-headed fellow-voyager standing motionless next to the male cypress, armed to the teeth in bronze. Now, for the first time, the sight of her made him feel relieved and secure.

The old man came out, panting, and the huge green-turbaned man went in. Hours later came the turn of the youth with the golden bands around his ankles, then that of the old man with the amber rosary. The son of Mary now remained all alone in the yard, waiting.

The sun was about to set. Two clouds were sailing in the sky. They stopped, laden with gold. A thin gilding of frost fell over trees, soil and the faces of men.

The old man with the amber rosary came out. Stopping for a moment on the threshold, he wiped his running eyes, nose and lips, then shuffled with drooping shoulders towards the street-door.

The son of Mary got up and turned to the male cypress. His companion lifted her foot, ready to follow behind him. He wanted to speak to her, to beg her to wait for him outside the door, to tell her that he wished to be alone, that he would not run away; but he knew his words would go to waste, and he remained silent. Tightening the strap around his middle, he raised his eyes and looked at the heavens. He hesitated, but a hoarse voice called angrily from within the chamber: "Is there anyone else? Come in!" It was Magdalene. Summoning all his strength, he went forward. The door was half-open and he entered, trembling.

Magdalene lay on her back, stark naked, drenched in sweat, her raven-black hair spread out over the pillow and her arms entwined beneath her head. Her face was turned towards the wall and she was yawning. Wrestling with men on this bed since dawn had tired her out. Her hair, nails and every inch of her body exuded smells of all nations, and her arms, neck and breasts were covered with bites.

The son of Mary lowered his eyes. He had stopped in the middle of the room, unable to go further. Magdalene waited without moving, her face turned towards the wall. But she heard no masculine grunts behind her, no one getting undressed, not even a panting breath. Frightened, she abruptly turned her face in order to see—and all at once uttered a cry, seized the sheet and wrapped herself up.

"You! You!" she shouted, covering her lips and eyes with her palms.

"Mary," he said, "forgive me!"

Magdalene burst into a fit of hoarse heart-rending laughter. You thought her vocal cords were about to snap into a thousand pieces.

"Mary," he repeated, "forgive me!"

And then she jumped up onto her knees, tightly enclosed in the sheet, and lifted her fist:

"Is this why you entered my yard, my young gallant? Is this why you mixed yourself in with my lovers: to hoax your way into my house in order to bring God the bogeyman down to me here on my hot bed? Well, you're late, my friend, very late; and as for your God, I don't want him—he's already broken my heart!"

She moaned and spoke at the same time, and her infuriated breast heaved up and down behind the sheet.

"He's broken my heart, broken my heart. . . ," she moaned again, and two tears welled up into her eyes and remained suspended on her long lashes. . . .

"Don't blaspheme, Mary. I'm to blame, not God. That's why I came: I want to beg your forgiveness."

But Magdalene exploded:

"You and your God have the identical snout; you're one and the same and I can't tell you apart. Sometimes I happen to think of him at night, and when I do—curse the hour!—it's with your face that he bears down on me out of the darkness; and when I chance to meet you on the street—curse the hour!—I feel that it's still God I see rushing directly for me."

She lifted her fist into the air:

"Don't bother me with God," she yelled. "Get out of here and don't let me see you again. There's only one refuge and consolation for me—the mud! Only one synagogue where I enter to pray and cleanse myself—the mud!"

"Mary, listen to me, let me speak, don't fall into despair. That's

94

exactly what I've come for, my sister: to pull you out of the mud. I have committed many sins—I'm on my way to the desert now to expiate them—many sins, Mary, but your calamity weighs on me the most."

Magdalene thrust her sharp nails towards the unexpected guest, maniacally, as though she wanted to tear open his cheeks.

"What calamity?" she shrieked. "I'm getting along fine, just fine; I don't need your holiness's compassion! I fight my own fight, all alone, and I ask no help from men, or from gods or devils either. I'm fighting to save myself, and save myself I will."

"Save yourself from what, from whom?"

"Not, as you think, from the mud, God bless it! That's where all my hopes are—in the mud. It's my road of salvation."

"The mud?"

"Yes, the mud: shame, filth, this bed, this body of mine, covered as it is with bites and bemired with the whole world's drivel, sweat and slime! Don't cast your covetous sheep's eye upon me like that. Keep your distance, coward! I don't want you here. You disgust me, don't touch me! In order to forget one man, in order to save myself—I've surrendered my body to all men!"

The son of Mary lowered his head.

"It's my fault," he repeated in a strangulated voice, and he clutched the strap which was tied around him, still splashed with blood. "Forgive me, my sister. It's my fault, but I shall pay off my debt."

Savage laughter again tore the woman's throat:

"You bleat away piteously: 'It's my fault. . . , it's my fault, my sister. . . , I shall save you. . . ,' but oh no, you don't lift your head like a man to confess the truth. You crave my body, and instead of saying so, which you wouldn't dare, you start blaming my soul and saying you want to save it. What soul, day-dreamer? A woman's soul is her flesh. You know it, you know it; but you don't have the courage to take this soul in your arms like a man and kiss it—kiss it and save it! I pity you and detest you!"

"You're possessed with seven devils, strumpet!" cried the youth now, who had turned fiery red with shame. "Seven devils. Yes, your unlucky father is right."

Magdalene shuddered. She angrily gathered her hair into a coil and tied it up with a ribbon of red silk. For a considerable time she did not speak, but finally her lips moved:

"Not seven devils, son of Mary, not seven devils—seven wounds. You must learn that a woman is a wounded doe. She has no other joy, poor thing, except to lick her wounds. . . ."

Her eyes filled with tears. She wiped them away with one sweep of her palm, then exploded in a frenzy:

"Why did you come here? What do you want from me, standing over my bed like that? Go away!"

The young man came one step closer.

"Mary, try to remember back to when we were still small children. . ."

"I don't remember! What kind of man are you? Still drivelling? You ought to be ashamed of yourself! You never had the courage to stand up by yourself like a man and not rely on anyone. If you're not hanging on to your mother's apron strings, you're hanging on to mine, or God's. You can't stand by yourself, because you're scared. You don't dare look deep into your own soul —or into your body for that matter—because you're scared. And now you're off to the desert to hide, to stick your snout into the sand—because you're scared! Scared, scared! Poor fellow, I detest you, I pity you, and whenever I bring you to mind, my heart cracks in two."

Unable to continue, she began to weep. Although she wiped her eyes rabidly, the tears, together with her make-up, ran more and more furiously and bemired the sheets.

The young man felt a spasm in his heart. Oh, if he could only lose his fear of God, could only clasp her in his arms, wipe away her tears, caress her hair and gladden her heart; then take her with him and leave!

If he was a man, truly, that was what he had to do to save her. What did she care about fasting, prayer and monasteries? No, these were not the way—how could they possibly save a woman? To take her from this bed, to leave, to open a workshop in a distant village, for the two of them to live like man and wife, have children, suffer and rejoice like human beings: that was the woman's way of salvation and the way in which the man could be saved with her—the only way!

Night was falling now. Far in the distance thunder rumbled; a flash of lightning entered through a crack in the door and ignited Mary's now-livid face, only to snuff it out again. New thunderclaps were heard, closer than before. The choking sky had come down and nearly touched the earth.

A great weariness suddenly overcame the youth. His knees sagged; he sat down cross-legged on the ground. The nauseating stench of musk, sweat and he-goats hit his nostrils. He stroked his throat with his palm so that he would not throw up.

He heard Mary's voice in the darkness: "Turn your head the other way. I want to get up to light the lamp, and I'm naked."

"I'm going to leave," said the youth, softly. Summoning up all his strength, he rose.

But Mary pretended that she had not heard. "Take a look in the yard, and if anyone's still there, tell him to go away."

The youth opened the door and put out his head. The air had become dark. Large scattered drops were being slung at the pomegranate-leaves; the sky hung over the earth, ready to fall. The old crone had taken her lighted grate and burrowed into the yard, where she stood glued to the trunk of the male cypress. The heavy drops began to come down harder and harder.

"No one," said the youth, quickly closing the door. The squall had now lashed out in full force.

Magdalene had jumped out of bed in the meantime and covered herself with a warm woollen shawl embroidered with lions and deer, presented to her that morning by a loving Ethiopian. Her shoulders and loins shuddered with delight at the sweet warmth of the garment. Stretching up on tip-toe, she unhooked the lamp from the wall.

"No one," the youth repeated, with gladness in his voice.

"The old lady. . .?"

"Under the cypress. It's a real squall."

Mary flew into the yard, discovered the lighted grate in the darkness, and approached.

"Grandma Noemi," she said, pointing towards the bolt of the street-door, "take your grate and your crabs and go home. I'll lock up. No one else tonight!"

"You've got your lover inside, eh?" hissed the old woman, vexed at losing her night-customers.

"Yes," Magdalene answered, "he's inside. Go!"

Grumbling, the old lady got up and gathered together her utensils.

"He's a real beauty, your ragamuffin," she mumbled softly with her toothless gums, but Mary, who was in a hurry, shoved her outside and barred the door. The heavens had opened; the whole sky was pouring into her yard. She uttered a shrill cry of joy, just as she used to do as a child every time she saw the first autumn rain. When she got inside, her shawl was drenched.

The youth stood in the middle of the room, unable to make up his mind whether to stay or go. Which was God's will? It was pleasant here, and warm; he had even become accustomed to the nauseating odour. Outside: wind, rain and cold. He knew no one in Magdala, and Capernaum was far away. Should he go, or stay? His soul swung back and forth like a ringing bell.

"It's coming down in buckets, Jesus. I bet you haven't eaten a thing today. Help me light the fire and we'll cook. . . ." Her voice was tender and attentive, like a mother's.

"I'm going to leave," said the youth, turning towards the door.

"Sit down and we'll eat together!" Magdalene ordered. "Does the thought disgust you? Are you afraid you'll pollute yourself by eating with a whore?"

The youth took logs and kindling from the corner, bent down by the stone jamb of the fireplace, in front of the two andirons, and lit the fire.

Magdalene's heart had grown calm. Smiling now, she filled a pot with water and placed it on the fire. From a sack hanging on the wall she took two heaping handfuls of de-eyed broad beans and threw them in. Then she knelt in front of the lighted fire and listened. Outside, the flood-gates of heaven had opened up.

"Jesus," she said quietly, "you asked me if I remembered when we were children and played together. . ."

But the young man, kneeling like Magdalene in front of the hearth, simply stared at the fire, his mind far away. He felt as though he had already reached the monastery in the desert, as though he had put on the white robe and begun to promenade in

98

the solitude; and his heart was a small happy goldfish swimming in the deep tranquil waters of God. Outside, the world was falling apart; within him: peace, love and security.

"Jesus," the voice next to him repeated, "you asked me if I remembered when we were children and played together. . ."

Magdalene's face, reflecting the light of the flames, glowed like red-hot iron. But the youth, submerged in the desert, did not hear.

"Jesus," the woman said again, "you were three and I was one year older. There were three steps leading to the door of our house and I used to sit on the highest one and watch you struggle for hours, unable to mount the first step. You fell, you got up again, and I did not even lift my little finger to help you. I wanted you to come to me, but not before you suffered greatly. . . . Do you remember?"

A devil, one of her seven devils, was goading her on to speak to the man and tempt him.

"Hours later you would finally manage to climb up the first step. Then you struggled to mount the second. . . , then the third —where I sat, motionless, waiting for you. And then. . ."

The youth gave a start and held out his hand.

"Be still," he shouted; "don't go further!"

But the woman's face gleamed and flickered; the flames licked her eyebrows, lips, chin and uncovered throat. She took a handful of laurel leaves, threw them in the fire, and sighed.

"Then you took me by the hand—yes, you took me by the hand, Jesus—and we went inside and lay down on the pebbles of the yard. We glued the soles of our feet together, felt the warmth of our bodies mix, rise from our feet to our thighs, from our thighs to our loins. Then we closed our eyes and. . ."

"Quiet!" the youth shouted again. He lifted his hand in order to cover her mouth, but restrained himself—he was afraid to touch her lips.

The woman sighed now and continued, lowering her voice to a murmur:

"Never in my whole life have I felt such sweetness." She paused, and then:

"It is that sweetness, Jesus, which I've been seeking ever since from man to man; but I have not found it. . . ."

99

The youth buried his face between his knees. "Adonai," he murmured, "Adonai, help!"

The warm peaceful chamber was silent except for the bubbling of the fragrant pot of beans, and the hissing of the fire as it devoured the wood. Outside, the male waters poured out of the skies with a roar and the earth opened its thighs and giggled.

"Jesus, what are you thinking about?" asked Magdalene, not daring now to face the man.

"I'm thinking about God," he answered in a strangulated voice, "about God, Adonai. . ."

As he spoke, he repented of having pronounced the sacred name in such a house as this.

Magdalene jumped up and paced back and forth between the fire and the door. Her mind had grown furious.

God is the great enemy, she was thinking, yes, God. He never fails to intrude; he is evil, jealous; he won't let a person be happy. . . . She stopped behind the door and cocked her ear. The heavens were bellowing. A whirlwind had arisen and the pomegranates in the yard knocked against one another and were ready to break.

"The rain has let up a little," she said.

"I'll go," replied the youth, rising.

"Eat first and put some strength into your body. Where can you go at such an hour? It's pitch-black outside and still raining."

She took down a round mat from the wall and spread it out on the floor. She removed the casserole from the fire, opened a small cupboard recessed in the wall and took out a toasted barley-roll and two earthenware soup plates.

"This is the prostitute's meal," she said. "Eat, you essence of piety, eat—if it doesn't disgust you."

The hungry youth did not hesitate to put out his hand. The woman tittered.

"Is that the way you eat?" she hissed. "Without saying grace? Hadn't you better give thanks to God for sending bread, broad beans and whores?"

Jesus' mouthful stuck in his throat.

"Why do you hate me, Mary?" he said. "Why do you tease me?

Look, tonight I am about to break bread with you; we have become friends again. Let bygones be bygones, and forgive me. That's why I've come."

"Eat, and stop your whining. If the forgiveness is not given, take it! You're a man."

She lifted her hand and divided the bread, laughing:

"Blessed be the name of Him who sends bread, broad beans and whores to the world—and pious guests!"

They remained kneeling one opposite the other under the light of the lamp, and said nothing more. Both were hungry, both had suffered much anguish on this day, and they ate to replenish their forces.

The rain outside began to subside. The sky had found relief, the earth was filled. There was no sound except the cackling laughter of the rivulets which ran happily down the village's cobbled streets.

They finished eating. The tiny cupboard also contained a sip of wine, which they drank, and several fully ripe dates for the sweet-tooth. For some time, both remained silent and watched the fire, which was about to go out. Their minds rose and fell, danced with the dying flames.

It was cold. The youth got up and put more wood on the fire; Magdalene took another handful of laurel leaves and threw them on top: perfume filled the room. She went to the door and opened it. A wind had arisen, the clouds had already scattered. Two large stars, freshly-bathed and immaculate, gleamed brilliantly over her yard.

"Is it still raining?" asked the youth, who stood again in the middle of the room, unable to make up his mind.

But Magdalene did not answer. She unrolled a mat, went to her trunk, took out sheets and thick woollen blankets—gifts from her lovers—and made up a bed in front of the fire.

"You'll sleep here," she said. "It's cold and windy out, and almost midnight. Where can you go? You'll catch your death of cold. Here's where you're going to sleep: next to the fire.

The youth shuddered.

"Here!"

"Are you afraid? Well, rest assured, my innocent dove, I won't bother you. No, I won't tempt you, I won't touch your virginity, my pet—such as it's worth!"

She put still more wood on the fire, and lowered the wick of the lamp.

"Pleasant dreams," she said. "Tomorrow we both have much to do. You'll set out along the road again, to seek your salvation; I'll set out along another road, my own, and I too will be seeking salvation. Each his own road, and we shall never meet again. . . . Good night."

She fell onto her mattress and thrust her face into the pillow, biting the sheets all night long to hold back her cries and tears. She was afraid that if the man who was sleeping next to the fire heard her, he would take fright and leave. All night long she listened to him breathe tranquilly, restfully, like an infant nursing at the breast; and she, lamenting softly within herself with tender protracted sighs, lay awake and lulled him to sleep like a mother.

The next day at dawn she looked out between half-closed eyelashes and saw him get up, secure the leather strap tightly about his waist, and open the door. There he halted. He wanted to leave, but at the same time he did not want to leave. Turning, he looked at the bed and took a hesitating step towards it. He leaned over it—it still was not very bright inside the room—he leaned over as though he wanted to find the woman and touch her. His left hand was thrust beneath the strap; with his right he covered his chin and mouth.

The woman lay on her back, motionless, her hair veiling her naked breasts. She watched him through her eyelashes, and her whole body trembled.

His lips moved:

"Mary. . ."

But as soon as he heard his own voice, he took fright. He reached the threshold with one bound, strode hurriedly across the courtyard and unbolted the door.

And then—jolting up from her mattress and throwing off the sheets—then Mary Magdalene began to weep.

VIII

THE monastery lay perched in the desert beyond the lake of Gennesaret, built of ash-red stones and wedged-in and hidden between huge ash-red rocks. Midnight. . . . Out of the sky the waters fell not in drops, but in floods. The hyenas, wolves and jackals howled, as did a pair of lions further away—infuriated by the repeated thunderclaps. Plunged in impenetrable darkness, the monastery was frequently striped by the lightning flashes: the God of Sinai seemed to be flogging it. The monks were fallen face downward in their cells, beseeching Adonai not to drown the earth once more. Hadn't he given his word to the patriarch Noah? Hadn't he stretched a rainbow from earth to heaven as a sign of friendship?

The only light was in the Abbot's cell. Joachim, the Abbot, sat beneath the seven-branched candelabrum in his elevated stall of cypress-wood and listened—skinny, short of breath, his white beard like a river, his arms crossed, eyes closed—listened to John, the young novice, who stood at the lectern and read to him from the prophet Daniel:

" 'A night vision fell upon me. I saw the four winds of heaven bound over the Great Sea. And four large beasts came up out of the sea and the one did not resemble the other. The first was like a lion and had the wings of an eagle. I beheld until its wings were uprooted and it was made to stand upright on its feet like a man; and a man's heart was wedged into its breast. And behold, there emerged a second beast and it resembled a bear; and someone said to it, Arise, devour much flesh. I looked and lo, a third beast. It resembled a leopard and had four wings on its back, like a bird. This beast had four heads, and dominion was given to it. . .' "

The novice felt uneasy and stopped. He no longer heard the Abbot sigh or drive his nails with agitation into the stall; no longer even heard him breath. Could he have died? For days and days now he had refused to put food into his mouth. He was angry with God and wanted to die. He wanted to die—that he made absolutely clear to the brothers—so that his soul might be unburdened of the body, might be relieved of this weight and enabled to ascend to heaven in order to find God. He had a complaint to settle with him: it was necessary for him to see him and talk to him. But the body was lead, it prevented his ascent. He decided therefore to send it about its business, to abandon it in the grave so that the true Joachim could ascend to heaven and tell God his grievance. This was his duty. Wasn't he one of the Fathers of Israel? The people had mouths, but no voice. They could not stand in front of God and relate their suffering. But Joachim could: he had no choice!

The novice turned and looked. Beneath the seven flames the Abbot's head—pitted like old worm-eaten wood, roughened by the sun and fasting: how it resembled the primordial rain-washed skulls of beasts which caravans sometimes encountered in the desert! What visions that head had seen, how many times heaven had opened up before it, how many times the bowels of hell! His mind was a Jacob's ladder on which all of Israel's anxieties and hopes climbed up and down.

Opening his eyes, the Abbot saw the novice standing before him, deathly pale. In the light of the menorah the blond fuzz on his cheeks glowed in all its virginity, and his eyes, swept away far into the distance, were full of affliction.

The Abbot's severe expression sweetened. He loved this well-formed youth whom he had snatched from old Zebedee, his father, and brought here to be delivered up to God. He liked his submissiveness and ferocity, the silent lips and insatiable eyes, his sweetness and quick intelligence. One day, he reflected, this boy will speak with God, will do what I could not do; and the two wounds which I have on my shoulder, he will transform into wings. I did not rise to heaven during my lifetime, he will during his.

The boy had come to the monastery once with his parents. It was to celebrate the Passover. The Abbot, a distant relation of old Zebedee's, received them merrily and sat them at his own table. John was about sixteen years old at the time. While he ate, bent over his food, he felt the Abbot's eye fall upon his scalp, push aside the bones, pass through the suture-lines of his skull, into the brain. Terrified, he looked up and the two glances joined in mid-air over the paschal table. . . . From that day on, neither fishing boats nor the lake of Gennesaret had been large enough for the boy. He sighed and withered away until one morning old Zebedee grew weary and shouted: "Your mind isn't on the fishing, it's on God. Well, go on, go to the monastery. I had two sons. God willed that I divide them with him, so let's divide them and be done with it—and let him have his way!". . .

The Abbot gazed at the boy who stood before him. He had intended to scold him, but as he looked at him, his expression sweetened.

"Why did you stop, my child?" he asked. "You abandoned the vision in the middle. One mustn't do that. He's a prophet, and prophets must be revered."

The boy turned fiery red, rolled the leathern scroll out on the lectern once more, and began again, chanting on one invariable note, to read:

"'After this I saw in my night visions a fourth beast, dreadful and sinister and terribly strong; and it had great iron teeth. It devoured and broke in pieces, and trampled the remainder with its feet. It did not resemble any of the other beasts; and it had ten horns. . .'"

"Stop!" shouted the Abbot. "That's enough!"

The cry frightened the boy, and the sacred text rolled down onto the flagstones. He picked it up, placed his lips to it and kissed it; then went and stood in the corner, his eyes riveted on his superior. The Abbot, his fingernails now clawed into the stall, was shouting:

"Daniel, all your prophecies have been fulfilled. The four beasts have passed over us. The lion with the wings of the eagle came and tore us open, the bear who feeds on Hebrew flesh came and ate us, the four-headed leopard came and bit us, east, west, north and south. The shameful beast with the iron teeth and the ten horns sits now above us: he has not come yet, has not fled. All the ignominy and fear you prophesied you would send us, Lord, you have sent—and we thank you! But you prophesied good things too. Why haven't you sent those? Why are you so tight-fisted where they are concerned? You've given us a liberal supply of calamities; now give us generously of your benefits! Where is the Son of man you promised us? . . . John, read!"

The boy moved away from the corner where he had been standing with the scroll under his shirt. Going up to the lectern, he began again to read. But his voice, like his superior's, had now grown fierce:

" 'I looked in my night visions and behold, one like a son of man came upon the clouds of heaven and approached the Ancient of days, and was brought near to him. And to him was given dominion and glory and the kingdom, and all peoples, nations and men of all tongues served him. His dominion is an everlasting dominion, that shall never end; and his kingdom is indestructible.' "

The Abbot, unable to restrain himself any longer, left his stall, took one step, then one more, reached the lectern, tripped and was about to fall, but managed to put his palm heavily down on the holy manuscript and steady himself.

"Where is the Son of man you promised us? Did you give us your word or didn't you? You can't deny it—here it is in writing!" He banged his hand angrily, exultantly on the prophecy. "Here it is in writing! John, read it again!"

But the Abbot could not wait. Before the novice had time to start, he seized the scripture, lifted it high into the light and began without looking, to cry out in a triumphant voice:

" 'To him was given dominion and glory and the kingdom, and all peoples, nations and men of all tongues served him. His dominion is an everlasting dominion, that shall never end; and his kingdom is indestructible.' "

He left the scroll open on the lectern and looked through the window at the darkness outside.

"Well, where is the Son of man?" he shouted, gazing into the blackness. "He isn't yours any more, seeing that you promised him to us—he's ours! Well, where is he! Why don't you give him dominion, glory and the kingdom so that your people, the people of Israel, can govern the whole universe? Our necks are stiff from watching the sky and waiting for it to open. When, when? Yes—why do you harp on it—we know well enough that one second for you is a thousand years for men. All right, but if you're just, Lord, you'll measure the time with man's measure, not with yours. That's what justice means!"

He started towards the window, but his knees sagged and he halted and thrust out his hands as though he wanted to steady himself on the air. The boy ran to support him, but the Abbot grew angry and nodded to him not to touch him. Calling up all his strength, he reached the window, leaned against the wall, extended his head as far as he could, and looked out. Darkness. . . . The flashes of lightning were fewer now, but the waters still thundered down upon the rocks which flanked the monastery. Every time the cacti were hit by lightning they seemed to whirl about and be transformed: they became a nation of mutilees with the leprous stumps of their arms lifted towards the sky.

Tensing body and soul, the Abbot listened. From afar in the distance came the howling of the wild game of the desert. The animals were not hungry, they were afraid. Close by, almost on top of them, a beast wrapped in fire and whirlwind bellowed and approached in the darkness. . . . The Abbot listened to the voices of the desert and as he listened suddenly he shuddered and turned. Some invisible being had entered his cell! He looked. The seven flames of the candelabrum flickered turbulently and were on the point of going out; the nine strings of the harp which was leaning unused in a corner vibrated wildly, as though some invisible hand had seized them in a fury in order to snap them. The Abbot began to tremble.

"John," he said softly, looking around him, "come here, close to me."

The boy flew out of his corner and approached.

"Command me, Father," he said, and he placed his knee on the ground, to prostrate himself.

"John, go and call the monks. I have something to tell them before I depart."

"Before you depart, Father?"

The boy shuddered. Two large black wings, beating in back of the old man, had caught his eye.

"I'm going," said the Abbot, and his voice suddenly seemed to come from beyond the other shore, "I'm going! Didn't you see the seven flames lurch and draw away from their wicks? Didn't you hear the nine strings of the harp vibrate madly, ready to snap? I'm going, John. Run and call the monks—I want to speak to them."

The boy bowed his head and disappeared. The Abbot remained standing in the middle of the cell under the seven-branched candelabrum. Now at last he was alone with God: he could speak his mind freely, with no fear of being overheard. He lifted his head calmly; he knew that God stood before him.

"I'm coming, I'm coming," he said to him. "Why do you enter my cell, why do you try to put out the light, shatter the harp and capture me? I'm coming, and not only of your will, but of my own. I'm coming. I hold in my hands the tables on which the complaints of my people are written. I want to see you and speak to you. I know you don't listen or at least pretend you don't listen, but I shall bang on your door until you open, and if you don't open (nobody's here now to hear me, so I'll speak freely) if you don't open your door, I shall break it down! You're fierce, you love fierce people—they alone you name your sons. Until now we have wept, prostrated ourselves and said: Your will be done! But we cannot last any longer, Lord. How long are we going to wait? You are fierce, you love fierce people—we shall become fierce. Our wills be done now—ours!"

As the Abbot spoke he kept his ear tensed so that he could hear whatever was in the air. But the rain had abated, the thunder had retreated into the distance: the claps were muffled and came from the east, far away over the desert. The seven flames burnt steadily above the old man's white head.

The Abbot waited in silence. He waited a considerable time for the flames to waver again, for the harp to quiver once more with fright. . . . Nothing! He shook his head. "The body of man is accursed," he murmured. "It's the body which always intrudes and refuses to allow the soul to see and hear the Invisible. Slay me, Lord. I want to be able to stand before you free of the dividing-wall of the flesh, so that when you speak to me I shall hear you!"

The door of the cell had opened noiselessly meanwhile and the untimely-awakened monks had filed in, dressed all in white. They stood against the wall like so many ghosts, and waited. They had heard the Abbot's last words, and the breath stuck in their throats. He's talking with God, they said to themselves, he's up-braiding God: now the thunderbolt will fall upon us! They stood against the wall, trembling.

The Abbot looked off into the distance. His eyes were some-where else—they did not see. The novice approached and pros-trated himself.

"They have come, Father," he said. He spoke softly, in order not to frighten him.

The Abbot heard his subordinate's voice. Turning, he saw the others. He moved from the centre of the cell, walking methodic-ally, slowly, holding his moribund body as straight as he was able. He reached the stall, mounted the low stool in front, and halted. The phylactery with the holy apophthegms which was around his arm came undone. The novice darted forward in time to retie it tightly, before it could be soiled by touching the ground on which we walk. The Abbot put out his hand and grasped the ivory-hilted abbot's crosier which was next to the stall. Feeling new strength, he tossed his head high and swept his eyes over the monks who were lined up against the wall.

"Friars," he said, "I have a few words to say to you—my last. Open your ears, and if anyone is sleepy, let him leave! What I am about to say is difficult. All your hopes and fears must wake up and alert their ears, in order to give me an answer!"

"We're listening, Holy Abbot," said Father Habakkuk, the oldest of the Abbot's suite, and he placed his hand over his heart.

"These are my last words, friars. You're all thick-headed, so I shall speak in parables."

"We're listening, Holy Abbot," Father Habakkuk repeated.

The Abbot bowed his head and lowered his voice:

"First came the wings and then the angel!"

He stopped, glanced at the monks one by one, then shook his head.

"Friars, why do you look at me like that, with open mouths? Father Habakkuk, you raised your hand and moved your lips. Do you have some objection?"

The monk put his hand to his heart.

"You said: 'First came the wings and then the angel.'. . . We never noticed those words in Scripture, Holy Abbot."

"How could you have noticed them, Father Habakkuk? Alas! your minds are still dim. You open the prophets and your eyes are able to see nothing but the letters. But what can the letters say? They are the black bars of the prison where the spirit strangles itself with screaming. Between the letters and the lines, and all around the blank margins, the spirit circulates freely; and I circulate with it and bring you this great message: Friars, first came the wings and then the angel!"

Father Habakkuk reopened his mouth:

"Our minds, Holy Abbot, are lamps which have gone out. Light them, light them so that we may enter into the parable, and see."

"In the beginning, Father Habakkuk, was the longing for freedom. Freedom did not exist, but suddenly, at the very depths of slavery, one man moved his manacled hands quickly, violently—as though they were wings; and then another, and another, and finally the entire people."

Questioning voices rang out joyfully: "The people of Israel?"

"Yes, friars, the people of Israel! This is the great and terrible moment which we are now passing through. The yearning for freedom has grown ferocious, the wings are beating wildly; the liberator is coming! Yes, friars, the liberator is coming, because ... Wait—this angel of freedom: what do you think he's made of? Of God's condescension and charity? Of his love? his justice? No, this angel is made of the patience, obstinacy and struggle of mankind!"

"You place a great obligation, an unbearable weight on man, Holy Abbot," old Habakkuk ventured to object. "Do you have that much confidence in him?"

But the Abbot ignored the objection. His mind was riveted on the Messiah.

"He is one of our sons," he cried. "That is why the Scriptures call him the Son of man! Why do you think thousands of Israel's men and women have coupled, generation after generation? To rub their backsides and titillate their groins? No! All those thousands and thousands of kisses were needed to produce the Messiah!"

The Abbot banged his crosier vigorously against the stall. "Take care, friars! He may come in the middle of the day, he may come in the middle of the night. Keep yourselves constantly prepared: bathed, hungry, wakeful. Woe is you if he finds you filthy, satiated or asleep!"

The monks herded one against the other and dared not look up to see the Abbot. They felt a wild flame flow out of the top of his head and attack them.

Coming down from his stall, the moribund advanced with firm steps towards the frightened herd of fathers. He held out his crosier and touched them one by one.

"Take care, friars!" he cried. "If the yearning is broken off for even an instant, the wings become chains again. Stay vigilant, fight, keep the torch of your soul burning day and night. Strike! Forge the wings! I'm going—I am in a hurry to speak to God. I'm going. . . . These are my final words: Strike! Forge the wings!"

Suddenly he stopped breathing, and the crosier slid out of his hand. Without a sound the old man fell tranquilly, gently down on his knees and rolled silently onto the flagstones. The novice uttered a cry and ran to help his superior. The monks moved away from the wall, stooped, laid the Abbot out on the stones, and lowered the seven-branched candelabrum and placed it next to his livid, immobile face. His beard gleamed; his white gown had opened, revealing the rough cassock with the sharp iron hooks, which swaddled the old man's bloody chest and flanks.

Father Habakkuk placed his hand over the Abbot's heart:

"He's dead."

"His deliverance has come," said someone else.

"The two friends have parted and returned to their homes," a third person whispered, "the flesh to the soil and the soul to God."

But while they talked and arranged to have water heated in order to wash him, the Abbot opened his eyes. The monks recoiled in terror and gazed at him. His face was resplendent, his thin long-fingered hands moved, his eyes were riveted ecstatically upon the air.

Father Habakkuk knelt and again placed his hand over the Abbot's heart.

'It's beating," he whispered; "he's not dead."

He turned to the novice, who was prostrate at the old man's feet, kissing them.

"Get up, John. Mount the fastest camel and race to Nazareth to bring old Simeon, the rabbi. He'll cure him. Quick, it's getting light!"

Day was breaking. The clouds had scattered; the satiated freshly-bathed earth gleamed and looked up at the heavens with gratitude. Two sparrow-hawks leapt into the sky and flew circles over the monastery to dry off.

Wiping away his tears, the novice went to the stable and chose the fastest camel, a young slender one with a white star on her forehead. He made her kneel, then mounted and let out a yodelling, throaty cry. The camel wrenched herself away from her foundations, stood up and with great strides started to race towards Nazareth.

The morning gleamed over the lake of Gennesaret. The water scintillated in the early light, muddy at the banks from the soil which the rains had washed down during the night, further on blue-green and further still, milky white. The sails of the fishing boats were stretched out to dry. Some boats were already in open waters: the fishing had begun. Rosy-white ringplovers perched happily on the quivering water. Black cormorants stood on the rocks, their round eyes pinned on the lake in case any fish should surface to rollick gleefully in the foam. Next to the shore a Capernaum drenched to the bone was awakening: cocks shook the water from their feathers, donkeys brayed, calves mooed tenderly . . . , and mixed in with these ill-matched sounds, the meaningful talk of human beings added security and gladness to the air.

Ten or so fishermen in an isolated cove, their large feet braced in the pebbles, were singing softly while they slowly, dexterously pulled in the nets. Over them stood old Zebedee, their loquacious and seven-times-cunning boss. He made out that he loved every one of them like a son and pitied them, but he did not give them a moment's rest. They were paid by the day, and voracious old gobble-jaws made sure they did not relax for even a second.

Bells chattered. A herd of goats and sheep bounded towards the shore. Dogs barked, someone whistled. . . . The fishermen turned to look, but old Zebedee rushed forward:

"It's Philip and his philipkins," he said with irritation. "As for us, back to work!"

He grabbed the rope himself and pretended to help.

Fishermen continually appeared from the village, loaded down with nets and followed by their wives, who carried the day's provisions balanced on their heads. Sunburnt boys lost no time in grasping the oars and rowing. They stopped every two or three strokes to bite the dry crusts they held in their hands. Philip stepped up onto a rock where he could be seen, and whistled. He wanted to chat, but old Zebedee frowned. Cupping his hands to his mouth, he shouted:

"Leave us alone, Philip. We've got work to do. Go somewhere else!"—and he turned him a cold shoulder.

"Let him go gab with Jonah, he's over there throwing his nets," he grumbled. "As for us, lads, we've got work to do!" Once more he seized a knot in the rope and began to pull.

The fishermen resumed their sad unvarying work-chant, and all had their eyes glued on the buoys of red gourds, which came continually closer.

But just as they were about to haul the womb of the net with its load of fish up onto the beach, they heard a dreary buzzing in the distance, all over the plain, accompanied by shrill cries like those of the dirge. Old Zebedee tensed his huge hairy ear in order to hear distinctly, and his men seized the opportunity and stopped work.

"What's happened, lads?" Zebedee asked. "That's the dirge, the women are lamenting."

"Some great man died," an aged fisherman answered him. "May God grant you a long life, boss."

But old Zebedee had already climbed up onto a rock. His rapacious eyes swept over the plain, where he could see men and women running to the fields, falling, getting up again—and raising the dirge. The whole village began to turn upside-down. Women passed by pulling out their hair, but behind them the men walked in silence, bowed down to the earth.

"What's up?" Zebedee yelled to them. "Hey, where are you going? Why are the women crying?"

But they hurried past him towards the threshing floors and did not answer.

"Hey, where are you going? Who died?" howled Zebedee, waving his hands. "Who died?"

A stocky man halted, puffing.

"The wheat!" he replied.

"Speak sensibly. I'm Zebedee, people don't joke with me. Who died?"

He was answered by cries which came from every direction:

"The wheat, the barley, the bread!"

Old Zebedee remained standing with gaping mouth. But suddenly he slapped his behind—he understood. "It's the flood," he murmured; "it washed the harvest off the threshing floors. . . . Well, let the poor complain, it's no concern of mine."

The cries now inundated the plain. Every soul in the village had come outdoors. The women fell on the threshing floors and rolled in the mud, hurrying to gather up the small amount of wheat and barley which had been left as sediment in the hollows and furrows. The arms of Zebedee's men fell useless to their sides: they had no strength to pull in the nets. Seeing them all gazing towards the plain with unemployed hands, Zebedee flew into a rage.

"To work!" he shouted, coming down from the rock. "Heave!" Once more he grasped the rope and pretended to pull. "We're fishermen, glory be to God, not farmers. Let the floods come. The fish are expert swimmers and don't drown. Two and two make four!"

Philip abandoned his flock and jumped from stone to stone. He wanted to talk.

"A new deluge, lads!" he shouted, appearing before them. "Stop for God's sake and let's talk. It's the end of the world! Just count up the calamities! Day before yesterday they crucified our great hope, the Zealot. Yesterday God opened the flood-gates of heaven—just exactly when the threshing floors were loaded—and away went our bread. And not very long ago one of my sheep had a two-headed lamb. . . . It's the end of the world, I tell you! For the love of God stop working and let's talk!"

But old Zebedee caught fire.

"Won't you get the hell out of here Philip and leave us alone," he yelled, the blood rising to his head. "Can't you see we've work to do. We're fishermen and you're a shepherd, so let the farmers complain—what do we care? . . . Men, your work!"

"And have you no pity, Zebedee, for the farmers who'll die of hunger?" objected the shepherd. "They're Israelites too, you know, our brothers; we're all one tree, all of us, and it's obvious that the ploughmen are the roots—if they dry out, so do we all. . . . And one thing more, Zebedee: if the Messiah comes and we've all died in the meantime, whom will he find to save? Answer me that if you can!"

Old Zebedee huffed and puffed. If you'd pinched his nostrils, he surely would have exploded.

"Go on, for the love of God, go back to your philipkins. I'm sick and tired of hearing about Messiahs. One comes along, he's crucified; along comes the next, he's crucified too. And haven't you learnt what message Andrew brought his father Jonah: it seems that wherever you go and wherever you stop, you find a cross. The dungeons are overflowing with Messiahs. . . . Ooo, enough's enough! We've been getting along just fine without Messiahs—they're nothing but a pain in the neck. Go on, bring me some cheese and I'll give you a pan-full of fish. You give me and I give you: that's the Messiah!"

He laughed and turned to his adopted sons.

"Step lively, my brave lads, so that we can light the fire, put on the chowder and eat. Look, the sun's risen a yard and we haven't done a thing."

But no sooner had Philip lifted his foot to go and join his flock, than he halted. A donkey, nearly perishing with a load which reached to its ears, appeared on the narrow path which hugged the shore of the lake, and behind the donkey was a colossus with bare feet, open shirt—and a red beard. He held a forked stick in his hand and prodded the beast: he was in a hurry.

"Look! I think it's old devil-hair himself, Judas Iscariot," said the shepherd, holding his ground. "He's started his rounds to the villages again to shoe mules and make pick-axes. Come on, let's see what he's got to say."

"A plague on him!" murmured old Zebedee. "I don't like his hair. I've heard that his ancestor Cain had a beard like that."

"The unfortunate fellow was born in the desert of Idumea," said Philip. "Lions still roam there, so better not pick an argument with him." He put two fingers into his mouth and began to whistle to the donkey-driver.

"Hello, Judas," he called, "glad to see you. Come over this way a bit so we can get a better look at you."

The redbeard spat and cursed. He did not like this shepherd-fellow, nor did he like Zebedee, that parasite—didn't like them at all. But he was a blacksmith, a man of need, and he approached.

"What news do you bring us from the villages along your route?" Philip asked. "What's happening on the plain?"

The redbeard stopped his donkey by pulling its tail.

"Everything's just fine and dandy," he answered with a dry laugh. "The Lord is exceedingly merciful, bless him! Yes, he loves his people! In Nazareth he crucifies the prophets, and here on the plain he sends a deluge and takes away his people's bread. Can't you hear the lamentations? The women are wailing for the wheat: you'd think it was their own sons."

"Whatever God does is right," Zebedee objected, vexed because all this talk was crippling the day's work. "I have confidence in him no matter what he does. When everyone drowns and I'm the only one to escape, God is protecting me. When everyone else is saved and I'm the only one to drown, God is protecting me then too. I have confidence, I tell you. Two and two make four."

When the redbeard heard these words he forgot that he was a day-labourer who lived from hand to mouth and had to rely on every one of these people for his livelihood. Fired up by his evil disposition, he spoke and did not mince his words:

"You have confidence, Zebedee, only because the Almighty lays a nice soft bed for you and your affairs. Your Worship has five fishing boats in his service; you have fifty fishermen as slaves, you feed them just exactly enough so they'll have strength to work for you and won't die of starvation—and all the while Your Highness stuffs his coffers and his larders, and his belly. Then you raise your hands to heaven and say: God is just, I have confidence in him! The world is beautiful—I hope it never changes! . . . Why don't you ask the Zealot who was crucified the other day why he struggled to free us; or the peasants whose whole year's supply of wheat God snatched away in one night—ask them! They're rolling in the mud right now picking it up grain by grain, and weeping. Or ask me: I go around the villages and see and hear Israel's suffering. How long? How long? Didn't you ever ask yourself that, Zebedee?"

"To tell you the truth," answered the old man, "I have no confidence in red hairs. You're from the stock of Cain, who murdered his brother. Go to the devil, my friend. I don't want to talk with the likes of you!"

This said, he turned his back on him.

The redbeard gave the donkey a swat with the forked stick. The beast drew up its head, slid back into the yoke, bolted forward and began to run.

"Never fear, old parasite," Judas murmured, "the Messiah will come to put everything in order."

When he had got around the rocks, he turned:

"We'll have a chance to discuss all this again, Zebedee," he shouted. "The Messiah will come one day, won't he? He will, and then, personally, he'll put every rascal in his place. You're not the only one who has confidence! See you again, boss—on the day of judgement!"

"Go to hell, redhair!" was Zebedee's reply. The womb of the net had finally become visible, and it was filled with giltheads and red mullets.

Philip stood between the two of them, unable to take sides. What Judas said was true, and courageous. The shepherd had often felt like smearing such words in old gobble-jaw's ugly puss or beating them over his head, but he had never had the courage. This unregenerate was a potent landlord, strong on land and sea. He owned every one of the meadows in which Philip grazed his goats and sheep—so how could the shepherd attack him? One had to be either a madman or a hero, and Philip was neither. He simply talked big, and much; and he never took an unnecessary chance.

He had remained silent therefore while the other two quarrelled, and was still standing by, bashful and irresolute. The fishermen

117

had now pulled in the nets. He bent down with them and helped fill the hampers. Even Zebedee was plunged waist-deep in the water, where he directed men and fish.

But while they all admired the overflowing hampers, completely elated, the redbeard's hoarse voice suddenly echoed from the rock opposite:

"Hey, Zebedee!"

Old Zebedee played deaf. Once more, the voice thundered:

"Hey, Zebedee, take my advice and go collect your son Jacob!"

"Jacob!" the old man cried out in a ferment. As far as his younger son was concerned, the damage was done: he had lost him. He did not want to lose this one too. He had no other son, and he needed him in his work. . . . "Jacob!" he called to Judas in a worried voice. "What do you have to say about Jacob, you confounded redhair?"

"I saw him on the road getting friendly with the cross-maker. They were having a pleasant chat!"

"What cross-maker, infidel? Speak clearly!"

"The son of the Carpenter, the one who builds crosses in Nazareth and crucifies the prophets. . . . Too late! Poor old Zebedee—Jacob's lost too. You had two sons. God snatched the one and the devil the other."

Old Zebedee stood with gaping mouth. A flying-fish bounded out of the water, winged over his head, then dived back into the lake and disappeared.

"A bad sign, a bad sign!" murmured the old man in a panic. "Is my son going to leave me like this, like the flying-fish, and disappear beneath deep waters?"

He turned to Philip.

"Did you see the flying-fish? Nothing that happens in the world is without its meaning. Tell me, what was the meaning of this fish? You shepherds. . ."

"If it had been a lamb, I'd be able to tell you, father Zebedee, even if I'd only seen its back. But fish are not in my department." He was angry because, unlike Judas, he lacked the courage to speak out like a man. "I'm off to see to my animals," he said. Putting his crook over his shoulders, he jumped from rock to rock and caught up with Judas.

"Wait, brother," he called to him. "I want to talk to you."

"Go to your sheep, coward," the redbeard answered him, without turning, "go to your sheep; keep your nose out of men's affairs. . . . And don't call me 'brother'. I'm no brother of yours!"

"Wait, I tell you. I have something to say to you. Don't get angry."

Judas halted now and eyed him with disdain.

"Why didn't you open your mouth? Why are you afraid of him? Can you still be afraid when you know what's happening, who is coming, where we are headed? Or maybe you haven't got wind of it yet. Well, poor devil, the time is near, the king of the Jews is approaching in all his glory—and woe be to cowards!"

"More, Judas, more," Philip implored. "Haul me over the coals, lift the forked stick you're holding and beat some self-respect into me. I'm fed up with always being afraid."

Judas approached him slowly and grasped his arm. "Does this come from the heart, Philip, or are you just speaking hollow words?"

"I'm fed up, I tell you. I was disgusted with myself to-day. Go in front, Judas, go in front and show me the way. I'm ready."

The redbeard looked around him and lowered his voice.

"Philip, can you kill?"

"Men?"

"Naturally. What did you think—sheep?"

"I haven't killed a man yet, but I'd be able to, yes, without a doubt. Last month I felled and killed a bull all by myself."

"A man's easier. Come with us."

Philip shuddered. He understood.

"Are you one of them. . . , one of the Zealots?" he asked, his face bathed in terror. He had heard a great deal about this awful brotherhood, the 'Saint Assassins' as it was called. They terrorized everyone, from Mount Hermon down to the Dead Sea, and even further south, as far as the desert of Idumea. Armed with crowbars, ropes and knives, they went about proclaiming: Don't pay tribute to the infidels. We have only one Lord, Adonai. Kill every Jew who disobeys the sacred Law, who laughs, speaks or works with the enemies of our God, the Romans. Strike, kill, clear the road so that the Messiah may pass! Cleanse the world, make ready the streets: he is coming!

They entered villages and cities in broad daylight to assassinate, without consulting anyone but themselves, a traitorous Sadducee or a bloodthirsty Roman. The landowners, priests and high priests trembled before them and called down the anathema: they were the ones who incited insurrections and brought out the Roman troops, with the result that massacres broke forth at regular intervals and rivers of Jewish blood were spilt.

"Are you one of them. . . , one of the Zealots?" Philip repeated in a hushed voice.

"Afraid, my brave friend?" asked the redbeard, laughing with scorn. "Don't be alarmed, we're not murderers. We're fighting for freedom, Philip, to emancipate our God, to emancipate our souls. Arise, the moment has come when you too can show the world that you're a man. Join us."

But Philip stared at the ground. He already regretted having been so effusive with Judas about such matters. Brave words are fine, he reflected. It's delightful to sit with a friend, to eat, drink, start weighty discussions, say "I shall do" and "I shall show. . . ." But on your guard, Philip, don't go any farther, or you'll find yourself in hot water.

Judas leaned over him and spoke to him in a changed voice. His heavy paw now touched Philip's shoulder gently and caressed it.

"What is the life of man? What is it worth? Nothing, if it isn't free. We're fighting for freedom, I tell you. Join us."

Philip was silent. If he could only get away! But Judas kept a firm hold on his shoulder.

"Join us! You're a man: decide! Do you have a knife?"

"Yes."

"Keep it on you at all times, under your shirt. You may need it at any minute. We're passing through difficult days, my brother. Don't you hear buoyant steps coming closer and closer? It's the Messiah, and he must not find the road closed. The knife is more of a help in this than bread. Here, look at me!"

He opened his shirt. Naked and gleaming next to the dark skin of his breast was a short double-bladed bedouin's dagger.

"If it hadn't been for Zebedee's scatter-brained son Jacob, I would have sunk it today into a traitor's heart. Yesterday before I left Nazareth the brotherhood condemned him to death. . ."

"Who?"

". . . and the lot of killing him fell to me."

"Who?" Philip asked again. He had grown afraid.

"That's my business," the redbeard replied abruptly. "Keep your nose out of our affairs."

"Don't you trust me?"

Judas swept his eyes about him, then leaned over and seized Philip by the arm.

"Listen well to what I'm going to say to you, Philip, and don't breathe a word of it to anyone—or you're done for! I'm on my way now to the desert, to the monastery. The monks called me to make some tools for them. In a few days, three or four, I'll be passing your camp again. Turn over well in your mind the words we exchanged. Keep mum, don't let out the secret to anyone. Decide all by yourself. If you're a man and you come to the right decision, I'll reveal to you who we plan to strike."

"Who? Do I know him?"

"Don't be in such a hurry. You're not one of the brothers yet." He held out his immense hand. "Farewell, Philip. You were a mere nothing until now; no one cared whether you were dead or alive. I was the same, a nothing, until the day I entered the brotherhood, but ever since then I've been a different person: I became a man. No more Judas the redbeard, the blacksmith who slaved like an ox with the sole purpose of nourishing these feet and this belly and this ugly snout. Now I'm working for a great purpose—do you hear?—for a great purpose; and whoever works for a great purpose, even if he's the humblest of the lot, he becomes great. Understand? That's all I'm going to say to you. Farewell!"

He poked his donkey and set off at a trot for the desert.

Philip remained all alone. Resting his chin on his crook, he watched Judas until he reached the other side of the rocks and disappeared.

Look here, this redbeard speaks well, he thought, well, and like a saint. A bit boastful perhaps, but who cares! As long as a fellow sticks to words, everything sails along just fine; but if he goes over to action. . . ? Watch out, Philip, poor devil. Think of your little sheep. This business will take some reflection. Best let it ride—and wait and see what happens.

He placed his crook over his shoulders—he had heard the bells of his goats and sheep—and hurried off, whistling.

Zebedee's adopted sons had made a fire meanwhile and put on water for the chowder. As soon as the water boiled they threw in rock-fish, limpets, sea-urchins, a dentex or two, and a green-haired stone to make the food smell of the sea. In a little while they would add the giltheads and red mullets, for how could they be satisfied with just rock-fish and limpets. The hungry fishermen squatted in a circle around the pot and waited anxiously, talking in low voices among themselves. The oldest leaned over to his neighbour.

"It was wonderful to see the blacksmith rub it in his face. Patience. The day will come when the poor will rise to the top and the rich sink to the bottom. That's the meaning of justice."

"Do you think that will ever happen?" replied the other, who had been consumed by hunger ever since his youth. "Do you think that will ever happen on this earth?"

"There's a God, isn't there?" the old man answered. "Yes, there is! And he's just, isn't he? He's got to be if he's God, hasn't he? He's just! So you see, it will happen. All we need, son, is patience —patience."

"Hey, what are you mumbling about over there," said Zebedee, who had caught some of it and grown suspicious. "You just worry about your work and forget about God. He knows better than you what he's about. Good lord, what next!"

They all immediately fell silent. The old fisherman got up, took the wooden spoon, and stirred the soup.

IX

THE hour the adopted sons lifted the nets to their shoulders and the morning fell over the lake, so virgin, it seemed to have come fresh from the hands of the Creator, the son of Mary was travelling along with Jacob, Zebedee's elder son. They had already left Magdala behind them. Now and then they stopped for a moment to comfort the women who were lamenting the lost wheat; then, conversing, they continued on. Jacob had also been caught by the squall. He had spent the night in Magdala, lodging at the house of a friend, and had risen before dawn to resume his journey.

He sloshed through the mud in the blue half-light, anxious to reach the lake of Gennesaret. The bitterness of all he had seen in Nazareth had already begun to settle down calmly within him. The crucified Zealot had become a distant memory and Jacob's mind was once again dominated by his father's fishing boats and men: by everyday concerns. He strode over the pits which had been scooped out by the rain. The trees dripped, half-smiling, half-weeping; the skies above him laughed, birds awoke—it was a glorious day. But as the light increased, he was able to see how the torrents had laid waste the threshing floors. The wheat and barley which had been stacked up ran now with the water in the road; the first farmer's and their wives had already poured out to the fields and begun the dirge. . . . Suddenly he saw the son of Mary, bent over with two old women on a devastated threshing floor.

He clenched his staff tightly and cursed. Nazareth jumped back into his mind, together with the cross and the crucified Zealot—and now, look! here was the cross-maker lamenting the lost wheat with the women! Jacob's soul was rough and unaccommodating. Loud-mouthed, rapacious, without compassion, he had taken all his father's characteristics and bore no resemblance either to his mother Salome, who was a saintly woman, or to John, his sweet, lovable brother. . . . Clenching his staff, he advanced angrily towards the threshing floor.

At the same moment the son of Mary, the tears still running down his cheeks, rose in order to go back to the road. The two old women held his hands, kissing him and not allowing him to leave. Who could possibly match this unknown wayfarer in finding the right words to comfort them?

"Don't cry, don't cry, I'll come back," he kept telling them as he gradually extricated his hands from the aged palms.

Jacob halted in his tracks and stood gaping with astonishment. The cross-maker's eyes glittered, brimming with tears. At one moment they gazed up at the rosy, elated heavens, at the next down at the earth and the stooping people who were scraping in the mud and lamenting.

"Can this be the cross-maker—this?" murmured Jacob, and he drew to one side, troubled. "His face shines like the prophet Elijah's!" The son of Mary had now stepped over the rim of the threshing floor. He saw Jacob, recognized him and put his hand over his heart in the sign of greeting.

"Where are you going, son of Mary?" said Zebedee's son, sweetening his tone. But before the other could reply, he added: "Let's go together. The road is long and calls for company."

The road is long and calls for company, the son of Mary repeated to himself, but he did not divulge his thought.

"Let's go," he said, and together, they started down the paved road to Capernaum.

They did not speak for some time. The women's laments rose up from every threshing floor. The old men, propped on their staffs, watched the wheat run off with the water. The farmers stood dark-faced and motionless in the middle of their mown and devastated fields. Some remained silent, others cursed.

The son of Mary sighed:

"Ach, if there was only one man who had the strength to starve to death so that the people would not die of hunger!"

Jacob glanced at him out of the corner of his eye.

"If you were able to become wheat," he scoffed, "so that the people could eat you and be saved, would you do it?"

"Who wouldn't?" said the son of Mary.

Jacob's hawk-like eyes flickered, as did his thick protruding lips. "Me," he answered.

The son of Mary was silent. The other took offence. "Why should I perish?" he growled. "It was God who sent the flood. What did I do wrong?" He looked fiercely at the sky. "Why did God do it? How did the people offend him? I don't understand—do you, son of Mary?"

"Don't ask, my brother: it's a sin. Until a few days ago I too asked, but now I understand. This was the serpent which corrupted the first creatures and made God banish us from Paradise."

"What do you mean by 'this'?"

"Asking questions."

"I don't understand," said Zebedee's son, and he quickened his pace.

He no longer cared for the cross-maker's company: his words weighed heavily on him, and his silences were even more unbearable than his words.

They came now to a small rise in the plain. Visible in the distance were the glittering waters of Gennesaret. The boats had already reached the middle and the fishing had commenced. The sun rose out of the desert, brilliantly red. On the shore of the lake a rich market-town gleamed in all its whiteness.

Jacob saw his boats in the distance and his mind filled with fish. He turned to his inconvenient companion.

"Where are you going, son of Mary," he asked. "Look, there's Capernaum."

The son of Mary bowed his head and did not reply. He was ashamed to say he was going to the monastery to become a saint.

Jacob gave his head a toss and eyed him. An evil thought had suddenly entered his mind.

"You'd rather not say, is that it?" he growled. "You're keeping it a secret, are you!"

Grabbing hold of his companion's chin, he raised his head. "Look into my eyes. Tell me: who's sending you?"

The son of Mary sighed. "I don't know, I don't know," he murmured. "It may be God, but it may be the. . ."

He hesitated. He was so frightened, the word stuck in his throat. What if he were truly being sent by the devil. . . ?

A dry laugh, filled with contempt, burst from Jacob's lips. He grasped him tightly by the arm and shook him with violence.

"The centurion," he bellowed softly, "your friend the centurion —is he the one who's sending you?"

Yes, that was it: the centurion must be sending him as a spy. New Zealots had cropped up in the mountains and the desert. They came down to the villages, got hold of the people secretly and spoke to them of revenge and liberty. The bloodthirsty centurion of Nazareth had unleashed a greased-palm spy of a Jew to every village. This fellow, this cross-maker, was without a doubt one of those spies.

Knitting his brows, Jacob shoved Jesus away from him. "Listen to me, son of the Carpenter," he said, lowering his voice, "here's where our ways part. You may not know where you're headed, but I do. All right, go now, but this won't be the last you'll see or hear of me. No matter where you lead me, poor devil, I'll follow you—and woe is you! That's all I've got to say; but mark my words, this road you've chosen: you won't leave it alive!"

This said, and without offering him his hand, he cascaded down the slope at a run.

Zebedee's adopted sons removed the copper cauldron from the fire and sat in a circle around it. First to dip in the wooden spoon was the boss himself. He chose the largest dentex and began to eat. But the oldest of the group put out his hand to prevent him.

"We forgot to say grace, boss," he reminded him.

Old Zebedee, still chewing his mouthful of food, lifted the wooden spoon and started to give thanks to the God of Israel for sending fish, grain, wine and oil to nourish the generations of the Hebrews and enable them to endure until the coming of the day of the Lord—when their enemies would be scattered, when all nations would fall prostrate at Israel's feet and worship her, when all gods would fall prostrate at the feet of Adonai and worship him. "That is why we eat, Lord, that is why we marry and have children, that is why we live—all for your sake!"

This said, he swallowed the dentex in one gulp.

While master and men ate and enjoyed the fruits of their labour, their eyes fixed on the lake—the mother that nourished them, suddenly Jacob appeared before them, puffing and covered with mud. The fishermen crowded together to make room for him, and old Zebedee, who was in a merry mood, cried: "Welcome to my first-born! You're in luck, sit down and eat. What news?"

No answer. The son knelt by his father's side, but did not extend his hand to the fragrant, steaming cauldron.

Old Zebedee turned his head timidly and looked at him. He knew this peevish taciturn son of his inside-out, and feared him. "Aren't you hungry?" he asked. "What kind of a face is that? Who've you been fighting with this time?"

"With God, devils and men," Jacob answered in a rage. "I'm not hungry!"

Ouch! he's come to spoil our chowder, Zebedee said to himself, but he strained to retain his good humour and change the subject. He slapped his son lovingly on the knee. "Hey, you rascal," he said, winking at him, "who were you talking with along the way?"

Jacob gave a start.

"So we have spies, have we? Who told you? . . . I wasn't talking with anyone!"

He got up, went to the lake, plunged in knee-deep and washed himself. Then he turned to the group, but as he saw how happy they were, all eating and laughing, he burst out:

"You eat and drink, and in Nazareth others are crucified for your sakes!"

Unable to stand the sight of them any more, he started towards the village, grumbling.

Old Zebedee watched him recede.

"My sons are a pain in the neck," he said, shaking his large head. "One turned out too soft and pious, the other too pigheaded: wherever he goes or stops, he's sure to start a row. A pain in the neck. . . . Neither of them developed into a true man: a little bit soft, a little bit against the grain; sometimes kind, sometimes a snapping dog; half devil, half angel—in short, a man!"

Sighing, he grabbed a gilthead to force the bitterness down. "Thank goodness we have the giltheads," he said, "and the lakes which make them and the God who makes the lakes."

"If you speak like that, boss, what must old Jonah say?" said the old man of the group. "The poor fellow sits on a rock every evening, looks towards Jerusalem and weeps for his son Andrew. He's another one of those clairvoyants. They say he discovered a prophet and goes the rounds with him, eating nothing but locusts and honey, and grabbing people to dunk them in the Jordan, apparently to wash away their sins.'

"And we're told to have sons to thrive!" said Zebedee. "Fetch me the gourd, men. There's still some wine, isn't there? My spirits need lifting!"

They heard heavy slow-moving footsteps on the pebbles. Some cumbersome beast seemed to be approaching in a rage. Old Zebedee turned.

"Welcome to Jonah, the good man!" he shouted. He sponged off his wine-stained beard, rose respectfully and offered him his place. "I've just been having it out with my sons and the gilt-heads. Come, try your hand at the giltheads and tell us what news from saint Andrew, your son."

An old fisherman appeared before them. He was short and stocky, barefooted, roasted by the sun; with cloudy, stale eyes, an immense head covered by curly white hair, and skin which had grown fish-like scales. Leaning forward, he stared at them one by one, looking for somebody.

"Who are you looking for, father Jonah?" Zebedee asked. "Are you too weary to speak?"

He gazed at his feet, his beard, his hair, all tangled and filled with fish-bones and seaweed, and at his thick chapped lips which opened and closed like those of a fish and made no sound. Zebedee wanted to laugh, but suddenly he was overcome by fright. A foolish suspicion darted through his mind. Terrified, he stretched forth both his hands as though he wished to prevent old Jonah from coming closer.

"Cripes! can you be the prophet Jonah?" he shouted, jumping to his feet. "Such a long time with us, and you've been hiding all the while? I adjure you in the name of Adonai: speak! Once I heard the holy Abbot of the monastery tell about the shark that swallowed the prophet Jonah and how, afterwards, the fish vomited and Jonah jumped out of its belly, a man as before. So help me God,

128

the way the Abbot described him to us he was just like you: sea-weed entwined in the hair of his head and chest, and his beard full of newborn crabs. No offence, Jonah, but I wager that if I feel under your beard I'll find crabs there."

The fishermen burst out laughing, but Zebedee continued to gaze at his old friend with terror in his eyes.

"Speak, man of God," he said to him. "Are you the prophet Jonah?"

Old Jonah shook his head. He couldn't recall being swallowed by any fish. It was possible, however. After so many years wrestling with the fish, what chance did he have to remember?

"It's him, it's him!" murmured old Zebedee, his eyes darting from side to side as though he wanted to escape. He knew that prophets were freakish men whom one must not trust. They disappeared into the air, the sea, or into fire—and afterwards, when you least expected them, lo! there they were in front of you! Had not Elijah risen to heaven mounted on fire? Yet he still lived and reigned, and on no matter what mountain-peak you scaled, there he was before you. The same was true of Enoch: immortal. And now, here was the prophet Jonah. He plays ignorant, Zebedee said to himself, he pretends to be a fisherman and the father of Peter and Andrew. Better tackle him with kindness: these prophets are an odd pig-headed lot, and if you don't watch out you'll find yourself in hot water. . . . He sweetened his voice:

"Beloved neighbour, father Jonah," he began, "you are looking for someone—is it Jacob? He returned from Nazareth but was tired, it seems, and went to the village. If you want to know about your son Peter, he says he's well and that you shouldn't worry: he's well, he's coming soon, he sends his best wishes. . . . Do you hear me, Jonah? Give me some sign."

He spoke sweetly to him and stroked his leathery shoulders. Who could tell, everything was possible, and this blockhead of a fisherman might be the prophet Jonah. So, best take care!

Old Jonah stooped, snatched a small sea-scorpion out of the cauldron, stuffed the whole thing into his mouth and began to chew it bones and all.

"I'm going," he mumbled, and he turned his back on them. Once more the pebbles began to crunch. A seagull skimmed over his head, flapped its wings and stopped for a moment as though its eye had caught sight of a crab under the fisherman's hair. But it uttered a hoarse cry, apparently from fear, and flew away.

"Watch out, lads," said old Zebedee. "I bet my bones he's the prophet Jonah. Two of you had better go help him now that Peter's away. Otherwise, who knows what will happen to us?"

Two great colossi got up and addressed their boss, half-joking, half-afraid:

"Zebedee, we hold you responsible for the consequences. The prophets are wild beasts. They open their mouths out of the blue and gobble you up to the last bone! All right, let's go. Farewell!"

Old Zebedee stretched with satisfaction—he had managed well with the prophet. Now he turned to the remaining adopted sons:

"Look alive, men, step lively, load the fish into the hampers and go round to all the villages. But be careful, the peasants are foxy, they're not like us fishermen—we're God's own! Give the least number of fish you possibly can and take the greatest possible amount of wheat (even if it's last year's), and of oil, wine, chickens, rabbits. . . . Do you understand? Two and two make four."

The adopted sons jumped up and began to fill the hampers.

In the distance, behind the rocks, a man appeared mounted on a racing camel. Old Zebedee shaded his eyes with his hand and looked.

"Hey, men," he cried, "here, have a look—do you think it's John, my son?"

The rider was now passing over the fine sand and approaching them.

"It's him, it's him!" the fisherman shouted. "Welcome to your son, boss!"

Now the rider was passing in front of them and waving his hand to greet them.

"John," cried the old father, "why in such a rush? Where are you going? Stop a minute and let us see you!"

"The Abbot is dying, I haven't time."

"What's the matter with him?"

"He doesn't want to eat, he wants to die."

"Why? Why?"

But the rider's words were lost in the air.

Old Zebedee coughed, thought for a moment and then shook his head.

"The Lord preserve us from sainthood," he said.

The son of Mary watched Jacob descend with angry strides towards Capernaum; then he collapsed to the ground, legs crossed, his heart filled with grievance. Why did he, who yearned so much to love and be loved, why did he awaken so much hatred in the hearts of men? It was his own fault; not God's, not men's, but his own. Why did he behave so cowardly, why did he choose a road to follow and then lack the courage to pursue it to its end? He was a cripple, a pitiful coward. Why didn't he dare take Magdalene as his wife, to save her from shame and death; and when God clawed him and commanded him to rise, why did he cling to the ground and refuse to get up? And now, why was he governed by fear and going to the desert to hide? Did he think God would not find him there as well as anywhere else?

The sun stood nearly above his head. The lamentation for the wheat had stopped. These tormented people were already used to calamities: they recalled that their wailing had never brought a cure, and were quiet. For thousands of years they had suffered injustice, gone hungry, been tossed about by forces both visible and invisible. But somehow they limped through life, always managing to make ends meet—and this had taught them patience.

A green lizard emerged from a squat bush. It had come out to sun itself. When it saw this terrifying man-beast above it, its heart took fright and began to thump, just below the neck; but the reptile nerved itself, glued the whole length of its body to the warm rock, shifted its round jet-black eye and gazed with confidence at the son of Mary, as though welcoming him or saying: I saw you were alone, so I came to keep you company. Rejoicing, the son of Mary held his breath so that he would not frighten the visitor; but while he watched it, feeling his own heart thump like the lizard's, two fuzzy butterflies, both black and splashed with red, fluttered down between them and flew back and forth from one to the other, not wanting to leave. They danced gleefully, frolicking in the sun, and at the very last alighted on the man's ensanguined kerchief with their proboscises over the red spots, as though they wished to suck up the blood. Feeling their caress on the top of his head, he recalled God's talons and it seemed to him that these and the butterfly-wings brought him the identical message. Ah, if only God could always descend to man not as a thunderbolt or a clawing vulture, but as a butterfly!

And just as he joined butterflies and God in his mind, he felt something tickle the soles of his feet. He looked down and saw a pre-occupied swarm of fat yellow-black ants filing hurriedly under his arches. Working in groups of twos or threes, they were carrying away the wheat in their roomy mandibles, one grain at a time. They had stolen it from the plain, right out of the mouths of men, and were transporting it now to their anthill, all the while praising God the Great Ant, who, ever solicitous for his Chosen People the ants, sent floods to the plain at precisely the right moment, just when the wheat was stacked upon the threshing floors.

The son of Mary sighed. Ants are God's creatures too, he reflected, and so are men, and lizards, and the grasshoppers I hear in the olive grove and the jackals who howl during the night, and floods, and hunger. . .

He heard someone puffing behind him. Terror took hold of him. He had forgotten her for such a long time, but she had not forgotten him. He could now feel her in back of him, seated cross-legged like himself and breathing heavily.

"The Curse is God's creature too," he murmured.

He felt completely enveloped in God's breath. It blew over him, sometimes warm and benevolent, sometimes savage, merciless. Lizard, butterflies, ants, Curse—all were God.

Hearing voices and bells along the road, he turned. A long camel-caravan laden with expensive merchandise was passing by, led by a humble donkey. This caravan must have started from Nineveh and Babylon, the rich river-valley of the patriarch Abraham, and come across desert transporting silks, spices, ivory and perhaps male and female slaves to the many-coloured ships of the Great Sea.

The procession filed by; it seemed to have no end. What riches these people have, the son of Mary thought, what marvels! Finally, at the caravan's tail, the rich black-bearded merchants appeared with their golden ear-rings, their green turbans and flowing white jellabs. They were passing in front of him now, rolling and pitching with the swaying jog of the camels.

The son of Mary shuddered. It suddenly occurred to him that they would stop at Magdala. Magdalene's door is open day and night and they will enter, he said to himself. . . . I must save you, Magdalene—oh, if I could only do it!—you, Magdalene, not the race of Israel: that I cannot save. I'm no prophet. If I open my mouth, I have no idea what to say. God did not anoint my lips with burning coals, did not cast his thunderbolt into my bowels to make me burn, rush frenzied into the streets and begin to shout. . . . I want the words to be his, not mine: I want nothing to do with them. I'll simply open my mouth, and he'll do the talking. No, I'm no prophet, I'm just a plain ordinary man who's scared of everything: I can't drag you out of the bed of shame, Magdalene, so I'm going to the desert, to the monastery, to pray for you. Prayer is all-powerful. They say that during the wars, as long as Moses kept his hands raised to heaven, the sons of Israel conquered, and as soon as he grew tired and lowered them, they were defeated. . . . Magdalene, I shall keep my hands raised to heaven for you day and night.

He looked up to see when the sun was going to set. He wanted to continue on in darkness so that he could get past Capernaum without being seen by a soul and then go around the lake and enter the desert. He was growing more and more anxious to arrive.

"Oh, if I could only walk over the waters and go directly across the lake!" he murmured, sighing once more.

The lizard was still sunning itself, glued to the warm rock. The butterflies had flown up high and disappeared into the light. The ants continued to transport the harvest. They shovelled it into their granaries, went hastily back to the fields and returned with new loads. The sun was ready to set. The passers-by grew scarcer, shadows lengthened; the evening fell upon trees and soil, gilding them. On the lake, the water was in perfect confusion: at the twinkling of an eye it altered its appearance—reddened, turned light violet, darkened. . . . One large star hung in the western skies.

Now night will come, the son of Mary reflected, now God's black daughter will arrive with her caravan of stars. . . ; and before the stars had a chance to come out and fill the sky, they filled his mind.

He had already begun to get ready to rise and resume his journey when he heard a horn behind him. A passer-by was calling him by name. He turned and in the thin light of the evening discerned someone signalling to him and mounting the slope, loaded down with an immense bundle. Who can it be? he asked himself, struggling to make out the wayfarer's features beneath the bundle. Somewhere he had seen that pale face and short scanty beard and those thin crooked shanks before. Suddenly he cried out:

"Is that you, Thomas? Have you started your circuit of the villages again?"

The wily cross-eyed pedlar stood in front of him now, panting. He placed his bundle on the ground and sponged the sweat from his pointed forehead and the tiny wry eyes whose ambivalent dance left you unable to tell whether they were rejoicing or scoffing.

The son of Mary liked him very much. He often saw him pass by his workshop on his way back from his rounds, the horn thrust under his belt. He would throw his bundle down on a bench and begin to talk about everything he had seen. He sneered, he laughed, he teased; he had faith neither in the God of Israel nor in any other god. They all jeer at us, he would say, they all jeer at us to make us slaughter kids for them, burn them sweet-incense and shout ourselves hoarse hymning their beauty. . . . The son of Mary listened to him and his constricted heart relaxed a little: he admired this roguish mind which despite all its poverty and all the slavery and misery of its race, found strength to conquer the slavery and the poverty by means of laughter and mockery.

And Thomas the pedlar liked the son of Mary. He looked upon him as a naive sheep, sickly and bleating, that was seeking God in order to hide behind his shadow.

"You're a sheep, son of Mary," he said to him regularly, splitting with laughter, "but you've got a wolf inside you and this wolf is going to eat you up!" Then from under his shirt he would take a handful of dates or a pomegranate or an apple he had stolen from the orchard, and treat him. . . .

"It's good to see you," he said now, as soon as he had caught his breath. "God loves you. Say, where're you going?"

"To the monastery," Jesus replied, pointing towards the lake.

"Well then, it's doubly good to see you. Turn back!"

"Why? God. . ."

But Thomas exploded:

"Do me a favour and don't start up again about God. Where he's concerned there are no boundaries. You walk all your life, this one and the next, trying to reach him, but the blessed fellow has no end. So forget about him and don't mix him up in our affairs. Listen to me: here we've got to deal with man—with dishonest, seven-times-shrewd man. To begin with, watch out for Judas the redbeard. Before I left Nazareth I saw him whispering with the mother of the crucified Zealot, then with Barabbas and two or three other knife-wielding cronies of his from the brotherhood. I heard them mention your name, so watch out, son of Mary: don't go to the monastery."

But Jesus bowed his head.

"Every living thing is in God's hands. He decides whom he wants to save, whom he wants to slay. What resistance can we offer? I shall go, and may God help me!"

"You'll go?" shouted Thomas in a rage. "But right now, right now as we talk, Judas is at the monastery with his knife hidden under his shirt. Do you carry a knife?"

The son of Mary shuddered.

"No," he said. "What use should I have for one?"

Thomas laughed.

"Sheep. . . , sheep. . . , sheep. . . ," he murmured. He picked up his bundle.

"Farewell. Do what you like. I tell you to turn back and you say, 'I shall go!' All right, go—and kick yourself afterwards when it's too late!"

With a twinkle in his tiny wry eyes he started back down the slope, whistling.

The night now fell in earnest. The ground darkened, the lake sank away; in Capernaum the first lamps were lit. The birds of the day had already buried their heads in their wings and gone to sleep; the night-birds, awakening, began to go out on the hunt.

This is a holy hour, a good time to leave, thought the son of Mary. No one will see me—so let's be off!

He recalled Thomas's words.

"Whatever God wills, that is what will happen," he murmured. "If God is the one who's pushing me to go find my murderer, then let me go quickly and be killed. That, at least, I am able to do, and I'm doing it." He turned and looked behind him.

"Let's go," he said to his invisible companion, and he set out towards the lake. . . .

The night was sweet, warm, damp; a gentle wind blew from the south, Capernaum smelt of fish and jasmine. Old Zebedee sat in the courtyard of his house with his wife Salome, under the large almond tree. They had finished their meal and were chatting. Inside, their son Jacob twisted and turned on his mattress. Tangled up in his mind and infuriating his heart were the crucified Zealot, the new injustice God had done the people in taking their wheat, and the son of Mary, who had sold himself as a spy. These thoughts did not let him sleep; and his father's chattering outside infuriated him that much more. Boiling over with rage, he jumped to his feet, went out into the yard and strode across the threshold.

Where are you going?" his mother called to him anxiously.

"To the lake to catch a breath of fresh air," he growled, and he vanished into the darkness.

Old Zebedee shook his head and sighed.

"The world isn't what it used to be, wife," he said. "Today the young folk are too big for their skins. They're neither birds nor fish, they're flying-fish. The sea is too small for them, so they fly into the air. But they can't last long there, so they plunge back down into the sea and then start all over again from the beginning. They've gone out of their minds. Why, just look at our son John, your darling. I'm for the monastery, he tells us. Prayers, fasting, God. . . .The fishing boat looks much too narrow to him—he can't possibly fit in. And now here's the other one, Jacob, who I thought had some sense in his head. Mark my words: he's fixed the rudder in the same direction. Didn't you see tonight how he got all heated up, ready to burst, and how the house was too small for him? All right, it doesn't matter to me, but who's going to look after my boats and the men? Is all my toil going to waste?

136

Wife, I'm troubled; bring me a little wine and a snack of octopus to restore my spirits."

Old Salome played deaf. Her old husband had drunk quite enough already. She tried to change the subject.

"They're young," she said. "Don't let it worry you, it will blow over."

"By gad, wife, you're right! You've got a fertile head on your shoulders. Why do I sit here getting a headache? That's it: they're young, it will blow over. Youth is a sickness, it passes. When I was young there were times when I too got all heated up and twisted and turned on my bed. I thought I was looking for God, but I was really looking for a wife—for you, Salome! I got married and calmed down. Our sons will do the same, so don't give it another thought! I'm content now. . . . Wife, bring me a snack and some octopus; and bring me a bit of wine, dear Salome—I want to drink to your health!"

In the adjoining neighbourhood, a little further on, old Jonah sat all alone in his cottage and mended his nets by the light of the lamp. He mended and mended, but his mind and thoughts were not on his dear departed wife, who had died on him this time a year before, nor on his nincompoop of a son Andrew, nor on that prize cow-brained nitwit, his other son Peter, who still went the rounds of the taverns of Nazareth, having left his father high and dry, old man that he was, to wrestle all alone with the fish. No, he was thinking of Zebedee's words and labouring under a great inquietude. Perhaps he really was the prophet Jonah. He looked at his hands, feet, thighs: all scales. Even his breath and sweat smelt of fish, and now he remembered that the other day when he wept on account of his wife, his tears had smelt of fish too. And sly old Zebedee was right about the crabs: once in a while he found some in his beard. . . . Perhaps he was the prophet Jonah after all. Ah! that explained why he was never in the mood to talk, why the words had to be dragged out of him with a grapnel, why he always stumbled and tripped when he walked on dry land. But when he plunged into the lake: what a relief that was, what joy! The water lifted him up in its bosom, caressed him, licked him, purred in his ear and spoke to him; and he, like the fish, answered it without words, and bubbles came out of his mouth!

I'm the prophet Jonah, without a doubt, he said to himself. I've been resurrected—the shark vomited me up again. But this time I've got a little sense in my head: I'm a prophet all right, but I pretend to be a fisherman and don't breathe a word to anyone— I don't want to find myself in hot water all over again. . . . He smiled with satisfaction at his own cunning. I managed it beautifully, he reflected. Look how many years no one got wind of it, not even me, until that devilish Zebedee came along. . . . Well, it's a good thing he opened my eyes. . . .

He left his tools on the floor, rubbed his hands together with satisfaction, opened a cupboard, took out a gourd-full of wine, tipped up his short fat scaly throat and began to drink, chuckling.

While the two contented old men drank in Capernaum, our night-owl journeyed along the shore of the lake, plunged deep in thought. He was not all alone: behind him he heard the sand crunching. In Magdalene's yard new merchants had dismounted and were now sitting cross-legged on the pebbles. They conversed quietly and munched dates and grilled crabs while they awaited their turns. At the monastery the monks had laid the Abbot out in the middle of his cell and were keeping the vigil. He still breathed; his protruding eyes stared at the opened door and his emaciated face was tensed: he seemed to be straining to hear something.

The monks looked at him and whispered among themselves:

"He's trying to hear whether or not the rabbi has arrived from Nazareth to cure him.". . .

"He's trying to hear whether or not the black wings of the archangel are coming near.". . .

"He's trying to hear the footsteps of the approaching Messiah.". . .

They whispered and looked at him, and the soul of each was prepared at that hour to welcome the miracle. They all strained their ears, but they heard nothing except the heavy blows of a hammer on the anvil. In the far corner of the courtyard Judas had lit his fires and was working through the night.

X

FAR away in Nazareth, Mary the wife of Joseph sat in her simple cottage. The lamp was lit, the door open. Hurriedly, she wound up the wool which she had spun. She had decided to rise and comb the villages in search of her boy. She wound and wound, but her mind was not on her work. Lonely and hopeless, it roamed the fields, visited Magdala and Capernaum, searched all around the shore of the lake of Gennesaret. She was seeking her son. He had run away again; once more God had prodded him with his ox-goad. Doesn't he pity him, she asked herself, doesn't he pity me? What have we done to him? Is this the joy and glory he promised us? Why, God, was it Joseph's staff which you made blossom, forcing me to marry an old man? Why did you cast your thunderbolt and plant in my womb this day-dreamer, this night-walker of an only son? The whole time I was pregnant the neighbours came and admired me. "Mary, you are blessed above all women," they said. I had blossomed, I was an almond tree covered with flowers from the roots to the highest branches. "Who is this flowering almond?" the passing merchants used to ask, and they stopped their caravans, got off their camels and filled my lap with gifts. Then, suddenly, a wind blew and I was stripped bare. . . . I fold my arms over my fallow breasts. Lord, your will has been done: you made me blossom, you blew, the petals fell away. Is there no hope I may blossom again, Lord? . . .

Is there no hope my heart may grow calm? her son asked himself early the next morning. He had gone around the lake and now he saw the monastery opposite him, wedged in among green-red rocks. As I proceed and near the monastery, my heart becomes more and more troubled. Why? Haven't I taken the right road, Lord? It's towards this holy retreat you've been pushing me, isn't it? Why then do you refuse to extend your hand and gladden my heart?

Two monks dressed all in white appeared at the monastery's

large door. They climbed up onto a rock and gazed out in the direction of Capernaum.

"Still no sign," said one of them, a half-crazy hunchback with a behind which nearly scraped the ground.

"He'll be dead by the time they arrive," said the other, a huge elephant of a man whose mouth, a shark-like slit, reached fully to his ears. "Go ahead, Jeroboam. I'll keep on the look-out here until the camel appears."

"Fine," said the delighted hunchback, sliding down from the rock. "I'll go and watch him die."

The son of Mary stood irresolutely on the monastery's threshold, his heart oscillating like a bell: should he enter or not? The cloister was circular and paved with flagstones. Not a single green tree graced the courtyard, not a flower, not a bird: only wild prickly-pears all round. Along the circumference of this round inhuman desolation were the cells, carved into the rock like tombs.

Is this the kingdom of heaven? the son of Mary asked himself. Is this where man's heart grows calm?

He looked and looked, unable to decide to cross the threshold. Two black sheep-dogs flew out of a corner and began to bark at him.

The stunted hunchback noticed the visitor and silenced the dogs with a whistle. Then he turned and scrutinized the new-comer from top to toe. The young man's eyes seemed full of affliction to him, the clothes he wore were very poor, and blood trickled from his feet. He felt sorry for him.

"Welcome, brother," he said. "What wind has tossed you out here into the desert?"

"God!" the son of Mary answered in a deep, despairing voice. The monk got frightened: he had never heard human lips pro-nounce God's name with such terror. Folding his arms, he said nothing.

After a short pause, the visitor continued:

"I've come to see the Abbot."

"Maybe you'll see him, but he won't see you. What do you want with him?"

"I don't know, I had a dream. . . . I've come from Nazareth."

"A dream?" said the half-crazy monk with a laugh.

"A terrible dream, Father. Since then my heart has had no peace. The Abbot is a saint; God taught him how to explain the languages of birds and dreams. That is why I came."

It had never entered his mind to come to this monastery to ask the Abbot to explain the dream he had on the night he constructed the cross: that wild chase in his sleep and the redbeard rushing in front and the dwarfs who followed him with their instruments of torture. But now as he stood irresolutely on the threshold, suddenly the dream tore across his mind like a flash of lightning. That's it! he shouted to himself. I've come because of the dream. God sent it in order to show me my road, and the Abbot is going to untangle it for me.

"The Abbot is dying," said the monk. "You've arrived too late, my brother. Go back."

"God commanded me to come," the son of Mary replied. "Is he capable of hoaxing his children?"

The monk cackled. He had seen a good deal in his lifetime and had no confidence in God.

"He's the Lord, isn't he? So, he does whatever comes into his head. If he wasn't able to inflict injustice, what kind of an Omnipotent would he be?"

He slapped the visitor on the back. He meant this slap to be a caress, but his huge paw was heavy, and it hurt the youth.

"All right, don't get worried," he said. "Here, step inside. I'm the guest-master."

They entered the cloister. A wind had arisen; the sand swirled over the flagstones. An opaque windstorm girded the sun. The air grew dark.

Gaping in the middle of the yard was a dried-out well. At other times it was filled with water, but now it had become filled with sand. Two lizards emerged to warm themselves on its corroded brim.

The Abbot's cell was open. The monk took his visitor by the arm.

"Wait here while I ask the brothers for permission. Don't budge."

He crossed his hands over his chest and entered. The dogs had placed themselves on either side of the Abbot's threshold.

Their necks stretched forward, they sniffed the air and yelped mournfully.

The Abbot lay stretched out in the middle of the cell, his feet towards the door. Around him the waiting monks dozed, exhausted by their all-night vigil. The moribund, stretched out as he was on his mat, kept his face continually tensed and his eyes open, riveted on the gaping doorway. The seven-branched candelabrum was still next to his face. It illuminated the polished arch of his forehead, the insatiable eyes, the hawk-like nose, the pale blue lips and the long white beard which reached his waist and covered the naked bony chest. The monks had thrown incense kneaded with dried rose-petals onto the lighted coals of an earthenware censer, and perfume invaded the air.

The monk entered, forgot why he had done so and squatted on the threshold, between the two dogs.

The sun had the door in its grasp now and was trying to enter to touch the Abbot's feet. The son of Mary stood outside, waiting. There was no sound save the whining of the two dogs and in the distance, the slow rhythmic blows of the sledge on the anvil.

The visitor waited and waited. The day advanced; they had forgotten him. There had been a frost during the night but now as he stood outside the cell he felt the delicious warmth of the morning sun enter his bones.

Suddenly the silence was broken by the voice of the monk who was doing sentry-duty on the rock:

"They're coming! They're coming!"

The monks in the Abbot's cell awoke with a start and flew outside, leaving the Abbot all alone.

Nerving himself, the son of Mary advanced two steps, timidly, and stopped on the threshold. Inside was the calm of death, of immortality. The Abbot's pale, slender feet gleamed, bathed in sunlight. A bee buzzed near the ceiling; a fuzzy black insect flitted about the seven lights, hopping from one to the next as though trying to select its crematorium.

Suddenly the Abbot stirred. Exerting all his strength, he raised his head—and at once the eyes popped out of his head, his mouth dropped open, his nostrils sniffed the air, twitching insatiably. The son of Mary put his hand to his heart, lips and forehead in the sign of greeting. The Abbot's lips moved:

"You've come. . . , you've come. . . , you've come. . . ," he murmured, so imperceptibly that the son of Mary did not hear. But a smile of unspeakable bliss spread over the Abbot's severe embittered face and straightway his eyes closed, the nostrils remained motionless, his mouth shut and the two hands which were crossed over his breast rolled one to the right the other to the left and rested on the ground with open upturned palms.

In the courtyard meanwhile, the two camels had knelt. The monks rushed forward to help the old rabbi dismount.

"Is he alive, is he still alive?" the young novice asked in anguished tones.

"He's still breathing," answered Father Habakkuk. "He sees and hears everything, but does not speak."

The rabbi entered first, followed by the novice with the precious wallet containing the healer's salves, herbs and magic amulets. The two black dogs, their tails between their legs, did not even turn their heads, Their necks were stretched out against the ground and they were yelping woefully, like humans.

The rabbi heard them and shook his head. I've come too late, he reflected, but he did not speak.

He knelt by the Abbot's side, leaned over his body and placed his hand on his heart. His lips were almost touching those of the Abbot.

"Too late," he whispered. "I've come too late. . . . Long may you live, Fathers!"

Crying out, the monks stooped and kissed the corpse, each according to his length of service, as prescribed by custom: Father Habakkuk the eyes, the remaining monks the beard and upturned palms, the novices the feet. And one of them took the Abbot's crosier from the empty stall and laid it next to the holy remains.

The old rabbi knelt and regarded him, unable to tear away his eyes. What was this triumphant smile? What meaning had the mysterious gleam around the closed eyes? A sun, an unsetting sun, had fallen over this face and remained there. What was this sun?

He looked about him. The monks, still on their knees, were paying homage to the deceased; John, his lips glued to the Abbot's

143

feet, wept. The old rabbi shifted his glance from one monk to the next as though questioning them; and suddenly his eye was caught by the son of Mary standing motionless and tranquil in the back corner of the cell, his hands crossed on his breast. But spread over the whole of his face was the same calm triumphant smile.

"Lord of Hosts, Adonai," whispered the terrified rabbi, "will you never cease tempting my heart? Help my mind now to understand—and decide!"

The next day an angry blood-red sun ringed by a dark tempest bounded out of the sand. A fiery east wind arose from the desert: the world turned black. The monastery's two ebony dogs tried to bark, but their mouths filled with sand and they remained still. The camels, glued to the ground, closed their eyes and waited.

Slowly, linked one to the next in a chain, the monks groped their way forward, struggling not to fall. Squashed together in a row and holding the Abbot's remains tightly in their arms so that the wind would not take him from them, they proceeded, going to bury him. The desert swayed: rose and fell like the sea.

"It's the desert wind, the breath of Jehovah," murmured John, leaning his entire body against the son of Mary. "It withers every green leaf, dries up every spring, fills your mouth with sand. We'll simply leave the sacred remains in a hollow, and the waves of sand will come to cover them up.

The moment they passed over the monastery's threshold the redbearded blacksmith, his hammer over his shoulder, rose up black and enormous out of the swirling mist and looked at them for an instant, but immediately disappeared, enveloped by the sand. The son of Zebedee saw this ogre in the middle of the sandstorm. Terrified, he clutched his partner's arm.

"Who was that?" he asked softly. "Did you see him?"

But the son of Mary did not reply. God arranges everything perfectly, and exactly as he desires, he reflected. Look how he brought Judas and me together—here in the desert, at the very ends of the earth. Well then, Lord, let your will be done.

Bent over, they advanced all together, planting their feet in the burning sand. They tried to block their mouths and nostrils with the edge of their robes, but the fine sand had already descended to their throats and lungs. The wind suddenly took hold of Father Habakkuk, who was in the lead. It twirled him around and threw him down. The monks, blinded by the clouds of sand, walked over him. The desert whistled, the stones jingled; old Habakkuk uttered a hoarse cry, but no one heard.

Why shouldn't Jehovah's breath be the cool breeze which comes to us from the Great Sea? the son of Mary was thinking. He wanted to ask his companion, but could not open his mouth. Why couldn't the wind of Jehovah fill the dried-out wells of the desert with water? Why couldn't the Lord love the green leaf and feel pity for men? Oh, if only one man could be found to approach him, fall at his feet and succeed, but before being reduced to ashes, in telling him of man's suffering, and of the suffering of the earth and of the green leaf!

Judas still stood in the low doorway of the isolated cell which the monks had given him as a workshop. Splitting with laughter, he watched the funeral procession which rolled and pitched, sank away and vanished at one moment, reappeared at the next. He had caught sight of the person he was hunting, and his dark eyes gleamed with pleasure. "Great is the God of Israel," he whispered. "He arranges everything beautifully. He has brought the traitor right to the point of my knife."

He went inside, stroking his moustache with delight. The cell was dark, but in a small furnace in the corner, the burning coals glowed fiercely. The low-rumped monk, half-saint, half-lunatic, was poking the fire, bellows in hand.

The blacksmith was in a good mood. "Hey, Father Jeroboam," he said, "is this what they call the wind of God? I like it, I like it very much. I would blow that way myself, if I were God."

The monk laughed. "I wouldn't blow at all—I'm worn out." He abandoned the bellows in order to sponge the sweat from his forehead and neck. Judas approached him.

"Will you do me a favour, Father Jeroboam?" he asked. "Yesterday a young man with a small black beard came as a guest to the monastery, a half-lunatic like Your Worship. He was barefooted and wore a red-spotted kerchief on his head."

"I was the first to see him," said the monk, putting on airs. "But my dear smith, he's no half-lunatic, he's as loony as they come! He says he had a dream and travelled from Nazareth so that the Abbot—may he rest in peace—could disentangle it for him."

"All right, then, listen: you're the guest-master, aren't you? Whenever anyone comes, isn't it you who fits up his cell, makes his bed, takes him to eat?"

"That's me, no doubt about it! It seems I'm hopeless in any other function, so they made me the guest-master. I wash, I sweep, and I feed the visitors."

"Fine! Put his bed in my cell tonight. I can't sleep alone, Jeroboam—how can I explain it to you? I have nightmares, Satan comes and tempts me, I'm afraid I'll be damned to hell. But as soon as I feel a human being breathing near me, I grow calm. Go on, do it. I'll give you a present: a pair of sheep-shears so you can trim your beard. You can barber the monks too. . . , and clip the camels—and no one will call you untalented any more. Do you hear what I say?"

"Bring me the shears!"

The blacksmith rummaged through his bag and extracted a pair of huge rusty scissors. The monk snatched them, brought them close to the light, opened them, closed them. . . . His admiration was endless.

"Lord, you are great, and wonderful are your works," he whispered, completely stupefied.

"Well. . . ?" said Judas, shaking him violently to wake him up.

"You shall have him tonight," the monk answered, and seizing the scissors, he left.

The others had returned already. They had not been able to go very far, for the wind of Jehovah twirled them around and threw them to the ground. They found a pit, rolled the carcass in and called for Father Habakkuk to say the prayer, but he was nowhere to be found, and the old rabbi of Nazareth bent over the pit and shouted to the evacuated soul-less flesh: "Dust you are, return to dust. The soul within you has fled, you are needed no longer, you have accomplished your duty. Flesh, you have accomplished your duty: you aided the soul to descend to its earthly exile, to walk for a few suns and moons over the sand and stones, to sin, to feel pain, to yearn for heaven, its fatherland, and for God, its father. Flesh, the Abbot no longer needs you: dissolve!"

Even while the rabbi spoke, a layer of fine sand was deposited over the Abbot's corpse: the face, beard and hands sank away. Still more clouds of sand arose, and the monks hurriedly retreated. The moment the half-crazy guest-master snatched his sheep-shears and left the blacksmith, the monks, blinded, their lips cracked, their armpits chafed, burrowed into the monastery, carrying old Habakkuk, whom they had found on the way back, half-buried in the sand.

The old rabbi brushed his eyes, mouth and neck with a damp cloth and squatted on the ground in front of the Abbot's empty stall. Through the bolted door he could hear the breath of Jehovah parch and obliterate the world. The prophets strode across his brain, from temple to temple. It was in fiery air such as this that they had cried out to God; and at the approach of the Lord of Hosts they must have felt a similar burning of their lips and eyes. "Of course! God is a scorching wind, a flash of lightning— I know that," he murmured. "He is not an orchard in bloom. . . . And the heart of man is a green leaf: God twists its stem and it withers. What can we do, how can we behave towards him to make his expression grow sweeter? If we offer him sacrificial lambs, he shouts: 'I don't want them, I don't want flesh, my hunger is satisfied only with psalms.'. . . If we open out mouths and begin to sing the psalms, he shouts: 'I don't want words. Nothing but the flesh of the lamb, of the son, of the only son, will satisfy my hunger!'"

The old rabbi sighed. Thinking about God had driven him furious and worn him out. He looked for a corner where he could lie down. The monks, exhausted from lack of sleep, had scattered to their cells to go to bed and dream about the Abbot. His spirit would roam the monastery for forty days, would enter their cells to see what they were doing, and to give them advice or scold them. They lay down therefore, both to rest and to see him in their sleep. The old rabbi turned and looked around him. He saw no one. The cell was empty except for the two black dogs. They had entered, had lain down on the flagstones, and were mournfully sniffing the deserted stall. Outside, the rabid wind beat on the door: it wanted to come in too.

But as the rabbi prepared to lie down next to the dogs, he discovered the son of Mary standing motionless in the corner, watching him. All at once the sleep fled from his drowsy eyelids. Troubled, he sat up and nodded to his nephew to approach. The youth seemed to have been waiting for the invitation. He came forward, a bitter smile quivering about his lips.

"Sit down, Jesus," said the rabbi. "I want to talk to you."

"I'm listening," the youth replied, and he knelt opposite him. "I want to talk to you too, Uncle Simeon."

"What are you seeking here? Your mother goes around the villages looking for you, and lamenting."

"She seeks me, I seek God. We shall never meet," answered the youth.

"You are heartless. You never loved your father and mother as a human being should."

"So much the better. My heart is a lighted coal. It burns whoever it touches."

"What's the matter with you? How can you talk like that? What is lacking in you?" said the rabbi, stretching forth his head to get a better look at the son of Mary. The youth's eyes were brimming with tears. "A hidden pain is devouring you, my boy. Confess it to me and relieve yourself. A pain hidden deep down—"

"One?" interrupted the youth, and the bitter smile spread over his entire face. "Not one, many!"

The heart-rending sound of this outburst terrified the rabbi. He placed his hand on the youth's knee, to give him courage.

"I'm listening, my boy," he said gently. "Bring your sufferings into the light, draw them up out of your bowels. They thrive in darkness, but light kills them. Don't be ashamed or afraid—speak!"

But the son of Mary had not the slightest idea how to begin or what to say: what to keep unrevealed deep in his heart, what to confess in order to relieve himself. God, Magdalene, the seven sins, the crosses, the crucified—all were passing through him and lacerating his insides.

The rabbi regarded him with a look of mute supplication, and patted his knee.

"Can't you, my child?" he said finally, in a low, tender voice. "Can't you?"

"No, Uncle Simeon, I cannot."

148

"Are you beset with many temptations?" he asked, his voice even softer now and tenderer.

"Many," answered the youth, with terror, "many".

"When I was young, my child," the rabbi said with a sigh, "I too suffered much. God tormented and tested me just as he does you: he wanted to see if I should bear up, and for how long. . . . I too had many temptations. I wasn't afraid of some—the ones with savage faces; but others, the tame ones, the ones full of sweetness: those I feared; and as you know, in order to find a respite I came to this monastery, just as you have done. But God did not give up the chase, and it was here, right here, that he caught me. He sent a temptation dressed like a woman. Alas, I fell before this temptation; and since then—perhaps that is what God wanted, perhaps that is why he tormented me—since then I have been tranquil, and so has God: we were reconciled, and now we are friends. In the same way, my child, you will become reconciled with God—and be cured."

The son of Mary shook his head. "I do not think I shall be cured so easily," he murmured. He remained silent, as did the rabbi next to him. They were both breathing rapidly, gasping.

"I don't know where to begin," said the youth, starting to rise. "I shall never begin: I'm too ashamed!"

But the rabbi kept a firm hold on the youth's knee. "Don't get up," he commanded, "don't go away. Shame is also a temptation. Conquer it—stay! I'm going to ask you some questions; I'll do the asking and you're going to be patient and answer me. . . . Why did you come to the monastery?"

"To save myself."

"To save yourself? From what? From whom?"

"From God."

"From God!" the rabbi cried out, troubled.

"He's been hunting me, driving his nails into my head, my heart, my loins. . . He wants to push me—"

"Where?"

"Over the precipice."

"What precipice?"

"His. He says I should rise up and speak. But what can I say? 'Leave me alone, I have nothing to say!' I shouted at him, but he refused. 'Aha! so you refuse, do you?' I said to him. 'All right, then: now I'll show you—I'll make you detest me, and then you'll leave me alone. . . .' I fell, therefore, into every conceivable sin."

"Into every conceivable sin?" cried the rabbi.

But the young man did not hear. He had been carried away by his indignation and pain.

"Why should he choose me? Doesn't he uncover my breast and look in? All the serpents are entwined and hissing there, hissing and dancing—all the sins. And above all—"

The word stuck in his throat. He stopped. Sweat spouted from the roots of his hair.

"And above all. . ." asked the rabbi, softly.

"Magdalene!" said Jesus, raising his head.

"Magdalene!"

The rabbi's face had grown pale.

"It's my fault, mine, that she took the road she did. I drove her to the pleasures of the flesh when I was still a small child—yes, I confess it. Listen, rabbi, if you want to be horrified. It must have been when I was about three years old. I slipped into your house at a time when no one was home. I took Magdalene by the hand; we undressed and lay down on the ground, pressing together the soles of our naked feet. What joy that was, what a joyful sin! From that time on Magdalene was lost; she was lost, she could no longer live without a man, without men. . ."

He looked at the old rabbi, but the other had placed his head between his knees, and did not speak.

"It's my fault, mine! mine!" the son of Mary cried, beating his chest. "And if it were only this!" he continued after a moment. "But ever since my childhood, rabbi, I've not only kept the devil of fornication hidden deeply within me, but also the devil of arrogance. Even when I was tiny—I could hardly walk at the time, I used to go along the wall, clinging to it to keep myself from falling—even then I shouted to myself—oh, what impudence! what impudence!—'God, make me God! God, make me God! God, make me God!'. . . And one day I was holding a large bunch of grapes in my arms and a gipsy woman passed by. She came over to me, squatted, and took my hand. 'Give me the grapes,' she said, 'and I'll tell you your fortune.' I gave them to her. She bent over and looked at my palm. 'O! O!' she cried, 'I see crosses—crosses and stars. . .' Then she laughed. 'You'll become king of the Jews!' she said, and went away. But I believed her and swaggered; and ever since then, Uncle Simeon, I haven't been in my right mind. You're the first person I've told, Uncle Simeon—until now I hadn't confessed it to a soul: ever since that day I haven't been in my right mind."

He was quiet for a moment, but then:

"I am Lucifer!" he screamed. "Me! Me!"

The rabbi unwedged his head from between his knees and clamped his hand over the young man's mouth.

"Be still!" he ordered.

"No, I won't be still!" said the overwrought youth. "Now I've started, and it's too late: I won't be still! I'm a liar, a hypocrite, I'm afraid of my own shadow, I never tell the truth—I don't have the courage. When I see a woman go by, I blush and lower my head, but my eyes fill with lust. I never lift my hand to plunder or to thrash or kill—not because I don't want to, but because I'm afraid. I want to rebel against my mother, the centurion, God—but I'm afraid. Afraid! Afraid! If you look inside me, you'll see Fear, a trembling rabbit, sitting in my bowels—Fear, nothing else. That is my father, my mother and my God."

The old rabbi took the youth's hands and held them in his own, in order to calm him. But Jesus' body was quivering convulsively.

"Do not be frightened, my child," the rabbi said, comforting him. "The more devils we have within us, the more chance we have to form angels. 'Angel' is the name we give to repentant devils—so have faith. . . . But I should like to ask you just one thing more: Jesus, have you ever slept with a woman?"

"No," the youth answered softly.

"And you don't want to?"

The youth blushed and did not breathe a word, but the blood was throbbing wildly at his temples.

"You don't want to?" the old man asked once more.

"I do," the youth answered, so softly that the rabbi could hardly hear.

But all at once he gave a start as though he had just woken up, and cried:

"No, I don't, I don't!"

"Why not?" asked the rabbi, who could find no other cure for the youth's pain. He knew from his own experience and from the multitudes of those possessed with demons who came to him cursing, frothing at the mouth and screaming that the world was too small for them: they married, and suddenly the world was no longer too small; they had children, and grew calm.

"It's not enough for me," the youth said in a steady voice. "I need something bigger."

"Not enough for you?" exclaimed the rabbi with surprise. "Well then, what do you want?"

Proud-gaited high-rumped Magdalene passed through the youth's mind, her breasts exposed, her eyes, lips and cheeks covered with make-up. She laughed and her teeth flashed in the sunlight; but as she wriggled up and down before him, her body changed, multiplied, and the son of Mary now saw a lake, which must have been the lake of Gennesaret, and around it thousands of men and women—thousands of Magdalenes—with happy up-lifted faces, and the sun fell upon them and they gleamed. But no, it was not the sun, it was himself, Jesus of Nazareth, who was bent over those faces and causing them to overflow with splendour. Whether from joy, desire, or salvation he could not distinguish: all he saw was the splendour.

"What are you thinking about?" asked the rabbi. "Why don't you answer me?"

The young man burst out, asking abruptly: "Do you believe in dreams, Uncle Simeon? I do; I believe in nothing else. One night I dreamt that invisible enemies had me tied to a dead cypress. Long red arrows were sticking into me from my head to my feet, and the blood was flowing. On my head they had placed a crown of thorns, and intertwined with the thorns were fiery letters which said: 'Saint Blasphemer.' . . . I am Saint Blasphemer, Rabbi Simeon. So you'd better not ask me anything else, or I'll start my blasphemies."

"Go ahead, my child—start," the rabbi said tranquilly, taking hold again of his hand. "Start your blasphemies and relieve yourself."

"There's a devil inside me which cries, 'You're not the son of

152

the Carpenter, you're the son of King David! You are not a man, you are the Son of man whom Daniel prophesied. And still more: The Son of God! And still more: God!' "

The rabbi listened, bowed over, and shudders passed through his ramshackle body. The youth's chapped lips were rimmed with froth; his tongue adhered to his palate: he could no longer speak. But what else was he to say? He had already said everything; he felt that his heart had been drained. Jerking his hands free of the rabbi's grip, he got up. Then he turned to the old man.

"Have you anything else to ask?" he said sarcastically.

"No," replied the old man, who felt all the strength flow out of him into the earth and perish. In his lifetime he had extracted many devils from the mouths of men. The possessed came from the ends of the earth and he cured them. Their devils, however, were small, and easy: devils of the bath, of anger, of sickness. But now . . . How could he wrestle with a devil like this?

Outside, the wind of Jehovah still beat on the door, trying to enter. There was no other sound. Not a jackal on the earth, nor a crow in the air. . . . Every living thing cowered in fear, waiting for the Lord's anger to pass.

XI

THE son of Mary leaned against the wall and shut his eyes. His mouth was bitter, poisonously bitter. The rabbi, his head once more wedged between his knees, meditated on hell and devils and the heart of man. . . . No, hell with its devils was not in the great pit below the earth, it was in the breasts of men, in the breast of the most virtuous, the most just. God was an abyss, man was an abyss—and the old rabbi did not dare open his heart to see what lay within.

They did not speak for some time. Deep silence. . . . Even the two black dogs had fallen asleep: they had grown tired of lamenting the deceased. Suddenly there was a sweet, piercing hiss from the yard. The half-mad Jeroboam jumped up, the first to hear it. The wind of Jehovah was always accompanied by this sweet hissing in the yard, and the monk bounded with delight whenever the sound reached his ears. The sun was setting, but the entire yard was still bathed in light and on the flagstones next to the dried-up well, the monk's eyes perceived a large snake, black with yellow patterns, lifting its swelled neck, vibrating its tongue, and hissing. Never in his life had Jeroboam heard a flute more seductive than this snaky throat. Now and then in the summertime, when he too dreamt of a woman, she appeared to him like this, like a snake which slid over the mat where he slept, put its tongue in his ear, and hissed. . . .

Tonight Jeroboam had once more flown out of his cell, and now, holding his breath, he approached the enflamed snake. It piped; he looked at it, looked at it, and began to pipe also and to feel the snake's warmth pass into his body. Then, little by little, other snakes emerged from the dried-up well or out of the sand, or from around the cacti: one with a blue hood, another green with two horns, others yellow, dappled, black. . . . Quickly, like water, they slid forward and joined the first snake, the decoy; they strung themselves all together, rubbed one against the next, licked each other: a snaky cluster of grapes hung in the middle of the yard, and Jeroboam opened his mouth and drooled. This is sex, he reflected. Men and women couple like this, and that is why God banished us from Paradise. . . . His humped unkissed body swayed back and forth in time with the snakes.

The rabbi heard the enticing sound, raised his head, and listened. God's fiery wind blows, he said to himself, and right in the middle of it, the snakes mate. The Lord puffs and wants to incinerate the world, and up come the snakes to make love! . . . For a moment the old man's mind succumbed to the enticement and wandered. But suddenly he shuddered. Everything is of God, he reflected, everything has two meanings, one manifest, one hidden. The common people comprehend only what is manifest. They say, "This is a snake," and their minds go no further; but the mind which dwells in God sees what lies behind the visible, sees the hidden meaning. These snakes which crept out today in front of the doors of this cell and began to hiss at precisely this moment, just after the son of Mary's confession, must assuredly have a deep concealed meaning. . . . But what is that meaning?

He rolled up into a ball on the ground, his temples throbbing. What was the meaning? Cold sweat flowed over his sun-baked face. Sometimes he glanced out of the corner of his eye at the pale youth next to him; sometimes, with eyes closed and mouth opened, he listened intently to the snakes outside. What was the meaning?

He had learnt the language of the birds from the great exorcist Josaphat, his former superior, who was Abbot when he came to the monastery to become a monk. He could interpret the sayings of swallows, doves and eagles. Josaphat had also promised to teach him the language of the snakes, but he died and took the secret with him. . . . These snakes tonight were doubtlessly bringing a message, but what was that message?

He rolled himself up again and squeezed his head between his hands: his mind was jingling. He writhed and sighed for a considerable time and felt white and black thunderbolts tear through his brain. What was the meaning? What was the message? Suddenly he uttered a cry. He got up from the ground, took the Abbot's crosier, and leaned on it.

"Jesus," he said in a low voice, "how does your heart feel?"

But the youth did not hear. He was plunged in unspeakable exultation. Tonight, after so many years, tonight, the night he had decided to confess and speak out, he was able for the first time to look into the darkness of his heart and distinguish, one by one, the serpents which were hissing within him. He gave them names, and as he did so, it seemed to him that they issued from his bowels and slid away outside, relieving him.

"Jesus, how does your heart feel?" the old man asked again. "Is it relieved?" He leaned over and took him by the hand. "Come," he said tenderly, and he put his finger to his lips.

He opened the door. He held Jesus by the hand, and they crossed the threshold. The audacious snakes, glued one to the next and holding on to the earth with nothing but their tails, had risen in the middle of the fiery swirl of sand and were dancing in a row, completely at the mercy of God's wind; and from time to time they stiffened and ceased moving, exhausted.

The son of Mary recoiled at the sight of them, but the rabbi squeezed his hand, held out the crosier and touched the edge of the snaky cluster.

"Here they are," he said softly, watching the youth and smiling. "They've fled."

"Fled?" asked the youth, perplexed. "Fled from where?"

"You feel your heart unburdened, don't you? They have fled from your heart."

The son of Mary stared with protruding eyes first at the rabbi, who was smiling at him, then at she snakes which, all in a clump, were now transferring themselves in a dance towards the dried-up well. He put his hand to his heart and felt it beating quickly, elatedly.

"Let's go inside," said the rabbi, taking him again by the hand. They entered and the rabbi closed the door.

"Glory be to God," he exclaimed with emotion. He looked at the son of Mary, and felt strangely troubled.

This is a miracle, he said to himself. The life of this boy who stands before me is nothing but miracles. . . . At one moment he wanted to hold his hands over Jesus' head and bless him, at the next to stoop and kiss his feet. . . . But he restrained himself. Had not God deceived him time after time until now? How many times, as he heard the prophets who had come forth lately from mountainside or desert, had he said: "This one is the Messiah!"? But God deceived him each time, and the rabbi's heart, which was ready to blossom, always remained a flowerless stump. So, he restrained himself. . . . I must test him first, he thought. Those were the serpents which were devouring him. They have fled and he has been cleansed. He is capable now of rising. He will speak to men—and then, we shall see.

The door opened and in came Jeroboam the guest-master with the two visitors' meagre supper of barley-bread, olives and milk. He turned to Jesus.

"I laid your sleeping-mat in another cell tonight so that you could have company."

But the minds of the two visitors were far away, and they did not hear. The snakes could be heard again, from the bottom of the well. They were piping, piping and gasping for breath.

"They're getting married," giggled the monk. "The wind of God blows, and they—a plague on them!—they don't get scared, they get married!"

He looked at the old man and winked, but the rabbi had begun to dip his bread into the milk and to chew. He wanted to gain strength, to transform the bread, olives and milk into intelligence so that he could speak to the son of Mary. The stunted hunchback eyed first the one, then the other, got bored, and left.

The two sat cross-legged facing one another, and ate in silence. The cell had grown dim. The stools, the Abbot's stall and the lectern, with the prophet Daniel still opened upon it, gleamed fuzzily in the darkness. The air of the cell still smelt of sweet-incense. Outside, the wind grew calm.

"The wind has subsided," the rabbi said at one point. "God has come and gone."

The youth did not reply. They've left, they've left, he was thinking, the serpents have fled from within me. . . . Perhaps that is just what God wanted, perhaps that it why he brought me here to the desert: to be cured. He blew, the serpents heard him, came out of my heart, and fled. . . . Glory be to God!

Having finished eating, the rabbi lifted his hands and gave thanks to God. Then he turned to his companion:

"Jesus, where is your mind? I am the rabbi of Nazareth. Do you hear me?"

"I hear you, Uncle Simeon," said the youth, coming out of his great torpor with a start.

"The hour is here, my child. Are you ready?"

"Ready. . . ? Ready for what?" asked Jesus, shuddering.

"You know very well—why do you ask me? Ready to stand up and speak."

"To whom?"

"To mankind."

"To say what?"

"Don't worry about that. You just open your mouth. God seeks nothing more from you. Do you love mankind?"

"I don't know. I see men and feel sorry for them, nothing else."

"That's enough, my child, that's enough. Rise up and speak to them. Your sorrows may then be multiplied, but theirs will be relieved. Perhaps that is why God sent you into the world. We shall see!"

"Perhaps that is why God sent me into the world?" the youth repeated. "How do you know, Father?" His soul left his body and hung on tenterhooks, awaiting the response.

"I don't. No one told me; but still, it's possible. I've seen signs. Once when you were a boy you took some clay and fashioned a bird. While you caressed it and talked to it, it seemed to me that this bird of clay grew wings and flew out of your grasp. . . . It's possible that this clay bird is the soul of man, Jesus, my child—the soul of man in your hands."

The youth got up and carefully opened the door. Putting out his head, he listened. The snakes were completely silent now—at last. Pleased, he turned to the old rabbi.

"Give me your blessing, Father, and do not say anything else to me. You've spoken quite enough; I cannot bear to hear more."

And after a pause: "I'm tired, Uncle Simeon, I'm going to bed. Sometimes God comes during the night and explains the events of the day. . . . Sleep well, Uncle Simeon."

The guest-master was waiting for him outside the door.

"Let's go," he said. "I'll show you where I put your bed. What's your name, my fine lad?"

"Son of the Carpenter."

"Mine's Jeroboam. I'm also called Brother Crackbrain, and also The Hunchback. So what! I keep my nose to the grindstone and gnaw the dry crust which God gave me."

"What dry crust?"

The hunchback laughed.

"Don't you understand, nitwit? My soul! And as soon as I get done—good night, pleasant dreams—along comes Charon and starts gnawing on me!"

He halted and opened a tiny squat door.

"Enter," he said. "There—in the back corner, to the left: your mat!" Guffawing, he pushed him through the doorway. "Sleep well, my fine lad, and pleasant dreams. But never fear, you'll dream about women—it's in the monastery air."

Splitting with laughter, he shut the door with a thunderous bang.

The son of Mary did not move. Darkness. . . . At first he distinguished nothing, but little by little half-transparent whitewashed walls began ever so imperceptibly to appear, a jug glittered in a niche along the wall; and in the corner, riveted upon him, were two sparking eyes.

He groped his way slowly forward, his arms stretched before him. His foot stumbled on the unfolded mat, and he stopped. The two eyes shifted, following him.

"Good evening, friend," the son of Mary greeted his companion, but no one replied.

Hunched up into a ball, his chin against his knees, his heavy gasping breaths reverberating throughout the cell, Judas leaned against the wall and watched him. Come. . . , come. . . , come. . . , he murmured within himself, the knife squeezed in his fist against his breast. Come. . . , come. . . , come. . . , he murmured, watching the son of Mary approach. Come. . . , come. . . , come. . . , he murmured, luring him.

His mind went back to the village where he was born, Kerioth, in far-away Idumea. He remembered that this was exactly how his uncle the exorcist had lured the jackals, rabbits and partridge he wanted to kill. He used to lie down on the ground, pin his burning eyes on the game and produce a hiss full of longing, entreaty and command: come. . . , come. . . , come. . . . The animal would immediately grow dizzy and start to creep, head bowed and out of breath, towards the hissing mouth. . . .

Suddenly Judas began to hiss—softly at first and with much tenderness, but all at once the sound grew stronger, became fierce and menacing, and the son of Mary, who had lain down to sleep, jumped up in terror. Who was this next to him? Who was hissing? He felt the odour of an incensed beast in the air, and understood.

"Judas, my brother, is that you?" he asked quietly.

"Crucifier!" growled the other, angrily stamping his heel on the ground.

"Judas, my brother," the youth repeated, "the crucifier suffers more than the crucified."

The redbeard lashed out and twirled his whole body around so that it faced the son of Mary.

"I swore to my brothers the Zealots and to the mother of the crucified that I would kill you. Welcome, cross-maker. I hissed, and you came."

He jumped to his feet, bolted the door and then returned to the corner and rolled himself up again into a ball, with his face turned towards Jesus.

"Did you hear what I said? Don't start your blubbering. Get ready!"

"I am ready."

"No shouting now! Quick! I want to get away while it's still dark."

"I'm delighted to see you, Judas, my brother. I'm ready. It wasn't you who hissed, it was God—and I came. His abounding grace arranged everything perfectly. You came just at the right moment, Judas, my brother. Tonight my heart was unburdened, purified: I can present myself now before God. I have grown tired of wrestling with him, grown tired of living. . . . I offer you my neck, Judas—I am ready."

The blacksmith groaned and knit his brows. He did not like, did not like at all—indeed it disgusted him to touch a neck which was offered undefended, like a lamb's. What he wanted was resistance, body-to-body grappling, and the kill to come at the very end as was appropriate for real men—after the blood had become heated: a just reward for the struggle.

The son of Mary waited, his neck stretched forward. But the blacksmith thrust out his huge hand and pushed him away.

"Why don't you resist?" he growled. "What kind of a man are you? Get up and fight!"

"But I don't want to, Judas, my brother. Why should I resist? What you want, I want; and surely God wants the same—that is why he put all the pieces together so perfectly. Don't you see: I departed for this monastery, you departed at the same moment; I arrived and right away my heart was cleansed: I prepared myself to be killed; you took your knife, huddled in this corner and prepared yourself to kill; the door opened, I entered. . . . What further signs could you possibly want, Judas, my brother?"

But the blacksmith did not speak. He chewed his moustache in a frenzy; his boiling blood circulating by fits and starts, rose to his head and fired his brain a bright red, rushed down again leaving it pale, then remounted. . .

"Why do you build crosses?" he thundered finally.

The young man lowered his head. That was his secret—how could he reveal it? How could the blacksmith give credence to the dreams which God sent him, or to the voices he heard when he was all alone, or the talons which nailed themselves into the top of his head and wanted to lift him to heaven? And he resisted and did not want to go—how could Judas understand that? He clutched sin, desperately, as a means of keeping himself on earth.

"I cannot explain it to you, Judas, my brother. Forgive me," he said contritely, "but I cannot."

The blacksmith shifted his position so that he could better distinguish the youth's face in the darkness. He looked at it avidly, then slowly drew back and leaned once again against the wall. What kind of person is this? he asked himself. I can't understand. I wonder if it's the devil who's guiding him—or God? In either case, damn him! he leads him with a sure hand. He doesn't resist, and that is the greatest resistance. I can't slaughter lambs; men, yes—but not lambs.

"You're a coward, you miserable wretch!" he burst out. "Ooo —why don't you go to hell! You're slapped on one cheek and you,

161

what do you do, you right away turn the other. You see a knife, and right away you stick out your neck. A man can't touch you without feeling disgusted."

"God can," the son of Mary murmured tranquilly.

The blacksmith twisted the knife in his fist, unable to make up his mind. For an instant he imagined he saw a halo of light trembling in the darkness over the youth's bowed head. Terror came over him, and the joints of his hands went slack.

"I may be thick-headed," he said to the son of Mary, "but speak —I'll understand. Who are you? What do you want? Where do you come from? What are these tales that surround you on every side: a flowering staff, a lightning flash, the fainting spells which seize you while you walk, the voices which you're said to hear in the darkness? Tell me, what is your secret?"

"Pity, Judas, my brother."

"For whom? Whom do you pity? Is it yourself, your own wretchedness and poverty? Or perhaps you feel sorry for Israel? Well, speak! Is it for Israel? That's what I want you to say, do you hear? That and nothing else. Are you being devoured by Israel's suffering?"

"By man's, Judas, my brother."

"Forget about 'man'. The Greeks who slaughtered us for so many years, curse them!—they're men. The Romans are men, and they're still slaughtering us and soiling the Temple and our God. Why care about them? It's Israel you should keep your sights on, and if you feel pity, it should be pity for Israel. All the others can go to the devil!"

"But I feel pity for the jackals, Judas, my brother, and for the sparrows, and the grass."

"Ha! Ha!" jeered the redbeard. "And for the ants?"

"Yes, for the ants too. Everything is God's. When I bend over the ant, inside his black shiny eye I see the face of God."

"And if you bend over my face, son of the Carpenter?"

"There too, very deep down, I see the face of God."

"And you don't fear death?"

"Why should I, Judas, my brother? Death is not a door which closes, it is a door which opens. It opens, and you enter."

"Enter where?"

"The bosom of God."

Judas sighed with vexation. This fellow just can't be caught, he reflected, he can't be caught, because he has no fear of death. . . . Propping his chin on his palm, he looked at Jesus and strained to come to a decision.

"If I don't kill you," he said finally, "what do you plan to do?"

"I don't know. Whatever God decides. . . . I should like to get up and speak to men."

"To tell them what?"

"How do you expect me to know, Judas, my brother? I'll open my mouth, and God will do the talking."

The halo of light around the youth's head grew brighter; his sad wasted face flashed like lightning and his large jet-black eyes seduced Judas with their unutterable sweetness. The redbeard felt troubled and lowered his eyes. I wouldn't kill him, he thought, if I were sure he would go out to speak and rouse the hearts of the Israelites, rouse them to attack the Romans.

"What are you waiting for, Judas, my brother?" asked the youth. "Or perhaps God did not send you to kill me; perhaps he wills something else, something unknown even to you, and you look at me and struggle to divine what it is. I am ready to be killed, and I am also ready to live. Decide."

"Don't be in a rush," the other answered dejectedly. "The night is long, we have plenty of time."

But after a pause, he shouted frantically: "A fellow can't even talk to you without getting himself in hot water. I ask you one thing and you answer another: I can't pin you down. My heart and mind were more certain before I saw you and listened to you than they are now. . . . Leave me alone. Turn your head the other way and go to sleep. I want to be alone so that I can digest all this and see what I'm going to do."

This said, he turned towards the wall, grumbling.

The son of Mary lay down on his mat and tranquilly crossed his hands.

Whatever God wants, that is what will happen, he reflected, and he closed his eyes with confidence.

An owl emerged from its hole in the rock facing them, saw that God's whirlwind had passed, flew to and fro silently and then

163

began to hoot tenderly, calling its mate. God has left, it called, we've escaped once more, dearest—come! . . . High above, the skylight of the cell had filled with stars. The son of Mary opened his eyes and was happy to see them. They moved slowly, disappeared; others arose. . . . The hours went by.

Judas twisted and turned, still cross-legged on his mat. Now and then he got up, gasping and murmuring, and went as far as the door, only to return again. The son of Mary watched him with half-closed eyes and waited. Whatever God wants, that is what will happen, he thought, and he waited. The hours passed by.

A camel in the stable adjacent to them neighed with fear; she must have seen a wolf or a lion in her sleep. Immense new stars mounted ferociously from the east, ordered like an army.

Suddenly a cock crowed in the still-deep darkness. Judas jumped up. With one stride he was at the door. He opened it violently, closed it behind him. His bare feet could be heard stamping heavily over the flagstones.

And then, the son of Mary turned and saw his faithful fellow-voyager. She was in the corner, erect and vigilant in the darkness.

"Forgive me, my sister," he said to her. "The hour has not yet come."

XII

THERE was a warm damp wind today which lifted large waves on the lake of Gennesaret. Autumn had already come and the earth smelt of vine leaves and overripe grapes. Men and women had poured out of Capernaum at dawn. The vintage was in its glory; the bunches of grapes, filled with their juice, lay waiting on the ground. The young girls, sparkling like the grapes, had eaten whole clusters and smeared their faces with must. The young men, panting in the full rage of youth, threw furtive glances at the giggling girls who were vintaging. In every vineyard there were shouts and fits of laughter. The girls grew bold and teased the boys, who became more and more heated and drew closer. The sly devil of the vintage ran to and fro pinching the women and splitting his sides with laughter.

Old Zebedee's spacious village house was wide open and buzzing. The wine press, on the left side of the yard, was being loaded with the contents of brimful hampers which the young men transported from the vineyards. Four giants, Philip, Jacob, Peter, and Nathanael, the village cobbler, a naive camel of a man, were washing their hairy shins and preparing to enter the press to tread the grapes. Every pauper in Capernaum was sure to have his tiny vineyard for the year's supply of wine, and each year he transported his crop to this press, trod the grapes and took back his share of the must. And old stuff-pocket Zebedee filled his own jars and barrels for the year with the commission he took for use of the press. He sat therefore on a raised platform with a long stick and a pen-knife in his hands and by means of notches marked the number of each person's hampers. But the owners also kept a record in their minds: they did not want to be cheated the day after next at the division of the must. Old Zebedee was predacious —nobody trusted him, and everyone had to have eyes in the back of his head.

The window of the inner house which gave onto the yard was open, and stretched on the divan was old Salome, the mistress of the house. She gazed outside and listened to all that went on in the yard; in this way she forgot the pains which tortured her knees and other joints. She must have been exceedingly beautiful in her youth—slim-boned, tall, with olive skin and large eyes: of a good stock. Three villages—Capernaum, Magdala and Bethsaida—had vied for her. Three suitors had set out at the same time and found her old father, the wealthy shipowner. Each came with a rich train of friends, camels and overflowing hampers. The shrewd old man carefully weighed in his mind the body, soul and fortune of each—and chose Zebedee, who wed her. She had pleased him, but now the exquisite girl had grown old, her beauty, eaten by time, had fallen away, and now and then, during the important festivals, her vigorous still-juicy husband made the rounds at night and played with the widows.

Today, however, old Salome's face was aglow. John her favourite son, had arrived the day before from the holy monastery. He was truly pale and skinny. Prayer and fasting had broken him, but she would keep him near her now and never let him go away again. She would nourish him with food and drink and he would grow strong, his cheeks would sparkle once more. God is good, she said to herself, and we worship his grace. Yes, he is good— but he must not want to drink the blood of our children. Fasting in moderation, prayer in moderation: that would be fine for both man and God, and they should arrange things in this way— sensibly. . . . She looked anxiously at the door, waiting for John, her baby, to return from the vineyards where he too was helping to bring in the vintage.

In the middle of the yard, beneath the large almond tree, which was heavy with fruit, Judas the redbeard was bent over, silent, swinging his hammer and fitting iron bands around the wine-barrels. If you looked at him from the right, his face was sullen and full of malice; if you looked at him from the left it was uneasy, and sad. Many days had passed since he fled like a thief from the monastery. During this time he had gone round the villages fitting up barrels for the new must. He would enter the houses, work, listen to the talk and register in his mind the words and deeds of each man, in order to inform the brotherhood of everything. . . . But where was the old redbeard—the rowdy, the wrangler! Ever since the day he left the monastery, he had been unrecognizable.

"Damn it, Judas Iscariot, open your mouth, devil-hair," Zebedee yelled at him. "What are you thinking about? Two and two make four—haven't you realized that yet? Open your mouth, you blessed ruffian, and say something. This is the vintage—no small matter. On a day like this everyone laughs, even the sullen black sheep."

"Don't lead him into temptation, Zebedee," Philip interrupted. "He went to the monastery; it seems he wants to don the robe. Haven't you heard? When the devil gets old, he becomes a monk!"

Judas turned and threw a venomous glance at Philip, but did not speak. He detested him. He wasn't a man: no, he was all words and no action, a prattler. At the last minute he'd become paralysed with fear and had refused to enter the brotherhood. "I have sheep," was his excuse. "I have sheep; how can I leave them?"

Old Zebedee burst out laughing and turned to the redbeard; "Take care, wretch," he shouted at him. "Monasticism is a contagious disease. Look out you don't catch it! . . . My own son escaped by a hair's breadth. My old lady got sick, bless her, and her pet learned about it. He had already finished his schooling in herbs with the Abbot, so he came home to doctor her. He won't leave here again, mark my words. Where to go? He's not insane, is he? There, in the desert, there's hunger, thirst, prostrations— and God. Here there's food, wine, women—and God. Everywhere God. So, why go look for him in the desert? What's your opinion, Judas Iscariot?"

But the redbeard swung his hammer and did not answer. What could he say to him? Everything came to this filthy dog just as he wanted it. How could he understand the next man's troubles? Even God, who wiped others off the face of the earth for the jump of a flea, flattered and coddled this swine, this parasite, this lickpenny, kept him from suffering the slightest harm, fell over him like a woollen cloak in the winter, like cool linen in the summer. Why? What did he see in him? Was the old bastard devoured with concern for Israel? Why, he wouldn't lift his little finger to help Israel—he loved the Roman criminals because they guarded his wealth. May God protect them, he said, for they maintain order.

167

If not for them the mob of ruffians and barefooted riff-raff would fall all over us, and that would be the last we'd see of our property. . . . But never fear, you old bastard, the hour will come. What God forgets and leaves undone the Zealots, bless them, will remember and do. . . . Patience, Judas, do not breathe a word. Patience. Jehovah Sabaoth's day will come!

Raising his turquoise eyes, he looked at Zebedee and saw him in the wine press, floating on his back in his own blood. His whole face smiled.

By this time the four giants had carefully scrubbed their legs and jumped into the press. Sunk up to the knees, they stamped and trampled the grapes, stooping to pick up whole fistfuls, which they ate, filling their beards with the stems. Sometimes they danced hand in hand, sometimes each screamed and jumped by himself. The smell of the must had made them drunk—and the must was not all: as they looked through the opened front door towards the vineyards they saw the girls bend over to pick up the grapes. Their beauty was visible even above the knees, and their breasts, like clusters of grapes, swung back and forth over the vine leaves.

The treaders saw them, and their minds grew turbid. This was not a wine press, that was not land and vineyard—but Paradise, with old Jehovah Sabaoth sitting on the platform holding a long stick and a pen-knife and marking his exact obligation to each: how many hampers of grapes each had brought and how many jugs of wine, day after tomorrow when they died, he would offer them—how many jugs of wine, how many cauldrons of food, how many women!

"On my honour," snapped Peter, "if God came this very moment and said to me: 'Hey, Pete, my little Pete, I'm in the best of moods today, ask me a favour, any favour, and I'll do it for you: what do you want?'—if he asked me that I should answer him, 'To tread grapes, Lord, to tread grapes for all eternity!'"

"And not to drink the wine, blockhead?" Zebedee rudely asked him.

"No, from the bottom of my heart: to tread the grapes!" He did not laugh; his face was serious and absorbed. He stopped treading for a moment and stretched in the sun. His upper body was bare, and tattooed over his heart was a large black fish. An artisan, formerly a prisoner, had tapped it on years before with a needle, so skillfully that you thought it moved its tail and swam happily, all tangled up in the curly hairs of Peter's chest. Above the fish was a small anchor with four crossed arms, each with a barb.

But Philip remembered his sheep. He did not like to plough the land, care for vineyards or tread grapes.

"Good God, Peter," he scoffed, "some job you found yourself —treading grapes for all eternity! I should have asked the Lord to make heaven and earth a green meadow full of goats and sheep. I should then milk them and send the milk flowing down the mountainside. It would run like a river and form lakes on the plain so that the poor could drink. And every night all of us should gather—all the shepherds, together with God the chief shepherd; we should light a fire, roast a lamb and tell stories. That is the meaning of Paradise!"

"A plague on you, moron!" grumbled Judas, and he threw another fierce glance at Philip.

The adolescents went in and out of the yard, naked, hairy, with a coloured rag around their loins. They listened to these disconnected discussions and laughed. They too had a Paradise inside them, but they did not confess what it was. They shovelled the hampers into the press and then with one bound were over the threshold and off to rejoin the pretty vintagers.

Zebedee parted his lips to add a clever remark, but remained standing with gaping mouth. A strange visitor had appeared at the door and was listening to them. He wore a black goat-skin which hung from his neck; his feet were bare, his hair dishevelled and his face yellow, like sulphur. His eyes were large, black, and fiery.

The feet ceased treading, Zebedee swallowed his witticism, and everyone turned towards the door. Who was this living corpse who stood on the threshold? The laughter came to a standstill. Old Salome appeared at the window, looked, and suddenly cried: "It's Andrew!"

"Good God, Andrew," shouted Zebedee, "just look at you! Are you returning to us from the underworld? Or maybe you're on you're way down there!"

Peter jumped out of the wine press, clasped his brother's hand without uttering a word, and looked at him with love and fright. Oh God, was this Andrew, Andrew the chubby young hero, the celebrated athlete, first in work and play? Was this the Andrew who had been engaged to flaxen-haired Ruth, the prettiest girl in the village? She had been drowned on the lake together with her father, one night when God raised a terrible wind, and Andrew had left in despair in order to surrender himself, bound hand and foot, to God. Who could tell, he thought. If I join God perhaps I shall find her with him. Obviously, he was seeking his fiancée, not God.

Peter stared at him in terror. He remembered how he had been when they surrendered him to God; and now, look how God had returned him to them!

"Hey," Zebedee shouted at Peter, "are you going to gape at him and finger him all day long? Let him come in; out there a wind might blow and knock him down! . . . Come in, Andrew my boy, bend over, take some grapes and eat. We have bread too, glory be to God. Eat and put some colour in your cheeks, because if your poor old father sees you in the state you're in, he'll be so scared he'll burrow right back into his shark!"

But Andrew raised his bony arm: "Aren't you ashamed of yourselves!" he shouted to them all. "Don't you fear God? The world is perishing, and you tread grapes here and laugh!"

"The saints preserve us, here's another one come to give us a hard time!" grumbled Zebedee, and now he turned to Andrew in a rage. "You won't leave us alone either, eh? We're stuffed to the gills, if you want to know. Is this what your prophet the Baptist proclaims? Well, you'd better tell him to change his tune. He says the end of the world has come, that the tombs will open and the dead fly out; he says God will descend—Second Coming!—to open the ledger, and then woe is us! . . . Lies! Lies! Lies! Don't listen to him, lads. On with our work! Tread the grapes!"

"Repent! Repent!" bellowed the son of Jonah. He shook himself out of his brother's embrace and stood in the middle of the yard, directly in front of old Zebedee, with his finger lifted towards the sky.

"For your own good, Andrew," said Zebedee, "sit down, eat,

drink a bit of wine and come to your senses. Poor thing, hunger has driven you mad!"

"Easy living has driven you mad, Zebedee," replied the son of Jonah. "But the ground is opening under your feet. The Lord is an earthquake; he'll swallow your wine press and your boats and you too, you and your confounded belly!"

He had caught fire. Shifting his eyes from side to side, he pinned them now on one, now on another, and shouted: "Before this must turns to wine, the end of the world will come! Put on hair shirts, spread ashes over your heads, beat your breasts and shout 'I have have sinned! I have sinned!' The earth is a tree, it has grown rotten, and the Messiah is coming with the axe!"

Judas stopped his hammering. His upper lip had rolled back and his sharp teeth gleamed in the sunlight. But Zebedee could control himself no longer.

"For the love of God, Peter," he shouted, "take him and get out of here. We've work to do. 'He's coming! . . . He's coming!' Sometimes he holds fire, sometimes a ledger and now—what next! —an axe. Why can't you leave us alone, you impostors, you deceivers of the people? This world is holding up fine, just fine— that's what I say! . . . Tread the grapes, men, and rest assured!"

Peter patted his brother tenderly on the back to calm him. "Be still," he said to him softly, "be still, Brother, don't shout. You're tired from your trip. Let's go home so that you can get some rest and so Father can see you and quiet his heart." He took him by the hand and slowly, carefully, guided his way as though he were blind. They went up the narrow street and disappeared.

Old Zebedee burst into laughter. "Eh, miserable Jonah, my poor old fish-profit, I shouldn't want to be in your shoes for all the world!"

But now it was old Salome's turn to open her mouth. She still felt Andrew's large eyes hanging over her and burning her. "Zebedee," she said, shaking her white-haired head, "mind what you say, old sinner. Do not laugh. An angel stands above us and writes. You will be paid in kind for your scoffing."

"Mother is right," said Jacob, who until now had kept his mouth locked. "You were within a hair's breadth of suffering the same thing with John, your pet; and as far as I can see, you're still not out of danger. He isn't helping with the vintage, so I'm told by the carriers, he's sitting with the women and slobbering about God and fasting and immortal souls. . . . I shouldn't want to be in your shoes either, Father!"

He laughed drily. He could not stomach his lazy pampered brother, and started furiously to stamp the grapes.

The blood rose to Zebedee's large head. He, in his turn, could not stomach his eldest son—they resembled each other too much. A quarrel would have broken out if at that moment Mary, the wife of Joseph of Nazareth, had not appeared at the door, leaning on John's arm. Her thin feet were bloody and covered with dust from her long journey. For days now she had abandoned her house and gone from village to village, weeping, in search of her unfortunate son. God had robbed him of his senses; he had departed from the ways of men. Sighing, the mother sang her son's dirge while he was still alive. She asked, asked everywhere if anyone had seen him: "He's tall, thin, barefooted; he was wearing a blue tunic and a black leather belt. Have you noticed him, perhaps?". . . No one had seen him, and it was only now, thanks to Zebedee's younger son, that she had got on his trail. He was at the monastery in the desert. He had donned the white robe and was prostrate, face down on the earth, praying. . . . John, feeling sorry for her, had revealed everything. Now, leaning on his arm, she entered Zebedee's yard for a bit of rest before she set out for the desert.

Old Salome rose majestically. "Welcome, Mary dear," she said. "Come inside."

Mary lowered her kerchief to her brows, bowed her head and passed through the yard with her eyes on the ground. Grasping her elderly friend's hand, she began to cry.

"It's a great sin for you to cry, my child," said old Salome. She placed her on the divan and sat down by her side. "Your son is in safety now, he's under God's roof."

"A mother's pain is heavy, Salome ma'am," Mary answered with a sigh. "God sent me but one boy, and he a blemished one."

Old Zebedee heard her complaint (he was not a bad man if you did not interfere with his profits) and came down from his platform in order to comfort her. "It's his youth, Mary," he said, "his youth. Don't worry about it—it will pass. Youth, bless it, is like wine, but we sober up soon enough and slide under the yoke without any more kicking. Your son will sober up too, Mary. Take my own son, the one you see before you: he's beginning now to get sober, glory be to God."

John blushed but did not say a word. He went inside to fetch a cup of cold water and some ripe figs to offer the visitor. The two women, sitting side by side, their heads touching, talked about the boy who had been swept away by God. They conversed in whispers so that the men would not hear them and by interfering spoil the deep feminine joy given them by pain.

"He prays and prays, your son tells me, Salome ma'am; he prostrates himself so much, his hands and knees have become all calloused. John says also that he doesn't eat, that he's melting away. He's begun to see wings in the air, too. It seems he even refuses to drink water, in order to see the angels. . . . Where can this affliction lead, Salome ma'am? Not even his uncle the rabbi can heal him, and think how many other people possessed with devils he has cured. . . . Why has God cursed me, Salome ma'am, what have I done to him?"

She leaned her head against her elderly friend's knees and began to weep.

John appeared with a brass cup filled with water, and five or six figs on a figleaf. "Don't cry, ma'am," he said to her, placing the figs in her lap. "A holy glimmer runs around your son's entire face. Not everyone sees it, but one night I did: I saw it licking his face and devouring it, and I was frightened. And after the Abbot died, father Habakkuk dreamt of him every night. He says he held your son by the hand and took him from cell to cell, pointing to him with his outstretched finger, not speaking, just smiling and pointing to him. . . . Finally father Habakkuk jumped out of bed in terror and roused the other monks. They struggled all together to disentangle the dream. What did the Abbot wish to tell them? Why did he point to their new guest and smile? Suddenly, the day before yesterday, the day I left, the monks were illumined by God and they untangled the dream. The dead man was instructing them to make your son Abbot. . . . Without losing a moment, the whole monastery-full of monks went and found your son. They fell at his feet and shouted that it was God's will he should become Abbot of the monastery. But your son refused. 'No, no, this is not my road,' he said. 'I am unworthy, I shall leave!' I heard his cries of refusal at noon, just as I left the monastery. The monks were threatening to lock him into a cell and place sentries in front of the door to prevent his escape."

"Congratulations, Mary," said old Salome, her aged face gleaming. "Fortunate mother! God blew into your womb and you don't even realize it!"

The woman loved by God heard and shook her head, unconsoled. "I don't want my son to be a saint," she murmured. "I want him to be a man like all the rest. I want him to marry and give me grandchildren. That is God's way."

"That is man's way," said John, softly, as though ashamed to offer an objection. "The other is God's way, the one your son is following."'

They heard voices and laughter from the direction of the vineyards. Two young, flushed carriers entered the yard.

"Bad news, bosses," they shouted, splitting with laughter. "It looks like Magdala's risen up. The people have taken stones and are hunting their mermaid in order to kill her!"

"What mermaid, lads?" yelled the treaders, stopping their dance. "Magdalene?"

"Yes, Magdalene, bless her! Two mule-drivers brought us the news as they went by. They said the bandit-chief Barabbas—phew! all fear and trembling he is!—they said he left Nazareth and invaded Magdala yesterday, Saturday."

"There's another one for you!" growled Zebedee in a rage. "A plague on him! He says he's a Zealot and will save Israel, him and his beastly snout. May he rot in hell, the filthy bastard! . . . Well?"

"Well, he went by Magdalene's house in the evening and found her yard full-up. The excommunicate was working on the holy Sabbath! This impiety was too much for him. In he rushes, yanks his knife out from under his shirt, the merchants draw their swords, the neighbours crowd in too, they all rush at each other and before you know it the yard turns into a tangled mass of arms and legs. Two of our men fell wounded; the merchants mounted their camels and ran for their lives. Barabbas broke down the door to find the lady in question and slaughter her. But where was Magdalene? She'd flown the coop, gone out through the back door, unseen! The whole village took up the hunt, but soon it got dark, and there was no chance of finding her. In the morning they scattered in every direction, searched, and got on her trail. It seems they found her tracks in the sand—and she's headed for Capernaum!"

"What luck if she comes, lads!" said Philip, licking his protruding goat-like lips. "She was the one thing missing from our Paradise. Yes, we forgot Eve, and now we'll certainly be delighted to see her!"

"Her water-mill is open on the Sabbath too, bless her!" said simple Nathanael, smirking craftily in his beard. He remembered how once, on the eve of the Sabbath, he had bathed, put on clean clothes and shaved. Then the Temptation of the bath came and took him by the hand. They went together to Magdala and made a bee-line for Magdalene's house—bless her! It was winter, business was bad, and Nathanael remained at her mill the whole of the Sabbath, all by himself—and ground. . . . He smiled with satisfaction. A great sin, one might say. Yes indeed, a great sin; but we place all our trust in God, and God forgives. . . . Calm, poor, harassed, unmarried, Nathanael spent his whole life sitting in front of a small bench in one corner of the village street making clogs for the villagers and thick sandals for the shepherds. What kind of a life was that! Once, therefore, one precious time in his whole life, he had thrown everything overboard and enjoyed himself like a man—even if it was on the Sabbath. As we said, God understands this sort of thing—and forgives. . . .

But old Zebedee scowled.

"Troubles! troubles!" he grumbled. "Do they always have to settle their rows in my yard? First prophets, then whores or weeping fishermen, and now Barabbases—this is too much!" He turned to the treaders:

"You, my fine lads, attend to your work. Tread the grapes!"

Inside the house old Salome and Mary the wife of Joseph heard the news, looked at each other and without saying a word, immediately bowed their heads. Judas abandoned his hammer and went to the street-door, where he leaned against the jamb. He had heard everything and had engraved it all in his mind. On his way to the door he threw a savage glance at old Zebedee.

He stood in the doorway and listened. He heard voices and saw a cloud of dust rise up. Men were running, women were screaming, "Catch her! Catch her!" and before the three men had time to jump out of the wine press or old stuff-pockets to slide down from his platform, Magdalene, her clothes in rags and her tongue hanging out of her mouth, entered the yard and fell at old Salome's feet.

"Help!" she cried. "Help! They're coming!"

Old Salome took pity on the sinner. She got up, closed the window, and told her son to bolt the door.

"Squat down on the ground," she said to Magdalene. "Hide yourself."

Mary the wife of Joseph leaned over and looked at this woman who had gone astray, looked at her with both sympathy and horror. None but honest women know how bitter and slippery honour is, and she pitied her. But at the same time this sinful body seemed to her a wild beast, shaggy, dark and dangerous. This beast had almost snatched away her son when he was twenty years old, but he had escaped by a hair's breadth. Yes, he escaped the woman, Mary thought, with a sigh, but what about God. . .

Old Salome placed her hand on Magdalene's burning head. "Why are you crying, my child?" she asked with compassion.

"I don't want to die," Magdalene replied. "Life is good. I don't want to die!"

Mary the wife of Joseph extended her hand now too. She did not fear her any longer, nor did she detest her. "Do not be afraid, Mary," she said, touching her. "God protects you; you won't die."

"How do you know, Mary, ma'am?" asked Magdalene, her eyes gleaming.

"God gives us time, Magdalene, time to repent," Jesus' mother replied with certainty.

But as the three women talked and were about to be united by pain, cries of "They're coming! They're coming! Here they are!" flowed forth from the vineyards and before old Zebedee could slide down again from his platform, huge incensed men appeared at the street-door and Barabbas, flushed and drenched with sweat, strode over the threshold, bellowing.

"Hey, Zebedee," he shouted, "we're coming in, with or without your permission—in the name of the God of Israel!"

This said, and before the old proprietor could open his mouth, Barabbas ripped the house-door off its hinges with one shove and seized Magdalene by her braids.

"Outside, whore! Outside!" he roared, hauling her into the yard. The citizens of Magdala entered at this point. They grabbed her, lifted her up, brought her amidst boos and fits of laughter to a pit near the lake, and threw her in. Then both men and women scattered all around and loaded their aprons and tunics with stones.

Old Salome meanwhile had jumped off her couch despite the pains which tortured her and had dragged herself into the yard in order to berate her husband.

"You should be ashamed of yourself," she shouted at him. "You let those rowdies set foot in your house and grab a woman right out of your hands, a woman who was seeking mercy from you."

She turned also to her son Jacob, who stood irresolutely in the middle of the yard.

"And you—you follow in your father's footsteps. Shame on you! Aren't you going to turn out any better; are you going to let profits be your God too? Go ahead, run! Run to protect a woman that an entire village wants to kill. An entire village! They should be ashamed of themselves!"

"Calm down, Mother, I'm going," answered her son, who feared no one in the whole world except his mother. Every time she turned upon him in anger he was overcome with fright because he felt that this wild severe voice was not hers, it was the ancient desert-roughened voice of the obstinate race of Israel.

Turning, Jacob nodded to Philip and Nathanael, his two companions. "Let's go!" he said. He searched all around the barrels in order to find Judas, but the blacksmith had gone.

"I'm coming too," said Zebedee, who felt irritated because he was afraid to stay alone with his wife. He bent over, picked up his club and followed his son.

Magdalene was screeching. Covered with wounds, she had collapsed into one corner of the pit and put up her arms to protect her head. The men and women stood around the rim and looked at her, laughing. Carriers and vintagers from all the vineyards of the vicinity had left their work and were approaching, the young men panting to see the famous body in its bloody halfnaked state; the girls because they hated and envied this woman who enjoyed all men while they had none.

Barabbas lifted his hand as a signal for the shouting to cease. He wanted to pronounce the decree and set the stoning in motion. At that moment Jacob appeared. He started to advance towards the bandit-chief Zealot, but Philip held him tightly by the arm.

"Where are you going?" he said. "Where are any of us going? We're a mere handful, and they're the whole village. We haven't a chance!"

But Jacob continued to hear his mother's savage voice within him.

"Hey, Barrabas, hey, cut-throat," he shouted, "you've come to our village to kill people, have you? Well, leave the woman alone; we'll judge her. The elders of Magdala and Capernaum will come to judge her; and her father the rabbi of Nazareth will come too. That's the Law!"

"My son is right," interrupted old Zebedee, who had arrived with his heavy club. "He's right, that's the Law!"

Barabbas swung his whole body around and stood directly in front of them. "The village elders have greased palms," he shouted, "and so has Zebedee. I don't trust them. I'm the Law, and if any one of you brave lads dares, let him come forward and match his strength with me!"

Men and women from Magdala and Capernaum swarmed around Barabbas, murder glittering in the pupils of their eyes. A troop of boys arrived from the village, armed with slings.

Philip grabbed Nathanael by the arm and stepped back. He turned to Jacob:

"Go, son of Zebedee, go on by yourself if you want—but as for us, we're staying put. Do you think we're crazy?"

"Aren't you ashamed of yourselves, cowards?"

"No, we're not. Go on, go on by yourself."

Jacob turned to his father, but Zebedee coughed.

"I'm an old man," he said.

"Well. . . ?" shouted Barabbas, guffawing.

Old Salome arrived, leaning on her younger son's arm. Behind them came Mary the wife of Joseph, her eyes filled with tears. Jacob turned, saw his mother, and quivered. In front of him was the terrifying cut-throat with the mob of frenzied peasants; behind him, his mother, savage and mute.

"Well. . . ?" Barabbas bellowed again, rolling up his sleeves.

"I won't make them ashamed of me!" murmured Zebedee's son. He stepped forward and at once Barabbas advanced directly at him.

"He'll kill him!" said the younger brother, trying to shake himself loose in order to run to Jacob's side. But his mother held him back.

"You keep quiet," she said. "Don't interfere."

But just as the two opponents were about to come to grips a happy cry was heard from the edge of the lake: "*Maran atha! Maran atha!*" A sunburned youth jumped in front of them, panting and waving his hands.

"*Maran atha! Maran atha!*" he shouted. "The Lord is coming!"

"Who's coming?" they all cried, circling him. "Who?"

"The Lord," answered the youth, and he pointed behind him towards the desert. "The Lord—there he is!"

Everyone turned. The sun was going down now, the heat was abating. A man could be seen climbing up from the shore. He was dressed all in white, like a monk from the monastery. The oleanders at the lake-front were in bloom and the white-robed man put out his hand, picked a red one and placed it between his lips. Two seagulls were walking on the pebbles; they stepped aside to let him pass.

Old Salome lifted her white-haired head and sniffed the air. "Who's coming?" she asked her son. "The wind has changed."

"My heart is ready to burst, Mother," the boy answered. "I think it's him!"

"Who?"

"Shh, don't talk!"

"And who are those people in back of him? Good grief, there's a whole army running behind him."

"They're the poor who glean the leavings of the vintage, Mother. They're not an army, don't be afraid."

179

And truly, the swarm of ragamuffins which began to appear in his train was like an army. They immediately scattered all through the harvested vineyards—men, women and children, with sacks and baskets—and began to search. Each year at the reaping, the vintage and the olive-harvest these flocks of hunger poured out of the whole of Galilee and collected the corn, grapes and olives which the landowners left for the poor, as ordered by the Law of Israel.

The man in white suddenly halted. The sight of the multitude had frightened him. I must leave! he said to himself, overwhelmed by the old fear. This is the world of men; I must leave, I must return to the desert, where God is. . . . Once more his fate hung on a delicate thread. Which way should he go—forward, or back?

Everyone about the pit stood motionless, watching him. Jacob and Barabbas still faced each other, with rolled-up sleeves. Even Magdalene lifted her head and listened. Life? Death? What was this silence? The wind had changed. Suddenly she jumped up, lifted her arms and cried: "Help!"

The man in white heard the voice, recognized it, and quivered. "It's Magdalene," he murmured. "Magdalene! I must save her!" He advanced rapidly towards the crowd, his arms spread wide.

The more he approached the people and perceived their anger-filled eyes and the dark tortured fierceness of their expressions, the more his heart stirred, the more his bowels flooded with deep sympathy and love. These are the people, he reflected. They are all brothers, every one of them, but they do not know it—and that is why they suffer. . . . If they knew it, what celebrations there would be, what hugging and kissing, what happiness!

He arrived finally and stepped up onto a rock, stretching out his arms to the left and right. One word, one joyful and triumphant word, spurted forth from deep within his bowels:

"Brothers!"

The astonished people looked at each other. No one replied.

"Brothers!"—the triumphant cry resounded again—"brothers, I am delighted to see you."

"Well, we're not delighted to see you, cross-maker!" Barabbas answered him, picking up a heavy stone from the ground.

"My boy!" someone shouted in a heart-rending voice, and Mary rushed out and embraced her son. She laughed, wept, caressed him; but he, without speaking, untwisted his mother's arms from about him and advanced towards Barabbas.

"Barabbas, my brother," he said, "I'm glad to see you. I am a friend; I bring a message of great joy."

"Don't come any closer," roared Barabbas, and he placed himself in front of Magdalene in order to hide her from the other's eyes. But she heard the beloved voice and jumped to her feet.

"Jesus," she screamed, "help!"

A single stride brought Jesus to the pit's brim. Magdalene had begun to climb up, gripping the rocks with her fingers and toes. Jesus stooped and held out his hand. She grasped it and he pulled her out. She collapsed onto the ground, puffing, and covered with blood.

Barabbas rushed over and stamped his foot down on her back. "She's mine!" he bellowed, raising the stone which he held in his hand. "I'll kill her—she polluted the Sabbath. Death!"

"Death! Death!" the people howled in their turn, afraid now that their sacrifice would escape.

"Death!" Zebedee cried out too as he saw the ragamuffins circle the newcomer, doubtlessly filling their heads with fancy ideas. Woe is us if paupers are allowed to do whatever they please. . . . "Death!" he shouted again, banging his club on the ground. "Death!"

Jesus restrained Barabbas's lifted arm. "Barabbas," he said, his voice tranquil and sad, "have you never disobeyed one of God's commandments? In your whole life have you never stolen, murdered, committed adultery or told a lie?"

He turned to the howling multitude and looked at each person, one by one, slowly.

"Let him among you who is without sin be the first to throw a stone!"

The mass stirred; one by one the people stepped back, struggling to escape this clawing look which was excavating their memories and vital organs. The men recalled all the lies they had uttered during their lifetimes, the acts of injustice they had committed, the wives of others they had bedded; the women lowered their kerchiefs, and the stones they held in their hands slid to the ground.

When old Zebedee saw the rabble about to emerge victorious, he flew into a rage. Once more Jesus turned to the people and stared at them one by one, stared into the very depths of their eyes.

"Let him among you who is without sin be the first to throw a stone."

"Me," snapped Zebedee. "Barabbas, give me your stone. Innocence has no fears: I'll throw it."

Barabbas was delighted. He gave him the stone and stepped to one side. Zebedee stood over Magdalene, holding the stone in his fist and judging its weight, in order to hit her squarely on the head. She had rolled herself up into a ball at Jesus' feet and was tranquil, for she felt that here she had no fear of death.

The infuriated ragamuffins looked at old Zebedee and one of them, the gauntest of the lot, jumped forward.

"Hey, Zebedee," he shouted, "there's a God, you know. Your hand will be paralysed—aren't you afraid? Think back: you never gobbled up the rights of the poor? You never in your life caused an orphan's vineyard to be sold at auction? You never stepped into a widow's house at night?"

As he listened, the old sinner felt the weight of the stone in his hand and restrained himself more and more. Suddenly he uttered a cry; his arm wilted abruptly and fell useless at his side. The large stone rolled out of his grasp and landed on his foot, breaking his toes.

The ragamuffins shouted for joy:

"Miracle! Miracle! Magdalene is innocent!"

Barabbas went wild; his pock-marked face puffed up fiery red. Darting at the son of Mary, he lifted his hand and slapped him. But Jesus calmly turned the other cheek.

"Hit the other one too, Barabbas, my brother," he said.

Barabbas's hand grew numb and his eyes popped out of his head. Who was this person? What was he—a ghost, a man, or a devil? Dumbfounded, he stepped back and gazed at Jesus.

"Hit the other cheek, Barabbas, my brother," the son of Mary incited him once more.

At this point Judas emerged from the shade of the fig tree where he had been standing off to one side, watching. He had seen everything but had not spoken. Whether or not Magdalene got killed made no difference to him, but he was pleased to hear Barabbas and the ragamuffins stand up against Zebedee and declaim his sins. When he saw Jesus appear at the lake-shore dressed in his new white robe, his heart had pounded. "Now it will become clear who he is, what he wants and what message he has for men," he had murmured, cocking his huge ear. But the very start, the very first word—"Brothers"—displeased him, and his expression soured. "He still hasn't put any sense into his head," he grumbled. "No, we're not all brothers. Israelites and Romans are not brothers, nor are Israelites among themselves. The Sadducees who sell themselves to Rome, the village chiefs—as many as cover up for the tyrant: they are not our brothers. . . . No, you've got off to a bad start, son of the Carpenter. Look out!" But when he saw Jesus offer the other cheek, without anger and with a superb inhuman sweetness, he became frightened. What is this man? he shouted to himself. This—this offering of the other cheek: only an angel could do that, only an angel—or a dog. . . .

He reached Barabbas now with one bound and seized him by the arm just as he was about to rush upon the son of Mary.

"Don't touch him," he said in a muffled voice. "Go home!"

Barabbas looked at Judas with astonishment. They were both in the same brotherhood; side by side they had often entered villages and cities and killed Israel's traitors. And now . . .

"You, Judas," he murmured, "you?"

"Yes, me. Go!"

Barabbas continued to hold his ground. Judas was his superior in the brotherhood and he could not oppose him; but his self-respect, on the other hand, did not let him budge.

"Go!" the redbeard commanded once more.

The bandit-chief lowered his head and threw a savage glance at the son of Mary. "You won't get away from me," he murmured, clenching his fist. "We shall meet again!"

Turning to his followers, he commanded them half-heartedly: "Let's go."

XIII

THE sun was about to touch the sky's foundations. The fever of the day wilted, the wind died down, the lake sparkled rose and blue. Several storks, still hungry, stood on one leg upon the rocks, their eyes pinned on the water.

The ragamuffins fixed their eyes on the son of Mary and waited, not wanting to leave. What were they waiting for? They had forgotten their hunger and nakedness, they had forgotten the malice of the landowners, who had lacked the goodness of heart to leave a few grapes on the vintaged vines in order to sweeten the throat of poverty. They had been going from vineyard to vineyard since the morning, and their baskets remained empty. The same had happened at the reaping: they had gone from field to field, their sacks hanging empty at their sides; and each evening their children waited for them with opened mouths! . . . But now—they did not know why or how—their baskets seemed suddenly to have been filled. They looked at the man in white in front of them, and could not bear to leave. . . . They waited. Waited for what? They themselves did not know.

The son of Mary returned their look. He too was waiting; he felt that all these souls were suspended from his neck. What did they want of him? What were they seeking? What could he give them, he who had nothing? He looked at them, looked at them, and for an instant lost courage and wanted to flee again, but was prevented by shame. What would become of Magdalene, who was clinging to his feet? And so many eyes gazing at him with yearning: how could he leave them unconsoled? To leave. . . ? But where to go? God was on every side. His grace pushed him where it pleased—no, not his grace, his power, his all-powerful power. The son of Mary now felt that this earth was his home—he had no other home; he felt that men were his desert—he had no other desert.

"Lord, your will be done," he murmured, bowing his head and surrendering himself to God's mercy.

An old man stood up among the ragamuffins and spoke: "Son of Mary, we are hungry, but it's not bread we ask of you. You are poor, like ourselves. Open your mouth, say a kind word to us, and we shall be filled."

A young man ventured: "Son of Mary, injustice is strangling us, our hearts can bear no more. You said you brought a kind word. Tell us that kind word; bring us justice!"

The son of Mary looked at the people. He heard the voice of freedom and hunger, and rejoiced. He felt that he had been awaiting this voice for years, this voice which had now come and called him by name. He turned to the people, his arms spread wide.

"Brothers," he said, "let us go!"

All at once, as though they too had been awaiting this call for years and had heard their true name for the first time, the people rejoiced and bellowed:

"Let us go! In God's name!"

The son of Mary took the lead; the rest moved off in one body. Next to the lake-front was a pitted hill, still pale-green despite the fiery heat of the summer sun, which beat down on it all day long. Now, in the sweetness of the evening, it was perfumed with thyme and savoury. Its summit must have been the site of some ancient heathen temple, for fragments of several carved capitals of columns still lay on the ground. The clairvoyant fishermen, fishing in the lake at night, regularly saw a white ghost sitting on the marble—and one night old Jonah even heard it weep. . . . It was towards this hill that they all marched as if in a trance, the son of Mary in front, and behind, the great family of the poor.

Old Salome turned to her younger son: "Carry me in your arms. We'll go too." She took Mary's hand.

"Don't cry, Mary," she said. "Didn't you see a glow around your son's face?"

"I have no son, I have no son," the mother replied, beginning to sob convulsively. "All those ragamuffins have sons, and I have none. . . ." She started towards the hill, wailing and lamenting. Now she was sure: her son had abandoned her for ever. When she ran to embrace him and take him home with her, he had looked at her with astonishment as though he did not know her;

and when she said to him, "I am your mother," he had put out his hand and pushed her away.

Old Zebedee saw his wife mount the hill with the multitude. Scowling, he grabbed his club, turned to his son Jacob and his son's two companions, Philip and Nathanael, and pointed to the noisy, agitated mob.

"They're famished wolves, damn them all! We'd better howl along with them so they won't take us for sheep and eat us. Let's follow behind—but remember, no matter what that windmill son of Mary tells them, we'll boo him. Do you hear! We musn't let him get the upper hand. Forward, all together, and look sharp!"

This said, he too started to climb the hill, as slow as a lame donkey.

Just then Jonah's two sons appeared. Peter held his brother by the arm and spoke to him tranquilly, tenderly, in order not to infuriate him. But the other was disturbed and kept his eyes on the swarms of people that were mounting, and on the man in white who led them.

"Who are they? Where are they going?" Peter asked Judas, who still stood in the street, unable to come to a decision.

"The son of Mary," the redbeard sneered.

"And the troup behind him?"

"The poor who glean the grapes after the vintage. They took one look and attached themselves to him. I think he's going up there to talk to them."

"What can he say? He couldn't even divide up hay for a pair of donkeys."

Judas shrugged his shoulders. "We'll see," he growled, and he too started up the hill.

Two swarthy amazons were returning from the vineyards, exhausted and overheated, each with a large basket of grapes balanced on her head. Envying the camaraderie of the others, they decided to join them to pass the time, and attached themselves to the rear of the procession.

Old Jonah, his net on his shoulders, was dragging himself towards his shack. He was hungry, and impatient to arrive. When he saw his sons and the crowd mounting the hill, he stopped open-mouthed, and gazed at them with round fish-like eyes. He did not think of anything; he did not ask himself who had died, who was getting married, or where so many people were going all in a group; he did not think of anything, he simply stared with gaping mouth.

"Come on, fish-prophet Jonah, let's go," Zebedee called to him. "It's a party! Seems like Mary Magdalene's getting married. Come on, let's go and have a good time!"

Jonah moved his thick lips. He was about to speak, but changed his mind. Giving a heave with his shoulder to adjust the net on his back, he went off towards his neighbourhood with heavy steps. A considerable time later, as he was at last nearing his hut, his mind, after many labour-pains, finally gave birth: "Go to the devil, Zebedee, you blockhead!" he grumbled; then, kicking open the door, he went in.

When Zebedee and his companions reached the top of the hill Jesus was sitting cross-legged on the capital of a column. He had not opened his mouth yet—he seemed to be waiting for them. The crowd of paupers was in front of him, the men cross-legged on the ground, the women standing in back, looking at him. The sun had set but Mount Hebron, to the north, still held the light at its summit and did not allow it to flee.

Jesus watched the light wrestle with the darkness, his hands crossed over his chest. At times he slowly drew his glance back onto the people's faces, which were turned directly towards him. They were wrinkled, sorrowful, shrunken by hunger; and the eyes, pinned upon him, looked at him with reproach, as though he was to blame.

As soon as he saw Zebedee and his men, he rose.

"Welcome," he said. "Gather round, all of you. My voice is not very strong. I want to speak to you."

Zebedee went in front in his capacity as village-elder and enthroned himself on a stone. To his right were his two sons and also Philip and Nathanael; to his left, Peter and Andrew. Old Salome and Mary the wife of Joseph stood among the women, further back. The other Mary, Mary Magdalene, was fallen at Jesus' feet, her face hidden in her palms. Judas waited under a tormented wind-gnarled pine tree, off to one side, and his hard blue eyes looked daggers at the son of Mary through the pine needles.

Jesus trembled secretly and struggled to find courage. This was the moment he had feared for so many years. It had come; God had conquered, had brought him by force where he wanted him—in front of men—in order to make him speak. And now, what could he say to them? The few joys of his life flashed through his mind, then the many sorrows, the contest with God, all that he had seen in his solitary wanderings—the mountains, flowers and birds, the shepherds who happily carried a stray sheep home on their shoulders, the fishermen throwing their nets to catch fish, the ploughmen sowing, reaping, winnowing the grain and then transporting the produce to their homes. . . . Heaven and earth opened and closed repeatedly within his mind: all the miracles of God—and he did not know which to choose first! He wanted to reveal them all, all! in order to console these inconsolables. . . . This world which unfolded before him was God's fairy-tale, full of princesses and ogres, just like the tale his grandmother used to recite to keep him from crying; and God leaned over the edge of heaven and narrated it to men.

He smiled and opened wide his arms.

"Brothers," he said in a trembling still-unsteady voice, "brothers, forgive me if I speak in parables. I am a simple illiterate man, poor and despised like yourselves. My heart has much to say, but my mind is unable to relate it. I open my mouth and without any desire on my part, the words come out as a tale. Forgive me, my brothers, but I shall speak in parables."

"We're listening, son of Mary," shouted the people, "we're listening!"

Once more Jesus opened his mouth:

"The sower went out to sow his field, and as he sowed, one seed fell on the road and the birds came and ate it. Another fell on stones, found no soil in which to be nourished, and withered away. Another fell on thorns, and the thorns grew up and choked it. Finally, another fell on good soil; it took root, sprouted an ear, brought forth grain and fed mankind. . . . He among you who has ears to hear, let him hear!"

No one spoke. They all looked at each other, bewildered. But old Zebedee, who sought a pretext for a brawl, jumped up.

"I'm sorry," he said, "but I don't understand. I have ears, glory be to God, I have ears and I'm listening—but I don't understand. What are you trying to say? Can't you put it a little more clearly?" He laughed sarcastically, and proudly stroked his white beard.

"Or by any chance, are you the sower?"

"Yes," Jesus replied with humility, "I am the sower."

"The Lord preserve us!" exclaimed the old chief, banging his club on the ground. "And we, to be sure, are the stones and thorns and fields where you sow, eh?"

"You are," the son of Mary answered, his voice still tranquil.

Andrew tensed his ear and listened. As he looked at Jesus his roused heart pounded furiously. It had pounded in this same way at the banks of the Jordan when he caught his first glimpse of John the Baptist—wrapped in the skins of animals, gnawed away by the sun, devoured so completely by prayer, vigils and hunger that nothing remained of him but two monstrous eyes—two live coals; and a larynx which cried "Repent! Repent!" When he shouted, great waves swelled up on the Jordan, the caravans halted, the camels were unable to proceed. But now here was this other man in front of him who smiled and whose voice was tranquil and wavering—a gawky bird he was, struggling to twitter for the first time; and his eyes, instead of burning, caressed. Andrew's heart winged back and forth between the two, completely bewildered.

Little by little, John moved away from his father's side and approached Jesus. He had almost reached the teacher's feet when Zebedee saw him and grew even more enraged than before. He was already sick and tired of false prophets. New ones sprouted up every day of the year and took the weight of the world upon their shoulders; and every single one of them, as though they had come to some previous understanding, attacked landlords, priests, and kings. Whatever was stable and good in this world, they wanted to demolish. And now—what next!—here was the barefooted son of Mary! Ah! thought Zebedee, I'd better wring his neck for him while it's still young and tender.

To find encouragement, he turned to see what the others were saying. He saw Jacob, his elder son, with wrinkled brow, but he could not tell whether from distress or anger; he saw his wife, who had come close now and was wiping her eyes; he shifted his glance to the ragamuffins and was terrified to see all of them, all of those famished paupers, staring at the son of Mary with opened mouths, like birds being fed by their mother.

"A plague on all beggars!" he grumbled as he slunk down next to his son. I'd best be still, he told himself. I'll only get myself in trouble.

A calm pathetic voice was heard. Someone sitting at Jesus' feet had begun to talk. The people who were stretched out behind sat up to see. It was Zebedee's younger son. He had crawled gradually to Jesus' feet and was speaking to him now, with his head bent up:

"You are the sower and we are the stones, the thorns and the field. But what is the seed you hold?"

His fuzzy virginal face was on fire, his black almond-shaped eyes gazed at Jesus in an agony, his chubby white body, all tremors, was stretched upwards and waiting. He had a foreboding that his whole life depended on the answer he would receive—this life, and the next.

Jesus had bent over in order to hear. He was silent for a considerable time as he listened to his heart and struggled to find the right word, the simple everyday immortal word. Hot sweat frosted his face.

"What is the seed you hold?" Zebedee's son anxiously repeated.

All at once, Jesus jerked himself erect, spread out his arms and leaned towards the multitude.

"Love one another!"—the cry escaped from his very bowels—"love one another!"

As he said this, he felt his heart become suddenly empty, and he collapsed onto the capital, exhausted.

Whispering arose. The people were roused. Many shook their heads; some laughed.

"What did he say?" asked an old man who was hard of hearing.

". . . that we should love one another."

"Impossible!" said the old man, growing angry. "Someone who's starving can't love a man whose stomach is full. The victim of injustice can't love his oppressor. Impossible! Let's go home!"

Judas leaned against the pine tree and stroked his red beard in a rage. "So, son of the Carpenter," he grumbled, "that's what you've come to tell us, is it? Is this the stupendous message you bring us? You want us to love the Romans, eh? Are we supposed to hold out our necks like you do your cheek, and say: 'Dear brother, slaughter me please'?"

Jesus heard the whispering, saw the scowling faces, the leaden eyes—and understood. Bitterness flowed over his face. Summoning up all his strength, he rose.

"Love one another! Love one another!" he repeated in a persistent, imploring voice. "God is love! I too used to think him savage, I too used to think that at his touch mountains fumed, men died. I hid in the monastery to escape; I fell on my face and waited. Now he'll come, I said to myself, now he'll fall on me like a thunderbolt. And one morning he did come, he blew over me like a cool breeze and said: 'Arise, my child'. . . and I arose, I came: here I am!"

He crossed his hands and bowed from the waist as though greeting the people before him.

Old Zebedee coughed and spat, squeezing his club.

"God a cool breeze!" he growled softly, infuriated. "Go to hell, you quack!"

The son of Mary continued to speak. He went down now among the people, looked at them one by one, besought them one by one. He marched up and down, his arms lifted to heaven.

"He is our Father," he said. "He will leave no pain unconsoled, no wound unhealed. However much we suffer pain and hunger in this world, by that much, and more, shall we be filled in heaven, shall we rejoice. . . ."

Tired, he went up again to the capital of the column and sat down.

"Pie in the sky when we die!" a voice shouted, and laughter broke out.

But Jesus was swept away by God, and did not hear.

"Blessed are those who hunger and thirst for righteousness," he now shouted.

"Righteousness isn't enough," interrupted one of the famished. "Righteousness isn't enough. We want bread!"

"Bread too," said Jesus, sighing, "bread too. . . . Blessed are those who hunger and thirst for righteousness, for they shall be filled. Blessed are those who mourn, for God will comfort them.

Blessed are the poor, the meek, the wronged. It is for them, for you, the poor, the meek and the wronged, that God has prepared the kingdom of heaven."

The two amazons, who stood with their baskets of grapes still on their heads, glanced rapidly at one another and without a word lowered their baskets and began, one to the right and the other to the left, to distribute the grapes to the poor. Magdalene, fallen at Jesus' feet, still did not dare lift her head and let the people see her face, but she secretly kissed the teacher's feet, which were buried in her hair.

Jacob's endurance gave out; he jumped up and left. Andrew was infuriated. He extricated himself from his brother's grasp and went and stood before Jesus.

"I've just come from the river Jordan in Judea," he shouted. "There a prophet proclaims: 'Men are chaff and I am the fire. I have come to burn up and purify the earth, to burn up and purify the soul so that the Messiah may come forth!' And you, son of the Carpenter, you preach love! Why don't you take a look around you? Everywhere: liars, murderers, robbers! All are dishonest—rich and poor, oppressed and oppressors, Scribes and Pharisees—all! all! I too am a liar, I too am dishonest, and so is my brother Peter over there, and so is Zebedee with his fat paunch: he hears 'love' and thinks of his boats and men and how to steal as much as he can from the wine press."

When old Zebedee heard this he flew into a rage. His blubbery nape turned fiery red, the veins of his neck swelled and he rushed forward with raised club, ready to strike. But Salome was in time to catch hold of his arm.

"Shame on you, shame on you," she said to him softly. "Come, let's go home."

"No barefooted beggars are going to get the upper hand here in my territory!" he yelled at the top of his voice, so that all could hear. Huffing and puffing, he turned to the son of Mary:

"And you, carpenter, don't go playing the Messiah with me, because woe is you, poor thing, you'll end up being crucified like the others—that's the way you'll forget your problems! But it's not you I pity, you good-for-nothing, it's the unlucky mother who has you for her only son."

He pointed to Mary, who had collapsed to the ground in a heap and was beating her head against the stones.

But the old man's anger was still not appeased. He continued to bang his club on the ground, and shouted:

"'Love,' he says, and forward everyone—you're all brothers, so grab what you can, everything's on the house! But can I love my enemy? Can I love the beggar who roams outside my yard, just itching to break down the door and rob me? 'Love,' he says—just listen to the cock-brain! Three cheers for the Romans! That's what I say, even if they're heathens. Three cheers! They keep order!"

This provoked the paupers to action. Bellowing furiously, they started towards Zebedee, and Judas bounded out from his pine tree. Old Salome was terrified. She silenced her husband by putting her hand over his mouth and then turned to the stormy intimidating multitude which was coming closer.

"Don't listen to him, my children. His rage makes him say one thing when he means another."

She turned to the old man. "Let's go," she said in a commanding tone.

She nodded also to her darling son who sat tranquil and happy at Jesus' feet.

"Come, my boy," she said. "It's dark."

"I'm going to stay, Mother," the youth answered.

Mary got up from the rocks where she had thrown herself. Wiping her eyes, she went forward with unsteady steps in order to fetch her son and bring him home. The unfortunate woman had been frightened both by the love which the poor had shown him and the threats hurled at him by the rich village-elder.

"I implore you in God's name not to listen to him," she said now to one, now to another as she went by. "He's ill. . . , ill. . . , ill. . . ."

Trembling, she approached her son. He now stood with crossed hands, gazing out over the lake.

"Come, my child," she said to him tenderly, "come, let's go home together. . . ."

He heard the voice, turned, and looked at her with surprise. He seemed to be asking who she was. . . .

"Come, my child," Mary repeated, clasping him around the waist. "Why do you look at me like that? Don't you know me? I am your mother. Come, your brothers are waiting for you in Nazareth, and your old father. . ."

The son shook his head. "What mother," he said calmly, "what brothers? My mother and brothers are here."

Holding out his hand, he indicated the ragamuffins and their wives, and redhaired Judas, who stood mutely in front of the pine tree and looked at him with rage.

"And my father. . ." He raised his finger towards heaven: "My father is God."

The eyes of this luckless victim of God's thunderbolt began to flow with tears. "Is there any mother in the whole world more miserable than I?" she said. "I had one son, one, and now. . ."

Old Salome heard the heart-rending cry. Leaving her husband, she retraced her steps and took Mary by the hand. But the other resisted, and turned once more to her son.

"You're not coming?" she cried. "This is the last time I'm going to say it to you: Come!"

She waited. The son was silent; he had again turned his face towards the lake.

"You're not coming?" the mother cried in a heart-rending voice. She lifted her hand.

"Aren't you afraid of a mother's curse?"

"I'm not afraid of anything," answered the son without turning. "And I'm not afraid of anyone, except God."

Mary's face became ferocious. She lifted her fist and even opened her mouth to utter the curse, but old Salome was in time to place her hand over the mother's lips.

"Don't! Don't!" she said. She clasped her around the waist and forcefully dragged her away. "Come, Mary, my child," she said, "come, let's go. I have something to tell you."

The two women started down the hill to Capernaum. Old Zebedee went in front in a rage, decapitating the thistles with his club. Salome spoke to Mary:

"Why are you crying, Mary, my child? Didn't you see them?"

Mary looked at her with surprise and held back her tears. "See what?" she asked.

"While he spoke, didn't you see blue wings, thousands of blue wings behind him? I swear to you, Mary, there were whole armies of angels."

But Mary shook her head in despair. "I didn't see anything," she murmured, "I didn't see anything. . . , anything." Then, after a pause: "What good are angels to me, Salome, ma'am? I want children and grandchildren to be following him, children and grandchildren, not angels!"

But old Salome's eyes were filled with blue wings. Putting out her hand, she touched Mary's breast and whispered to her as though confiding a great secret: "You are blessed, Mary, and blessed is the fruit of your womb."

But Mary was inconsolable. She shook her head and followed behind, weeping.

The infuriated ragamuffins, meanwhile, had encircled Jesus. They uttered threats, beat their staffs on the ground, waved their empty baskets in the air.

"Death to the rich!" they shouted. "You spoke well, son of Mary—death to the rich!"

"Go in the lead and we'll burn down Zebedee's house."

"No, let's not burn it," others objected. "Let's break in and divide up his wheat, oil, wine and the coffers-full of expensive clothes. . . . Death to the rich!"

Jesus waved his arms in despair. "I didn't say that! I didn't say that!" he shouted. "I said: Brothers, love!"

But the poor were driven wild by hunger: how could they listen!

"Andrew is right," they yelled. "First fire and the axe, then love!"

Andrew heard this, standing at Jesus' side, but his head was bowed in thought, and he did not reply. When his teacher in the desert spoke, he was thinking, his words fell on men's heads like stones and crushed them. But this man next to him portioned out his words to men like bread. . . . Who was right? Which of the two roads led to the world's salvation—force, or love?

While all this was spinning in his mind he felt two hands on his scalp. Jesus had drawn near and gently placed his palms on the top of Andrew's head. The fingers were beautifully supple and so very long that whatever they grasped, they embraced—they had spread out over Andrew's entire head. Andrew did not budge. He felt the suture lines of his skull open and an unutterable honey-thick sweetness flow in, descend to his brain, reach his mouth, neck and heart, continue to his loins, ramify to the very soles of his feet. He rejoiced with his whole body, his whole soul—deeply, with the very roots of his being, like a thirsty tree that is watered. He did not speak. If only these hands above him would never go away! Now, after so much struggle, he finally felt security and inner peace.

A short distance away, Philip and simple Nathanael, the two inseparable friends, were having words.

"I like him," said the gangling cobbler. "His words are as sweet as honey. Would you believe it: listening to him, I actually licked my chops!"

The shepherd was of a different opinion. "I don't like him. He says one thing and does another; he shouts 'Love! Love!' and builds crosses and crucifies!"

"That's all over and done with, I tell you, Philip. He had to pass that stage, the stage of crosses. Now he's passed it and taken God's road."

"I want works!" Philip insisted. "The itch has begun to attack my sheep. Let him come first to say a blessing over them. If they're cured, then I'll believe in him. Otherwise, he can go you know where with the rest of his kind. Why shake your head? If he wants to save the world, let him start with my sheep."

Night fell and covered lake, vineyards and the faces of men. David's wain appeared in the sky. In the east a red star hung like a drop of wine over the desert.

Jesus suddenly felt tired and hungry. He wanted to be alone. The people gradually recalled the journey home, and their houses and the small children who awaited them. Their daily cares crushed down on them again. This was a flash of lightning—they had let themselves be swept away, but now it had passed and they had been recaptured by the wheel of everyday need. Singly, and in pairs—furtively, like deserters—they slipped away and left.

Overcome by melancholy, Jesus lay down on the ancient marble. No one held out his hand to bid him good-bye, no one asked him if he was hungry or if he had a place to spend the night. His face turned towards the darkening earth, he heard the hurried steps recede, recede. . . , and then die out. Suddenly all was quiet. He lifted his head: no one. He looked around him: darkness. The people had left. Around him, nothing but the stars above; within him, nothing but fatigue and hunger. . . Where could he go? At which door could he knock? He curled up again on the ground, feeling reproachful and aggrieved. "Even the foxes have lairs in which to sleep," he murmured, "and I have none." He closed his eyes. A smarting cold had come down with the night, and he was shivering.

Suddenly he heard a groan from behind the marble and then muffled weeping. Opening his eyes, he perceived a woman crawling towards him on all fours in the darkness. When she arrived she unplaited her hair and began to sponge his feet, which had been cruelly lacerated by the stones. He recognized her by her scent.

"Magdalene, my sister," he said, placing his hand on her warm perfumed head, "Magdalene, my sister, return to your home and sin no more."

"Jesus, my brother," she said, kissing his feet, "let me follow in your shadow until I die. Now I know what love is."

"Return to your home," Jesus repeated. "When the hour comes, I shall call you."

"I want to die for you, my child."

"Do not be impatient, Magdalene. The hour will come, but it has not come yet. I will call you when it does. Now, go."

She was about to object when she heard his voice again, and this time it was extremely stern:

"Go!"

Magdalene began to descend the hill. Her light steps were audible for a short while; then, little by little, they were snuffed out and nothing remained but the smell of her body in the air. But the night breeze blew and carried this way too.

The son of Mary now remained completely alone. Above him: God, his ebony night-face splashed with stars. Jesus cocked his ear as though he wanted to hear a voice in the starry darkness. He waited. . . . Nothing. He wanted to open his mouth and ask the Invisible: Lord, are you pleased with me? but did not dare. He wanted to say many things to the Invisible, but did not dare. He was terrified by the abrupt silence which closed in upon him. Surely the Lord must be displeased with me, he suddenly thought, shuddering. But why am I to blame, Lord? I've told you, how many times have I told you: I cannot speak! But you have pushed me more and more, sometimes laughing, sometimes frowning with anger; and this morning at the monastery when the monks chased me in order to make me Abbot—unworthy that I am—and bolted all the doors to prevent my escape, you opened a tiny hidden gate for me, you dug your talons into my hair and threw me down here in front of this immense crowd. "Speak," you ordered me, "the hour has come!" But I kept my lips squeezed tight and said nothing. You shouted, but I said nothing. Finally your patience gave out and you darted forward and opened my mouth. I did not open it, you opened it for me—by force; you anointed it not with lighted coals as you are accustomed to anoint the lips of your prophets, no, not with lighted coals, but with honey! And I spoke. My heart was angry, it incited me to cry: God is fire!—yes, just like your prophet the Baptist—God is fire, he's coming! Men without law, without justice, without honour: where will you hide? He is coming! . . . That's what my heart tried to make me shout, but you anointed my lips with honey and instead, I cried: "Love! Love!"

"Lord, O Lord," he murmured, "I cannot fight with you. To-night I surrender my arms. Your will be done!"

As soon as he said this, he felt relieved. Lowering his head to his breast like a drowsy bird, he closed his eyes and slept. Straight-way it seemed to him that he withdrew an apple from under his shirt, split it, removed a seed and planted it in front of him in the ground. No sooner had he done so than the seed germinated, pushed up through its covering of earth, formed a stem, sprouted branches, leaves, flowers—and produced fruit: hundreds of red apples. . . .

The stones shifted; a man's footsteps were heard. Jesus' sleep took fright and fled. He raised his eyelids and saw someone standing before him. Happy that he was no longer alone, he calmly, mutely welcomed the man's warm presence.

The night-visitor came forward and knelt.

"You must be hungry," he said. "I've brought you bread, honey and fish."

"Who are you, my brother?"

"Andrew, the son of Jonah."

"They all abandoned me and left. Yes, it is true that I am hungry. How is it, my brother, that you remembered me and brought me bread, honey and fish, all the riches of God? Nothing is wanting but the kind word."

"I bring you that too," said Andrew, the darkness giving him courage. Jesus did not see the youth's trembling hands, nor the two tears which rolled down his pale cheeks.

"That first—the kind word first," said Jesus, holding out his hand to him and smiling.

"Rabboni, my Master. . . ," whispered the son of Jonah, and he stooped and kissed his feet.

XIV

TIME is not a field, to be measured in rods, nor a sea, to be measures in miles; it is a heart-beat. How long did this betrothal last? Days? Months? Years? Jolly and compassionate, the son of Mary went from village to village with the good word on his lips, from village to village, mountain to mountain, or sometimes by rowboat from one shore of the lake to the other, dressed in white like a bridegroom. And the Earth was his betrothed. As soon as he lifted his foot, the ground he had trodden filled with flowers. When he looked at the trees, they blossomed. The moment he set foot in a fishing-boat, a favourable wind puffed out the sail. The people listened to him, and the clay within them turned to wings. The entire time this betrothal lasted, if you lifted a stone you found God underneath, if you knocked at a door, God came out to open it for you, if you looked into the eye of your friend or your enemy, you saw God sitting in the pupil and smiling at you.

The indignant Pharisees shook their heads. "John the Baptist fasts and weeps," they scolded, glaring at him with leaden eyes; "he threatens, and does not laugh. But you—wherever there is a merry wedding, you're first and foremost. You eat, drink and laugh with the rest, and the other day at a marriage in Cana you were not ashamed to dance with the young ladies. Who ever heard of a prophet laughing and dancing?"

But he smiled.

"Pharisees, my brothers, I am not a prophet, I am a bridegroom."

"A bridegroom?" the Pharisees howled, going through the motions of tearing their clothes.

"Yes, Pharisees, my brothers, a bridegroom. Forgive me, but I know no other way to describe it to you.". . .

He would turn to his companions, John, Andrew and Judas, to the peasants and fishermen who abandoned their fields and boats in order to run and hear him, seduced by the sweetness of his face, and to the women, who came with their infants in their arms.

"Rejoice and exult while the bridegroom is still among you," he would tell them. "The days will also come when you shall be widows and orphans, but place your trust in the Father. Look at the faith of the birds of the air. They neither sow nor reap, and yet the Father feeds them. Consider the flowers of the earth. They do not spin or weave, but what king could ever dress in such magnificence? Do not be concerned about your body, what it will eat, what it will drink or wear. Your body was dust and it will return to dust. Let your concern be for the kingdom of heaven and for your immortal soul!"

Judas listened to him and knit his brows. He was not interested in the kingdom of heaven. His great concern was for the kingdom of the earth—and not the whole earth, either, but only the land of Israel, which was made of men and stones, not of prayer and clouds. The Romans—those barbarians, those heathens—the Romans were trampling over this land. First they must be expelled; then we can worry about kingdoms of heaven.

Jesus saw the redbeard's frown and from the wrinkles which stormed his forehead read his hidden thoughts.

"Heaven and earth are one, Judas, my brother," he would say, smiling at him; "stone and cloud are one, the kingdom of heaven is not in the air, it is within us, in our hearts. I talk about that, about the heart. Change your heart, and heaven and earth will embrace, Israelites and Romans will embrace, all will become one."

But the redbeard kept his indignation within him, brooding over it and forcing himself to be patient and wait. He does not know what he's talking about, he grumbled to himself. He lives in a dream-world and hasn't the slightest idea of what goes on around him. . . . My heart will change only if the world about me changes. Only if the Romans disappear from the land of Israel will I find relief!

One day Zebedee's younger son turned to Jesus. "Forgive me, rabbi," he said, "but I find I don't love Judas. When I go near him a dark force gushes out of his body, thousands of tiny tiny needles which wound me; and the other day at dusk I saw a black angel whisper something in his ear. What did he say?"

"I have a foreboding of what he said," Jesus answered with a sigh.

"What? I'm scared, rabbi. What did he say?"

"You will learn when the time comes. I myself still do not know exactly."

"Why do you take him with you, why do you let him follow you night and day? And when you speak to him, why is your voice sweeter than it is when you speak to us?"

"That is how it must be, John, my brother. He has the greater need for love.". . .

Andrew followed the new teacher, and day by day the world changed for him, grew sweeter. Not the world: his heart! Eating and laughter were no longer sins, the earth became firm underfoot, the sky leaned over it like a father and the day of the Lord was not a day of wrath and conflagration, not the end of the world —it was harvest, vintage, weddings, dancing: the perpetual renewal of the earth's virginity. Every daybreak was a renascence; each morning, God renewed his promise to hold the world in his sacred palm.

As the days went by, Andrew grew calm. He made friends with laughter and food; his pale cheeks reddened. In the evening or at noontime when he stretched out under a tree to eat, or when they were feted in some house by friends, and Jesus, as was his habit, blessed and divided the bread, Andrew's entrails took this bread and immediately transubstantiated it into love and laughter. . . . He still sighed now and then however, when he remembered his family and friends.

"What will become of Jonah and Zebedee?" he asked one day, his eyes lost in the distance. The two old men seemed to him at the ends of the earth. "And what about Jacob and Peter? Where are they, in what surroundings are they now suffering?"

"We shall find them all," Jesus answered with a smile, "and each one of them will find us. Do not be sad, Andrew. The Father's courtyards are wide, there is room for all."

One evening Jesus entered Bethsaida. The children took olive branches and palm leaves and ran out to greet him. Doors opened, housewives emerged. Abandoning the housework, they ran behind him to hear the good word. Sons lifted paralysed parents to their shoulders; grandchildren led blind grandfathers by the hand. Men with bulging muscles dragged along those who were possessed with devils and ran behind him so that he might place his hand on the heads of these maniacs and cure them.

It chanced that this was the day when Thomas the pedlar made his rounds of the village. Staggering under his load of spools of thread, combs, women's wonder-working cosmetics, bronze bracelets and silver ear-rings, he was tooting his horn and hawking his wares when Jesus saw him. A sudden puff of wind. . . ; he was no longer Thomas the cross-eyed merchant. In his hand he held a carpenter's level. He was surrounded by swarms of people, in some far-away country. Labourers were hauling stones and cement, masons were building a large temple, an imposing edifice with marble columns. . . , and Thomas the master-builder ran here and there with his level, checking their work. . . . Jesus blinked, Thomas blinked in return—and suddenly he found himself before him once again, loaded down as before with his wares. His sly crossed eyes danced roguishly.

Jesus placed his hand on the pedlar's head.

"Thomas, come with me. I shall load you with other wares: the spices and ornaments of the soul. Your rounds will then take you to the ends of the earth, and you will hawk your new wares and portion them out to men."

"I'd rather sell these first," said the shrewd merchant, chuckling, "and then. . . , well, let's wait and see what happens." He swelled his shrill voice and began on the spot to hawk his combs, threads and wonder-working cosmetics. . . .

An old village-notable, very rich, cruel and dishonest, stood in his doorway, his hands against the jambs, and stared with curiosity at the approaching multitude. The mass of children, running in front and waving their palm leaves and olive branches in the air, knocked on the doors and shouted: "He's coming, he's coming, the son of David is coming!" They were followed by a man dressed in white, with hair which spilled down onto his shoulders. Tranquil and smiling, he extended his hands to the left and the right as though blessing the houses. The men and women who ran behind him vied to see who would touch him and acquire strength and sanctity. Further behind came the blind and the paralysed, and new doors continued to open and new crowds to appear.

The old notable felt uneasy. "Now who is this?" he asked, grasping the door-jambs securely lest the mob rush inside and plunder his wealth.

Someone stopped and answered him. "It's the new prophet, Ananias. This man in white who you see before you holds life in one hand, death in the other, and portions them out just as he pleases. A word to the wise, Ananias: flatter him, treat him well."

When old Ananias heard this, he became terrified. He had many troubles weighing on his soul, and at night he often woke up with a start to find himself struck dumb with fear. In his nightmares he seemed to be roasting, plunged up to the neck in the flames of hell. . . . Perhaps this man could save him. Everything in the world is sorcery, he reflected, and this man is a sorcerer. . . . So, let's set the table for him, let's invest a little money to feed him, and perhaps he'll perform a miracle.

Having made the decision, he stepped out into the middle of the road and placed his palm over his heart.

"Son of David," he said, "I am old Ananias, a sinner, and you are a saint. When I learnt that you deigned to set foot in our village, I had tables set so that you could dine. Come in, please, if you'll be so kind. As we all know, it's for us sinners that saints come into the world, and my home is thirsting for sanctity."

Jesus stopped. "What you say pleases me, Ananias. I'm glad to meet you!"

He entered the rich village-house. The slaves arranged the tables in the courtyard and brought pillows. Jesus reclined, and on either side of him reclined John, Andrew, Judas, and also sly Thomas, who pretended to be a disciple in order to eat. The old proprietor enthroned himself opposite them, searching in his mind for a subtle way in which to direct the conversation to the subject of dreams and get the exorcist to exorcize his nightmares. The food was brought, and also two pitchers of wine. The people stood outside and watched them eat and talk about God, the weather and the vineyards. When they had finished their food and drink the slaves brought kettles and basins. The guests washed their hands and prepared to rise. At this point old Ananias's endurance gave out. I went to the expense of giving him a meal, he said to himself. He ate and drank—he and his suite. Now it is only right that he should pay.

"Teacher, I have nightmares," he said. "I learnt that you are considered to be a great exorcist. I did all that I could for you; now, let Your Holiness do something for me: take pity on me and exorcize my dreams. They say that you speak and exorcize with parables. Tell me a parable, therefore. I shall understand its meaning and be cured. Everything in the world is sorcery, isn't it? Well then, perform your sorcery."

Jesus smiled and looked into the old man's eyes. This was not the first time he had seen the rapacious jaws, the fat napes and quick-moving eyes of the glutted. They made him shudder. These people ate, drank and laughed, thought the whole world belonged to them; they stole, danced, whored—and had not the slightest idea that they were burning in the fires of hell. It was only at rare times, in sleep, that they opened their eyes and saw. . . . Jesus looked at the old glutton, looked at his flesh, his eyes, his fear—and once more, the truth inside him became a tale.

"Open your ears, Ananias," he said, "and open your heart, for I shall speak."

"I have opened my ears and I have opened my heart. I am listening, praised be God."

"Once, Ananias, there was a rich man who was unjust and dishonest. He ate and drank, dressed himself in silks and purple, and never gave as much as a green leaf to his neighbour Lazarus, who was hungry and cold. Lazarus crawled under the tables to gather up the crumbs and lick the bones, but the slaves threw him out. He sat on the threshold and the dogs came and licked his wounds. Then came the appointed day and both of them died. One went to the eternal fire, the other to the bosom of Abraham. One day the rich man lifted his eyes and saw his neighbour Lazarus laughing and rejoicing in Abraham's bosom. 'Father Abraham, father Abraham,' he cried, 'send Lazarus down, let him moisten the tip of his finger in order to cool my mouth—I am roasting!' But Abraham answered him: 'Think back to the days when you ate and drank and enjoyed the fat of the land while he was hungry and cold. Did you ever give him as much as a green leaf? Now it is his turn to enjoy himself, and yours to burn for ever and ever.' "

Jesus sighed and was quiet. Old Ananias stood with opened mouth, waiting to hear more. His lips had become dry, his throat parched. He looked at Jesus, imploring him with his eyes.

"Is that all?" he asked, his voice trembling. "Is that all, is there nothing more?"

"Served him right!" Judas said with a laugh. "Whoever over-eats and overdrinks on earth will vomit everything up in Hades."

But Zebedee's younger son leaned over to Jesus' chest.

"Rabbi," he said softly, "your words have not unburdened my heart. How many times have you instructed us to forgive our enemies! You must love your enemy, you told us, and if he wrongs you seven and seventy-seven times, you must do good to him seven and seventy-seven times. This, you said, is the only way hatred can be discharged from the world. . . . But now. . . ? Is God unable to forgive?"

"God is just," interrupted the redbeard, throwing a sarcastic glance at old Ananias.

"God is perfect goodness," John objected.

"Does this mean there is no hope?" stammered the old proprietor. "Is the parable finished?"

Thomas got up, took a stride towards the street-door, and stopped.

"No, milord, it's not finished," he scoffed. "There's more."

"Speak, my child, and you shall have my blessing."

"The rich man's name is Ananias!" said Thomas. He grabbed his bundle of wares and was suddenly outside in the middle of the street, where he stood and guffawed with the neighbours.

The blood rose to the old notable's large head and his eyes grew dim like the setting sun.

Jesus put out his hand and stroked his beloved companion's curly hair. "John," he said, "all have ears, and heard; all have minds, and judged. God is just, they said, and they were unable to go beyond. But you have a heart as well, and you said: Yes, God is just, but this is not enough. He is also perfect goodness. The parable cannot stand as it is, it must have a different ending."

"Pardon me, rabbi," said the youth, "but that was exactly what my heart felt. Man forgives, I said to myself. Is it possible then that God does not? No, it is impossible. The parable is a great blasphemy and cannot stand as it is. It must have a different ending."

"It does have a different ending, John beloved," said Jesus, smiling. "Listen, Ananias, and you will be reassured; listen, you who are in the yard, and you, neighbours, who laugh in the street. God is not only just, he is good; and he is not only good, he is also the Father. When Lazarus heard Abraham's words he sighed and addressed God in his mind: 'God, how can anyone be happy in Paradise when he knows that there is a man—a soul—roasting for all eternity? Refresh him, Lord, that I may be refreshed. Deliver him, Lord, that I may be delivered. Otherwise I too shall begin to feel the flames.' God heard his thought and was glad. 'Lazarus, beloved,' he said, 'go down, take the thirster by the hand. My fountains are inexhaustible. Bring him here so that he may drink and refresh himself, and you refresh yourself with him.'. . . 'For all eternity?' asked Lazarus. 'Yes for all eternity,' God replied."

Jesus got up without a further word. Night had overwhelmed the earth. The people dispersed; men and women returned to their wretched huts, whispering to one another. Their hearts had been filled. Can the word give nourishment? they asked themselves. Yes, it can—when it is the good word!

Jesus held out his hand to take leave of the old proprietor, but Ananias fell at his feet.

"Rabbi," he murmured, "forgive me!" and he burst into tears.

That same night, under the olive trees where they had lain down to sleep, Judas went and found the son of Mary. He could not calm himself. He had to see him and speak to him so that they could lay their cards down on the table and make everything perfectly clear. When, at the house of that criminal Ananias, he had rejoiced at the rich man's punishment in hell and clapped his hands and shouted "Served him right!" Jesus had looked at him out of the corner of his eye for a long time, secretly, as though scolding him, and this glance still tortured him. It was imperative therefore that they clear up their accounts. Judas did not like half-baked words or secret glances.

"Welcome," said Jesus. "I've been waiting for you."

"Son of Mary, I don't fit in with the others," the redbeard started straight off. "I don't have the virginity and goodness of John, your darling, and I'm not a scatter-brained day-dreamer like Andrew, who changes his mind with every breeze that blows. I am a wild uncompromising beast. I was born out of wedlock and my mother threw me into the wilderness, where I suckled on the milk of the wolf. I became rough, rigid, and honest. Whoever I love—I'm dirt under his feet; whoever I hate—I kill."

As he spoke, his voice grew hoarse. His eyes threw sparks into the darkness. Jesus placed his hand on the terrible head in order to calm it. But the redbeard shook off this hand of peace.

Weighing his words one by one, he continued: "I am even able to kill someone I love, if I see him slip away from the true path."

"Which is the true path, Judas, my brother?"

"The deliverance of Israel."

Jesus closed his eyes and did not reply. The two flames which were being slung at him out of the darkness burned him, as did Judas's words. What was Israel? Why only Israel? Weren't we all brothers?

The redbeard waited for an answer, but the son of Mary did not speak. Judas grasped him by the arm and shook him as though trying to wake him up. "Do you understand?" he asked. "Did you hear what I said?"

"Yes, I understand," Jesus answered, opening his eyes.

"I've spoken to you without beating about the bush because I want you to know who I am and what I desire, so that you can give me an answer. Do you wish me to come with you, or don't you? I want to know."

"I want you to come, Judas, my brother."

"And you'll let me speak my mind freely, you'll let me object, say 'no' when you say 'yes'? Because—I'll tell you so there will be no doubt in your mind—everyone else may listen to you with gaping mouth, but not me! I'm no slave, I'm a free man. That's the way things are, and you'd better make the best of it."

"But freedom, Judas, is exactly what I want too."

The redbeard gave a start. Grasping Jesus' shoulder, he shouted with fiery breath: "You want to free Israel from the Romans?"

". . . to free the soul from sin."

Judas snatched his hand away from Jesus' shoulder in a frenzy and banged his fist against the trunk of the olive tree. "This is where our ways part," he growled, facing Jesus and looking at him with hatred. First the body must be freed from the Romans, and later, the soul from sin. That is the road. Can you take it? A house isn't built from the roof down, it's built from the foundation up."

"The foundation is the soul, Judas."

"The foundation is the body—that's where you've got to begin. Watch out, son of Mary. I've said it once and I say it again: watch out, take the road I tell you. Why do you think I go along with you? Well, you'd better learn: it's to show you your way."

Andrew was under the neighbouring olive tree. He heard talk in his sleep and awoke. Listening intently, he made out the rabbi's voice and one other, raucous and full of anger. He quivered like a startled deer. Could people have come during the night to annoy the rabbi? Andrew knew that wherever the teacher went he left behind him many women and young men, and whole flocks of the poor, who loved him; but also many notables, many of the rich and old, who hated him and wanted his downfall. Could these criminals have sent some hooligan to harm him? He crept forward in the darkness on all fours, towards the voices. But the redbeard heard the creeping and rose to his knees.

"Who's there?" he called.

Andrew recognized the voice. "Judas, it's me, Andrew," he answered.

"Go back to bed, son of Jonah, we've got private business."

"Go to sleep, Andrew, my child," Jesus said also.

Judas lowered his voice now. Jesus felt the redbeard's heavy breath on his face.

"You'll remember that I disclosed to you in the desert that the brotherhood commissioned me to kill you. But at the very last minute I changed my mind, put the knife back into its sheath and ran away from the monastery at dawn, like a thief."

"Why did you change your mind, Judas, my brother? I was ready."

"I wanted to wait."

"To wait for what?"

Judas was silent for a moment. Then, suddenly:

"To see if you were the One awaited by Israel."

Jesus shuddered. He leaned against the trunk of the olive tree, his whole body trembling.

"I don't want to rush into this and kill the Saviour; no, I don't want that!" Judas cried out, wiping his brow, which had suddenly become drenched with sweat. "Do you understand?" he screamed, as though someone were strangling him. "Do you understand: I don't want that!"

He took a deep breath.

"He might not even know it himself, I said. Best be patient and let him live awhile, let him live so that we can see what he says and does; and if he isn't the One we're waiting for, there's always plenty of time to get rid of him. . . . That's what I said to myself, that's why I let you live."

He puffed for some time, scooping out the soil with his big toe. Suddenly he grabbed Jesus by the arm. His voice was hoarse and despairing:

"I don't know what to call you—son of Mary? son of the Carpenter? son of David? As you can see, I still don't know who you are—but neither do you. We both must discover the answer, we both must find relief! No, this uncertainty cannot last. Don't look at the others—they follow you like bleating sheep; don't look at the women, who do nothing but admire you and spill tears. After all, they're women: they have hearts and no minds, and we've no use for them. It's we two who must find out who you are and whether this flame that burns you is the God of Israel or the devil. We must! We must!"

Jesus trembled all over. "What can we do, Judas, my brother? How can we discover the answer? Help me."

"There is a way."

"How?"

"We'll go to John the Baptist. He will be able to tell us. He shouts 'He's coming! He's coming!' doesn't he? Well then, as soon as he sees you, he'll understand whether or not you're the one who is coming. Let's go: you'll calm your nerves, and I'll find out what I have to do."

Jesus plunged into a profound meditation. How many times had this anxiety taken possession of him, how many times had he fallen face down on the ground, shaken with convulsions and foaming at the mouth! People thought him deranged, possessed with a devil, and they hurried by, frightened. But he was in the seventh heaven; his mind had fled its cage, ascended, knocked on God's door and asked: Who am I? Why was I born? What must I do to save the world? Which is the shortest road—is it perhaps my own death?

He raised his head. Judas's whole body was bent over him.

"Judas, my brother," he said, "lie down next to me. The Lord will come in the form of sleep and carry us away. Tomorrow, God-willing, we'll start off bright and early to find the prophet of Judea, and whatever God desires, that is what will take place. I am ready."

"I am ready too," said Judas, and they lay down, one next to the other.

They both must have been extremely tired, for they slept instantaneously and the next morning at dawn, Andrew, who was the first to awake, found them fast asleep in one another's arms.

The sun fell upon the lake and illuminated the world. The redbeard took the lead, blazing trail. Jesus followed with his two faithful companions, John and Andrew. Thomas, who still had wares to sell, remained behind in the village. I like what the son of Mary says, the artful pedlar spun in his brain, which was trying to make the best of both sides of the situation. The poor will eat and drink their fill for all eternity—as soon as they kick the bucket. That's fine, but meanwhile, look what happens to us here below! Watch out, Thomas you wretch, watch out—don't get stuck in either place. To be on the safe side the best thing is to load your basket with two kinds of wares: on the very top, for all to see— the combs and cosmetics; underneath, on the bottom, for grade-A customers—the kingdom of heaven. . . . He giggled, swung the bundle once more onto his back and at daybreak tooted his horn, raised his high voice and began his rounds of the lanes of Bethsaida, hawking his earthly wares.

In Capernaum, Peter and Jacob had got up at dawn to pull in

the nets. The mesh was already full of twitching fish which flashed in the sunlight. At any other time the two fishermen would have rejoiced to feel their nets so heavy, but today their minds were far away, and they did not speak. They were silent, but within themselves both had picked a quarrel, now with fate, which kept them tied generation after generation to this lake, now with their own minds which calculated, recalculated, and did not let their hearts take wing. What kind of a life is this! they shouted to themselves. To throw the nets, catch fish, eat, sleep: and at the break of each new day to start the same old hand to mouth existence all over again—all day long, all year long, for the whole of our lives! How long? How long? Is this how we shall die? ... They had never thought about this until now. Their hearts had always been tranquil; they had followed the age-old way without complaint. This was how their parents had lived and their grandparents back for thousands of years—around this same lake, wrestling with the fish. One day they crossed their stiffened hands and died, and then their children and grandchildren came and, without complaint, took the identical road. ... These two, Peter and Jacob, had got along fine until now, they too had no complaint. But lately, suddenly, their surroundings had grown narrow and they were suffocating. ... Their gaze now was far away, out beyond the lake. Where? Towards what? They themselves did not know; all they knew was that they were suffocating.

And as if this torment was not enough, each day saw passers-by come with fresh news: corpses were revived, the paralysed walked, blind men saw the light. ... "Who is this new prophet?" the passers-by would ask the two fishermen. "Your brothers are with him, so you must know. We hear he's not the son of the Carpenter of Nazareth, but the son of David. Is this true?" But Peter and Jacob would shrug their shoulders and bend once again over the nets. They felt like weeping, to relieve themselves. Sometimes, after the passers-by had receded into the distance, Peter would turn to his comrade:

"Do you believe these miracles, Jacob?"

"Pull the nets and keep quiet!" the loud-mouthed son of Zebedee would reply, and giving a heave, he would bring the loaded net an arm's length closer.

This day too, a carter passed by at dawn with additional news:

"They say the new prophet ate in Bethsaida at old pinch-fist Ananias's house. As soon as he finished eating and the slaves brought him water and he washed his hands, he drew near to Ananias, whispered something in his ear—and all at once the old man's mind turned upside-down, he burst into tears and began to divide his goods among the poor."

"What did he whisper to him?" asked Peter, his eyes lost once more in the distance, far beyond the lake.

"Ah, if only I knew!" laughed the carter, "I would hammer it into the ear of every rich man, so that the poor might have a chance to breathe. . . . Farewell," he called, continuing on his way, "and good fishing!"

Peter turned to speak to his companion, but immediately changed his mind. What could he say to him? More words? Hadn't he had enough of them by now? He felt like smashing the whole works down on the ground, like getting up in disgust and going away for ever. Yes, he would go away! Jonah's hut was too small for him now, and so was this washbasin of water, this lake of Gennesaret. "This isn't living," he murmured; "it just isn't living! I'll go away!"

Jacob turned. "What are you mumbling about?" he asked. "Be still!"

"Nothing, damn it, nothing!" Peter answered, and he started furiously to pull in the nets.

At that instant the solitary figure of Judas appeared at the summit of the green hill where Jesus had first spoken to men. He held a crooked stick cut along the road from a wild kermes-oak, and banged it on the ground as he marched. The three other companions appeared after him. Out of breath, they halted for a moment on the summit to survey the world below them. The lake glittered happily; the sun caressed it, and it laughed. The fishing boats were red and white butterflies on the water. Above them flew the winged fishermen, the seagulls. Capernaum buzzed in the distance. The sun had risen high: the day was in its glory.

"Look, there's Peter!" said Andrew, pointing to the beach, where his brother was pulling in the nets.

"And Jacob!" John said with a sigh. "They still can't wrench themselves away from the world."

Jesus smiled. "Do not sigh, beloved companion," he said. "Lie down here, all of you, and rest. I shall go down and bring them."

He began the descent with quick, buoyant steps. He's like an angel, John thought, admiring him. Nothing is missing but the wings. . . . Stepping from stone to stone, he descended. When he reached the shore he slowed his pace and approached the two fishermen, who were leaning over their nets. He stood behind them and looked at them for a long time without moving. He looked at them, his mind empty of thoughts; but he felt himself being drained: a force was escaping from inside him. Everything grew light, hovered in the air, floated above the lake like a cloud; and the two fishermen grew light also and hovered in the air, and their net with its contents was apotheosized: this was no longer a net, these were no longer fish—they were people, thousands of happy dancing people. . . .

Suddenly the two fishermen felt a tingling on the top of their heads, a strange, sweet numbness. They jumped up and turned with fright. Behind them Jesus stood motionless and silent, watching them.

"Forgive us, rabbi!" cried Peter, mortified.

"Why, Peter? What have you done that I should forgive you?"

"Nothing," Peter murmured. And suddenly: "Do you call this living? I'm sick of it!"

"So am I!" said Jacob, and he smashed the net down on the ground.

"Come," said Jesus, extending his hands to both of them. "Come, I shall make you fishers of men."

He took each by the hand and stepped between them. "Let us go," he said.

"Shouldn't I say good-bye to my father?" asked Peter, remembering old Jonah.

"Do not even look back, Peter. We haven't time. Let's go."

"Where?" said Jacob, halting.

"Why do you ask? No more questions, Jacob! Come!"

Old Jonah, all this time, was cooking, bent over the grate and waiting for his son Peter so that they could sit down together and eat. Only one son—the Lord preserve him—remained to him now. Peter was a sensible lad, a good manager; the other, Andrew, the old man had long ago written off the books. He followed first this charlatan, then that one, and left his aging father all by himself to mend the nets and wrestle with the winds and the confounded boat, besides cooking and taking care of the house—he had been fighting with these domestic devils ever since the death of his wife. But Peter—my blessing upon him, Jonah reflected—Peter stands by me and gives me strength. . . . He sampled the food. Ready. He glanced at the sun. Almost noon. "I'm hungry," he grumbled, "but I won't eat until he comes." Crossing his hands, he waited. . . .

Zebedee's house, further along, was open. Baskets and jugs filled the yard; in the corner was the still. These were the days when the raki which had been distilled from the grape-skins and stems left in the wine press was being drawn off, and the whole house smelt of alcohol. Old Zebedee and his wife were having their dinner at a small table under the despoiled vine arbour. Old Zebedee mashed the food as best he could with his toothless gums and talked about developing his business. For a long time now he'd had his eye on the cottage of old Nahum, his next-door neighbour, who was in debt to him and had not the wherewithal to pay. Next week, God-willing, Zebedee planned to put the house up for auction. For years now he had longed to get it so that he could knock down the dividing wall and widen his yard. He had a wine press, but he wanted an olive press also, so that the whole village could come to him to extract its olive oil, and he could take out a percentage and fill his own jars for the year. But where was the wine press to fit? At all costs he must get Nahum's house. . . . Old Salome heard his words, but her mind was on John, her beloved. Where could he be? What was this honey that dripped from the new prophet's lips? She wanted so much to see him again, to hear him speak once more and bring God down into the hearts of men! My son did well, she reflected, he took the right road, and I give him my blessing. . . . She recalled the dream she had had a few days earlier in which she pulled open the door and slammed it behind her, leaving this house with its wine presses and bursting larders in order to follow the new prophet. . . . I ran behind him,

215

barefooted and hungry, she thought, and for the first time in my life, I understood the meaning of happiness. . . .

"Are you listening to me?" demanded old Zebedee, who saw his wife's eyes momentarily droop. "Where is your mind?"

"I'm listening," Salome replied, and she looked at him as though she had never seen him before.

At that moment the old man heard familiar voices in the street. He raised his eyes.

"There they are!" he shouted. Seeing the man in white, flanked by his own two sons, he flew to the doorway, his mouth still full of food.

"Hey, boys," he shouted, "where are you headed? Is this the way to pass my house? Stop!"

He was answered by Peter, while the others went on ahead:

"We've got a job on our hands, Zebedee."

"What job?"

"A very involved, complicated job," said Peter, and he burst out laughing.

The old man's eyes popped out of his head. "You too, Jacob, you too?" he cried, swallowing his mouthful unchewed. With his throat torn in two he went inside and looked at his wife.

"Say good-bye to your sons, Zebedee," she said, shaking her head. "He's taken them from us."

"Jacob too?" said the old man, not knowing what to think. "But he had some sense in his head. It's impossible!"

Salome did not speak. What could she say to him? How could he understand? No longer hungry, she got up, placed herself in the doorway and watched the happy company take the royal highway which followed the Jordan towards Jerusalem. She lifted her aged hand and spoke softly, so that her husband would not hear:

"My blessing upon you all.". . .

At the exit of the village they encountered Philip, who had led his sheep to the edge of the lake to graze. He had climbed high up on a red rock and using his staff as a support was bending forward to admire his shadow, a black ripple on the blue-green waters of the lake below. When he heard the crunching of pebbles beneath him on the road, he stood up straight.

"Hallo!" he shouted, recognizing the passers-by. "Hey, can't you see me? Where are you headed?"

"For the kingdom of heaven!" shouted Andrew. "Are you coming?"

"Look here, Andrew, speak sensibly, will you? If you're on your way to Magdala for the wedding, I'm with you. Nathanael invited me too, you know. He's marrying off his nephew."

"Won't you go further than Magdala?" Jacob yelled at him.

"I have sheep," Philip answered. "Where can I leave them?"

"In God's hands," said Jesus without turning.

"The wolves will eat them!"

"Let them!" shouted John.

Good God, those fellows have gone completely mad, the shepherd concluded; and he whistled to gather together his flock.

The companions marched along. Judas, carrying his crooked staff, again took the lead. He was in the greatest hurry to arrive. The hearts of the others were joyous. They whistled like the blackbirds and laughed as they went. Peter approached Judas, the leader, the only one whose expression was sombre. He did not whistle, did not laugh; he led the way, anxious to arrive.

"Judas, tell me once and for all where we're going," Peter said to him softly.

Half of the redbeard's face laughed: "To the kingdom of heaven."

"Stop joking for God's sake and tell me where we're going. I'm afraid to ask the teacher."

"To Jerusalem."

"Ouch! Three days' march!" said Peter, pulling at his grey hairs. "If I'd only known, I would have brought my sandals, and a loaf of bread and a gourd-full of wine, and my stick."

This time the whole of the redbeard's face laughed. "Ah, poor Peter," he said, "the ball is rolling now and can't be stopped. Say good-bye to your sandals and your bread and wine and stick. We've left—can't you understand that, Peter—we've left the world; left the land and the sea, and gone into the air!" He leaned over to Peter's ear:

"There's still time. . . . Go!"

"How can I go back now?" said Peter, and he spread his arms and turned them in every direction as though he were hemmed in and suffocating. "All this seems tasteless to me now," he said, pointing to the lake, the fishing boats and the houses of Capernaum.

"Agreed!" said the redbeard, shaking his large head. "Well then, stop your grumbling, and let's go!"

XV

FIRST the village dogs picked up his scent and began to bark. Soon the children were running to Magdala with the news: "He's coming! He's coming!"

"Who, boys, who?" the villagers asked, opening their doors.

"The new prophet!"

The thresholds filled with women young and old; the men abandoned their work, the sick jumped for joy and prepared to crawl out to touch him. He had already won a great name for himself in the vicinity of the lake of Gennesaret. His gifts and powers had been proclaimed from village to village by the epileptics, the blind and the paralysed whom he had cured.

"He touched my darkened eyes and I saw the light."

"As soon as he ordered me to throw down my crutches and walk, I began to dance."

"Whole armies of demons were feeding on my insides. He lifted his hand and commanded them: 'Be gone, go to the pigs!' Straightway they bounded out of my bowels, kicking, and entered the pigs that were grazing on the shore. The animals went mad. One climbed on top of the other and they hurled themselves into the water and drowned."

When Magdalene heard the good news she came out of her cottage. She had not appeared at her door since the day the son of Mary ordered her to return home and sin no more. She had wept and cleansed her soul with tears, had struggled to erase the past from her mind, to forget everything—the shame, the joys, the all-night vigils—and be born again with a virgin body. For the first few days she beat her head on the ground and wailed, but in time she grew calm, her pain abated, the nightmares which had tormented her disappeared, and now, every night, she dreamt that Jesus came, opened her door like the man of the house and sat down in the yard under the blossoming pomegranate tree. He had travelled a great distance and was tired, covered with dust, and much embittered by men. Every evening Magdalene would heat water, wash his holy feet and then, letting out her hair, wipe them dry. And he, he would relax, smile, and chat with her. She never remembered what he said, but when she awoke in the morning she jumped out of bed buoyant and exhilarated; and the last few days she had begun—in a low voice, so that the neighbours would not hear—to chirp sweetly like a goldfinch. . . . Now, hearing from the children's shouts that he was coming, she leapt up, lowered her kerchief to hide all of her much-kissed face except her two large all-black eyes, unbolted the door and went out to receive him.

This evening the village was all astir. Young girls had begun to don their jewellery and make ready their lamps for the wedding. Nathanael's nephew was getting married. A cobbler like his uncle, he was a chubby brown over-grown child with a nose like a cudgel. The bride, covered with a veil so thick that you could see only the two eyes which bored through it and the large silver rings on her ears, sat on a raised armchair in the middle of her home, waiting for the gentlemen guests and the village girls with their lighted lamps, waiting for the rabbi to come to unroll the Scriptures and read the blessing, waiting, finally, for the moment when everyone would decamp and she would remain all alone with her cudgel-nose.

Nathanael heard the children shout, "He's coming, he's coming!" and ran out to invite his friends to the wedding. He found them sitting by the well at the entrance to the village, drinking water to quench their thirst. Magdalene was kneeling in front of Jesus. She had washed his feet and was now wiping them dry with her hair.

"Tonight my nephew is getting married," he said. "If you'll be so kind, please come to the wedding. We'll drink the wine made from the grapes I trod in Zebedee's yard this summer."

He turned to Jesus. "We hear a great deal about your sanctity, son of Mary. Do me the honour of coming to bless the new couple so that they will give birth to sons, for Israel's glory."

Jesus rose. "The joys of men please us," he replied. "Companions, let us go."

He grasped Magdalene's hand and helped her up. "Join us, Mary," he said.

Feeling in good spirits, he took the lead. He liked festivities. He loved the people's glowing faces; he loved to see the young marry and keep the fires burning in the hearth. Plants, beetles, birds, animals, men—all are sacred, he reflected as he proceeded to the wedding, all are God's creatures. Why do they live? They live to glorify God. May they continue to live, therefore, for ever and ever!

The freshly-bathed girls already stood in their white robes outside the closed richly-ornamented door. They held their lighted lamps in their hands while they sang the ancient wedding-songs which praised the bride, teased the groom and called on God to deign to come in and join the rest of the company. A wedding was taking place, an Israelite was being married, and the two bodies which would couple that night might engender the Messiah. . . . The girls sang to deceive the time, for the groom was late. They were waiting for him to come and throw open the door so that the ceremony could begin.

But while they were singing, Jesus appeared with his train. The virgins turned. As soon as they saw Magdalene their song came to an abrupt standstill and they recoiled, glowering. What business had this slut among virgins? Where was the old village chief to bar her? The wedding was soiled! The married women turned also and eyed her fiercely; wave after wave of movement could be seen in the murmuring crowd of invitees, the respectable householders, who were also waiting outside the closed door. Magdalene, however, was resplendent, a lighted torch. Standing like this by Jesus' side, she felt her soul newly virgin and her lips unkissed. Suddenly the crowd made way and the village chief, a tiny desiccated old man whose nose dripped venom, came up to Madgalene, touched her with the end of his staff and nodded for her to leave.

Jesus felt the envenomed glances of the people on his hands, face and uncovered chest. His body became inflamed, as though pricked by countless invisible thorns. Looking at the old chief, the honest wives, the scowling men and flustered virgins, he sighed. How long would the eyes of men remain blind and fail to see that we all were brothers?

The murmur had now grown intense; the first threats already resounded in the darkness. Nathanael went up to speak to Jesus but the teacher calmly pushed him aside and making his way through the crowd, approached the virgins. Lamps swayed; room was made for him to pass. He stopped in their midst and raised his hand:

"Virgins, my sisters, God touched my mouth and confided a kind word to me to present to you on this holy wedding night. Virgins, my sisters, open your ears, open your hearts; and you, my brothers, be quiet, for I shall speak!"

They all turned, uneasy. From his voice the men divined that he was angry, the women that he was sad. No one spoke. The two blind musicians in the courtyard of the house could be heard tuning their lutes. Jesus raised his hand:

"Virgins, my sisters, what do you suppose the kingdom of heaven is like? It is like a wedding. God is the bridegroom and the soul of man is the bride. A wedding takes place in heaven, and the whole of mankind is invited. Forgive me, my brothers, but God speaks to me thus, in parables, and it is in parables that I shall speak now:

"There was to be a wedding in a certain village. Ten virgins took their lamps and went out to receive the bridegroom. Five were wise and took along flasks filled with oil. The other five were foolish and carried no extra oil with them. They stood outside the house of the bride and waited and waited, but the bridegroom was late and they grew tired and slept. At midnight there was a cry, 'Behold, the bridegroom is coming! Run out to receive him!' The ten virgins jumped up to fill their lamps, which were about to go out. But the five foolish virgins had no more oil. 'Give us a little oil, sisters,' they said to the wise virgins, 'for our lamps are going out.' But the wise replied, 'We haven't any left for you. Go and get some.' And while the foolish virgins ran to find oil, the bridegroom arrived, the wise virgins went in, and the door was shut.

"A little while later the foolish virgins returned, their lamps lit, and began to pound on the door. 'Open the door for us!' they cried and pleaded. But inside, the wise virgins laughed. 'It serves you right,' they answered them. 'Now the door is closed. Go away!' But the others wept and begged, 'Open the door! Open the door!' And then. . ."

Jesus stopped. Once more he surveyed the old chief, the guests, the honest housewives, the virgins with the lighted lamps. He smiled.

"And then. . ." said Nathanael, who was listening with gaping mouth. His simple, sluggish mind had begun to stir. "And then, rabbi, what was the outcome?"

"What would you have done, Nathanael," Jesus asked, pinning his large bewitching eyes on him, "what would you have done if you had been the bridegroom?"

Nathanael was silent. He still was not entirely clear in his mind what he would have done. One moment he thought to send them away. The door had definitely been closed, and that was what the Law required. But the next moment he pitied them and thought to let them in. . . .

"What would you have done, Nathanael, if you had been the bridegroom?" Jesus asked again, and slowly, persistently, his beseeching eyes caressed the cobbler's simple, guileless face.

"I would have opened the door. . . ," the other answered in a low voice so that the old chief would not hear. He had been unable to oppose the eyes of the son of Mary any longer.

"Congratulations, friend Nathanael," said Jesus happily, and he stretched forth his hand as though blessing him. "This moment, though you are still alive, you enter Paradise. The bridegroom did exactly as you said: he called to the servants to open the door. 'This is a wedding,' he cried. 'Let everyone eat, drink and be merry. Open the door for the foolish virgins and wash and refresh their feet, for they have run much.' "

Tears welled up between Magdalene's long eyelashes. Ah, if she could only kiss the mouth that uttered such words! Simple Nathanael glowed from head to toe as though he were actually in Paradise already. But old poison-nose, the village chief, lifted his staff:

"You're going contrary to the Law, son of Mary," he screeched.

"The Law goes contrary to my heart," Jesus calmly replied.

He was still speaking when the groom made his appearance, bathed, perfumed, a green wreath over his thick head of curly hair. A few drinks had put him in the best of moods, and his nose was dazzling. With one thrust he threw open the door. The guests flowed in behind him, and Jesus entered also, holding Magdalene by the hand.

"Which are the foolish virgins, which the wise?" Peter asked John in a low voice. "What did you make of it?"

". . . that God is our Father," replied the son of Zebedee.

The rabbi arrived and performed the ceremony. Afterwards, bride and groom placed themselves in the middle of the house and the guests filed by, kissing them and expressing the wish that they might give birth to a son who would rescue Israel from its slavery. Then the lutes started to play, the guests danced and drank, and Jesus and his companions danced and drank with them. The hours passed, and when the moon rose they resumed their journey. It was autumn now, but the great heat of the days had not abated, and it was delightful to travel in the moist coolness of the night.

Their faces directed towards Jerusalem, they proceeded. They had drunk, and everything appeared transformed. Their bodies had grown buoyant, like souls; they walked with winged feet, with the Jordan on their left and on their right, lying tame and fertile under the moonlight, the plain of Zabulon, tired and satisfied this year too, after having once more fulfilled the obligation which God had entrusted to it for centuries and centuries: to lift up the grain to the height of a man, to load down the vines with grapes and the olive trees with olives. It lay now, tired and satisfied, like a mother who had just given birth to her child.

"What a joy this is, brothers!" Peter said over and over again. His delight in this nocturnal march and in the sweetness of the camaraderie was insatiable. "Is it real? Is it a dream? Have we been bewitched? The way I am, I feel like singing a song, or else I'll burst!"

"All together!" cried Jesus. He went in front, tipped up his head, and was the first to begin. His voice was weak, but pleasant and full of passion. To its right and left were the voices of John and Andrew, melodious and tender. For some time these three high voices chirped their graceful vibrato all alone. They were so mellifluous, your heart skipped a beat: they can't keep it up, you said to yourself. So much honey will surely make them dizzy and sick, one after the other. But the voices spurted forth out of a very deep spring and every time they were about to falter, steadied themselves again. Suddenly—what joy! what strength!—the baritones of Peter, Jacob and Judas shook the air, heavy, triumphant and full of virility; and all together, each with his own grace and force, the companions lifted high to the heavens the jubilant psalm of the sacred journey:

> *O, there is nothing better or sweeter*
> *than brothers journeying together.*
> *It is like the holy oil which runs down*
> *from the beard of Aaron;*
> *It is like the dew of Hermon,*
> *which falls on the mountains of Zion.*
> *There, God sends the blessing, and life*
> *for evermore.*

The hours passed, the stars dimmed, the sun rose. Leaving the red soil of Galilee behind them, they entered black-soiled Samaria.

Judas halted. "Let's change our route," he proposed. "This is a heretical and accursed land. Let's cross the Jordan bridge and go along the other bank. It's a sin to touch those who transgress the Law. Their God is contaminated and so is their water and their bread. A mouthful of Samaritan bread, my mother used to tell me, is a mouthful of pork. Let's change our route!"

But Jesus took Judas calmly by the hand and they continued on together. "Judas, my brother," he said to him, "when the pure man touches the soiled man, the soiled man becomes pure. Do not object. We have come for them, for sinners. What need do the righteous have of us? Here in Samaria a kind word may save a soul—a kind word, Judas, a good deed, a smile at the Samaritan who goes by. Do you understand?"

Judas glanced furtively around him to be sure the others could not hear. "This is not the way," he said softly, "no, it is not the way. But I'll be patient until we reach the wild ascetic. He will judge. Until then, go where you like, do what you like. I won't leave you."

He passed his crooked staff over his shoulders and walked on ahead, all by himself.

The others conversed as they marched. Jesus spoke to them of love, the Father, the kingdom of heaven. He explained which souls were the foolish virgins, which the wise, what the lamps were and what the oil, who the bridegroom was and why the foolish virgins not only entered his house, as did the wise, but were the only ones to have their tired feet washed by the servants. As the four companions listened, their minds widened, received all that was being said to them, and their hearts grew firm. Sin now appeared to them like a foolish virgin standing with her extinguished lamp, imploring and weeping before the door of the Lord. . .

They marched and marched. The skies above them clouded over and the face of the earth grew dark. The air smelt of rain.

They arrived at the first village, at the foot of Gerizim, the holy mountain of their forefathers. At the entrance to the village, surrounded by date-palms and reeds, was the age-old well of Jacob. It was here that the patriarch had come with his sheep to draw water and drink. The stone lip of the well was eaten away by the ropes which had rubbed over it for generations and generations.

Jesus felt tired. The stones had cut his feet; they were bleeding. "I shall stay here," he said. "You go into the village and knock at the doors. Some good soul will be found to give us a loaf of bread as alms; and some woman will come to the well and draw water for us to drink. Have faith in God, and in men."

The five left, but on the way, Judas changed his mind. "I'm not going into a contaminated village," he said, "and I'm not going to eat contaminated bread. I'll stay here under this fig tree and wait for you."

Jesus had lain down meanwhile in the shade of the reeds. He was thirsty, but the well was deep: how was he to drink? He inclined his head and gave himself up to thought. He had placed a difficult road before him. His body was weak, he grew tired, his knees sagged, he did not have the strength to support his soul. He fell, but straightway God always blew a cool light breeze over him, his body found strength again and he got up and continued on. . . . For how long? Until death? Until beyond death?

While he reflected on God, man and death, the reeds stirred and a young woman wearing bracelets and ear-rings and carrying a jug on her head approached the well and placed her jug down on the brim. Jesus saw her through the reeds let out the rope she was carrying, lower the bucket, draw up water and fill the jug. His thirst increased.

"Woman," he said, emerging from the reeds, "give me a drink."

The woman was startled by his sudden appearance in front of her.

"Do not be afraid," he said. "I am an honest man. I'm thirsty, give me a drink."

"How is it," she replied, "that you, a Galilean—I can tell by your clothes—ask a drink of me, a Samaritan?"

"If you knew who it was that says to you, 'Woman, give me a drink' you would fall at his feet and ask him to give you immortal water to drink."

The woman was perplexed. "You have neither rope nor bucket, and the well is deep. How could you draw up water to give me a drink?"

"He who drinks of the water of this well will thirst again," Jesus answered, "but he who drinks the water that I shall give him will not thirst again for all eternity."

"Sir," the woman then said, "give me this water so that I will not thirst again for all eternity or have to come here every day to the well."

"Go, call your husband," Jesus said to her.

"I have no husband, sir."

"You are right in saying, 'I have no husband,' for you have had five husbands until now, and he whom you have at present is not your husband."

"Sir, are you a prophet?" the woman asked, filled with admiration. "Do you know everything?"

Jesus smiled. "Is there anything you wish to ask me? Speak freely."

"Yes, there is one thing I would like you to answer for me, sir. Until now our fathers have worshipped God on this holy mountain, Gerizim. Now you prophets say that we ought to worship God only in Jerusalem. Which is right? Where is God found? Enlighten me."

Jesus bowed his head and did not speak. This sinful woman,

so tortured by her solicitude for God, deeply agitated his heart. He struggled for her sake, struggled within himself to find the right words to console her. Suddenly he lifted his head. His face was gleaming.

"Woman, keep what I shall tell you deep in your heart. The day will come—it has already come—when men will worship God neither on this mountain nor in Jerusalem. God is spirit, and spirit must be worshipped only in spirit."

The woman was confused. She leaned over and looked anxiously at Jesus. "Can you be. . . ," she asked, slowly and in a trembling voice, "can you be the One we're waiting for?"

"Whom are you waiting for?"

"You know. Why do you want me to pronounce his name? You know it. My lips are sinful."

Jesus leaned his head against his breast. He seemed to be listening to his heart, as though he expected it to give him the answer. The woman, bending over him, waited feverishly.

But while the two of them, both troubled, stood in silence, happy voices were heard and the disciples appeared, triumphantly waving a loaf of bread. Finding the teacher with an unknown woman, they halted. Jesus was delighted to see them, for now he was saved from having to answer the woman's terrible question. He nodded to the companions to approach.

"Come," he called. "This good woman has come from the village, sent by God to draw water for us to drink."

The companions approached, all except Judas, who stepped aside in order to avoid being contaminated by Samaritan water.

The woman tipped her jug and the thirsty men drank. She refilled the jug, placed it skilfully on her head and proceeded towards the village, thoughtful and silent.

"Rabbi, who was that woman?" Peter asked. "You were talking together as though you'd known each other for years and years."

"She was one of my sisters," Jesus answered. "I asked her for water because I was thirsty, and it was her thirst that was quenched."

Peter scratched his thick skull. "I don't understand," he said.

"It doesn't matter," Jesus replied, patting his friend's grey

228

head. "Don't be impatient. You will understand in time, bit by bit. . . . Right now we're hungry: let's eat!"

They stretched out beneath the date-palms. Andrew began to relate how they entered the village and started asking for alms:

"We knocked at the houses and were hooted and chased from door to door. Finally, at the opposite end of the village a·tiny old woman half-opened her door and looked carefully up and down the street. Not a soul in sight. . . . She handed us a loaf of bread on the sly and immediately shut the door. We grabbed it and ran for our lives."

"It's a shame we don't know the old woman's name," said Peter. "We could ask God to remember her."

Jesus laughed. "Don't feel bad on that account, Peter," he said. "God knows her name."

Jesus took the bread, blessed it, gave thanks to God for having put the old woman there to give it to them, and then divided it into six large pieces, one for each of the companions. But Judas pushed his portion away with his staff and turned aside his face. "I don't eat Samaritan bread," he said; "I don't eat pork."

Jesus did not argue with him. He knew that Judas's heart was hard and that for it to soften, time was needed—time and skill and much love.

"We shall eat," he said to the others. "Samaritan bread becomes Galilean when eaten by Galileans, and pork becomes the flesh of men when eaten by men. So, in God's name!"

Laughing, the four companions ate with relish. Samaritan bread tasted delicious, like all bread, and they were elated. After the meal they crossed their hands. They were tired, and they slept— all except Judas, who remained awake and struck the ground with his stick as though thrashing it. Hunger is better than shame, he reflected, and this consoled him.

The first drops of rain began to beat against the reeds. The sleepers jumped to their feet.

"It's the first rain," said Jacob. "The earth is going to quench its thirst."

But as they began to consider where to find a cave in which to shelter themselves, a wind arose from the north and chased away the clouds. The skies cleared. They resumed their march.

The figs which remained on the fig trees gleamed in the damp air. The pomegranate trees were loaded with fruit. The companions reached out, picked some pomegranates and refreshed themselves. The farmers were lifting their heads from the ground. They looked with amazement at the Galileans. What business had they in Samaria? Why were they mixing with Samaritans and eating their bread and picking fruit from their trees? They'd better get out of our sight, but quick! One old man could not bear it. He left his orchard and stood before them.

"Hey, Galileans," he shouted, "your unlawful law hurls the anathema on the sanctified land which you now tread. So, what are you doing on our soil? Out of our sight!"

"We are going to holy Jerusalem to worship," Peter answered him, and he stopped in front of the old man and bulged out his chest.

"You should worship here, apostates, on Gerizim, the mountain trodden by God," the old man thundered. "Haven't you ever read the Scriptures? It was here at the foot of Gerizim, under the oak trees, that God appeared to Abraham. He showed him the mountains and the plains from one end to the other, from Mount Hebron to Idumea and the Land of Midian, and said, 'Behold the Promised Land, a land that flows with milk and honey. I gave you my word I would present it to you, and present it to you I will.' They shook hands and sealed the agreement. . . . Do you hear, Galileans? That is what the Scriptures say. Whoever wants to worship, therefore, ought to worship here in this holy land and not in Jerusalem, which murders the prophets!"

"Every land is holy, old man," Jesus said with a calm voice. "God is everywhere, old man, and we are all brothers."

The other turned, astonished. "Samaritans and Galileans too?"

"Samaritans and Galileans too, old man—and Judeans. . . . All!"

Stroking his beard, the old man fell deep into thought. He examined Jesus from head to toe.

"God and the devil too?" he asked finally. He spoke in a lowered voice so that the invisible powers would not hear.

Jesus was terrified. Never in his life had he been asked if God's mercy was so great that one day he would forgive even Lucifer and welcome him back into the kingdom of heaven.

"I don't know, old man," he replied, "I don't know. I am a man, and my concern is for men. What's beyond is God's affair."

The old man did not speak. Still stroking his beard and still deep in thought, he watched the strange passers-by proceed, two by two, and disappear under the trees.

Night fell; a cold wind arose. They found a cave and burrowed in, huddling all together in a ball to keep warm. A left-over piece of bread remained for each, and they ate. The redbeard went out, collected wood and lit a fire. This revived the companions, and they sat in a circle, silently watching the flames. They heard the whistling of the wind, the howling of the jackals, the far-away muffled thunderclaps which rolled down from Mount Gerizim. Through the opening of the cave a large comforting star could be seen in the sky, but soon clouds came and covered it up. The companions closed their eyes and leaned their heads on each other's shoulders. John secretly threw the woollen cloak he was wearing over Jesus' back, and all of them, squeezed closely together like bats, slept.

The next day they entered Judea. They observed a gradual change in the trees. The road was now lined with yellow-leafed poplars, locusts heavy with fruit, and ancient cedars. The region was rocky, arid, rough; even the peasants who appeared in the low dark doorways were made of flint. Now and then a blue wild-flower, humble and graceful, emerged from between the rocks; and sometimes in the mute loneliness, deep in a ravine, a partridge cackled. It must have found a sip of water to drink, Jesus thought as he heard it, and he felt the bird's warm breast in his palm and rejoiced.

As they came closer to Jerusalem the land grew fiercer and fiercer. God changed too. The earth here did not laugh, as it did in Galilee, and God himself, like the villages and the people, was made of flint. The heavens which in Samaria had tried for a moment at least to rain and refresh the earth, here were red-hot iron. The panting companions marched forward in this deep furnace. When nightfall came again they saw a large group of tombs cut into the rocks and shining in all their blackness. Thousands of their ancestors had decomposed inside and turned again to stone. They burrowed into the empty tombs, lay down and went to sleep early, in order to be fresh for their entry into the holy city the next day.

Jesus was the only one who did not sleep. He roamed the tombs, listening intently to the night. His heart was uneasy. Inside him were obscure voices, a great wailing, as though thousands of suffering men were shouting. . . . Towards midnight the wind stopped and the night grew silent. And then, in this silence, a heart-rending cry tore through the air. At first he thought it was a hungry jackal, but then he understood, with terror, that it was his own heart.

"Dear God," he murmured, "who is shouting within me? Who is weeping?"

Fatigued, he too entered one of the tombs, crossed his hands, and gave himself up to God's mercy. At dawn he had a dream. It seemed that he was with Mary Magdalene, and that both of them were flying tranquilly and noiselessly above a large city, just grazing the rooftops. When they reached the edge of the city the very last door opened, and a huge old man appeared. He had a flowing beard and blue eyes which shone like stars. His sleeves were rolled up; his hands and arms were covered with mud. Lifting his head and seeing them fly above him, he shouted: "Stop, I have something to tell you." They stopped.

"What, old man? We're listening."

"The Messiah is he who loves the whole world. The Messiah is he who dies because he loves the whole world."

"Nothing else?" asked Madgalene.

"Isn't that enough for you?" the old man shouted angrily.

"May we enter your workshop?" Magdalene asked.

"No. Can't you see that my hands are all covered with clay? Inside I am constructing the Messiah."

Jesus awoke with a start. His body was truly weightless; he felt he was flying. Day broke. The companions had already risen and their eyes leapt from rock to rock, hill to hill, in the direction of Jerusalem.

They set out, anxious to arrive. They marched and marched, but the mountains in front of them always seemed to recede and the road to become longer and longer.

"I don't think we'll ever get to Jerusalem, brothers," said Peter in despair. "What is happening to us? Don't you see—she gets further and further away."

"She comes closer and closer," Jesus answered him. "Courage, Peter. We take a step to find Jerusalem, and she takes a step to find us. Like the Messiah."

"The Messiah?" asked Judas, turning abruptly.

"The Messiah is coming," Jesus said in a deep voice. "You know very well, Judas, my brother, whether or not we are going in the right direction to find him. If we do a good or noble deed. if we pronounce a kind word, the Messiah quickens his pace and approaches. If we are dishonest, evil, afraid of everything, the Messiah turns his back on us and moves further away. The Messiah is a Jerusalem in motion, brothers. Jerusalem is in a hurry, and so are we. Let's move fast and find her! Have faith in God and in the immortal spirit of man!"

Encouraged, they all quickened their pace. Judas again went in front, his whole face happy now. He speaks well, he said to himself as he marched. Yes, the son of Mary is right. The old rabbi shouts the same thing at us: salvation depends on us. If we cross our hands the land of Israel will never be delivered. If we all take up arms, we shall see freedom. . . .

Judas continued on, talking to himself. But suddenly he stopped, confused. "Who is the Messiah?" he murmured. "Who? Is it perhaps the entire people?"

Grains of sweat began to run down his fiery brow. Is it perhaps the entire people? This was the first time this thought had come to him, and he felt troubled. Can the Messiah be the entire people? he asked himself over and over. But then, what need have we for all these prophets and false prophets? Why must we grope in an agony, trying to see which one is the Messiah? That's it, the people are the Messiah—I, you, every one of us. The only thing we have to do is take up arms!

He started marching again, waving his club in the air; and while he proceeded, playing happily with his new thought as with the club, suddenly he uttered a cry. In front of him, flashing on a double-peaked mountain, was Holy Jerusalem, beautiful, white and proud. He did not shout to the others, who were coming up behind him. He wanted to enjoy the sight by himself as long as he could. Palaces, towers and castle-doors glittered in the pupils of his blue eyes; and in the very centre, protected by God, was the Temple, all gold, cedar and marble.

The remaining companions caught up, and they too shouted for joy.

"Come, let us sing the beauty of our Lady," suggested Peter, the good singer. "Ready men, all together now!"

All five began to dance in a circle around Jesus, who stood motionless in the centre and started the sacred hymn:

> I was glad when they said to me,
>   "Arise, let us go to the house of the Lord!"
> My feet have stopped before
>   your courtyards, O Jerusalem.
>
> Jerusalem, stoutly-built fortress,
>   peace be within your strong towers,
>   happiness within your palaces.
> For my brethren and companions' sake,
>   peace, peace be upon you, Jerusalem!

XVI

STREETS, rooftops, courts, squares: Jerusalem was entirely clothed in green. It was indeed the great autumn festival and the Jerusalemites had constructed thousands of tents from olive and vine branches, palm boughs, pine and cedar as prescribed by the God of Israel in remembrance of the forty years which their forefathers had spent under tents in the wilderness. The harvest and vintage were finished, the year had ended, and the people had suspended all their sins around the neck of a black, well-fed billy-goat and, stoning him, had chased him out into the desert. Now they felt greatly relieved. Their souls were purified, a new year had begun, God had opened a new ledger, and for eight days they would eat and drink under the green tents and sing the glories of the God of Israel who blessed the harvest and the vintage and also sent them the billy-goat to bear their sins. He too was a God-sent Messiah: he bore all the sins of the people, perished of hunger in the desert—and with him perished their sins.

The wide courtyards of the Temple overflowed with blood. Every day flocks of burnt-offerings were slaughtered. The holy city stank from the smell of meat, dung and drippings. The sacred air echoed with horns and trumpets. The people over-ate, over-drank, and their souls grew heavy. The first day was all psalms, prayers and prostrations; and Jehovah, invisible, strode joyously into the tents and celebrated too, eating and drinking with his people. Several had seen him with their own eyes smacking his lips and wiping his beard. But starting with the second and third days, the excessive meat and wine went to the heads of the people. The dirty jokes and the laughter and the bawdy tavern-songs began, and men and women coupled shamelessly in broad daylight, at first within the tents, and then openly in the roads and on the green grass. In every neighbourhood the celebrated prostitutes of Jerusalem appeared, plastered with make-up and smeared with aromatic oil. The simple farmers and fishermen who had come from the ends of the Land of Canaan to adore the holy of holies fell into these accomplished arms and were flabbergasted. They had never dreamt that a kiss could involve such art and such savour.

Holding his breath, Jesus strode hurriedly, angrily, through the streets and over the dead-drunk people who were rolling on the ground. The smells and filth and the shameless guffawing nauseated him. "Quickly, quickly!" he exhorted his companions. Holding his right arm around John and his left around Andrew, he proceeded.

But Peter was continually halting, encountering pilgrims from Galilee who offered him a glass of wine, a bite to eat, and engaged him in conversation. He would call Judas, Jacob would come too —they did not wish to give grounds for complaint to any of their friends. But the three in front were in a hurry. They continually called the tarriers and made them start out again.

"Good God, the teacher won't let us breathe freely like human beings," grumbled Peter, who had already fallen into a gay mood. "What have we got ourselves into?"

"And where have you been all this time, my poor Peter?" said Judas, shaking his head. "Do you think we've come here to have a good time? Do you think we're going to a wedding?"

But while they were running, they heard a hoarse voice from one of the tents: "Hey, Peter, son of Jonah, you lousy Galilean— you pass by, we practically knock our heads together and you don't even notice. Stop a minute to have a drink. It'll clear your sight and you'll be able to see me!"

Peter recognized the voice and stopped. "Halloo! Nice to bump into you, Simon, you filthy Cyrenian!" He turned to his two companions:

"Lads, this time we can't escape: let's stop and have a drink. Simon is a famous drunkard, keeper of a celebrated inn near the gate of David. He deserves to be hanged and have his head impaled on a stake, but he's a nice fellow all the same, and we ought to do him the honour."

And truly, Simon was a good fellow. In his youth he had shipped out from Cyrene and opened a tavern, and every time Peter came to Jerusalem he put up at his house. The two of them ate and drank, talked, joked, sometimes broke out into a song, sometimes into

236

a brawl, became friends again, drank some more, and then Peter would wrap himself up in a thick blanket, lie down on a bench, and fall asleep. Simon was sitting now under his tent of entwined vine-branches, a jug under his arm and a bronze cup in his hand. He was drinking, all by himself.

The two friends embraced. They were both half-drunk, and each felt so much love for the other that his eyes filled with tears. After the initial shouts and hugs and repeated toasts were over, Simon began to laugh.

"I bet my bones you're on your way to get baptized," he said. "You're doing the right thing, I give you my blessing. The other day I was baptized myself, and I don't regret it. It's quite satisfying."

"And have you noticed any improvement?" asked Judas, who was eating, not drinking. His mind was full of thorns.

"What can I say to you, my friend? It's been years since I was in the water. Water and I are at sword's points. I'm made for wine, water is for the toads. But the other day I said to myself: Look here, why not go and get baptized? The whole world is going, and it's certain that among the newly-enlightened there'll be a few who drink wine. They can't all be imbeciles, so I'll be able to make a few acquaintances and to hook some clients. Everyone knows my tavern at the David-gate. . . . Well, to make a long story short, I went. The prophet is a savage untamed beast—how can I describe him? Flames fly out of his nostrils—God protect me! He grabbed me by the neck and dunked me into the water up to my beard. I screamed. He was going to drown me, the infidel! But I survived, came out—and here I am!"

"And have you noticed any improvement?" Judas repeated.

"I swear to you by my wine that the bath did me a lot of good, yes, a lot of good. I felt relieved. The Baptist says I was relieved of my sins. But—just between you and me—I think I was relieved of a few grease-spots, because when I came out of the Jordan, there was a film of oil on top of the water an inch deep."

He burst out laughing, filled his cup, drank; and then Peter and Jacob drank too. He refilled his cup and turned to Judas:

"And you, blacksmith, don't you drink? It's wine, you blessed idiot, not water."

"I never drink," answered the redbeard, pushing away the cup.

Simon's eyes popped: "Are you one of them. . . ?" he asked in a low voice.

"Yes, one of them," said Judas, and with one flourish of his hand he cut the conversation short.

Two painted women passed, stopped for a moment and winked at the four men.

"Nor women?" asked Simon, bewildered.

"Nor women," Judas again drily replied.

"What then, poor fellow?" shouted Simon, who could bear this no longer. "Why did God make wine and women, can you tell me? To while away his own time, or for us to while away ours?"

At that moment Andrew came up at a run. "Come quickly," he shouted. "The teacher is in a hurry."

"What teacher?" asked the innkeeper. "The one dressed all in white, the barefooted one?"

But the three companions had already left, and Simon the Cyrenian, standing disconcerted outside his tent, the empty cup still in his hand and the jug under his arm, watched them and shook his head. "This must be another Baptist, another lunatic. Bah, they've been sprouting up lately like mushrooms. Let's drink to his health," he said, filling the cup. "May God give him some sense!"

Meanwhile, Jesus and the companions had reached the great courtyard of the Temple. Halting, they washed their hands, feet and mouths in order to enter the Temple and worship. They glanced quickly around them: tiers, one after the other, all crowded with men and animals; well-shaded arcades, columns of white and blue marble girded with golden vine-branches and grapes; and on every side, sheds, tents, carts, money-changers, barbers, wine-sellers, butchers. The air resounded with shouts, brawls and laughter, and the house of the Lord stank from sweat and filth.

Jesus put his palm over his nose and mouth. He looked all around him, but God was nowhere. " 'I hate, I despise your festivities. I am nauseous from the stench of the fatted calves you slaughter for me. Take away from me the tumult of your psalms and your lutes . . .' " It was no longer the prophet, nor God, but the heart of Jesus which was upside-down and crying out. Suddenly he felt faint. Everything disappeared. The heavens opened and an angel with hair of fire rushed forth, his feet lashing out into the air. With smoke and flames rising from the hair of his head, he climbed onto a black rock in the middle of the courtyard and pointed his sword towards the proud gold-saddled Temple. . .

Jesus staggered. He steadied himself on Andrew's arm. Opening his eyes, he saw the Temple and the noisy people. The angel had hidden himself in the great light. Jesus extended his arms towards his companions:

"Forgive me," he said, "but I cannot last. I shall faint. Let us go."

"Without worshipping?" said Jacob, scandalized.

"We worship within ourselves, Jacob," said Jesus. "Each of our bodies is a temple."

They left. Judas went in the lead, tapping his stick on the ground. He can't endure filth, blood and shouting, he was thinking. He isn't the Messiah.

A wild, throbbing Pharisee, stretched out face-down on the last step of the Temple, was ravenously kissing the marble, and bellowing. Thick strings of talismans stuffed with terrifying texts from Scripture hung around his neck and arms. Repeated prostrations had made his knees calloused like a camel's; and his face, neck and breast were covered with open, running wounds: every time this tempest of God threw him down, he would seize sharp stones and mutilate himself.

Andrew and John quickly stepped in front of Jesus so that he would not see the Pharisee. Peter came up to Jacob and leaned over to his ear. "You know him. He's Jacob, the eldest son of Joseph the Carpenter. He makes his rounds selling talismans and every two minutes his evil spirit takes hold of him, and he rolls on the ground and literally murders himself."

"Is he the one who's hunting the master so ravenously?" asked Jacob, stopping for a moment.

"Yes. He says he's a disgrace to their house."

They went out by the Gold Door of the Temple, passed through the Cedron Valley and began to march towards the Dead Sea. On their right they passed the garden and olive grove of Gethsemane.

239

The sky above them was white and burning. They reached the Mount of Olives. The world had sweetened a bit. Light dripped from every leaf of the olive trees; flocks of crows dashed one after the other towards Jerusalem.

Andrew, his arm around Jesus, was speaking about his former master the Baptist. The closer he came to his lair, the more he breathed in, with terror, the prophet's leonine breath.

"He is the veritable Elijah. He rushed down from Mount Carmel to heal man's soul once more with fire. One night, with my own eyes, I saw the fiery chariot circle over his head; another night I saw a crow bring in its beak a lighted coal for him to eat. . . . One day I took courage and asked him, 'Are you the Messiah?' He shook as though he'd stepped on a snake. 'No', he answered with a sigh, 'I am the ox who draws the plough. The Messiah is the seed.' "

"Why did you leave his side, Andrew?"

"I wanted to find the seed."

"Have you found it?"

Andrew pressed Jesus' hand to his heart and blushed violently. "Yes," he answered, but he spoke so softly that Jesus did not hear.

They descended slowly, out of breath, towards the Dead Sea. The sun poured flames over them until their heads rattled. In front of them the mountains of Moab towered higher and higher, an arid wall. Behind them, lime-white, were the mountains of Idumea. The road wound and descended more and more. They were entering a deep well, and they all held their breath.

We're going down to the Inferno. . . , they were all thinking, and they could smell the tar and brimstone.

The light blinded them. They groped their way forward, their feet lacerated, their eyes burning. They heard bells: two camels passed—not camels, but mirages which melted away in the violent heat.

"I'm afraid," whispered Zebedee's younger son. "This is the Inferno."

"Courage," Andrew answered him. "Haven't you heard that Paradise is at the heart of the Inferno?"

"Paradise?"

"You'll see shortly."

The sun finally went down. The mountains of Moab turned dark purple, the mountains of Idumea, pink—bringing comfort to the eyes of men. Suddenly, at a twist in the road, their sight was refreshed—their sight and their bodies, as though they had stepped into cool water. What were those unexpected meadows directly in front of them, right in the sand; what were those waters which chuckled, and the pomegranates charged with fruit and the white, shaded cottages? The air was suddenly perfumed with jasmine and rose.

"Jericho," Andrew shouted happily. "They have the sweetest dates in the whole world here, and the most miraculous roses: if they wither, all you do is dip them in water and they revive."

The night fell abruptly. The first lamps had already been lit.

"To travel, watch the darkness fall, arrive in a village, see the first lamps lit and have nothing to eat, nor anywhere to sleep, and to let everything depend on God's grace and the goodness of men —this, I think, is one of the greatest and purest joys in the world," said Jesus, stopping to enjoy fully this holy moment.

The village dogs scented the strangers and began to bark. Doors opened; lighted lamps appeared, searched the darkness and then returned inside. The companions went to all the doors, knocked, were cheerfully offered here a slice of bread or a pomegranate, there a handful of grapes or of green olives. They amassed all these alms from God and man, reclined in the corner of an orchard, ate, and immediately fell asleep. And all night long in their dreams they heard the desert shifting, lulling them to sleep like the sea. But Jesus, in his sleep, heard trumpets—and the walls of Jericho came tumbling down.

It was nearly midday when the companions, deathly pale, their tongues hanging out, reached the accursed Dead Sea. Fish that descended the current of the Jordan perished as they touched it; the few squat trees on its banks were like standing bones. The water was leaden, thick, motionless. If you were pious and you leaned over it, you could see two rotted whores, Sodom and Gomorrah, embracing on the black bottom.

Jesus got up on a rock and gazed into the distance: desolation. The earth was burning, the mountains had melted away. He took

Andrew by the arm and asked him, "Where is John the Baptist? I see no one. . . , no one. . . ."

"Over there behind the reeds," Andrew replied, "the river becomes calm. The water forms a pool and the prophet baptizes. Let's go find him; I know the way."

"You're tired, Andrew. Stay with the others. I'll go by myself."

"He's savage. I'll accompany you, rabbi."

"I want to go by myself, Andrew. Stay here."

He started towards the reeds, his heart pounding strongly. He placed his hand over it and patted it to make it calm. A new flock of crows appeared from the desert and flew hurriedly towards Jerusalem.

Suddenly he heard someone walking behind him. He turned. It was Judas.

"You forgot to call me," said the redbeard, smiling caustically. "This is the most difficult hour, and I want to be with you."

"Come," Jesus said.

They went forward silently, Jesus in front, Judas behind. They pushed aside the reeds and plunged their feet into the lukewarm river slime. A black snake gave a start, slid onto a rock and lifted its head and neck. It looked at them with its tiny, cunning eyes and hissed, half its body glued to the rock, half standing erect. Jesus stopped for a moment and waved his hand amicably at the snake, as though bidding it welcome. Judas lifted his oaken club, but Jesus put out his arm and restrained him.

"Don't hurt it, Judas my brother," he said. "It too does its duty —by biting."

The heat was roaring and the south-wind which blew from the Dead Sea carried a heavy stench of rotting carcasses. Jesus now began to hear a wild, hoarse voice. Now and then he was able to distinguish a few words: "Fire. . . , axe. . . , barren tree. . . ," and then, louder: "Repent! Repent!" All at once a large multitude burst into shouts and wailing. Jesus went forward slowly, craftily, as though approaching the cave of a wild beast. He pushed aside the reeds: the noise increased. Suddenly he bit his lips to prevent himself from screaming—for there he was, standing on his reed-like legs upon a rock which rose above the waters of the Jordan. Was this a man, a locust, the angel of Hunger, or the archangel of

Revenge? Wave after wave of bellowing men broke upon the rocks—Ethiopians with painted fingernails and eyelashes, Chaldeans with thick brass rings in their noses, Israelites with long greasy sideburns. Frothing at the mouth, the south-wind shaking him like a reed, the Baptist was shouting, "Repent! Repent! The day of the Lord has come! Roll on the ground, bite the dust, howl! The Lord of Hosts has said: 'On this day I shall command the sun to set at noon; I shall crush the horns of the new moon and spill darkness over heaven and earth. I shall reverse your laughter, turn it into tears, and your songs into lamentation. I shall blow, and all your finery—hands, feet, noses, ears, hair—will fall to the ground.' "

Judas strode forward and took Jesus by the arm. "Do you hear? Do you hear? Look! That's how the Messiah speaks! He is the Messiah!"

"No, Judas, my brother," Jesus answered, "he who holds the axe and opens the way for the Messiah speaks in that way, but the Messiah does not." He bent down, broke off a sharp green leaf and passed it between his teeth.

"He who opens the way is the Messiah," the redbeard growled. He pushed Jesus in order to make him emerge from the reeds and show himself.

"Move ahead, let him see you," he ordered. "He will judge."

Jesus came out in the sunlight, took two hesitating steps, stumbled, and stopped, his eyes glued to the prophet. His whole soul had become a gaze which explored the prophet, ran over his reed-like legs and up to his fiery head and then still higher, to the full invisible stature. The Baptist's back was turned. He felt the vehement stare ransacking his entire body, grew angry, swung completely around and half-closed his two round hawk-like eyes in order to see better. Who was this silent motionless young man dressed all in white and staring at him? Somewhere, sometime, he had seen him. Where? When? He struggled in an agony to remember. Could it have been in a dream? He often dreamt about men dressed similarly all in white. They never talked to him, but simply stared and waved their hands as if greeting him or saying good-bye. Then the cock of the dawn would crow and they would turn into light and disappear.

Suddenly the Baptist, still looking at him, cried out. He remembered: one day at exactly noon he had lain down on the bank of the river and taken out the Prophet Isaiah, written on a goat skin. All at once stones, water, people, reeds and river vanished; the air filled with fires, trumpets and wings, the words of the prophet opened like doors, and the Messiah stepped forth. He remembered that he was dressed all in white, thin, gnawed by the sun, barefooted and, like this man, he held a green leaf between his teeth!

The ascetic's eyes filled with joy and fear. He tumbled down from his rock and approached, stretching forth his gnarled neck.

"Who are you? Who?" he asked, his terrible voice trembling.

"Don't you know me?" said Jesus, advancing one more step. His own voice was trembling: he knew that his fate depended on the Baptist's reply.

It's him, him, the Baptist was thinking. His heart thumped furiously and he could not, dared not, decide. Once more he stretched forward his neck: "Who are you?" he asked again.

"Haven't you read the Scriptures?" Jesus answered in a voice sweet yet complaining, as though he were scolding him. "Haven't you read the prophets? What does Isaiah say? Forerunner, don't you remember?"

"Is it you, you?" whispered the ascetic. He put his hands on Jesus' shoulders and examined his eyes.

"I have come. . . ," Jesus said hesitatingly, then stopped, unable to breathe, unable to continue. It was as if he were putting forth his foot and searching to see whether or not he could take a further step without falling down. . .

The savage prophet leaned on top of him and examined him silently. He wondered if he had ever heard the wonderful, terrifying words which had escaped Jesus' lips.

"I have come. . . ," the son of Mary repeated, so softly that not even Judas, who was on the alert behind them with cocked ear, could hear. This time the prophet gave a start. He had understood.

"What?" he said, and the hairs of his head stood on end.

A crow passed over them and uttered a hoarse cry like that of a drowning man who was mocking something, or laughing. The Baptist became angry. He bent over to pick up a stone to throw at the bird. The crow had flown away but he continued to look for it, rejoicing in the passage of time—for in this way his mind gradually grew calm. . . . Rising, he said tranquilly:

"Welcome." He looked at him, but there was no love in his eyes.

Jesus' heart shook. Were his ears jangling or was it true that the prophet had bid him welcome? If true, how astonishing, how joyful, how frightening!

The Baptist glanced around him, swept his eyes over the river Jordan, the reeds, and the people who, kneeling in the mud, were openly confessing their sins. He hurriedly embraced his kingdom and bid it farewell. Then he turned to Jesus: "Now I can depart."

"Not yet, Forerunner. First you must baptize me." Jesus' voice had become sure, decisive.

"I? You are the one who must baptize me, Lord. . ."

"Don't talk so loud. They might hear us. My hour has not yet come. Let us go!"

Judas was straining his ears to hear, but he made out only a murmur, a joyous, dancing murmur as though from the union of two streams of running water.

The crowd which had assembled on the shore made way. Who was this pilgrim who, having thrown off his white robe, was clothed in sunlight? Who was this man, that without confessing his sins, entered the water with such nobility and assurance. The Baptist in the lead, they both thrust their way into the blue stream. The Baptist climbed onto a rock which jutted out above the face of the water. Jesus stood next to him on the sandy riverbed, the water embracing his body up to the chin.

The moment the Baptist lifted his hand to pour water over Jesus' face and to pronounce the blessing, the people cried out: the flow of the Jordan had abruptly ceased. Schools of multicoloured fish floated up from every direction, circled Jesus and began to dance, folding and unfolding their fins and shaking their tails, and a shaggy elf in the form of a simple old man entwined with seaweed rose up from the bottom of the river, leaned against the reeds, and with mouth agape and eyes popping from joy and fear, stared at all that was going on in front of him.

The people, viewing such wonders, were stricken dumb. Many fell face-down on the shore to hide their eyes. Others shivered in the violent heat. One, seeing the old man emerge from the deep all covered with mud, shouted: "The Spirit of the Jordan!" and fainted.

The Baptist filled a deep shell and with trembling hand began to pour water over Jesus' face. "The servant of God is baptized. . . ," he began. But he stopped: he did not know what name to give.

He turned to ask Jesus; but just as everyone, stretched on tiptoe, expected to hear the name, wings were heard to descend from the heavens and a white-feathered bird—was it a bird, or one of Jehovah's Seraphim?—darted forward and balanced itself on the head of the baptized. It remained motionless for several moments, then suddenly circled three times above him. Three wreaths of light glowed in the air and the bird uttered a cry as though proclaiming a hidden name, a name never heard before. The heavens seemed to be answering the Baptist's mute question.

The people's ears buzzed, their minds reeled. There were words together with the beating of wings. The voice of God? The voice of the bird? It was a strange miracle. . . . Jesus tensed his whole body, trying to hear. He had a presentiment that here was his true name, but he could not distinguish what it was. All he heard were many waves breaking within him, many wings and great, bitter words. He raised his eyes. The bird had already bounded towards the summit of the heavens and become light within the light.

The Baptist, whose years in the desert and in cruel solitude had enabled him to master the language of God, was the only one who understood. Today is baptized, he whispered to himself, trembling, the servant of God, the son of God, the Hope of mankind!

He signalled the waters of the Jordan to resume their flow. The sacrament was over.

XVII

THE sun came out of the desert like a lion and beat at all the doors of Israel. From every Jewish home the savage morning prayer rose up to the stiff-necked God of the Hebrews: "We hymn you and glorify you, our God and God of our fathers. Almighty and terrible, you are our help and support. Glory to you, Immortal, glory to you, defender of Abraham. Who can vie with you in strength, O King, with you, who slay, resurrect and bring deliverance? Glory to you, Deliverer of Israel! Destroy and crush and scatter our enemies, but quickly, while we are still alive!"

Sunrise found Jesus and John the Baptist sitting above the Jordan in the hollow of a precipitous rock. All night long the two of them had held the world in their hands, deliberating what to do with it. Sometimes one took it, sometimes the other. The one's face was severe and decisive: his arms went up and down as though he was actually holding an axe and striking. The other's face was tame and irresolute, his eyes full of compassion.

"Isn't love enough?" he asked.

"No," answered the Baptist angrily. "The tree is rotten. God called to me and gave me the axe, which I then placed at the roots of the tree. I did my duty. Now you do yours: take the axe and strike!"

"If I were fire, I would burn; if I were a wood-cutter, I would strike. But I am a heart, and I love."

"I am a heart also, that's why I cannot endure injustice, shamelessness or infamy. How can you love the unjust, the infamous and the shameless? Strike! One of man's greatest obligations is anger."

"Anger? said Jesus, his heart objecting. "Aren't we all brothers?"

"Brothers?" the Baptist replied sarcastically. "Do you think love is the way of God—love? Look here—"

He stretched forth his bony, hairy hand and pointed to the Dead Sea, which stank like a rotting carcass.

"Have you ever bent over to see the two whores, Sodom and Gomorrah, at her bottom? God became angry, hurled fire, stamped on the earth: dry land turned to sea and swallowed up Sodom and Gomorrah. That is God's way—follow it. What do the prophecies say? 'On the day of the Lord blood will flow from wood, the stones of the houses will come to life, will rise up and kill the house-owners!' The day of the Lord has set out and is coming. I was the first to discern it. I uttered a cry, took God's axe, placed it at the root of the world. I called, called, called for you to come. You came, and now I shall depart."

He grasped Jesus' hands as though he were placing a heavy axe in them. Jesus drew back, frightened. "Be patient a little longer, I beg of you," he said. "Don't hurry. I shall go speak to God in the desert. There his voice can be heard more clearly."

"So can the voice of Temptation. Take care—Satan is lying in wait for you, his army all in order. He knows very well that you mean life or death for him. He shall fall upon you with all his wildness and all his sweetness. Take care. The desert is full of sweet voices—and death."

"Sweet voices and death cannot deceive me, friend. Trust in me."

"I do. Alas, if I didn't! Go, talk with Satan, talk with God too, and decide. If you are the One I have been awaiting, God has already made the decision, and you cannot escape. If you are not, what do I care if you perish? Go ahead, and we'll see. But quickly; I don't want to leave the world all alone."

"The wild dove that beat its wings above me while I was being baptized: what did it say?"

"It was not a wild dove. The day will come when you shall hear the words it pronounced. But until then, they will hang over you like swords."

Jesus rose and held out his hand. "Beloved Forerunner," he said, his voice shaking, "farewell—perhaps for ever."

The Baptist pressed his lips to Jesus' lips and held them there. His mouth was a live coal, and Jesus' lips were scorched. "It is

248

to you I finally render my soul," he said, tightly squeezing Jesus' tender hand. "If you are the One I've been waiting for, hear my last instructions, for I think I shall never see you again on this earth, never again."

"I'm listening," Jesus whispered, shuddering. "What instructions?"

"Change your expression, strengthen your arms, make firm your heart. Your life is a heavy one. I see blood and thorns on your brow. Endure, my brother and superior; courage! Two roads open up in front of you, the road of man, which is level, and the road of God, which ascends. Take the more difficult road. Farewell! And don't feel afflicted at partings. Your duty is not to weep, it is to strike. Strike! and may you have a steady hand! That is your road. Both ways are the daughters of God, do not forget that. But Fire was born first and Love afterwards. Let us begin therefore with Fire. Forward, and good luck!"

The sun had already risen high. Caravans from the Arabian desert appeared bringing new pilgrims with multi-coloured turbans on their shaven heads. Some had crescent-shaped talismans made from boars' teeth which they wore suspended around their necks; others had tiny bronze goddesses—all hips; and others, necklaces made from the teeth of their enemies. They were wild beasts of the east who had come to be baptized. The Baptist saw them, uttered a piercing cry and rushed down from the rock. The camels knelt on the mud of the Jordan and the voice of the desert was heard to resound mercilessly: "Repent, repent. The day of the Lord has come!"

Meanwhile, Jesus found his companions. They were sitting on the river-bank, silent and afflicted, waiting for him. It was now three days and three nights that he had not appeared, three days and three nights that the Baptist had abandoned his baptizing to talk to him. He spoke on and on, and Jesus listened with bowed head. What was he saying, bearing down over him like a vulture; and why was the one so wild and the other so sad? Judas paced up and down in a rage, puffing. As soon as night fell, he secretly approached the rock to hear. The two of them were talking, cheek to cheek. Judas cocked his ear but could distinguish only a murmur, a rapid murmur, as from running water. One was giving, the other receiving, being filled, as though the son of Mary was a jug propped up under a tap. The redbeard slid down from the rock in a frenzy, and once more began to pace in the darkness. "Shame on me, shame on me," he grumbled, "to let them deliberate about Israel while I am absent! The Baptist should have entrusted his secret to me, should have given me the axe. I am the only one who feels Israel's pains. I am able to use the axe; he, the clairvoyant, is not. He shamelessly proclaims that we are all brothers, injured and injurers, Israelites and Romans and Greeks, devil take them!"

He lay down at the foot of the rock, far from the other companions, whom he did not wish to see. For a moment he fell asleep and seemed to hear the Baptist's voice and scattered, disparate words: "Fire," "Sodom and Gomorrah," "Strike!" He jumped up. Once awake, however, he heard nothing but the night-birds and the jackals and the murmur of the Jordan in the reeds. . . . He went down to the river and plunged his flaming head into the water to extinguish the fire. "He'll come down from the rock, won't he?" he murmured. "He will, and then I shall learn his secret, whether he likes it or not!"

When he saw Jesus approach, therefore, he jumped up, as did the other companions. They ran out joyfully to receive him, touched his shoulders, his back, caressed him; and John's eyes filled with tears—a deep wrinkle was now engraved in the middle of the master's forehead.

Peter could not contain himself. "Rabbi," he said, "why did the Baptist talk to you for days and nights? What did he tell you to make you so sorrowful? Your face has changed."

"His days are few," answered Jesus. "Stay with him, all of you, and be baptized. I am leaving."

"Where are you going, rabbi?" cried out Zebedee's younger son, taking hold of Jesus' tunic. "We'll all come with you."

"I am going by myself to the desert, where no company is needed. I'm going there to speak with God."

"With God?" said Peter, covering his face. "But then you'll never return!"

"I shall return," said Jesus with a sigh. "I must return. The world is suspended by a single thread. God will give me instructions, and I shall return."

"When? How many days will you be absent again? Look how you're leaving us!" they all shouted, holding on to him so that he would not go. But Judas stood apart, silent, and looked at them with scorn. "Sheep. . . , sheep. . . ," he grumbled. "I thank the God of Israel that I am a wolf."

"I shall return when God wishes, brothers. Farewell. Stay here and wait for me. Until then, good-bye!"

The brothers stood petrified and watched him move slowly towards the desert. He did not walk now as before, when he hardly touched the ground, but heavily, thoughtfully. He picked a reed to lean upon, mounted the arched bridge, stopped at its middle, and looked down. On all sides he saw pilgrims immersed in the muddy current of the river, their sun-blackened faces shining happily. Opposite them, on the shore, others still beat their breasts and confessed their sins to the air, watching with inflamed eyes for the Baptist to signal their turn to plunge into the holy water. Sunk hip-deep in the Jordan, the wild ascetic baptized the people in whole flocks, then, angrily, without love, pushed them towards the shore, whence new flocks followed behind them. His pointed jet-black beard shone in the sun, as did his fuzzy hair, which had never been cut; and continued shouts came from his wide, massive, eternally-opened mouth.

Jesus swept his eyes over the river, the people, and in the distance the Dead Sea, the mountains of Arabia, the desert. He leaned over and saw his shadow undulating with the current towards the Dead Sea.

How nice it would be, he thought, to sit at the edge of the river and watch the water flow towards the sea with the trees, birds, clouds, and at night the stars all reflected in it and flowing too; how nice if I could roll along also and not be devoured by this care for the world. . . .

But he shook himself, banished the temptation, pulled himself away from the bridge and, descending with quick steps, disappeared behind the bleak rocks. The redbeard stood on the shore keeping constant watch over him. He saw him disappear and, fearing that he might escape, rolled up his sleeves and followed behind, overtaking him just as he was about to enter the endless sea of sand.

"Son of David, stop!" he called to him. "Why are you leaving me like this?"

Jesus turned. "Judas, my brother," he said supplicatingly, "do not come further. I must be alone."

"I want to learn your secret!" said Judas, advancing.

"Don't be in a hurry. You will learn it when the time comes. But I'll tell you this much, Judas, my brother: be happy, everything is going well!"

"'Everything is going well' isn't enough for me. A wolf's hunger isn't appeased with words. Maybe you don't know that, but I do."

"If you love me, be patient. Look at the trees. Are they in a hurry to ripen their fruit?"

"I'm not a tree, I'm a man," the redbeard objected, coming closer. "I'm a man, and that means a thing which is in a hurry. I go by my own laws."

"The law of God is the same, whether for trees or men, Judas."

The redbeard ground his teeth. "And what is that law called?" he asked sarcastically.

"Time."

Judas stood still and clenched his fist. He did not accept this law. Its pace was excessively slow, whereas he had not a moment to lose. The depths of his being held to another law, his own, opposite to that of Time.

"God lives for many years," he shouted. "He is immortal, he can be patient therefore and wait. But I'm human, a thing, I tell you, that's in a hurry. I don't want to die before I see what I have now only in my mind—not only see it, but touch it with my hands!"

"You shall see it," answered Jesus, waving his hand to calm him. "You shall see and touch it, Judas, my brother—have faith. Good-bye! God is waiting for me in the desert."

"I'll come along."

"The desert is not big enough for two. Go."

The redbeard growled and bared his teeth like a sheep-dog that hears his master's voice. Head bowed, he turned around and marched heavily over the bridge, talking to himself. He remembered when he roamed the mountains with Barabbas—God bless him!—and the other rebels. What an atmosphere of ferocity and freedom. What a splendid leader of cut-throats was the God of Israel! That was the kind of leader he needed. Why did he follow this clairvoyant who was scared of blood and shouted "Love! Love!" like a panting teen-aged girl? But let's be patient, Judas reflected, and see what he brings back from the desert!

Jesus had now entered the desert. The more he advanced, the more he felt he had gone into a lion's cave. He shuddered, not from fear, but from a dark inexplicable joy. He was happy. Why? He could not explain it. Suddenly he remembered, remembered a dream he had one night when he was still a child hardly able to talk. It seemed thousands of years ago: the earliest dream he was able to recall. . . . He had worked his way into a deep cave and found a lioness who had given birth and was suckling her cubs. When he saw her, he grew hungry and thirsty, lay down and began to suckle with the lion-cubs. Afterwards it seemed that they all went out to a meadow and began to play in the sun, but while they were frisking, Mary, his mother, appeared in his dream, saw him with the lions, and screamed. He awoke and turned angrily to his mother, who was sleeping at his side. Why did you wake me up? he shouted at her. I was with my brothers and my mother!

Now I understand why I am happy, he reflected. I am entering my mother's cave, the cave of the lioness, of solitude. . . .

He heard the disquieting hiss of snakes, and of the burning wind which blew between the rocks, and of the invisible spirits of the desert.

Jesus bent over and spoke to his soul: "My soul, here you will show whether or not you are immortal."

Hearing steps behind him, he cocked his ear. There was the crunching of sand. Someone was walking towards him, calmly, surely. I forgot her, he thought, shuddering, but she did not forget me. She is coming with me, my Mother is coming with me. . . . He knew very well that it was the Curse, but he had been calling her Mother to himself now for such a long time. . .

He marched on, forcing his thoughts elsewhere. He recalled the wild dove. A savage bird seemed to be imprisoned within him— or was it his soul rushing to escape? Perhaps it had escaped, perhaps the wild dove which chirped and flew circles over him the whole time he was being baptized was his soul, not a bird or a Seraph, but his own soul.

This was the answer. He started out again, calm. He heard the footsteps behind him crunching the sand—but his heart was steady now, he could at last endure everything with dignity. Man's soul, he reflected, is all-powerful, it can take on whatever appearance it likes. At that instant it became a bird and flew over me. . . . But as he marched tranquilly along, suddenly he cried out and stopped. The thought had come to him that perhaps the dove was an optical illusion, a buzzing in his ear, a whirling of the air—because he remembered how his body had gleamed, light and omnipotent, like a soul, how whatever he wanted to hear he had heard, whatever he wanted to see he had seen. . . . He had built castles in the air. "O God, O God," he murmured, "now that we shall be alone, tell me the truth, do not deceive me. I am weary of hearing voices in the air."

He advanced and the sun advanced with him. It had finally reached the top of the sky, directly above his head. His feet were burning in the fiery sand. He spied around him to find some shade, and as he did so, he heard wings flapping above him and saw a flock of crows rush into a pit where there was a stinking black object in the process of decay.

Holding his nose, he approached. The crows had fallen upon the carcass, planted their claws in it and begun to eat. When they saw a man approach they flew away angrily, each with a mouthful of flesh in its talons. They circled in the air, calling to the intruder to go away. Jesus leaned over, saw the opened belly, the black, half-stripped hide, the short knotted horns, the strings of amulets around the putrid neck. . .

"The goat!" he murmured with a shudder, "the sacred goat that bore the people's sins. He was chased from village to village, mountain to mountain, and finally to the desert, where he perished. . . ."

He bent over, dug in the sand as deeply as he could with his hands, and covered the carcass.

"My brother," he said, "you were innocent and pure, like every animal. But men, the cowards, made you bear their sins, and killed you. Decompose in peace; feel no malice against them. Men,

254

poor weak creatures, have not the courage to pay for their sins themselves: they place them upon one who is sinless. My brother, requite their sins. Farewell!"

He resumed his march but stopped after a few moments, troubled. Waving his hand, he called: "Until we meet again!"

The crows began to pursue him maniacally. He had deprived them of the tasty carcass and now they were following him, waiting for him to perish in his turn and for his belly to split open so that they could eat. What right did he have to do them this injustice. Had not God designed crows to eat carcasses! He must pay!

Night was coming at last. Tired, he squatted on a rock which was as large and round as a millstone. "I shall go no further," he murmured. "Here on this rock I shall set up my bulwark and do battle." The darkness flowed abruptly down from the sky, rose up from the soil, covered the earth. And with the darkness came the frost. His teeth chattering, he wrapped himself in his white robe, curled up into a ball and closed his eyes. But as he closed them, he grew frightened. He recalled the crows, heard the famished jackals begin to howl on every side, felt the desert prowling around him like a wild beast. . . . Afraid, he reopened his eyes. The sky had filled with stars, and he felt comforted. The Seraphim have come out to keep me company, he said to himself. They are the six-winged lights which sing psalms around God's throne, but they are far away, so very far away that we cannot hear them. . . . His mind illuminated by star-light, he forgot his hunger and cold. He too was a living thing, an ephemeral beacon in the darkness; he too sang hymns to God. His soul was a small pharos, the humble poorly-dressed sister of the angels. . . . Thinking of his high extraction, he took heart, saw his soul standing together with the angels around God's throne; and then, peacefully and without fear, he closed his eyes and slept.

When he awoke he lifted his face towards the east and saw the sun, a terrible blast-furnace, rising above the sand. That is God's face, he reflected, putting his palm over his eyes so that he would not be dazzled. "Lord," he whispered, "I am a grain of sand, can you see me in this desert? I am a grain of sand which talks and breathes and loves you—loves you and calls you Father.

I possess no weapon but love. With that I have come to do battle. Help me!"

He rose. With his reed he inscribed a circle around the rock where he had slept.

"I shall not leave this threshing-floor," he said loudly, so that the invisible forces which were lying in wait for him could hear, "I shall not leave this threshing floor unless I hear God's voice. But I must hear it clearly, I won't be satisfied with the usual unsteady hum or twittering or thunder; I want him to speak to me clearly, with human words, and to tell me what he desires from me and what I can, what I must, do. Only then will I get up and leave this threshing floor to return to men, if that is his command, or to die, if that is his will. I'll do whatever he wishes, but I must know what it is. . . . In God's name!"

He knelt on the rock with his face towards the sun, towards the great desert. He closed his eyes, remassed those of his thoughts which had lingered at Nazareth, Magdala, Capernaum, Jacob's well and the river Jordan, and began to put them in battle-array. He was preparing for war.

With his neck tensed and his eyelids closed, he sank within himself. He heard the roar of water, the rustling of reeds, the lamentations of men. . . . From the river Jordan came wave after wave of cries, terror and far-away visionary hopes. . . . First to stand up in his mind were the three long nights he had spent on the rock with the wild ascetic. In full armour, they rushed to the desert to enter the war at his side.

The first night jumped down on top of him like a monstrous locust with cruel wheat-yellow eyes and wings, breath like the Dead Sea, and strange green letters on its abdomen. It clung to him; its wings began furiously to rend the air. Jesus cried out and turned. The Baptist was standing next to him with his bony arm pointing in the heavy darkness towards Jerusalem.

"Look. What do you see?"

"Nothing."

"Nothing? In front of you is holy Jerusalem, the whore. Don't you see her? She sits and giggles on the Roman's fat knees. The Lord cries: 'I do not want her. Is this my wife? I do not want her!' I too, like a dog at the Lord's feet, bark: 'I do not want her!' I walk around her towers and walls and bark at her: 'Whore! Whore!' She has four great fortress-gates. At the first sits Hunger, at the next Fear, at the third Injustice, and at the fourth, the northern one, Infamy. I enter, go up and down her streets; I approach her inhabitants and examine them. Regard their faces: three are heavy, fat, over-satiated; three thousand emaciated from hunger. When does a world disappear? When three masters overeat and a people of three thousand starves to death. Look at their faces once more. Fear sits on all of them, their nostrils quiver, they scent the day of the Lord. Regard the women. Even the most honest glances secretly at her slave, licks her chops and nods to him: *Come*! . . . I have unroofed their palaces. Look. The king holds his brother's wife on his knee and caresses her nakedness. What do the Holy Scriptures say? 'He who looks at the nakedness of his brother's wife—death!' It is not he, the incestuous king, who will be killed, however, but I, the ascetic. Why—because the day of the Lord has come!"

The whole of that first night Jesus sat at the Baptist's feet and watched Hunger, Fear, Injustice and Infamy go in and out of Jerusalem's four opened gates. Over the holy prostitute the clouds were gathering, full of anger and hail.

The second night the Baptist once more stretched forth his reed-like hand and with a thrust, pushed through time and space:

"Listen. What do you hear?"

"Nothing."

"Nothing! Don't you hear Iniquity, the bitch who has climbed shamelessly up to heaven and is barking at the Lord's door? Haven't you been through Jerusalem, haven't you seen the yelping priests, high priests, Scribes and Pharisees who surround the Temple. But God endures the earth's impudence no longer. He has risen, he is tramping down the mountainsides and coming. In front of him is Anger, behind him are heaven's three bitches, Fire, Leprosy and Madness. Where is the Temple with the proud gold-inlaid columns which supported it and proclaimed: Eternal! Eternal! Eternal! Ashes the Temple, ashes the priests, high priests, Scribes and Pharisees, ashes their holy amulets, their silken cassocks and golden rings! Ashes! Ashes! Ashes! . . . Where is Jerusalem? I hold a lighted lantern, I search in the mountains, in the

Lord's darkness; I shout, 'Jerusalem! Jerusalem!'... Deserted, completely forsaken: not even a crow answers—the crows have eaten, and left. I wade knee-deep in the skulls and bones; tears come to my eyes, but I push the bones away and banish them. I laugh, bend down and choose the longest one, make a flute and hymn the glory of the Lord."

The whole of the second night the Baptist laughed, stood in God's darkness and admired Fire, Leprosy and Madness. Jesus grasped the prophet's knees:

"Cannot salvation come to the world by means of love?" he asked. "By means of love, joy, mercy?"

The Baptist, without even turning to look at him, replied:

"Haven't you ever read the Scriptures? The Saviour crushes our loins, breaks our teeth, hurls fire and scorches the fields—all in order to sow. And he uproots the thorns, stink-weeds and nettles. How can you wipe out falsehood, infamy and injustice from the world if you do not eradicate the liars, the unjust, the wicked? The earth must be cleansed—don't pity it—it must be cleansed, made ready for the planting of new seed."

The second night passed. Jesus did not speak. He was awaiting the third night: perhaps the prophet's voice would sweeten.

The third night the Baptist twisted and turned upon the rock, uneasy. Without laughing, without talking, he examined Jesus with anguish, searched his arms, hands, shoulders and knees, then shook his head and remained quiet, sniffing the air. Illuminated by the starlight, his eyes stood out, glistening sometimes green, sometimes yellow; and sweat mingled with blood ran from his sun-baked forehead. Finally at daybreak, when the white dawn fell upon them, he took Jesus' hand, looked into his eyes, and frowned. "When I first saw you emerge from the reeds by the Jordan and come directly towards me," he said, "my heart bounded like a young calf. Can you think how Samuel's heart leapt up when he first saw the red-haired beardless shepherd, David? That is how my heart leapt. But the heart is flesh and loves the flesh, and I have no faith in it. Last night I examined you, smelt you as though seeing you for the first time—but I could not find peace. I looked at your hands. They were not the hands of a wood-chopper, of a saviour. Too soft, too merciful. How could they swing the axe? I looked at your eyes. They were not a saviour's eyes—too full of sympathy. I got up and sighed. Lord, I murmured, your ways are dark and oblique, you are capable of sending a white dove to burn up the world and turn it into ashes. We watch the heavens, expecting a thunderbolt, an eagle, or a crow—and you give us a white dove. What use is there of questioning, of resisting? Do what you like!" He spread out his arms and hugged Jesus, kissed him on his right shoulder, then on his left. "If you are the One I've been waiting for," he said, "you have not come in the form I imagined you would. Was it all for nothing then that I carried the axe and placed it at the root of the tree? Or can love also wield an axe?" He reflected for a moment. "I cannot judge," he murmured finally. "I shall die without seeing the result. It does not matter, that's my lot: a hard one—and I like it!" He squeezed Jesus' hand. "Go, and good luck. Go talk with God in the desert. But come back quickly, so that the world will not remain all alone."

Jesus opened his eyes. The river Jordan, the Baptist and the baptized, the camels and the lamentations of the people—all flared up in the air and were snuffed out. The desert now stretched before him. The sun had risen high and was burning: the stones steamed like loaves of bread. He felt his insides being mowed down by hunger. "I'm hungry," he murmured, looking at the stones, "I'm hungry!" He remembered the bread which the old Samaritan woman had presented them. How delicious it had been, sweet like honey! He remembered the honey, split olives and dates he was treated to whenever he passed through a village; and the holy supper they had when, kneeling on the shore of Lake Gennesaret, they removed the grill, with its row of sweet-smelling fish, from the andirons. And afterwards, the figs, grapes and pomegranates came to his mind, agitating him still further.

His throat was dry and parched from thirst. How many rivers flowed in the world! All these waters which bounded from rock to rock, rolled from one end of the land of Israel to the other, ran into the Dead Sea and disappeared—and he had not even a drop to drink! He thought of these waters and his thirst increased. He felt dizzy, his eyes fluttered. Two cunning devils in the shape of young rabbits emerged from the burning sand, stood up on their hind legs and danced. They turned, saw the eremite, screamed happily and began to hop towards him. They climbed onto his knees and jumped to his shoulders. One was cool, like water, the other warm and fragrant, like bread; but as he longingly put out his hands to grasp them, with a single bound they vanished into the air.

He closed his eyes and recollected the thoughts which hunger and thirst had dispersed. God came to his mind: he was neither hungry nor thirsty any more. He reflected on the salvation of the world. Ah, if the day of the Lord could only come with love! Was not God omnipotent? Why couldn't he perform a miracle and by touching men's hearts make them blossom. Look how each year at the Passover bare stems, meadows and thorns opened up at his touch. If only one day men could awake to find their deepest selves in bloom!

He smiled. In his thoughts the world had flowered. The incestuous king was baptized, his soul cleansed. He had sent away his sister-in-law Herodias and she had returned to her husband. The high priests and noblemen had opened their larders and coffers, distributed their goods to the poor; and the poor in their turn breathed freely once more and banished hate, jealousy and fear from their hearts. . . . Jesus looked at his hands. The axe which the Forerunner had surrendered to him had blossomed: a flowering almond-branch was now in his palm.

The day concluded with this feeling of relief. He lay down on the rock and fell asleep. All night long in his sleep he heard water running, small rabbits dancing, a strange rustling, and two damp nostrils examining him. . . . It seemed to him that towards midnight a hungry jackall came up and smelt him. Was this a carcass, or wasn't it? The beast stood for a moment unable to make up its mind. And Jesus, in his sleep, pitied it. He wanted to open his breast and give it food, but restrained himself. He was keeping his flesh for men.

He woke up before dawn. A network of large stars covered the sky; the air was fluffy and blue. At this hour, he reflected, the cocks awake, the villages are roused, men open their eyes and look through the skylight at the radiance which had come once more. The infants awake in their turn, the bawling begins and the mothers approach, holding forth their full breasts. . . . For an instant the world undulated over the desert with its men and houses and cocks and infants and mothers—all made from the morning frost and breeze. But the sun would now rise to swallow them up! . . . The eremite's heart skipped a beat. If only I could make this frost everlasting! he thought. But God's mind is an abyss, his love a terrifying precipice. He plants a world, destroys it just as it is about to give fruit, and then plants another. He recalled the Baptist's words: "Who knows, perhaps love carries an axe. . . ," and shuddered. He looked at the desert. Ferociously red, it swayed under the sun, which had risen angrily today, zoned by a storm. The wind blew, the smell of pitch and sulphur came to his nostrils. He thought of Sodom and Gomorrah—palaces, theatres, taverns, prostitutes—plunged in the tar. Abraham had shouted: Have mercy, Lord, do not burn them. Are you not good? Take pity therefore on your creatures. And God had answered him: I am just, I shall burn them all!

Was this then God's way? If so, it was a great impudence for the heart—that clod of soft mud—to stand up and shout: Stop! . . . What is our duty? he asked himself. It is to look down, to find God's tracks in the soil and follow them. I look down, I clearly see God's imprint on Sodom and Gomorrah. The entire Dead Sea is God's imprint. He trod, and palaces, theatres, taverns, brothels —the whole of Sodom and Gomorrah—was engulfed! He will tread once more, and once more the earth—kings, high priests, Pharisees, Sadducees—all will sink to the bottom.

Without realizing it, he had begun to shout. His mind was wild with fury. Forgetting that his knees were unable to support him, he tried to rise, to set out on God's trail, but he collapsed supine onto the ground, out of breath. "I am unable, don't you see me?" he cried, lifting his eyes towards the burning heavens. "I am unable, why do you choose me? I cannot endure!" And as he cried out, he saw a black mass on the sand before him: the goat, disembowelled, its legs in the air. He remembered how he had leaned over and seen his own face in the leaden eyes. "I am the goat," he murmured. "God placed him along my path to show me who I am and where I am heading. . . ." Suddenly he began to weep. "I don't want. . . , I don't want. . . ," he murmured, "I don't want to be alone. Help!"

And then, while he was bowed over and weeping, a pleasant breeze blew, the stench of the tar and the carcass disappeared and a sweet perfume pervaded the world. The eremite heard water, bracelets and laughter jingling in the distance and approaching. His eyelids, armpits and throat felt refreshed. He lifted his eyes. On a stone in front of him a snake with the eyes and breasts of a woman was licking its lips and regarding him. The eremite stepped back, terrified. Was this a snake, a woman, or a cunning demon of the desert? Such a serpent had wrapped itself around the forbidden tree of Paradise and seduced the first man and woman to unite and give birth to sin. . . . He heard laughter and the sweet wheedling voice of a woman:

"I felt sorry for you, son of Mary. You cried: 'I don't want to be alone. Help!' I pitied you and came. What can I do for you?"

"I don't want you, I didn't call you. Who are you?"

"Your soul."

"My soul!" Jesus exclaimed, and he closed his eyes, horrified.

"Yes, your soul. You are afraid of being alone. Your great-grandfather Adam had the same fear. He too shouted for help. His flesh and soul united, and woman emerged from his rib to keep him company."

"I don't want you, don't want you! I remember the apple you fed to Adam, I remember the angel with the scimitar!"

"You remember, and that's why you're in pain and you cry out and cannot find your way. I shall show it to you. Give me your hand, don't look back, don't recall anything. See how my breasts take the lead. Follow them, my spouse. They know the way perfectly."

"You are going to lead me also to sweet sin and the Inferno. I'm not coming. Mine is another road."

The serpent giggled derisively and showed her sharp poisonous teeth. "Do you wish to follow God's tracks, the tracks of the eagle—you worm! You, son of the Carpenter, wish to bear the sins of an entire race! Aren't your own sins enough for you? What impudence to think that it's your duty to save the world!"

"She's right. . . , she's right. . . , the eremite thought, trembling. What impudence to wish to save the world!

"I have a secret to tell you, dear son of Mary. . . ," said the snake in a sweet voice, her eyes sparkling. She slid down from the rock like water and began, richly-decorated, to roll towards him. She arrived at his feet, climbed onto his knees, curled herself up and with a spring reached his thighs, loins, breast and finally leaned against his shoulder. The eremite, despite himself, inclined his head to hear her. The snake licked Jesus' ear with her tongue. Her voice was seductive and far-away: it seemed to be coming from Galilee, from the edge of Lake Gennesaret.

"It's Magdalene. . . , it's Magdalene. . . , it's Magdalene. . ."

"What?" said Jesus, shuddering. "What about Magdalene?"

". . . it's Magdalene you must save!" the snake hissed imperatively. "Not the Earth—forget about the Earth. It's her, Magdalene, you must save!"

Jesus tried to shake the serpent away from his head, but she thrust herself forward and vibrated her tongue in his ear. "Her body is beautiful, cool and accomplished. All nations have passed over her, but it has been written in God's hand since your childhood that she is for you. Take her! God created man and woman to match, like the key and the lock. Open her. Your children sit huddled together and numb inside her, waiting for you to blow away their numbness so that they may rise and come out to walk in the sun. . . . Do you hear what I'm telling you? Lift your eyes, give me some sign. Just nod your head, my darling, and this very hour I shall bring you, on a fresh bed—your wife."

"My wife?"

"Your wife. Look how God married the whore Jerusalem. The nations passed over her, but he married her to save her. Look how the prophet Hosea married the whore Gomer, daughter of Debelaim. In the same way, God commands you to sleep with Mary Magdalene, your wife, to have children and save her."

The serpent had now pressed its hard cool round breast against Jesus' own, and was sliding slowly, tortuously, wrapping itself around him. Jesus grew pale, closed his eyes, saw Magdalene's firm, high-rumped body wriggling along the shores of Lake Gennesaret, saw her gaze towards the river Jordan and sigh. She extended her hand—she was seeking him; and her bosom was filled with children: his own. He had only to twitch the corner of his eye, to give a sign, and all at once: what happiness! How his

263

life would change, sweeten, become more human! This was the way, this! He would return to Nazareth, to his mother's house, would become reconciled with his brothers. It was nothing but youthful folly—madness—to want to save the world and die for mankind. But thanks to Magdalene, God bless her, he would be cured, he would return to his workshop, take up once more his old beloved craft, once more make ploughs, cradles and troughs; he would have children and become a human being, the master of a household. The peasants would respect him and stand up when he passed. He would work the whole week long and on Saturday go to the synagogue in the clean garments woven for him of linen and silk by his wife Magdalene, with his expensive kerchief over his head, his golden wedding ring on his finger; and he would have his stall with the elders, would sit and listen peacefully and indifferently while the seething half-insane Scribes and Pharisees sweated and shivered to interpret the Holy Scriptures. . . . He would snigger and look at them with sympathy. Where would they ever end up, these theologians! He was interpreting Holy Scripture quietly and surely by taking a wife, having children, by constructing ploughs, cradles, and troughs. . . .

He opened his eyes and saw the desert. Where had the day gone! The sun was once more inclining towards the horizon. The serpent, her breast glued to his own, was waiting. She hissed tranquilly, seductively, and a tender, plaintive lullaby flowed into the evening air. The entire desert rocked and lullabied like a mother.

"I'm waiting. . . , I'm waiting. . . ," the snake hissed salaciously. "Night has overtaken us. I'm cold. Decide. Nod to me, and the doors of Paradise will be opened to you. . . . Decide, my darling. Magdalene is waiting. . . ."

The eremite felt paralysed with fear. As he was about to open his mouth to say Yes, he felt someone above looking down on him. Terrified, he lifted his head and saw two eyes in the air, two eyes only, black as night and two white eyebrows which were moving and signalling to him: No! No! No! Jesus' heart contracted. He looked up again beseechingly, as if he wished to scream: Leave me alone, give me permission, do not be angry! But the eyes had grown ferocious and the eyebrows vibrated threateningly.

"No! No! No!" Jesus then shouted, and two large tears rolled from his eyes.

All at once the serpent writhed, unglued herself from him and with a muffled roar, exploded. The air was glutted with the stench.

Jesus fell on his face. His mouth, nostrils and eyes filled with sand. His mind was blank. Forgetting his hunger and thirst, he wept—wept as though his wife and all his children had died, as though his whole life had been ruined.

"Lord, Lord," he murmured, biting the sand, "Father, have you no mercy? Your will be done: how many times have I said this to you until now, how many times shall I say it in the future? All my life I shall quiver, resist and say it: Your will be done!"

In this way, murmuring and swallowing the sand, he fell asleep; and as the eyes of his body closed, those of his soul opened and he saw the spectre of a serpent as thick as the body of a man and extending in length from one end of the night to the other. She was stretched out on the sand with her wide bright-red mouth opened at his side. Opposite this mouth hopped an ornate trembling partridge struggling in vain to open its wings and escape. It staggered forward uttering small weak cries, its feathers raised out of fear. The motionless serpent kept her eyes glued on it, her mouth opened. She was in no hurry for she was sure of her prey. The partridge advanced little by little directly towards the opened mouth, stumbling on its crooked legs. Jesus stood still and watched, trembling like the partridge. . . . At daybreak the bird had at last reached the gaping mouth. It quivered for a moment, glanced quickly around as though seeking aid; then suddenly stretched forth its neck and entered head-first, feet together. The mouth closed. Jesus was able to see the partridge, a ball of feathers and meat and ruby-coloured feet, descend little by little towards the dragon's belly.

He jumped up, terrified. The desert was a mass of swelling rose-coloured waves.

The sun was rising. "It is God," he murmured, trembling. "And the partridge is. . ."

His voice broke. He did not have the strength to complete his reflection. But inside himself he thought:

265

. . . man's soul. The partridge is man's soul!

He remained plunged in this reflection for hours. The sun came up, set the sand on fire; it pierced Jesus' scalp, went inside him and parched his mind, throat and breast. His entrails were suspended like bunches of left-over grapes after the autumn vintage. His tongue had stuck to his palate, his skin was peeling off, his bones emerging; and his finger-tips had turned completely blue.

Time, within him, had become as small as a heartbeat, as large as death. He was no longer hungry or thirsty; he no longer desired children and a wife. His whole soul had squeezed into his eyes. He saw—that was all: he saw. But at precisely noon his sight grew dim, the world vanished and a gigantic mouth gaped somewhere in front of him, its lower jaw the earth, its upper jaw the skies. Trembling, he dragged himself slowly forward towards the opened mouth, his neck stretched forward. . .

The days and nights went by like flashes of white and black lightning. One midnight a lion came and stood in front of him, proudly shaking its mane. Its voice was like a man's:

"Welcome to my lair, victorious ascetic. I salute the man who conquered the minor virtues, the small joys, and happiness! We don't like what's easy and sure, our sights are on difficult things. Magdalene isn't a big enough wife for us, we wish to marry the entire Earth. Bridegroom, the bride has sighed, the lamps of the heavens are lit, the guests have arrived: let us go."

"Who are you?"

"Yourself—the hungry lion inside your heart and loins that at night prowls around the sheepfolds, the kingdoms of this world, and weighs whether or not to jump in and eat. I rush from Babylon to Jerusalem, from Jerusalem to Alexandria, from Alexandria to Rome, shouting: I am hungry, everything is mine! At daybreak I re-enter your breast and shrink; the terrifying lion becomes a lamb. I play at being the humble ascetic who desires nothing, who seems able to live on a grain of wheat, a sip of water, and on a naive accommodating God whom he tries to flatter with the name of Father. . . . But secretly, in my heart, I am ashamed; I grow fierce and yearn for nightfall when I can throw off my sheepskin and begin once more to roar, roam the night and stamp my four feet down on Babylon, Jerusalem, Alexandria and Rome."

266

"I don't know who you are. I never desired the kingdom of this world. The kingdom of heaven is sufficient for me."

"It is not. You deceive yourself, friend. It is not sufficient for you. You don't dare gaze within yourself, deep within your loins and heart—to find me. . . . Why do you look askance and think ill of me? Do you believe I am Temptation, an emissary of the Sly One, come to mislead you? You brainless hermit, what strength can external temptation have? The fortress is taken only from within. I am the deepest voice of your deepest self, I am the lion within you. You have wrapped yourself in the skin of a lamb to encourage men to approach you, so that you can devour them. Remember, when you were a small child a Chaldean sorceress looked at your palm. 'I see many stars,' she said, 'many crosses. You shall become king.'. . . Why do you pretend to forget? You remember it day and night. Rise, son of David, and enter your kingdom!"

Jesus listened with bowed head. Little by little he recognized the voice, little by little he recalled having heard it sometimes in his dreams and once when he was a child and Judas had thrashed him, and one other time when he had left his house and roamed the fields for days and nights pinched by hunger, then returned shamefully home to be greeted with hoots by his brothers, lame Simon and pious Jacob, who were standing in the doorway. Then, truly, he had heard the lion roar inside him. . . . And hardly the other day, when he carried the cross to the Zealot's crucifixion and passed before the stormy crowd, everyone looking at him with disgust and moving out of his path, the lion had again jumped up within him, and with such force that he was thrown down.

And now, in this forsaken midnight—look! the bellowing lion inside him had come out and stood before him. It rubbed itself against him, vanished and re-appeared as though going in and out of him, and playfully tapped him with its tail. . . . Jesus felt his heart grow more and more ferocious. The lion is really right, he thought. I've had enough of all this. I'm fed up with being hungry, with wanting to play at humility, with offering the other cheek only to get it slapped. I'm tired of flattering this man-eating God with the name of Father in order to cajole him to be more gentle;

tired of hearing my brothers curse me, my mother weep, men laugh when I go by; sick of going barefooted, of not being able to buy the honey, wine and women I see when I pass by the market, and of finding courage only in my sleep to have God bring them to me, so that I can taste and embrace the empty air! I'm sick of it all! I shall rise, gird myself with the ancestral sword—am I not the son of David?—and enter my kingdom! The lion is right. Enough of ideas and clouds and kingdoms of heaven. Stones and soil and flesh—that is my kingdom!"

He rose. Somewhere he found the strength to jump up and gird himself, gird himself interminably with an invisible sword, bellowing like a lion. He was ready. "Forward!" he cried. He turned, but the lion had disappeared. He heard pulsating laughter above him and a voice: "Look!". . . A flash of lightning knifed through the night and stood fixed, motionless. Under it were cities with walls and towers, houses, roads, squares, people; and all around, plains, mountains, sea. Babylon was to the right, Jerusalem and Alexandria to the left, and across the sea was Rome. Once more he heard the voice: "Look!"

Jesus raised his eyes. A yellow-winged angel dropped head-first from the sky. Lamentations were heard: in the four kingdoms the people lifted their arms to heaven, but their hands fell off, gnawed away by leprosy. They parted their lips to cry *Help!* and their lips fell, devoured by leprosy. The streets filled with hands and noses and mouths.

And while Jesus cried with upraised arms: "Mercy, Lord, have pity on mankind!" a second angel, dapple-winged, with bells around his feet and neck, fell head-first from heaven. All at once laughter and guffawing broke out over the entire earth: struck down by madness, the lepers were running helter-skelter. Whatever remained of their bodies had burst into peals of laughter.

Trembling, Jesus blocked his ears so that he would not hear. And then a third angel, red-winged, fell like a meteor from the sky. Four fountains of fire rose up, four columns of smoke, and the stars were extinguished for want of air. A light breeze blew, scattering the fumes. Jesus looked. The four kingdoms had become four handfuls of ashes.

The voice sounded once more: "These, wretch, are the king-

268

doms of this world which you are setting out to possess; and those are my three beloved angels: Leprosy, Madness and Fire. The day of the Lord has come—my day, mine!" With this last clap of thunder the lightning disappeared.

The dawn found Jesus with his face plunged in the sand. During the night he must have rolled off his stone and wept and wept, for his eyes were swollen and smarting. He looked around him. Could this endless sand be his soul? The desert was shifting, coming to life. He heard shrill cries, mocking laughter, weeping. Small animals resembling rabbits, squirrels and weasels, all with ruby-red eyes, were hopping towards him. It is Madness, he thought, Madness, come to devour me. . . . He cried out and the animals disappeared; an archangel with the half-moon suspended from his neck and a joyous star between his eyebrows towered up before him and unfurled his green wings.

Jesus shaded his eyes against the dazzling light. "Archangel. . . ," he whispered.

The archangel closed his wings and smiled. "Don't you recognize me?" he said. "Don't you remember me?"

"No, no! Who are you? Go further away, archangel. You're blinding me."

"Do you remember when you were a small child still unable to walk, you clung to the door of your house and to your mother's clothes so that you would not fall, and shouted within yourself, shouted loudly: 'God, make me God! God, make me God! God, make me God!' "

"Don't remind me of that shameless blasphemy. I remember it!"

"I am that inner voice. I shouted then; I shout still, but you're afraid and pretend not to hear. Now, however, you are going to listen to me, like it or not. The hour has come. I chose you before you were born—you, out of the whole of mankind. I work and gleam within you, prevent you from falling into the minor virtues, the small pleasures, into happiness. Behold how just now when Woman came into the desert where I brought you, I banished her. The kingdoms came, and I banished them. *I* did, I, not you. I am reserving you for a destiny much more important, much more difficult.

"More important. . . , more difficult. . . ?"

"What did you long for when you were a child? To become God. That is what you shall become!"

"I? I?"

"Don't shrink back, don't moan. That is what you shall become, what you have already become. What words do you think the wild dove threw over you at the Jordan?"

"Tell me! Tell me!"

" 'You are my son, my only son!' That was the message brought you by the wild dove. But it was not a wild dove, it was the archangel Gabriel. I salute you, therefore: Son, only son of God!"

Two wings beat within Jesus' breast. He felt a large rebellious morning-star burning between his eyebrows. A cry rose up within him: I am not a man, not an angel, not your slave, Adonai—I am your son, I shall sit on your throne to judge the living and the dead. In my right hand I shall hold a sphere—the world—and play with it. Make room for me to sit down!

He heard peals of laughter in the air. Jesus gave a start: the angel had vanished. He uttered a piercing cry, "Lucifer!" and fell prone onto the sand.

"See you again," said a mocking voice. "We shall meet again one day—soon!"

"Never, never, Satan!" Jesus bellowed with his face buried in the sand.

"See you soon!" the voice repeated. "At this Passover, miserable wretch!"

Jesus began to wail. His tears fell in warm drops on the sand, washing, rinsing, purifying his soul. Towards evening a cool breeze blew, the sun became gentle and coloured the distant mountains pink. And then Jesus heard a merciful command, and an invisible hand touched his shoulder.

"Stand up, the day of the Lord is here. Run and carry the message to men: I am coming!"

XVIII

HOW quickly he traversed the desert, reached the Dead Sea, went around it and once more entered ploughed land and air thick with the respiration of men! He did not walk unaided—where could he have found the strength? Two invisible hands were holding him up by the armpits. The thin cloud which appeared over the desert thickened, blackened, invaded the sky. There was a clap of thunder, followed by the first drops of rain. The land grew dark, roads vanished, and suddenly the cataracts of heaven were released. Jesus cupped his palms. They filled with water, and he drank. He halted, wondering which way to go. Lightning tore through the air. For an instant the face of the earth glittered a pale blue-yellow, then suddenly plunged back again into darkness. Which was the way to Jerusalem, which to John the Baptist? And what about his companions, waiting for him in the reeds by the river? "God," he whispered, "enlighten me, throw a thunderbolt, show me my road!" As he spoke, a flash incised the heavens directly in front of him. God had given him a sign, and he proceeded with assurance in the direction shown him.

It was pouring. The male waters of heaven spouted down and united with the rivers and lake, the female waters of earth. Land, sky and rain became one; they were pursuing him, directing him towards mankind. He slopped through the mud, became tangled in roots and branches, traversed pits. In the gleam of a lightning flash he saw a pomegranate-tree heavy with fruit. He cut off a pomegranate: his hand was filled with rubies, his throat was refreshed. He took another, then another; he ate, and blessed the hand that had planted the tree. With new strength he set out again and marched and marched. Darkness. Was it day? Was it night? His feet became heavy with mud; he seemed to be lifting the entire earth at each step. Suddenly in the gleam of a lightning-flash he saw before him a small village high up on a hill. The lightning ignited the white houses, then blew them out. His heart jumped for joy. Men were sitting in those houses—brothers. He desired to touch a human hand, to breathe in human exhalation, to eat bread, drink wine, talk. How many years he had longed for solitude, roamed through the fields and mountains, spoken with the birds and wild game, not wanting to see men! But now, what a joy it would be to touch a human hand!

He quickened his pace and started up the cobbled ascent. He found strength, for now he knew where he was going, where the road which God had shown him would lead. As he mounted, the clouds thinned out and a bit of sky appeared. The sun became visible just as it was setting. He heard the village cocks crowing, the dogs barking, the women on the roofs of their houses shouting to each other. Blue smoke rose from the chimneys. He could smell the burning wood.

"Blessed is the seed of man. . . ," he murmured as he passed the first house of the village and heard human conversation within.

Stones, water and houses were shining—no, not shining: laughing. The parched earth had quenched its thirst. The deluge had frightened both animals and men; but then the clouds began to scatter, revealing deep-blue sky, and the sun which had disappeared returned once more and brought reassurance to the world. Jesus, drenched and happy, went through the narrow gurgling lanes. A young girl appeared, pulling a large-uddered goat to pasture.

"What is the name of your village?" Jesus smilingly asked her.

"Bethany."

"And at which door may I knock to find a place to sleep. I'm a stranger here."

"Wherever you find an open door, enter," the girl replied with a laugh.

Wherever you find an open door, enter. This is a kind-hearted, hospitable village, Jesus reflected, and he went forward to find the open door. The alleys had become small rivers but the largest stones rose above the water. Jesus proceeded by hopping from stone to stone. The house-doors were completely black from the rain, and closed. He turned at the first corner. A small arched door, painted indigo, stood wide open. A young woman, short and chubby, with a fat chin and thick lips, was standing in the doorway. Another young woman could be seen inside the palely-lit house. She was sitting at the loom, weaving and singing softly.

Jesus approached, stopped at the threshold and placed his hand over his heart in the sign of greeting.

"I am a foreigner," he said, "a Galilean. I am hungry and cold, and I have no place to sleep. I am an honest man. Allow me to spend the night in your home. I found the door open and entered. Excuse me."

The young woman turned, her hand still full of chicken-feed. She regarded him from head to foot tranquilly, then smiled.

"We're at your service," she said. "Welcome. Come in."

The weaver extricated herself from the loom and appeared in the yard. She was thin-boned and pale, with her black braids tied in a double bun on her head. Her eyes were large, fuzzy and sad. Around her frail neck she wore a necklace of turquoises as a charm against the evil eye. She looked at the visitor and blushed.

"We're alone," she said; "our brother Lazarus isn't here. He went to the Jordan to be baptized."

"And what difference does it make if we're alone?" said the other. "He won't eat us. Come inside, my good man. Don't listen to her, she's scared of her own shadow. We'll call the villagers to keep you company, and the elders will come also to ask you who you are, where you're going and what news you bring us. So, if you please, enter our poor house. . . . What happened to you? Are you cold?"

"I'm cold, hungry and sleepy," answered Jesus, striding across the threshold.

"All three will be remedied, have no fears," she said. "Now, I want you to know that I'm called Martha, and this is my sister Mary. And you?"

"Jesus of Nazareth."

"A good man?" Martha laughed, teasing him.

"Yes, good," he answered, his expression severe. "Good, to the best of my ability, Martha, my sister."

He entered the cottage. Mary lit the lamp and hooked it in place, illuminating the room and its immaculate whitewashed walls. There were two trunks of embossed cypress-wood, several stools, and along the wall a long wooden platform with mattresses and pillows. The loom stood in one corner; in the other were two small earthenware jars for the olives and oil. The jug of cool water was on its shelf to the right of the entrance. Next to it a long linen towel hung on a peg. The house smelt of cypress-wood and quince. At the back was a wide unlit fireplace with the cooking utensils suspended all around it.

"I'll light a fire so that you can dry off. Sit down." Martha found a stool and placed it for him in front of the hearth, then raced to the courtyard and brought in an armful of vine twigs, laurel branches and two logs of olive-wood. She squatted, arranged the kindling into a little hut, and ignited it.

Crouching, his head between his two palms, his elbows on his knees, Jesus watched. What a holy ceremony it is, he reflected, to arrange wood and light a fire on a cold day: the flame comes like a merciful sister to warm you. And to enter an alien house, hungry and tired, and to see two other sisters, strangers, come and comfort you. . . . His eyes filled with tears.

Martha got up, went to the larder and brought bread, honey and a brass pot of wine which she placed at the stranger's feet.

"This is the appetizer," she said. "Now I'll fix the casserole so that you can taste something hot and renew your strength. I imagine you've come a long way."

"From the ends of the earth," he answered. He bent eagerly towards the bread, olives and honey. What marvels they were, what joys! How generously God sent them to men! He ate and ate, blessing the Lord.

Mary, all the while, stood next to the lampstand and silently watched first the fire, then the unexpected guest, then her sister who, swept away by the joy of having a man in her house and serving him, had sprouted wings.

Jesus raised the pot of wine and looked at the two women. "Martha and Mary, my sisters," he said, "you must have heard of the flood in the time of Noah. All men were sinful, and everyone drowned except the few virtuous men who boarded the ark and were saved. Mary and Martha, I swear to you that if there is another flood, and if it is up to me to invite you to enter the new ark, I shall do so, my sisters, because this evening a poorly-dressed unknown barefooted guest appeared at your door, you lit a fire for him and he was warmed, you gave him bread and he was filled, you spoke a kind word to him and the kingdom of heaven came down and entered his heart. I drink to your health, my sisters. I'm delighted to meet you!"

Mary drew near and sat down at his feet. "I can't hear enough of your voice, stranger," she said, blushing terribly. "Speak more."

Martha put the casserole on the fire, set the table and drew cool water from the well in the yard. Then she sent a young neighbour to announce to the three village-elders that she would like them (if they would be so kind) to call at her house, because a visitor had come to her and her sister.

"Speak more," Mary repeated, seeing Jesus quiet.

"What do you wish me to say, Mary?" Jesus asked. He lightly touched her black braids. "Silence is good. It says everything."

"Silence does not satisfy a woman. Women, poor things, need a kind word."

"Don't listen to her. Not even a kind word satisfies a woman," interrupted Martha, who was feeding the lamp with oil now so that it would last, for the elders were coming and would engage the visitor in profound discussions. "Not even a kind word satisfies poor womankind. A woman wants to hear her husband shake the house with his tread, she wants to suckle a baby in order to soothe her breast. . . . She wants many things, Jesus of Galilee, many—but what do you men know about such matters!"

She tried to laugh, but could not. She was thirty years old and unmarried.

They remained silent, listening to the fire devour the olive-logs and lick the earthenware casserole which was bubbling away. The eyes of all three were lost in the flames. Finally Mary spoke:

"If you could only know how much goes through a woman's mind while she sits and weaves! If you knew you would pity her, Jesus of Nazareth."

"I do know," said Jesus, smiling. "I too was once a woman, in another life, and I used to weave."

"And what did you think about?"

"God. Nothing else, Mary, just God. And you?"

Mary did not answer, but her breast swelled. Martha heard their conversation and sighed, but restrained herself from speaking. Finally she could endure it no longer.

"Never fear," she said, her voice suddenly harsh, "Mary and I, and all the unmarried women of the world, think of God. We hold him on our knees like a husband."

Jesus bowed his head and did not speak. Martha removed the casserole from the fire. The supper was ready. She went to the larder to bring the earthenware dishes so that she could serve the meal.

"I want to tell you something which struck my mind once while I was weaving," said Mary, whispering so that her sister would not hear her from the larder. "I too was thinking of God on that day, and I spoke to him: 'God,' I said, 'if you ever deign to enter our poor house, you will be its master, and we shall be the guests. And now. . ." She choked, and was silent.

"And now?" said Jesus, leaning forward to hear.

Martha appeared with the plates.

"Nothing," Mary whispered, getting up.

"Come and eat," said Martha. "The elders will be here any minute. They mustn't find us still eating."

All three knelt. Jesus took the bread, lifted it high and pronounced the blessing so warmly and with such pathos that the two astonished sisters turned and stared at him. But when they saw him they were terrified, for his face shone and the air behind his head was afire and quivering. Mary put forth her hand.

"Lord," she cried, "you are the master and we the guests. Command us!"

Jesus lowered his head so that they would not see how troubled he was. This was the first cry, the first time a soul had recognized him.

They rose from the low table just as the doorway darkened and a gigantic old man appeared on the threshold. His beard flowed like a river; he was large-boned, his arms firm, his breast as hairy as a ram's. He held a crooked staff which was taller than he was and which he used not to lean upon, but to beat others and keep the village in order.

"Welcome to our poor house, Father Melchezidek," said both women, curtsying.

He entered, and a second old man appeared on the vacant threshold. This one was thin, with a long horse-like head and no

276

teeth. Flames darted out of his tiny eyes, and it was impossible to look at him for very long. The snake's poison is supposed to be behind its eyes; behind this man's eyes was fire, and behind the fire a twisted, perverse mind.

The women curtsied, welcomed him, and he too went inside. Behind him appeared the third old man, blind, stumpy, fat as a pig. He held his staff before him: its eyes guided him and prevented him from stumbling. He was a good soul. He loved to joke, and when he judged the villagers, he did not have the heart to punish a single one of them. "I am not God," he would say. "He who judges will be judged. Mend your arguments, my children, so that I don't get into trouble in the next world!" Sometimes he paid the restitution out of his own pocket, sometimes he went to prison himself in order to save the offender. Some called him a fool, some a saint; and old Melchezidek could not bear the sight of him—but what could he do: he was dealing with a man descended from the priestly race of Aaron, and the most potent householder of the village.

"Martha," said Melchezidek, whose staff reached the ceiling-beams, "where is the stranger who has entered our village?"

Jesus rose from the corner by the chimney where he had remained, silently watching the fire.

"You?" said the old man, examining him from head to toe.

"Yes, me," Jesus replied. "I come from Nazareth."

"Galilean?" gummed the second old man, the venomous one. "Nothing good can come out of Nazareth. The Scriptures declare it."

"Don't scold him, father Samuel," interrupted the blind elder. "True, the Galileans are prattlers, idiots and provincial boors—but they're honest. Our guest this evening is an honest man. I can tell from his voice."

He turned towards Jesus: "Welcome, my child."

"Are you a merchant?" asked old Melchezidek. "What do you sell?"

While the elders talked, the established men of the village—the reputable landowners—came in through the opened door. They had learnt of the arrival of a stranger, had donned their finery and

277

come to pass the time by welcoming him, seeing where he was from and what he had to say. They entered, and knelt on the ground behind the three elders.

"I don't sell anything," said Jesus. "I used to be a carpenter in my village, but I abandoned my work, left my mother's house and dedicated myself to God."

"You did well to escape from the world, my child," said the blind man, "but take care, for now, poor fellow, you've got yourself mixed up with a bad devil, this God. How will you escape from him?" He burst into laughter.

Hearing this, old Melchezidek was ready to explode with malicious rage. But he remained silent.

"Monk?" the second elder hissed derisively. "You're another one of those Levites, are you? A Zealot? False prophet?"

"No, no, father," Jesus replied, troubled, "no, no!"

"What then?"

The village ladies were now entering with all their jewellery in order to see the stranger and to be seen by him. Was he old, young, handsome? What did he sell? Or could he be a suitor for the hand of those beautiful but aging girls Martha and Mary? It was centuries since a man had embraced them: they would go insane, poor things. . . . Let's go and see!

They adorned themselves, came, and stood in a row behind the men.

"What, then?" the old viper asked once more.

Jesus suddenly felt a chill and held his hands in front of the fire. His clothes, still wet, steamed. For some time he was silent, thoughtful. This is a good moment to speak out, he was thinking, a good moment to reveal the word which the Lord confided to me and to awaken the God that sleeps within these men and women who destroy themselves in the pursuit of vain cares. They ask me what I sell. I shall answer: the kingdom of heaven, the salvation of the soul, life everlasting. Let them give the very clothes off their backs to buy this Great Pearl. He glanced rapidly around him, saw the faces in the lamplight and in the glow of the fire: rapacious, cunning, aged by petty man-devouring cares, shrivelled from fear. He pitied them and wanted to stand up and speak, but this night he was so very tired. It was many days since he had slept in the house of a human being or had rested his head on a pillow. Sleepy, he leaned against the smoky chimney-wall and closed his eyes.

"He's tired, my lords," Mary interrupted and she looked beseechingly at the old men. "Do not torment him. . . ."

"Right!" growled Melchezidek. Leaning on his staff, he began to get up and leave. "You're absolutely right, Mary. We've been talking to him as though we were his judges. We forget. . ."—he turned to the second elder—"you forget, father Samuel, that the angels frequently come down to earth dressed like paupers, with but one humble tunic and no staff, purse or shoes—just like this man. It is well, therefore, that we take heed and bear ourselves towards the stranger as we should towards an angel. That's simply good sense."

"That's also simply asinine," the blind elder snapped again, guffawing. "I say we should consider every man an angel, every man, yes, even old Samuel!"

Old venom-nose flew into a rage. He was ready to open his mouth, but on reflection changed his mind. The blind buzzard was rich, he might have need of him one day. Best play deaf—that was simply good sense.

The sweet glow of the fire fell on Jesus' hair, tired face and uncovered chest; threw sudden blue beams over his curly raven-black beard.

"He's delicious, even if poor," said the ladies to one another, stealthily. "Did you notice his eyes? They're the sweetest I've ever seen, sweeter even than my husband's when he holds me in his arms."

"I've never viewed any so wild," interrupted another. "All fear and terror. You feel like leaving everything and taking to the hills."

"And did you see Martha just eating him up with her eyes, dear? Poor thing, she'll go crazy tonight."

"But he eyed Mary on the sly," another lady said. "The two sisters will have it out tonight, mark my words. I'm their neighbour, I'll hear the yelling."

"Let's go," commanded old Melchezidek. "It was a waste of time to take the trouble of coming. The visitor is sleepy. Get up,

279

elders, let us go!" He began to push aside both men and women with his staff so that he could pass through.

But just as he reached the door hurried footsteps were heard in the yard and a pale man rushed inside and crumpled down in a heap in front of the fire, out of breath. The two terrified sisters fell upon him and hugged him.

"Brother," they cried, "what has happened to you? Who is chasing you?"

Melchezidek stopped and touched the newcomer with his staff. "Lazarus, son of Manacheim," he said, "if it's bad news you bring, let the women leave and the men remain, so that we may hear it."

"The king seized John the Baptist and cut off his head!" shouted Lazarus in a single breath.

He stood up, trembling. He was jaundiced, the colour of soil, with flabby gourd-like cheeks; and his faded green eyes glittered in front of the fire like those of a wild cat.

"Our evening hasn't gone to waste after all," the blind elder said contentedly. "In the time which elapsed from the morning, when we awoke, until now, when we are about to go to sleep, something at least has finally happened: the world has moved. Let us therefore sit ourselves down on the stools and listen. I like news, even if it's bad."

He leaned towards Lazarus. "Speak, if you please, my good fellow. Tell us when, how and why this misfortune took place. Put everything in its proper order and don't rush—it will while away our time. Catch your breath. . . . We're listening."

Jesus had risen with a start. He looked at Lazarus, his lips quivering. This was a new sign sent him by God. The Forerunner had left the world, was no longer needed. He had prepared the way and departed, his duty done. . . . My hour has come. . . , my hour has come, Jesus thought, shuddering; but he remained silent, his eyes riveted upon Lazarus's pale-green lips.

"He murdered him, did he?" growled old Melchezidek, angrily banging his staff on the ground. "What a state we've come to, when incestuous lechers kill saints, and debauchees ascetics! It's the end of the world!"

Overcome with fright, the women began to scream. The blind elder pitied them:

280

"You exaggerate, Melchizedek," he said. "The world stands firm on its feet. Ladies, don't be afraid."

"The throat of the world is cut," whined Lazarus, tears streaming from his eyes. "The voice of the desert has been snuffed out. Who now will call to God for us sinners? The world is orphaned!"

"One must not lift his hand against authority," hissed the second elder. "No matter what the powers-that-be do, close your eyes and don't look—for God looks. The Baptist should have minded his own business. . . . Serves him right!"

"Are we slaves?" thundered Melchizedek. "Can you tell me why God gave men hands? I'll tell you why: so that they could lift them against tyrants!"

"Be quiet, Fathers, so that we may hear how this evil took place," said the blind elder, irritated. "Speak, Lazarus!"

"I was on my way to get baptized with all the rest," Lazarus began. "I hoped it might improve my health. As you know, I haven't been very well recently. In fact, I've been getting worse and worse. I feel dizzy, my eyes puff up, and my kidneys. . ."

"All right, all right, we know all that," scoffed the blind elder. "Come to the point!"

"I reached the Jordan and was by the bridge where the crowd assembles to be baptized. I heard cries and weeping and said to myself, It's nothing, probably just the people tearfully confessing their sins. I went forward a bit, and what do I see but men and women fallen on their faces in the river-mud, lamenting. . . . I ask: 'What's up, brothers? What are you crying about?'

" 'The Prophet's been murdered!'

" 'By whom?'

" 'The criminal, the transgressor—Herod!'

" 'How, when?'

" 'He was drunk and his shameless step-daughter Salome was dancing in front of him stark naked. Her beauty drove the old lecher out of his senses. He sat her on his knee and asked what she wanted him to give her. Half his kingdom? She said no. What did she want, then? She said John the Baptist's head. You shall have it, he told her, and he had it brought her on a silver platter.' "

Exhausted by his speech, Lazarus collapsed once more to the ground. No one spoke. The lamp sputtered, flickered, was about to go out. Martha rose and refilled it with oil. It grew bright again.

"It's the end of the world," old Melchizedek repeated after a long pause. All this time he had been silently stroking his beard and weighing the world's iniquity and shamelessness. News frequently came from Jerusalem that the idolaters were soiling the holy Temple. Every morning the priests slaughtered a bull and two lambs as a sacrifice not to the God of Israel but to the godless, execrable Roman emperor. The wealthy opened their doors in the morning, saw on their doorsteps men who had died of hunger during the night, lifted up their silken robes and stepped over the corpses to go and parade along the arcades around the Temple. . . . Melchizedek weighed everything in his mind, and decided: it was truly the end of the world. He turned to Jesus.

"And you, what do you have to say about all this?"

Jesus replied in a voice which had suddenly become so exceedingly deep that they all turned and stared at him: "I come from the desert where I saw them. Yes, three angels have already departed from the heavens to fall upon this earth. I saw them with my own eyes, visible at the edge of the sky. They are coming. The first is Leprosy, the second Madness, and the third, the most merciful, Fire. And I heard a voice: 'Son of the Carpenter, construct an ark, place therein as many virtuous men as you find, but quickly!' The day of the Lord is here—my day. I am coming!"

The three elders shrieked. The rest of the men got up from the ground where they had been sitting with crossed legs. Their teeth were chattering. The women, stricken dumb, turned in one body towards the door. Mary and Martha went and stood next to Jesus, as though seeking his protection. Had he not sworn to take them into the ark? The time had come.

Old Melchizedek wiped away the sweat which was running from his white temples.

"The stranger speaks the truth," he shouted, "the truth! Listen, brothers, to this miracle: When I got up this morning, I unrolled the Holy Scriptures as I always do and I chanced upon the words of the Prophet Joel: 'Blow the trumpet of Zion; may the holy mountain resound. Let all who inhabit the earth tremble, for the day of the Lord is coming, a day of clouds and darkness. Before

Him—fire; behind Him—flames. They shall rush like horses, they shall clatter like chariots of war over the stones. And at the tops of the mountains the flames will crackle, as when they pour over the reeds and devour them. . . . Such is the day of the Lord!' I read this terrible message two or three times and began, barefooted, to chant it in my yard. Then I fell on my face and cried: 'Lord, if you plan to come soon, send me a sign. I must prepare myself, I must pity the poor, open my larders and pay for my sins. . . . Send a thunderbolt, a voice or a man to warn me, so that I'll be in time!' "

He turned to Jesus: "You are the sign. God sent you. Do I have time? When will the heavens open, my child?"

"Each second which passes, father," Jesus replied, "is a heaven ready to open. At every instant, Leprosy, Madness and Fire advance one more step. Their wings are already touching my hair."

Lazarus had opened wide his faded green eyes and was staring at Jesus. He took an unsteady step forward.

"Are you by any chance Jesus of Nazareth?" he asked. "They say that as the executioner seized the cleaver to cut off the Baptist's head, the Prophet stretched out his hand towards the desert and cried: 'Jesus of Nazareth, leave the desert, return to mankind. Come, do not forsake the world.' If you are Jesus of Nazareth, blessed is the ground on which you walk. My house is sanctified; I am baptized and cured. I fall and worship your feet!"

Having said this, he prostrated himself in order to kiss Jesus' feet, which were covered with bruises.

But sly old Samuel quickly pulled himself together. His mind had tottered for a moment, but he rapidly resteadied himself on his feet. We find in the prophets whatever our hearts desire, he reflected. On one page the Lord is in a frenzy against his people and lifts his fist to crush them; on the next, he is all milk and honey. We find the prophecy which matches our morning mood—so, let's not lose any sleep over it. . . . He shook his horse-like head and smirked in his beard, but said nothing. Let the people be afraid. It's good for them. Without fear . . . The poor are more numerous and more muscular. . . . We're lost!

He kept silent therefore, and gazed contemptuously at Lazarus, who was kissing the visitor's feet and speaking to him:

"If the Galileans I met at the Jordan are your disciples, rabbi, they gave me a message in case I should meet you: They're going to leave, and will wait for you in Jerusalem, at the David-gate, in the tavern of Simon the Cyrenian. They got frightened evidently at the slaying of the Prophet and have fled in order to hide. The persecution has begun."

The women, meanwhile, pulled at their husbands, trying to get them to depart. They understood everything. This foreigner, they told themselves, has the viper's eye. He looks at you and you go out of your mind. He speaks and the world comes tumbling down. . . . Let's get away!

The blind elder took pity on them. "Courage, my children," he cried. "I hear monstrous things, but don't be afraid. Everything will fall peacefully in place once more—you shall see. The world is steady, it has a good foundation and will stand as long as God stands. Don't listen to those who can see; listen to me, a blind man, who therefore can see better than all of you. The race of Israel is immortal. It signed an agreement with God; God affixed his seal and presented us with the entire earth. So, don't be afraid. It's almost midnight—let's go to bed!" He put forth his staff and made a line for the door.

The three elders left first. Next went the rest of the men; lastly, the women—emptying the house.

The two sisters laid the visitor's bedding on the wooden platform. Mary went to her trunk and took out the silk and linen sheets meant for her wedding night. Martha brought the satin feather-quilt which she had kept untouched so many years, awaiting the long-desired night when it would cover both her and her husband. She also brought fragrant herbs—basil and mint—and filled his pillow to overflowing.

"He'll sleep tonight like a bridegroom," said Martha with a sigh. Mary sighed also, but did not speak. Close your ears, God, she murmured to herself. The world is good despite my sighs. Yes, good; but I'm so afraid of loneliness, and I like this visitor so very much. . ."

The sisters went into the small inner room and lay down on their hard mats. The two men were on the wooden platform, one at each end, their feet touching. Lazarus was happy. What an air of sanctity and beatitude hung over the entire house! He breathed tranquilly, deeply, pushed the soles of his feet lightly against the holy soles and felt a mysterious force, a divine certitude, rising and branching out through his whole body. His kidneys no longer pained him, his heart stopped palpitating, his blood flowed peacefully, contentedly from head to toe and irrigated the afflicted, jaundiced body.

This is the real baptism, he was thinking. This night I, the house, my sisters—all were baptized. The river Jordan came to our house.

But how could the two sisters close their eyes! It had been years since a strange man slept in their house. Visitors always lodged with one of the village notables, never descended to their humble out-of-the-way cottage; and besides, their queer sickly brother did not like company. But tonight, what an unexpected joy! With quivering nostrils they smelt the air. How it had changed, how perfumed it was—not with basil and mint, but with the odour of a man!

"He says God sent him to build the ark, and he's promised to put us in. . . . Do you hear me, Mary, or are you asleep?"

"I'm not asleep," Mary replied. She was holding her breasts in her palms, for they pained her.

"Dear God," Martha continued, "let the end of the world come soon, so that we can enter the ark with him. I'll serve him, that won't bother me; and you, Mary, will be his companion. The ark will sail on and on for ever, and I shall serve him perpetually, and you will sit perpetually at his feet and be his companion. That is how I imagine Paradise to be. You too, Mary?"

"Yes," Mary replied, closing her eyes.

They talked and sighed. Jesus, meanwhile, was sitting up, though still in a deep sleep. He felt that he was not asleep at all, but rather standing body and soul in the Jordan, refreshed. The desert sand was being removed from his body and the virtues and vices of mankind from his soul—leaving it again virgin. Suddenly it seemed to him in his sleep that he had come out of the Jordan, taken a green untrodden path and entered a dense orchard full of blossoms and fruit. And it seemed he was no longer himself, Jesus the son of Mary of Nazareth, but rather Adam, the first man to be created. He had issued from God's hands at precisely that moment —his flesh was still fresh clay—and had lain down on the flowering grass to dry off in the sun so that his bones might congeal, colour come to his face and the seventy-two joints of his body tighten and enable him to stand up and walk. While he lay and ripened under the sun birds fluttered over his head, flew from tree to tree, promenaded on the springtime grass. They conversed among themselves, twittered, looked at this new creature who lay on the grass, examined him with curiosity. Each had his say and then continued on; and he, versed in their language, rejoiced to hear them.

The peacock, proudly fanning out its feathers, strolled up and down, threw oblique, seductive glances at this Adam stretched on the ground, and explained to him: "I used to be a hen, but I loved an angel and became a peacock. Is there any bird more beautiful than I am? None!" The turtle-dove flew from tree to tree, lifted its throat to heaven and cried: "Love! Love! Love!" And the thrush: "Among all the birds, only I sing and keep warm in the thickest of frosts." The swallow: "If not for me, the trees would never blossom." The cock: "If not for me, morning would never come." The lark: "At dawn when I fly up into the sky to sing, I say good-bye to my children because I never know if I shall return from my song still alive." The nightingale: "Don't look at me as I am now, in my poor clothes. I too had large gleaming wings, but I turned them into song." And a long-nosed blackbird came and clung to the shoulder of the first-created man, bent over to his ear and spoke to him softly, as though entrusting a great secret to him:

"The doors of heaven and hell are adjacent, and identical: both green, both beautiful. Take care, Adam! Take care! Take care!"

Exactly then, at dawn, with the blackbird's song in his mind— Jesus awoke.

XIX

GREAT things happen when God mixes with man. Without man, God would have no mind on this Earth to reflect upon his creatures intelligibly and to examine, fearfully yet impudently, his wise omnipotence. He would have on this Earth no heart to pity the concerns of others and to struggle to beget virtues and cares which God either did not want, or forgot, or was afraid to fashion. He breathed upon man, however, giving him the power and audacity to continue creation.

But man, without God, born as he is unarmed, would have been obliterated by hunger, fear and cold; and if he survived these, he would have crawled like a slug midway between the lions and lice; and if with incessant struggle he managed to stand on his hind legs, he would never have been able to escape the tight, warm, tender embrace of his mother the monkey. . . . Reflecting on this, Jesus felt more deeply than he had ever felt before, that God and man could become one.

He had set out in the early morning along the road to Jerusalem. God was to his left and to his right. He could touch him with his elbows. They were travelling together, both with the identical concern. The world had gone astray. Instead of ascending to heaven it was descending to hell. The two of them together, God and the Son of God, would have to toil to bring it once more onto the correct road. That was why Jesus hurried so. He ate up the road with long strides, anxious to meet his companions so that the struggle could begin. The sun, rising from the Dead Sea, the birds struck by the new light and singing, the trembling leaves of the trees, the white road which rolled to the walls of Jerusalem and drew him with it—all were shouting at him: Hurry! Hurry! We are perishing!

"I know, I know," Jesus answered. "I know, and I am coming!"

The same morning, just after dawn, the companions were sliding along, next to the walls of Jerusalem's still-deserted lanes; not all together, but scattered in twos—Peter with Andrew, Jacob with

John, and Judas by himself in the lead. Afraid, they ran, glancing out of the corners of their eyes in every direction to see if they were being followed. The fortress-gate of David rose up before them. They took the first alley on the left and stole into the tavern of Simon the Cyrenian.

The fat stoop-shouldered innkeeper was still half-asleep, having just risen from his bed of straw. His eyes and nose were red and swollen, for he had sipped wine with his drunken patrons until all hours of the night, had sung, brawled, and gone to bed terribly late. Now, sluggish and in a bad humour, he was cleaning the counter, sponging away the remains of the celebration. Though on his feet, he was still not awake: it seemed to him that he had begun in a dream to clean the counter, sponge in hand. . . . But as he laboured between slumber and wakefulness, he heard panting men enter his tavern. He turned. His eyes still smarted, his mouth was bitter, his beard full of the shells of roasted pumpkin-seeds.

"Damn it, who's there?" he growled hoarsely. "Leave me alone, will you! You've come in bright and early to eat and drink, eh? Well, I'm not in the mood. Scram!"

But his shouting gradually woke him up, and little by little he began to recognize his old friend Peter and the other Galileans. He came forward, examined them closely, and burst out laughing:

"Bah, what snouts do I see here! Stick your tongues back in your mouths, boys. Grab your belly-buttons before they burst from fear. Aren't you a proud lot, my brave Galileans!"

"For God's sake, Simon, don't stir up the whole world with your shouting," Peter answered him, putting his hand over Simon's mouth. "Close the door. The king killed John the Baptist, haven't you realized that yet? He cut off his head and put it on a platter. . . ."

"He did well by him. The Baptist chewed off his ears with this business about his sister-in-law. Who cares! He's the king, let him do what he likes. And afterwards—just between friends—he chewed off my ears too with his 'Repent! Repent!'. . . Bah, I just want to be left alone!"

"But they say he's going to kill all the baptized—put them to the sword. And we're baptized. . . . Don't you understand?"

"Who told you to get baptized, blockheads! Serves you right!"

"But you were baptized too, wine-jug!" Peter scolded him. ' 'You told us yourself. So, why scream at us?"

"That wasn't the same thing, you make-believe fishmonger. I'm not baptized. You call that baptism? I dove in the water, went for a swim. Everything the fake prophet chanted went in one ear and out the other, as it does with anyone who has any sense. But you, you morons. . . These quacks tell you they can milk a billy-goat into a sieve, and you're the very first to believe them. They command you to dive into the water and—pluff! in you go and catch your death of pneumonia. They say not to kill your fleas on the Sabbath—it's a very great sin. So you don't kill them, and they kill you. Don't pay the head-tax! You don't pay and snap! off goes your head. Serves you right! Sit down now and we'll have a drink. You need steadying down and I waking up!"

Two fat barrels loomed black in the recesses of the tavern. On one was painted a cock in red oils, on the other, in grey-black, a pig. He filled a pitcher of wine from the barrel with the cock, found six glasses and plunged them into a tub of filthy water in order to clean them. The smell of the wine hit him, and he awoke.

A blind man appeared at the tavern door. Putting his staff between his legs, he began to tune an ancient lute while coughing drily and spitting to clear his throat. This was Eliakim, who had been a camel-driver in his youth. One day at noon, however, while he was traversing the desert, he saw a naked woman washing herself in a pit of water under a date tree. Instead of turning his face away, the saucy fellow pinned his eyes on the beautiful Bedouin. It was just his luck that her husband was squatting behind a rock and had lit a fire for cooking. Seeing the camel-driver approach his wife and devour her nudity with his gaze, he rushed out with two live coals and extinguished them in the offender's eyes. . . . From that day on, the unfortunate Eliakim threw himself into psalm and song. He went the rounds of Jerusalem's taverns and homes with his lute, sometimes hymning the kindness of God, sometimes singing the nudity of women. He would receive a piece of dry bread, a handful of dates, a couple of olives, and then continue on his way.

He tuned his lute, cleared his throat, raised his voice, and with melismatic elaboration began to sing his favourite psalm:

Have mercy on me, O God, according to your great mercy;

And according to the multitude of your compassions, blot out my iniquity.

At that moment the innkeeper appeared with the pitcher of wine and the wine-glasses. He heard the psalmody and went wild:

"Enough! Enough!" he exploded. "You're another one who chews off my ears. Always the same tune: 'Have mercy on me. . . , have mercy on me. . .' Go to hell! Bah, was I the one who sinned? Was I the one who lifted my eyes to see someone else's wife at her bath? God gave us eyes so that we should keep them closed— don't you understand that yet? Well, serves you right. Go on, get out of here. Go bother someone else!"

The blind man once more took up his staff, squeezed the lute under his arm, and departed without breathing a word.

" 'Have mercy on me, O God. . . , have mercy on me, O God. . . ,' " trilled the irritated innkeeper. "David made eyes at other people's wives, this eyeless idiot did the same—and we are the ones who have to suffer for it. . . . O God, I just want to be left alone!"

He finally filled the glasses. They drank. He refilled his own and downed it.

"I'm off now to put a lamb's head into the oven for you. Grade A! A mother would steal it from the mouth of her babe!" He flew into the yard, where there was a small oven which he had built all by himself; brought twigs and vine-branches, lit the oven, thrust in the pan with the lamb's head, then returned to his company. He was dying for wine and talk.

But the companions were not in the mood. Crowded together by the fire, they would mumble a few words half-heartedly, then once more become mute. It was as though they were walking over burning coals. They stared at the door, anxious to leave. Judas got up and went and stood on the threshold. He detested the sight of these cowards who were all upside-down with fear. Look how they had run, how fast they had reached Jerusalem from the Jordan; look how they'd gone, their hearts in their mouths, and burrowed into this out-of-the-way tavern! And now, their ears sticking up like rabbits', they trembled and stood on tiptoe, ready to flee. . . . To hell with you, brave Galileans, he said to himself. Thank you, God of Israel, for not fashioning me in their image. I was born in the desert; I'm made of bedouin granite, not of soft Galilean soil. Every one of you fawned on him and was lavish with oaths and kisses; while now: 'Don't fail me, legs!' —all you want is to save your own hides. But I—the savage, the devil, the cut-throat—I shall not abandon him. I shall wait here until he returns from the Jordan desert, in order to see what he has to say; and then I shall make my decision. . . . I don't care about my own hide. Only one thing torments me, and that's the suffering of Israel.

He heard a low-voiced argument within the tavern. He turned.

"I say we should go back to Galilee where there's security," said Peter. "Don't forget our lake, boys!" He sighed. He saw his green boat flowing over the blue surge, and his heart swelled. He saw the pebbles, the oleanders, the nets loaded with fish. Tears came to his eyes. "Let's go, lads," he said, "come on, let's go!"

"We gave him our word we'd wait for him in this tavern," said Jacob. "It's only right we keep our promise."

"We can arrange matters," suggested Peter, "by instructing the Cyrenian to tell him, if he comes, that—"

"No, no!" Andrew objected. "How can we forsake him in this wild city? We'll wait for him here."

"I say we should return to Galilee," Peter repeated obstinately.

John grasped the others' hands and shoulders. "Brothers," he besought them, "think of the Baptist's final words. He raised his arms under the executioner's sword and shouted: 'Jesus of Nazareth, leave the desert. I am departing. Return to mankind. Come, do not forsake the world!' Those words have a deep significance, friends. God forgive me if I utter a blasphemy, but. . ."

His heart stopped. Andrew clasped his hand:

"Speak, John. What terrible presentiment is it that you don't dare reveal?"

"But if our master is the. . . ," he stammered.

"Is what?"

John's voice was soft, gasping, full of terror:

". . . the Messiah!"

They all shook. The Messiah! They had been with him for such a long time, and the idea had never entered their heads! At first they had taken him for a good man, a saint who was bringing love to the world; then for a prophet, not a wild one like the prophets of old, but gay and domesticated. He was lowering the kingdom of heaven to earth: in other words, he was bringing justice and a comfortable, contented way of life. He called the ancestral God of Israel 'Father', and no sooner did he do so than hard-necked, obstinate Jehovah sweetened and everyone became his child. . . . But now, what was this word which had escaped John's lips— Messiah! In other words: the sword of David, Israel's omnipotence, war! And they, the disciples, his first followers: they were great lords, tetrarchs and patriarchs around his throne! As God had angels and archangels surrounding him in heaven, so they, the disciples, were the ethnarchs and patriarchs upon the earth! Their eyes gleamed.

"I take back what I said, lads," exclaimed Peter, blushing terribly. "I shall never leave him!"

"Nor I!"

"Nor I!"

"Nor I!"

Judas spat angrily and banged his fist on the door. "You damned stalwarts!" he screamed at them. "As long as you believed him sickly and weak, you couldn't get away fast enough. But now that you smell grandeur: 'I shall never leave him!' One day every single one of you will forsake him—mark my words—while I alone shall not betray him. Simon of Cyrene, be my witness!"

The innkeeper had been listening to them and sniggering behind his drooping moustache. He caught Judas's eye.

"Bah, just look at them! And they want to save the world!"

But his nostrils caught a smell from the oven. "The head is burning!" he shouted, and with one bound he was in the yard.

The bewildered companions looked at each other.

"So, that's why the Baptist froze when he saw him," said Peter, tapping his forehead.

Once they got started, their minds swelled and swelled:

"And did you all see the dove over his head while he was being baptized?"

"It wasn't a dove, it was a flash of lightning."

"No, no—a dove. It was cooing."

"It wasn't cooing, it was talking. I heard it with my own ears say: 'Saint! Saint! Saint!' "

"It was the Holy Spirit!" said Peter, his eyes filling with wings of gold. "The Holy Spirit came down from heaven and we all turned to stone, don't you remember! I wanted to take a step and go closer, but my foot was numb—how could I move! I wanted to scream, but my lips would not part. The winds stood still; reeds, river, men, birds—every single thing turned to marble from fear. The Baptist's hand was the only moving thing: slowly, slowly, it baptized. . . ."

"I didn't see anything and I didn't hear anything," said Judas, incensed. "Your eyes and ears were drunk."

"You didn't see, redbeard, because you didn't want to see," Peter rebuked him.

"And your lordship, straw-beard, saw because you wanted to see. You had an appetite to see the Holy Spirit, so it was the Holy Spirit you saw. And what's more, now you make these numb-skulls see it too. You'll have to answer for the consequences."

Jacob, so far, had been chewing his fingernails and listening, without speaking. Now, however, he could contain himself no longer.

"Wait a minute, lads," he said; "don't explode like gunpowder. Come, let's discuss this thing sensibly. Do you really think the Baptist said those words before they cut off his head? It seems very unlikely to me. First of all, which one of us was there to hear him? And then there's this also: even if he said the words to himself, he would never have voiced them—because he'd have known the king would hear about it, would send spies to find out who this man was, this Jesus in the desert, would catch him and cut off his head as well. As my old man says, two and two make four. So, let's not allow our heads to get too swelled."

But Peter became angry. "Two and two make fourteen, that's my opinion, and damn it! let logic and our brains say what they will. Give us something to drink, Andrew. We'll drown our minds in order to clear our sight!"

A tall ungainly man with shrunken cheeks, barefooted, wearing a white sheet wrapped about him and a string of amulets around his neck, rushed into the tavern and put his palm to his breast in the sign of greeting.

"Farewell, brothers. I'm leaving, going to God. Do you have any commissions to place with me?"

Without waiting for an answer, he departed at a run and entered the next house.

At this moment the innkeeper appeared with the platter, and a delicious aroma invaded the room. His eye fell on the gangling lunatic.

"Have a good trip," he called to him. "Send our kindest regards! . . . There's another one for you!" he laughed. "Bah, it's true the end of the world has already come: the place is full of maniacs. This one says he saw God two nights ago when he went out to take a piss. From that moment on, how could he deign to live! He even refuses to eat. 'I've been invited to heaven,' he says; 'I'll eat there.' Well, he's dressed himself in his shroud and is going a quick round of all the doors. He accepts commissions, says good-bye, and leaves. . . . You see what happens when you get too close to God! Take care lads—I say it for your own good —don't go too near him. I worship his grace, but from a distance. Keep clear!"

He placed the platter with the lamb's head in the middle of the table. His lips, eyes and ears were laughing.

"Fresh head!" he called. "John the Baptist! Eat hearty!"

John felt nauseous and drew back. Andrew, who had put out his hand, held it in the air. The head, posed on the tray, looked at them one by one, dimly, with its wide-opened motionless eyes.

"Simon, your scoundrel," exclaimed Peter, "you'll disgust us and we won't be able to touch it! How can I pick out the eyes now? I'd love them as an appetizer, but it'll be just like eating the eyes of the Baptist."

The innkeeper burst into laughter.

"Don't worry, dear Peter," he said, "I'll eat them myself—but not before the dainty tongue, bless it! which shouted: Repent! Repent! the end of the world has come! Unfortunately, his own end came first, poor thing."

He took out a knife, sliced away the tongue and downed it in one gulp. Then he bolted a full glass of wine, and sat admiring his two barrels.

"All right, forget it, lads. I feel sorry for you. I'll change the subject so that the Baptist's head will go out of your minds and you'll be able to eat the lamb's. . . . Well then, can you imagine who painted that gem of a cock and a pig that you admire there on the barrels? Your gracious host, with his own hands, if you please. And can you guess why a cock and a pig? How could you, you idiotic Galileans! I must therefore disentangle the mystery for you and enlighten your infinitesimal brains!"

Peter looked at the head and licked his chops, but still did not dare put out his hand to remove the eyes and eat them. The Baptist was continually in his mind. The Prophet's eyes had gaped in the same way when they regarded mankind.

"So, listen," continued the innkeeper, "and enlighten, as I say, your infinitesimal brains. . . . When God finished the world (why did the bloke go to all that trouble anyway) and washed the mud off his hands, he called all the new-born creatures and proudly asked them: 'Say, birds and beasts, how do you like the world I built? Do you find anything wrong with it?' They all straightway began to bleat, bray, moo, meow, and twitter: 'Nothing! Nothing! Nothing!'

" 'Bless you,' said God. 'By my faith, I don't find a single defect either. My hands deserve congratulations.' But he glimpsed the cock and the pig who, heads bowed, were not breathing a word. 'Halloo! pig,' shouted God, 'and you, Your Excellency the cock, why don't you speak? Maybe the world I created doesn't please you? Perhaps something is missing?' But they still did not say a word. The devil, you can be sure, had hissed instructions into their ears: 'Tell him that something is indeed missing—a low-growing plant which makes grapes that you crush, put in barrels and turn into wine.'

" 'Look here, beasts, why don't you speak?' God shouted again, raising his gigantic hand. And then at last the two of them (the devil gave them courage) lifted their heads. 'Mastercraftsman, what can we say to you? Congratulations to your hands: your world is fine—knock wood! But it lacks one low-growing plant which makes grapes which you crush, put in barrels and turn into wine.'

" 'Ah, so that's it! Now I'll show you, you scoundrels,' said God in a fit of temper. 'It's wine you want from me, is it, and drunkenness and brawls and vomiting? Let the vine be born!' He rolled up his sleeves, took some mud, fashioned a vine-plant, planted it. 'Whoever overdrinks,' he said, 'hear my curse: may he have the mind of a cock and the snout of a pig!' "

The companions burst out laughing, forgot the Baptist and buried their faces in the roast head. Judas was first and foremost. He split the skull in two and filled his hands with lamb-brains. When the innkeeper saw the pillage he became frightened. They won't even leave me a bone, he thought.

"Say, lads," he shouted, "it's fine for you to eat and drink, but don't forget the late John the Baptist. Ah, his poor head!"

They all froze with their portions in their hands; and Peter, who had chewed the eye and was getting ready to swallow it, choked. It would be disgusting to swallow it, but such a pity to spit it out. What should he do? Of them all, only Judas was not bothered. The innkeeper filled the glasses.

"May his name be long enshrined in our memories. Alas! his poor decapitated head. . . . But here's to yours, lads!"

"And to yours, you old fox," said Peter, gulping down the eye.

"Don't worry," answered the innkeeper, "I'm not a bit afraid. I keep my nose out of God's business and I don't give a damn about saving the world! I'm an innkeeper, not an angel or arch-angel like your worships. At least I've saved myself from that fate." With this, he grabbed what was left of the head.

Peter opened his mouth but suddenly his breath was taken away: a huge man, wild and pock-marked, had appeared on the threshold and was looking inside. The companions drew back into a corner. Peter hid behind Jacob's broad shoulders.

"Barabbas!" growled Judas, scowling. "Come in."

Barabbas bent his thick neck and perceived the disciples in the half-light. His ugly face laughed sarcastically: "I'm delighted to find you, my lambs. I've gone half-way to China to dig you out."

The innkeeper got up, grumbling, and brought him a cup.

"You're just the one we needed, Captain Barabbas," he murmured. He bore a grudge against him because every time he came to the tavern he became drunk, began brawls with the Roman soldiers who passed by—and it was the innkeeper who got into trouble. "Don't start your old tricks again, pig-cock!"

"Listen, as long as the impure tread the land of Israel, I keep my fists up—so get any other idea out of your head. Bring food, lousy horse-hide!"

The innkeeper pushed forward the platter of bones. "Eat. You've got teeth like a dog's: they break bones."

Barabbas emptied his cup in one gulp, twisted his moustache and turned to the companions. "And where is the good shepherd, my lambs? I have an old account to settle with him." His eyes were spitting fire.

"You're drunk before you even start drinking," Judas said to him severely. "Your valiant exploits have already caused us enough bother. Cut it out!"

"What do you have against him?" John dared to ask. "He's a holy man. When he walks he looks at the ground so that he won't step on the ants."

"So that an ant won't step on him, you mean. He's afraid. Is he a man?"

"He rescued Magdalene from your claws, and now you cry over spilt milk," Jacob had the courage to say.

"He crossed me," Barabbas growled, his eyes growing cloudy, "he crossed me, and he's going to pay for it!"

But Judas grabbed him by the arm and took him to one side. He spoke to him softly, hurriedly, with anger:

"What business do you have here? Why did you leave the mountains of Galilee? The brotherhood chose them for your hideout. Others are assigned here in Jerusalem."

"Are we fighting for freedom or aren't we?" Barabbas objected in a rage. "If we are, I'm free to do whatever enters my head. I came to see for myself about this Baptist with his signs and great wonders. Maybe he's the One we've been waiting for, I said to myself. If so, let him come without more delay, take the lead, and begin the slaughter. But I arrived too late: they'd already cut off his head. . . . Judas, you're my leader—what have you got to say?"

"I say you should get up and leave. Don't mix in other people's business."

"I should leave? Are you serious? I came because of the Baptist and I hit upon the son of the Carpenter. I've been hunting him for ages, and now that God has set him right in front of my nose, you say I should give him up?"

"Leave!" Judas commanded him. "That's my business. Don't stick your hand in it."

"What's your purpose? The brotherhood, for your information, want him rubbed out. He's an emissary of the Romans: they pay him to shout about the kingdom of heaven so that the people will be hoaxed into forgetting the earth and our slavery. But you, now. . . . What's your purpose?"

"Nothing. I have my own account to settle. Beat it!"

Barabbas turned and threw a last glance at the companions, who were listening with cocked ears.

"See you soon, my lambs," he shouted at them maliciously. "No one gets away this easily from Barabbas. You'll see, we'll talk the matter over again." He disappeared in the direction of the David gate.

The innkeeper winked at Peter. "He's given him his orders," he said to him softly. "Call that a brotherhood! They kill one Roman and the Romans kill ten Israelites. Not ten, fifteen! Watch out, lads!"

He leaned over to Peter and hissed in his ear: "Listen to me: don't trust Judas Iscariot. These redbeards. . ."

But he stopped. The redbeard had just reseated himself on his stool.

John was troubled. He got up, stood in the doorway and looked up and down. The teacher was nowhere in sight. The day had begun; the streets were filled with people. Beyond the David-gate all was forsaken: pebbles, ashes, not a single green leaf—nothing but standing white stones: tombstones. The air stank from the carcasses of dogs and camels. . . . So much wildness frightened John. Everything here was stone: stone the faces of men, stone their hearts, stone the God they worshipped. Where was the Merciful Father that the teacher had brought them! Oh, when would the beloved master appear so that they could return to Galilee!

Peter rose. His endurance had given out. "Brothers, let's go! He won't come."

"I hear him approaching. . . ," whispered John timidly.

"Where do you hear him, clairvoyant?" said Jacob, who did not care for his brother's dream-phantasies. Like Peter, he was impatient to find the lake and his boats once more. "Where do you hear him, can you tell me?"

"In my heart," the younger brother answered. "It is always the first to hear, the first to see. . ."

Jacob and Peter shrugged their shoulders, but the innkeeper snapped: "Don't scoff. The boy is right. I've heard say that— Wait, the thing they call Noah's ark, what do you think it is? Man's heart, of course! Inside sits God with all his creatures. Everything drowns and goes to the bottom while it alone sails over the waters with its cargo. This heart of man knows everything—yes! don't laugh—everything!"

Trumpets blared, a din arose, the people in the streets made way. The companions became suspicious and flew to the door. Beautiful, nimble adolescents were conveying a litter decorated in gold; and lying inside stroking his beard was a blubbery notable complete with clothes of silk, golden rings and a face greasy with easy living.

"Caiaphas, the high goat-priest!" said the innkeeper. "Hold your noses, lads. The first part of the fish to stink is the head." He squeezed his nostrils and spat. "He's on his way again to his garden to eat, drink and play with his women and pretty boys. Confound it, if I were only God. . . . The world hangs from a single thread. I would cut that thread—yes, by my wine!—I would cut it and let the world go to the devil!"

"Let's leave," Peter said again. "It's not safe here. My heart has eyes and ears too. 'Leave,' it shouts to me, 'Leave, all of you, you miserable creatures!' "

He said that he heard his heart and as he said so he actually did hear it. Terrified, he jumped up and grasped a staff which he found in a corner. Seeing him the others all jumped up too. His terror was contagious.

"Simon, you know him. If he comes, tell him we've gone off to Galilee," Peter instructed.

"And who's going to pay," said the innkeeper anxiously. "The head, the wine. . ."

"Do you believe in the next life, Simon of Cyrene?" asked Peter.

"Of course I do."

"Well, I give you my word I'll pay you there. If you want, I'll put it in writing."

The innkeeper scratched his head.

"What? Don't you believe in the afterlife?" said Peter severely.

"I believe, Peter. Damn it, I believe—but not quite that much. . . ."

XX

BUT while they were talking, a blue shadow suddenly fell over the threshold. They all recoiled. Jesus stood in the doorway, his feet bloody, his clothes covered with mud, his face unrecognizable. Who was it: the sweet teacher or the savage Baptist? His hair fell in twisted plaits down to his shoulders, his skin was now baked and roughened, his cheeks sunken and his eyes grown so large they invaded his entire face. His forcefully-clenched fist, his hair, cheeks and eyes were identical with those of the Baptist. The open-mouthed disciples looked at him silently. Could the two men have joined and become one?

He killed the Baptist, he. . . , he. . . , thought Judas as he stepped aside to let the disquieting newcomer pass. He observed how Jesus strode over the threshold, how he stared at each of them severely, how he bit his lips. . . . He's taken everything from him, everything; he's plundered his body, Judas reflected. But his soul, his wild words? He'll talk now, and we shall see. . . .

They were all quiet for some time. The atmosphere of the tavern changed. The innkeeper crouched silently in the corner and stared goggle-eyed at Jesus, who came forward slowly, biting his lips. The veins in his temples had swelled. Suddenly they all heard his wild hoarse voice. The companions shuddered, for this was not his own voice, it was the voice of the fearful prophet, the Baptist.

"You were leaving?"

No one answered. They had formed a bulwark, one behind the other.

"You were leaving?" he repeated angrily. "Speak, Peter!"

"Rabbi," Peter answered in an unsure voice, "John heard your footsteps in his heart and we were just going out to welcome you. . . ."

Jesus frowned. He was overcome by bitterness and anger, but restrained himself.

"Let us go," he said, turning towards the door. He saw Judas, who was standing off to one side looking at him with his hard blue eyes.

"Are you coming, Judas?" he asked him.

"I'm with you to the death. You know that."

"Not enough! Do you hear, not enough. Till beyond death! . . . Let us go!"

The innkeeper flew out from his cramped position between the wine-barrels. "Good luck, lads," he cried, "and good riddance! Have a nice trip, Galileans, and when the happy time comes and you enter Paradise, don't forget the wine I treated you to—and the head!"

"You have my word," Peter answered him, his face serious and afflicted. He felt ashamed at having lied to the teacher out of fear. Jesus' angry frown was a sure sign he had detected the lie. He was silently scolding him: Peter, coward, liar, traitor! Confound it, when will you become a man? When will you conquer fear? When will you cease turning—windmill!

Peter stood in the tavern's entrance-way, waiting to see in which direction the master would go. But Jesus, motionless, had cocked his ear and was listening to a bitter monotonous melody sung by high, cracked voices from beyond the gate of David. It was the lepers. They had strewn themselves in the dust and were holding out the stumps of their arms to the passers-by while softly singing the majesty of David and the mercy of God, who had given them leprosy to enable them to pay for their sins here on earth, so that tomorrow in the future life their faces would shine like suns for ever and ever.

Jesus grew bitter. He turned towards the city. The stores, workshops and taverns had opened; the streets had filled with people. How they ran and shouted, how the sweat poured from their bodies! He heard a fearful bellowing from horses, men, horns and trumpets: the holy city seemed to him a frightful beast, sick, its entrails filled with leprosy, madness and death.

The bellowing in the streets continued to increase, the men to run here and there. What is their hurry, Jesus asked himself. Why are they running, where are they going? He sighed. All, all—to hell!

He was troubled. Was it his duty to stay here in this cannibalistic city, to climb upon the roof of the Temple and shout, "Repent, the day of the Lord has come"? These unfortunate panting people who ran up and down the streets had more need of repentance and comforting than the serene fishermen and plowmen of Galilee. I'll stay here, thought Jesus. Here I shall first announce the destruction of the world, and the kingdom of heaven!

Andrew could not retain his sorrow. He approached Jesus. "Rabbi," he said. "They seized the Baptist and killed him!"

"It does not matter," Jesus calmly replied. "The Baptist had sufficient time to do his duty. Let us hope, Andrew, that we shall have enough to do ours!" He saw the eyes of the Forerunner's former disciple fill with tears. "Don't be sad, Andrew," he said to him, patting his shoulder. "He did not die. The only ones who die are those who are too late to become immortal. He was not too late. God granted him time."

As he said this, his mind was enlightened. Truly, everything in this world depended on time. Time ripened all. If you had time, you succeeded in working the human mud internally and turning it into spirit. Then you did not fear death. If you did not have time, you perished. . . . Dear God, Jesus silently implored, give me time, that is all I ask of you. Give me time. . . . He felt he still had much mud within him, much of man. He was still subject to anger, fear, jealousy; when he thought of Magdalene his eyes grew misty; and just last night, as he secretly gazed at Lazarus's sister Mary. . .

He blushed from shame and immediately made his decision: he would leave this city. The hour of his death had not yet come; he was still not ready. . . . Dear God, he again implored, give me time, time and nothing else. . . . He nodded to the companions:

"Come, my partisans, let us return to Galilee. In God's name!"

The companions raced towards the lake of Gennesaret like aching, hungry horses returning to the beloved stable. Judas the redbeard was again in the lead. He was whistling. He had not felt his heart so contented for years. The teacher's face, voice and fierceness since his return from the desert pleased him immensely. He killed the Baptist, he said over and over again to himself. He took him with him; lamb and lion joined and became one. Can the Messiah be lamb plus lion, like the ancient monsters? . . . He marched along, whistling and waiting. This silence can't last, he reflected. One of these nights before we reach the lake, he will open his mouth and speak. He'll tell us the secret: what he did in the desert, whether or not he saw the God of Israel, and what the two of them talked about. Then I shall judge.

The first night passed. Jesus, without speaking, looked at the stars. Around him, the tired companions slept. But Judas's blue eyes sparkled in the darkness. . . . He and Jesus sat up all night, one opposite the other, but did not utter a word.

At dawn they started out again. They left the stones of Judea behind them and reached the white soil of Samaria. Jacob's well was deserted: not a single woman came to draw water and refresh them. They passed rapidly over the heretical soil and then saw their beloved mountains—snow-capped Hermon, graceful Tabor, holy Carmel.

The day grew dim. They lay down under a thickly-foliaged cedar and watched the sunset. John pronounced the evening prayer: "Open your doors to us, Lord. The day declines, the sun falls, the sun disappears. We come to your doors, Lord. Open them to us. Eternal, we beseech you, forgive us. Eternal, we beseech you, have mercy upon us. Eternal, save us!"

The air was dark blue. The sky had lost the sun and not yet found the stars. Unadorned, it fell upon the earth. Jesus' supple, long-fingered hands, pressed against the soil, shone white in the uncertain half-light. Within him, the evening prayer was still circulating and doing its work. He heard the trembling hands of men beat desperately on the doors of the Lord, but the doors did not open. The men were knocking and shouting. What were they shouting?

He closed his eyes in order to hear distinctly. The birds of the day had returned to their nests, the night-birds had not yet opened their eyes. The villages of mankind were far away: you heard neither the tumult of men, nor the barking of dogs. The companions mumbled the evening prayers, but they were sleepy and the holy words sank within them without reverberation. Inside him, however, Jesus heard men beat on the doors of the Lord—on his own heart. They were beating on his warm human heart and crying: "Open! Open! Save us!"

Jesus grasped his breast as though he too were knocking at his heart and begging it to open. And while he struggled, believing himself all alone, he felt someone watching him from behind. He turned. Judas's cold inflamed eyes were pinned upon him. Jesus shuddered. This redbeard was a proud untamable beast. Of all the companions, he felt him the closest to him, and yet the farthest away. It seemed that he need explain himself to none other, only to him. He held out his right hand.

"Judas, my brother," he said, "look: what am I holding?"

Judas strained his neck in the half-light in order to see.

"Nothing," he answered. "I don't see anything."

"You will see it shortly," said Jesus smiling.

"The kingdom of heaven," said Andrew.

"The seed," said John. "Rabbi, do you remember what you told us by the lake the first time you parted your lips and spoke to us? 'The sower has come out to sow his seed. . .' "

"And you, Peter?" Jesus asked.

"Master, what can I say to you? If I ask my eyes: nothing. If I ask my heart: everything. Between the two, my mind swings like a bell."

"Jacob?"

"Nothing. Forgive me, rabbi, but you're not holding a single thing."

"Look!" said Jesus, and he violently lifted his arm. And as he lifted it high and brought it forcefully down, the companions became frightened. Judas was so happy he blushed a bright rose and his whole face gleamed. He grasped Jesus' hand and kissed it.

"Rabbi," he shouted, "I saw! I saw! You're holding the Baptist's axe!"

But straightway he felt ashamed and angry because he had not been able to restrain his joy. He withdrew again and leaned against the trunk of the cedar. Jesus' voice was heard, tranquil and grave:

"He brought it to me and placed it at the roots of the rotted tree. That is why he was born: to bring it to me. He could do no more. I came, stooped, picked up the axe—that is why I was born. Now begins my own duty: to chop down the rotted tree. . . . I believed I was a bridegroom and that I held a flowering almond-branch in my hand, but all the while I was a wood-chopper. Do you remember how we danced and promenaded in Galilee, proclaiming the beauty of the world, the unity of heaven and earth, and how Paradise would presently open up for us to enter? Friends, it was all a dream. Now we are awake."

"Is there no kingdom of heaven, then?" Peter cried out, terrified.

"There is, Peter, there is—but within us. The kingdom of heaven is within us, the Devil's kingdom is without. The two kingdoms fight. War! War! Our first duty is to chop down Satan with this axe."

"Which Satan?"

"This world about us. Courage, friends—I invited you to war, not to a wedding. Forgive me, for I did not know myself. But whoever among you thinks of wife, children, fields, happiness— let him leave! There is nothing to be ashamed of. Let him rise, say good-bye to us quietly, and leave with our blessing. There is still time."

He was silent. He swept his eyes over the companions. No one moved. The Evening Star, like an immense drop of water, rolled behind the cedar's black boughs. The night-birds shook their dark wings and awoke. A cool breeze flowed down from the mountains. And suddenly, in the sweetness of the eventide, Peter jumped forward and shouted:

"Rabbi, I'm with you in this war cheek by jowl—to the death!"

"Those are boastful words, Peter, and I don't like them. We're passing along a difficult road. Men will oppose us, Peter—for who desires his own salvation? When did a prophet ever rise up to save the people and the people not stone him to death? We're marching along a difficult road. Hold on to your soul for dear life, Peter—it must not escape. The flesh is weak, don't trust it. . . . Do you hear? It's you I'm talking to, Peter."

Peter's eyes suddenly brimmed with tears. "Don't you have faith in me, rabbi?" he murmured. "The man you look at in that way and do not trust: one day he will die for you."

Jesus put his hand on Peter's knee and stroked it.

"It's possible. . . , possible. . . ," he murmured. "Forgive me, dearest Peter."

He turned to the others. "John the Baptist baptized with water," he said, "and they killed him. I shall baptize with fire. I am making that clear to you tonight so that you'll know it and won't complain to me when the dark times crush down upon us. Before we even set out, I'm informing you which way we're headed: towards death—and after we die, immortality. This is the way. Are you ready?"

The companions grew numb. This voice was severe. It no longer frolicked and laughed; it was calling them to arms. In order to enter the kingdom of heaven, then, would they have to go by way of death? Was there no other road? They were simple men, poor illiterate day-labourers, and the world was rich and all-powerful—how could they take up arms against it? If only the angels could descend from heaven and come to their aid! But none of the disciples had ever seen an angel walk on earth and help the poor and despised. They remained silent therefore, secretly measuring and remeasuring the danger. Judas watched them out of the corner of his eye and chuckled with pride. He alone did not calculate. He went to war despising death, caring nothing for his body and less for his soul. He had but one great passion, and it would be a supreme joy to destroy himself for that passion's sake.

Peter finally opened his mouth. He was the first to speak:

"Rabbi, will angels come down from heaven to help us?"

"We are God's angels on earth, Peter," Jesus replied. "There are no other angels."

"But do you think we can manage all by ourselves, master?" asked Jacob.

Jesus rose. The bridge of his nose was quivering.

"Go away," he shouted. "Abandon me!"

"I won't forsake you, rabbi," cried John. "I'm with you to the death!"

"Me too, rabbi," Andrew exclaimed, and he hugged the teacher's knees.

Two large tears rolled from Peter's eyes, but he did not speak; and Jacob, who was a strapping young man, bowed his head in shame.

"And you, Judas, my brother?" Jesus asked, seeing the mute redbeard gaze savagely at all the rest.

"I don't bother with words," Judas blustered," and I don't blubber like Peter. As long as you hold the axe, I'm with you. You abandon it: I abandon you. I'm not following you, as you very well know. I'm following the axe."

"Aren't you ashamed to talk like that to the rabbi?" said Peter.

But Jesus was glad. "Judas is right," he said. "Friends, I follow the axe myself."

They all stretched out on the ground, their backs against the cedar. In the sky the stars multiplied.

"From this moment onward," Jesus said, "we unfurl God's banner and set out for war. A star and a cross are embroidered on the flag of the Lord. God be with us!"

They were all silent. They had made their decisions; their hearts had become valorous.

"I shall speak once more in parables," Jesus said to the companions, who had finally been swallowed up by the darkness. "One last parable before we depart for battle. . . . Know that the earth is fastened on top of seven columns, and the columns on water, and the water on clouds and the clouds upon the winds, and the winds on the tempest, and the tempest on a thunderbolt. And the thunderbolt rests at God's feet, like an axe."

"I don't understand," said John, blushing.

"John, son of the Thunderbolt!" Jesus replied, caressing his beloved companion's hair. "You will understand when you grow old and go to become an ascetic on an island and the heavens open above you and your mind catches fire!"

He was silent. It was the first time he had so clearly seen what God's thunderbolt was: a burning axe at the feet of the Lord; and hanging from this axe like a string of beads were the tempest, wind, cloud and water: the entire earth. Though he had lived for years with men, for years with the Holy Scriptures, no one had ever revealed to him this terrible secret. What secret: that the thunderbolt is the Son of God, the Messiah. It was the Messiah who was going to cleanse the world!

"Fellow partisans," he said—and Peter perceived two flames, like horns, suddenly fly out from his forehead—"I went to the desert, as you know, to meet God. I was hungry, thirsty, broiling hot. I sat curled up on a rock and called God to appear. Wave after wave of devils pounded over me, broke, frothed and then turned around and flowed back. First were the devils of the body, then the devils of the mind and lastly the all-powerful devils of the heart. But I held God before me as a shield of bronze, and the sand around me filled with fragments of claws and teeth and horns. And than I heard a great voice above me: 'Rise, take the axe brought you by the Forerunner, strike!' "

"Will no one be saved?" Peter cried. But Jesus did not hear.

"All at once my arm grew heavy as if someone had wedged an axe into my grasp. I started to get up, but as I did so I heard the voice once more: 'Son of the Carpenter, a new flood is lashing out, not of water this time, but of fire. Build a new ark, select the saintly, and place them inside!' The selection has begun, friends. The ark is ready, the door is open still. Enter!' "

They all stirred. Creeping forward, they swarmed around Jesus as if he were the ark and they were trying to go in.

"And I heard the voice again: 'Son of David, as soon as the flames subside and the ark casts anchor in the New Jerusalem—mount your ancestral throne and govern mankind! The old earth will have vanished, the old sky will have disappeared. A new heaven will stretch itself over the heads of the saints. The stars—and the eyes of men—will shine seven times brighter than ever before.' "

"Rabbi," Peter again cried, "all of us who have fought the fight with you must not die before we see that day and sit to the right and left of your throne!"

But Jesus did not hear. Plunged in the fiery vision of the desert, he continued:

"And for the last time I heard the voice over my head: 'Son of God, receive my blessing!' "

Son of God! Son of God! each one shouted to himself, but no one dared open his mouth.

All the stars had now appeared. They were hanging low tonight, half-way between sky and men.

"And now, rabbi," Andrew asked, "where do we begin our military life?"

"God," Jesus answered, "took earth from Nazareth and fashioned this body of mine. It is therefore my duty to begin the war in Nazareth. It is there that my flesh must commence its transformation into spirit."

"And afterwards we'll go to Capernaum," said Jacob, "to save my parents."

"And then to Magdala," suggested Andrew, "to get poor Magdalene and put her in the ark too."

"And then to the whole world!" shouted John, pointing to the east and west.

Peter heard them and laughed. "I'm wondering about our bellies," he said. "What'll we eat in the ark? I suggest that we take along only edible animals. Goodness gracious, what use have we for lions and gnats?"

He was hungry, and his mind and thoughts were on food. The others all laughed.

"All you can think about is dinner," Jacob scolded him. "We're speaking here about the salvation of the world."

"The rest of you have the same thought I have," Peter objected, "but you won't admit it. I say frankly whatever comes into my head, whether good or bad. My mind goes round and round, and I go round and round with it. That's why the gossips call me Windmill. Am I right, rabbi, or am I not?"

Jesus' face brightened into a smile. An old story came to his mind:

"Once upon a time there was a rabbi who desired to find someone who could blow the horn so skillfully and loud that the faithful would hear and come to the synagogue. He announced therefore that all good horn-blowers should present themselves for an audition. The rabbi himself would choose the best. Five came—the most skilled in town. Each took the horn and blew. When they all had finished, the rabbi questioned them one by one: 'What do you think of, my child, when you blow the horn?' The first said, 'I think of God.' The second: 'I think of Israel's deliverance.' The third: 'I think of the starving poor. . . .' The fourth: 'I think of orphans and widows. . . .' One only, the shabbiest of the lot, stayed behind the others in a corner and did not speak. 'And you, my child,' the rabbi asked him, 'what do you think of when you blow the horn?' 'Father,' he answered blushing, 'I am poor and illiterate and I have four daughters. I'm unable to give them dowries, poor things, so that they can get married like everyone else. When I blow the horn, therefore, I say to myself: God, you see how I toil and slave for you. Send four husbands, please, for my daughters!' 'Have my blessing,' said the rabbi. 'I choose you!' ''

Jesus turned to Peter and laughed. "Have my blessing, Peter," he said. "I choose you. You have food on your mind, and you talk about food. When you have God on your mind you'll talk about God. Bravo! That's why men call you Windmill. . . . I choose you. You are the windmill which will grind the wheat into bread so that men may eat."

They had one piece of bread. Jesus divided it. Each man's share was only a mouthful, but the rabbi had blessed it, and they were filled. Afterwards, they leaned against one another's shoulders, and slept.

All things sleep, relax and grow during the night—even stones, water and souls. When the companions awoke in the morning, their souls had branched out and invaded every inch of their bodies, filling them with assurance and joy.

They started out before dawn. The air today was cool. Clouds gathered—it was an autumn sky. Late-journeying cranes flew by, carrying the swallows towards the south. The carefree disciples ate up the road: heaven and earth had joined in their hearts, and even the humblest stone glistened, filled with God.

Jesus marched all alone in front. His mind was sluggish; it hung on the mercy of God. He knew that he had finally burned his bridges behind him and could no longer turn back. His fate marched in front and he was following it. Whatever God decided, that was what would take place. . . His fate? Suddenly he again heard the mysterious footsteps which had been mercilessly following him for such a long time. He strained his ears and listened. They were rapid, heavy, decisive. But now they were not behind him, they were in front, guiding him. . . . It's better, he reflected, better. Now I can no longer lose my way. . . .

Rejoicing, he lengthened his stride. It seemed to him that the feet were hurrying, so he hurried too. He advanced, whispering "Onward! Onward!" to the invisible guide; stumbled forward over rocks, jumped ditches, ran. Suddenly he uttered a cry. He felt a horrible pain in his hands and feet, as though he had been pierced by nails. He collapsed onto a rock, the sweat pouring over him in cold granules. . . . For a moment his head swam. The earth sank away from under his feet and a fierce dark ocean spread itself out before him. It was deserted but for a tiny red skiff which sailed bravely along, its sails puffed out, ready to burst. . . . Jesus looked and looked, then smiled: "It is my heart," he murmured, "it is my heart. . . ." His head became steady again, the pains subsided; and when his disciples arrived, they found him tranquilly seated on the rock and smiling.

"Onward lads, faster!" he said, and he rose.

XXI

IT is said that the Sabbath is a well-fed boy at rest on God's knees. With him rest the waters, birds refrain from building their nests, and men do not work. They dress, ornament themselves and go to the synagogue to watch the rabbi unroll the holy scroll with its Law of God written in red and black letters and to hear the learned search every word, every syllable and discover —with great art—the will of God.

It is the Sabbath today. At this very moment the faithful are leaving the synagogue of Nazareth, their eyes still dazzled by the visions which Simeon, the old rabbi, called up before them. The light in their eyes is so strong, they all stumble like blind men. They disperse throughout the village square and promenade slowly under the tall date-palms to recover their equilibrium.

Today the rabbi had let the Scriptures fall open according to chance. They opened to the prophet Nahum. He placed his finger, again according to chance, and it fell upon the following sacred text: "Behold, upon the mountain are heard the feet of him who brings good tidings!" The old rabbi read these words, re-read them, worked up steam:

"It's the Messiah!" he screamed. "He's coming. Look around you, look within you. The signs of his coming are everywhere. Within us: wrath, shame, hope, and the cry: We've had enough! . . . And outside: look! Satan sits on the throne of the Universe. He holds and caresses man's rotted body on one knee; on the other, man's prostituted soul. The years which the prophets prophesied have come—and it is God who speaks through the mouths of the prophets. Open the Scriptures. What do they say? 'When Israel is hurled from its throne and our holy soil is trodden by barbarian feet, the end of the world will have come!' And what more do the Scriptures say: 'The last king will be dissolute, unlawful, atheistic; his children will be unworthy. And the crown will slip from Israel's head.' The dissolute and unlawful king came: Herod! I saw him with my own eyes when he called me to Jericho to heal him. I took along my secret herbs—I knew all about such lore—

and went. I went, and from that day on, I have not been able to eat meat, for I saw his putrescent flesh; I have not been able to drink wine, for I saw his blood filled with worms. I have retained his stench in my nostrils for over thirty years. . . . He died, his carcass rotted. His sons came: trivial unworthy dregs. The royal crown slid from their heads. . . .

"The prophecies, therefore, have been fulfilled: the end of the world is here! A voice resounded by the Jordan: 'He's coming!' A voice resounds within us: 'He's coming!' Today I opened the Scriptures and the letters drew together and cried, 'He's coming!' I've grown old, my eyes are dim, my teeth have fallen out, my knees grown slack. I rejoice! I rejoice because God gave me his word: 'Simeon,' he said, 'you shall not die before you see the Messiah.' Thus the nearer I come to death, the nearer to us comes the Messiah. Courage, my children. There is no slavery, no Satan, there are no Romans. There is only the Messiah, and he is coming! Men, strap on your arms: this is war! Women, light the lamps, the bridegroom arrives! We do not know the hour or exact moment— it may be today, it may be tomorrow. Keep the vigil! I hear the stones of the near-by mountains shift under his feet. He's coming! Go out, perhaps you will see him!"

The people went out and dispersed under the tall date-palms. The rabbi's words were extremely disorganized and his auditors struggled to forget them completely so that the roaring flames would subside and their souls could once more dispose themselves around cares still at hand. . . . And while they promenaded, anxiously awaiting the hour of noon when they could return to their homes and by talking, arguing and eating forget the sacred words—look! there with his torn clothes, barefooted, his face a flash of lightning, was the son of Mary. The four disciples flocked timidly behind him; and bringing up the rear, dark-eyed and unsociable, was Judas the redbeard.

The burghers were astonished. Where did this riff-raff come from—and wasn't that the son of Mary in the lead?

"Look how he walks. He puts out his arms and flaps them like wings. God has swelled his head and he's trying to fly."

"He's mounting a rock and gesturing. He's going to speak."

"Let's go for the laughs!"

Jesus had indeed stepped onto a rock in the middle of the square. Laughing, the people gathered round, glad that this clairvoyant had appeared. Now they would be able to forget the rabbi's grave words. "This is war," he had told them. "Keep the vigil, he's coming!" He had been booming this hymn into their ears for years and years, and they were sick of it. Now, thank God, the son of Mary would help them relieve their minds.

Jesus waved his arms, signalling them all to gather round him. The place filled with beards, skull-caps and striped robes. Some of the crowd were munching dates to deceive their hunger, others sunflowers, and the oldest and most god-fearing were telling long chaplets with beads made of tiny knots of blue cloth, each containing a text from the Holy Scriptures.

Jesus' eyes flashed. Though he was in front of such a great multitude, his heart felt no fear. He parted his lips:

"Brothers," he shouted, "open your ears, open your hearts, hear the words I shall speak. Isaiah cried: 'The spirit of the Lord has flowed over me, he chose me to bring good tidings to the poor, he sent me to proclaim freedom to the slaves and light to the blind!' The prophesied day has come, brothers. The God of Israel has sent me to bring the good tidings. He anointed me out in the Judean desert, and from there I come! He entrusted me with the great secret. I received it and came across plains and mountains—didn't you hear my footsteps upon the hills?—I ran here to the village of my birth to announce the happy news for the first time. What happy news? The kingdom of heaven has come!"

An old man with a double hump like a camel's lifted his chaplet and cackled:

"Vague words, the words you speak, son of the Carpenter, vague, groundless words. 'Kingdom of heaven,' 'justice,' 'freedom,' and 'grab what you can, boys, it's all for the taking.' I've had enough! ... Miracles, miracles! I want you to do something here and now. Perform some miracles to make us believe in you. Otherwise, shut up!"

"Everything is a miracle, old man," Jesus replied. "What further miracles do you want? Look below you: even the humblest blade of grass has its guardian angel who stands by and helps it to grow. Look above you: what a miracle is the star-filled sky! And

315

if you close your eyes, old man: what a miracle the world within us! What a star-filled sky is our heart!"

They heard him, astonished, one turning to the next:

"Isn't this the son of Mary? how does he talk with such authority?"

"It's a devil speaking through his mouth. Where are his brothers to tie him up so that he won't bite anyone?"

"He's opened his mouth again. Ssh!"

"The day of the Lord has come, brothers. Are you ready? You have few hours left. Call the poor and portion out your belongings. What do you care about the goods of this earth? The fire is coming to burn them up! Before the kingdom of heaven: the kingdom of fire. On the day of the Lord the stones of the houses of the rich will stand up and crush the inhabitants; the pieces of gold in the coffers of the rich will exude sweat, and over the prosperous will flow the sweat and the blood of the poor. The heavens will open, flood and fire will pour down, and the new ark will float above the flames. I hold the keys and I open the ark and select. My brothers of Nazareth, I begin with you. You are the first I invite. Come, enter. The flames of God have already begun to descend!"

"Boo! Boo! The son of Mary has come to save us!" hooted the crowd amid fits of laughter. Several people bent down, filled their hands with stones, and waited.

A running figure appeared at the edge of the square. It was Philip, the shepherd. He had made a dash as soon as he heard of his friends' arrival. His eyes were swollen and enflamed as from much weeping, and his cheeks had sunk away. The very day he said good-bye to Jesus and the companions by the lake and laughingly called to them: "I'm not coming, I have sheep, where can I leave them?" bandits had rushed down from Lebanon and seized him, leaving him nothing but his shepherd's staff. He kept it still and went from village to village, mountain to mountain, an unthroned king, still seeking his flock. He cursed and threatened, sharpened a wide dagger and said that he was going to journey to Lebanon. But at night when he was all alone, he wept. . . . He ran now to join his old friends and tell them about his suffering so that all of them could set out together for Lebanon. He heard the laughing and booing. "What's going on over there?" he murmured. "Why are they laughing?" He came closer. Jesus had now grown furious:

"What are you laughing at," he shouted. "Why are you gathering stones to strike the son of man? Why do you brag about your houses and olive groves and vineyards? Ashes! Ashes! And your sons and daughters: ashes! And the flames, the great bandits, will rush down from the mountains to seize your sheep!"

"What bandits, what sheep?" grumbled Philip, who was listening with his chin resting on his staff. "What are these flames he's bringing us now?"

While Jesus spoke, more and more of the soil-coloured people of the slums arrived. They had heard of the appearance of a new prophet for the poor and had run. It was said that in one hand he held heavenly fire to burn up the rich, and in the other a pair of scales for portioning out their goods to the poor. He was a new Moses, the bringer of a new, juster, Law. The people stood and listened to him, enthralled. It had come, it had come! The kingdom of the poor had come!

But as Jesus again parted his lips to speak, four arms fell upon him, seized him and brought him down from the rock. A thick rope was quickly wrapped around him. Jesus turned and saw the sons of Joseph, his own brothers Simon the lame and Jacob the devout.

"Go on home, home—inside! You're possessed with devils!" they screamed, rabidly dragging him along.

"I have no home. Release me. This is my home, these are my brothers!" cried Jesus and he pointed to the crowd.

"Go home, go home!" The burghers also shouted, laughing. One of them lifted his arm and slung the stone he was holding. It grazed Jesus' forehead: the first drop of blood flowed. The old man with the double hump screeched:

"Death! Death! He's a sorcerer, he's casting spells over us, he's calling the fire to come and roast us—and it will come!"

"Death! Death!" was heard on every side.

Peter raced forward. "Shame on all of you," he cried. "What has he done to you? He's innocent!"

A young stalwart flew at him: "It looks like you're on his side, eh!" He grabbed him by his Adam's apple.

317

"No! No! I'm not!" screamed Peter, fighting to unfasten the huge hand from his throat.

The other three of Jesus' companions were scared out of their wits. Jacob and Andrew stood by, taking stock of their forces; John's eyes filled with tears. But Judas opened a way through the crowd with his arms, pulled the two frenzied brothers away from the rabbi, and undid the rope.

"Scram!" he shouted at them, "or you'll have to deal with me. Off with you!"

"Go to your own town if you want to be boss!" screeched Simon the lame.

"I'm boss wherever my fists are, short-leg!" He turned to the four disciples: "Aren't you ashamed of yourselves, denying him already! Forward! Form a circle around him so that no one can touch him!"

The four were ashamed. The paupers and ragamuffins jumped forward, shouting: "Brothers, we're on your side! Let's murder them!"

"And I'm with you too," cried a wild voice. Philip flourished his staff and pushed aside the crowd in order to pass through. "I'm coming too!"

"Welcome, Philip," the redbeard answered him. "Come, join us! The poor and the wronged—all together!"

When the burghers saw these slum-dwellers rebelling against them, they flew into a frenzy. The son of the Carpenter has come to put ideas into the heads of the poor, to turn the established order of the world upside-down. Didn't he say he was bringing a new Law? Death! Death!

They flared up and charged, some with staffs, some with knives, some with stones. The old ones remained on the side and shrieked encouragement. Jesus' friends made their bulwark behind the plane-trees at the edges of the square; others rushed out into the open. Jesus himself went forward and stood between the two opposing camps. He spread his arms and shouted: "Brothers! Brothers!" but no one listened to him. The stones were now being slung with fury and the first of the wounded were already groaning.

A woman flew out from a narrow street. A purple kerchief was wrapped tightly around her face, covering all but half of her mouth, and her large black eyes which were submerged in tears.

"For God's sake, don't kill him!" she cried in her high voice.

"Mary, his mother!" people murmured.

But how could the old men pity the mother at this point: they had become rabid. "Death! Death!" they howled. "He's come to awaken the people, to incite a rebellion, to divide our goods among the barefooted rabble. Death!"

The opponents had now come to grips. Joseph's two sons rolled on the ground, howling. Jacob had seized a stone and cracked open their heads. Judas stood with drawn dagger in front of Jesus, allowing no one to approach. Philip remembered his sheep. Unable to restrain himself any longer, he blindly swung his staff at his opponents' heads.

"In God's name," Mary's voice was again heard, "he's sick! He's gone out of his senses. Have pity on him!"

But her cry was drowned in the uproar. Judas had now seized the strongest of the stalwarts and was stepping on him, his knife at his throat. But Jesus arrived in time to pull back the red-beard's arm.

"Judas, my brother," he cried, "no blood! no blood!"

"What then—water?" shouted the redbeard, enraged. "Have you forgotten that you hold an axe? The hour has come!"

Even Peter had grown ferocious, incited by the blows he received. He grasped a huge heavy stone and fell upon the old men. Mary entered the very centre of the brawl and approached her son. She took his hand:

"My child," she said, "what has happened to you? How did you descend to this? Return home to wash, change your clothes and put on your sandals. You've made yourself all dirty, my son."

"I have no home," he said. "I have no mother. Who are you?"

The mother began to weep. Digging her nails into her cheeks, she spoke no more.

Peter slung his stone. It crushed the foot of the old man with the double hump. The victim bellowed with pain and hobbled away, going through the alleyways towards the rabbi's house. But at that moment the rabbi appeared, panting. He had heard the uproar and had jumped up from his table, where with face buried in the Holy Scriptures he had been toiling to extract God's will from the words and syllables. But when he heard the tumult he took up his crosier and ran to see what was happening. He had encountered several of the wounded along the way and learnt everything. He now pushed aside the crowd and reached the son of Mary.

"What is all this, Jesus?" he said severely. "Is this you, the bearer of love? Is this the kind of love you bring? Aren't you ashamed?"

He turned to the crowd:

"My children, return to your homes. This is my nephew. He's sick, unfortunate man; he's been sick for years. Do not bear any malice against him for what he has said, but forgive him. It is not he who speaks, but someone else who uses his mouth."

"God!" Jesus exclaimed.

"You keep quiet," the rabbi snapped, and he touched him reprovingly with his crosier.

He turned once more to the crowd:

"Leave him alone, my children. Bear no grudge against him, for he knows not what he says. All—rich and poor—we are all seeds of Abraham. Do not quarrel amongst yourselves. It's noontime, return to your homes. I shall cure this unfortunate man."

He turned to Mary. "Mary, go home. We'll come presently."

The mother threw a final glance at her son, a glance of great longing, as though she was saying good-bye to him for ever. She sighed, bit her kerchief, and disappeared into the narrow lanes.

While the people were murdering each other clouds had covered the heavens; rain was preparing to fall and refresh the earth. A wind arose, the stems of the last leaves of the plane- and fig-trees separated from their branches and the leaves scattered over the ground. The square had emptied. Jesus turned to Philip and held out his hand:

"Philip, my brother, welcome."

"I'm glad to see you, rabbi," the other replied, squeezing Jesus' hand and surrendering his crook to him.

"Take this to lean on," he said.

"Come, fellow-partisans," said Jesus, "let us go. Shake the dust from your feet. Farewell, Nazareth!"

"I'll keep you company until the edge of the village so that no one bothers you," the old rabbi said.

He took Jesus' hand and they went in the lead together. The rabbi felt Jesus' palm burning in his grasp.

"My son," he said, "don't take the care of others upon yourself. They will devour you."

"I have no cares of my own, Father. Let those of others devour me!"

They reached the end of Nazareth. The orchards came into view, and beyond, the fields. The disciples in back had stopped for a moment to wash their wounds in a spring. With them were a good number of the paupers and cripples, plus two blind men— all chattering and waiting for the new prophet to perform his miracles. They were excited and merry, as though returning from a great battle.

But the four disciples marched along in silence. Uneasy, they were hurrying to approach the rabbi so that he could comfort them. Nazareth, the master's home, had hooted and banished them: the great campaign had started off badly! And if we're chased out of Cana too, they were thinking, and out of Capernaum and everywhere else around the lake of Gennesaret, what will become of us? Where will we go? To whom will we proclaim the word of God? Since the people of Israel refuse us and hoot us, to whom shall we turn? To the infidels?

They looked at Jesus, but no one opened his mouth to speak. Jesus saw the fear in their eyes, however, and took Peter's hand.

"Peter, man of little faith," he said, "a black beast with bristling hair sits shrivelled up and trembling inside the pupils of your eyes. It is Fear, Peter, Fear. Are you afraid?"

"When I'm far from you, rabbi, yes, I am afraid. That's why I've come close; that's why all of us have come close. Speak to us and steady our hearts."

Jesus smiled. "When I bend far down into my soul," he said, "I don't know how and why the truth always issues from within me in the form of a parable. So, friends, once more I shall speak to you in parables:

"A great nobleman once commanded a rich dinner to be made ready in his palace for his son's marriage. As soon as the bulls were slain and the tables set, he sent his servants to announce to those who were invited: 'Everything is ready. If it so pleases you, come to the wedding.' But each of the invited found a pretext for not coming: 'I bought a field which I must go to see,' said one. 'I'm newly-married myself and can't come,' said the next. 'I purchased five pairs of oxen and I'm off to try them out,' the next gave as his excuse. . . . The servants returned and said to their master: 'None of the invited is able to come. They all say they're busy.' The nobleman became angry. 'Run quickly to the squares and cross-roads, gather together the poor, lame, blind and deformed and bring them here. I invited my friends but they refused. I shall therefore fill my house with the uninvited so that they may eat, drink and rejoice at the wedding of my son.' "

Jesus stopped. He had begun calmly, but the more he spoke the more he thought of the Nazarenes and Jews, and wrath flamed up between his eyes. The disciples looked at him with surprise.

"Who are the invited, who the uninvited, what marriage is it? Forgive us, rabbi, but we don't understand," said Peter, scratching his thick head in despair.

"You will understand," said Jesus, "when I summon the invited to enter the ark and they refuse because they say they have fields, vineyards and wives and because their eyes, ears, lips, nostrils and hands are five pairs of oxen which are tilling—tilling what? The bottomless pit!"

He sighed. Looking at the companions, he felt completely forsaken.

"I speak," he murmured, "but to whom? To the air. I am the only one who listens. When shall the desert grow ears in order to hear me?"

"Forgive us, rabbi," Peter repeated, "but our minds are clods of mud. Have patience: they will blossom."

Jesus turned and looked at the rabbi, but the old man was staring at the ground. He had a foreboding of the terrible hidden meaning, and his aged lashless eyes were brimming with tears.

At the end of Nazareth, in front of a wooden shed, stood the customs officer who collected the duties. Matthew was his name. All merchants who entered or left the village had to pay tax to the Romans. He was short, stout, jaundiced; his hands yellow and soft, his fingers inky, nails black; he had long hairy ears and a high voice like a eunuch's. The whole village found him disgusting and hated him. No one would shake hands with him, and everyone who passed by the shed looked the other way. Did not the Scriptures say: "It is our duty to pay tax only to God, not to men"? This man was a publican, a tax-collector in the tyrant's service. He trampled the Law, made a living from illegality. The air around him was polluted for seven miles. "Move quickly, lads," Peter said. "Hold your breath. Turn away your faces!"

But Jesus stopped. Matthew, standing outside the shed, was holding his quill pen between his teeth. He breathed rapidly, not knowing what to do. He was afraid to stay where he was, yet he did not want to go inside the shed. For ages now he had longed for a close view of the new prophet who proclaimed that all men were brothers. Wasn't it he who one day said: "God loves the sinner who repents more than he who never sinned?" And another day, hadn't he said: "I came to the world not for the righteous, but for sinners: it is with them I like to speak and eat"? And another day when he was asked, "Rabbi, what is the name of the true God?" he answered: "Love".

For many a day and night Matthew had turned these words over and over in his heart, saying with a sigh: "When shall I see him, when shall I fall at his feet!" And now, there he was in front of him, yet Matthew was ashamed to lift his eyes to look at him. He stood motionless, head bowed, and waited. What was he waiting for? The prophet would go away now, and he would lose him forever.

Jesus took a step towards him and said, "Matthew" so quietly and sweetly that the publican felt his heart melt, and raised his eyes. Jesus was standing in front of him, looking at him. His regard was tender and all-powerful: it descended to the officer's very bowels, brought peace to his heart and enlightenment to his mind. His vital organs had been shivering, but now the sun fell over them and warmed them. What joy this was, what certainty, what friendship! Was the world then so simple and salvation so easy?

Matthew went inside, closed his ledgers, put a blank one under his arm, wedged his bronze ink-well into his belt and placed his quill behind his ear. Next, he removed a key from his belt, locked the shed and tossed the key into a garden. As soon as he had finished, he approached Jesus with trembling knees. He stopped. Should he go forward, or not? Would the teacher offer him his hand? He raised his eyes and looked at Jesus as if imploring him to have pity. . . . Jesus smiled at him and offered his hand:

"Welcome, Matthew. Come with me."

The disciples felt troubled and stepped to one side. The old rabbi bent over to Jesus' ear. "My child," he said, "a publican! It's a great sin. You must listen to the Law."

"Father," Jesus replied, "I listen to my own heart."

They had advanced beyond Nazareth. Passing the orchards, they reached the fields. A cold wind was blowing. Mount Hermon gleamed in the distance, sprinkled with the first snow.

The rabbi took Jesus' hand once more. He wanted to talk to him before they separated. . . . But what could he say? Where should he begin? Jesus claimed that in the Judean desert God entrusted him with the fire in one hand and the seed in the other. He said he would burn up this world and then plant a new world. . . . The rabbi regarded him stealthily. Should he believe him? Did not the Scriptures say that God's Elect would be despised and rejected by men, like a withered tree which has sprouted among stones? It was possible therefore, possible that this man was the One. . . .

The rabbi leaned against Jesus. "Who are you?" he asked softly, so that the others should not hear.

"You've been with me such a long time, uncle Simeon—from the hour of my birth—and you still haven't recognized me?"

The old man's heart stood still. "It's more than my mind can hold," he murmured, "more than it can hold. . . ."

"And your heart, uncle Simeon?"

"My child, I do not listen to my heart. It leads one to the abyss."

"To God's abyss—to salvation," said Jesus, looking sympathetically at the old man. And in a moment: "Father, don't you remember the dream the prophet Daniel had about the race of Israel one night in Babylon? The Ancient of days was sitting on his throne, his clothes white as snow, the hair of his head like the white fleece of a ram. His throne was made of flames, and a river of flames flowed at his feet. The Judges were enthroned to his left

324

and right. Then the heavens opened up and upon the clouds descended: —who? Do you remember, Father?"

"The Son of man," answered the old rabbi, who had been nourishing himself on this dream for generations. There were even nights when he dreamt the same dream himself.

"And who is the Son of man, Father?"

The old rabbi's knees gave way. He looked at the youth, terrified.

"Who?" he whispered, hanging on Jesus' lips. "Who?"

"I," Jesus replied tranquilly, and he placed his hand on the old man's head, as if blessing him.

The old rabbi wanted to speak, but could not open his mouth.

"Farewell, Father," said Jesus, holding out his hand. "You must be a happy man, Simeon, for God kept his word and deemed you worthy of seeing, before your death, what you longed to see all your life."

The rabbi stood and gazed at him with protruding eyes. . . . What was all this around him: thrones, wings, and the Son of man upon the clouds? Was he dreaming? Was he the prophet Daniel? Were the doors of the future opening before him and enabling him to look in? He was not standing on soil, but on clouds; and this young man who held out his hand and smiled was not the son of Mary, he was the Son of man!

Feeling dizzy, he drove his crosier into the ground and propped himself up on it so that he would not fall. Then he looked, looked at Jesus who, holding his shepherd's staff, was passing under the autumn trees. The heavens had darkened; the rain could no longer hold itself in the sky: it fell. The old rabbi's clothes became drenched and stuck to his body. Water ran down from his hair. Though shivering, he remained motionless in the middle of the road. Jesus, followed by his companions, had already disappeared behind the trees, but as the old rabbi stood in the wind and the rain he saw them, ragged and barefooted, still going forward and mounting. . . . Where were they going? In which direction? Would these barefooted illiterate ragamuffins set fire to the world? The designs of the Lord are a great abyss. . .

"Adonai," he whispered, "Adonai. . . ," and his tears began to flow.

325

XXII

ROME sits upon the nations with her all-powerful insatiable arms spread wide and receives the boats, caravans, gods and produce of all the world and all the sea. While believing in no god she fearlessly and with ironic condescension receives all gods into her courts: from far-away fire-worshipping Persia, Mithras the sun-faced son of Ahuramazda, mounted on the sacred bùll which is soon to die; from the many-uddered land of the Nile, Isis, who in springtime upon the blossoming fields seeks the fourteen pieces of her husband and brother Osiris, whom Typhon dismembered; from Syria, amidst heart-rending lamentations, exquisite Adonis; from Phrygia, stretched out on a bier and covered with faded violets, Attis; from shameless Phoenicia, Astarte of the thousand husbands: all the gods and devils of Asia and Africa; and from Greece, white-topped Olympus, and black Hades.

She receives all the gods; she has opened roads, freed the sea of pirates and the land of bandits, brought peace and order to the world. Above her is no one, not even God. Under her—everyone. Gods and men: all are citizens and slaves of Rome. Time and Space are richly-illuminated scrolls rolled up in her fist. I am eternal, she vaunts, caressing the two-headed eagle which, having folded its blood-stained wings, reposes at the feet of its mistress. What splendour, what irremovable joy to be omnipotent and immortal, thinks Rome; and a wide fat smile flows over her fleshy rouged face.

Contented, she smiles. . . , and forgets. For whom has she opened up the routes of land and sea, for whom has she toiled for so many ages to bring safety and peace to the world? This never even crosses her mind. She conquered, made laws, became rich, stretched herself over the entire universe—for whom, for whom?

For the barefooted man who at this moment, followed by a swarm of ragamuffins, is proceeding along the deserted road from Nazareth to Cana. He has nowhere to sleep, nothing to wear or eat. All his larders, horses and rich silks are still in heaven—but they have begun to descend.

Holding his shepherd's staff he marches with bloody feet amidst dust and stones. Sometimes he halts, leans on the staff and without speaking sweeps his eyes along the mountains and then above the peaks to a light: God, who sits on high and keeps watch over men. He raises his staff, salutes him, and then resumes his journey. . . .

They finally reached Cana. At the well outside the village a pale young woman with swelling womb was happily drawing water and filling her jug. They recognized her. It was the girl whose marriage they had gone to in the summer. They had expressed their wish at that time that she might have a son.

"Our wish has been fulfilled," Jesus said to her, smiling. She blushed and asked if they were thirsty. They were not, so she put the jug on her head, went into the village, and disappeared.

Peter took the lead and began to knock at all the doors, running from threshold to threshold. A mysterious drunkenness had swept him away. Dancing, he shouted, "Open up! Open up!"

The doors opened and women appeared. Night was falling; the farmers were returning from their fields. "What's up, friend?" they asked, surprised. "Why are you pounding on the doors?"

"The day of the Lord has come," Peter answered. The deluge, men! We carry the new ark. All believers: enter. Behold! the master holds the key. Step lively now!"

The women became frightened. The men approached Jesus, who was sitting on a rock now and inscribing crosses and stars in the soil with his staff.

The sick and the lame from the whole village gathered round him.

"Rabbi, touch us so that we may be healed. Say a kind word to make us forget that we are blind, crippled, and leprous."

A tall aristocratic old lady dressed all in black cried, "I had a son and they crucified him. Raise him from the dead!"

Who was this noble old woman? The astonished farmers turned. No one from their village had been crucified. They looked to see where the voice came from—but the old lady had disappeared into the twilight.

Bowed over the soil, Jesus inscribed crosses and stars and

listened to a trumpet of war which was descending the hill opposite. Heavy, rhythmic marching was heard and suddenly bronze shields and helmets flashed in the light of the evening sun. The villagers turned; their faces grew dark.

"The confounded hunter is returning from the chase. He's gone out again to catch rebels."

"He brought his paralysed daughter to our village to be cured, so he says, by the pure air. But the God of Israel keeps a ledger and records and does not forgive. The soil of Cana shall bury her!"

"Don't shout, wretches—here he is!"

Three horsemen passed before them. In the middle was Rufus, the centurion of Nazareth. Spurring his mount, he approached the crowd of peasants.

"Why have you assembled?" he shouted, lifting his whip. "Disperse!" His face was afflicted. In several months' time he had grown old; his hair was turning grey. He had been broken by his pangs of grief for his only daughter, who one morning had suddenly found herself paralysed in her bed. As he charged and dispersed the villagers, he glimpsed Jesus sitting off to one side on a stone. Suddenly his face lit up. He spurred his horse and approached him.

"Son of the Carpenter," he said, "you have come from Judea—welcome! I've been looking for you."

He turned to the villagers. "I have something to say to him. Go away!"

He saw the disciples and paupers who had followed from Nazareth, recognized several, and frowned.

"Son of the Carpenter," he said, "you have helped crucify others, take care you don't get crucified yourself. Do not touch the people, do not put ideas into their heads. My hand is heavy, and Rome is immortal."

Jesus smiled. He knew very well that Rome was not immortal, but he did not speak.

The grumbling farmers had dispersed. They stood off at a distance and stared at the three rebels—a tall old man with a forked beard, and his two sons—who had been captured by the legionaries and were now being transported, loaded in chains. All three, with heads held high, gazed over the Roman helmets, trying to see the crowd, but they saw nothing, nothing except the God of Israel, erect in the air, and angry.

Judas recognized them. He had once fought side by side with them. He nodded, but they, blinded by God's splendour, did not see him.

"Son of the Carpenter," said the centurion, bending low while still mounted on his horse, "there are gods who hate and kill us, others who do not deign to look down and see us, still others who are well-disposed and exceedingly merciful, and who heal the sicknesses of unfortunate mortals. Son of the Carpenter, to which of these categories does your God belong?"

"There is one God," Jesus answered. "Do not blaspheme, centurion!"

Rufus shook his head. "I don't intend to get into a theological discussion with you," he said. "I detest the Jews and if you don't mind my saying so, all of you incessantly harp on God. The only thing I wanted to ask you was this: can your God—"

He stopped. He was ashamed to condescend to ask a favour of a Jew.

But straightway a narrow virginal bed arose in his mind and lying upon it, motionless, the pale body of a young girl with two large green eyes which looked at him, looked at him, and implored him. . .

He swallowed his pride and leaned even further over on his saddle. "Son of the Carpenter, can your God heal the sick?"

He looked agonizedly at Jesus.

"Can he?" he asked again, seeing Jesus silent.

Jesus slowly rose from the rock where he was sitting, and approached the rider.

" 'The fathers have eaten sour grapes, and the children's teeth are set on edge.' Such is the law of my God."

"Unjust!" shouted the centurion with a shudder.

"No, just!" Jesus contradicted him. "Father and son are of the same root. Together they rise to heaven, together they descend to hell. If you strike one, both are wounded; if one makes a mistake, both are punished. You, centurion, hunt and kill us, and the God of Israel strikes down your daughter with paralysis."

"Son of the Carpenter, those are heavy words. I happened once

329

to hear you speak in Nazareth, and your words then seemed sweeter than what would be suitable for a Roman. But now. . ."

"Then the kingdom of heaven was talking, now the end of the world. Since the day you heard me, centurion, the Just Judge seated himself on his throne, opened his ledgers and called for Justice, who came, sword in hand, and stood next to him."

"Is yours then one more God who goes no further than Justice?" shouted the exasperated centurion. "Is that where he stops? What then was the new message of love you proclaimed last summer in Galilee? My daughter doesn't need God's justice, she needs his love. I seek a God who surpasses justice and who can heal my child. That's why I've moved every stone in Israel to find you. . . . Love—do you hear? Love, not justice."

"Merciless loveless centurion of Rome: who puts these words into your savage mouth?"

"Suffering, and my love for my child. I seek a God who will cure my child, that I may believe in him."

"Blessed are those who believe in God without requiring miracles."

"Yes, blessed. But I am a hard man and not easily convinced. I saw many gods in Rome—we've got thousands locked up in cages—and I've had enough of them!"

"Where is your daughter?"

"Here. She's in a garden at the highest point in the village."

"Let us go."

The centurion braced himself and jumped off his horse. He and Jesus marched in front. Behind them at a distance came the disciples, and further back still, the crowd of peasants. At that instant Thomas, rapturously happy, emerged from behind the legion's rear guard. He had been going behind the soldiers, selling them his wares at an immense profit.

"Hey, Thomas," the disciples shouted at him, "you're still not coming with us, eh? Now you'll see the miracle and believe."

"I've got to see first," Thomas answered, "—and to touch."

"Touch what, you shrewd merchant?"

"The truth."

"Does truth have a body? What's this you're piping, block-head!"

"If it has no body, what do I want with it?" said Thomas, laughing. "I need to touch things. I don't trust my eyes or my ears, I trust my hands."

They reached the highest part of the village and entered a cheery whitewashed house.

A girl of about twelve years of age was lying on a white bed, her two large green eyes open. When she saw her father her face lit up. Her soul shook violently, trying to lift the paralysed body, but in vain; and the joy on her face went out. Leaning over, Jesus took the girl's hand. All his strength assembled in his palm—all his strength and love and mercy. Without speaking, he pinned his eyes onto the two green eyes and felt his soul flow impetuously from the tips of his fingers into the girl's body. She looked at him ardently, her lips just parted, and smiled.

The disciples tiptoed into the room with Thomas first and foremost, his sack of wares over his back and his horn under his belt. The peasants scattered throughout the garden and narrow lane. Everyone was holding his breath and waiting. The centurion, leaning against the wall, watched his daughter and struggled to hide his anguish.

Little by little the girl's cheeks began to redden, her chest swelled, she was permeated by a sweet tingling which passed from her hand to her heart, and from her heart to the very soles of her feet. Her entrails rustled and stirred like the leaves of a poplar caught in a gentle breeze. Jesus felt the girl's hand beat like a heart and return to life in his grasp. Only then did he open his mouth and speak.

"Rise, my daughter!" he gently commanded.

The girl moved peacefully, as though recovering from numbness; stretched herself, as if waking up; then, propping her hand against the bed, lifted her body—and with one jump was in her father's arms. Thomas's swivel-eyes popped out of his head. He extended his hand and touched the girl, apparently wishing to make sure she was real. The disciples were astonished and frightened. The crowd, which had swarmed around, bellowed for an instant and then, terrified, became immediately mute. You heard nothing but the girl's refreshing laughter as she hugged and kissed her father.

Judas approached the master, his face angry and evil.

"You dissipate your strength on unbelievers. You help our enemies. Is this the end of the world you've brought us? Are these the flames?"

But Jesus, hovering far away in dark skies, did not hear him. He had been frightened more than anyone else at the sight of the girl jumping out of her bed. The disciples, unable to contain their joy, formed a circle and danced around him. So—they had done well to abandon everything and join him. He was the real thing: he performed miracles. Thomas placed a scale in his mind and weighed. On one tray he put his wares, on the other the kingdom of heaven. The trays oscillated for some time, and finally stood still. The kingdom of heaven was the heavier. Yes, it was an excellent risk: I give five, I might get a thousand. Forward, then, in God's name!

He approached the master. "Rabbi," he said, "for your precious sake I'll portion out my wares to the poor. Please don't forget it tomorrow when the kingdom of heaven arrives. I'm sacrificing everything to come with you, for today I saw and touched the truth."

But Jesus was still far away. He heard but did not answer.

"I'm going to keep only my horn," continued the former merchant, "so that I can blow it to assemble the people. We're selling new wares, immortal ones—and free!"

The centurion, holding his daughter in his arms, came up to Jesus. "Man of God," he said, "you revived my daughter. What favour can I do for you?"

"I freed your daughter from the chains of Satan," Jesus answered. "You, centurion, free those three rebels from the chains of Rome."

Rufus bowed his head and sighed. "I cannot," he murmured sadly, "truly, I cannot. I took an oath to the Roman Emperor, just as you took an oath to the God you worship. Is it right to betray our oath? Ask me any other favour you desire. I'm leaving for Jerusalem the day after tomorrow, and I want to do this favour for you before I go."

"Centurion," Jesus replied, "one day we shall meet in holy Jerusalem at a difficult hour. I shall ask the favour of you at that time. Until then, be patient."

He placed his hand on the girl's blonde hair and kept it there for a long time. He closed his eyes, felt the warmth of the head, the softness of the hair, the sweetness of womanhood.

"My child," he said at last, opening his eyes, "I am going to tell you something which I don't want you to forget. Take your father by the hand and lead him to the true road."

"Which is the true road, man of God?" the girl asked.

"Love."

The centurion gave orders. Food and drink were brought, tables set.

"Be my guests," he said to Jesus and the disciples. "Tonight you shall eat and drink in this house, for I celebrate my child's resurrection. I have not been happy for years. Today my heart is filled to overflowing with joy. Welcome!"

He leaned over to Jesus. "I owe a great debt of gratitude to the God you worship," he said. "Give him to me so that I can send him to Rome along with the other gods."

"He'll get there on his own," Jesus answered, and he went out to the yard in order to breathe.

Night fell. The stars began to mount the sky. Below in the tiny village the lamps were lit and the eyes of the people gleamed. This evening their everyday talk rose one degree higher than usual, for they sensed that God, like a kind lion, had entered their village.

The tables were set. Jesus sat down among his disciples and divided the bread, but did not speak. Within him, his soul still anxiously flapped its wings as though it had just escaped an immense danger or completed a great and unexpected exploit. The disciples around him did not speak either, but their hearts bounded for joy. All these ends of the world and kingdoms of heaven were not dreams and mere excitement, they were the truth; and the dark-complexioned, barefooted youth next to them who ate, spoke, laughed and slept like other men, was truly the apostle of God.

When the meal ended and all the others lay down to sleep, Matthew knelt below the lamp, drew out the virgin notebook from under his shirt, took his quill from behind his ear, leaned over the blank pages and remained meditating for a long time. How should he begin? Where should he begin? God had placed him next to this holy man in order that he might faithfully record the words he said and the miracles he performed, so that they would not perish and that future generations might learn about them and choose, in their turn, the road of salvation. Surely, that was the duty God had entrusted to him. He knew how to read and write; therefore he had a heavy responsibility: to catch with his pen all that was about to perish and by placing it on paper, to make it immortal. Let the disciples detest him, let them not want to frequent his presence because once he was a publican. He would show them now that the repentant sinner is better than the man who has never sinned.

He plunged his quill into the bronze ink-well and heard a rustling of wings to his right. An angel seemed to come to his ear and dictate. With a sure, rapid hand he started to write: "The Book of the Generation of Jesus Christ, son of David, son of Abraham. Abraham begot. . ."

He wrote and wrote until the east began to glow bluish-white and the first cock was heard to crow.

They departed, with Thomas and his horn in the lead. He tooted, and the village awoke. "Farewell," he shouted, "see you soon in the kingdom of heaven." Jesus came behind with the disciples and the mob of ragamuffins and cripples from Nazareth who still followed him, augmented now by new ones from Cana. They were waiting. He can't possibly forget us, they said to themselves. The blessed hour will come when he'll turn towards us too, and rid us of hunger and disease. . . . Today Judas remained at the end of the procession. He had found a set of large travelling-bags and he halted before each door and spoke to the housewives in a half-beseeching, half-threatening voice. "On our side, we work for you, poor things, so that you can be saved. On your side, you can help us—keep us from starving to death. You must know that even saints have to eat to get strength to save mankind. Some bread, cheese, raisins, dates, a handful of olives: no matter what it is, God writes it down and repays you in the next world. You give one split olive and he'll repay you with a whole orchard."

And if any housewife dallied in opening her larder, he shouted at her:

"Why so tight-fisted, lady? Tomorrow, day after tomorrow, maybe even tonight the heavens will open, the fire will fall and of all your goods nothing will be spared except what you give to us. If you're saved, you miserable creature, you'll owe it to the bread and olives and bottle of oil you gave me!"

The frightened women opened their larders, and by the time Judas reached the edge of the village his sacks were overflowing with alms.

Winter had begun; the earth shivered. Many trees, standing completely bare, were cold. Others—the olive, date, cypress—were blessed by God and retained their finery intact summer and winter. Similarly with men: all the poor were cold, like the bald trees. . . . John had thrown his woollen robe over Jesus and now, shivering, was in a hurry to reach Capernaum in order to open his mother's trunks. Old Salome had woven many things in her lifetime and her heart was noble and generous. He would portion out warm clothes to the companions, and devil care if old lickpenny Zebedee grumbled. It was Salome, with her obstinacy and sweetness, who governed the house.

Philip was hurrying too, his thoughts on his bosom friend Nathanael, hunched over as he was all day long in Capernaum, sewing up and patching sandals and moccasins. His life was being lost in this way. Where could he find time to lift his mind to God, to lean Jacob's ladder against the heavens, and mount! Oh, when will I get there, Philip thought, to unveil the great secret to the poor wretch, so that he too can be saved!

They took a turning, leaving Tiberias behind them on their left—Tiberias, despised by God, with its Baptist-murdering tetrarch condemned to the fires of hell. Matthew approached Peter to ask him everything he remembered about the river Jordan and the Baptist, so that he could write it all down event by event; but Peter recoiled and turned his face aside to avoid inhaling the publican's breath. Saddened, Matthew wedged the partly-filled notebook under his arm. He lagged behind and finding two carters who went to and from Tiberias, questioned them in order to learn —and to set down in his book—how the wicked murder took place. Was it true that the tetrarch became drunk and that his stepdaughter Salome danced before him naked. . . ? Matthew

335

had to learn all the details in order to immortalize them in writing.

They had by this time arrived at the large well outside Magdala. Clouds had covered the sun: a pale darkness fell over the face of the earth. Black threads of rain hung down, joining sky and soil. . . . Magdalene lifted her eyes to her skylight and saw the heavens blacken. "Winter is upon us," she murmured; "I must move quickly." She twirled the bobbin and began with great speed to spin the choice wool she had found. She intended to weave a warm cloak for her beloved so that he would not be cold. From time to time she glanced towards the yard and admired her grand pomegranate with its burden of fruit. She was guarding the pomegranates and not cutting them, for she had vowed them all to Jesus. God is exceedingly merciful, she reflected. One day my beloved will again pass through this narrow street and then I shall fill my arms with pomegranates and place them at his feet. He will bend over, take one and refresh himself. . . . While spinning, and admiring the pomegranate-tree, she turned her life over in her mind. It began and ended with Jesus, the son of Mary. What sorrow, what joy she had had! Why had he left her, opening her door on that final night to flee like a burglar? Where had he gone? Was he still wrestling with shadows instead of digging the soil, fashioning wood or fishing the sea; instead of having a wife (women too were God's creatures) and sleeping next to her? Ah, if he would only pass once more through Magdala so that she could run and place her pomegranates at his feet, to refresh him!

While she meditated on all this and rotated the bobbin with her quick skilled hand, she heard cries and tramping in the street and the sound of a horn—halloo! wasn't it cross-eyed Thomas the pedlar—and then she heard a shrill voice:

"Open, open your doors. The Kingdom of heaven is here!"

Magdalene jumped up, her heart leaping for joy. He had come! He had come! Cold and warm shudders passed through her entire body. Forgetting her kerchief, she rushed out, her hair flowing down to her shoulders. She went through the yard and appeared on the doorstep. Then she saw the Lord. Uttering a joyous cry, she fell at his feet. "Rabbi, rabbi," she purred, welcome!"

She had forgotten the pomegranates and her vow. She hugged

the sacred knees, and her blue-black hair, which still smelt from its old accursed perfumes, spilt out over the ground.

"Rabbi, rabbi, welcome," she purred, and she dragged him gently towards her poor house.

Jesus bent over, took her by the hand and lifted her up. Bashful and enchanted, he held her just as an inexperienced bridegroom holds his bride. His body rejoiced from its very roots. It was not Magdalene he had lifted from the ground, but the soul of man—and he was its bridegroom. Magdalene trembled, blushed, spread her hair over her bosom to hide it. Everyone looked at her with astonishment. How she had pined away, lost her colour! Purple rings circled her eyes, and her firm full mouth had withered like an unwatered flower. As she and Jesus walked hand in hand they felt they were dreaming. Instead of treading the earth they were floating in the air and proceeding. Was this a wedding? Was the ragged multitude which followed behind, filling the whole street, their marriage procession? And the pomegranate-tree which was visible in the yard with its burden of fruit: was it a kind spirit or a household goddess, or perhaps a simple thrice-fortunate woman who had given birth to sons and daughters and now stood in the middle of her yard and admired them?

"Magdalene," Jesus said softly, "all your sins are forgiven, for you have loved much."

She leaned over, wonderfully happy. She wanted to say, I am a virgin! but she was so overjoyed, she could not open her mouth.

She ran, pillaged the pomegranate-tree, filled her apron and made a tower of the cool red fruit at the Beloved's feet. What happened next was precisely what she had so ardently desired. Jesus bent down, took a pomegranate, opened it, filled his hand with seeds, and refreshed his throat. Then the disciples stooped in their turn. Each took a pomegranate and refreshed himself.

"Magdalene," Jesus said, "why do you look at me with such troubled eyes, as though you were saying good-bye to me?"

"My Beloved, I have been saying hello and good-bye to you every single instant since the day I was born." She spoke so softly that only Jesus and John, who were close to her, could hear.

After a moment's silence, she continued: "I must look at you, because woman issued from the body of man and still cannot

337

detach her body from his. But you must look at heaven, because you are a man, and man was created by God. Allow me to look at you therefore, my child."

She pronounced these momentous words, "My child!" in such a low voice that not even Jesus heard her. But her own breast filled out and stirred as though she were giving suck to her son.

A murmur arose in the crowd. New invalids suddenly arrived and occupied the entire yard.

"Rabbi," said Peter, "the people are grumbling and impatient."

"What do they want?"

"A kind word; a miracle. Look at them."

Jesus turned. In the turbulent air of the squall which was coming he perceived a multitude of half-opened mouths full of longing, and of eyes which were gazing at him with anguish. An old man came forward through the crowd. His eyelashes had fallen out: his eyes were like two wounds. Around his skeleton-like neck hung ten amulets, each containing one of the Ten Commandments. He leaned on his forked staff and stood himself in the doorway.

"Rabbi," he said, his voice all grievance and pain, "I am one hundred years old. Hanging around my neck, constantly before me, are God's Ten Commandments. I have not disobeyed a single one of them. Every year I go to Jerusalem and offer a sacrificial ram to holy Sabaoth. I light candles and burn sweet-incense. At night instead of sleeping, I sign psalms. I look sometimes at the stars, sometimes at the mountains—and wait, wait for the Lord to descend so that I may see him. That is the only recompense I desire. . . . I've waited now for years and years, but in vain. I have one foot in the grave, yet I still have not seen him. Why, why? Mine is a great grievance, rabbi. When shall I see the Lord; when shall I find peace?"

As he spoke he grew continually angrier. Soon he was banging his forked staff down on the ground and shouting.

Jesus smiled. "Old man," he replied, "once upon a time there was a marble throne at the eastern gate of an important city. On this throne sat a thousand kings blind in the right eye, a thousand kings blind in the left eye, and a thousand kings who had sight in both eyes. All of them called God to appear so that they might see him, but all went to their graves with their wishes unfulfilled. When the kings had died, a pauper, barefooted and hungry, came and sat on the throne. 'God,' he whispered, 'the eyes of man cannot bear to look directly at the sun, for they are blinded. How then, Omnipotent, can they look directly at you? Have pity, Lord; temper your strength, turn down your splendour so that I, who and poor and afflicted, may see you!' Then—listen old man!— God became a piece of bread, a cup of cool water, a warm tunic, a hut, and in front of the hut, a woman giving suck to an infant. The pauper stretched forth his arms and smiled happily. 'Thank you, Lord,' he whispered. 'You humbled yourself for my sake. You became bread, water, a warm tunic and my wife and son in order that I might see you. And I did see you. I bow down and worship your beloved·many-faced face!' "

No one spoke. The old man sighed like a buffalo and putting forth his forked staff, disappeared into the crowd. Next, a young man, newly-married, lifted his fist and shouted, "They say you hold fire to burn up the world—to burn up our homes and children. Is this the kind of love you claim to bring us? Is this the justice: fire?"

Jesus's eyes filled with tears. He pitied this newly-married youth. Truly, was this the justice he brought: fire? Was there no other way to attain salvation?

"Tell us clearly what we have to do to be saved," cried a house-owner who then elbowed his way through the gathering in order to come close for the answer, since he was hard of hearing.

"Open your hearts," thundered Jesus, "open your larders, divide your belongings among the poor! The day of the Lord has come! Whoever stingily retains a loaf of bread, a jar of oil or a strip of land for his final hours will find that bread and that jar and that earth hanging around his neck and dragging him down to hell."

"My ears are buzzing," said the house-owner. "Excuse me if I leave, but I feel dizzy."

He went off in a rage towards his rich villa. "Listen to that! Divide our belongings among the scabby rabble! Is that justice? Damn him to hell." Mumbling to himself and cursing, he continued on.

Jesus watched him disappear. "Wide is the gate of hell," he said with a sigh, "wide the road and strewn with flowers. But the gate to God's kingdom is narrow, the way uphill. While we live we may choose, for life means freedom. But when death comes, what's done is done and there is no deliverance."

"If you want me to believe in you," shouted a man with crutches, "perform a miracle and heal me. Shall I enter the kingdom of heaven lame?"

"And I leprous?"

"And I with only one arm?"

"And I blind?"

The cripples moves forward in one body and stood threateningly in front of him. Losing all sense of restraint, they began to shout. A blind old man lifted his staff:

"Cure us," he howled, "or you won't leave our village alive!"

Peter ripped the staff out of the old man's hands. "With a soul like yours, buzzard-eyes, you'll never see the light!"

The cripples drew together and became ferocious. The disciples became ferocious in their turn and placed themselves next to Jesus. Magdalene, terrified, put out her hand to bolt the door, but Jesus stopped her.

"Magdalene, my sister," he said, "this is an unfortunate generation—all flesh. Habits, sins, and fat crush their souls. I push away flesh, bones and entrails to find the soul, and I find nothing. Alas, I think the only cure is fire!"

He turned to the multitude. His eyes were now dry and pitiless.

"Just as we scorch the fields before sowing, in order for the good seed to thrive, so shall God scorch the earth. He has no mercy for thorns, tares or tarragon. That is the meaning of justice. Farewell!"

He turned to Thomas. "Blow your horn. We're leaving!"

He put forth his staff. The benumbed people made way and he passed through. Magdalene ran into her house, seized her kerchief and—leaving the wool half-spun, the earthenware pot on the mantle and the poultry unfed in her yard—tossed the doorkey into the middle of the road; then without looking back, silent and tightly wrapped in her kerchief, she followed the son of Mary.

XXIII

THE night was in its infancy when they arrived at Capernaum. The squall had passed over their heads. The north wind had blown and pushed it towards the south.

"We'll all sleep at our house," said Zebedee's two sons. "It's big, and there's room for everyone. That's where we'll set up camp."

"And old Zebedee?" said Peter, laughing. "He wouldn't give a drop of water to an angel."

John reddened. "Trust in the master," he said. "His breath will have a good effect on him, you'll see."

But Jesus did not hear. He was marching in front, his eyes filled with the blind, the lame, and the leprous. . . . Ah, if I could only blow on every soul, he thought, and cry to it, Awake! Then, if it did awake, the body would become soul and be cured.

As they entered the large market-town, Thomas inserted the horn between his lips in order to blow. But Jesus put out his hand. "Don't," he said. "I'm tired. . . ." And indeed, his face was pale and the flesh around his eyes had turned blue. Magdalene knocked at the first door to ask for a cup of water. Jesus drank and recovered his strength.

"I owe you a cup of cool water, Madgalene," he said to her with a smile.

He remembered what he had said to the other woman, the Samaritan, at Jacob's well.

"I shall repay you with a cup of immortal water," he added.

"You gave it to me a long time ago, rabbi," Magdalene answered with a blush.

They passed by Nathanael's cottage. The door was open and the master of the house stood in the yard under his fig tree. Pruning-hook in hand, he was removing the tree's dead branches. Philip quickly cut himself off from the group of travellers and entered.

"Nathanael," he said, "I have something to tell you. Stop your pruning." He went into the house. Nathanael followed and lit the lamp. "Forget your lamps, your fig trees and your house," Philip said to him, "and come."

"Where?"

"Where? But haven't you heard the news? The end of the world is here! Today or tomorrow the heavens will open and the world will be reduced to ashes. Move quickly and enter the ark so that you can be saved."

"What ark?"

"The bosom of the son of Mary, the son of David—our rabbi from Nazareth. He's just returned from the desert, where he met God. The two of them talked and decided on the destruction and salvation of the world. God placed his hand on our rabbi's hair. 'Go and choose who is to be saved,' he said. 'You are the new Noah. Look, here is the key to the ark so that you can open and close it,' and he gave him a key of gold. He has it hanging around his neck, but the human eye cannot see it."

"Speak clearly, Philip. I'm all confused. When did all these wonders take place?"

"Just now, I tell you, in the Jordan desert. They killed the Baptist, and his soul went into our rabbi's body. To see him, you wouldn't recognize him. He's changed—grown wild, and sparks fly from his hands. Why, just now at Cana he touched the paralysed daughter of the centurion of Nazareth, and all at once she jumped up and started to dance. Yes, I swear it by our friendship! We mustn't lose any time. Come!"

Nathanael sighed. "Look here, Philip, I was so well set up, I had so many orders. Look, look at all these sandals and moccasins waiting to be finished. My business was sailing full speed ahead, and now. . ." He threw a lingering glance around him, looked at his beloved tools, the stool on which he sat and patched, the cobbler's knife, the awls, the waxed string, the wooden tacks. . . . He sighed again.

"How can I leave them?" he murmured.

"Don't worry, you'll find tools of gold up above. You'll mend the golden sandals of the angels, you'll have eternal, innumerable orders. You'll sew, you'll rip, you won't lack work. Only move quickly, come and say to the master: 'I'm with you!'—nothing else. I'm with you and I'll follow you wherever you go—to the death!' That's what we've all sworn."

"To the death!" said the cobbler, shuddering. His body was huge, but he had the heart of a miller.

"It's just a way of speaking, poor thing," the shepherd said to reassure him. "That's what we've all sworn, but don't be afraid—we're headed for majesty, not for death. This man, my friend, is not a man. No, he's the Son of man!"

"It's not the same, eh?"

"The same? Aren't you ashamed to say that? Didn't you ever hear anyone read the prophet Daniel? Son of man means Messiah, in other words, King! He's going to sit on the throne of the Universe very soon, and we—as many as were clever enough to join him—are going to divide up the honours and the wealth. You won't walk barefooted any more. You'll wear golden sandals and the angels will stoop to tie your laces. Nathanael, I tell you it's a good deal. Don't let it slip out of your hands. What more need I say than to inform you that Thomas joined us. He smelt something good, the rascal, gave the very shirt off his back to the poor, and ran. So, you run too. He's at Zebedee's house now. Come on, let's go!"

But Nathanael held back, unable to decide. "Look here, Philip, you'll have to answer for the consequences," he said at last. "And I warn you: if I find the going rough, I leave for good. I'm ready for anything, short of getting myself crucified."

"All right, all right," said Philip, "we'll both make ourselves scarce in that case. Do you think I've gone completely mad? . . . Agreed? Let's go!"

"Well, then—in God's name!" He locked the door, put the key under his shirt, and the two of them departed arm in arm for Zebedee's house.

Jesus and the disciples sat warming themselves in front of the lighted fire while old Salome went in and out, overjoyed. All her illnesses had disappeared. She went in and out, setting the table, and her pride in her sons and in serving the holy man who would bring the kingdom of heaven was insatiable. John leaned over

343

and whispered into his mother's ear. By glancing at the disciples he made her notice how they shivered, dressed as they were in summer linens. The mother smiled, went inside, opened her trunks and took out woollen clothes. Then, quickly—before her husband's return—she divided them up among the companions. The thickest robe, one of brilliantly white wool, she threw tenderly over Jesus' shoulders. He turned and smiled at her.

"Bless you, mother Salome," he said. "It is right and just that you should care for the body. The body is the camel on which the soul mounts in order to traverse the desert. Care for it, therefore, so that it will be able to endure."

Old Zebedee came in and looked at the unexpected visitors. He greeted them half-heartedly, then sat down in a corner. These gangsters (that is what he called them) did not please him at all. Who invited them to come and take over his home? And his lavish wife had already laid them out a magnificent feast! Curse the day this new fanatic sprouted up. It wasn't bad enough that he had stolen both his sons! No, besides that there were the arguments all day long with his idiotic wife, who took the two boys' part. They had acted well, she said. This man was a true prophet: he would become king, throw out the Romans and sit on Israel's throne. Then John would be enthroned to his right, Jacob to his left—great lords, not fishermen in rowboats, but great important lords! Why, do you think they should rot away their entire lives here on the water? . . . Day and night Zebedee was nagged with this—and more—by the old idiot, who would bang her foot on the floor and shout. Sometimes he cursed and smashed whatever happened to be in front of him; sometimes he gave up in despair and went off to roam the edge of the lake like a madman. In the end he had given himself up to drink. . . . And now—what next!—all these gangsters had transported themselves to his house: nine immense mouths; and they had with them that expert a thousand times kissed—that Magdalene. They sat themselves down in a circle around the table, and did not even turn to look at him—him, the master of the house—or to ask his permission. So that's what we've come to! Was it for these parasites that he and his ancestors had slaved for so many years? He flew into a rage and jumping up, shouted:

"Just a minute my fine fellows—whose house is this, yours or mine? Two and two make four. Will you tell me, please?"

"It's God's,' answered Peter, who had downed quite a few drinks and was in a merry mood. "God's, Zebedee. Haven't you heard the news? Nothing anymore is yours or mine, everything is God's."

"The law of Moses. . ." Zebedee began, but Peter interrupted him before he could work up steam:

"What do I hear—the law of Moses? That's done with, Zebedee, finished, gone for a nice long walk and never coming back. Now we have the Law of the Son of man. Understand? We're all brothers! Our hearts have broadened, and with our hearts the law has also broadened. It now embraces the whole of mankind. The entire world is the Promised Land. The frontiers are gone! I, the very man you see before you, Zebedee, shall go proclaim the word of God to the nations. I'll get clear to Rome—yes, don't laugh— and I'll grab the emperor by his Adam's apple, knock him down and sit myself on the throne. And why not! As the master said, we're no longer your kind of fishermen. We don't catch fish— we're fishers of men. And a word to the wise: flatter us, bring us plenty of wine and food, because one day—and quickly too— we'll be great lords. You give us one dry piece of bread, and we'll repay you with a whole oven-full in a few days. And what loaves! Immortal! You'll eat and eat, and they'll never be consumed."

"Poor fellow, I already see you crucified upside-down," growled Zebedee, who had slunk away again to his corner. Listening to Peter's words he had gradually begun to feel afraid. I'd better keep my mouth shut, he thought. You never know what will happen. The world is a sphere, and turns. It's just possible that one day these madmen. . . Let's play it safe then, to be on the inside!

The disciples laughed in their beards. They knew perfectly well that Peter was in a merry mood and joking; but inside themselves —though they still were not drunk enough to speak out—they secretly spun the same thoughts. Impressiveness, rank, clothes of silk, golden rings, abundant food—and to feel the world under the Jewish heel: that was the kingdom of heaven.

Old Zebedee took another drink and mustered up courage.

"And you, teacher," he said, "aren't you going to open your mouth? You started all this, and now you sit back cool as a cucumber while we others sweat it out. . . . Look here, can you tell me in the name of your God why I should see my goods scattered and not scream about it?"

"Zebedee," Jesus answered, "there was once a very rich man who reaped, vintaged, gathered in the olives, stuffed his jugs, ate, filled himself and then lay down on his back in his yard. 'My soul,' he said, 'you have many belongings. Eat, drink and be merry!' But as he said this a voice was heard from the sky: 'Fool, fool— this night you shall surrender your soul to hell. What will you do with all the goods you have amassed?'. . . Zebedee, you have ears, you hear what I say to you; you have a mind, you understand what I mean. May this voice of heaven be above you, Zebedee, night and day!"

The old proprietor lowered his head and did not speak again.

Just then the door opened and Philip appeared on the threshold. Behind him, an immense gawky bean-stalk, was Nathanael. His heart no longer chimed two bells at once; he had made his decision. He approached Jesus, stooped and kissed his feet.

"My master," he said, "I am with you to the death."

Jesus placed his hand on the curly buffalo-like head. "Welcome, Nathanael. You make sandals for everyone else and go barefoot yourself. That pleases me very much. Come with me!" He seated him at his right and handed him a slice of bread and a cup of wine. "To become mine," he said, "eat this mouthful of bread and drink this cup of wine."

Nathanael ate the bread, drank the wine and all at once felt strength flow into his bones and soul. The wine rose like the sun and permeated his mind. Wine, bread and soul became one.

He was sitting on hot coals. He wanted to speak but was too bashful.

"Speak, Nathanael," the master said to him. "Open your heart and relieve yourself."

"Rabbi," he replied, "I want you to know that I've always been poor; I've lived and eaten from day to day and have never had time to study the Law. I'm blind, rabbi. Forgive me. . . . That's what I want you to know. I've had my say and I feel better."

Jesus caressingly touched the newly-enlightened man's broad shoulders.

"Don't sigh, Nathanael," he said, laughing. "Two paths lead to God's bosom. One is the path of the mind, the other the path of the heart. . . . Listen to the story I shall tell you:

"A poor man, a rich man and a rake died on the same day and appeared before God's tribunal at the same hour. None of them had ever studied the Law. God frowned and asked the poor man, 'Why didn't you study the Law while you were alive?'

" 'Lord,' he answered, 'I was poor and hungry. I slaved day and night to feed my wife and children. I didn't have time.'

" 'Were you poorer than my faithful servant Hillel?' God asked angrily. 'He had no money to pay to enter the synagogue and hear the Law being explained, so he climbed onto the roof, stretched himself out and listened through the skylight. But it snowed and he was so absorbed in what he heard that he did not realize it. In the morning when the rabbi entered the synagogue he saw that it was dark. Raising his eyes, he discovered a man's body over the skylight. He mounted to the roof, dug away the snow and exhumed Hillel. He took him in his arms, carried him down, lit a fire, and brought him back to life. Then he gave him permission to enter and listen after that without paying, and Hillel became the famous rabbi whom the whole world has heard of. . . . What do you have to say to that?'

" 'Nothing, Lord,' murmured the poor man, and he began to weep.

"God turned to the rich man. 'And you, why didn't you study the Law while you were alive?'

" 'I was too rich. I had many orchards, many slaves, many cares. How could I manage?'

" 'Were you richer,' God snapped, 'than Harsom's son Eleazar, who inherited a thousand villages and a thousand ships? But he abandoned them all when he learnt the whereabouts of a sage who was explaining the Law. What do you have to say for yourself?'

" 'Nothing, Lord,' the rich man murmured in his turn, and he too began to weep.

"God then turned to the rake. 'And you, my beauty, why didn't you study the Law?'

347

" 'I was exceedingly handsome and many women threw themselves at me. With all the amusement I had, where could I find time to look at the Law?'

" 'Were you handsomer than Joseph, who was loved by the wife of Putiphar? He was so beautiful that he said to the sun, "Shine, sun, so that I may shine." When he unfolded the Law the letters opened up like doors and the meaning came out dressed in light and flames. What do you have to say?'

" 'Nothing, Lord,' murmured the rake, and he too began to weep.

"God clapped his hands and called Hillel, Eleazar and Joseph out from Paradise. When they had come, he said: 'Judge these men who because of poverty, wealth, and beauty did not study the Law. Speak, Hillel. Judge the poor one!'

" 'Lord,' answered Hillel, 'how can I condemn him? I know what poverty means, I know what hunger means. He should be pardoned!'

" 'And you, Eleazar?' said God. 'There is the rich one. I hand him over to you!'

" 'Lord,' replied Eleazar, 'how can I condemn him? I know what it is to be rich—death! He should be pardoned!'

" 'And you, Joseph? It's your turn. There is the handsome one!'

" 'Lord, how can I condemn him? I know what a struggle it is, what a terrible martyrdom, to conquer the body's loveliness. He should be pardoned!' "

Jesus paused, smiled, and looked at Nathanael. But the cobbler felt uneasy.

"Well, what did God do next?" he asked.

"Just what you would have done," Jesus answered with a laugh.

The simple cobbler laughed too. "That means I'm saved!" He seized both the master's hands and squeezed them hard. "Rabbi," he shouted, "I understand. You said there were two paths leading to God's bosom, the path of the mind and the path of the heart. I took the path of the heart and found you!"

Rising, Jesus went to the door. A strong wind had come up and the lake was bellowing. The stars in the heaven were innumerable fine grains of sand. He recalled the desert, shuddered, and closed the door. "Night is a great gift from God," he said. "It is the Mother of man and comes quietly and tenderly to cover him. It rests its cool hand on his forehead and effaces the day's cares from his body and soul. Brothers, it is time to surrender ourselves to night's embrace."

Old Salome heard him and rose. Magdalene also got up from the corner by the fire where, bowed over, she had been happily listening to the Beloved's voice. The two women laid out the mats and brought covers. Jacob went to the yard, carried in an armful of olive-logs and heaped them on the fire. Jesus, standing erect in the middle of the house with his face turned towards Jerusalem, lifted his hands and in a deep voice pronounced the evening prayer: "Open your doors to us, O Lord. The day goes down; the sun falls, the sun disappears. Eternal, we come to your doors. We implore you: pardon us. We implore you: have mercy upon us. Save us!"

"And send us nice dreams, Lord," Peter added. "In my sleep, Lord, let me see my aged green boat all new and with a red sail!" He had drunk much and was in a jolly mood.

Jesus lay down in the centre, surrounded by the disciples. They occupied the entire length and breadth of the house. Zebedee and his wife, finding no room, went to an outbuilding; and with them went Magdalene. The old man grumbled. He was deprived of his comforts. Turning in a rage to his wife, he said in a loud voice, so that Magdalene would hear:

"What next! Thrown out of my own house by a pack of foreigners. Look what we're reduced to!"

But the old lady turned to the wall and did not answer him.

This night Matthew again remained awake. He squatted under the lamp, removed the partly-filled notebook from under his shirt and began to compose—how Jesus entered Capernaum, how Magdalene joined them; and the parable told by the master: There was once a very rich man. . . . When he finished writing he blew out the lamp and then he too went to bed, but a little to one side, because the disciples still had not become accustomed to his breath.

No sooner had Peter closed his eyes than he fell asleep. Straightway an angel came down from heaven, quietly opened his temples and entered him in the form of a dream. A great crowd seemed to be assembled on the shore of the lake. The teacher stood there too, admiring a brand new boat, green with a red sail, which was drifting in the water. On the rear part of her prow gleamed a great painted fish, identical with the fish that was tattooed on Peter's chest. "Who does that beautiful boat belong to?" Jesus asked. "It's mine," Peter proudly replied. "Go, Peter, take the rest of the companions and sail out to the middle so that I can admire your courage!"

"With pleasure, rabbi," said Peter. He detached the cable. The rest of the companions jumped in. A favourable wind blew over the stern, the sail swelled out and they reached the open sea singing.

But suddenly a whirlwind arose. The boat twirled around, her creaking hull ready to crack. She started to ship water and sink. The disciples, fallen face-down on the deck, raised a great lament. Peter seized hold of the mast and shouted, "Rabbi, rabbi, help!" and lo! there in the thick darkness he perceived the white-clad rabbi walking towards them over the waters. The disciples lifted their heads and saw him. "A ghost! a ghost!" they cried out, trembling. "Don't be afraid," Jesus said to them, "it's me!" Peter answered him, "Lord, if it is really you, order me also to walk on the waves and to come and meet you."

"Come!" Jesus ordered him. Peter jumped out of the boat, stepped on the waves and began to walk. But when he saw the enraged sea he became paralysed with fear. He started to sink. "Lord, save me," he screamed, "I'm drowning!" Jesus put out his hand and pulled him up. "Man of little faith," he said, "why were you afraid? Have you no confidence in me? Look!" He raised his hand over the waves and said, "Be still!" and all at once the wind subsided, the waters became calm. Peter burst into tears. His soul had been put to the test this time also, and once more it had emerged with disgrace.

Uttering a loud shout, he awoke. His beard was sprinkled with tears. He sat up on the mat, leaned his back against the wall and sighed. Matthew, who was still awake, heard him.

"Why did you sigh, Peter?" he asked.

For a second Peter resolved to play deaf and not answer him. To be sure, he did not relish conversations with publicans. But the dream was choking him and he felt he had to pull it out from within him in order to find relief. He therefore crawled near to Matthew and began to relate it to him, and the more he related, the more he embroidered. Matthew listened insatiably, recording it all in his mind. Tomorrow at daybreak, God-willing, he would copy it into his book.

Peter finished, but within his breast his heart still pitched, just like the boat in the dream. Suddenly he shook with fright.

"Could the master really have come in the night and taken me with him to the open sea in order to test me? Never in my life have I seen a sea more alive, a boat more real or fear more palpable. Perhaps it wasn't a dream. . . . What do you think, Matthew?"

"It most certainly wasn't a dream. This miracle definitely took place," Matthew answered, and he began to turn over deeply in his mind how he could set it down the next day on paper. It would be extremely difficult because he was not entirely sure it was a dream, nor was he entirely sure it was the truth. It was both. The miracle happened, but not on this earth, not on this sea. . . . Elsewhere—but where?

He closed his eyes to meditate and find the answer. But sleep came, and took him along.

The next day there was a continuous downpour with strong winds, and the fishermen did not set sail. Shut up in their huts they mended their nets and talked about the odd visitor who was lodging at old Zebedee's. It seemed he was John the Baptist resuscitated. Immediately after the executioner's stroke the Baptist bent down, picked up his head, replaced it on his neck and was off in a flash. But to prevent Herod from catching him again and once more cutting off his head, he went and entered the son of the Carpenter of Nazareth and they became one. Seeing him, you went out of your mind. Was he one, or two? It was bewildering. If you looked him straight in the face, he was a simple man who smiled at you. If you moved a bit, one of his eyes was furious and wanted to eat you, the other encouraged you to come closer. You approached and grew dizzy. Without knowing what was happening to you, you abandoned your home and children and followed him!

An old fisherman heard all this and shook his head. "This is what happens to those who don't get married," he said. "All they want to do is save the world, by hook or by crook. The sperm rises to their heads and attacks their brains. For God's sake, all of you: get married, let your forces loose on women and have children in order to calm yourselves!"

Old Jonah had heard the news the previous evening and had waited and waited in his shack. This can't last, he thought. Surely my sons will come to see if I'm dead or alive. He waited the whole night, hoped and then lost hope, and in the morning put on the high captain's boots which were made when he got married and which he only wore on great occasions, encased himself in a torn oilcloth and went off in the rain towards the house of his friend Zebedee. Finding the door open, he entered.

The fire was lit. Ten or so men and two women sat cross-legged in front of the fire. He recognized one of the women—it was old Salome. The other was young. He had seen her somewhere, but he could not remember where. The house was in half darkness. He recognized his two sons Peter and Andrew when they turned momentarily and their faces were illuminated by the fire-glow. But no one heard him come in and no one turned to see him. All were listening with heads thrust forward and mouths agape to someone who faced directly towards him. What was he saying? Old Jonah, all ears, opened his mouth and listened. Now and then he caught a word: "justice," "God," "kingdom of heaven. . . ." The same—year in, year out! He was sick of it. Instead of telling you how to catch a fish, mend a sail, caulk a boat, or how to avoid getting cold, wet or hungry—they sat there and spoke about heaven! Confound it, didn't they have anything to say about the earth and the sea? Old Jonah became angry. He coughed so that they would hear him and turn around. No one turned. He raised his huge leg and brought his captain's boot thundering down—but in vain. They were all hanging on the lips of the pale speaker.

Old Salome was the only one who turned. She looked at him but did not see him. Old Jonah went forward therefore and squatted in front of the fireplace, just behind his two sons. Putting out his huge hand he touched Peter on the shoulder and shook him. Peter turned, saw his father, placed his finger to his lips in a signal for him not to speak, and once again turned his face towards the pale youth just as though this was not Jonah, his own father, just as though it was not months since he had seen him last. First Jonah felt aggrieved, then angry. He took off his boots (which had begun to pinch him) so that by throwing them in the teacher's face he could silence him at long last and be able to talk to his children. He had already lifted the boots and was swinging them to gather momentum when he felt a restraining hand behind him. Turning, he saw old Zebedee.

"Get up, Jonah," his friend whispered into his ear. "Let's go inside. Poor fellow, I've got something to tell you."

The old fisherman put his boots under his arm and followed Zebedee. They entered the inner part of the house and sat down side by side on Salome's trunk.

"Jonah," Zebedee began, stammering because he had drunk too much in an attempt to drown his rage, "Jonah, my much-buffeted friend, you had two sons—write them off. I too had a pair of sons, and I wrote them off. It seems their father is God, so why are we butting in? They look at us as if to ask, 'Who are you, greybeard?'. . . It's the end of the world, my poor Jonah!

"At first I got angry too. I felt like grabbing the harpoon and throwing them out. But afterwards I saw there was no solution, so I crawled back into my shell and handed the keys over to them. My wife sees eye to eye with them, poor thing. She's getting a little senile, you know. So mum's the word, old Zebedee, and mum's the word, old Jonah—that's what I wanted to tell you. What's the use of kidding ourselves? Two and two make four: we're licked!"

Once more old Jonah put on his boots and wrapped himself in his oilskin. Then he gazed at Zebedee to see if he had anything more to say. He had not, so Jonah opened the door, looked at the sky, looked at the earth: darkness like pitch; rain, cold. . . . His lips moved: "We're licked," he grumbled, "we're licked. . . ," and he splashed through the mud back towards his shack.

While Jonah went puffing along, the son of Mary held his palms out to the fire as if praying to the spirit of God which, hidden in the flames, gives warmth to men. His heart had opened up; he held out his palms and spoke:

"Think not that I have come to abolish the law and the prophets. I have come not to abolish the old commandments but to extend them. You have seen inscribed on the tables of Moses: You shall not kill! But I say to you that whoever is even angry with his brother and lifts his hand against him, or only speaks an unkind word to him, will be hurled down into the flames of hell. You have seen inscribed on the tables of Moses: You shall not commit adultery! But I say to you that whoever even looks at a woman lustfully has already committed adultery in his heart. The impure glance brings the lecher down to hell. . . .

"The old law instructs you to honour your father and your mother; but I say, Do not imprison your heart within your parents' home. Let it emerge and enter all homes, embrace the whole of Israel from Mount Hermon to the desert of Idumea and even beyond: east and west—the entire Universe. Our father is God, our mother is Earth. We are half soil and half sky. To honour your father and your mother means to honour Heaven and Earth."

Old Salome sighed. "Your words are hard, rabbi, hard for a mother."

"The word of God is always hard," Jesus replied.

"Take my two sons," the old mother murmured, crossing her hands. "Take them, they are yours."

Jesus heard the orphaned mother and felt that all the sons and daughters of the world were suspended from his neck. He recalled the black he-goat he had seen in the desert with all the sins of the people enclosed in blue amulets and hanging from its neck. Without speaking, he leaned towards old Salome, who had given him her two sons. He seemed to be saying to her, Look, here is my neck, hang your sons around it. . . .

He threw a handful of vine-branches onto the fire. The flames swept over them. For a long time Jesus watched the fire hissingly consume the branches, then he turned again to the companions.

"He who loves father and mother more than me is not worthy to come with me; and he who loves son or daughter more than me is not worthy to come with me. The old commandments are no longer large enough to hold us, neither are the old loves."

He paused for a moment, then continued: "Man is a frontier, the place where earth stops and heaven begins. But this frontier never ceases to transport itself and advance towards heaven. With it the commandments of God also transport themselves and advance. I take God's commandments from the tables of Moses and extend them, make them advance."

"Does God's will change then, rabbi?" asked John, surprised.

"No, John beloved. But man's heart widens and is able to contain more of God's will."

"Forward, then," shouted Peter, jumping up. "Why are we sitting? Let's go proclaim the new commandments to the world."

"Wait for the rain to stop so we don't get wet!" hissed Thomas mockingly.

Judas shook his head, infuriated. "First we've got to chase out the Romans," he said. "We must liberate our bodies before we liberate our souls—each in its proper order. Let's not start building from the roof downwards. First comes the foundation."

"The foundation is the soul, Judas."

"I say the foundation is the body!"

"If the soul within us does not change, Judas, the world outside us will never change. The enemy is within, the Romans are within, salvation starts from within!"

Judas jumped up, boiling. For a long time he had kept his heart from crying out. He had listened and listened, storing everything in his breast, but now he could bear it no longer.

"First throw out the Romans!" he shouted again, choking. "First the Romans!"

"But how can we throw them out?" asked Nathanael, who had begun to feel uneasy and to cast sidelong glances at the door. "Will you tell us how, Iscariot?"

"Revolution! Remember the Maccabees! They expelled the Greeks. It's our turn now, it's time for new Maccabees to expel the Romans. Afterwards, when everything is in our own hands again, we can settle about rich and poor, injured and injurer."

No one spoke. The disciples were not sure which of the two roads to take. They gazed at the teacher and waited. He was looking thoughtfully at the flames. . . . When would men understand that only one thing exists in both the visible and invisible worlds—the soul.

Peter rose. "Excuse me," he said, "but these are complicated discussions and I don't understand them. Experience will teach us which is the foundation. Let's wait and see what happens. Master, give us the authority to go out by ourselves in order to bring the Good News to men. When we return we'll talk it all over again."

Jesus raised his head and swept his eyes over the disciples. He nodded to Peter, John and Jacob. They came forward and he placed his hands heavily on their heads.

"Go, with my blessing," he said. "Proclaim the Good News to men. Do not be afraid. God will hold you in his palm and keep you from perishing. Not a single sparrow falls from the sky without his will, and you are worth many sparrows. God be with you! Come back quickly, and may thousands of souls be suspended from your necks. You are my Apostles."

The three apostles received the blessing. Opening the door, they went out into the tempest, and each took a different road.

The days went by. Zebedee's yard filled with people in the morning and emptied in the evening. The sick, the lame and those possessed with devils came from every direction. Some wept, others grew furious and shouted at the Son of man to perform a miracle and cure them. Wasn't this why God had sent him? Let him appear then in the courtyard! . . . Hearing them day after day Jesus became sad. He would go out to the yard and touch and bless each one, saying. "There are two kinds of miracles, my brothers, those of the body and those of the soul. Have faith only in the miracles of the soul. Repent and cleanse your souls, and your flesh will be cleansed. The soul is the tree. Sickness, health, Paradise and the Inferno are its fruits."

Many believed and as soon as they believed felt their blood spurt up and fill their benumbed bodies. They threw away their crutches and danced. Others, as Jesus leaned his hand against their extinguished eyes. felt light flow out from the tips of his fingers. They raised their eyelids and shouted with joy, for now they saw the world!

Matthew kept his quill ready and his eyes and ears open. He did not allow even a single word to fall to the ground, but collected everything and placed it on paper. And thus little by little, day by day, the Gospel—the Good News—was composed. It took root, threw out branches and became a tree to bear fruit and nourish those born and yet to be born. Matthew knew the Scriptures by heart. He noticed how the teacher's sayings and deeds were exactly the same as the prophets, centuries earlier, had proclaimed; and if once in a while the prophecies and Jesus' life did not quite match, it was because the mind of man was not eager to understand the hidden meaning of the sacred text. The word of God had seven levels of meaning, and Matthew struggled to find at which level the incompatible elements could find their mates. Even if he occasionally matched things by force, God forgives! Not only would he forgive, he desired this. Every time Matthew took up his quill, did not an angel come and bend over his ear to intone what he was to write?

Today was the first time Matthew clearly understood where to start and how the life and times of Jesus had to be taken in hand. First of all, where he was born and who his parents and grandparents were, for fourteen generations. He was born in Nazareth to poor parents—to Joseph the carpenter and Mary, daughter of Joachim and Anne. . . . Matthew took up his quill and called silently upon God to enlighten his mind and give him strength. But as he began to inscribe the first words on the paper in a beautiful hand, his fingers stiffened. The angel had seized him. He heard wings beat angrily in the air and a voice trumpeted in his ear, "Not the son of Joseph! What says the prophet Isaiah: 'Behold, a virgin shall conceive and bear a son.' . . . Write: Mary was a virgin. The archangel Gabriel descended to her house before any man had touched her, and said: 'Hail Mary, full of grace, the Lord is with you!' Straightway her bosom bore fruit. . . . Do you hear? That's what you're to write. And not in Nazareth; no, he wasn't born in Nazareth. Do not forget the prophet Micah: 'And you, Bethlehem, tiny among the thousands of Judah, from you shall come forth One who is to be ruler in Israel, and his root is from of old, from the days of eternity.' . . . Jesus was therefore born in Bethlehem, and in a stable. What says the infallible psalm: 'He took him from the stable where the lambs were suckling, in order to make him shepherd of the flock of Jacob.' Why do you stop? I have freed your hand—write!" But Matthew grew angry. He turned towards the invisible wings at his right and growled softly, so that the sleeping disciples would not hear him: "It's not true. I don't want to write, and I won't!" Mocking laughter was heard in the air, and a voice: "How can you understand what truth is, you handful of dust? Truth has seven levels. On the highest is enthroned the truth of God, which bears not the slightest resemblance to the truth of men. It is this truth, Matthew Evangelist, that I intone in your ear. . . . Write: 'And three Magi, following a large star, came to adore the infant. . .' "

The sweat gushed from Matthew's forehead. "I won't write! I won't write!" he cried, but his hand was running over the page, writing.

Jesus heard Matthew's struggle in his sleep, and opened his eyes. He saw him bent over and gasping under the lamp, the squeaking quill running furiously over the page, ready to break.

"Matthew, my brother," he said to him quietly, "why are you groaning? Who is above you?"

"Don't ask me, rabbi," he replied, his quill still racing over the paper. "I'm in a hurry. Go to sleep."

Jesus had a presentiment that God must be over him. He closed his eyes so that he would not disturb the holy possession.

XXIV

THE days and nights passed by. One moon came and went; the next came. Rain, cold, fires in the hearth; saintly vigils in old Salome's house. . . . Capernaum's poor and aggrieved came each evening after the day's work in order to hear the new Comforter. They arrived poor and unconsoled; they returned to their wretched huts rich and comforted. He transplanted their vineyards, boats and joys from earth to heaven; explained to them how much surer heaven was than earth. The hearts of the unfortunate filled with patience and hope. Even Zebedee's savage heart began to be tamed. Little by little Jesus' words penetrated him, lightly inebriating his mind. This world thinned out and over his head hovered a new world made of eternity and imperishable wealth. In this odd new world Zebedee and his sons and old Salome and even his five caiques and full coffers would live evermore. Best not grumble therefore when he saw these uninvited guests day and night in his house or sitting around his table. It would come, the recompense would come.

In mid-winter the sun-drenched halcyon days arrived. The sun gleamed, warmed the bare bones of the earth and duped the almond-tree in the middle of Zebedee's yard: it thought that spring had come and began to put out buds. The kingfishers had been awaiting these warm merciful days, for they wished to entrust their eggs to the rocks. All the rest of God's birds procreate in the spring, the kingfisher in mid-winter. God pitied them and promised to allow the sun to come up warm several days in the winter, just for their sakes. Rejoicing, these nightingales of the sea flew now over the waters and rocks of Gennesaret and warbled their thanks to God for having once more kept his word.

During these lovely days the remaining disciples scattered to the fishing-caiques and near-by villages so that they too could try their wings. Philip and Nathanael set out overland to meet with their friends the farmers and shepherds and proclaim the word of God to them. Andrew and Thomas went to the lake to catch the fishermen. Unsociable Judas departed all by himself towards the mountain to let the anger filter out of his system. Much of the master's behaviour pleased him but there were some things he simply could not stomach. Sometimes the wild Baptist thundered through Jesus' mouth, but sometimes the same old son of the Carpenter still bleated: Love! Love! . . . What love, clairvoyant? Whom to love? The world has gangrene and needs the knife—that's what I say!

Matthew was the only one who stayed in the house. He did not want to leave, for the teacher might speak, and Matthew must not let his words be carried away by the winds; he might perform some miracle, and Matthew must see it with his own eyes in order to recount it. And then again, where could he go, to whom could he talk? No one would come near him, because once upon a time he had been a dirty publican. He therefore remained in the house and from his corner glanced stealthily at Jesus, who sat in the yard under the budding almond tree. Magdalene was at his feet and he was speaking to her softly. Matthew strained his huge ear to catch a word, but in vain. All he could do was watch the rabbi's severe afflicted face and his hand, which every so often skimmed Magdalene's hair.

It was the Sabbath and pilgrims had set out in the early morning from distant villages—farmers from Tiberias, fishermen from Gennesaret, shepherds from the mountains—to hear the new prophet speak to them about Paradise, the Inferno, unfortunate mankind, and God's mercy. They would take him—the sun was out, it was a splendid day—and bring him up to the green mountainside where they could strew themselves on the warm grass to listen to him, and perhaps they might even fall sweetly asleep on the springtime turf. They assembled therefore outside in the road, for the door was shut, and shouted for the teacher to emerge.

"Magdalene, my sister," said Jesus, "listen, the people have come to fetch me."

But Magdalene, lost within the rabbi's eyes, did not hear. And of all that he had been telling her for such a long time, she had heard nothing. She rejoiced solely in the sound of his voice: the voice told her everything. She was not a man, she had no need for words. Once she had said to him, "Rabbi, why do you talk to me about the future life? We are not men, to have need of another, an eternal life; we are women, and for us one moment with the man we love is everlasting Paradise, one moment far from the man we love is everlasting hell. It is here on this earth that we women live out eternity."

"Magdalene, my sister," Jesus repeated to her, "the people have come to fetch me. I must go." He got up and opened the door. The road was full of ardent eyes and shouting mouths, and of the groaning sick who were stretching out their hands. . . . Magdalene appeared at the door and put her hand over her mouth so that she would not scream. "The people are wild beasts, wild bloodthirsty beasts who will devour him," she murmured as she watched him calmly go in the lead, with the crowd behind him bellowing. . . .

Jesus advanced with great calm strides towards the mountain which rose above the lake, the mountain where he had once opened his arms to the multitude and cried: Love! Love! But between that day and this his mind had grown fierce. The desert had hardened his heart; he still felt the Baptist's lips like two lighted coals upon his mouth. The prophecies flashed on and off within him, the divine inhuman shouts came back to life and he saw God's three daughters, Leprosy, Madness and Fire, tear through the heavens and descend.

When he reached the summit of the hill and opened his mouth to speak, the ancient prophet bounded up from within him, and he began to shout:

" 'The fearful army comes bellowing from the ends of the earth; terrible and quick-moving, it comes. Not one of the warriors limps from fatigue, not one is sleepy or ever sleeps. Not a single waistband is slack or a single shoe-thong broken. The arrows are sharp, the bow-strings taut: the horses' hoofs are hard stones, the chariot-wheels are whirlwinds. It roars menacingly like a lioness. Whomever it catches is lifted up in its teeth and can be saved by no one!' "

"What army is this?" shouted an old man whose white hair was standing on end.

"What army is this? Do you ask, you deaf, blind, foolish people!" Jesus lifted his hand to heaven. "It is the army of God, wretches! From a distance God's warriors seem to be angels, but up close they are flames. I myself took them for angels this past summer on this very rock where I now stand—for angels, and I cried: Love! Love! But now the God of the desert has opened my eyes. I saw. They are flames! 'I can endure you no longer,' shouts God. 'I am coming down!' Lamentation is heard in Jerusalem and in Rome, lamentation upon the mountains and at the tombs. The earth weeps for its children. God's angels descend to the scorched earth, search with their lamps to discover where Rome was, where Jerusalem. Between their fingers they crumble the ashes and smell them. . . . This must have been Rome, they say, this Jerusalem; and they toss the ashes to the winds."

"Is there no salvation?" cried a young mother, squeezing her baby to her breast. "I'm not talking for myself, but for my son."

"There is!" Jesus answered her. "In every flood God contrives an ark and entrusts to it the leaven of the future world. I hold the key!"

"Who'll be saved as leaven? Whom will you save? Do we have time?" cried another old man, and his lower jaw trembled.

"The Universe passes before me and I choose. On one side, all those who overate, overdrank, overkissed. On the other, the starving and oppressed of the world. These, the starving and oppressed, I choose. They are the stones with which I shall build the New Jerusalem."

"The New Jerusalem?" shouted the people, their eyes shining.

"Yes, the New Jerusalem. I did not know it myself until God confided the secret to me in the desert. Love comes only after the flames. First this world will be reduced to ashes and then God will plant his new vineyard. There is no better fertilizer than ashes."

"No better fertilizer than ashes!" echoed a hoarse joyous voice which seemed like his own, only deeper and happier. Surprised, Jesus turned and saw Judas behind him. He felt afraid, for the redbeard's face flashed lightning, as if the coming flames had already fallen over him. He rushed forward and clasped Jesus' hand.

"Rabbi," he whispered with unexpected tenderness, "my rabbi. . ."

Never in his life had Judas spoken so tenderly to anyone. He felt ashamed. He stooped and pretended to ask something, though he himself did not know what; then, finding a small premature anemone, he pulled it up by the roots.

In the evening when Jesus returned and sat down once more on his stool in front of the hearth and stared into the fire, he suddenly felt that his inner God was in a hurry and would allow him to wait no longer. He was overcome by sorrow, exasperation, and shame. Once more today he had spoken and waved the flames over the heads of the people. The simple fishermen and farmers had been frightened for a moment, but had then immediately regained their composure and quieted down. All these threats seemed to them like a fairy-tale, and several of them had fallen asleep on the warm grass, lulled by his voice.

Uneasy and silent, he watched the fire. Magdalene stood in the corner and looked at him. She wanted to speak but did not dare. At times a woman's speech gladdens a man, at times it makes him furious. Magdalene knew this and remained silent.

There was no sound. The house smelt of fish and rosemary. The window facing the courtyard was open. Somewhere near-by some medlar-trees must have bloomed, for their aroma, sweet and peppery, entered with the evening breeze.

Jesus got up and closed the window. All these springtime perfumes were the breath of temptation; they were not the proper atmosphere for his soul. It was time to leave and find the air which suited him. God was in a hurry.

The door opened. Judas entered and flitted his blue eyes around the room. He saw the teacher with his eyes pinned on the fire; saw high-rumped Magdalene, Zebedee, who had fallen asleep and was snoring, and under the lamp, the scrivener scratching away and filling his paper with blots. . . . He shook his head. Was this their great campaign? Was this the way they were setting out to conquer the world? One clairvoyant, one secretary, one woman of questionable morals, a few fishermen, one cobbler, one pedlar—and all taking their ease at Capernaum! He curled himself up in a corner. Old Salome had already set the table.

"I'm not hungry," he growled, "I'm sleepy," and he shut his eyes so that he would not see the others, who presently sat down to dinner. A moth came in through the door, beat its wings around the flame of the lamp, went for a moment and fluttered in Jesus' hair, then began to circle the room.

"We're going to have a visitor," said old Salome. "We'll be pleased to see him."

Jesus blessed the bread, divided it, and they began to eat. No one spoke. Old Zebedee, who had been awakened for the meal, felt suffocated by so much silence. He could stand it no longer.

"Talk, lads!" he said, banging his fist down on the table. "What's wrong? Is there a corpse in front of us? Haven't you heard: whenever three or four sit down and eat and do not talk about God, they might as well be sitting at a funeral supper. The old rabbi of Nazareth—God bless him—told me that once, and I still remember it. So speak, son of Mary. Bring God again into my house! Excuse me if I call you son of Mary, but I still don't know what to call you. Some call you the son of the Carpenter, others the son of David, son of God, son of man. Everyone is confused. Obviously the world has not yet make up its mind."

"Old Zebedee," Jesus answered, "countless armies of angels fly around God's throne. Their voices are silver, gold, clear running water, and they praise God—but from a distance. No angel dares come too close, except one."

"Which?" asked Zebedee, opening wide his well-wined eyes.

"The angel of silence," Jesus answered, and spoke no more.

The master of the house choked, filled his cup with wine, and emptied it in one gulp.

This visitor is certainly a kill-joy, he said to himself. You feel like you're sitting at table with a lion. . . . No sooner had this thought come to him than he became frightened, and got up.

"I'm going to find old Jonah so that we can talk a bit like human beings," he said, making for the door. But at that instant some light footsteps were heard in the yard.

"Look, here's our visitor," said old Salome, rising. They all turned. On the threshold stood the old rabbi of Nazareth.

How he had aged and melted away! There remained of him nothing but a few bones wrapped in a sun-baked hide—just enough to give the soul something to catch hold of so that it would not fly away. Lately the rabbi had been unable to sleep, and when he sometimes did fall asleep, at dawn, he would have a strange and recurring dream: angels, flames. . . , and Jerusalem in the form of a wounded, howling beast which had scrambled up Mount Zion. The other day at dawn he had dreamt the dream again and his endurance had given out. He jumped up, left his house, reached the fields, traversed the plain of Esdrelon. God-trodden Carmel towered before him. The prophet Elijah would surely be standing at its summit. It was he who dragged the rabbi onward and gave him the strength to mount. The sun went down when the old man reached the top of the mountain. He knew that three great upright rocks stood as an altar on the scared summit and that around them were the bones and horns of the sacrifices. But as he approached and raised his eyes, he uttered a cry: the stones were gone! This evening three men with gigantic bodies stood on the summit. They were dressed all in white, like snow, and their faces were made of light. Jesus, the son of Mary, was in the centre. To his left stood the prophet Elijah clutching burning coals in his fists; to his right Moses with twisted horns and holding two tables inscribed in letters of fire. . . . The rabbi fell on his face. "Adonai! Adonai!" he whispered, trembling. He knew that Elijah and Moses had not died, and that they would reappear on earth on the fearful day of the Lord. It was a sign that the end of the world had come. They had appeared—there they were!—and the rabbi shook with fear. He raised his eyes to look . . . Gleaming in the dusk were the three gigantic sun-drenched rocks.

The rabbi had been opening the Scriptures for many years, for many years he had breathed in the breath of Jehovah. He had learnt how to find God's hidden meaning behind the visible and the invisible—and now he understood. He raised his crosier from the ground—where did his ramshackle body find such strength?— and set out for Nazareth, Cana, Magdala, Capernaum—every-where! in order to find the son of Mary. He had heard of his return from the desert of Judea, and now as he followed his trail throughout Galilee he saw how the farmers and fishermen had already begun to compose the new prophet's legend: what miracles he performed, what words he uttered, which stone he stood on to speak, and how the stone was suddenly covered with flowers. . . . He questioned an old man whom he met on the road. The old man lifted his hands to heaven. "I was blind. He touched my eyelids and gave me my sight. Though he instructed me not to say a word about it, I'm making the rounds of the villages, telling everyone."

"And can you inform me where he is now to be found, old man?"

"I left him at Zebedee's house, in Capernaum. Step lively to catch him before he ascends to heaven."

The rabbi stepped lively, was overtaken by nightfall, found old Zebedee's house in the dark, and entered. Old Salome jumped up to welcome him.

"Salome," the rabbi said, striding over the threshold, "peace be on this house, and may the wealth of Abraham and Isaac fall to its owners."

He turned and was dazzled by the sight of Jesus.

"Many birds pass over me and bring me news of you," he said. "My child, the road you have taken is rough and exceedingly long. God be with you!"

"Amen!" Jesus answered in a grave voice.

Old Zebedee put his hand to his heart and greeted the visitor. "What wind blows you to my house, father?" he asked.

But the rabbi—perhaps he did not hear—sat down next to the fire without replying. He was tired, cold and hungry—but he had no desire to eat. Two or three routes stretched before him, and he did not know which to take. . . . Why had he set out and come? To reveal his vision to Jesus. But if this vision was not from God? The rabbi knew very well that the Tempter could take on God's face in order to delude men. If he disclosed what he had seen to Jesus, the demon of arrogance might take possession of his soul, and then he would be lost and he, the rabbi, would have to answer for it. Should he guard his secret and follow him wherever he went? But was it right for him, the rabbi of Nazareth, to follow this most bold of revolutionaries, a man who boasted he would bring a new law? Just now on his way, had he not found Cana in confusion because of something Jesus had said which was contrary to the Law? It seemed that on the holy Sabbath he had gone to the fields and had seen someone at work clearing ditches and irrigating his garden. "Man," he had said to him, "if you know what you are doing, may joy descend upon you; if you know not, may you be cursed, for you transgress the Law." When the old rabbi heard this, he felt troubled. This rebel is dangerous, he reflected. Look sharp, Simeon, or you'll find yourself damned—and at your age!

Jesus came and sat down beside him. Judas was lying on the ground; he had closed his eyes. Matthew had gone to his place under the lamp and was waiting, pen in hand. But Jesus did not speak. He watched the fire devour the wood and felt the rabbi next to him puffing as though he was still on the road.

Meanwhile old Salome made up a bed for the rabbi. He was an old man, he must have a soft mattress and a pillow. She also placed a small pitcher of water next to the bed so that he would not be thirsty during the night. Old Zebedee saw that the new visitor had not come for him. Taking his cudgel, he went out to find Jonah in order to breathe the breath of a human being again—his house was filled with lions. Magdalene and Salome withdrew to the inner rooms so that Jesus and the rabbi could be alone. They had a presentiment that the two men had weighty secrets to discuss.

But Jesus and the rabbi did not talk. They both understood perfectly that words can never empty and relieve the heart of man. Only silence can do that, and they kept silent. The hours went by. Matthew fell asleep with the quill in his hand; Zebedee returned after having had his fill of talk and lay down next to his old wife. It was midnight. The rabbi had had his fill also—of silence. He got up.

"We said a good deal tonight, Jesus," he whispered. "Tomorrow we shall resume!" He drew towards his bed with sagging knees.

The sun rose and mounted in the sky. It was almost noontime, but the rabbi still had not opened his eyes. Jesus had gone to the lake-shore to talk with the fishermen. He climbed into Jonah's boat to give him a hand with the fishing. Judas walked around aimlessly, all by himself like a sheepdog.

Old Salome leaned over the rabbi to try to hear if he was still breathing. He was. "Glory be to God, he is still alive," she murmured. She was about to go away when the old rabbi opened his eyes, saw her leaning over him, understood, and smiled:

"Don't be afraid, Salome," he said. "I'm not dead. I can't die yet."

"We've both grown old," Salome replied severely. "We're

travelling further and further from men and are approaching God. No one can know the hour or the moment. It's a sin, I believe, to say, 'I can't die yet.' "

"I can't die yet, dear Salome," the rabbi insisted. "The God of Israel gave me his word: 'You will not die, Simeon, unless you have seen the Messiah!' "

But as he said this his eyes opened wide with fear. Could he already have seen the Messiah? Could Jesus be the Messiah? Was the vision on Carmel a vision sent by God? If so, the time had come for him to die! A cold sweat bathed his whole body. He did not know whether to rejoice or to begin to wail. His soul rejoiced: the Messiah had come! But his ramshackle body did not want to die. . . . Panting, he got up, crawled to the door, sat down on the threshold to sun himself, and fell deep into thought.

Jesus returned towards nightfall, exhausted. He had fished with Jonah all day long. The boat overflowed with fish and Jonah, overjoyed, opened his mouth to speak but then changed his mind and waded knee-deep into the mass of twitching fish, looked at Jesus—and laughed.

That same night the disciples returned from the near-by villages. They squatted around Jesus and began to relate everything they had seen and done. Deepening their voices in order to frighten the farmers and fishermen, they had proclaimed the coming of the day of the Lord; but their auditors had continued to mend their nets tranquilly or to dig their gardens. Now and then they shook their heads, said, "We'll see. . . , we'll see. . ." and then changed the subject.

While the disciples were relating this, lo! the three Apostles suddenly returned. Judas, who was silent and sitting off to one side, could not contain his laughter when he saw them.

"What's this mess you're in, apostles!" he shouted, "Poor devils, they must have beaten you silly!"

And truly, Peter's right eye was swollen and running, John's cheeks were full of scratches and blood, and Jacob limped.

"Rabbi," said Peter with a sigh, "the word of God is a lot of trouble, a lot of trouble indeed!"

They all laughed, but Jesus looked at them thoughtfully.

"They did beat us silly," continued Peter, who was in a hurry to reveal everything and relieve his mind. "At first we said each one should take his own road. But then we were afraid, each one alone, and the three of us reunited and began the preaching. I climbed up on a rock or in a tree in the village square, clapped my hands or put my fingers in my mouth and whistled, and the people assembled. John spoke whenever there were plenty of women. That's why his cheeks are all scratched. When the men were in the majority, Jacob, with his deep voice, took over; and if he grew too hoarse, I got up and spoke. What did we say? The same things you say. But they received us with rotten lemons and boos because we brought, as they said, the ruin of the world. They fell on us, the women with their nails, the men with their fists, and now look, just look at the state we're in!"

Judas guffawed again, but Jesus turned and with a severe look closed the impudent mouth.

"I know that I send you as lambs among wolves," he said. "They will revile you, stone you and call you immoral because you make war on immorality; they will slander you, saying you want to abolish faith, family and fatherland because our faith is purer, our house wider and our fatherland the whole world! Gird yourselves well, comrades. Say good-bye to bread, joy and security. We are going to war!"

Nathanael turned and glanced anxiously at Philip. But Philip signalled to him as if to say: Don't be afraid—he talks that way just to test us. . . .

The old rabbi was very tired. He had lain down again on his bed, but his mind was wide open: he saw and heard everything. He had made his decision now, and felt tranquil. A voice rose up within him—his own? God's? perhaps it was both—and commanded him: Simeon, wherever he goes, follow him!

Peter prepared to re-open his mouth. He had more to tell, but Jesus put out his hand.

"That's enough!" he said.

He rose up. Jerusalem arose before his eyes: savage, full of blood and at the height of despair—which is where hope begins. Capernaum vanished along with its simple fishermen and peasants. The lake of Gennesaret sank away within him. Zebedee's house narrowed—the four walls approached each other and touched him. Suffocating, he went and opened the door.

Why did he stay here and eat, drink, have the fire lit for him and the table set noon and night? He was spending his time aimlessly. Was this how he intended to save the world? Wasn't he ashamed of himself?

He went into the yard, There was a warm wind which carried the smell of budding trees. The stars were strings of pearls around the neck and arms of the night. Below, at his feet, the earth tingled as though countless mouths were suckling at its breasts.

He turned his face towards the south, towards holy Jerusalem. He seemed to be listening intently and to be trying in the darkness to discern her hard face of blood-stained stones. And while his mind, ardent and despairing, flowed like a river past mountain and plain and was at last about to touch the holy city, suddenly it seemed to him that he saw a huge shadow stir in the yard under the budding almond tree. All at once something darker than night itself (that was how he was able to distinguish it) arose in the black air. It was his gigantic fellow-voyager. In the still night he could clearly hear her deep breathing, but he was not afraid. Time had accustomed him to her breath. He waited, and then slowly, commandingly, a tranquil voice from under the almond tree said, "Let us go!"

John had appeared at the doorway, troubled. He thought he heard a voice in the darkness. "Rabbi," he whispered, "whom are you talking to?"

But Jesus entered the house, put out his hand and took his shepherd's staff from the corner.

"Friends," he said, "let us go!" He marched towards the door without looking back to see if anyone was following him.

The old rabbi jumped out of his bed, tightened his belt and seized his crosier. "I'm coming with you, my child," he said, and he was the first to start for the door.

Old Salome was spinning. She rose also. She placed the distaff on her trunk and said, "I'm coming too. Zebedee, I leave you the keys. Farewell!" She unbelted the keys from around her waist and surrendered them to her husband. Then she wrapped herself tightly in her kerchief, surveyed her home and with a nod of her head bid it good-bye. Her heart had suddenly become that of a twenty-year-old girl.

Magdalene rose also, silent and happy. The agitated disciples got up and looked at each other.

"Where are we headed?" asked Thomas, hooking his horn onto his belt.

"At this time of night? Why in such a hurry? Won't tomorrow morning do?" said Nathanael, and he glanced sullenly at Philip.

But Jesus, with long strides, had already passed through the yard and begun his march towards the south.

THE foundations of the world were shaken because man's heart was shaken, crushed under the stones which men call Jerusalem, under the prophecies, the Second Comings, the anathemas, under the Pharisees and Sadducees, the rich who ate, the poor who were hungry, and under the Lord Jehovah, from whose beard and moustaches the blood of mankind had been running for centuries upon centuries into the abyss. No matter where you touched this God, he bellowed. If you said a kind word to him he lifted his fist and shouted, "I want meat." If you offered a lamb or your first-born son as a sacrifice, he screamed, "I don't want meat. Do not rend your clothes, rend your hearts. Turn your flesh into spirit, your spirit into prayer, and scatter it to the winds!"

Man's heart was crushed under the six hundred and thirteen written commandments of the Hebrew Law, plus the thousands of unwritten ones—yet it did not stir; under Genesis, Leviticus, Numbers, Judges and Kings—yet it did not stir. And then suddenly at the most unexpected moment a light breeze blew, not from heaven, but from below, on earth, and all the chambers of man's heart were shaken. Straightway Judges, Kings, the prophecies, anathemas, Pharisees, Sadducees and the stones which men call Jerusalem cracked, tottered and began to tumble down— at first within the heart, then in the mind and finally upon the earth itself. Haughty Jehovah once again tied on his leather master-craftsman's apron, once again took up his level and rule, went down to earth and personally began to help demolish the past and along with men, to build the future. But before anything else, he began the Temple of the Jews at Jerusalem.

Jesus went every day and stood on the blood-sprinkled paving stones. He looked at this overloaded Temple and felt his heart hammer against it and pull it down. It continued to stand, how-ever, gleaming in the sun like a golden-horned garlanded bull. The walls were veneered right up to the roof in white marble streaked with sea-blue: the Temple seemed to float upon a turbulent ocean. In front of him hung three tiers of chambers, one on top of the next. The lowest and widest was for the idolators, the middle one was for the people of Israel, and the highest for the twenty thousand Levites who washed and sandpapered, lit and extinguished the lamps, and cleaned the Temple. Day and night seven kinds of incense were burnt. The smoke was so thick that the goats sneezed seven miles away.

The humble ark which enclosed the Law, the ancestral ark their nomadic forefathers had transported across the desert, had moored itself to this summit of Zion, put out roots, sprouted up, dressed itself in cypress-wood, gold and marble—and become a Temple. At first the savage desert-god did not deign to inhabit a house, but so much did he like the smell of the cypress-wood and incense and the savour from the slaughtered beasts, that one day he lifted his foot and entered.

It was now two months since Jesus' arrival from Capernaum. Each day he went and stood in front of the Temple and looked at it; each day he seemed to see it for the first time. It was as though each morning he expected to find it crumbled to the ground and to be able to trample over it from end to end. He had no desire to see it any longer, nor did he fear it. In his heart it had already been destroyed. One day when the old rabbi asked him why he did not go in to worship, he shook his head and answered, "For years I circled the Temple, now the Temple is circling me."

"Jesus, those are boastful words," the rabbi objected, thrusting his aged head against his breast. "Aren't you afraid?"

"When I say 'I'," Jesus answered, "I do not speak of this body —which is dust; I do not speak of the son of Mary—he too is dust, with just a tiny tiny spark of fire. 'I' from my mouth, rabbi, means God."

"That is a still more terrible blasphemy!" cried the rabbi, covering his face.

"I am Saint Blasphemer, and don't forget it," Jesus replied with a laugh.

One day when he saw his disciples standing before the imposing building in open-mouthed admiration, he became angry.

"You find the Temple astonishing, don't you?" he said to them

373

sarcastically. "How many years were needed to build it? Twenty years? Ten thousand workmen? In three days I shall destroy it. Regard it well—for the last time. Say good-bye to it, for there shall not be left here one stone upon another that will not be thrown down!"

The frightened disciples stepped back. Could something have gone wrong with the teacher's mind? He had become so abrupt and strange lately, so obstinate. Odd, vacillating winds were blowing over him. Sometimes his face gleamed like the rising sun and everything around him was made to dawn; at other times his look was dark, his eyes despairing.

"Don't you feel sorry for it, rabbi?" John ventured.

"For what?"

"The Temple. Why do you want to demolish it?"

"So that I can build a new one. I shall build a new one in three days. But first of all, this one must vacate the land."

He took the shepherd's staff which Philip had presented him and banged it down on the paving. The wind of anger was now blowing over him. He looked at the Pharisees who were stumbling along and lacerating themselves against the walls, apparently blinded by the excessive splendour of God. "Hypocrites," he shouted at them, "if God took a knife and tore open your hearts, out would bound snakes, scorpions and filth!" The Pharisees heard, became frantic, and secretly decided to block this fearless mouth with dirt.

The old rabbi put his palm over Jesus' lips to silence him.

"Are you courting death?" he asked him one day, his eyes brimming with tears. "Don't you realize that the Scribes and Pharisees run continually to Pilate and demand your head?"

"I know, Father," Jesus replied, "but I know still more, still more. . . ."

Bidding Thomas sound the horn, he mounted his usual platform on Solomon's Porch and once more began to proclaim, "It has come, the day of the Lord has come!". . . Every day from morning till sunset he shouted in order to oblige the heavens to open up and hurl down their flames—because, as he well knew, man's voice is an all-powerful charm. You cried, "Come!" to the fire or the dew, to the Inferno or to Paradise, and it came. Similarly, he was calling Fire. It would purify the earth, would open the way for the appearance of Love. Love's feet are always pleased to step on ashes. . . .

"Rabbi," Andrew asked him one day, "why don't you laugh any more, why aren't you joyful like before? Why have you grown continually more ferocious?"

But Jesus did not answer. What could he say, and how could Andrew's naive heart understand? This world, he reflected, must be destroyed right down to its roots if the new world is to be planted. The old Law must be torn down, and it is I who shall tear it down. A new Law must be engraved on the tables of the heart, and it is I who shall engrave it. I shall widen the Law to make it contain friends and enemies, Jews and idolators: the Ten Commandments will burst into bloom! That is why I have come here to Jerusalem. It is here that the heavens will open. What will descend from heaven—the great miracle, or death? Whichever God desires. I am ready to ascend to heaven or to be hurled down into hell. Lord, decide!

The Passover was approaching. An unexpected vernal sweetness had flowed over the hard face of Judea. The routes of land and sea had opened up, and worshippers arrived from the four corners of the Jewish world. The bellowing tiers of the Temple stank from human beings, slaughtered animals, and dung.

Today a great number of the ragged and the lame had assembled outside Solomon's Porch. With pale hungry faces and burning eyes they looked maliciously at the well-fed Sadducees and at the rich merry burghers and their wives, who were weighted down with bracelets of gold.

"How long do you think you're going to laugh?" someone growled. "We'll soon cut your throats. The teacher said so: the poor will kill the rich and divide up their goods."

"You didn't hear very well, Manasses," snapped a pale man with sheep-like eyes and hair. "Poor and rich won't exist any more, they'll all be one. That's what the kingdom of heaven means."

"Kingdom of heaven," an ungainly bean-stalk of a man interrupted, "means that the Romans get out. A kingdom of heaven with Romans isn't possible."

"You understood nothing of what the teacher said, Aaron,"

replied a venerable man with rabbit-like lips. He shook his bald head. "Israelites and Romans, Greeks and Chaldeans don't exist—nor do Bedouins. We're all brothers!"

"We're all ashes!" shouted someone else. "That's what I understood; I heard it with my own ears. The teacher said, 'The heavens will open. The first flood was of water, this one will be of fire. All —rich and poor, Israelites and Romans: ashes!' "

" 'The olive tree will be shaken, but two or three olives will remain at the top, three or four on the highest branches.' The prophet Isaiah said that. . . . Courage, men. We'll be the remaining olives. All we have to do is keep the teacher close by, so that he doesn't get away from us!" These words were pronounced by a man with skin the colour of a charred pot, and round popping eyes which stared at the white dust-filled road to Bethany. "He's late today," he grumbled, "he's late. . . . Take care, lads! Don't let him get away from us!"

"Where can he go?" asked old rabbit-lip. "God told him to do battle in Jerusalem, and it's here he'll do battle!"

The sun was in the middle of the sky. The paving steamed; the stench increased with the torrid heat. Jacob the Pharisee appeared, his arms loaded with amulets. He was publishing the special grace of each: these cured smallpox, colic and erysipelas; these expelled demons; the most powerful and expensive killed your enemies. . . . He noticed the ragamuffins and cripples, recognized them. His envenomed mouth cackled maliciously: "Go to the devil!" and he spat three times into the air to be rid of them.

While the ragamuffins bickered, each one twisting the teacher's words in accordance with the longing of his own heart, a huge and venerable man with a long stick bolted in front of them, sweating, covered with dust, his wide still-unwrinkled face glistening.

"Melchizedek!" cried old rabbit-lip. "What's the good news from Bethany? Your face is all lit up!"

"Rejoice and exult, men!" shouted the old notable. Weeping continually, he began to embrace them all. "A corpse has been resurrected; I saw it with my own eyes. He got up out of the tomb and walked! They gave him water and he drank, they gave him bread and he ate and spoke!"

"Who? Who was resurrected, who was resurrected?" they all

376

demanded, falling upon the old chieftain. People in the neighbouring arcades heard. Men and woman ran. Several Levites and Pharisees also came near. Barabbas was going by; his ear caught the uproar, and he too joined the crowd. Melchizedek was delighted to see such a great multitude hanging on his lips. He leaned on his staff and proudly began to speak:

"Lazarus, the son of Eliakim. Does anyone know him? He died a few days ago and we buried him. One day went by, two, three—we forgot him. Suddenly, on the fourth day, we hear shouting in the street. I race outside and see Jesus, the son of Mary of Nazareth, with Lazarus's two sisters prostrate and kissing his feet, lamenting for their brother. 'If you'd been with him, rabbi, he wouldn't have died,' they screamed, wailing all the while and pulling out their hair. 'Bring him back from Hades, rabbi. Call him and he'll come!' Jesus took them both by the hand and lifted them up.

" 'Let us go,' he said.

"We all ran behind them until we came to the grave. There Jesus stopped. All the blood went to his head, his eyes rolled and disappeared, only the whites remained. He brought forth such a bellow you'd have thought there was a bull inside him, and we all got scared. Then suddenly while he stood there, trembling all over, he uttered a wild cry, a strange cry, something from another world. The archangels must shout in the same way when they're angry. . . . 'Lazarus,' he cried, 'come out!' And all at once we hear the earth in the tomb stir and crack. The tombstone begins to move; someone is gradually pushing it up. Fear and trembling . . . Never in my life have I feared death as much as I feared that resurrection. I swear that if I was asked what I wanted to see more, a lion or a resurrection, I would say a lion."

"Lord have mercy upon us! Lord have mercy upon us!" the people shouted, weeping. "Speak, father Melchizedek, speak!"

"The woman shrieked, many of the men hid themselves behind rocks, and we who remained trembled. The tombstone rose little by little. We saw two yellow arms and then a head all green, cracked and full of dirt; finally the skeleton-like body wrapped in the shroud. . . . It put forward one foot, then the other, and came out. It was Lazarus."

377

The old chieftain stopped to wipe away the sweat with his wide sleeve. All around him the people were howling. Some wept, others danced. Barabbas raised his huge hairy hand:

"Lies! lies!" he shouted. "He's commissioned by the Romans and cooked all this up with Lazarus. Down with traitors!"

"Shut your mouth!" bellowed a savage voice behind him. "What Romans?"

They all turned and immediately recoiled. Rufus the centurion was coming towards Barabbas with his whip held high. A pale blonde-haired girl grasped his arm. She had been standing and listening to old Melchizedek the whole time, the tears running from her large green eyes. Barabbas slid away into the assembled humanity and disappeared, and behind him ran Jacob the Pharisee with his amulets. He overtook him behind a column. There the two of them, their heads glued together, began to chatter: bandit and Pharisee became brothers. Barabbas spoke first.

"You think it's true?" he asked anxiously.

"What?"

"What they say: that he revived a corpse. . ."

"Listen well to what I'm going to tell you. I'm a Pharisee, you're a Zealot. Until now I always said Israel would be saved only with prayer, fasting and the holy Law. But now. . ."

"Now?" asked the Zealot, his eyes flashing.

"Now, Zealot, I'm beginning to see things your way. Prayer and fasting aren't enough. A knife has got to be put to work here. Do you understand me?"

Barabbas guffawed. "You're asking me? There's no better prayer than the knife. Well. . . ?"

"Let's start with him."

"Who? Speak clearly."

"Lazarus. It's of the first importance that we lower him once more into the ground. As long as the people see him they'll say, 'He was dead and the son of Mary resurrected him.' In this way the false prophet's glory will spread. . . . You're right, Barabbas, he's commissioned by the Romans to shout. 'Don't bother about the kingdom of the earth,' he says, 'keep your eyes on heaven!' And thus—while we waste our time looking at the sky—the Romans will sit on our necks. Understand?"

"Well. . . ? Do you want us to do away with him too, even if he's your brother?"

"He's no brother of mine, I want no part of him!" shouted the Pharisee, pretending to tear his robes. "I hand him over to you!"

This said, he pulled himself away from the column and began once more to hawk his talismans. He had wound Barabbas up well, and was content.

The crowd of paupers outside Solomon's Porch gave up hope of seeing Jesus arrive and began to disperse. Old Melchizedek purchased two white doves to offer as sacrifices in order to thank the God of Israel for taking pity on his people at last and sending them, after so many years, a new prophet.

The stones were on fire. The faces of the people vanished in the excessive light. Suddenly a cloud of dust arose on the road from Bethany. Happy cries; the whole village had closed up shop and was coming. First to appear were the children with palm-branches and laurels. Behind the palm-branches came Jesus, his face gleaming; further back the disciples, red-faced and sweating as though each one had personally raised a man from the dead; and last of all, completely hoarse from shouting, the Bethanites. They were all rushing to the Temple. Jesus mounted the stairs two at a time, passed the first tier and reached the second. A savage light gushed from his face and hands; and no one could go near him. For an instant the old rabbi, who was running breathlessly behind him like the others, tried to cross into the invisible arena surrounding the master, but straightway he drew back, as though licked by flames.

Jesus had just issued from God's kiln and his blood was still furiously bubbling. He still could not believe it, nor did he want to: was the power of the soul so great? Could it order the mountains, *Come!* and indeed move them? Could it tear apart the earth and bring forth the dead, destroy the world in three days and rebuild it in three days? But if the strength of the soul was so all-powerful, then all the weight of perdition or salvation fell upon the shoulders of mankind; the borders of God and man joined. . . . This was a terrifying, dangerous thought, and Jesus' temples drummed.

He had left Lazarus standing in his shroud over the tomb and had departed with unusual haste for the Temple of Jerusalem. It was the first time he had felt so invincibly that this world must at last see its end and that a new Jerusalem must rise from the tombs. The moment had come. This was the sign he had been waiting for. The hopelessly rotted world was a Lazarus. The time had come for him to cry out, "World, arise!" He had the obligation; and most frightening of all, as he now realized: he also had the strength. It was no longer possible for him to escape by saying, I am unable! He was able, and if the world failed to be saved, the entire sin must fall on him.

The blood rose to his head. On every side he saw the stares of the oppressed and the ragamuffins, who had all of their hopes pinned on him. Uttering a savage cry, he jumped onto a platform. The people swarmed around him. Smirking, the rich and well-fed stopped too, in order to hear. Jesus turned, saw them, and raised his fist.

"Listen, you who are rich," he shouted; "listen, lords of this world: Injustice, infamy and hunger can last no longer! God rubbed my lips with burning coals and I cry out: How long will you recline on beds of ivory and on soft mattresses? How long will you eat the flesh of the poor and drink their sweat, blood and tears? 'I can stand you no longer!' cries my God. The fire is approaching, the dead are being raised, the end of the world has come!"

Two huge ragamuffins seized him and lifted him above their heads. The multitude gathered round, waving palm leaves. Steam rose from the prophet's fiery head.

"I have come not to bring peace to the world, but a sword. I shall throw discord into the home, the son shall lift his hand against the father, the daughter against her mother, the daughter-in-law against her mother-in-law—for my sake. Whoever follows me abandons all. He that seeks on this earth to save his life, shall lose it; and he that for my sake loses this temporary life, shall gain life for all eternity."

"What does the Law say, rebel?" shouted a wild voice. "What do the Holy Scriptures say, Lucifer?"

"What say the great prophets Jeremiah and Ezekiel?" Jesus answered, his eyes glistening. "I shall abolish the Law engraved on the tables of Moses and shall engrave a new Law in man's heart. I shall remove the heart of stone which men now have, and give them a heart of flesh; and in this heart I shall plant a new Hope! It is I who engrave the new Law in the new hearts, and I am also the new Hope! I extend love; I open God's four great doors, the East, West, North and South, for all nations to enter. The bosom of God is not a ghetto, it embraces the entire world! God is not an Israelite, he is immortal Spirit!"

The old rabbi hid his face in his hands. He wanted to shout: Jesus, be quiet, this is a great blasphemy! but was too late. Wild cries of joy broke out. The poor howled with delight; the Levites booed, and Jacob the Pharisee tore his robes and spat into the air. The old rabbi gave up in despair. Weeping, he departed. "He's finished," he murmured as he went, "finished! What devil, what god shouts from within him?"

He went along, so fatigued that he stepped all over his feet. During all these days and weeks that he had been running behind Jesus, battling to understand who he was, his ramshackle body had completely melted away. Nothing was left now but a sun-baked hide wrapped around bones to which the soul clung and waited. Was this man the Messiah whom God had promised him, or wasn't he? All the miracles he performed could also be performed by Satan, who could even resurrect the dead. The miracles therefore did not give the rabbi sufficient basis to pass judgment; nor did the prophecies. Satan was a sly and exceedingly powerful archangel. In order to deceive mankind he was capable of making his words and actions fit the holy prophecies to perfection. For these reasons the rabbi lay in bed at night unable to sleep and begged God to take pity on him and to give him a sure sign. . . . What sign? The rabbi understood perfectly: death, his own death. When he brought this sign to mind, he shuddered.

He stumbled along in a cloud of dust. Bethany appeared at the top of the hill, fully devoured by the sun. Puffing, he began the ascent.

Lazarus's house was open. The villagers ran in and out in order to see and touch the resuscitated man, to listen carefully for his respiration, to discover if he could speak and if he was really alive —or if, perhaps, he was a ghost! Fatigued and reticent, Lazarus sat in the darkest corner of the house, for light bothered him. His legs, arms and belly were swollen and green, like those of a four-day corpse. His bloated face was cracked all over and it exuded a yellowish-white liquid which soiled the white shroud which he continued to wear: it had stuck to his body and could not be removed. In the beginning he had stunk terribly, and those who came close held their noses; but little by little the strench decreased until now he smelt only of earth and incense. From time to time he shifted his hand and removed the grass which had become tangled in his hair and beard. His sisters Martha and Mary were cleansing him of the soil and of the small earthworms which had attached themselves to him. A sympathetic neighbour had brought him a chicken and old Salome, squatting by the fireplace, was at present boiling it so that the resurrected man could drink the broth and regain his strength. The peasants came and stayed just a few moments to examine him attentively and speak to him. He answered their questions wearily with a laconic yes or no; and then others came from the village or the surrounding towns. . . . Today the blind village-chief came too. He put out his hand and fingered him avidly. "Did you have a pleasant time in Hades?" he asked laughing. "You're a lucky fellow, Lazarus. Now you know all the secrets of the underworld. But don't reveal them, wretch, or you'll drive everyone up here crazy. . . ." He leaned over to his ear and half-joking, half-trembling, asked: "Worms, eh? Nothing but worms. . . ?" He waited a considerable time, but Lazarus did not answer. The blind man became enraged, took his staff, and left.

Magdalene stood in the doorway and gazed down the road which led to Jerusalem. Her heart was crying like a small infant. All these nights she had been having bad dreams: she saw Jesus marry, and that meant death. The night before, it seemed she dreamt of him as a flying-fish which opened its fins, jolted out of the water and fell onto the land. It flapped spasmodically on the pebbles of the beach, struggling in vain to open its fins once more. Suffocating, its eyes began to grow dim. It turned and looked at her, and she all but perished in an effort to grasp it and replace it in the ocean. When she bent down and took it in her hand, however, it was dead. But all the time she held it, lamenting and bathing it in her tears, it grew, filled her embrace and became a dead man.

"I won't let him return to Jerusalem. . . , I won't let him.". . . She sighed and gazed down the white road in case he should appear.

But it was not Jesus who appeared on the road from Jerusalem. Instead, Magdalene saw her old father, all bent over and stumbling. Poor shrunken old man, she thought. In the awful state he's in, why does he want to follow our rabbi wherever he goes, like an aged faithful dog. I hear him get up at night, go out into the yard, prostrate himself and cry to God, "Help me, give me a sign!" But God allows him to torture himself, apparently punishing him because he loves him: and in this way the poor man is comforted.

She watched him mount now, supporting himself on his crosier. He frequently halted, looked back towards Jerusalem and stretched wide his arms, to catch his breath. . . . All these days that father and daughter were together at Bethany they both forgot the past and spoke to one another again. Seeing that his daughter had abandoned the evil road, the rabbi forgave her. He knew that all sins are washed away by tears, and Magdalene had wept much.

The old man arrived, breathless. Magdalene stepped aside so that he could go through the door, but he stopped and imploringly took her hand. "Magdalene, my child," he said, "you are a woman: your tears and caresses have great power. Fall at his feet, beg him not to return to Jerusalem. The Scribes and Pharisees grew even more ferocious today. I saw them talk secretly among themselves, poison dripping from their lips. They are plotting his death."

"His death!" exlcaimed Magdalene, and her heart felt crushed. "But can he die, Father?"

The old rabbi looked at his daughter and smiled bitterly. "We always speak that way about those we love," he murmured, and then was silent.

"But the rabbi is not a man like all the rest; no, he's not!" Magdalene said in despair. "He's not! he's not!" she repeated over and over again, in order to charm away her fears.

"How do you know?" asked the old man. His heart leapt up because he believed in the presentiments of women.

"I know," Magdalene answered. "Don't ask me how. I'm sure of it. Do not be afraid, Father. Who will dare touch him now that he's raised Lazarus?"

"Now that he has raised Lazarus, they're more frantic than ever. Earlier, they listened to his preaching and shrugged their shoulders. But now that the miracle has been made known, the people have found courage. 'He's the Messiah,' they shout; 'he revives the dead, his power is from God—let's go and join him.' Today men and women took palm branches and ran behind him. The cripples lifted their crutches and threatened; the poor became unruly. . . . The scribes and Pharisees see all this and fly into a maniacal rage. 'If we leave him a little while longer, we're done for,' they say, and they go incessantly to Annas, and from Annas to Caiaphas and from Caiaphas to Pilate—digging his grave. . . . Magdalene, my child, clasp his knees, don't let him ever enter Jerusalem again. We must all go back to Galilee!"

He recalled a sombre pock-marked face. "Magdalene," he said, "on my way here I saw Barabbas roaming about, his face as dismal as Charon's. When he heard my steps he hid himself in the bushes. That is a bad sign!"

His weak body went slack. His daughter took him in her arms and brought him inside. She fetched him a stool, and he sat down. She knelt at his side.

"Where is he now?" she asked. "Where did you leave him, Father?"

"At the Temple. He shouts and his eyes throw out flames: he'll set the holy building on fire! And what words, my God, what blasphemies! He says he'll abolish the Law of Moses and bring a new Law. He won't go to meet God at the top in Sinai, he'll meet him in his own heart."

The old man lowered his voice. "Sometimes, my child," he said, trembling, "I fear I'm going out of my mind. Or perhaps Lucifer—"

"Silence!" Magdalene commanded, and she placed both her hands over the old man's lips. . . .

They were still talking when the disciples, one behind the other, appeared at the door. Magdalene jumped up and looked, but Jesus was not among them.

"And the rabbi," she asked in a heart-rending voice, "where is the rabbi?"

"Don't be afraid," Peter answered her with a sullen expression. "He's coming right away."

Mary jumped up too. She left her brother and anxiously approached the disciples. Their faces were dark and troubled, their eyes dull. She leaned against the wall.

"The rabbi?" she murmured weakly.

"He's coming presently, Mary, he's coming. . . ," answered John. "If anything happened to him, would we leave him?"

The sulking disciples scattered throughout the house, one far away from the next.

Matthew drew his papers out from under his shirt and prepared to write.

"Speak, Matthew," said the old rabbi. "Say something, and you'll have my blessing."

"My Father," answered Matthew, "just now as we were returning all together, Rufus the centurion overtook us at the gate of Jerusalem. 'Stop,' he cried, 'I have orders for you!' We were all paralysed with fear. But the rabbi gave his hand tranquilly to the Roman. 'Welcome, friend,' he said, 'what do you want with me?'

" 'It's not me,' Rufus answered, 'but Pilate who wants you. Come with me, please.'

" 'I'm coming,' Jesus said calmly, and he turned his face towards Jerusalem.

"But we all fell upon him. 'Rabbi, where are you going?' we cried. 'We won't let you leave!'

"The centurion came between us and said, 'Don't be afraid, I give you my word he means well.'

" 'Go,' the master commanded us, 'and do not fear. The hour has not yet come.'

"But Judas interrupted. 'I'll come with you, master; I won't leave you.'

" 'Come,' said the master. 'I won't leave you either.' Off they went towards Jerusalem, the two in front and Judas behind like a sheep-dog."

While Matthew spoke, the disciples, without a word, approached and knelt on the floor.

"Your faces are troubled," said the rabbi. "You are hiding something from us."

"We have other worries, Father, other worries. . . ," Peter mumbled, and he fell once more into silence.

And indeed just now, along their way, evil demons had entered them. The raising of the dead had commenced. Evidently the day of the Lord was coming near; the master would mount his throne. The time had therefore come for them to divide up the spoils. It was there, in the dividing, that the disciples had begun to quarrel.

"I shall sit on his right hand, he loves me the most," said one. They all dashed forward and shouted:

"No, me! me!"

"Me!"

"Me!"

"I was the first to call him rabbi!" said Andrew.

"He comes more often to my dreams than to yours," Peter objected.

"He calles me 'beloved'," said John.

"And me!"

"And me!"

Peter's blood began to boil. "Step back—all of you!" he shouted. "Just the other day didn't he say to me, 'Peter, you are the rock, and upon you I shall build the new Jerusalem'?"

"He didn't say 'the new Jerusalem!' I have his words written down here," exclaimed Matthew, tapping the note book under his shirt.

"What did he say to me then, scribbler? That's what I heard!" said Peter angrily.

"He said: 'You are Peter, and upon this rock I shall build my church.' . . . My church, not Jerusalem—there's a big difference!"

"And what else did he promise me?" Peter shouted. "Why did you stop? It goes against your interests to continue, eh? What about the keys. . . ? Well, speak!"

Matthew, not very eagerly, took his notebook, opened it and read: " 'And I shall give you the keys of the kingdom of heaven. . .' "

"Go on! Go on!" Peter shouted triumphantly.

Matthew swallowed his saliva and bent again over his notebook.

" 'And whatever you bind upon earth shall be bound in heaven; and whatever you loose on earth shall be loosed in heaven. . . .' There—that's all!"

"And does it seem a mere trifle to you? I—listen, all of you—I hold the keys; it's I who open and close the gates of Paradise. If I want, I let you in; if I don't, I don't!"

At that point the disciples went wild and certainly would have come to blows if they had not already neared Bethany. But they felt ashamed in front of the villagers and swallowed their anger. Their faces, however, were still completely dark.

XXVI

MEANWHILE, Jesus marched along with the centurion, followed by Judas the sheep-dog. They entered the narrow twisting alleyways of Jerusalem and proceeded in the direction of the Temple, towards the tower which was Pontius Pilate's palace. The centurion was the first to speak.

"Rabbi," he said with emotion, "my daughter is marvellously well and thinks of you always. Every time she learns you're speaking to the people she secretly leaves our house and runs to hear you. Today I held her tightly by the hand. We were together, listening to you at the Temple, and she wanted to run to kiss your feet."

"Why didn't you let her?" Jesus asked. "One instant is enough to save the soul of man. Why did you let that instant go to waste?"

A Roman girl kiss the feet of a Jew! Rufus thought with shame, but he did not speak.

With a short whip which he held in his hand he forced the noisy crowd to make way for him. It was so hot you almost swooned, and there were clouds of flies. The centurion felt nauseated as he breathed in the Jewish air. He had been in Palestine so many years, yet he still was not accustomed to the Jewry. . . . They were passing now through the bazaar-ground, which was covered with straw mats. It was cooler here, and they slowed their pace.

"How can you talk to this pack of dogs?" the centurion asked.

Jesus blushed. "They are not dogs," he said, "but souls, sparks of God. God is a conflagration, centurion, and each soul a spark which should be revered by you."

"I am a Roman," answered Rufus, "and my God is a Roman. He opens roads, builds barracks, brings water to cities, arms himself in bronze and goes to war. He leads, we follow. The body and the soul you talk about are one and the same to us, and above them is the seal of Rome. When we die both soul and body die together —but our sons remain. That is what we mean by immortality. I'm sorry, but what you say about kingdoms of heaven seems just a fairy-tale to us."

After a pause, he continued: "We Romans are made to govern men, and men are not governed by love."

"Love is not unarmed," said Jesus, looking at the centurion's cold blue eyes, his freshly-shaven cheeks and fat short-fingered hands. "Love too makes war and runs to the assault."

"It isn't love, then," said the centurion.

Jesus lowered his head. I must find new wineskins, he reflected, if I'm to pour in new wine. New wineskins, new words. . .

At last they arrived. Towering before them, at once fortress and palace, was the tower which guarded within the haughty Roman Governor, Pontius Pilate. He detested the Jewish race and held a perfumed handkerchief in front of his nostrils whenever he walked in the lanes of Jerusalem or was compelled to speak with the Hebrews. He believed neither in gods nor in men—nor in Pontius Pilate, nor in anything. Constantly suspended around his neck on a fine golden chain was a sharpened razor which he kept in order to open his veins when he became weary of eating, drinking and governing, or when the emperor exiled him. He often heard the Jews shout themselves hoarse calling the Messiah to come and liberate them—and he laughed. He would point to the sharpened razor and say to his wife, "Look, here is my Messiah, my liberator." But his wife, without answering him, would turn away her head.

Jesus halted outside the tower's great door. "Centurion," he said, "you owe me a favour. Do you remember? The time has come for me to demand it of you."

"Jesus of Nazareth, to you I owe all the joy of my life," Rufus answered. "Speak. What I can, I'll do."

"If they seize me, if they put me in prison, kill me—do not do anything to save me. . . . Will you give me your word?"

They were now passing through the tower-gates. The guards lifted their hands and saluted the centurion.

"Is what you ask of me a favour?" said Rufus, astonished. "I don't understand you Jews."

Two huge negro guards stood outside Pilate's door.

"Yes, a favour, centurion," said Jesus. "Do you give me your word?"

Rufus nodded to the negroes to open the door.

Pilate sat reading on a raised throne which was decorated with grossly-carved eagles. Crisp, clean-shaven, with low forehead, hard grey eyes and sword-straight narrow lips, he lifted his head to look at Jesus, who was standing in front of him.

"Are you Jesus of Nazareth, king of the Jews?" he hissed teasingly, putting the perfumed handkerchief to his nostrils.

"I am not a king," Jesus answered.

"What? Aren't you the Messiah, and isn't it the Messiah that your fellow-countrymen the Abrahamites have been waiting for over so many generation—waiting for him to free them, to sit on the throne of Israel and to throw out us Romans? Why then do you say you're not a king?"

"My kingdom is not on earth."

"Where, then: on the water, in the air?" said Pilate, bursting into laughter.

"In heaven," Jesus calmly replied.

"Fine," said Pilate. "You can take heaven as a present, but don't touch the earth!"

He removed the thick ring he was wearing on his thumb, lifted it high into the light and looked at the red stone. Carved upon it was a skull surrounded by the words, "Eat, drink and be merry, for tomorrow you die."

"I find the Jews disgusting," he said. "They never wash themselves, and they have a God in their own image: long-haired, unwashed, grasping, boastful, and vindictive as a camel."

"Know that this God has already lifted his fist over Rome," Jesus said, again calmly.

"Rome is immortal," Pilate answered, yawning.

"Rome is the huge statue which the prophet Daniel saw in his vision."

"Statue? What statue? Whatever you Jews yearn for while you're awake, you see in your sleep. You live and die with visions."

"That is the way man begins his campaign—with visions. Little by little the shade thickens and solidifies, the spirit dons flesh and descends to earth. The prophet Daniel had his vision, and because he had it: that's that!—the spirit will take on flesh, descend to earth and destroy Rome."

"Jesus of Nazareth, I admire your audacity—or is it idiocy? It seems that you don't fear death, and that's why you speak with such freedom. .... I like you. Well, tell me about Daniel's vision."

"One night the prophet Daniel saw a huge statue. Its head was of gold, its breast and arms of silver, its stomach and thighs of bronze. Its shins were of iron, but its feet, at the very bottom, were of earth. Suddenly an invisible hand slung a stone at the earthen feet and shattered them; and immediately the entire statue—gold, silver, bronze and iron—rolled to the ground. . . . The invisible hand, Pontius Pilate, is the God of Israel, I am the stone, and the statue is Rome."

Pilate yawned once more. "I understand your game, Jesus of Nazareth, king of the Jews," he said wearily. "You insult Rome in order to make me angry, so that I'll crucify you and you'll swell the ranks of the heroes. You prepared everything very cleverly. You've even started, I hear, to revive the dead: yes, you're clearing the road. Later on, in the same way, your disciples will spread the word that you didn't die, that you were resurrected and ascended to heaven. . . . But my dear rascal, you've missed the boat. Your tricks are out of date, so you'd better find some new ones. I'm not going to kill you, I'm not going to make a hero of you. You're not going to become God—so get the idea out of your head."

Jesus did not speak. Through the open window he watched Jehovah's immense Temple flash in the sun like a motionless maneating beast with multi-coloured flocks of men moving and entering its black gaping jaws. Pilate played with his delicate golden chain and did not speak either. He was ashamed to ask a favour of a Jew, but he had promised his wife he would and now had no choice.

"Is that all?" Jesus asked. He turned towards the door.

Pilate rose. "Don't leave," he said, "I have something to tell you—that's why I called you here. My wife says she dreams about you every night. Because of you she hardly dares close her eyes. She says you complain to her that your compatriots Annas and Caiaphas seek your death and you beg her every night to speak to me and convince me not to let them kill you. Last night my wife screamed, woke up with a start and began to cry. It seems she pities you (I don't know why: I keep my nose out of female nonsense). Well, she fell at my feet to make me call you and tell you to go away and save yourself. . . . Jesus of Nazareth, the air of Jerusalem isn't good for your health. Return to Galilee! I don't want to use force—I'm telling you as a friend. Return to Galilee!"

"Life is war!" Jesus answered in the same resolute, always-tranquil voice, "and you know it because you're a soldier and a Roman. But what you don't know is this: God is the commander and we his soldiers. From the moment that man is born, God shows him the earth and upon the earth a city, village, mountain, sea or desert, and says to him, 'Here you shall wage war!' Governor of Judea, one night God seized me by the hair, lifted me up, brought me to Jerusalem, set me down in front of the Temple and said, 'Here you shall wage war!' I am no deserter, Governor of Judea—it is here that I shall wage my war!"

Pilate shrugged his shoulders. He already regretted that he had asked the favour and revealed a household secret to a Jew. As was his habit, he went through the motions of rinsing his hands.

"Do as you please," he said. "I wash my hands of the whole matter. Go!"

Jesus raised his arm and took his leave. But as he was crossing the threshold, Pilate called to him teasingly, "Hey, Messiah, what is this fearful news I hear you bring the world?"

"Fire," Jesus replied, again tranquilly, "fire, to cleanse the earth."

"Of Romans?"

"No, of unbelievers. Of the unjust, the dishonourable, the satiated."

"And then. . . ?"

"And then on the scorched, purified earth, the new Jerusalem shall be built."

"And who is going to build the new Jeusalem?"

"I am."

Pilate burst into laughter. "Well, well, I was right when I told my wife you were as crazy as they come. You must visit me now and again—it will help me pass the time. All right now: go! I'm tired of you."

He clapped his hands. The two colossal negroes entered and showed Jesus to the door.

Judas was waiting anxiously outside the tower. Some hidden worm had been eating the master lately. Each day his face grew more wrinkled and fierce, his words sadder and more threatening. He often went and stayed all alone for hours on Golgotha, a hill outside of Jerusalem where the Romans crucified insurgents; and to the degree he saw the priests and high priests around him grow frantic and dig his grave, by so much—and even more—did he assault them and call them venomous adders, liars, hypocrites who trembled at the thought of swallowing a mosquito and then went ahead and swallowed a camel! Every day he stood from dawn to dusk outside the Temple and uttered wild words as though deliberately seeking his death; and the other day when Judas asked him when he would finally throw off the lamb-skin so that the lion could appear in all its glory, Jesus shook his head, and never in his life had Judas seen a bitterer smile on human lips. From that time on, Judas had not left his side. Even when he saw him mount Golgotha, he went secretly behind lest some hidden enemy lift his hand against him. . . .

Judas paced up and down outside the accursed tower and glanced fiercely at the motionless Roman guards with their armour of brass and heavy boorish faces; and at the godless standard behind them which, with its eagles, waved back and forth at the top of a high pole. What did Pilate want with him, he asked himself; why had he called him? Judas knew—the Zealots of Jerusalem kept him informed—that Annas and Caiaphas went continually in and out of this tower and that they accused Jesus of wanting to start a revolution in order to chase out the Romans and make himself king. But Pilate did not agree. "He's completely insane," he would say, "and he doesn't mix himself up in Rome's business. I once purposely sent men to ask him, 'Does the God of Israel want us to pay taxes to the Romans—what's your opinion?' And he, quite truly, quite intelligently, answered: 'Render to Caesar the things that are Caesar's, and to God the things that are God's!' . . . He's not as crazy as a saint," Pilate would say, laughing, "he's crazed by saintliness. If he steps on your religion, punish him—I wash my hands of the whole affair. But he does not concern Rome." This is what he always told them, and then he sent them away. But now. . . . Could he have changed his mind?

Judas halted and leaned against the wall opposite the tower, nervously clenching and unclenching his fists.

Suddenly he gave a start. Trumpets blared, the crowd made way. Four Levites arrived and gently placed a gold-inlaid litter in front of the tower door. The silken curtains parted and light-skinned Caiaphas, wearing a yellow all-silk gown, slowly descended. He was so fat that globs of blubber formed cocoons around his eyes. The heavy double doors opened exactly as Jesus was coming out, and the two men met face to face on the threshold. Jesus halted. He was barefooted, his white tunic full of patches. Perfectly motionless, he stared deeply into the high priest's eyes. The other lifted his heavy eyelids, recognized him, eyed him rapidly from head to toe. His goatish lips parted:

"What do you want here, rebel?"

But Jesus, still motionless, stared down on him severely with his large afflicted eyes.

"I'm not afraid of you, high priest of Satan," he replied.

"Throw him out!" Caiaphas screamed at his four litter-bearers. He proceeded into the courtyard, a fat bow-legged pigmy whose immense behind nearly scraped the ground.

The four Levites closed in on Jesus, but Judas dashed forward. "Hands off!" he bellowed. Shoving them aside, he took the teacher by the arm.

"Come," he said, "let's go."

Judas pushed through camels, men and sheep, clearing a path so that Jesus could proceed. They strode under the city's fortified gate, descended into the Cedron Valley, climbed up the opposite side and took the road to Bethany.

"What did he want with you?" Judas asked, squeezing the master's arm in an agony.

"Judas," Jesus answered after a deep silence, "I am now going to confide a terrible secret to you."

Judas bowed his redhaired head and waited with gaping mouth.

"You are the strongest of all the companions. Only you, I think, will be able to bear it. I have said nothing to the others, nor will I. They have no endurance."

Judas blushed with pleasure. "Thank you for trusting me, rabbi," he said. "Speak. You'll see: I won't make you ashamed of me."

"Judas, do you know why I left my beloved Galilee and came to Jerusalem?"

"Yes," Judas answered. "Because it is here that what is bound to happen must happen."

"That's right, the Lord's flames will start from here. I can no longer sleep. I wake with a start in the middle of the night and look at the sky. Hasn't it opened yet? Aren't the flames flowing down? Daylight comes and I run to the Temple, speak, threaten, point to the sky, command, beseech, invoke the fire to descend. But my voice is always lost. The heavens remain closed, mute, and tranquil above me. And then suddenly one day. . ."

His voice broke. Judas leaned on top of him in order to hear, but could detect only stifled breathing and the rattling of Jesus' teeth.

"Go on! Go on!" Judas gasped.

Jesus caught his breath and continued. "One day as I was lying all alone on the top of Golgotha, the prophet Isaiah rose up in my mind—no, no, not in my mind: I saw his entire body in front of me on the rocks of Golgotha, and he was holding a goat-skin sewn up and inflated, and it looked just like the black he-goat I met in the desert. There were letters on the hide. 'Read!' he commanded, stretching out the goat-skin in the air in front of me. But as I heard the voice, prophet and goat disappeared and only the letters remained—in the air, black with red capitals."

Jesus lifted his eyes into the light. He had turned pale. He squeezed Judas's arm and clung to him. "There they are!" he whispered, terrified. "They've filled the air!"

"Read!" said Judas, who was also trembling.

Panting, Jesus began hoarsely to spell out the words. The letters were like living beasts: he hunted them and they resisted. Continually wiping away his sweat, he read: " 'He has borne our faults; he was wounded for our transgressions, our iniquities bruised him. He was afflicted, yet he opened not his mouth. Despised and rejected by all, he went forward without resisting, like a lamb that is led to the slaughter.' "

Jesus spoke no more. He had turned deathly pale.

"I don't understand," said Judas, standing still and shifting the pebbles with his big toe. "Who is the lamb being led to slaughter? Who is going to die?"

"Judas," Jesus slowly answered, "Judas, my brother, I am the one who is going to die."

"You?" said Judas, recoiling. "Then aren't you the Messiah?"

"I am."

"I don't understand!" Judas repeated, and he lacerated his toe on the stones.

"Don't shout, Judas. This is the way. For the world to be saved, I, of my own will, must die. At first I didn't understand it myself. God sent me signs in vain: sometimes visions in the air, sometimes dreams in my sleep; or the goat's carcass in the desert with all the sins of the people around its neck. And since the day I quit my mother's house, a shadow has followed behind me like a dog or at times has run in front to show me the road. What road? The Cross!"

Jesus threw a lingering glance around him. Behind him was Jerusalem, a mountain of brilliantly white skulls; in front of him, rocks and a few silver-leafed olive trees and black cedars. The sun, filled with blood, had begun to set.

Judas was uprooting hairs from his beard and tossing them away. He had expected a different Messiah, a Messiah with a sword, a Messiah at whose cry all the generations of the dead would fly out of their tombs in the valley of Joshaphat and mix with the living. The horses and camels of the Jews would be resuscitated at the same time, and all—infantry and cavalry—would flow forth to slaughter the Romans. And the Messiah would sit on the throne of David with the Universe as a cushion under his feet, for him to step on. . . . This, this was the Messiah Judas Iscariot had expected. And now. . .

He looked fiercely at Jesus and bit his lips to prevent an unkind word from escaping them. He began again to shift the pebbles, this time with his heels. Jesus saw him and pitied him.

"Take courage, Judas, my brother," he said, sweetening his voice. "I have done so. There is no other way: this is the road."

"And afterwards?" asked Judas, staring at the rocks.

"I shall return in all my glory to judge the living and the dead."

"When?"

"Many of the present generation will not die before they have seen me."

"Let's go!" said Judas. He increased his pace. Jesus panted behind him, toiling to keep up. The sun was at last about to tumble down behind the mountains of Judea. Far away, from the Dead Sea, the first wakening jackals could be heard.

Judas rolled on ahead, bellowing. Within him was an earthquake: everything falling away. He had no faith in death—that seemed to him the worst road of all; resurrected Lazarus, who appeared to him deader and filthier than all the dead, made him nauseous; and the Messiah himself—how could he possibly manage in this fight with Charon? . . . No, no, Judas had no faith in death as a way.

He turned. He wanted to object, to throw out the grave words which were burning on his tongue. Perhaps they would make Jesus change his route and not go by way of death. As he turned, however, he uttered a cry of terror. An immense shadow fell from Jesus' body. It was not the shadow of a man, but of a huge cross. He grasped Jesus' hand.

"Look!" he said, pointing.

Jesus shuddered.

"Quiet, Judas, my brother. Do not speak."

And thus, silently, arm in arm, they began to mount the gentle incline to Bethany. Jesus' knees sagged and Judas held him up. They did not speak. Once Jesus leaned over, picked up a warm stone and held it for a long time tightly in his palm. Was this a stone, or the hand of some beloved man? He looked around him. All the soil, which had died during the winter: how it sprouted grass now, how it blossomed!

"Judas, my brother," he said, "do not be sad. Look how the wheat comes to the earth; how God sends rain and the earth swells and the ears of grain rise from the foamy soil to feed man-

397

kind. If the grain of wheat did not die, would the ears ever be resurrected? It is the same with the Son of man."

But Judas was not consoled. Without speaking, he continued to climb. The sun fell behind the mountains; the night rose up from the soil. The first lamps were already flickering at the top of the hill.

"Remember Lazarus. . . ," Jesus said. But Judas felt nauseated and hurried on, spitting.

Martha lit the lamp. Lazarus put his hand in front of his eyes—the light still wounded him. Peter took Matthew by the arm and the two of them sat down under the lamp. Old Salome had found a bundle of black fleece and was spinning, thinking of her two sons. My goodness, would the day never come when she would see them in their splendour, a ribbon of gold in their hair, and when the whole lake of Gennesaret would be theirs? . . .

Magdalene had started down the path. The teacher was late. Her suffering was so intense, she seemed no longer able to fit into the house, and she had gone down the road in the hope of meeting her beloved. The disciples, squatting in the yard, glanced out of the corners of their eyes at the street-door and did not speak. Anger was still boiling inside them. The whole house was peaceful; not a breath could be heard. It was just the moment for Peter, who had been longing for days to see what the publican wrote in his notebook each evening. Tonight, after his quarrel with the others, he could wait no longer: he had to know what Matthew said about him. These scribblers were a shameless lot and he had better take care he was not being ridiculed for future generations. If Matthew dared do such a thing, he would throw the book—pen and all—into the fire. Yes, this very evening! . . . He took the publican's arm cajolingly and the two of them knelt down under the lamp.

"Read to me please, Matthew," he requested. "If you must know, I want to learn what you write about the teacher."

Matthew was delighted to hear this. He slowly removed the notebook from its position next to his breast. He had just wrapped it in an embroidered lady's kerchief presented him by Lazarus's sister Mary. Now he carefully unwrapped it as though it were something alive and wounded. He opened it. His body began to pitch forward and back; he gathered momentum and started, half-reading half-chanting, to recite:

" 'The book of the generation of Jesus Christ, son of David, son of Abraham. Abraham begot Isaac. And Isaac begot Jacob. And Jacob begot Judas and his brothers. And Judas begot Phares and Zara. . .' "

Peter closed his eyes and listened. The generations of the Hebrews passed before him: from Abraham to David, fourteen generations; from David to the Babylonian captivity, fourteen generations; from the Babylonian captivity to Christ, fourteen generations. . . . What a multitude, what an innumerable, immortal army! And what immense joy, what pride to be one of the Jews! Peter inclined his head against the wall and listened. The generations marched by, reached the time of Jesus. Peter listened. How many miracles had taken place, and he had never even had a whiff of them! So. . . , Jesus was born at Bethlehem, and his father was not Joseph the carpenter but was the Holy Spirit, and three Magi had come and worshipped him; and at the Baptism, what were those words thrown down from heaven by the dove? He, Peter, had not heard them. Who told them to Matthew, who wasn't even there? Little by little Peter no longer heard the words, he heard only a lulling music, monotonous and sad—and then, gently, he fell asleep. . . . There, in his sleep, he heard both music and words with perfect clarity. Each word seemed to him in his sleep like a pomegranate—like those pomegranates he had eaten the year before at Jericho. They burst open in the air and from inside flew out sometimes flames, sometimes angels, wings and trumpets. . . .

Suddenly in the deep sweetness of sleep he heard a tumult of happy cries. He awoke with a start. In front of him he saw Matthew, still reading, the notebook on his knees. He remembered, felt ashamed at having fallen asleep, flew into the publican's arms, and kissed him on the mouth.

"Forgive me, brother Matthew," he said, "but while I was listening to you I entered Paradise."

Jesus appeared at the door, followed by Magdalene. She was radiant with joy. Flames flew from her lips, eyes and bare neck.

When Jesus saw Peter hugging and kissing the publican, his expression sweetened. He pointed to the two embracing men.

"That." he said, "is the kingdom of heaven."

He approached Lazarus, who attempted to rise. But his loins creaked and he was afraid they would break. He sat down again. Extending his arm, he touched Jesus' hand with his fingertips. Jesus shuddered. Lazarus's hand was extremely cold, and black, and it smelt of soil.

Jesus went out again into the yard in order to breathe. This resurrected man still tottered between life and death. God had not yet been able to conquer the rottenness within him. Never had death shown its true strength as it did in this man. Jesus was overcome with fear and intense sadness.

Old Salome, her distaff under her arm, approached him and stood on tiptoe to whisper secretly in his ear:

"Rabbi," she began. He bent over to hear her.

"Speak, Salome."

"Rabbi, when you go up to heaven, I have a favour to ask of you. You've seen how much we have done for you. . ."

"Speak, Salome. . ." Jesus' heart suddenly constricted. When, he asked himself, would men realize that good deeds never condescend to accept recompense.

"Now that you are going to mount your throne, my child, place my sons John and Jacob one at your right hand and one at your left."

Biting his lips so that he would not speak, Jesus stared at the ground.

"Did you hear, my child? John. . ."

Jesus took a long stride and entered the house. He saw Matthew next to the lamp, still holding the open notebook on his knees. He stopped. Matthew's eyes were closed: he was still submerged in all that he had read.

"Matthew," said Jesus, "bring your notebook here. What do you write?"

Matthew got up and handed Jesus his writings. He was very happy.

"Rabbi," he said, "here I recount your life and works, for men of the future."

Jesus knelt under the lamp and began to read. At the very first words, he gave a start. He violently turned the pages and read with great haste, his face becoming red and angry. Seeing him, Matthew huddled fearfully in a corner and waited. Jesus skimmed through the notebook and then, unable to control himself any longer, stood up straight and indignantly threw Matthew's Gospel down on the ground.

"What is this?" he screamed. "Lies! lies! lies! The Messiah doesn't need miracles. He is the miracle—no other is necessary! I was born in Nazareth, not in Bethlehem—I've never even set foot in Bethlehem, and I don't remember any Magi. I never in my life went to Egypt; and what you write about the dove saying 'This is my beloved son' to me as I was being baptized—who revealed that to you? I myself didn't hear clearly. How did you find out, you, who weren't even there?"

"The angel revealed it to me," Matthew answered, trembling.

"The angel? What angel?"

"The one who comes each night I take up my pen. He leans over my ear and dictates what I write."

"An angel?" Jesus said, disturbed. "An angel dictates, and you write?"

Matthew gathered courage. "Yes, an angel. Sometimes I even see him, and I always hear him: his lips touch my right ear. I sense his wings wrapping themselves around me. Swaddled in the angel's wings like an infant, I write; no, I don't write—I copy what he tells me. What did you think? Could I have written all those miracles by myself?"

"An angel?" Jesus murmured again, and he plunged into meditation. Bethlehem, Magi, Egypt, and "you are my beloved son": if all these were the truest truth. . . ? If this was the highest level of truth, inhabited only by God. . . ? If what we called truth, God called lies. . . ?

He did not speak. Bending down, he carefully gathered together the writings he had thrown on the ground, and gave them to Matthew, who rewrapped them in the embroidered kerchief and hid them under his shirt, next to the skin.

"Write whatever the angel dictates," Jesus said. "It is too late for me to—" But he left his sentence unfinished.

Meanwhile, the disciples formed a circle around Judas in the yard and asked him to tell them what Pilate wanted with the rabbi. But Judas, without even turning to look at them, broke away and stood at the street-door. He detested the sight and sound of them; he could speak only with the rabbi now. A terrible secret joined the two of them and separated them from the rest. . . . Judas looked at the night which had devoured the world, and at the first stars above him, small icon-lamps which were just beginning to glow.

"God of Israel," he murmured within himself, "help me, or I'll go out of my mind."

Magdalene felt uneasy, and went and stood next to him. He started to leave, but she seized the edge of his tunic.

"Judas, you can reveal the secret to me without fear. You know me."

"What secret? Pilate wanted him in order to tell him to be careful. Caiaphas. . ."

"Not that, the other."

"What other? You're burning up again, Magdalene. Your eyes are lighted coals." He laughed half-heartedly. "Cry, cry. Your tears will put them out."

But Magdalene bit into her kerchief and tore it with her teeth. "Why should he have chosen you," she murmured, "you, Judas Iscariot?"

The redbeard became angry now. He squeezed his hand around Magdalene's arm. "Who, Mary of Magdala, did you wish him to choose—windmill Peter, or that idiot John. . ., or could it be that you wanted to be chosen yourself—you, a woman? I am a piece of flint from the desert: I stand up against wear. That's why he chose me!"

Magdalene's eyes filled with tears. "You are right," she murmured. "I'm a woman, a creature maimed and wounded. . . ." She went inside and huddled into a ball next to the fire.

Martha had set the table for supper. The disciples came in from the yard and knelt. Lazarus had drunk the chicken broth. It became blood inside him, and he no longer stared at the floor. Little by little with the air, light and nourishment, his fissured body was becoming caulked and strengthened.

The inner door opened and the old rabbi appeared, pale and airy, like a ghost. He leaned heavily on his crosier because his knees refused to support him any more. When he saw Jesus he signalled that he wanted to speak to him. Jesus rose, took hold of the old man, seated him, and then sat down himself next to Lazarus.

"Father," he said, "I also want to speak to you."

"I have a complaint against you today, my child," said the old rabbi, looking at him with stern tenderness. "I say it openly in front of everyone. Let all—men and women—hear us; and Lazarus, who rose from the grave and must know many secrets. Let everyone hear us and judge."

"What can men know?" Jesus replied. "An angel—ask Matthew —flies inside this house and listens. Let him judge. What is your grievance, Father?"

"Why do you wish to abolish the sacred Law? Until now you respected it, just as it is right that a son should respect his old father. But today in front of the Temple, you hoisted your own banner. How far is this rebellion in your heart going to lead?"

"To love, Father; to the feet of God. There it will find support and repose."

"Can't you reach that far with the sacred Law? Don't you know what our holy Scriptures say? The Law was written nine hundred and fourteen generations before God built the world. But it wasn't written upon parchment, because at that time no animals existed to give up their hides; nor on wood, for there were no trees; nor upon stone: there still were no stones. It was written in black flames upon white fire on the left arm of the Lord. It was in accordance with this sacred Law, I want you to know, that God created the world."

"No! no!" Jesus cried, unable to control himself any longer. "No!"

The old rabbi tenderly took his hand. "Why do you shout like that, my child?"

Jesus felt ashamed, and blushed. The reins had escaped his hands and he could no longer manage his soul. It was as though he were covered with wounds from head to toe. No matter where you touched him, no matter how lightly, he always screamed with pain.

He had screamed this time too, and then become calm. He took the old rabbi's hand, and lowered his voice:

"The holy Scriptures, Father, are the pages of my heart. I have torn up all the other pages."

But as he spoke he changed his mind: "Not I . . . , not I, but God, who sent me."

The old rabbi, sitting as he was next to Jesus, so close that their knees touched, felt an unbearable fiery force spurt out of Jesus' body; and as a strong wind suddenly blew through the opened window and extinguished the lamp, the rabbi saw in the darkness, all splendour like a column of fire, the son of Mary standing erect in the centre of the room. He looked to the right and left in case Moses and Elijah should again be present, but saw neither of them. Jesus was alone in his splendour, and his head reached the cane-lathed ceiling and set it aglow. Just as the old rabbi was about to scream, Jesus stretched out his arms. He had become a cross now and was being licked by the flames.

Martha got up and relit the lamp. Everything immediately returned to order. Jesus was still sitting with bowed head, thinking. The rabbi glanced around: no one else had seen anything in the darkness. The others had all placed themselves around the table and were tranquilly arranging themselves for dinner. God holds me in his hands and plays, thought the rabbi. Truth has seven levels. He brings me up and down from level to level, and I grow dizzy. . . .

Jesus was not hungry and did not sit down to eat. Nor did the old rabbi. The two of them remained next to Lazarus, who had closed his eyes and seemed to have fallen asleep. But he was not sleeping, he was thinking. What was this dream he had had? Had he died, he wondered, had he been laid under the earth, and had he then suddenly heard a terrible voice: "Lazarus, come out!" and had he jumped up in his shroud and awaked to find himself wrapped in the very shroud he had seen in his dream? Or perhaps it was not a dream. Could he really have descended to Hades?

"Why did you bring him out of the tomb, my child?"

"I didn't want to," Jesus answered softly, "I didn't want to, Father. When I saw him lift up the tombstone I became terrified. I wanted to run away, but was too ashamed. I stayed there and trembled."

I can endure everything," said the rabbi, "everything, except the stench of a rotting body. I've seen one other horrible body. It decomposed while it still lived, ate, talked and sighed. King Herod, a great soul condemned to hell. . . . He killed beautiful Mariana, the woman he loved; killed his friends, his generals, his sons. He conquered kingdoms, built towers, palaces, cities and the holy Temple of Jerusalem, richer even than Solomon's ancient Temple. He inscribed his name deeply on the stones in bronze and in gold: he thirsted for immortality. Then suddenly at the height of his glory God's finger touched him on the neck, and all at once he began to rot. He was always hungry. He ate ceaselessly but was never filled. His intestines were one lingering, putrid wound; he was so hungry, the jackals heard his bellowing in the night and trembled. His belly, feet and armpits began to swell. Worms emerged from his testicles—they were the first to rot. The stench was so great that no human being could come close to him. His slaves fainted. He was carried to the warm springs at Callirhoe near the Jordan, and he became worse. They plunged him in warm oil, and he became worse. At that time I had a reputation for curing and exorcizing diseases. The king was told this, and he called for me. They had him then at Jericho, in the gardens, and his stench reached from Jerusalem to the Jordan. The first time I approached him I fainted. I made salves and anointed him. Secretly I lowered my head and vomited. Is this a king? I asked myself. Is this what man is: filth and stench? And where is the soul to put things in order?

The rabbi spoke extremely softly. It was not right for the others to hear such words while they ate. Jesus listened, bowed over in despair. This was precisely the favour he wished to ask of the rabbi this evening: to talk to him about death, so that he could find strength. He ought at this time to have death always in front of him, in order to get used to it. But now . . . He wanted to put forth his hand to stop the old rabbi, to shout at him: That's enough! but at this point, how could he hold the old man back.

The rabbi could not wait to recount all the filth, to draw it out of his memory and cleanse himself.

"My salves were worthless; the worms ate them too. But a devil was still enthroned in that filth and he gave orders. He commanded all the rich and powerful of Israel to assemble, and he penned them up in his courtyard. As he was dying he called for his sister Salome. 'As soon as I give up the ghost,' he said, 'kill them all, so that they won't rejoice at my death!' He perished. Herod the Great perished, the last king of Judah. I hid behind the trees and began to dance. The last king of Judah had perished—the blessed hour had come, the blessed hour which Moses prophesied in his Testament: 'At the end there will come a king debauched and dissipated, his sons unworthy; and out of the west will come barbarous armies and a king to occupy the Holy Land. And then, it will be the end of the world!' That's what the prophet Moses predicted. It has all taken place. The end of the world has come."

Jesus gave a start. It was the first time he had heard this prophecy. "Where is it written?" he shouted. "Who is the prophet? This is the first I hear of it!"

"Not many years ago in a cave of the Judean desert a monk found an ancient parchment in a clay jar. He unrolled it and saw at the top in red letters: 'The Testament of Moses'. Before he died the great patriarch had called his successor, Joshua, son of Nun, and dictated to him all that was going to happen in the future. And lo! we've reached the years he prophesied. The debauched king was Herod, the barbarous armies the Romans; and as for the end of the world, if you lift your head, you'll see it coming in through the door.

Jesus rose. The house constricted him. He went past between the companions who were eating, free of cares, and emerged into the yard. There, he lifted his head. The moon, large and sorrowful, was at that moment rising from behind the mountains of Moab. It was at last about to become entirely full and to issue in the Passover.

He gazed at it, astonished, as though he saw it for the first time in his life. What is this moon, he asked himself, this moon which rises from the mountains and makes the frightened dogs thrust their tails between their legs and bark at it? It mounts, silent in the terrifying silence, and drips venom. The heart of man becomes a pit which fills with venom. . . . Jesus felt an envenomed tongue over his cheeks and neck and arms, a tongue which licked him, which wrapped his face and body in a white light, a white shroud.

John had a presentiment of the master's suffering. He came out into the yard and saw him, his whole body submerged in moonlight. Speaking softly so that he would not frighten him, he said, "Rabbi. . ." and approached on tiptoe.

Jesus turned and looked at him. The tender beardless adolescent vanished, and an old man, a very old man, stood in the middle of the yard under the moon. He held a blank book open in one hand and in the other a quill, long, like a copper-tipped lance. And his all-white beard flowed down to his knees.

"Son of Thunder," Jesus cried, drawn out of himself, "write: 'I am the Alpha and the Omega, he who was, is, and shall be, the Lord of Hosts.' Did you hear a loud voice like a trumpet?"

John was terrified. The rabbi's mind had begun to totter! He knew that the moon inebriates—that was why he had come out into the yard: to get him and bring him indoors. But alas! he had arrived too late. "Be still, rabbi," he said. "I am John, whom you love. Let's go inside. This is Lazarus's house."

"Write!" Jesus again commanded. " 'There are seven angels around God's throne, each with a trumpet in his mouth.' Do you see them, son of Thunder! Write: 'The first angel fell to the earth, hail and fire, mixed with blood. One third of the earth was burnt up, one third of the trees, one third of the green grass. The second angel sounded his trumpet. A mountain of fire fell into the sea, and one third of the sea became blood, one third of the fish died; one third of the sailing ships sank. The third angel sounded his trumpet: a great star fell from heaven and one third of the rivers, lakes and fountains were poisoned. The fourth sounded his trumpet: one third of the sun became dark, and one third of the moon, and of the stars. The fifth sounded his trumpet: another star hurled forth, the Abyss opened and out poured clouds of smoke and in the smoke? locusts which flowed, not over the grass or trees, but over men; and their hair was long like women's hair, and their teeth like lions' teeth. They wore iron armour and their wings thundered like many-horsed chariots rushing into battle. The sixth angel sounded his trumpet. . ."

But John could stand it no longer. He burst into tears and fell at Jesus' feet. "My rabbi," he cried, "be still. . . , be still. . ."

Jesus heard the weeping, quivered, bent over and saw the beloved disciple at his feet.

"John beloved," he said, "why do you cry?"

John was ashamed to reveal that for a moment, under the moon, the teacher's mind had tottered. "Rabbi," he said, "let's go inside. The old man is asking what happened to you, and the disciples want to see you."

"And is it because of that you weep, John beloved? . . . Let us go in."

He entered and sat down once more next to the old rabbi. He was extremely tired. His hands were sweating; he was burning up —yet shivering. The old rabbi gazed at him, frightened.

"My child, do not look at the moon," he said, clasping Jesus' dripping hand. "They say that it is the nipple of Satan's chief love, the Night, and flows with—"

But Jesus' mind was on death.

"Father," he said, "I believe you spoke badly about death. Death does not wear Herod's face. No, it is a great lord, the keeper of God's keys, and it opens the door. Try to recall other deaths, Father, and comfort me."

The disciples had finished their meal. They cut short their chattering in order to listen. Martha cleared away; the two Marys collapsed at Jesus' feet. From time to time the one glanced stealthily at the other's arms, bosom, eyes, mouth and hair, anxiously calculating who was the more beautiful.

"My child, you are right," said the old man. "I spoke badly of God's black archangel. He always wears the face of the moribund. If Herod dies, he becomes Herod; but if a saint dies, his face shines like seven suns. A great lord, he comes with his chariot and lifts the saint from the ground and brings him up to heaven. Do you want to see the face you will have in eternity? Then look to see how death appears before you at the last hour."

They all listened open-mouthed and each, within his mind, anxiously weighed his own soul. For a long time silence fell over them all, as though each one was struggling to see the face of his death.

Finally Jesus opened his mouth and spoke. "Once, Father, when I was twelve years old, I went to the synagogue and listened to you relate the prophet Isaiah's martyrdom and death to the people of Nazareth. But that was years ago, and I've forgotten it. Tonight I have a great desire to hear about his end once more, so that my soul may be soothed and I may become reconciled with death: for you have made my soul extremely angry with your talk of Herod, Father."

"Why do you want us to talk only about death this evening, my child? Is this the favour you wished to ask of me?"

"Exactly. There is none greater." He turned to the disciples. "Do not fear death, comrades. May it be blessed! If death did not exist, how could we reach God and remain with him for ever? Truly I say to you, death holds the keys and opens the door."

The old rabbi looked at him with surprise. "Jesus, how can you speak with such love and sureness about death? It's been a long time since I've heard your voice so tender."

"Tell us about the prophet Isaiah's death, and you'll see that I am right."

The old rabbi shifted his position to avoid touching Lazarus.

"Iniquitous King Manasseh forgot the commands of his father, God-fearing Hezekiah; Satan entered and took possession of him. Manasseh could no longer bear to hear Isaiah, the voice of God. He therefore sent assassins all over Judea to find him and cut his throat so that he would speak no more. But Isaiah was in Bethlehem. Hidden inside a huge cedar, he prayed and fasted in order to make God take pity on Israel and save her. One day a Samaritan, a man outside the Law, passed by as the hand of the prophet, who was praying, emerged from the tree. The lawless Samaritan saw it and straightway ran to the king and informed him. The prophet was seized and led to the king. 'Bring the saw used to cut down trees, and saw him in two!' the accursed man ordered. They laid him down. Two men took hold of the two handles and began to saw. 'Disown your prophecies,' shouted the king, 'and I'll grant you your life!' But Isaiah had already entered Paradise, and no longer heard the voices of this earth. 'Deny God,' the king shouted again, 'and I'll have my subjects fall at your feet and adore you.'

" 'You have no power,' the prophet then answered him, 'except to kill my body. You cannot touch my soul, nor can you smother my voice. Both are immortal. The one goes up to God; the other, my voice, shall remain evermore on the earth and preach.' When he had spoken Death came in a chariot of fire, with a crown of gilded cedar in his hair, and took him."

Jesus got up, his eyes shining, A chariot of fire hung over him.

"Friends," he said, looking at the disciples one by one, "beloved fellow-voyagers: if you love me, listen to the words I shall speak to you tonight. You must always be tightly girded and ready —those who have sandals, with sandals, those who have staffs, with staffs, ready for the great journey. What is the body? The tent of the soul. 'We are taking up our tents and leaving!' you should say at every instant, 'We are leaving, returning to our homeland.' What homeland? Heaven!

"Friends, here is the final word I wish to say to you tonight. When you find yourselves in front of a beloved tomb, do not begin to weep. Keep ever in your minds this great consolation: Death is the door to immortality, there is no other door. Your beloved did not die—he became immortal."

XXVII

ALL day long, starting at the heavenly daybreak, but even more so during the night when no one observed, spring had been gradually pushing aside rocks and soil and rising from the land of Israel. In one night the plains of Sharon in Samaria and Esdrelon in Galilee filled with yellow daisies and wild lilies; and short-lived anemones—large drops of blood—sprouted amongst the sullen rocks of Judea. Protruding crab-like eyes appeared on the vines. In each of these rose-green buds the unripe clusters, the mature grapes and the new wine gathered momentum to burst forth; and still deeper, in the heart of each bud, were the songs of men. A guardian angel stood by each tiny leaf and helped it grow. You thought the first days of creation were returning, when each word of God which fell upon the freshly-turned soil was full of trees, wild-flowers and greenery.

This morning at the foot of holy mount Gerizim, the Samaritan woman was again filling her pitcher at Jacob's well and looking down the road to Galilee, as though she still longed to see the pale youth who had once spoken to her about immortal water. And now that it was spring, this pleasure-loving widow had revealed even more of the two mounds of her sweaty bosom.

This springtime night the immortal soul of Israel metamorphosed, became a nightingale which perched in the open window of each young unmarried Jewess and kept her awake until dawn with its singing. Why do you go to bed all alone? it twittered, scolding her. Why do you think I gave you long hair and two breasts and round wide hips? Arise, put on your jewelry, lean out of your window. Place yourself on your threshold at the break of dawn, take your pitcher and go to the well, flirt with the unmarried Jews you meet on your way, and with them, make children for me. We Hebrews have many enemies, but as long as my daughters give me children, I am immortal. I hate the unploughed fields and ungrafted trees of the land of Israel—and the virgins.

In the desert of Idumea, at God-protected Hebron, around the all-holy tomb of Abraham, the Hebrew children awoke early in the morning and played at being the Messiah. They constructed bows out of osiers and shot arrows made of cane into the sky, shouting for the Messiah—the king of Israel—to descend at last with a long sword and helmet of gold. They made a throne for him to sit on by spreading a lamb-skin over the sacred tomb. They composed a special song for him, they clapped their hands for him to appear—and suddenly, from behind the tomb there were cheers and the sound of drums and out came the strutting bellowing Messiah with beard and moustache of corn-tassals, and a ferocious painted face. He held a long sword made of a date-branch and struck the children one by one on the neck. They all fell down, massacred.

Day was also breaking at Lazarus's house in Bethany, but Jesus had not yet closed his eyes. His anguish had refused to subside; no road opened before him except one: death. The prophecies speak about me, he was thinking. I am the lamb who shall take upon himself the sins of the world and be slaughtered at this Passover. Well then, let the lamb be slaughtered one hour sooner. The flesh is weak; I have no faith in it. At the last minute it may turn coward. Let death come now while I still feel my soul to be standing erect. . . . Oh, when will the sun rise so that I can go to the Temple. I must put an end to everything—today!

The decision made, his mind felt somewhat soothed. He closed his eyes, fell asleep, and had a dream: the sky seemed to be an orchard enclosed by a rail fence and full of wild animals. He too was a wild animal and was frisking with the rest, and in his frisking he jumped over the rails and fell onto the ground. When the people saw him they became terrified. The women screamed and collected their children from the streets so that the beast would not eat them. The men seized lances, stones and swords, and began the hunt. . . . Blood was running all over him when suddenly he fell prone onto the ground. Then it seemed that judges accumulated around him in order to judge him. They were not men, however, but foxes, dogs, hogs and wolves. They judged him, condemning him to death. But as they led him to be executed, he remembered that he could not die: he was a heavenly beast, and immortal. And as he remembered this a woman took his hand, and it was Mary Magdalene. She brought him out of the city to the fields. "Do not go to heaven," she said to him. "Spring is here; stay with us." . . . They marched and marched, until the border of Samaria. There the Samaritan woman appeared, her jug on her shoulder. She offered it to him and he drank; afterwards, she too took his hand and brought him, without speaking, as far as the border of Galilee. Then his mother emerged from under the ancient flowering olive-trees. She was wearing a black kerchief and weeping. When she saw the wounds, the blood all over him and the crown of thorns in his hair she lifted her hands: "As you scathed me," she said to him, "may God scathe you. You placed my name on the tongues of men: the whole world is buzzing. You lifted your hand against the Fatherland, the Law, the God of Israel. Didn't you fear God, weren't you ashamed before men? Had you no thought for your mother and father? My curse upon you!" Having said this, she vanished.

He awoke with a jolt, drenched in sweat. Around him the disciples were stretched out, snoring. Outside in the yard the cock crowed. Peter heard it and half-opened his eyes. He saw Jesus standing up. "Rabbi," he said, "when the cock crowed, I was dreaming. You seemed to have taken two crossed boards. In your hands they became a lyre and bow, and you were playing and singing. The wild beasts assembled from the ends of the earth to hear you. . . . What does it mean? I'll ask the old rabbi."

"The dream does not end there, Peter," Jesus answered. "Why were you in such a hurry to wake up? The dream continues further."

"Further? I don't understand. Maybe you dreamt it yourself, rabbi—all of it?"

"When the beasts heard the song they rushed forward and devoured the singer."

Peter's eyes popped. His heart had a presentiment of the meaning, but his mind stood still. "I don't understand," he said.

"You will understand," Jesus replied, "on another morning when you again hear the cock crow."

He nudged the companions one by one with his foot. "Wake up, lazy-bones," he said. "We have much to do today."

"Are we leaving?" Philip asked, rubbing his eyes. "I say we should return to Galilee, to safety."

Judas ground his teeth, but did not speak.

In the inner room the women awoke, and began to chatter. Old Salome came out to light the fire. The disciples had already gathered in the yard. They were waiting for Jesus, who was bent over the rabbi, talking to him in a low voice. The old man, gravely ill, was bed-ridden in the back corner of the house.

"Where are you going now, my child?" the rabbi asked. "Where are you leading your army? Once more to Jerusalem? Will you again lift your hand to pull down the Temple? As you know, the word becomes act when it issues from a great soul—and yours is a great soul. You are liable for what you say. If you declare the Temple will be destroyed, one day it will indeed be destroyed. So, measure your words!"

"I do, Father. The whole world is in my mind when I speak. I choose what will stay and what will not. I take the responsibility upon myself."

"Oh, if I could only keep alive long enough to see who you are! But I'm old. The world has become a phantasm which roams around my head and wants to enter. But all the doors are blocked."

"Try to last a few days longer, Father. Until the Passover. Hold on to your fleeing soul for dear life, and you shall see. . . . The hour has not yet come."

The rabbi shook his head. "When will that hour come?" he complained. "Has God deceived me? What happened to his promise? I'm dying, I'm dying, and where is the Messiah?" He clutched Jesus' shoulders with all the strength which remained to him.

"Last until the Passover, Father. You'll see that God keeps his word!" Jesus extricated himself from the old man's grip, and went out into the yard.

"Nathanael," he said, "and you, Philip: go to the end of the village, to the very last house. There you'll find a donkey and her colt tied to the door-hasp. Untie her and bring her here. If anyone asks you where you're taking her, answer: 'The rabbi needs her and we'll bring her back again.' "

"We're going to get ourselves into trouble," Nathanael whispered to his friend.

"Let's go," Philip said. "Do what he tells you, come what may!"

Matthew had taken up his pen first thing in the morning and was all eyes and ears. God of Israel, he reflected, look how the whole structure is just as the prophets, with divine illumination, assembled it! What does the prophet Zacharias say: 'Rejoice and exult, daughter of Zion, shout for joy, daughter of Jerusalem. Look, your king comes to find you, humble and mounted on an ass—though he is a conqueror!' "

"Rabbi," Matthew said to test the master, "it appears you're tired and can't go to Jerusalem on foot."

"No, I'm not tired," Jesus replied. "Why do you ask? I suddenly had a desire to ride there."

"You should ride on a white horse!" Peter interrupted. "You're the king of Israel, aren't you? So, you must enter your capital on a white horse."

Jesus threw a hurried glance at Judas and did not answer.

In the meantime Magdalene had come out and placed herself in the doorway. There were bags under her eyes, for she had not slept the whole night. Leaning against the doorpost, she regarded Jesus, regarded him deeply, inconsolably, as though taking leave of him for ever. She wanted to tell him not to go, but her throat seemed blocked. Matthew saw her open and close her mouth without being able to sound a word, and he understood. The prophets do not allow her to speak, he reflected. They do not allow her to hinder the rabbi from accomplishing what they prophesied. He will mount the ass and go to Jerusalem whether Magdalene wants it or not, whether he himself wants it or not. It is written!

At that moment Philip and Nathanael arrived, happily pulling behind them, on one rope, the mother with her saddleless foal. "It turned out just as you said, rabbi," exclaimed Philip. "Mount now, and let's go."

Jesus turned to look at the house. The women stood and watched with crossed hands, sad but mute. Old Salome and the two sisters, with Magdalene in front. . .

"Is there a whip in the house, Martha?" Jesus asked.

"No, rabbi," Martha replied. "There is only our brother's ox-goad."

"Give it to me."

The disciples had laid their clothes upon the docile animal to make a soft seat for the teacher, and on top of these, Magdalene threw a red blanket of her own weaving, decorated along the edges with small black cypresses.

"Are you all ready?" Jesus asked. "Is everyone in good heart?"

"Yes," answered Peter, who went in front. Holding the animal's rein, he led the way.

The Bethanites heard the group pass and opened their doors.

"Where are you off to, lads? Why is the prophet riding today?"

The disciples leaned over and confided the secret to them: "He's off today to sit on his throne."

"What throne, fellow?

"Ssh, it's a secret. The man you see before you is the king of Israel."

"Really! Let's go with him," shouted the young women, and more and more people swarmed around.

The children cut palm-branches and went in front, happily chanting: "Blessed is he who comes in the name of the Lord!" The men took off their coats and spread them along the road for him to pass over. How they ran! What a spring this was! How tall the flowers had grown this year; how the birds sang and flew behind the procession, towards Jerusalem!

Jacob leaned over to his brother. "Our mother spoke to him yesterday. She said he should seat us to his left and right now that he's going to mount the throne of glory. But he didn't answer her. Maybe he got angry. She said his face seemed to darken."

"Of course he got angry," John replied. "She shouldn't have done it."

"What, then? Should he leave us like we are and—who knows— give precedence to Judas Iscariot? Did you notice how all these days the two of them have been talking secretly together? They seem inseparable. Be careful, John. Go and speak to him yourself so we don't suffer any loss. The hour has come for the division of the honours."

But John shook his head. "My brother," he said, "look how afflicted he is. It's as though he were going to his death."

I would like to know what is destined to happen now, thought

Matthew as he marched by himself behind the others. The prophets don't explain it very well. Some say the throne, others death. Which one of the two prophecies will he untangle? No one can interpret a prophecy except after the event. It's only then that we understand what the prophet meant. So. . . , let's be patient and wait and see what happens—just to be sure. We'll write it all down tonight when we return.

By this time the good news had taken wing and reached the near-by villages and the huts scattered throughout the olive groves and vineyards. The peasants ran from every direction and placed their cloaks or kerchiefs on the ground for the prophet to pass over. . . . There were also many of the lame, the sick, and the ragged. From time to time Jesus turned his head and looked behind him at his army. Suddenly he felt an immense loneliness. He turned and cried: "Judas!" but the unsociable disciple was at the very end and did not hear.

"Judas!" Jesus shouted again, desperately.

"Here!" the redbeard replied. He pushed aside the other disciples in order to pass through.

"What do you want, rabbi?"

"Stay next to me, Judas. Keep me company."

"Don't worry, rabbi, I won't leave you," He took the rope from Peter's hand and began to lead.

"Do not abandon me, Judas, my brother," Jesus said once more.

"Why should I abandon you, rabbi? Haven't we already decided all that?"

At last they came close to Jerusalem. The holy city, brilliantly white in the merciless sun, towered before them on Mount Zion. They passed through a tiny hamlet and from one end to the other heard a dirge, tranquil and sweet like warm springtime rain.

"Whom are they lamenting? Who died?" asked Jesus with a shudder. But the villagers who ran behind him laughed:

"Don't be troubled, master. No one died. The village girls are singing a dirge while they turn the hand-mill."

"But why?"

"To get used to it, master. To know how to lament when the time comes."

They climbed up the cobbled lane and entered the cannibalistic city. Noisy richly-bedecked flocks from all the ghettos of the world—each bringing its local smells and filth—were hugging and kissing each other: the day after next was the immortal festival, and all Jews were brothers! When they saw Jesus mounted on the humble ass with the crowd behind him waving palm-branches, they laughed:

"Now who in the world is this?"

But the cripples, the diseased and the ragamuffins lifted their fists and threatened: "Now you'll see! This is Jesus of Nazareth, the king of the Jews!"

Jesus dismounted and hurriedly climbed the steps of the Temple, two by two. He reached Solomon's Porch, stopped, and looked around him. Stalls had been set up. Thousands of people were selling, buying, bargaining, arguing, hawking their wares: merchants, money-changers, innkeepers, prostitutes. Jesus' bile rose to his eyes; a sacred rage took possession of him. He lifted the ox-goad and swept down upon each of the wine-stands, refreshment stalls and workshops; overturned the tables, stuck the tradesmen with his goad. "Away! Out of here! Out of here!" he shouted, brandishing the ox-goad and advancing. Within him was a quiet, bitter entreaty: Lord, Lord, what you have decided must happen, let it happen—but quickly. I ask no other favour of you. Quickly —now while I still have strength.

The mob rushed behind him; it too frantically screamed, "Out of here! Out of here!" and looted the stalls. Jesus halted at the royal arcade, above the Cedron Valley. Smoke rose from his entire body, his long raven-black hair stormed over his shoulders, his eyes threw out flames. "I have come to set fire to the world," he shouted. "In the desert John proclaimed, 'Repent! Repent! The day of the Lord is coming near!' But I say to you: you no longer have time to repent. It has come, it has come. I am the day of the Lord! In the desert John baptized with water; I baptize with fire. I baptize men, mountains, cities, boats. I already see the fire engulfing the four corners of the earth, the four corners of the soul—and I rejoice. The day of the Lord has come: my day!"

"Fire! Fire!" shouted the mob. "Bring fire, burn up the world."

The Levites grabbed lances and swords. Jacob, the brother of

Jesus, took the lead, his amulets hanging around his neck. They rushed out to seize Jesus. But the people became ferocious; the disciples mustered up courage and in one body, bellowing, rushed to join the others in the fray. High up in the Palace tower the Roman sentries watched them and laughed.

Peter grabbed a lighted torch from one of the stalls. "After them, brothers," he shouted. "Fire, lads. The hour has come!"

Much blood would then have been spilt in God's courtyard if the Roman trumpets had not resounded menacingly from Pilate's tower. And the great high priest Caiaphas emerged from the Temple and ordered the Levites to put down their arms. He had personally and with much skill dug a trap into which the insurgent would fall without fail—and without clamour.

The disciples encircled Jesus and looked at him with anguish. Would he or would he not give the sign? What was he waiting for? How long would he wait? Why was he delaying, and why, instead of raising his hand in a signal to heaven, was he staring at the ground? He, to be sure, need be in no hurry, but they—they were poor men who had sacrificed everything, and the time had come for them to be repaid.

"Decide, rabbi!" said Peter, red-faced and sweating. "Give the sign!"

Jesus, motionless, had closed his eyes. Sweat ran in drops from his forehead. Your day is approaching, Lord, he said over and over to himself; the end of the world has come. I know that I shall bring it, I—but by dying. . . . Repeating this again and again, he found courage.

John came up to him too. He touched his shoulder and pushed him to make him open his eyes. "If you don't give the sign now," he said, "we're finished. What you've done today means death."

"It means death," Thomas joined in, "and for your information we don't want to die."

"Die!" cried Philip and Nathanael, startled. "But we came here to reign!"

John leaned close to Jesus' breast. "What are you thinking about, rabbi?" he asked.

But Jesus pushed him away. "Judas, come here beside me," he said, and he supported himself on the redbeard's sturdy arm.

"Courage, rabbi," Judas whispered. "The hour has come; we mustn't let them be ashamed of us."

Jacob stared with hatred at Judas. Earlier, the master would not even turn to look at him, and now, what was this friendship and secret whispering? "They're cooking up something, the two of them. What do you say, Matthew?"

"I don't say anything. I listen to what all of you say and do, and I write. That's my job."

Jesus squeezed Judas's arm. Suddenly he felt dizzy. Judas supported him. "Are you tired, rabbi?" he asked.

"Yes, I'm tired."

"Think of God and you'll feel refreshed," the redbeard replied.

Jesus recovered his balance and turned to the disciples. "Come, let us go," he said.

But the disciples stood still. They did not want to leave. Where? Again to Bethany? And for how long? . . . They had had enough of this shuttling back and forth.

"I think he's teasing us," Nathanael remarked softly to his friend. "I'm not budging!" Having said this, he followed the rest of the disciples, who had started to go sullenly back towards Bethany.

Behind them, the Levites and Pharisees guffawed. A youngish Levite, ugly and round-shouldered, slung a lemon-rind which struck Peter square in the face.

"Nice throw, Saul! You hit the bull's-eye!"

Peter started to turn around to charge the Levite, but Andrew held him back. "Be patient, my brother," he said. "Our turn will come."

"When? Damn it, when, Andrew?" Peter grumbled. "Can't you see the mess we're in?"

Humiliated and silent, they took to the road. The crowd behind them had dispersed, cursing. No one followed them any more, no one laid out his ragged garment for the rabbi to walk upon. Philip dragged the donkey now, while Nathanael, behind, held the tail. Both were in a hurry to return the animal to its master so that they would not get into trouble. The sun was burning; a warm breeze blew, clouds of dust rose up and suffocated them. As they approached Bethany, there in front of them was Barabbas with two savage huge-moustached companions.

"Where are you taking your master?" he shouted. "Mercy on us! he's scared right out of his pants."

"They're taking him to resurrect Lazarus!" replied Barabbas's companions, bursting into guffaws.

When they reached Bethany and entered the house they found the old rabbi breathing his last. The women were kneeling around him, silently and motionlessly watching him depart. They knew that there was nothing they could do to bring him back. Jesus approached and placed his hand on the old man's forehead. The rabbi smiled but did not open his eyes.

The disciples squatted in the yard with a bitter taste in their mouths. They did not speak. Jesus nodded to Judas.

"Judas, my brother, the hour has come. Are you ready?"

"I ask you again, rabbi: why did you choose me?"

"You know you're the strongest. The others don't bear up. . . . Did you go speak to the high priest Caiaphas?"

"Yes. He says he wants to know when and where."

"Tell him the eve of the Passover after the pascal dinner, at Gethsemane. Try to be brave, Judas, my brother. I'm trying too."

Judas shook his head and without speaking, went out to the road in order to wait for the moon to rise.

"What happened at Jerusalem?" old Salome asked her sons. "What happened to you that makes you so silent?"

"I think, Mother, that we've built our house on sand," Jacob answered. "The damage is done!"

"And the rabbi, the grandeur, the silks threaded with gold, the thrones?. . . Did he deceive me, then?" The old lady looked at her sons and clapped her hands, but neither of them answered her.

The moon emerged from behind the Moabite mountains, sad and fully round. Hesitant, it stopped for a moment at the moutains' crest, looked at the world and then all at once made its decision, pulled away from the peaks and began to rise. Lazarus's dark hamlet, as though it had suddenly been whitewashed, gleamed a brilliant white.

At daybreak the disciples swarmed around the teacher. He did not speak, but looked at them one by one as though seeing them for the first, or the last, time. Towards midday he opened his mouth: "Friends, I desire to celebrate the sacred Passover with you. On a day such as this our ancestors departed, left the land of slavery behind them and entered the freedom of the desert. We also, for the first time on this Passover, come out of another slavery and enter another freedom. He who has ears to hear, let him hear!"

No one spoke. These words were obscure. What was the new slavery, what the new freedom? They did not understand. After a few moments Peter said, "There's one thing I do understand, rabbi. Passover without lamb is impossible. Where will we find the lamb?"

Jesus smiled bitterly. "The lamb is ready, Peter. At this very moment it is proceeding all by itself to the slaughter so that the world's poor may celebrate the new Passover. Don't worry therefore about the lamb."

Lazarus, who had been sitting silently in the corner, got up, placed his skeleton-like hand over his breast and said, "Rabbi, I owe my life to you and bad as it is, it's still better than the darkness of Hades. I shall therefore bring you the Passover lamb as a gift. A friend of mine is a shepherd on the mountain. Good-bye, I'm going to him."

The disciples looked at him with astonishment. Where did this living dead-man find the strength to get up and move towards the door! The two sisters fell upon him to prevent his leaving, but he pushed them aside, took a cane to lean upon, and strode over the threshold.

He proceeded through the village lanes. The doors along his passage opened. The frightened, surprised women emerged and marvelled that his spindle-shanks could walk, that his sagging middle did not break! Though he was in pain he took heart and now and then struggled to whistle in order to show how indubitably he had been rejuvenated. But his lips could not quite join. He therefore abandoned the whistling and began, with a serious expression, to ascend the mountain's slope, towards his friend's sheepfold.

He had not advanced a stone's throw, however, when from out

of the flowering broom up jumped Barabbas in front of him. How many days had he roamed the village waiting for this moment, waiting for the confounded resurrected fellow to stick his nose out of his house so that he could do away with him. He must prevent men from seeing him and being reminded of the miracle. The son of Mary, since the day he resuscitated him, had certainly amassed a great following; therefore Lazarus must be dispatched back into the grave and gotten rid of once and for all.

"Damned hell-deserter," he shouted at him, "how nice to meet you! What say, did you have a nice time down there, by God! Which is better, life or death?"

"Six of one, half a dozen of the other," Lazarus answered. He started to pass by, but Barabbas put out his arm and blocked the way.

"Excuse me, my dear ghost," he said, "but Passover is coming, I don't have a lamb, and this morning, so that I too could celebrate the Passover, I swore to God that in place of a lamb I would slaughter the first living thing I happened to meet along the road. Well, you're in luck. Stick out your neck: you're about to become a sacrifice to God."

Lazarus started to scream. Barabbas seized him by the Adam's apple, but was immediately overcome with fright. He had caught hold of something exceedingly soft, like cotton. No—softer, like air. His fingernails went in and came out again without drawing a single drop of blood. Maybe he's a ghost, he thought, and his heavily pock-marked face grew pale.

"Does it hurt?" he asked.

"No," Lazarus answered, sliding out of Barabbas' grip in order to escape.

"Stop!" Barabbas growled, seizing him now by the hair. But the hair, together with the scalp, remained in his hand. Lazarus's skull flashed yellowish-white in the sunlight.

"Damn you!" Barabbas murmured, trembling. "Blast it! are you a ghost?" He clutched Lazarus's right arm and shook it violently. "Say you're a ghost and I'll let you go."

But as he shook the arm, it came off in his hand. Terror took hold of him. He threw the decayed arm into the flowering broom and spat, nauseated. He was so terrified, the hair on his head stood on end. He grabbed his knife. He wanted to finish him off in a hurry, to be rid of him. He took hold of him carefully by the nape of the neck, propped his throat against a stone and began the slaughter. He sliced and sliced but the knife did not penetrate. It was like cutting through a tuft of wool. Barabbas's blood ran cold. Am I slaughtering a corpse? he asked himself. He started to go down the hill in order to flee, but saw Lazarus still moving and was afraid his goddamned friend might find him and resurrect him again. Conquering his fear, he seized him at both ends and— just as we wring out a wet garment before hanging it up on the line —twisted him and gave him a snap. His vertebrae uncoupled and he separated at the middle into two pieces. These Barabbas hid under the broom; then he departed at a run. He ran and ran. It was the first time in his life he had been afraid. He dared not look back. "Ach," he murmured, "if I can only get to Jerusalem in time to find Jacob! He'll give me a talisman to exorcize the demon!"

In Lazarus's house, meanwhile, Jesus was bending over the disciples, struggling to throw a little light into their minds so that what they were about to see would not frighten them into dispersing.

"I am the road," he told them, "as well as the house towards which one heads. I am also the guide, and he whom one goes out to meet. You must all have faith in me. No matter what you see, do not be afraid, for I cannot die. Do you hear—I cannot die."

Judas had remained all by himself in the yard. He was uprooting the pebbles with his big toe. Jesus frequently turned to look at him, and an inexpressible sorrow spread over his face.

"Rabbi," John complained, "why do you always call him to stay near you? If you look into the pupils of his eyes you'll see a knife."

"No, John beloved," Jesus answered, "not a knife—a cross."

The disciples gazed at each other, disturbed.

"A cross!" John exclaimed, falling on Jesus' breast. "Rabbi, who is being crucified?"

"Whoever leans over those eyes and looks in will see his face on the cross. I looked, and I saw my face."

But the disciples did not understand. Several laughed.

"It's a good thing you told us, rabbi," snapped Thomas. "As for me, I won't look into the redbeard's eyes as long as I live!"

"Your children and grandchildren will, Thomas," Jesus said. He glanced through the window at Judas, who was standing now on the doorstep, gazing towards Jerusalem.

"Your words are obscure, rabbi," Matthew complained. "How do you expect me to record them in my book?" All this time, he had been holding his pen in the air, unable to understand anything or to write.

"I don't speak in order for you to write, Matthew," Jesus answered bitterly. "You clerks are rightly called cocks: you think the sun won't come up unless you crow. I feel like taking your pen and papers and throwing them into the fire!"

Matthew quickly gathered together his writings and shrank away.

Jesus' rage did not abate. "I say one thing, you write another, and those who read you understand still something else! I say: cross, death, kingdom of heaven, God. . . , and what do you understand? Each of you attaches his own suffering, interests and desires to each of these sacred words, and my words disappear, my soul is lost. I can't stand it any longer!"

He rose, suffocating. Suddenly he felt his mind and heart being filled with sand.

The disciples cowered. It was as though the rabbi still held the ox-goad and pricked them, as though they were sluggish oxen who refused to move. The world was a cart to which they were yoked; Jesus goaded them on, and they shifted under the yoke but did not budge. Looking at them, Jesus felt drained of all his strength. The road from earth to heaven was a long one, and there they were, motionless.

"How long will you have me with you?" he cried. "Those who guard within yourselves a grave question, hurry and ask it. Those who have a tender word to say to me, say it quickly: it will do me good. Say it, so that after I have gone you will not complain that you missed the opportunity to utter a kind word to me, that you never made me realize how much you loved me. Then, it will be much too late."

The women listened. They were heaped up in a corner, their chins wedged between their knees. From time to time they sighed. They understood everything, but could say nothing. Suddenly Magdalene uttered a cry. She was the first to have the presentiment, and the funeral lamentation broke out within her. She jumped up and went into the inner room. Searching under her pillow, she found the crystal flagon she had brought with her. It was full of Arabian perfume which a former lover had given her in payment for one night. As she followed Jesus she carried it always with her, poor wretch, saying to herself: God is great, who knows but the day will come when I shall wash the hair of my beloved in this precious scent; the day might come when he'll wish to stand next to me as a bridegroom. Such were the hidden longings of her bosom; but now behind her beloved's body she saw death—not Eros, death. It too, like a marriage, required perfumes. She removed the crystal flagon from under her pillow, placed it in her bosom and began to weep. Holding the flagon to her breast and rocking it like an infant, she wept quietly, so that she would not be heard. Then she wiped her eyes, went out and fell at Jesus' feet. Before he could lean over to lift her up, she crushed the flagon and the fragrant myrrh flowed over the holy feet. Then, weeping, she let out her hair and wiped the perfumed feet. With the remaining perfume she washed the beloved head. Straightway she again collapsed at the rabbi's feet and kissed them.

The disciples were provoked.

"It's a shame to let so much expensive perfume go to waste," said Thomas, the merchant. "If we'd sold it, we'd have been able to feed many of the poor."

"To dower orphans," said Nathanael.

"To buy sheep," said Philip.

"It's a bad sign," John murmured, sighing. "With such perfumes the corpses of the rich are anointed. You shouldn't have done it, Mary. If Charon smells his beloved aroma and comes. . .?"

Jesus smiled. "You will always have the poor with you," he said, "but you will not always have me. It does not matter therefore if a flagon of perfume has been wasted for my sake. There are times when even Prodigality mounts to heaven and sits next to her well-born sister, Nobility. You, John beloved: do not feel oppressed. Death always comes. It is better that it come when the hair is perfumed."

The house had the fragrance of a rich tomb. Judas appeared and glanced rapidly at the rabbi. Could he have revealed the secret to the disciples? Were they anointing the moribund with funeral myrrh? But Jesus smiled.

"Judas, my brother," he said, "the swallow flies faster in the air than the deer moves on land; and faster than the swallow moves the mind of a man; and faster than the mind of a man, the heart of a woman." When he had spoken, he indicated Magdalene with his eyes.

Peter opened his mouth: "We have said many things, but have forgotten the most significant. Where in Jerusalem, rabbi, shall we have our Passover? I say we should go to Simon of Cyrene's tavern."

"God has arranged it differently," said Jesus. "Get up, Peter. Take John and go to Jerusalem. You'll see a man there with a pitcher on his shoulder. Follow him. He will enter a house. You enter also and say to the owner, 'Our master sends greetings and asks you: Where are the tables laid so that I may eat the Passover supper with my disciples?' And he will reply: 'My compliments to your master. Everything is ready. We look forward to seeing him.'"

The disciples stared at each other, wide-eyed in admiration, like infants.

"Are you serious, rabbi?" asked Peter, goggle-eyed. "Everything ready? The lamb, the skewer, the wine—everything?"

"Everything," Jesus answered. "Go. Have faith. We sit here and talk, but God does not sit and does not talk. He works for men."

At that moment they heard a feeble rale from the back corner of the house. They all turned, ashamed. All that time, they had forgotten the old rabbi in his death-agony! Magdalene ran with the three other women behind her. The disciples reached the bedside. Jesus again placed his palm on the old man's icy mouth. The other opened his eyes, saw him and smiled. Then he moved his hand, signalling the men and women to leave. When they were alone, Jesus bent over and kissed his mouth, eyes and forehead. The old man looked into his eyes, his face radiant.

"I saw the three again—Elijah, Moses and you. I'm sure now. . . . I'm going!"

"God bless you, Father. Are you pleased?"

"Yes. Let me kiss your hand."

He seized Jesus' hand and glued his icy lips to it for a long time. He looked at him ecstatically, mutely, saying good-bye to him. But in a moment, he spoke:

"When will you also come—there, above?"

"Tomorrow, on the Passover. I'll see you then, Father!"

The old rabbi crossed his hands.

"Release your servant now, O Lord," he murmured. "My eyes have seen my Saviour!"

XXVIII

THE sun had reached the horizon and, brilliantly red, was about to set. At the opposite end of the sky a bluish-white glow had already appeared in the east. Soon the paschal moon would emerge, enormous and mute. The pale rays of the sun still entered the house, fell obliquely over Jesus' thin face, caught the foreheads, noses and hands of the disciples and going into the corner, caressed the old rabbi's calm happy now-immortal face. Mary sat at her loom. She was in a deep shadow and no one saw the tears which ran peacefully down her cheeks and chin and onto the half-woven cloth. The house was still fragrant; Jesus' fingertips dripped with myrrh.

Suddenly, while they sat there in silence, each one feeling more and more heart-stricken as the night approached, a swallow came like a sword-thrust through the window, circled three times over their heads, peeped joyously, turned again towards the sun and left like a dart. They hardly had time to see its white belly and serrated wings.

As though this was the mysterious sign he had been waiting for, Jesus rose. "The time has come," he said.

He threw a lingering glance around him at the fireplace, the work-tools, household utensils, lamp, water-jug, loom; then at the four women—old Salome, Martha, Magdalene, and Mary the weaver; lastly at the white old man who had entered the life ever-lasting.

"Farewell," he said, waving his hands.

None of the three younger women was able to answer. But old Salome said, "Don't look at us like that, my child. You seem to be saying good-bye to us for ever."

"Farewell," Jesus repeated. He approached the women and placed his palm first on Magdalene's hair, next on Martha's. The weaver then rose and came near. She too bowed her head. They felt as though he was blessing and embracing them, as though he

429

was going to take the three of them with him—always. But then all three abruptly began the dirge.

They went out into the yard. The disciples followed behind him. On the hedge of the yard, above the well, a honeysuckle had blossomed. Now that night had fallen, its perfume spilled forth. Jesus put out his hand, picked a flower and passed it between his teeth. May God give me strength, he prayed within his heart, may God give me strength to hold this tender flower between my teeth all through the great throes of crucifixion and not bite into it!

On the threshold of the street-door he stopped once more, lifted his hand and cried in a deep voice:

"Women, farewell!"

None of them answered. Their lamentations resounded in the courtyard.

Jesus took the lead, and the group started along the road to Jerusalem. The full moon rose from the mountains of Moab; the sun set behind the mountains of Judea. For a moment the two great jewels of the sky stopped and looked at each other. Then the one mounted, the other sank down.

Jesus nodded to Judas, who came and marched by his side. The two of them must have had secrets to exchange, for they spoke softly. Sometimes Jesus would lower his head, sometimes Judas; and each carefully weighed his words of response to the other, as though each word were a gold piece.

"I'm sorry, Judas, my brother," Jesus said, "but it is necessary."

"I've asked you before, rabbi—is there no other way?"

"No, Judas, my brother. I too should have liked one. I too hoped and waited for one until now—but in vain. No, there is no other way. The end of the world is here. This world, this kingdom of the Devil, will be destroyed and the kingdom of heaven will come. I shall bring it. How? By dying. There is no other way. Do not quiver, Judas, my brother. In three days I shall rise again."

"You tell me this in order to comfort me and make me able to betray you without rending my own heart. You say I have the endurance—you say it in order to give me strength. No, the closer we come to the terrible moment. . . , no, rabbi, I won't be able to endure!"

"You will, Judas, my brother. God will give you the strength,

430

as much as you lack, because it is necessary—it is necessary for me to be killed and for you to betray me. We two must save the world. Help me."

Judas bowed his head. After a moment he asked, "If you had to betray your master, would you do it?"

Jesus reflected for a long time. Finally he said, "No, I'm afraid I wouldn't be able to. That is why God pitied me and gave me the easier task: to be crucified."

Jesus took him by the arm and spoke to him softly, enticingly. "Do not abandon me; help me. Didn't you speak to the high priest Caiaphas? The Temple-slaves who'll seize me, aren't they ready and armed? Hasn't everything, Judas, happened just as we planned? Let us therefore celebrate the Passover tonight all together, and I shall give you a sign to get up and go fetch them. The dark days are only three; they will pass by like lightning, and on the third day we shall exult and dance all together—at the resurrection!"

"Will the others know?" Judas asked, pointing with his thumb to the flock of disciples in back.

"I'll tell them tonight. I don't want them to offer any resistance when the soldiers and Levites seize me."

Judas wrinkled his lips in contempt. "They offer resistance! Where did you find them, rabbi? One is worse than the next."

Jesus lowered his head and did not reply.

The moon rose and flowed over the earth, anointing stones, trees and men. Dark blue shadows fell on the land. In back the disciples, flocked together, talked and bickered. Some licked their chops at the thought of the banquet, some spoke with concern of Jesus' piercing words; and Thomas remembered the poor old rabbi:

"It's all over with him. Here's to our turn!"

"What, will we die too?" said Nathanael, surprised. "Didn't we say we were headed for immortality?"

"Right, but it seems we first have to go by way of death," Peter explained to him.

Nathanael shook his head. "We're taking a bad route to immortality," he grumbled. "Mark my words, we'll find it mighty unpleasant down there in hell!"

White and diaphanous like a ghost, Jerusalem now towered all moon-lit in the air before them. The houses, in the moonlight, seemed to be detached and suspended above the ground. A din compounded of men singing psalms and animals being slaughtered rose more and more clearly into the night.

Peter and John stood waiting at the eastern fortress-gate. Their faces flashing under the brilliant moon, they ran out happily to receive them. "Everything happened just as you said it would, rabbi. The tables are set. Dinner is served!"

"And if you ask for the master of the house," John added, laughing, "he prepared everything and then disappeared."

Jesus smiled. "That is the supreme hospitality: for the host to disappear."

They all quickened their pace. The streets were full of people, lighted lanterns, and myrtles. The Passover psalm resounded triumphantly from behind the closed doors:

> *When Israel went forth from Egypt,*
> *   when the house of Jacob was delivered from the barbarians,*
> *The sea looked and fled,*
> *   Jordan reversed its course;*
> *The mountains skipped like rams,*
> *   the hills like lambs.*
> *What ailed you, sea, that you fled,*
> *   and you, Jordan, that you turned front to back?*
> *What ailed you, mountains, that you skipped like rams,*
> *   and you, hills, like lambs?*
> *Tremble before the Lord, O Earth,*
> *   before the God of Israel,*
> *Who with his touch turns the rocks into lakes;*
> *   and stones spout cool waters!*

As the disciples marched through the streets they too began to chant the Passover psalm. Peter and John went in front and led them. All, with the exception of Jesus and Judas, had forgotten their cares and fears and were running towards the waiting tables.

Peter and John halted, pushed open a door marked with a fingerprint made with the blood of the slain lamb, and entered. Jesus and the hungry procession followed. Passing through the yard, they climbed up a stone staircase to the upper storey. The tables were set. Three seven-branched candelabra illuminated the lamb, wine, unleavened bread, hors d'oeuvres and even the staffs they were supposed to hold as they ate, as though they were ready to depart on a long journey.

"We're delighted to meet you!" said Jesus. He lifted his hand and blessed the invisible host.

The disciples laughed. "Whom are you greeting, rabbi?"

"The Invisible," Jesus answered, and he looked at them severely.

He tied a large towel around his waist, took water, knelt, and began to wash the disciples' feet.

"Rabbi, I'll never agree to let you wash my feet!" Peter cried.

"Peter, if I do not wash your feet, you will not join me in the kingdom of heaven."

"Well in that case, rabbi, wash not only my feet, but my hands and head too."

They seated themselves around the tables. They were famished, but no one dared put out his hand. The teacher's face was stern this evening and his lips embittered. He looked at the disciples one by one: at Peter on his right, John on his left—all; and opposite him, at his grave, unaccommodating accomplice with the red beard.

"First of all," he said, "we must drink the salt water, to remember the tears which our fathers shed in the land of slavery."

He took the pitcher with the salt water and started by filling Judas's glass to overflowing, then poured a few sips into the glasses of the others, and lastly filled his own brimful.

"May we remember the tears, the pain and the anguish men suffer for the sake of freedom!" he said, and he emptied his brimful glass in a single gulp.

The others drank with contorted mouths. Like Jesus, Judas emptied his glass in one gulp, He showed it to the master and turned it upside-down. Not a single drop remained.

"You're a brave warrior, Judas," Jesus said, smiling. "You can endure even the most severe bitterness."

He took the unleavened bread and divided it. Next, he served the lamb. Each one put out his hand and took his share of the bitter herbs prescribed by the Law: oregano, bay, and savoury.

Then, red gravy was poured over the meat in remembrance of the red bricks which their ancestors manufactured during their captivity. They ate hurriedly, as the Law prescribed, and each one grasped his staff and kept one foot raised in the air, prepared to depart.

Jesus watched them eat, not eating himself. He too held his staff and kept his right foot in the air, ready for a great journey. No one spoke. The only sounds were from the clacking of jaws, the clinking of wine glasses, and tongues licking the bones. The moon entered through the skylight above them. Half of the tables were brightly illuminated, half plunged in purple darkness.

After a deep silence Jesus opened his mouth: "Passover, my faithful fellow-voyagers, means passage—passage from darkness to light, from slavery to freedom. But the Passover that we celebrate tonight goes even further. Tonight's Passover means passage from death to eternal life. I go in the lead, comrades, and clear the way for you."

Peter shuddered. "Rabbi," he said, "you're speaking about death again, and again your words are a double-edged knife. If any calamity hangs over you, speak freely. We're men."

"It's true, rabbi," said John. "Your words are bitterer than these bitter herbs. Have pity and speak to us clearly."

Jesus took his still-untouched portion of bread and divided it mouthful by mouthful among the disciples.

"Take it and eat," he said. "This is my body."

He also took his glass of wine, which was still full, and passed it from mouth to mouth. They all drank.

"Take it and drink," he said. "This is my blood."

Each of the disciples ate his mouthful of bread and drank his sip of wine. Their minds reeled. The wine seemed to them thick and salty, like blood; the portion of bread descended like a burning coal into their very bowels. Suddenly, terrified, they all felt Jesus take root within them and begin to devour their entrails. Peter leaned his elbows on the table and began to weep. John bent over to Jesus' breast:

"You want to depart, rabbi, you want to depart. . . , to depart. . . ," he mumbled over and over, unable to utter anything more.

434

"You're not going anywhere!" Andrew yelled. "The other day you said, 'Let him who has no knife sell his cloak to buy one!' We'll sell our clothes, we'll arm ourselves; and then let Charon come in—if he dare—to touch you!"

"You shall all abandon me," Jesus said uncomplainingly. "All."

"I never!" shouted Peter, wiping away his tears.

"Peter, Peter, before the cock crows, you will deny me three times."

"I? I?" Peter bellowed, beating his chest with his fists. "I deny you? I'm with you to the death!"

"To the death!" groaned all the disciples, jumping to their feet in a trance.

"Sit down," Jesus said tranquilly. "The hour has not yet come. This Passover I have a great secret to confide to you. Open your minds, open your hearts, do not let yourselves be afraid!"

"Speak, rabbi," John murmured, his heart trembling like a reed.

"You have eaten? You are no longer hungry? The body is filled? Will it finally allow your soul to listen in peace?"

Trembling, they all hung on Jesus' lips.

"Beloved companions," he cried, "farewell! I depart!"

The disciples cried out, fell upon him and held him so that he would not leave. Many were weeping. But Jesus turned calmly to Matthew.

"Matthew, you know the Scriptures by heart. Get up and in a strong voice tell them Isaiah's prophetic words in order to steady their hearts. You remember: 'He grew up in the eyes of the Lord like a small, frail tree. . .' "

Rejoicing, Matthew jumped to his feet. He was stoop-shouldered, bow-legged, desiccated, and his long slender fingers were endlessly smudged; but suddenly—how straight he stood! His cheeks caught fire, his neck swelled, and the words of the prophet echoed in the high-ceilinged attic, full of bitterness and strength:

> He grew up in the eyes of the Lord like a small, frail tree
>   which sprouts out of unwatered ground.
> He had neither beauty nor lustre that we should turn
>   our eyes to see him;
>   his face had nothing to please us.

He was despised and rejected by men,
  a man of sorrows, and acquainted with grief.
We turned away our faces and esteemed him not.

But he took upon himself all our pains;
He was wounded for our transgressions,
  he was bruised for our iniquities;
And with his stripes we are healed.

He was scourged, and he was afflicted,
  yet he opened not his mouth;
Like a lamb that is led to the slaughter,
  he opened not his mouth. . . .

"That's enough," said Jesus, sighing. He turned to the companions:

"It is I," he said quietly. "The prophet Isaiah is speaking about me: I am the lamb that is being led to the slaughter, and I shall not open my mouth." After a pause, he continued: "They have been leading me to the slaughter ever since the day of my birth."

The amazed disciples stared at him, with gaping mouths, struggling to understand what he had told them; and suddenly, all together, they hid their faces against the tables and raised the dirge.

For a moment even Jesus lost heart. How could he abandon these wailing companions? He lifted his eyes and looked at Judas. But the other's hard blue eyes had been pinned on Jesus for a long time. He had divined what was happening inside the master and how easily love could paralyse his strength. The two glances joined and wrestled in the air for a split-second, the one stern and merciless, the other beseeching and afflicted. A split-second only—and straightway Jesus shook his head, smiled bitterly at Judas, and turned again to the disciples.

"Why do you weep?" he asked them. "Why are you afraid of Death? He is the most merciful of God's archangels, the one who loves man the most. It is necessary that I be martyred and crucified, and that I descend to hell. But in three days I shall jolt out of my tomb, ascend to heaven and sit next to the Father."

"Are you going to leave us again?" John shouted, weeping. "Take us with you to hell and heaven, rabbi!"

"The task on earth is also a heavy one, John beloved. You must all stay here on the soil, and work. Fight, here on the earth; love, wait—and I shall return!"

Jacob had already become reconciled to the rabbi's death and was spinning in his mind what they would do when they were left on earth without him.

"We cannot oppose God's will and the will of our master. As the prophets tell us, rabbi, it is your duty to die, ours to live: to live so that the words you spoke shall not perish. We'll establish them firmly in new Holy Scriptures, we'll make laws, build our own synagogues and select our own high priests, Scribes and Pharisees."

Jesus was terrified. "You crucify the spirit, Jacob," he shouted. "No, no, I don't want that!"

"This is the only way we can prevent the spirit from turning into air and escaping," Jacob countered.

"But it won't be free any more; it won't be spirit!"

"That doesn't matter. It will look like spirit. For our work, rabbi, that's sufficient."

A cold sweat flowed over Jesus. He threw a quick glance at the disciples. No one lifted his head to object. Peter looked at Zebedee's son with admiration. His was a creative mind: he'd taken on all the shining traits of his father, the captain; and now you would see—he was going to set everything in order for the master himself. . . . Jesus, despairing, lifted his hands. He seemed to be asking for help.

"I shall send you the Comforter, the spirit of truth. He will guide you."

"Send us the Comforter quickly," John cried, "so that we won't be led astray and fail to find you again, rabbi!"

Jacob shook his hard obstinate head. "It too—this spirit of truth you're talking about—it too will be crucified. You must realize, rabbi, that the spirit will be crucified as long as men exist. But it doesn't matter. Something is always left behind, and that, I tell you, is enough for us."

"It's not enough for me!" Jesus shouted in despair.

Jacob felt troubled when he heard this painful cry. He approached and took the master's hand. "Yes, it's not enough for you, rabbi," he said. "That is why you are being crucified. Forgive me for contradicting you."

Jesus placed his hand on the obstinate head. "If God wills it thus, let the spirit be eternally crucified upon this earth, and may the cross be blessed! Let us bear it with love, patience and faith. One day it will turn to wings on our shoulders."

They did not speak. The moon was now high in the heavens and a funereal light spilled over the tables. Jesus crossed his hands.

"The day's work is done," he said. "What I had to do, I did; what I had to speak, I spoke. I think I have done my duty. Now I cross my hands."

He nodded opposite him to Judas, who rose, tightened his leather belt and grasped his crooked staff. Jesus waved his hand at him, as though saying good-bye.

"Tonight," he said, "we shall be praying under the olive trees of Gethsemane, past the Cedron Valley. Judas, my brother: go—with God's blessing. God be with you!"

Judas parted his lips. He wanted to say something, but changed his mind. The door was open. He rushed out, and his large feet were heard stamping heavily down the stone stairs.

Peter felt uneasy. "Where is he going?" he asked. He started to get up in order to follow him, but Jesus held him back.

"Peter, the wheel of God has begun to roll. Do not step in the way."

A breeze had arisen. The flames on the seven-branched candelabra flickered. Suddenly there was a vehement gust of wind and the candles went out. The entire moon entered the chamber. Nathanael was frightened and leaned over to his friend:

"That wasn't the wind, Philip. Someone came in. Oh God! do you think it was Charon?"

"And what do you care if it was!" the shepherd answered him. "He isn't looking for us." He slapped the back of his friend, who still had not recovered his equilibrium.

"Big ships, big storms," he said. "Thank God we're only rowboats and walnut shells."

The moon had seized Jesus' face and devoured it. Nothing

remained but two pitch-black eyes. John was frightened. He stealthily held his hand to the rabbi's face to see if it still existed. "Rabbi," he murmured, "where are you?"

"I haven't left yet, John beloved," Jesus replied. "I was lost for a moment because I thought of something an ascetic on holy mount Carmel once told me: 'I was immersed in the five troughs of my body,' he said, 'like a pig.'

" 'And how were you saved, grandfather?' I asked him. 'Was it a great struggle?'

" 'Not at all,' he answered me. 'One morning I saw a flowering almond tree and was saved. . .'

"A flowering almond tree, John beloved: that is how death appeared to me for an instant just now."

He rose. "Let us go," he said. "The hour has come." He took the lead. The disciples followed, deep in thought.

"Let's leave," Nathanael whispered to his friend. "I smell complications."

"I've been thinking of the same thing myself," Philip answered, "but let's take Thomas too."

They searched in the moonlight to find Thomas, but he had already disappeared into the alleyways. They remained by themselves in the rear. As soon as the group reached the Cedron Valley they allowed the others to outdistance them and then ran for their lives.

Jesus descended the Cedron Valley with those who remained, climbed up the opposite side and took the path which led to the olive grove of Gethsemane. How many times he had stayed awake all night under those ancient olive trees and talked about God's mercy and the iniquities of men!

They halted. The disciples had eaten and drunk a great deal this evening and were sleepy. They cleaned the soil by pushing away the stones with their feet, and then made themselves ready to lie down.

"Three are missing," said the master, searching around him. "What happened to them?"

"They left," Andrew said angrily.

Jesus smiled. "Do not condemn them, Andrew. You will see: one day all three shall return, and each will be wearing a crown made of thorns, which is the most royal of crowns—and unwithering!" When he had spoken he leaned against an olive tree, for he suddenly felt greatly fatigued.

The disciples had already lain down. They found large stones for pillows and made themselves comfortable.

"Come, rabbi, lie down with us," said Peter, yawning. "Andrew will keep watch."

Jesus drew his body away from the tree. "Peter, Jacob and John," he said, "come with me!" His voice was full of affliction and command.

Peter pretended not to hear. He stretched out on the ground and yawned again, but Zebedee's two sons took him by the hands and lifted him up.

"Let's go," they said. "Aren't you ashamed?"

Peter approached his brother. "Who knows what will happen, Andrew. Give me your knife."

Jesus marched in front. They left the olive trees behind and reached open land. Opposite them gleamed Jerusalem, dressed all-white in the moonlight. The sky above was milky, and starless. The full moon, which earlier they had seen rise in such a hurry, now hung stationary in the centre of the sky.

"Father," Jesus murmured, "Father who are in heaven, Father who are on the earth: the world you created is beautiful, and we see it; beautiful too is the world which we do not see. I don't know—forgive me—I don't know, Father, which is the more beautiful."

He stooped, took up a handful of soil and smelt it. The aroma went deep down into his bowels. There must have been pistachio nearby, and the ground smelt of resin and honey. He rubbed the soil against his cheek, neck and lips.

"What perfume," he murmured, "what warmth, what brotherhood!"

He began to weep. He held the soil in his palm, not wanting to part with it ever. "Together," he murmured, "together we shall die, my brother. I have no other companion."

Peter had stood enough. "I'm exhausted," he said. "Where's he taking us? I'm not going further. I'm going to lie down right here."

But as he searched around him to find a comfortable hollow in which to stretch out, he saw Jesus coming slowly down upon them. He immediately recovered his strength and went out before the others to meet him.

"It's almost midnight, rabbi," he said. "This is a good place for us to sleep."

"My children," Jesus said, "my soul is mortally sad. You go back and lie down under the trees while I stay here in the open to pray. But I beg of you, do not sleep. Stay awake tonight and pray with me. Help me, my children, help me to pass through this difficult hour."

He turned his face towards Jerusalem. "Go now. Leave me alone."

The disciples drew a stone's throw away and thrust themselves under the olive trees. But Jesus fell to the ground with his face glued to the soil. His mind, heart and lips could not be separated from the earth—they had become earth.

"Father," he murmured, "here I am fine: dust with dust. Leave me. Bitter, exceedingly bitter, is the cup you have given me to drink. I don't have the endurance. If it is possible, Father, remove it from my lips."

He remained silent, listening. Perhaps he would hear the Father's voice in the blackness. He closed his eyes. Who could tell—God was good, the Father might appear inside him and smile compassionately and nod to him. He waited and waited, trembling. He heard nothing, saw nothing. All alone, he looked around him, became frightened, jolted upright and went to find the companions in order to steady his heart. He found all three asleep. He pushed Peter with his foot, then John, then Jacob.

"Aren't you ashamed of yourselves?" he said to them bitterly. "Can't you bear up just a short while, to pray with me?"

"Rabbi," said Peter, unable to keep his eyelids from falling, "the soul is ready and willing but the flesh is weak. Forgive us."

Jesus returned to the open space and fell upon his knees on the rocks.

"Father," he cried again, "bitter, exceedingly bitter is the cup you have given me. Remove it from my lips."

As he spoke he saw above him in the moonlight an angel, stern and pale, coming down. His wings were made of the moon and between his palms he held a silver chalice. Jesus hid his face in his hands and collapsed to the ground.

"Is this your response, Father? Have you no mercy?"

He waited a short time. Little by little he timidly separated his fingers to see if the angel was still above him. The heavenly visitor had come still lower, and the chalice was now touching his lips. He shrieked, threw out his arms and fell supine onto the ground.

When he came to, the moon had moved a hand's breadth from the summit of the heavens and the angel had dissolved into the moonlight. In the distance, on the road to Jerusalem, he saw scattered, moving lights—apparently from burning torches. Were they coming towards him? Were they going away from him? Once more he was overcome by fear—and by the longing to see men, to hear a human voice, to touch hands he loved. He departed at a run to find the three companions.

All three were again asleep, their serene faces floating in a bath of moonlight. John had Peter's shoulder as a pillow, Peter Jacob's breast. Jacob supported his black-haired head on a stone. His arms were spread wide as if he was embracing the heavens, and his gleaming teeth shone through his raven-black moustache and beard. He must have been having a pleasant dream, for he was laughing. Jesus took pity on them and this time refrained from pushing them awake. Walking on tiptoe, he retraced his steps. Then he fell once more on his face and began to weep.

"Father," he said, so softly it seemed he did not wish God to hear, "Father, your will be done. Not mine, Father—yours."

He rose and looked again in the direction of the Jerusalem road. The lights had now come closer. He could clearly see the quivering shadows around them and the flashing of bronze armour.

"They're coming. . . , they're coming. . . ," he murmured, and his knees gave way beneath him. Exactly at that moment a nightingale appeared and perched in a small young cypress opposite him. It swelled its throat and began to sing. It had become drunk from the immense moon, the vernal perfumes, the damp warm night. Inside it was an omnipotent God, the same God that created heaven, earth and the souls of men. Jesus lifted his head and listened intently. Could this God who loved the soil, cool embraces, and the tiny breasts of the birds really be the true God of men? Suddenly, in reply to the bird's invitation, another nightingale bounded up from the very depths of his soul and it too began to hymn the eternal pains and joys: God, love, hope. . .

It sang, and Jesus trembled. He had not realized that such riches were inside him, nor so many delectable, unrevealed joys and sins. His insides blossomed; the nightingale became entangled in the flowering branches and could not, did not, wish to flee ever again. Where to go? Why should it leave? This earth was Paradise. . . . But as Jesus, following the double song, entered Paradise without losing his body, hoarse voices were heard, lighted torches and bronze panoplies came near, and amidst the glare and the smoke he seemed to descry Judas: two strong arms which clasped him and a red beard which pricked his face. He screamed and lost consciousness for a moment—so it seemed to him—but not before he felt Judas's heavy-breathed mouth glued to his own and heard a hoarse, despairing voice:

"Hail, rabbi!"

The moon was now about to touch the whitish-blue mountains of Judea. A damp freezing wind arose and Jesus' nails and lips turned blue. Jerusalem towered blind and deathly pale in the moonlight.

Jesus turned and looked at the soldiers and Levites.

"Welcome to the envoys of my God," he said. "Let us go!"

Suddenly, amidst the tumult, he discerned Peter drawing his knife to cut off the ear of one of the Levites.

"Put your knife in its sheath," he ordered. "If we meet the knife with the knife, when will the world ever be free of stabbings?"

XXIX

THEY seized Jesus. Hooting him, they dragged him over the rocks, through the clumps of cypresses and olive trees, down into the Cedron Valley, into Jerusalem and finally to Caiaphas's Palace, where the Council was assembled and waiting to judge the rebel.

It was cold. The servants warmed themselves before fires they had lit in the courtyard. Levites constantly issued from within with reports. The evidence brought against Jesus was enough to make the hair stand on end: this recipient of the divine malediction had uttered such-and-such blasphemies concerning the God of Israel, such-and-such concerning the Law of Israel; and he said he was going to tear down the Holy Temple and sow it with salt!

Peter, heavily bundled up, slid into the yard. Keeping his head bowed, he held his hands before the fire, warmed himself, and listened tremblingly to the reports. A maidservant came by and halted when she saw him.

"Hey, old man," she said, "why are you hiding from us? Lift your head so that we can see you. I think you were with him."

Several Levites heard her words and approached. Peter was afraid. He raised his hand.

"I swear I don't know the man!" he said, and he drew towards the door.

Another maidservant passed by, saw him trying to leave, and put out her hand. "Hey old man, where are you going? You were with him! I saw you!"

"I don't know the man," Peter cried once more. Pushing the girl aside, he continued on. But at the door two Levites stopped him. They grabbed him by the shoulders and shook him violently.

"Your accent betrays you," they shouted. "You're a Galilean, one of his disciples!"

Then Peter began to swear and curse, and he shouted: "I don't know the man!"

At that moment the cock of the yard crowed. Peter groaned loudly. He remembered the rabbi's words: "Peter, Peter, before the cock crows, you will deny me three times." . . . He went out to the street, collapsed onto the ground and burst into tears.

Day was breaking. The sky turned blood-red. A pale Levite flew out of the Palace in an uproar.

"The High Priest is rending his clothes. What do you think the criminal just said: 'I am the Christ, the Son of God!' All the Elders jumped up. They're ripping their clothes and shouting, 'Death! Death!' "

Another Levite appeared. "Now they're going to take him and lead him to Pilate. He's the only one who has the right to kill him. Make way for them to pass. The doors are opening!"

The doors opened and out came Israel's nobility. First, walking slowly, the overwrought high priest Caiaphas. Behind him—a mass of beards, sly malformed eyes, toothless mouths and evil tongues—the Elders. They were all staggering from rage, and steaming. Behind them: Jesus, tranquil and sad. Blood ran from his head, for they had struck him.

Hoots, laughter and cursing broke out in the yard. Peter jumped up and supported himself against the jamb of the street-door, his tears flowing. "Peter, Peter," he murmured, "coward, liar, traitor! Rise up and shout: 'I am with him!' even if they kill you." He advised his soul, excited it; but his body, motionless, leaned against the door-post and trembled. On the threshold Jesus tripped and stumbled forward. Putting out his hand to catch hold somewhere, he found Peter's shoulder. The other turned to marble and did not breathe a word, did not stir. He felt the rabbi's hand hooked into him, not letting him go. It was not fully light out yet, and Jesus did not turn in the bluish darkness to see what he had grasped to prevent himself from falling. He regained his balance and—behind the Elders, and surrounded by soldiers—started out once more towards the palace tower.

Pilate had awakened, washed, anointed himself with aromatic oil, and was pacing nervously back and forth on the high solarium of his tower. He had never liked this Passover day. The Jews, drunk with their God, would work themselves into a frenzy, come

445

to blows again with the Roman soldiers—and this year another massacre might break out, which was not in the best interests of Rome. This Passover he had an additional worry. The Hebrews would by all means crucify the poor Nazarene, the crazy one. . . . Disgraceful race!

Pilate clenched his fist. He was overcome by an obstinate desire to save this imbecile, not because he was innocent (*innocent*: what did that mean?) nor because he pitied him (alas! if at this point he began to pity the Jews. . .), but in order to enrage the disgraceful Hebrew race.

Pilate heard a great tumult beneath the tower windows. He leaned out and saw that his yard had filled with Jewry. He could also see the maniacal multitude which filled the porches and tiers of the Temple to overflowing. Armed with staffs and slings, the crowd shoved, kicked and hooted Jesus, whom the Roman soldiers were guarding and pushing towards the immense tower door.

Pilate went inside and sat down on his coarsely-sculptured throne. The door opened. The two colossal negroes pushed Jesus in. His clothes were in tatters and his face covered with blood, but he held his head high, and in his eyes gleamed a light, calm and far-removed from men. Pilate smiled.

"Once more I see you before me, Jesus of Nazareth, king of the Jews. It seems they want to kill you."

Jesus gazed through the window at the sky. His mind and body had already departed. He did not speak. Pilate became angry.

"Forget the sky," he yelled. "You'd better look at me! Don't you know I've got the authority to release you, or crucify you?"

"You have no authority over me whatever," Jesus calmly replied. "No one has but God."

Below, there were maniacal cries: "Death! Death!"

"Why are they so rabid?" Pilate asked. "What have you done to them?"

"I proclaimed the truth to them," Jesus answered.

Pilate smiled. "What truth? What does *truth* mean?"

Jesus' heart constricted with sorrow. This was the world, these the rulers of the world. They ask what truth is, and laugh.

Pilate stood before the window. He remembered that just yesterday they had seized Barabbas for the murder of Lazarus. It

446

was an established custom for the Romans to release a prisoner on the day of the Passover.

"Whom do you want me to release to you," he shouted, "Jesus the king of the Jews or Barabbas the bandit?"

"Barabbas! Barabbas!" howled the people.

Pilate called the guards and pointed to Jesus. "Scourge him," he ordered, "place a crown of thorns on his head, wrap him in a scarlet cloth and give him a long reed to hold as a sceptre. He is a king—dress him like a king!"

He had devised to present him to the people in this pitiful state, hoping they would feel sorry for him.

The guards seized him, bound him to a column and began to thrash him and spit on him. They plaited him a crown of thorns and thrust it onto his head. The blood spurted from his forehead and temples. They threw a scarlet cloth over his back, passed a long reed through his fingers, then brought him back to Pilate. When the Roman saw him, he could not keep from laughing.

"Welcome to His Majesty!" he said. "Come, let me show you to your subjects."

He took him by the hand and they went out onto the terrace.

"Behold the man!" he shouted.

"Crucify him! Crucify him!" the people began to howl.

Pilate ordered a basin and a pitcher of water brought him. He leaned over and washed his hands in front of the crowd.

"I wash and rinse my hands," he said. "It is not I who spill his blood; I am innocent. May the sin fall on you!"

"His blood be on our heads and on the heads of our children!" the people bellowed.

"Take him," Pilate said, "and don't bother me any more!"

They seized him, loaded the cross on his back, spit at him, beat him, kicked him towards Golgotha. The cross was heavy. Staggering, he looked about him. Perhaps he would discover one of the disciples and nod to him so that he might take pity on him. He looked and looked. No one. He sighed.

"Blessed is death," he murmured. "Glory be to God!"

The disciples, meanwhile, had burrowed into Simon the Cyrenian's tavern. They were waiting for the crucifixion to be over

447

and night to fall so that they could escape without being seen. Squatting behind the barrels, they listened with cocked ears to the happy throngs which passed by outside in the street. The whole city—men and women—had begun to run towards Golgotha. The people had enjoyed a fine Passover, had eaten more than enough meat, drunk more than enough wine; and now here was the crucifixion to while away their time.

The people ran; the disciples listened to the noise in the street, and trembled. Now and then John's muffled weeping could be heard. At times Andrew rose and paced up and down the tavern uttering threats. Peter cursed and vilified himself for being a coward and not having the courage to race outside to be killed along with the master. . . . How many times he had sworn to him: "With you, rabbi, to the death!" But now that death had appeared, he had burrowed behind the barrels.

Jacob grew furious. "John," he said, "stop your bawling—you're a man. And you, gallant Andrew, don't twist your moustache. Sit down. Sit down, all of you. Let's come to a decision. Suppose he's really the Messiah. . . . With what kind of faces will we appear before him if he is resurrected in three days' time? Did you ever think about that? What do you say, Peter?"

"If he's the Messiah, we're done for—that's what I say," answered Peter hopelessly. "I told you, I already denied him three times."

"But if he isn't the Messiah, we're still done for," said Jacob. "What do you say Nathanael?"

"I say we should get out of here. Whether he's the Messiah or not, we're done for."

"And leave him like this, unprotected? How can your hearts endure that?" said Andrew, starting to rush towards the door.

But Peter caught hold of his tunic. "Sit down, wretch, before I break you into a thousand pieces! Let's find another solution."

"Hypocrites and Pharisees!" Thomas hissed. "What solution? Let's speak out and not blush over it: we made a transaction, we sank in all our capital. Yes: business! Why look daggers at me—that's what we did, we transacted a little business. You give me and I give you. I gave my wares—combs, spools of thread, pocket-mirrors—in exchange for the kingdom of heaven. All of you did the same. One gave his boat, another his sheep, a third his peace of mind. And now the whole affair has gone to the devil. We're bankrupt, our capital has disappeared down the drain. Look out we don't lose our lives in the bargain. What advice do I give, then? Go while the going's good!"

"Agreed!" shouted both Philip and Nathanael. "Go while the going's good!"

Peter turned anxiously to Matthew, who was sitting off to one side. He had been listening with cupped ear, not breathing a word. "For God's sake, Matthew," Peter said, "don't write all this down. Play deaf. Don't make us ridiculous for all eternity!"

"Don't worry, I know what I'm doing," Matthew answered. "I see and hear a lot, but I select. . . . A word, however, for your own good: Come to a noble decision; show how brave you are—so that I can write about it and you poor fellows can be glorified. You are apostles, and that's no small matter!"

Just then Simon the Cyrenian shoved open the tavern door and entered. His clothes were torn, his face and chest full of blood, his right eye swollen and running. Cursing and groaning, he threw off the rags that remained to him, plunged his head into the tub he used to clean the wine-glasses, grabbed a towel and wiped his chest and back, all the while bellowing and spitting. Then he put his mouth to the tap of the barrel and drank. Hearing a disturbance behind the barrels, he leaned over. When he saw the pile of huddling disciples, he went wild.

"Out of my sight, filthy dogs!" he screamed at them. "Bah! Is this the way you stick by your chief! Ducking out of battle, eh! Lousy Galileans, lousy Samaritans, lousy bastards!"

"God knows our souls were willing," Peter ventured, "but our bodies—"

"Shut up, jabber-jaws! Bah! When the soul is willing, the body doesn't mean a thing. All becomes soul, even the club in your hand, the coat on your back, the stones you walk over—all, all! Look, cowards, look at me: black and blue, my clothes in tatters, my eyeballs ready to fall out of my head. Why?—the devil take you, filthy disciples!—because, damn it, I defended your master, I fought the whole population—me, me, the innkeeper, the lousy Cyrenian! And why did I do it? Was it because I believed he was the Messiah and tomorrow he'd make me great and important? Not a bit; no, not a single bit. It was because my confounded self-respect got hold of me—and I'm not sorry, either!"

He paced up and down, tripped over the stools, spat, cursed. Matthew was sitting on hot coals. He wanted to learn what happened at Caiaphas's palace, what at Pilate's, what the teacher said, what the people shouted. . . , so that he could record it all in his book.

"If you believe in God, Simon, my brother," he said, "quiet down and tell us what happened: how, when and where; and if the teacher spoke. . . ."

"He certainly did speak!" Simon answered. " 'Damn you to hell, disciples,—that's what he said. Well—write! Why are you looking at me? Grab your pen and write: 'Damn you to hell!' "

Lamentations arose from behind the barrels. John was rolling on the ground and screeching, and Peter was beating his head against the wall.

"If you believe in God, Simon," Matthew begged him again, "tell the truth so that I can write it down. Can't you understand that at this moment the future of the whole world depends on what you say?"

Peter was still beating his head against the wall.

"Blast it, don't get desperate, Peter," the innkeeper said to him. "I'll tell you what you can do to win glory for all eternity. Listen: soon they're going to lead him by here—I already hear the noise. Get up, open the door like a man, go take the cross from him and put it on your own shoulders. It's heavy, curse it, and your god is very delicate, and exhausted."

Laughing, he shoved Peter with his foot. "You'll do it? I want to see some action, here and now!"

"I would do it, I swear to you, if there weren't such a crowd," Peter whined. "They'll make mincemeat out of me."

The enraged innkeeper spat. "Go to hell—all of you!" he shouted. "Will none of you do it? You, Nathanael bean-stalk. . . ? You, Andrew cut-throat. . . ? No one, no one? Pfoul to the devil with you all! Ah, my poor Messiah, what sterling generals you chose to help you conquer the world! You'd have done better choosing me—me! I may deserve to be hanged and have my head displayed on a stake, but I've got a little self-respect all the same, and when a fellow's got self-respect it doesn't matter if he's a drunkard, a robber or a liar: he's still a man. When you've got no self-respect—you might be an innocent dove, but pfou! you're not worth a miserable shoe-patch!"

Spitting again, he opened the door and stood on the threshold, puffing.

The streets had filled with people. Men and women were running, shouting: "He's coming! The king of the Jews is coming. Boo! Boo!"

The disciples burrowed again behind the barrels. Simon whirled around: "Bah! Don't you have any self-respect? You're not going out to see him, eh? Won't you even give the poor fellow the consolation of a glimpse of his disciples? All right, then—I'll go out, I'll wave to him. 'It's me,' I'll say, 'me, Simon the Cyrenian—present!'"

With one bound he was in the road.

The multitude passed by, wave after wave. In front, Roman cavalry; behind, Jesus bearing the cross. Blood ran over him and his clothes hung in tatters. He no longer had the strength to walk. His face pitched more and more forward; he continually stumbled, ready to fall, and they continually set him up straight again and kicked him onward. In back ran the lame, the blind and the maimed, enraged because he had not healed them. They cursed him and struck him with their crutches and canes. He frequently looked around him. Would none of the beloved companions appear? What had happened to them?

Outside the tavern he turned and saw the innkeeper waving his hand at him. His heart rejoiced. He started to nod his head to say good-bye to him, but tripped on a stone and collapsed to the ground, the cross over his back. He groaned with pain.

The Cyrenian rushed forward, lifted him up, took the cross and loaded it upon his own back. Then he turned and smiled at Jesus. "Courage," he said to him. "I'm here, don't be afraid."

They left by the gate of David and started up the slope which led to the summit of Golgotha—Golgotha: all stones, thorns and bones. Here the rebels were crucified, their remains left to the vultures. The air stank from carrion.

The Cyrenian put down the cross. Two soldiers began to dig and embed it between the rocks. Jesus sat-down on a stone and waited. The sun hung high above them; the heavens were white, burning—and closed. Not a flame, not an angel, not even a small sign that someone there above was watching the events below on earth. . . . And while he sat and waited, crumbling a small clod of earth between his fingers, he felt someone standing before him, looking at him. Raising his head calmly, without haste, he saw and recognized her.

"Welcome, faithful fellow-voyager," he murmured. "Here the journey ends. What you wanted has been accomplished; what I wanted has also been accomplished. All my life I toiled to turn the Curse into a blessing. I've done it, and we are friends now. Farewell, Mother!". . . He waved his hand languidly at the savage shade.

Two soldiers grabbed him by the shoulders.

"Get up, Your Majesty," they shouted at him. "Mount your throne!"

They undressed him, revealing his thin body. It was covered with blood.

The heat was intense. The people, tired of shouting themselves hoarse, watched mutely.

"Let him drink some wine to gain strength," a soldier suggested. But Jesus pushed away the cup and extended his arms to the cross.

"Father," he murmured, "your will be done."

The blind, the leprous and the maimed now began to howl:

"Liar! Cheat! Deceiver of the people!"

"Where is the kingdom of heaven, where are the ovens with the loaves?" howled the ragamuffins, and they barraged him with lemon-peels and stones.

Jesus spread wide his arms and opened his mouth to cry: Brothers! but the soldiers seized him and hoisted him up onto the cross. Then they called the gipsies with the nails—but as the hammers were lifted and the first blow was heard, the sun hid its face; as the second was heard, the sky darkened and the stars appeared: not stars, but large tears which dripped onto the soil.

The crowd was overcome with fright. The horses on which the Romans were mounted became ferocious. Rearing, they began to gallop furiously and trample the Jewry. Then earth, sky and air suddenly grew mute, as at the beginning of an earthquake. Simon the Cyrenian fell prone onto the stones. The world had shaken many times under his feet, and he was terrified.

"Alas! now the earth will open up and swallow us all," he murmured.

He lifted his head and looked around him. The world seemed to have fainted. Deathly pale, it was now just barely visible in the bluish darkness. The heads of the people had vanished and only their eyes—black holes—bored through the air. A thick flock of crows which had scented the blood and rushed to Golgotha now fled in terror. A feeble gasp of complaint descended from the cross and the Cyrenian, tying his heart into a knot so that he would not weep, lifted his eyes and looked. Suddenly he uttered a cry. Jesus was not being nailed to the cross by gipsies! No, a multitude of angels had come down from heaven, holding hammers and nails in their hands. They flew around Jesus, swung the hammers happily and nailed the hands and feet; some tightly bound the victim's body with stout cord so that he would not fall; and a small angel with rosy cheeks and golden curls held a lance and pierced Jesus' heart.

"What is this?" murmured the Cyrenian, trembling. "God himself, God himself is crucifying him!"

And then—never in his life had the Cyrenian experienced such intense fear or pain—a great heart-rending cry, full of complaint, tore the air from earth to heaven:

ELI . . . , ELI . . .

The sufferer was unable to continue. He wanted to but could not: he had no more breath.

The Crucified inclined his head—and fainted.

453

XXX

HIS eyelids fluttered with joy and surprise. This was not a cross, it was a huge tree reaching from earth to heaven. Spring had come: blossoms covered the entire tree; and at the very very end of each branch a bird sat over the brink and sang. . . . And he—he stood erect, his whole body leaning against the flowering tree. He lifted his head and counted: one, two, three. . .

"Thirty-three," he murmured. "As many as my own years. Thirty-three birds, and all singing."

His eyes expanded, burst their bounds, covered his entire face. He could see the world in bloom in every direction, without turning. His ears, two sinuous sea-shells, received the blasphemies, weeping and tumult of the world and turned them into song. And from his heart, pierced by a lance, the blood flowed.

There was no wind, but the compassionate tree shed its flowers, one by one, onto his thorn-entangled hair and bloody hands. And as he struggled amidst the sea of twitterings to remember who he was and where he was, the air suddenly whirled, congealed—and an angel stood before him. . . . At that moment, day broke.

He had seen many angels, both while asleep and while awake, but he had never seen an angel like this. What warm human beauty, what soft curly fluff on his cheeks and upper lip! And the eyes— how they played friskily, full of passion, like those of a young man or woman in love. His body was·supple and firm, a blue-black disquieting fluff enwrapped his legs, from the shins to the rounded thighs; and his armpits smelt of beloved human sweat.

Jesus was disconcerted. "Who are you?" he asked him, his heart pounding.

The angel smiled and his whole face became sweet, like the face of a man. He folded his two wide green wings as though he did not want to frighten Jesus too much.

"I am just like yourself," he answered. "Your guardian angel. Have faith."

His voice was deep and caressing, compassionate and familiar—

just like the voice of a man. The voices of the angels Jesus had heard until now had been severe, and they had always scolded him. Rejoicing, he looked imploringly at the angel and waited for him to speak again.

The angel divined this and inclined smilingly to the man's desire. "God sent me to bring sweetness to your lips. Men have given you much bitterness to drink; the heavens have done the same. You have suffered and struggled. In your whole life you have seen not one day of gladness. Your mother, brothers, disciples; the poor, the maimed, the oppressed—all, all abandoned you in the last terrible moment. You remained upon a rock in the darkness, completely alone and undefended. And then God the Father took pity on you. 'Hey there, why are you sitting?' he called to me. 'Aren't you his guardian angel? Well, go down and save him. I don't want him to be crucified. Enough's enough!'

" 'Lord of Hosts,' I answered him, trembling, 'didn't you send him to earth to be crucified in order to save mankind? That's why I sit here undisturbed: I thought that such was your will.'

" 'Let him be crucified in a dream,' God answered. 'Let him taste the same fear, the same pain.' "

"Guardian angel," cried Jesus, grasping the angel's head with both his hands so that he would not lose him, "guardian angel, my boy: I'm bewildered—wasn't I crucified?"

The angel placed his all-white hand on Jesus' agitated heart in order to calm it.

"Quiet down, don't be disturbed, beloved," he said to him, and his bewitching eyes fluttered. "No, you weren't crucified."

"Was the cross then a dream—and the nails, the pain, the sun which became dark?"

"Yes, a dream. You lived your entire Passion in a dream. You mounted the cross and were nailed to it in a dream. The five wounds in your hands, feet and heart were inflicted in a dream, but with such force that, look! the blood is still flowing. . . ."

Jesus gazed around him in a trance. Where was he? What was this plain with its flowering trees and water? And Jerusalem? And his soul? He turned to the angel and touched his arm. How cool his flesh was, how firm!

"Guardian angel, my boy," he said, "as you speak my flesh finds relief, the cross becomes the shadow of a cross, the nails shadows of nails, and the crucifixion floats in the sky above me, like a cloud. . . ."

"Let us go," said the angel, and he began to stride nimbly over the blossoming meadow. "Great joys await you, Jesus of Nazareth. God left me free to allow you to taste all the pleasures you ever secretly longed for. . . . Beloved, the earth is good—you'll see. Wine, laughter, the lips of a woman, the gambols of your first son on your knees—all are good. . . . We angels (would you believe it?) often lean over, up there in heaven, look at the earth—and sigh."

His huge green wings fluttered and embraced Jesus. "Turn your head," he said. "Look behind you."

Jesus turned his head—and what did he see? High in the distance, the hill of Nazareth gleamed in the rising sun, the fortress-gates were open, and a multitude of thousands—all great lords and ladies—was coming out. They were dressed in gold and mounted on white horses. Waving in the air were standards of snowy-white silk decorated with golden lilies. The procession descended between flowering mountains, passed by royal castles, forded rivers, wound in and out, hugging the hillsides. He heard a din compounded of laughter, shrill conversations, and from behind the thick clumps of trees, sweet sighs. . . .

"Guardian angel, my boy," said Jesus, bewildered, "what is this multitude of noblemen? Who are these kings and queens? Where are they going?"

"It's a royal marriage-procession," the angel replied with a smile. "They are going to a wedding."

"Who is getting married?"

"You," he answered. "This is the first joy I give you."

Jesus' blood flowed up to his head. Suddenly he conjectured who the bride would be, and his flesh rejoiced. He was in a hurry now. "Let's go," he said.

He immediately felt that he too had mounted a white horse saddled and bridled in gold. He looked at himself. A blue feather was waving at the top of his head, and his poor tunic with its thousands of patches had become all velvet and gold.

"My boy, is this the kingdom of heaven I announced to men?" he asked.

"No, no," the angel replied, laughing. "This is the Earth."

"How did it change so much?"

"It did not change, you did. Once upon a time your heart did not want the earth: it went against her will. Now it wants her—and that is the whole secret. Harmony between the earth and the heart, Jesus of Nazareth: that is the kingdom of heaven. . . . But why waste our time with words? Come, the bride is waiting."

The angel now mounted a white horse and they set out. Behind him the mountains neighed with the royal cavalcade which was descending. The laughter of the women had increased. The birds, beating their wings in the air, were drawing everything towards the south. "He's coming," they sang, "he's coming, he's coming!" Jesus' heart was also a bird. Perched on the top of his head, it twittered, "I'm coming, I'm coming, I'm coming!"

But while he was galloping, suddenly, in the midst of his great exaltation, he remembered his disciples. Looking behind him, he examined the mass of lords and ladies, searched to find them—and did not find them. He glanced at his companion with surprise.

"And my disciples?" he asked. "I don't see them. Where can they be?"

He was answered with mocking laughter: "Dispersed."

"Why?"

"Fear."

"Even Judas?"

"All! All! They returned to their caiques, hid themselves in their cottages. They swear they never saw you, don't know you. . . . Don't look behind you any more. Forget about them. Look in front."

The inebriating perfume of flowering lemon-trees invaded the air.

"Here we are," said the angel, dismounting. His horse turned into light and vanished.

A deep lowing of complaint, all suffering and sweetness, resounded from within the olive grove. Jesus felt troubled: his own bowels seemed to be calling out. He looked. Tied to the trunk of an olive tree was a gleaming full-rumped bull, black with white forehead. His tail was held high, and a nuptial crown rested on his horns. Jesus had never seen such power, such brilliance, such hard

457

muscles, nor eyes so dark, so full of virility. He was frightened. This is not a bull, he reflected, it is one of the dark, deathless faces of Almighty God.

The angel stood near him and smiled cunningly. "Don't be afraid, Jesus of Nazareth. It's a bull, a young virgin bull. Look how swiftly he moves his tongue and licks his moist nostrils, how he lowers his head and butts the olive tree, anxious to fight with it, how he shakes himself in order to break the rope and escape. . . . Look down there in the meadow: What do you see?"

"Heifers, young heifers. . . . They're grazing."

"They're not grazing, they're waiting for the young bull to break the rope. Listen once more how he bellows. What tenderness, what supplication, what power! Truly, like a dark and wounded god. . . . Why has your face grown fierce, Jesus of Nazareth? Why do you look at me with those dark, unlaughing eyes?"

"Let us go," Jesus bellowed softly. His voice was all tenderness, supplication and power.

"First I'll release the bull," answered the angel, laughing. "Don't you feel sorry for him?"

He approached and untied the rope. For a moment the chaste beast did not move. But suddenly he understood: he was free. With a bound he rushed towards the meadow.

At precisely that instant Jesus heard the tinkling of bracelets and necklaces from within a lemon-orchard. He turned. Mary Magdalene, crowned with lemon-blossoms, was standing before him, bashful and trembling.

Jesus rushed forward and took her in his arms.

"Magdalene, beloved Magdalene," he cried, "oh how many, how very many years I've longed for this moment! Who stepped between us and refused to leave us free—God? . . . Why are you crying?"

"Because of my great joy, Beloved; because of my great longing. Come!"

"Let us go. Lead me!"

He turned to say good-bye to his companion, but the angel had vanished into the air. Behind them, the great royal cortege of lords, ladies, kings, white horses and white lilies had also vanished. Below in the meadow, the bull was mounting the heifers.

"Whom are you looking for, Beloved? Why do you gaze behind you? Only we two remain in the world. I kiss the five wounds on your feet, your hands, your heart. What joy this is, what a Passover! The whole world has been resurrected! Come."

"Where? Give me your hand; lead me. I trust you."

"To a dense orchard. You're being hunted, they want to seize you. Everything was ready—the cross, the nails, the mob, Pilate. . . , but suddenly an angel came and snatched you away. Come—before the sun mounts and they see you. They've grown rabid: they want your death."

"What have I done to them?"

"You sought their good, their salvation. How can they ever pardon you for that! Give me your hand, beloved. Follow the woman. She, always sure, finds the way."

She took his hand. Her fiery-red veil swelled as she walked hastily under the flowering soon-fruitful lemon trees. Her fingers, entwined in those of the man, were burning hot, and her mouth smelt of lemon-leaves.

Out of breath, she stopped for a moment and looked at Jesus. He shuddered, for he saw her eye frolic seductively, cunningly, like the eye of the angel. But she smiled at him.

"Don't be afraid, Beloved. For years and years I've had something on the tip of my tongue, but I never had the courage to reveal it to you. Now I shall do so."

"What is it? Speak without fear, Beloved."

"If you're in the seventh heaven and a passer-by requests a glass of water of you, descend from the seventh heaven in order to give it to him. If you are a holy saint and a woman requests a kiss of you, descend from your sanctity in order to give it to her. Otherwise you cannot be saved."

Jesus seized her, threw back her head and kissed her on the mouth.

They both turned deathly pale. Their knees gave way. Unable to go further, they lay down under a flowering lemon-tree and began to roll on the ground.

The sun came and stood above them. A breeze blew; several lemon-flowers fell on the two naked bodies. A green lizard cemented itself to a stone opposite and watched them with its round motionless eyes. Now and then the bull could be heard bellowing in the distance, rested now and satiated. A gentle drizzle cooled the two burning bodies and drew out the odour of the soil.

Purring, Mary Magdalene hugged the man, kept his body glued to hers.

"No man has ever kissed me. I have never felt a man's beard over my lips and cheeks, nor a man's knees between my knees. This is the day of my birth! . . . Are you crying, my child?"

"Beloved wife, I never knew the world was so beautiful or the flesh so holy. It too is a daughter of God, a graceful sister of the soul. . . . I never knew that the joys of the body were not sinful."

"Why did you set out to conquer heaven, and sigh, and seek the miraculous water of eternal life? I am that water. You have stooped, drunk, found peace. . . . Are you still sighing, my child? What are you thinking about?"

"My heart is a withered rose of Jericho which revives and opens up again when placed in water. Woman is a fountain of immortal water. Now I understand."

"Understand what, my child?"

"This is the road."

"The road? What road, dearest Jesus?"

"The road by which the mortal becomes immortal, the road by which God descends to earth in human shape. I went astray because I sought a route outside of the flesh; I wanted to go by way of the clouds, great thoughts, and death. Woman, precious fellow-worker of God: forgive me. I bow and worship you, Mother of God. . . What shall we name the son we are going to have?"

"Take him to the Jordan and baptize him as you please. He's yours."

"Let's call him Paraclete, the Comforter!"

"Shh, I hear someone coming through the trees. It must be my faithful little negro. I told him to keep watch so that no one would come near. Here he is!"

"Saul, ma'am."

The boy's brilliantly white eyes danced; his chubby body was frothing all over like that of a horse after a gallop. Magdalene jumped up and placed her hand over his mouth.

"Quiet!"

She turned to Jesus. "Beloved husband, you're tired. Sleep. I shall return quickly."

But Jesus had already closed his eyes. A sweet sleep had flowed over his eyelids and temples, and he did not see Magdalene go away under the lemon trees and disappear down the deserted road.

But his mind jolted up. Leaving his body on the ground to sleep, it started out after Magdalene. Where was she going? Why had her eyes suddenly filled with tears and the world grown dim? His mind, like a hawk, flew over those eyes and did not let her escape.

The scared young negro stumbled along in front. They passed the olive grove. The sun still had not set. They entered the meadow. The heifers were stretched out on the grass, chewing their cud. They went down into a shady, rocky ravine where they heard dogs barking and the panting voices of men. Terror took hold of the young negro. "I'm leaving," he said, and ran off.

Magdalene remained all alone. She looked around her. Rocks, flint, a few brambles. A wild, barren fig-tree protruded horizontally from the face of the cliff. Two ravens—sentries on the vantage-point of a jutting rock—caught sight of Magdalene and began to screech as though calling their mates.

She heard the sound of stones being dislodged. Men were climbing the cliff. A black, red-spotted dog appeared, its tongue hanging out. The ravine became filled, like a cemetery, with cypresses and palms.

A calm, satisfied voice was heard: "Welcome."

Magdalene turned around. "Who spoke? Who greeted me?"

"I did."

"Who are you?"

"God."

"God! Let me cover my hair and hide my breasts. Turn away your face, Lord; you must not see my nakedness—I'm ashamed. Why did you bring me into this savage wilderness? Where am I? I see nothing but cypresses and palms."

"Exactly! Death and immortality.... Great Martyr, I've brought you precisely where I want you. Prepare yourself for death, Magdalene, so that you may become immortal."

"I don't want to die. I don't want to become immortal. Let me continue to live on the earth, and afterwards, turn me into ashes."

"Death is a caravan laden with spices and perfumes. Do not be afraid, Magdalene. Mount the black camel and enter the desert of heaven."

"Oh! Who are those frenzied travellers who emerged from behind the cypresses?"

"Don't be afraid, Magdalene, they are my camel-drivers. Shade your eyes with your hand. Don't you see the black camel they are leading, the one with the red velvet saddle in which you'll ride? Do not resist."

"Lord, I'm not afraid of death, but I have a complaint to make. Just now, for the first time, my flesh and soul were considered worthy of having the same mouth; for the first time, both of them were kissed—and must I die?"

"This is an excellent moment for you to die, Magdalene. You won't find a better one, so do not resist."

"Oh! What are those cries, threats and peals of laughter I hear? Lord, do not abandon me. They're coming to kill me!"

She heard the voice, still calm and satisfied, but far away now in the distance:

"Magdalene, you have attained the highest joy of your life. You can go no higher. Death is kind. . . . Until we meet again, First Martyr!"

The voice disappeared. From a bend in the ravine the mob of frenzied Levites and bloodthirsty slaves of Caiaphas emerged with knives and hatchets. They saw Magdalene, and cleavers, dogs and men fell upon her.

"Mary Magdalene, whore!" they howled in fits of laughter.

A black cloud covered the sun; the earth grew dark.

"I'm not, I'm not!" the unfortunate woman cried out. "I was, but am not. Today I was born!"

"Mary Magdalene, whore!"

"I was, but I'm not now, I swear it. Don't kill me. Mercy! Who are you, you with the bald head, the fat belly, the crooked legs—you, the hunchback? Don't touch me!"

"Mary Magdalene, whore! I am Saul. The God of Israel sent me from Damascus and gave me the authority to kill him."

"To kill whom?"

"Your lover!"

462

He turned to his gang. "On her, lads! She's his lover, she'll know. Tell us where you've hidden him, strumpet!"

"I won't!"

"I'll kill you!"

"In Bethany!"

"Liar! We've just come from there. You've got him hidden somewhere near here. The truth now!"

"Let go of my hair! Why do you want to kill him? What has he done to you?"

"Whoever lifts his hand against the holy Law—death!"

While the hunchback spoke he looked at her passionately and came closer and closer, his breath on fire. Magdalene fluttered her eyelids.

"Saul," she said, "look at my breasts, my arms, my throat. Wouldn't it be a shame if they perished? Don't kill them!"

Saul came still closer. His voice was smothered, hoarse:

"Confess where he is and I won't kill you. I like your breasts, your arms, your neck. Pity your beauty and confess! Why do you look at me like that? What are you thinking?"

"I was just thinking, Saul (and sighing)—just thinking what miracles you would perform if God suddenly flashed within you and you saw the truth! To conquer the world my beloved needs disciples like you—not fishermen, pedlars and shepherds, but flames like yourself, Saul!"

"Conquer the world! Does he want to conquer the world? How? Speak, Magdalene, because that's just what I want to do."

"With love."

"With love?"

"Saul, listen to what I'm going to tell you. Send the others away—I don't want them to hear. This man you're hunting and want to kill is the son of God, the Saviour of the world, the Messiah! Yes, by the soul which I shall render to God!"

A skinny, tubercular Levite with a scanty grey beard hissed, "Saul, Saul, her arms are wolf-snares: beware!"

"Go away!"

He turned again to Magdalene: "With love? I too want to conquer the world. I go down to the ports, see the ships leaving— and my heart burns. I want to reach the ends of the earth, but not as a beggarly slave of a Jew: no, as a king, with my sword! But how? It's impossible. I feel so wretched I want to kill myself. In the meantime I find relief by killing others."

He was quiet for a moment and then, coming still closer to the woman:

"Where is your master, Magdalene?" he asked in a gentle tone. "Tell me so that I can go find him and speak with him. I want him to tell me what love is, and which kind of love will conquer the world. . . . Why are you crying?"

"Because I do want to reveal to you where he is. I want the two of you to meet. He is all sweetness, you all fire. Together, you will conquer the world. But I don't trust you; no, I don't trust you, Saul—and that's why I'm crying."

She was still speaking when a stone whistled through the air and broke her jaw.

"Brothers—in the name of the God of Abraham, Isaac and Jacob—strike!" howled the consumptive Levite. It was he who had seized the first stone and had struck her.

The heavens thundered. In the distance the setting sun was bathed in blood.

"Here's for her thousand-kissed mouth!" howled one of Caiaphas's slaves. Magdalene's teeth scattered on the ground.

"Here's for her belly!"

"And for her heart!"

"And for the bridge of her nose!"

Magdalene buried her head in her breast to protect it. Blood gushed from her mouth, her breasts, her womb. The death-rale commenced.

The hawk beat its wings. Its round eyes had seen everything. Uttering a piercing cry it returned, found its body still lying under the lemon trees, and entered. Jesus' eyelids fluttered; a large drop of rain fell on his lips. He awoke and sat up on the rich mortuary soil, lost in thought. What had he just dreamt? He could not remember. Nothing remained in his mind but stones, a woman, and blood. . . . Could the woman have been Magdalene? Her face rippled, flowed like water, would not stay fixed so that he could see it. As he struggled to distinguish it the stones and blood seemed

464

to turn into a loom, and now the woman was a weaver sitting before her machine and singing. Her voice was exceedingly sweet, and full of complaint.

Above his head the lemons gleamed all gold between the dark leaves of the lemon tree. He pressed his palms into the damp soil and felt its coolness and vernal warmth. He glanced quickly around him: no one was watching. Leaning over, he kissed the earth.

"Mother," he said softly, "hold me close, and I shall hold you close. Mother, why can't you be my God?"

The lemon-leaves stirred, there were light footsteps on the damp earth, an invisible blackbird whistled. Jesus raised his eyes and saw his green-winged guardian angel standing before him, pleased and merry. The curly fuzz on his body glittered in the oblique rays of the setting sun.

"Hello," Jesus said. "Your face is sparkling. What more good news do you bring me? I have faith in you: the green of your wings is like the grass of the earth."

The angel laughed and folded his wings. Squatting next to him he crumpled a lemon-flower and smelt it ardently, then gazed at the western sky, which was now the colour of sour cherries. A gentle breeze rose from the earth and all the leaves of the lemon tree rustled joyously and danced.

"How happy you human beings must be!" he said. "You are made of soil and water, and everything on the earth is made of soil and water. That's why you all match: men, women, meat, vegetables, fruit. . . . Aren't you of the same soil, the same water? Everything wants to join together. Why, just now on my way I heard a woman calling you."

"Why was she calling me? What does she want?"

The angel smiled. "Her water and soil are calling your water and soil. She sits at her loom, weaving and singing. Her song pierces the mountains, spills over the plain—seeking you. Listen. In a moment it will come here, here to the lemon trees. Quiet: there it is. Do you hear? I thought she was singing, but she is not singing—she is lamenting. Listen carefully. What do you hear?"

"I hear the birds returning to their nests. It's getting dark."

465

"Nothing else? Try with all your might. Let your soul escape your body so that it may hear."

"I hear! I hear! The voice of a woman, far away, far away. . . . She's lamenting, but I can't catch the words."

"I hear them perfectly. Listen to them yourself. What is she lamenting?"

Jesus rose and exerted all his strength: his soul escaped. It arrived at the village, entered the house and stopped in the courtyard.

"I hear. . . ," Jesus said, putting his finger to his lips.

"Speak."

> *Tomb of silver, tomb of gold, gilded tomb,*
> *Eat not the red lips, eat not the black eyes,*
> *Eat not his tiny nightingale-voiced tongue. . .*

"Do you recognize the singer, Jesus of Nazareth?"

"Yes."

"It's Mary, the sister of Lazarus. She is still weaving her trousseau. She thinks you are dead, and weeps. Her snowy throat is uncovered, her necklace of turquoises bears down upon her bosom. Her whole body is wet with sweat—and smells: smells like bread freshly removed from the oven, like the ripe quince, like soil after a rain. Get up. Let us go and console her."

"And Magdalene?" Jesus cried, frightened.

The angel took him by the arm and sat him down once more on the ground.

"Magdalene," he said tranquilly. "Oh yes, I forgot to tell you: she's dead."

"Dead?"

"She was killed. Hey, where are you going, Jesus of Nazareth, with your fists all clenched like that? Whom are you off to murder —God? It was he who killed her. Sit down! The All-holy threw an arrow, pierced her at the highest peak of her happiness—and now she remains above, immortal. Can there be a greater joy for a woman? She will not see her love fade, her heart turn coward, her flesh rot away. I was there the whole time he was killing her, and I saw what happened. She lifted her hands to heaven and shouted, 'Thank you, God. This is what I wanted!' "

But Jesus flared up:

"Only dogs have such a longing for submission—dogs, and angels! I'm not a dog and I'm not an angel. I'm a man, and I shout: Unjust! Unjust! Almighty, it was unjust of you to kill her. Even the most boorish of wood-choppers trembles to cut down a tree in bloom, and Magdalene had blossomed from her roots right up to the topmost branches!"

The angel took him in his arms and caressed his hair, shoulders, knees; spoke to him quietly, tenderly. It became dark at last. A breeze blew; the clouds scattered and a large star appeared. It must have been the Evening Star.

"Be patient," he said to him; "submit, do not despair. Only one woman exists in the world, one woman with countless faces. This one falls; the next rises. Mary Magdalene died, Mary sister of Lazarus lives and waits for us, waits for you. She is Magdalene herself, but with another face. Listen. . . . She sighed again. Let us go and comfort her. Within her womb she holds—holds for you, Jesus of Nazareth—the greatest of all joys: a son—your son. Let us go!"

The angel stroked his friend tenderly and slowly lifted him from the ground. The two now stood together under the lemon trees. Above them, the Evening Star went down, laughing.

Little by little Jesus' heart softened. In the humid half-darkness the faces of Mary Magdalene and Mary sister of Lazarus were mixing, becoming one. . . . The night arrived, all perfume, and covered them.

"Come," mumbled the angel, placing his round, fuzzy arm about Jesus' waist. His breath smelt of nutmeg and damp soil. Jesus leaned his head against him, closed his eyes and breathed in deeply. He wanted the breath of the guardian angel to descend to his very bowels.

Smiling, the angel unfolded one of his wings. The night was accompanied by a heavy frost, and he wrapped his thick green wings around Jesus so that he would not be cold. Once more the woman's lament, like a peaceful springtime drizzle, was audible in the damp air:

Tomb of silver, tomb of gold. . .

"Let us go!" said Jesus, and he smiled.

467

XXXI

ALL night long Jesus skimmed over the ground wrapped in the green wings and hugging the angel tightly around the waist. A large moon had climbed into the sky. It was odd tonight, and merry. On it, instead of seeing Cain slay Abel, you saw a wide, happy mouth, two peaceful eyes and two well-nourished cheeks bathed in light: the fully circular face of a night-roaming woman in love. The trees fled; the night-birds spoke like humans. The mountains opened, drew the two nocturnal wanderers within and closed again behind them.

What happiness this is: to fly, skimming over the earth just as we do in our dreams! Life has become a dream. Can this be the meaning of Paradise? . . . He wanted to ask the angel but remained quiet, for he feared that by speaking he might wake himself up.

He looked around him. How very light the spirits of the stones, the air, the mountain had become: as when you sit with friends, your heart heavy, and the cool wine comes and you drink; and little by little your mind lightens, hovers, sails above your head, becomes a rosy cloud; and the world, all gold and air, is reflected on it upside-down. . .

Once more he started to turn in order to speak to the angel, but the other placed his finger on his lips, smiled at him, and gently told him to be still.

They must have neared some village, for the cocks were announcing the daybreak. The moon had now rolled behind the mountains and dawn peacefully illuminated the world. The earth grew sober, time became sensible again. Mountain, village and olive grove went back and stood once more where God had placed them to await the end of the world. Here was the beloved road, there the compassionate village of Bethany amidst its olives, figs and vineyards. There too was the refreshing house of friendship with the holy loom and the lighted fire and the two sisters, the two sleepless flames. . . .

"Here we are," said the angel.

Smoke was rising from the flue on the roof. The two sisters must have already awoke and lit the fire.

"Jesus of Nazareth," said the angel, unwrapping his wings from around him, "the two sisters lit a fire, did the milking first thing in the morning, and are now preparing the milk for you. On our way, didn't you want to ask me the meaning of Paradise? Thousands of small joys, Jesus of Nazareth. To knock at a door, to have a woman open it for you, to sit down in front of the fire, to watch her lay the table for you; and when it is completely dark, to feel her take you in her arms. . . . That is the way the Saviour comes: gradually—from embrace to embrace, son to son. That is the road."

"I understand," said Jesus. He stopped in front of the indigo-coloured door and grasped the knocker, but the angel held him back.

"Don't be in a hurry," he said. "Listen, we'd better not separate any more. I'm afraid to leave you all alone and undefended—so I'll come with you. I'll turn myself into a negro boy, the one you saw under the lemon trees, and you can say I'm a young slave who runs errands for you. I don't want you to take the wrong road again and get lost."

No sooner had he spoken than a negro boy stood before Jesus. His head reached the man's knees, he had broad white teeth, two golden rings in his ears; and he was holding a basket filled to overflowing.

"Here, master," he said with a smile. "Gifts for the two sisters. Silk clothing, ear-rings, bracelets, fans made of precious feathers —the complete feminine armour. Now you can knock at the door."

Jesus knocked. He heard the sound of clogs in the yard and then a sweet voice called, "Who's there?"

Jesus blushed scarlet. He recognized the voice: it was Mary's. The door opened and the two sisters fell at his feet.

"Rabbi, we worship your Passion, we salute your holy resurrection. Welcome!"

"Allow me to touch your breast, rabbi, to see if it's really you," said Mary.

"Mary, he's flesh, real flesh," Martha exclaimed, "flesh—like us. Don't you see? And look, there's his shadow on our doorstep."

469

Jesus listened, and smiled. He felt the two sisters touching him, smelling him, rejoicing.

"Martha and Mary, twin flames: it's fine to see you. Tranquil, humble, courteous house of men: it's fine to see you. We are still alive, we still hunger, act and weep. Glory be to God!"

While still talking and greeting the two sisters, he entered the house.

"It's fine to see you, fireplace and loom and kneading-trough, and table and pitcher and beloved lamp! Faithful servants of woman, I bow and worship your grace. When woman arrives at the gate of Paradise she will stop and ask, 'Lord, will my companions enter too?'

" 'What companions?' God will ask her.

" 'Here—the trough, cradle, lamp, pitcher and loom. If they don't go in, neither do I.'

"And good-hearted God will laugh:

" 'You're women, can I refuse you a favour? Enter, all of you. Paradise is so full of troughs, cradles and looms, I have no place left for the saints.' "

The two women laughed. Turning, they saw the small negro with the overflowing basket.

"Rabbi, who is this boy?" Mary asked. "I like his teeth."

Jesus sat down in front of the hearth. They brought milk, honey and whole-wheat bread. Jesus' eyes filled with tears.

"The seven heavens were not big enough for me," he said, "nor the seven great virtues nor the seven great ideas. And now, what miracle is this, my sisters? A tiny house is big enough for me, and a mouthful of bread, and the simple words of a woman!"

He marched up and down the house as its master, brought in an armful of vine-branches from the yard, fed the fire. The flames leapt up. He bent over the well, drew water and drank. He put out his hands, placed them on the shoulders of Martha and Mary and took possession of them.

"Dearest Martha and Mary," he said, "I shall change my name. They killed your brother, whom I raised from the dead. I shall come and sit in the place where he sat, here in the corner; I shall take his ox-goad, I shall plow, sow and harvest his fields. When I return in the evening my sisters will wash my weary feet and lay the table for me. Then I shall sit by the fire, on his stool. My name is Lazarus.

While he spoke the small negro bewitched him with his large eyes. The more he looked at him, the more Jesus' face changed, as did his whole body: head, chest, thighs, hands and feet. He grew more and more to resemble Lazarus, a ripe, mature Lazarus, all health and strength, with a bull-neck, sunburnt chest and huge gnarled hands. The two sisters watched this metamorphosis in the half-light and trembled.

"I've changed body. I've changed soul. Hello! I proclaim war against poverty and fasting. The soul is a lively animal, it wants to eat. This mouth beneath my beard and moustache is the soul's mouth, the only mouth the soul has. . . . I declare war against chastity. An infant sits mute and numb in the womb of every woman. Open the doors and let him out! He who does not beget, murders. . . . Are you crying, Mary?"

"How else can I respond, rabbi? We women have no other answer."

Martha opened wide her arms. "We women," she said, "are two arms incurably open. Come in, my rabbi. Sit down. Command. You are the master of the house."

Jesus' face shone. "I've finished wrestling with God," he said. "We have become friends. I won't build crosses any more. I'll build troughs, cradles, bedsteads. I'll send a message to have my tools brought from Nazareth; I'll have my embittered mother come too, so that she can bring up her grandchildren and feel some sweetness on her lips at last, poor thing."

One of the women leaned her bosom against his knees, the other took his hand and would not let it go. In front of the fire the small negro had propped his cheek on his knees and was pretending to sleep. But from between his long eyelashes his black eye watched Jesus and the two women and a sly, contented smile spread across his face.

Mary, her bosom leaning against Jesus' knees, was speaking:

"I was sitting at the loom, rabbi, working your Passion—a cross, with thousands and thousands of swallows all around—into a white blanket. I was shuttling the black and red threads and singing a dirge; and you heard me, pitied me and came."

471

Martha waited quietly for her sister to finish. Then she commenced:

"I know nothing except how to knead bread, wash clothes and say yes. Those are my only graces, rabbi. I have a premonition that you'll choose my sister as your wife, but allow me to breathe in the air of married life along with you: allow me to make and air your beds and take charge of all the household needs."

She stopped, sighed, and then:

"The girls of our village sing a song, a very bitter song. They sing it in the springtime, the days when the birds sit on their eggs. Instead of reciting it, let me sing it to you so that you'll understand, because it's bitterness lies in the tune:

> *Ho, you! beardless stalwarts—*
> *I'm weary of selling, of selling myself*
> *And finding no buyer.*
> *I offer all at a bargain, including myself:*
> *First come, first served!*
>
> *Whoever gives me a swallow's egg,*
> *I shall grant him my lips;*
> *Whoever gives me an eagle's egg,*
> *I shall grant him my breasts;*
> *And whoever gives me a stab,*
> *I shall grant him my heart!*

Her eyes filled with tears. Mary entwined her arms around the man's waist as though she feared he was going to be taken from her. Martha felt a knife pierce her heart, but she gathered up courage and spoke again:

"Rabbi, I want to say just one thing more to you, and then I'll get up and leave you with Mary. Once there was a robust landowner named Boaz who lived near here, in Bethlehem. It was summer and his slaves had reaped, threshed, winnowed and made stacks on the threshing floor, the wheat on the right, the chaff on the left. He lay down between the two stacks and went to sleep. In the middle of the night a poor woman named Ruth came quietly, in order not to wake him, and sat at his feet. She was a childless widow, and had suffered much. The man felt the warmth of her body at his feet. He lowered his hand, searched, found her and raised her to his breast. . . . Do you understand, rabbi?"

"Yes. Speak no more."

"I'm leaving," said Martha, and she rose.

The two remained alone. Taking a mat and the blanket which was decorated with the cross and the swallows, they went up to the roof of the house. A merciful cloud covered the sun. They hid under the embroidered blanket so that God would not see them, and began to caress each other. . . . Once, the cover slipped off for a moment and Jesus opened his eyes. He saw the negro boy sitting on the edge of the roof. He was holding a shepherd's pipe and piping, his eyes staring far off in the direction of Jerusalem. . . .

The next day the whole village stopped by to admire the new Lazarus. The small negro ran errands, drew water from the well, milked the ewes, helped Martha to start the fire and then curled up on the doorstep and played his pipe. Loaded with gifts of ears of maize, milk, dates or honey, the villagers came to greet the strange visitor who looked so much like Lazarus. They saw the negro on the doorstep, teased him, and laughed. He laughed too.

The blind village-chief entered, put out his hand and examined Jesus' knees, thighs and shoulders. Then he shook his head and burst out laughing.

"Humph! are you all blind?" he yelled at the villagers who had filled the yard. "This isn't Lazarus. His breath doesn't smell the same, his flesh is kneaded differently, and his bones are held firmly together by plenty of meat. A cleaver couldn't separate them."

Jesus sat in the yard, braided together truths and lies, and laughed: "Don't be afraid, lads, I'm not Lazarus. It's all over with him. It's just that my name is Lazarus, Master Lazarus—I'm a carpenter. An angel with green wings led me to this house and I entered." He looked at the negro, who had doubled up with laughter.

Time ran on like immortal water, and irrigated the world. The grain matured, the grapes began to glisten, the olives filled with oil, the blossoming pomegranate-trees bore fruit. Autumn overtook them, winter arrived—and their son was born. Lying-in after the birth, Mary the weaver admired the newborn with no end of admiration: "My God, how did this miracle issue from my womb? I drank of the immortal water," she would say with a smile. "I drank of the immortal water: I shall not die!"

It is deep night, and raining. Welcoming heaven into its bowels, the gaping earth turns it into mud. Master Lazarus, stretched out in the deep of night amidst half-finished cradles and troughs on the wood-shavings of his workshop, listens to the thunder and thinks about his new-born son and about God. He is pleased. It is the first time that God has entered his mind in the form of a child. In the adjoining room he hears him cry and laugh; hears him dance at his mother's feet. Is God then so close, he thinks, stroking his black beard. Are the rosy soles of his feet so tender, is he so ticklish; does he laugh so easily, this Almighty God, when the fingers of man caress him?

The small negro yawned. He had pretended to be asleep in the other corner, next to the door. Hearing the mother cuddle the newborn, he smiled with satisfaction. Now in the night, when no one saw him, he had become an angel again and was relaxing, his green wings spread over the shavings.

"Jesus, are you awake?" he whispered in the darkness.

Jesus pretended not to hear. It pleased him immensely to remain silent and listen to the newborn in the quiet of the night. But he smiled. He had become much endeared to this negro. All day long the boy ran errands for him and helped him shape the wood. Then in the evening when the day's work was finished, he sat on the doorstep and piped for him. Listening, Jesus would forget the day's toil; and when the first star appeared they would all sit down together at the same table to eat, and the negro would chuckle and joke ceaselessly, teasing poor Martha and embarrassing her on account of her virginity.

"Out in my homeland Ethiopia," he would say, laughing and eyeing Martha coquettishly, "we don't hide our inner longings and fret our hearts out as do you Jews, we discuss our desires honestly, openly, and act on them. If I want to eat a banana—who cares if it's my own or someone else's—I eat it. If I want to go for a swim, I go for a swim. If I want to kiss a woman, I kiss her. And our God doesn't scold us, either. He's a black and he loves the blacks. He wears golden rings in his ears and he too does whatever

474

he pleases. He is our big Brother: we both have the same mother—Night."

"Does your God die?" Martha asked one evening, to tease him.

"So long as a single negro is alive, our God will not die!" the negro answered, stooping to tickle the sole of Martha's foot.

Each night as soon as the lamp was extinguished the guardian angel unfolded his wings in the darkness and laid himself down next to his companion. They spoke together in whispers so that no one would hear, and the angel gave advice for the following day. Then he became the negro boy again, crept over the wood shavings to his place, and went to sleep.

But tonight he could not sleep. "Jesus, are you awake?" he repeated, raising his voice. When he saw that he received no answer he jumped up, came close to Jesus and gave him a push.

"Ho! Master Lazarus, I know you're not asleep Why don't you answer?"

"I don't want to talk. I'm happy," said Jesus, closing his eyes.

"Are you satisfied with me!" asked the angel, with pride. "Have you any complaint?"

"None, my boy, none. . . ." His heart grew warm, rose up: "What an evil road I took to find God," he murmured, "what a forsaken incline, all cliffs and precipices! I called and called, my voice rebounded from the uninhabited mountain and I thought it was an answer!"

The angel laughed:

"Alone, you cannot find God. Two persons are needed, a man and a woman. You didn't know that—I taught it you; and thus, after so many years of seeking God, you finally found him—when you joined Mary. And now you sit in the darkness, you listen to him laugh and cry, and you rejoice. . . ."

"That is the meaning of God," Jesus murmured; "that is the meaning of man. This is the road." He again closed his eyes.

His former life flashed through his mind, and he sighed. Extending his arm, he found the angel's hand. "My guardian angel," he said tenderly, "if you had not come, my boy, I would have been lost. Stay near me always."

"I shall, don't be afraid. I won't leave you . . . . I like you."

"How long with this happiness last?"

"As long as I'm with you and you're with me, Jesus of Nazareth."

"For all eternity?"

The angel laughed. "What is *eternity*? Haven't you been able yet to get rid of big words, Jesus of Nazareth, of big words, big ideas, kingdoms of heaven? Does this mean that even your son hasn't succeeded in curing you?" He banged his fist on the ground. "Here is the kingdom of heaven: earth. Here is God: your son. Here is eternity: each moment, Jesus of Nazareth, each moment that passes. Moments aren't enough for you? If so, you must learn that eternity will not be either."

He was silent. Light footsteps were heard in the yard. Bare feet approached.

"Who's there?" Jesus asked, getting up.

"A woman," answered the angel with a smile. He went and unbolted the door.

"What woman?"

The angel shook his finger as though scolding him. "I told you once before—have you forgotten? There is only one woman in the world; one, with innumerable faces. One of those faces is coming. Get up to greet it. I am leaving."

He slid into the shavings like a snake and vanished.

The bare feet halted outside the door. Turning towards the wall, Jesus closed his eyes and pretended to be asleep. A hand pushed open the door and a woman slid inside, holding her breath. She went forward slowly, reached the corner where Jesus lay, and without talking or making any noise, rolled herself up at his feet.

Jesus felt a warmth rise from the soles of his feet to his knees, thighs, heart and neck. He lowered his hand, found the tresses and examined the woman's face, throat and breasts in the darkness. She stooped, all expectation and submission, and did not speak; but her flesh trembled and her entire body was covered with a frosty sweat.

The man spoke softly, tenderly, full of compassion:

"Who are you?"

The woman trembled and did not speak. Jesus was sorry he asked, for once again he had forgotten the angel's words. Of what importance was her name, where she came from, or the shape, colour, beauty or ugliness of her face? It was the feminine face of the earth. Her womb was smothering her: many sons and daughters were within, suffocating and unable to emerge. She had come to the man so that he might open a way for them. Jesus' heart overflowed with compassion.

"I am Ruth," the woman murmured, trembling.

"Ruth? What Ruth?"

"Martha."

XXXII

DAYS went by, months, years. In the house of Master Lazarus the sons and daughters multiplied, and Martha and Mary competed to see who would give birth to the most. The man wrestled, sometimes in the workshop with pine, kermes-oak and cypress, throwing them down and forcing them into tools for men; sometimes in the fields with winds, moles, and nettles. In the evening he would return, exhausted, to sit in his yard, and his women would come and wash his feet and calves, light a fire, lay the table for him and open wide their arms. And then, just as he worked the wood, liberating the cradles which were within it, just as he worked the land, liberating the grapes and ears of grain which were within it, so too he worked the women and liberated from within them: God.

What happiness this is, Jesus reflected, what profound correspondence between body and soul, between earth and man! ... And Martha and Mary held out their hands and touched the man they loved and the children which issued from their wombs and resembled him, touched them to see if they and all this joy and sweetness were real. So much happiness seemed much too much to them, and they trembled. . . . One night Mary had a horrible dream. She got up, went into the yard and saw Jesus, who had washed himself and was sitting contentedly on the ground, his palms pressed into the soil. She went near him and sat down at his side. "What are dreams, rabbi?" she asked him softly. "What are they made of? Who sends them?"

"They are neither angels nor devils," Jesus answered her. "When Lucifer started his revolt against God, dreams could not make up their minds which side to take. They remained between devils and angels, and God hurled them down into the inferno of sleep. . . . Why do you ask? What did you dream, Mary?"

But Mary burst into tears and did not answer. Jesus stroked her hand. "As long as you keep it within you, Mary, it will eat away your insides. Bring it out into the light so that you can be rid of it."

Mary wanted to begin but was so afraid, she could hardly breathe. Jesus caressed her, gave her courage.

"The whole night the moon was so bright I could not sleep. But at dawn I must have fallen asleep, because I saw a bird—No, it wasn't a bird: it had six fiery wings—it must have been one of the seraphim that surround God's Throne. He came, fluttered silently around me and then suddenly rushed down and wrapped his wings about my head. He put his beak into my ear and spoke to me. . . . Rabbi, I prostrate myself, I kiss your feet. Order me to be quiet!"

"Courage, Mary. I'm with you, aren't I? Why are you afraid? . . . Well, he spoke to you. What did he say?"

"That all this, rabbi, is. . ."

Once again she could not breathe. She grasped Jesus' knees and squeezed them forcefully between her arms.

"That all this is. . . Is what, dearest Mary?"

"A dream." She burst into tears.

Jesus shuddered. "A dream?"

"Yes, rabbi. All this a dream. . ."

"What do you mean by *all this*?"

"You, me, Martha, our embraces at night, the children. . . .All, all—all lies! Lies created by the Tempter to deceive us! He took sleep, death and air and fashioned them into—Rabbi, help me!"

She rolled to the ground, quivered convulsively for a moment and then suddenly became stiff. Martha ran out with some rose vinegar and chafed her temples. Mary came to, opened her eyes and seeing Jesus, clutched his feet.

"She moved her lips, rabbi," said Martha. "Bend down. She wants to say something to you."

Jesus leaned over and raised her head. She moved her lips.

"What did you say, beloved Mary? I could not hear."

Mary called up all her strength: "And that you, rabbi. . . ," she murmured.

"That I. . . ? Speak!"

". . . were crucified!" She said this and then once more rolled to the ground in a swoon.

They laid her on her bed. Martha stayed with her. Jesus opened

479

the door and went out to the fields. He was suffocating. He heard footsteps behind him. Turning, he saw the young negro.

"What is it?" he shouted at him angrily. "I want to be alone."

"I'm afraid to leave you alone, Jesus of Nazareth," the negro replied, his eyes glistening. "This is a difficult moment. Your mind might waver."

"That's just what I want. There are times when my confounded mind hinders my sight."

The negro laughed. "Are you a woman? Do you believe in dreams? Let the ladies cry. They're females; they can't endure great joy—so they cry. But we, we endure, don't we?"

"Yes. Be quiet!"

They went along quickly and climbed up onto a green hill. Anemones and yellow daisies were scattered in the grass. The earth smelt of thyme. Jesus could see his house between the olive trees. Peaceful smoke rose from the roof, and Jesus' soul felt relieved. The women have recovered their forces, he reflected. They have squatted before the hearth and lit a fire. . . . Let's go back without breathing a word," he said to the negro. "They're women: have pity on them."

Days went by. One evening a strange half-drunk wayfarer appeared. It was the Sabbath and Jesus was not working. He sat on the doorstep holding his youngest son and youngest daughter on his knees, playing with them. It had rained in the morning, but the weather cleared in the afternoon and now thin cherry-coloured clouds floated towards the west. Between them the sky was solid green, like a meadow. Two cooing doves were on the roof. Mary sat at Jesus' side, her breasts pendulent and full.

The wayfarer halted, glanced maliciously at Jesus and laughed.

"Ho, Master Lazarus," he said, stammering, "well, you've certainly had good luck! The years run past your door and depart while you sit like the patriarch Jacob with his two wives Leah and Rachel. You've got two wives yourself—Martha and Mary. The one, so I hear, is in charge of the house and the other is in charge of you; while you are in charge of everything: wood, land, wives—and God. But show yourself a little, stick your nose out of your door, shade your eyes against the sun and gaze out over the world to see what's going on. . . . Have you ever heard of Pilate, Pontius Pilate? May his bones roast in tar!"

Jesus recognized the half-drunk wayfarer and smiled.

"Simon of Cyrene, man of God and wine: welcome! Take a stool and sit down. Martha, a cup of wine for my old friend."

The wayfarer sat down on the stool and took the cup between his palms.

"All the world knows me," he said proudly. "Everyone has come to do worship in my tavern. You must have too, Master Lazarus—but don't change the subject. I was asking you if you'd heard of Pilate, Pontius Pilate. Did you ever see him?"

The negro appeared. He leaned against the doorpost and listened.

"A thin cloud passes across my mind," said Jesus, struggling to remember. "Two cold eyes, ash-grey like a hawk's; a laugh full of mockery, a gold ring. . . I don't remember anything else. Oh, yes —a silver basin he had brought to him so that he could wash his hands. Nothing else. It must have been a dream, the hoar-frost of the mind. Up came the sun and it vanished. . . . But now that you remind me of him, Cyrenian, I do remember: he tormented me greatly in my sleep."

"Curse him! I've heard that in God's eyes dreams weigh more heavily than the reality of the day. Well, God punished Pilate. He's been crucified!"

Jesus uttered a cry: "Crucified!"

"Why get excited? Serves him right! They found him yesterday, at dawn—crucified. It seems his mind began to totter. He couldn't sleep. He would get out of bed, find a basin and wash his hands all night long, shouting, 'I wash and rinse my hands, I am innocent!' But the blood remained on his hands, and he would get more water and wash them again. . . . Then he would go out and roam Golgotha. He could find no rest. Every night he ordered his two faithful negro slaves to beat him with his own whip. He gathered thorns, made them into a crown, pushed it onto his head—and the blood flowed."

"I remember. . . , I remember. . . ," Jesus murmured. From time to time he glanced stealthily at the negro boy who, leaning against the door-post, was listening intently.

481

"Afterwards he fell to drink and went the rounds of the taverns. He came to mine too, drank, became a cock and a pig. . . . His wife got disgusted and abandoned him. Then orders came from Rome to dismiss him. . . . Are you listening, Master Lazarus? Why do you sigh?"

Jesus stared at the ground and did not reply. The boy refilled Simon's cup. "Quiet!" he hissed softly in his ear. "Go away!"

But Simon became angry. "Why should I be quiet! . . . To make a long story short, yesterday at dawn your friend Pilate was found at the top of Golgotha, crucified!"

Jesus suddenly felt a stab in his heart as though he was being pierced with a lance; and the four blue marks on his hands and feet swelled and turned red.

Mary saw him grow pale. She approached and stroked his knees. "Beloved," she said, "you are tired. Come inside and lie down."

The sun had set; the air grew cool. The Cyrenian, now completely drunk, was tired of talking. He fell asleep. The negro seized his arm, raised him with one heave and dragged him out of the village.

"You were delirious," he said to him angrily, pointing to the road to Jerusalem. "Leave!"

The boy returned anxiously to the house. Jesus, stretched out in his workshop, had his eyes pinned on the skylight. Martha was arranging the dinner. Mary suckled the youngest child and silently watched Jesus. The negro boy entered, his eyes still flashing with anger.

"He's gone," he said. "He was completely drunk; he didn't know what he was saying."

Jesus turned and looked at the negro in an agony. He bit his lips so that they would not dare part and speak. Once more he turned to the negro. He seemed to be asking his aid. But the boy put the finger to his lips and smiled at him.

"Go to sleep," he said, "go to sleep. . ."

Jesus closed his eyes. His lips relaxed, the wrinkles in his forehead disappeared, and he slept. The next day at dawn when he awoke, he felt joy and relief, as though he had escaped from a great danger. The negro had also awakened. Chuckling to himself, he was putting the workshop in order.

"What are you laughing at?" asked Jesus, winking at him.

"I'm laughing at mankind, Jesus of Nazareth," he answered in a low voice, so that the women would not hear. "What terrors your wretched minds have to pass at every moment! Sheer cliffs to the right, sheer cliffs to the left, sheer cliffs behind you. No passage but in front, and there: a string stretched out over the abyss!"

"For a moment," said Jesus, laughing also, "my mind stumbled on your string and all but fell. But I escaped!"

The women entered and the talk took a different turn. The fire was lit; the day began. A mob of laughing children flew into the yard and set about playing blindman's buff.

"Mary, do we have so many children?" said Jesus, laughing. "Martha, the yard is full. We've either got to enlarge the house or stop giving birth."

"We'll enlarge the house," answered Martha.

"They're almost ready to climb the walls and trees of the yard like field-mice and squirrels. We've declared war on death, Mary. Blessed be the organs of women. They are full of eggs, like those of fish, and each egg is a man. Death will not overcome us."

"No, death will not overcome us, beloved. You just take care of yourself and stay well," Mary replied.

Jesus was in a good mood and wanted to tease her. Besides, Mary pleased him very much this morning, only half-awake as she was, and standing before him combing her hair.

"Mary," he said, "don't you ever think about death, don't you seek God's mercy, don't you worry what will become of you in the next world?"

Mary shook her long hair and laughed. "Those are a man's concerns," she said. "No, I don't seek God's mercy. I'm a woman, I seek mercy from my husband. And I don't knock at God's door either, asking like a beggar for the eternal joys of Paradise. I hug the man I love and have no desire for any other Paradise. Let's leave the eternal joys to the men!"

"The eternal joys to the men?" said Jesus, caressing her bare shoulder. "Beloved wife, the earth is a narrow threshing-floor. How can you lock yourself up in that space and not want to escape?"

"A woman is happy only inside boundaries. You know that, rabbi. A woman is a reservoir, not a spring."

Martha entered at a run. "Someone's looking for our house," she said. "Short and fat, hunchbacked, with a head bald like an egg. He's tripping all over his crooked pegs and will be here in a minute."

The negro also rushed in, panting. "I don't like his looks. I'm going to shut the door in his face. He's another one who'll turn everything upside-down."

Jesus eyed the boy fiercely. "What are you afraid of?" he asked. "Who is he that you should fear him? Open the door!"

The negro winked at him. "Chase him away!" he said to him softly.

"Why? Who is he?"

"Chase him away," the negro repeated, "and don't ask any questions."

Jesus became angry. "Am I not free? Can't I do what I please? Open the door."

By this time feet were heard in the road. They halted and there was a knock at the door.

"Who's there?" Jesus asked, running into the yard.

A high, cracked voice replied, "One sent by God. Open!"

The door opened. A squat fat hunchback, still young, but bald, stood on the threshold. His eyes were spitting fire. The two women, who had run to see him, recoiled.

"Rejoice and exult, brothers," said the visitor, opening wide his arms. "I bring you the Good News!"

Jesus looked at him, struggling to remember where he had seen him. Cold shivers ran up and down his spine. "Who are you? I think I've met you somewhere. At Caiaphas's palace? At a crucifixion?"

Sneering, the young negro, who was rolled up in one of the corners of the yard, said, "It's Saul, bloodthirsty Saul!"

"Are you Saul?" Jesus asked, horrified.

"I was, but I'm not bloodthirsty Saul any more. I've seen the true light, I am Paul. I was saved—glory be to God!—and now I've set out to save the world. Not Judea, not Palestine, but the whole world! The Good News I carry needs oceans and distant cities: spaciousness. Don't shake your head, Master Lazarus; don't laugh, don't mock. Yes, I shall save the world!"

"My fine lad," Jesus replied, "I've already come back from where you're headed. I remember that when I was young like you, I too set out to save the world. Isn't that what being young means —to want to save the world? I went around barefooted, in rags, girded with a strap which was full of nails, like the ancient prophets. I shouted, 'Love! Love!' and a lot more I no longer wish to remember. They barraged me with lemon peels, beat me up, and I was a hair's breadth from getting myself crucified. My fine lad, the same will happen to you!"

He had gathered momentum. Forgetting his role as Master Lazarus, he was revealing his secret to a stranger.

The terrified negro came between them to detour the conversation.

"Don't talk to him, master. I have something to ask him; let me speak with him."

He turned to the stranger. "Isn't it you, hell-fiend, who most unjustly murdered Mary Magdalene? Your hands are dripping with blood. Get out of our respectable yard!"

"You? You?" said Jesus, shuddering.

"Yes, me," Paul answered with a deep sigh. "I beat my breast, tear my clothes and cry, 'I have sinned! I have sinned!' I received letters with instructions to kill anyone who violated the Law of Moses. I had killed everyone I could and was returning to Damascus when suddenly a flash of lightning shot out of the sky and threw me to the ground. The great brilliance blinded me: I saw nothing. But I heard a reproachful voice above my head: 'Saul, Saul, why do you pursue me? What have I done to you?'

" 'Who are you, Lord,' I cried.

" 'I am Jesus whom you pursue. Arise, go into Damascus, and there my faithful will tell you what you must do.' I jumped up, trembling. My eyes were open, but I saw nothing. My companions took me by the hand and brought me into Damascus. And one of Jesus' disciples, Ananias—God bless him—came to the cottage where I was lodging. He placed his hand on my head and prayed: 'Christ, give him his sight so that he may travel over the whole world and proclaim The Gospel!' As he spoke, the scales fell from my eyes. I received my sight and was baptized. I was baptized, I became Paul, the apostle to the Nations. I preach—on land, on sea—I preach the Good News. . . . Why do you look at me like that, your eyes popping out of your head? Master Lazarus, why have you got up in such a tumult?"

His fists clenched, and frothing at the mouth, Jesus paced the yard. He saw the pale women standing in the corner; he saw the children screaming and clutching their mothers. "Go inside," he ordered them, "leave us alone!" The overwrought negro came up to speak to him, but he pushed him angrily aside. "Am I not free?" he said. "I've stood enough; I'm going to speak!"

He turned to Paul. "What Good News?" he bellowed with trembling voice.

"Jesus of Nazareth (you must have heard of him) was not the son of Joseph and Mary, he was the son of God. He came down to earth and took on human flesh in order to save mankind. The wicked priests and Pharisees seized him, brought him to Pilate and crucified him. But on the third day he rose from the dead and ascended to heaven. Death was conquered, brothers, sins were forgiven, the Gates of Heaven opened up!"

"Did you see this resurrected Jesus of Nazareth?" Jesus bellowed. Did you see him with your own eyes? What was he like?"

"A flash of lightning—a flash of lightning which spoke."

"Liar!"

"His disciples saw him. They were gathered together after the crucifixion in an attic and the doors were shut. Suddenly he came and stood in their midst and said to them, 'Peace be unto you!' They all saw him and were dazzled, but Thomas was not convinced. He placed his finger inside his wounds and gave him some fish, which he ate. . . ."

"Liar!"

But Paul had worked up steam. His eyes flashed; his crooked body had stretched itself up straight.

"He wasn't born of a man: his mother was a virgin. The angel Gabriel descended from heaven, said 'Hail, Mary' and the Word fell like seed into her womb. That's how he was born."

"Liar! Liar!"

Astonished, Paul remained immobile. The negro rose and bolted

486

the door. The neighbours, hearing the cries, had half-opened their doors and cocked their ears. The two frightened wives had reappeared in the yard, but the negro had penned them up again inside. Jesus was swelling with rage; he could no longer calm his heart. Approaching Paul, he grabbed him by the shoulders and shook him violently.

"Liar! Liar!" he shouted. "I am Jesus of Nazareth and I was never crucified, never resurrected. I am the son of Mary and of Joseph the Carpenter of Nazareth. I am not the son of God, I am the son of man—like everyone else. What blasphemies you utter! What affronteries! What lies! Is it with such lies, swindler, that you dare save the world?"

"You, you?" murmured Paul, bewildered. While Master Lazarus spoke, frothing at the mouth, Paul had noticed blue marks like nail-wounds on his hands and feet, and a further wound over his heart.

"Why are you rolling your eyes?" cried Jesus. "Why do you stare at my hands and feet? Those marks you see were stamped on me by God during my sleep. By God—or by the Tempter: I still can't understand which. I dreamt I was on the cross and in pain, but I cried out, awoke, and my pain disappeared. What I should have suffered while awake, I suffered while asleep—and escaped!"

"Quiet! Quiet!" bellowed Paul, grasping his temples for fear they would burst.

But how could Jesus remain silent! He felt as though these words had been encased in his breast for years. Now his heart had opened and they were gushing out. The negro clung to his arm. "Quiet! Quiet!" he said to him, but Jesus threw him to the ground with one shake and turned to Paul.

"Yes, yes. I'll tell everything. I must find relief! What I should have suffered while awake, I suffered in my sleep. I escaped; I came to this tiny village under another name and with another body. Here I lead the life of a man: I eat, drink, work and have children. The great conflagration subsided, I too became a kind tranquil fire; I curl up in the fireplace, and my wife cooks the children's meals. I set sail to conquer the world but cast anchor in this tiny domestic trough. And that's that—I have no complaints. I am son of man, I tell you, not son of God. . . . And don't go around the whole world to publish lies. I shall stand up and proclaim the truth!"

Now it was Paul's turn to explode.

"Shut your shameless mouth!" he shouted, rushing at him. "Be quiet, or men will hear you and die of fright. In the rottenness, the injustice and poverty of this world, the Crucified and Resurrected Jesus has been the one precious consolation for the honest man, the wronged man. True or false—what do I care! It's enough if the world is saved!"

"It's better the world perish with the truth than be saved with lies. At the core of such a salvation sits the great Worm: Satan."

"What is 'truth'? What is 'falsehood'? Whatever gives wings to men, whatever produces great works and great souls and lifts us a man's height above the earth—that is true. Whatever clips off man's wings—that is false."

"You won't keep quiet, will you, son of Satan! The wings you talk about are just like the wings of Lucifer."

"No, I won't keep quiet. I don't give a hoot about what's true and what's false, or whether I saw him or didn't see him, or whether he was crucified or wasn't crucified. . . . I create the truth, create it out of obstinacy and longing and faith. I don't struggle to find it— I build it. I build it taller than man and thus I make man grow. If the world is to be saved, it is necessary—do you hear—absolutely necessary for you to be crucified, and I shall crucify you, like it or not; it is necessary for you to be resurrected, and I shall resurrect you, like it or not. For all I care you can sit here in your miserable village and manufacture cradles, troughs and children. If you want to know, I shall compel the air to take your shape. Body, crown of thorns, nails, blood. . . The whole works is now part of the machinery of salvation—everything is indispensable. And in every corner of the earth, innumerable eyes will look up and see you in the air—crucified. They will weep, and the tears will cleanse their souls of all their sins. But on the third day I shall raise you from the dead, because there is no salvation without a resurrection. The final, the most horrible enemy is death. I shall abolish death. How? By resurrecting you as Jesus, son of God—the Messiah!"

"It's not true. I'll stand up and shout that I wasn't crucified, didn't rise from the dead, am not God! . . . Why do you laugh?"

"Shout all you want. I'm not afraid of you, I don't even need you any more. The wheel you set in motion has gathered momentum: who can control it now? To tell you the truth, while you were talking there I felt for a minute like falling upon you and strangling you just in case you might accidentally reveal your identity and show poor mankind that you weren't crucified. But I calmed down immediately. Why shouldn't he shout? I asked myself. The faithful will seize you, will throw you on the pyre for a blasphemer and burn you!"

"I said only one word, brought only one message: Love. Love —nothing else."

"By saying 'Love' you let loose all the angels and demons that were asleep within the bowels of mankind. 'Love' is not, as you think, a simple, tranquil word. Within it lie armies being massacred, burning cities, and much blood. Rivers of blood, rivers of tears: the face of the earth has changed. You can cry now as much as you like; you can make yourself hoarse yelling: 'I didn't want to say that—that is not love. Do not kill each other! We're all brothers! Stop!' . . . But how, poor wretch, can they stop? What's done is done!"

"You laugh like a devil."

"No, like an apostle. I shall become your apostle whether you like it or not. I shall construct you and your life and your teachings and your crucifixion and resurrection just as I wish. Joseph the carpenter of Nazareth did not beget you; I begot you—I, Paul the scribe from Tarsus in Cilicia."

"No! No!"

"Who asked you? I have no need of your permission. Why do you stick your nose in my affairs?"

Jesus collapsed onto the drying-platform of the yard and sank his head between his knees, hopeless. How could he come to grips with this demon?

Paul stood over the prostrate Jesus and addressed him scornfully: "How can the world be saved by you, Master Lazarus? What uplifted example do you offer the world to make it follow you? With you, will it surpass its own nature, will its soul sprout wings? If the world wants to be saved, it will listen to me—me!"

He looked around him. The yard was deserted. Curled up in

one corner, his brilliantly white eyes rolling, the negro was howling like a chained-in sheep-dog. The women were in hiding; the neighbours had fled. But Paul—as though, to his eyes, the yard was a great boundless square filled with people—mounted the platform with one hop and began to preach to the invisible multitude.

"Brothers, lift up your eyes. Look! On one side, Master Lazarus; on the other, Paul, the servant of Christ. Choose! If you go with him, with Master Lazarus, you will lead a life of poverty, bound to the treadmill; you will live and die as sheep live and die—they leave behind them a little wool, a few bleats and a great deal of dung. If you come with me: love, struggle, war—we shall conquer the world! Choose! On one side, Christ, the son of God, the salvation of the world; on the other, Master Lazarus!"

He had caught fire. He swept his round eagle-eyes over the invisible multitudes. His blood was boiling. The walls of the yard crumbled down; the negro boy and Master Lazarus vanished. He heard a voice in the air:

"Apostle of the nations, great soul, you who knead falsehood with your blood and tears and turn it into truth: take the lead and guide us. How far will we go?"

Paul opened wide his arms. Embracing the whole world, he cried: "As far as man's eye can reach. Even further. As far as man's heart can reach! The world is large—glory be to God! Beyond the land of Israel are Egypt, Syria, Phoenicia, Asia Minor, Greece and the large wealthy islands of Cypress, Rhodes and Crete. Further away: Rome. Still further, with their long blond tresses and double-edged hatchets: the Barbarians. . . . What joy to set out early in the morning, the wind of the mountains or the sea in our faces, to hold the Cross, to plant it in the rocks and in the hearts of men—and to take possession of the world! What joy to be shunned, beaten, thrown in deep pits and killed—all for the sake of Christ!"

He came to himself and quieted down. The invisible multitude vanished into the air. He turned and saw Jesus, who was leaning now against the wall listening to him, aghast.

"For the sake of Christ. . . Not you, Master Lazarus, but the true Christ—my Christ!"

Unable to control himself any longer, Jesus burst into sobs.

The young negro approached him. "Jesus of Nazareth," he said softly, "why are you crying?"

"Secret companion," Jesus murmured, "how can anyone see the only way the world can be saved, and not be forced to weep?"

Paul now descended from the platform. The scanty hair on his head was steaming. He took off his sandals, banged them to remove the dust and turned towards the street-door.

"I have shaken the dust of your house from my sandals," he said to Jesus who stood, abashed, in the middle of the yard. "Farewell! Here's to good food, good wine, nice kisses, Master Lazarus —and a fine old age! And don't dare interfere with my work. If you do, you're finished—do you hear, Master Lazarus: finished! But you mustn't get the wrong idea. It's been delightful meeting you. I've freed myself, and that's just what I wanted: to get rid of you. Well, I did get rid of you and now I'm free, I'm my own boss. Farewell!"

This said, he unbolted the door and with one bound was in the main road to Jerusalem.

"What a rush he's in!" said the negro, going to the doorway and watching him with angry eyes. "He's rolled up his sleeves and is running like a famished wolf, running to eat up the world."

He turned in order to enwrap Jesus in his craft, to conjure away the dangerous spirit which had come from the heavens to bother him. But Jesus had already stridden over the threshold. He stood in the middle of the road and with anguish and longing, watched the wild apostle recede at a run into the distance. Terrible memories and yearnings which he had completely forgotten now rose up within him.

The negro was frightened, and grasped him by the arm. "Jesus," he said softly, commandingly, "Jesus of Nazareth, your mind is wavering. What are you looking at? Come inside!"

But Jesus, silent and pale, jerked his arm and shook away the angel's hand.

"Come inside," the other repeated angrily. "You'd better listen to what I say: you know well enough who I am."

"Leave me alone!" Jesus thundered, his eyes glued on Paul, who was finally about to disappear at the end of the road.

"Do you want to go with him?"

"Leave me alone!" Jesus thundered once more. His teeth were chattering: he had felt a sudden chill.

"Mary," the negro called, "Martha!" He held Jesus tightly around the waist so that he would not escape.

The two women heard and ran, with the mob of children behind them. The near-by doors opened; the neighbours emerged and formed a circle around Jesus, who stood in the middle of the road, pale as a sheet. Suddenly his eyelids dropped and quietly, gently, he rolled to the ground.

He felt himself being lifted up, put to bed, felt his temples being sprinkled with an essence of orange-flowers, smelt the rose-vinegar which was held before his nose. He opened his eyes, saw his two wives and smiled. When he glimpsed the negro boy, he clasped his hand.

"Take hold of me well," he said; "do not let me leave. I am fine here where I am."

XXXIII

JESUS sat under the ancient vine arbour in his yard, his white beard flowing over his uncovered chest. It was the day of the Passover. He had bathed, scented his hair, beard and armpits, and changed into clean clothes. The door was shut; there was no one near him. His wives, children and grandchildren laughed and played in the back part of the house; the negro, who had climbed the eaves at dawn, gazed towards Jerusalem, silent and angry.

Jesus looked at his hands. They had grown extremely fat and gnarled. The blue-black desiccated veins stood out, and on the back of each hand the old mysterious wound had begun to fade and disappear. . . . He shook his white, coarse-featured head and sighed.

"How quickly the years have gone by, how I've aged! And not only I, but my wives and the trees of my yard and the doors and windows and the stones I step on. . ."

Frightened, he shut his eyes and felt Time run like water from its high source—his mind—down through his neck, breast, loins and thighs, and flow out finally through the soles of his feet.

Hearing footsteps in the yard, he opened his eyes. It was Mary. She had seen him plunged in meditation and had come and seated herself at his feet. Jesus placed his hand on her hair, the raven-black hair which now, like his, had turned white. An inexpressible tenderness took possession of him. In my hands she became white, he reflected, in my hands she became white. . . . He bent over and spoke to her:

"Do you remember, beloved Mary, do you remember how many times the swallows have come since the blest day I crossed the threshold of your house as its master, and since I made my way, as husband, into your womb? How many times have we sown together, reaped, vintaged and gathered the olives? Your hair has turned white, Mary dearest, and so has the hair of courageous Martha."

"Yes, beloved, we have turned white," Mary answered. "The

493

years go by. . . . We planted this vine whose shade we're sitting under now, we planted it the year that accursed hunchback came, the one who threw a spell over you and made you faint—do you remember? How many years have we been eating these grapes?"

The negro slid down from the edge of the roof without a sound and stepped in front of them. Mary got up and left. She did not like this strange adopted child. He did not grow, he did not age; he was not a man, but he was a spirit, an evil spirit that had entered the house and would not leave again. And she did not like his derisive frolicking eyes, nor his secret conversations with Jesus during the night.

The negro approached, his eyes all mockery. His teeth were flashing, sharp and white.

"Jesus of Nazareth," he said softly, "the end is near."

Surprised, Jesus turned. "What end?"

The negro put his finger to his lips. "The end is near," he repeated. He squatted opposite Jesus and looked at him, laughing.

"Are you leaving me?" Jesus asked, and he suddenly felt strangely glad and relieved.

"Yes, the end has come. Why are you smiling, Jesus of Nazareth?"

"Have a nice trip. I've got from you what I wanted: I don't need you any more."

"Is this the way you say good-bye to me? Can you be so ungrateful? All my years of toil for your sake, all my efforts to give you every joy you desired: were these efforts in vain?"

"If your purpose was to smother me in honey like a bee, your pains have gone to waste. I've eaten all the honey I wanted, all I could, but I did not dip in my wings."

"What wings, clairvoyant?"

"My soul."

The negro guffawed maliciously. "Wretch, do you think you have a soul?"

"I have. And it doesn't need guardian angels or negro boys: it is free."

The guardian angel went wild with rage.

"Rebel!" he howled. He pulled up a stone from the courtyard, crumbled it between his palms and scattered the dust into the air.

"All right," he said, "we shall see," and he drew towards the door, cursing.

Wild cries, wailing, lamentation. . . Horses neighed, the highway filled with flocks of running people. "Jerusalem is burning!" they shouted. "They've taken Jerusalem! We're lost!"

The Romans had beseiged the city for months, but the Israelites placed their hopes in Jehovah. They were secure. The holy city could not burn, the holy city had no fears; an angel with a scimitar stood at each of her gates. And now. . .

The women dashed into the street, screaming and pulling their hair. The men tore their clothes and shouted for God to appear. Jesus rose, took Mary and Martha by the hand, brought them inside and bolted the door.

"Why do you cry?" he said to them compassionately. "Why do you resist God's will? Listen to what I shall tell you, and do not be afraid. Time is a fire, beloved wives. Time is a fire, and God holds the spit. Each year he rotates one paschal lamb. This year the paschal lamb is Jerusalem, next year it will be Rome, the following year—"

"Be quiet, rabbi," Mary screamed. "You forget that we're women, and weak. . . ."

"Forgive me, Mary," said Jesus. "I forgot. When the heart takes the uphill road it forgets, and has no mercy."

While he spoke, heavy steps were heard outside in the street. There was the sound of gasping breasts, and thick staffs knocked loudly on the door.

The negro jumped up, seized the bolt of the door, looked at Jesus and smiled mockingly.

"Shall I open?" he asked, hardly able to restrain his laughter. "It's your old companions, Jesus of Nazareth."

"My old companions?"

"You shall see them!" said the negro, and he threw the door wide open.

A cluster of tiny old men appeared in the doorway. Deteriorated and unrecognizable, they crept into the yard, one leaning against the other. It seemed as though they were glued together and could not be torn apart.

Jesus advanced one pace and stopped. He wanted to extend his hand to bid them welcome, but suddenly his soul felt crushed by an unbearable bitterness—by bitterness, indignation and pity. He clenched his fists and waited. There was a heavy effluvium from charred wood, singed hair and open wounds. The air stank. The negro had climbed up onto the horse-block. He watched them and laughed.

Taking one step more, Jesus turned to the old man who crept in the lead. "You, in front," he said, "come here. Stand still while I push away the ruins of time and see who you are. My heart pounds, but this hanging flesh, these eyes filled with discharge—I do not know them."

"Don't you recognize me, my rabbi?"

"Peter! Are you the rock on which, once upon a time in the folly of my youth, I wanted to build my church? How you've degenerated, son of Jonah! No longer a rock, but a sponge full of holes!"

"The years, my rabbi. . ."

"What years? The years are not to blame. As long as the soul stands erect it holds the body high and does not allow the years to touch it. Your soul has declined, Peter, your soul!"

"The troubles of the world came upon me. I married, had children, received wounds, saw Jerusalem burn. . . . I'm human: all that broke me."

"Yes, you're human and all that broke you. . .," Jesus murmured with sympathy. "Poor Peter, in the state the world's in today, you have to be both God and the devil to endure."

He turned to the next one, who emerged from behind Peter's shoulder.

"And you?" he said. "They cut off your nose: your face has become a skull—all holes. How do you expect me to recognize you? Go on, old companion, speak—say 'Rabbi!' and perhaps I shall remember who you are!"

The ramshackle form uttered a tremendous cry: "Rabbi!" and then lowered its head and was still.

"Jacob! Zebedee's eldest son, the massive colossus, the mind set solidly foursquare!"

"His remains, rabbi," said Jacob, snivelling. "A wild storm

crippled me. The keel cracked, the hull opened, the mast fell. . . .
I return to port a wreck."

"What port?"

"You, rabbi."

"What can I do for you? I am not a shipyard where you can be caulked. What I shall say, Jacob, is hard, but just: the only port for you is the bottom of the sea. As your father used to say, two and two make four."

He was suddenly overcome with indignation and intense sorrow. He turned to a second chaplet of old men:

"And you three? Ho! you, you, the gawky bean-stalk: once upon a time weren't you Nathanael? You've grown flabby. Just look at your bloated dangling backside, belly and double chins! What did you do with your firm muscles, Nathanael? You are nothing but the skeleton of a three-storeyed house now. Yes, only scaffolding remains, but do not sigh—that is enough, Nathanael, to get you to heaven."

But Nathanael became angry. "What heaven? It wasn't bad enough I lost my ears, fingers, and one eye! No, besides that, everything you pounded into us: the pomp, strutting, majesty, kingdoms of heaven—the whole lot was drunkenness and now we've sobered up! . . . What do you think, Philip? Am I right?"

"What can I say, Nathanael," sighed a tiny old man lost in the middle of the pile. "What can I say, brother! It's I who have to answer for your joining us!"

Jesus shook his head sympathetically and took the hand of this tiny old man they called Philip. "I fell hopelessly in love with you, Philip, best of all shepherds, because you had no sheep. You possessed only the shepherd's crook and you herded the air. At night you took out the winds and put them to pasture. In your imagination you lit fires, in your imagination you set up the great cauldrons, boiled the milk and sent it flowing from the top of the mountain down to the plain, so that the poor could drink. All your wealth was within your heart. Outside: poverty, hootings, solitude and hunger. That is what it means to be my disciple! And now. . . Philip, Philip, best of all shepherds, how you've fallen! You longed, alas! for real sheep, sheep whose wool, whose flesh, you could grasp in your hand—and you perished!"

"I get hungry," Philip replied. "What do you expect me to do?"

"Think of God and you shall be filled!" Jesus answered, and then suddenly his heart hardened again.

He turned to a hunched-over old man who had collapsed into the watering-trough and remained there, shivering. He lifted the rags which covered him, pushed aside his eyebrows, but could not understand who he was. When he searched under the hair, however, he found a large ear with an age-old broken quill behind it. He laughed.

"Welcome to the immense ear," he said, greeting him. "Huge, erect, full of hairs, it used to quiver like a rabbit's, all fear, curiosity and hunger. . . . Welcome to the inky fingers and the inkstand-heart! Do you still fill papers with blots, Matthew, my scribe? The quill, completely broken, is still behind your ear. Did you wage war using this as your lance?"

"Why do you jeer at me," said the other with a bitter taste on his lips. "Will you never stop ridiculing us? Think of the magnificence with which I began to write your Life and Times. I too would have become immortal, along with you. And now. . . : the peacock has lost his feathers. It wasn't a peacock, it was a chicken. What a shame I worked so hard!"

Jesus suddenly felt his knees go slack. He bowed his head; but then, quickly, angrily, he raised it and pointed his finger threateningly at Matthew.

"Quiet!" he said. "How dare you!"

An emaciated cross-eyed old man appeared between Nathanael's legs and chuckled. Jesus turned, saw him and recognized him immediately.

"Thomas, my seven-month babe, welcome! Where did you sow your teeth? What did you do with the two hairs you had on your scalp? And from what goat did you uproot that greasy little beard which hangs from your chin? Two-faced seven-eyed all-cunning Thomas, is it you?"

"In person! Only the teeth are missing—they fell out along the way; and the two hairs. Everything else is in order."

"The mind?"

"A true cock. It mounts the dung-heap knowing well enough it isn't the one who brings the sun, but it crows nevertheless every morning and brings it—because it knows the right time to crow."

"And did you fight too, hero of heroes, to save Jerusalem?"

"Me fight? Am I stupid? I played the prophet."

"The prophet? So the tiny ant-mind grew wings? Did God blow upon you?"

"What has God got to do with this? My intellect, all by itself, found the secret."

"What secret?"

"What being a prophet means. Your holiness also knew it once, but I think you've forgotten."

"Well, sly Thomas, remind me—it might come in handy again. What is a prophet?"

"A prophet is the one who, when everyone else despairs, hopes. And when everyone else hopes, he despairs. You'll ask me why. It's because he has mastered the Great Secret: that the Wheel turns."

"It's a dangerous thing for a man to talk with you, Thomas," Jesus said, winking at him. "Inside your tiny, quick-moving crossed eyes I perceive a tail, two horns—and a spark of burning light."

"True light burns, rabbi—you know that, but you pity mankind. The heart takes pity: that's why the world finds itself in darkness. The mind does not take pity: that's why the world is on fire. . . . Ah, you nod to me to be still. You're right, I'll be still. We mustn't uncover such secrets in front of these simple souls. None of them has any endurance, except one: Him!"

"Who is that?"

Thomas dragged himself as far as the street-door and pointed, without touching him, to a colossus who stood on the threshold like a withered, lightning-charred tree. The roots of his hair and beard were still red.

"Him!" he said, shrinking back. "Judas! He's the only one who still holds himself erect. Take care, rabbi. He's full of vigour, and unyielding. Speak to him gently, ingratiate yourself with him. Look, his obstinate skull is steaming with rage."

"Well then, to avoid getting bitten let's catch this desert-lion by sending a tame lion after him. Have we descended to this!" He raised his voice: "Judas, my brother, Time is a royal man-eating

499

tiger. He is not satisfied with men: he also devours cities, king-doms, and (forgive me, God) even gods! But you he has not touched. Your rage has refused to boil away; no, you have never made your peace with the world. I still perceive the unyielding knife by your breast, and in your eyes hate, wrath and hope, the great fires of youth. . . . Welcome!"

"Judas, can't you hear?" murmured John, who had collapsed at Jesus' feet. He was unrecognizable, with a white beard and two deep wounds on his cheeks and neck. "Can't you hear, Judas? The master is greeting you. Greet him in return!"

"He's pig-headed and obstinate as a mule," said Peter. "He bites his lips to keep himself from talking."

But Jesus had fixed his eyes on his old savage companion and was speaking to him sweetly:

"Judas, the chattering messenger-birds passed over the roof of my house and let fall the news, which then dropped into my yard. It seems you took to the mountains and made war against tyrants, both native and foreign. Then you went down to Jerusalem, seized the traitorous Sadducees, tied red ribbons around their necks and slaughtered them like lambs on the altar of the God of Israel. You're a great, gloomy, desperate soul, Judas. Since the day we separated you haven't seen a single day of gladness. Judas, my brother, I've missed you very much. Welcome!"

John's terrified eyes regarded Judas, who was still biting his lips to prevent himself from speaking. "Dense smoke never ceases to curl up over his head," he murmured, and he dragged himself back to the others.

"Take care, rabbi," said Peter. "He looks at you from every angle, and weighs where he is going to fall upon you first!"

"I'm speaking to you, Judas, my brother," Jesus continued. "Can't you hear? I greet you, but you don't place your hand over your heart and say 'I'm glad to see you!' Has Jerusalem's suffering stricken you dumb? Do not bite your lips. You're a man, bear up, don't burst into lamentations. You did your duty bravely. The deep wounds in your arms, breast, face—all in front—proclaim that you fought like a lion. But what can a man do against God? Fighting to save Jerusalem, you were fighting against God. In his mind the holy city was reduced to ashes years ago."

"Look, he's come a step forward," murmured Philip, frightened. "He's sunk his head into his shoulders, like a bull. Now he'll charge."

"Let's move to the sidelines, lads," said Nathanael. "Now he's raising his fist."

"Rabbi, rabbi, be careful!" called Martha and Mary, coming forward.

But Jesus tranquilly continued to speak. His lips, however, had begun to tremble just perceptibly.

"I too fought as well as I could, Judas, my brother. In my youth I set out, like a youth, to save the world. Afterwards, when my mind had matured, I stepped into line—the line of men. I went to work: plowed the land, dug wells, planted vines and olives. I took the body of woman into my arms and created men—I conquered death. Isn't that what I always said I would do? Well, I kept my word: I conquered death!"

Judas suddenly lashed out, pushed aside Peter and the women, who had placed themselves in front of him, and uttered a great savage cry:

"Traitor!"

They all turned to stone. Jesus grew pale and placed his hands on his breast.

"Me? Me, Judas?" he murmured. "You've uttered a grave word, take it back!"

"Traitor! Deserter!"

The tiny old men turned yellow and started for the door. Thomas had already reached the street. The two women jumped forward.

"Brothers, don't leave," Mary cried. "Satan has raised his hand against the rabbi. He's going to strike him!"

Peter was slinking towards the door to escape. "Where are you going," said Martha, grabbing him. "Will you deny him again— again?"

"I'm not getting mixed up in this," said Philip. "Iscariot has a mighty arm, and I'm old. Let's go, Nathanael."

Judas and Jesus were now standing face to face. Judas's body steamed. It smelt of sweat and putrescent wounds.

"Traitor! Deserter!" he bellowed again. "Your place was on the cross. That's where the God of Israel put you to fight. But you got cold feet and the moment death lifted its head, you couldn't get away fast enough! You ran and hid yourself in the skirts of Martha and Mary—coward! And you changed your face and your name, you fake Lazarus, to save yourself!"

"Judas Iscariot," Peter interrupted at that point (the women had given him courage), "Judas Iscariot, is that the way one talks to the rabbi? Don't you have any respect?"

"What rabbi?" howled Iscariot, brandishing his fist. "Him? But don't you have eyes to see with, minds to judge with? Him, a rabbi? What did he tell us, what did he promise us? Where is the army of angels which was supposed to come down to save Israel? Where is the cross which was supposed to be our springboard to heaven? As he faced the cross this fake Messiah went dizzy and fainted. Then the ladies got hold of him and installed him to manufacture children for them. He says he fought, fought courageously. Yes, he swaggers about like the cock of the roost. But your post, deserter, was on the cross, and you know it. Others can reclaim barren lands and barren women. Your duty was to mount the cross—that's what I say! You boast that you conquered death. Woe is you! Is that the way to conquer death—by making children, mouthfuls for Charon! Mouthfuls for Charon! That's what a child is—a mouthful for Charon! You've turned yourself into his meat market and you deliver him morsels to eat. Traitor! Deserter! Coward!"

"Judas, my brother," Jesus murmured, beginning now to tremble all over, "Judas, my brother, speak more affectionately..."

"You broke my heart, son of the Carpenter," bellowed Judas; "how do you expect me to speak to you affectionately? Sometimes I want to scream and wail like a widow and bang my head against the rocks! Curse the day you were born, the day I was born, the hour I met you and you filled my heart with hopes! When you used to go in the lead and draw us along behind you and speak to us about heaven and earth, what joy that was, what freedom, what richness! The grapes seemed as big as twelve-year-old boys. With a single grain of wheat we were filled. One day we had five loaves of bread: we fed a crowd of thousands, and twelve baskets-full remained. And the stars: what splendour, what an outpouring of light in the sky! They weren't stars, they were angels. No, they weren't angels, they were us—us, your disciples, and we rose and set, and you were in the centre, fixed like the north star, and we were all around you, dancing! You took me in your arms—do you remember?—and begged: 'Betray me, betray me. I must be crucified and resurrected so that we can save the world!' "

Judas stopped for a moment and sighed. His wounds had reopened and begun to drain. The little old men, glued again one to the next, struggled with bowed heads to remember and to bring themselves back to life.

A tear popped into Judas's eye. Crushing it angrily, he resumed his shouting. His heart was still not empty.

" 'I am the lamb of God,' you bleated, 'I go to the slaughter so that I may save the world. Judas, my brother, do not be afraid. Death is the door to immortality. I must pass through this door. Help me!' And I loved you so much, I trusted you so much that I said 'Yes' and went and betrayed you. . . . But you. . . , you. . ."

Foam gushed from his lips. Grasping Jesus by the shoulder, he shook him forcefully, glued him to the wall. He began again to bellow:

"What business do you have here? Why weren't you crucified? Coward! Deserter! Traitor! Was that all you accomplished? Have you no shame? I lift my fist and ask you: Why, why weren't you crucified?"

"Quiet! Quiet!" Jesus begged. The blood began to run from his five wounds.

"Judas Iscariot," Peter interrupted again, "have you no pity? Don't you see his feet, his hands? Put your hand to his side if you don't believe. It's bleeding."

Judas forced himself to laugh. Then he spit on the ground and shouted:

"Eh, son of the Carpenter you're not putting anything over on me, no! Your guardian angel came during the night. . ."

Jesus shook.

"My guardian angel. . . ?" he murmured with a shudder.

"Yes, your guardian angel: Satan. He stamped the red spots on your hands, feet and side so that you could deceive the world and be deceived yourself. Why are you looking at me like that? Why don't you answer? Coward! Deserter! Traitor!"

Jesus closed his eyes. He felt faint but managed to keep himself on his feet. "Judas," he said, his voice trembling, "you were always intractable and wild, you never accepted human limits. You forget that the soul of man is an arrow: it darts as high as it can towards heaven, but always falls back down again to earth. Life on earth means shedding one's wings."

Hearing this, Judas became frantic. "Shame on you!" he screamed. "Is that what you've come to, you, the son of David, the son of God, the Messiah! Life on earth means: to eat bread and transform the bread into wings, to drink water, and to transform the water into wings. Life on earth means: the sprouting of wings. That's what you told us—you, traitor! They're not my words, they're yours. In case you forgot, I'm reminding you of them!

"Where are you, Matthew, scribe? Come here! Open your weighty papers—you always carry them next to your heart, the same way I carry my knife. Open your writings. They've been devoured by time, moths and sweat, but quite a few words can still be seen. Open your writings, Matthew, and read so that the gentleman in question may hear and remember. One night an important notable of Jerusalem, Nicodemus by name, came to him secretly and asked, 'Who are you? What is your work?' And you, son of the Carpenter, you answered him—remember!—'I forge wings!' As you said that we all felt wings shoot out from our backs. And now what have you come to, you plucked cock! You whine away and say: 'Life on earth means shedding one's wings.' Ugh! out of my sight, coward! If life isn't all lightning and thunder what do I want with it? Don't come near me, Peter, you windmill; nor you, gallant Andrew. Don't screech, women. I won't bother him. Why lift my hand against him? He's dead and buried. He still stands up on his feet, he talks, he weeps—but he's dead: a carcass. Let God forgive him—God, because I cannot. May Israel's blood, tears and ashes fall upon his head!"

The endurance of the tiny old men gave out and they all collapsed in one heap onto the ground. Their memories reawakened; they had begun to feel young again, to remember the kingdom of heaven, the thrones, the majesty. Suddenly they broke out into the dirge. Groaning and wailing, they beat their foreheads against the stones.

All at once Jesus too burst into sobs. He cried, "Judas, my brother, forgive me!" and started to rush into the redbeard's arms. But Judas jumped back, put out his hands and would not let him come near. "Don't touch me," he shouted. "I don't believe in anything any more, I don't believe in anyone. You broke my heart!"

Jesus stumbled. He turned, searching for something to catch hold of. The women, fallen prone on the ground, were pulling out their hair and screaming; the disciples were looking up at him with anger and hatred. The negro boy had disappeared.

"I am a traitor, a deserter, a coward," he murmured. "Now I realize it: I'm lost! Yes, yes, I should have been crucified, but I lost courage and fled. . . . Forgive me, brothers, I cheated you. . . . Oh, if I could only relive my life from the beginning!"

He had collapsed to the ground while speaking and was now banging his head on the pebbles of the yard.

"Comrades, my old friends, say a kind word to me, comfort me. I perish, I am lost! I hold out my hand. Does no one of you rise to place his palm in mine or to say a kind word to me? No one? No one? Not even you, John beloved? Not even you, Peter?"

"How can I speak, what is there to say?" wailed the beloved disciple. "What was the witchcraft you threw over us, son of Mary?"

"You deceived us," said Peter, wiping away his tears. "Judas is right, you broke your word. Our lives have gone to waste."

All at once from the pile of tiny old men there arose a unified whining din:

"Coward! Deserter! Traitor!"

"Coward! Deserter! Traitor!"

And Matthew lamented: "All my work gone for nothing, nothing, nothing! How masterfully I matched your words and deeds with the prophets! It was terribly difficult, but I managed. I used to say to myself that in the synagogues of the future the faithful would open thick tomes bound in gold and say, 'The lesson for today is from the holy Gospel according to Matthew!' This thought gave me wings, and I wrote. But now, all that grandeur has gone up in smoke and you—you ingrate! you illiterate! you traitor!—you're to blame. You should have been crucified. Yes, if only for my sake, so that these writings might have been saved, you should have been crucified!"

Once more the unified whining din arose from the heap of tiny old men:

"Coward! Deserter! Traitor!"

"Coward! Deserter! Traitor!"

At that moment Thomas rushed in from the doorway, "Rabbi," he cried, "I won't leave you now that everyone is abandoning you and calling you traitor! No, I won't abandon you, not I, not Thomas the prophet. We said the Wheel turns. That's why I won't leave your side. I'm waiting for the Wheel to turn."

Peter rose. "Let's go!" he shouted. "Judas, step in front, lead us!"

Gasping, the tiny old men got up. Jesus was stretched out on the ground, face down, his arms spread wide. He filled the entire yard. They held their fists over him and shouted:

"Coward! Deserter! Traitor!"

"Coward! Deserter! Traitor!"

One by one they shouted:

"Coward! Deserter! Traitor!"—and vanished.

Jesus rotated his eyes with anguish, and looked. He was alone. The yard and house, the trees, the village doors, the village itself—all had disappeared. Nothing remained but stones beneath his feet, stones covered with blood; and lower, further away, a crowd: thousands of heads in the darkness.

He tried with all his might to discover where he was, who he was and why he felt pain. He wanted to complete his cry, to shout LAMA SABACTHANI. . . . He attempted to move his lips, but could not. He grew dizzy and was ready to faint. He seemed to be hurling downward and perishing. . . .

But suddenly, while he was falling and perishing, someone down on the ground must have pitied him, for a reed was held out in front of him, and he felt a sponge soaked in vinegar rest against his lips and nostrils. He breathed in deeply the bitter smell, revived, swelled his breast, looked at the heavens and uttered a heart-rending cry: LAMA SABACTHANI!

Then he immediately inclined his head, exhausted.

He felt terrible pains in his hands, feet and heart. His sight cleared; he saw the crown of thorns, the blood, the cross. Two golden ear-rings and two rows of sharp brilliantly-white teeth flashed in the darkened sun. He heard a cool mocking laugh, and rings and teeth vanished. Jesus remained hanging in the air, alone.

His head quivered. Suddenly he remembered where he was, who he was and why he felt pain. A wild indomitable joy took possession of him. No, no, he was not a coward, a deserter, a traitor. No, he was nailed to the cross. He had stood his ground honourably to the very end; he had kept his word. The moment he cried ELI ELI and fainted, Temptation had captured him for a split-second and led him astray. The joys, marriages and children were lies; the decrepit degraded old men who shouted coward, deserter, traitor at him were lies. All—all were illusions sent by the Devil. His disciples were alive and thriving. They had gone over sea and land and were proclaiming the Good News. Everything had turned out as it should, glory be to God!

He uttered a triumphant cry: IT IS ACCOMPLISHED!

And it was as though he had said: Everything has begun.

TRANSLATOR'S NOTE
on the Author and his Language

*T*HE LAST TEMPTATION is the summation of the thought and experience of a man whose entire life was spent in the battle between spirit and flesh. Out of the intensity of Kazantzakis' struggle, and out of his ability to reconcile opposites and unite them in his own personality, came art which succeeded in depicting and comprehending the full panorama of human experience.

If the scope of Kazantzakis' art was remarkable, even more remarkable was the scope and diversity of his life. He was an intellectual—the author of treatises on Nietzsche, Bergson and Russian literature, the student of Buddhism, the translator into Modern Greek of Homer, Dante and Goethe—but at the same time he knew and loved ordinary uneducated people, and it was to them that he always gave his greatest allegiance. Though he travelled over most of the world, restless and uprooted in a self-imposed exile, his native Crete remained his true spiritual home, and his devotion to it and to the peasantry into which he was born in 1883 (his father dealt in feeds and kept a small farm), gave his writings that sense of the "spirit of place" which is such an important ingredient of great literature. It was in Crete that he first came to know the shepherds, farmers, fishermen, innkeepers and peasant entrepreneurs who people his novels; it was in Crete too that he first experienced revolutionary ardour, his childhood being spent in an atmosphere where dare-devil hard-drinking heroism was the highest virtue, a virtue best exemplified for the boy by his own father. But when this ardour exploded in 1897 into an uprising against the Turks, young Kazantzakis, who was evacuated to Naxos, suddenly found himself in an atmosphere quite opposite to the one in which he had grown up: he was placed in a school run by Franciscan monks. There, studying French and Italian, he received his introduction to western thought. More important, he was introduced to a new virtue, contemplation, and to the heroism of a very different kind of father—Christ.

These early experiences set the pattern for a lifetime in which Kazantzakis, constantly torn between the need for action and for ascetic withdrawal, was to search untiringly for his true father, his true saviour—for the meaning of his, and our, existence.

His greatest ascetic fervour came after he had taken his degree at the University of Athens and then for two years studied philosophy with Henri Bergson in Paris. He decided to travel to Mt. Athos in Macedonia, famous for its ancient monasteries and its exclusion of all females—cows and hens as well as women. Kazantzakis remained on the Holy Mountain for six months, alone in a tiny monastery, trying through spiritual and bodily exercises to achieve direct contact with the Saviour. Unsuccessful, he decided to renew his allegiance to a saviour he had already found during his studies in Athens and Paris: Nietzsche.

He was thereafter to renounce Nietzsche for Buddha, then Buddha for Lenin, then Lenin for Odysseus. When he returned finally to Christ, as he did, it was to a Christ enriched by everything that had come between.

He was able to return to Christ with conviction precisely because he experienced in his own right the temptations which Christ rejected as false saviours. The same young man who shut himself up in a cell on the mountain where no female has penetrated since the tenth century, also came to know the joys of the hearth, for he married in 1911, and if he and his wife eventually began to live a great deal apart, the price in terms of loneliness which his spiritual searchings exacted from him is movingly attested to in his letters. (The marriage ended in divorce; Kazantzakis remarried in 1945.)

He was also confronted, like Jesus, with the temptation of violent revolution in the cause of freedom. His knowledge of the heroism of the Cretan revolutionaries had left in him a fervent admiration for the active life, plus a desire to participate in it, and in 1917 this desire was whetted by two things: the Russian Revolution, and his association in a Peloponnesian mining venture with a dynamic man named George Zorbas—an experience immortalized in Kazantzakis' novel *Zorba the Greek* (1946), the principal theme of which is the conflict between action and contemplation. Two years later, having been appointed Director General of the Greek Ministry of Welfare, Kazantzakis had an opportunity to visit Russia, together with Zorbas, in an effort to secure the repatriation of Greek refugees in the Caucasus. The seeds were planted for his short-lived faith in the Bolsheviks.

This faith did not blossom, however, until the middle twenties. At the beginning of the decade he was still unsettled, still searching for his saviour. Although the author of numerous verse plays, and of translations from Bergson, Darwin, Eckermann, William James, Maeterlinck, Nietzsche and Plato, he still did not know the ultimate direction of his life. In Paris he had been tremendously impressed by Bergson's vitalism: the life force which can conquer matter; he had also been so swept away by Nietzsche's idea of man making himself, by his own will and perseverance, into the superman, that he had gone on a pilgrimage to all the towns in Germany where Nietzsche had lived. Nietzsche, he later said, taught him that the only way a man can be free is to struggle—to lose himself in a cause, to fight without fear and without hope of reward. These lessons helped prepare him for his next saviour but one, Lenin.

Buddha intervened. In 1922 while staying in Vienna (where, incidentally, he had the opportunity to observe the mysteries of psychoanalysis) Kazantzakis embraced the doctrine of complete renunciation, of complete mutation of flesh into spirit. Buddha, like Christ, was for Kazantzakis a superman who had conquered matter; Under this influence, and feeling a great turmoil in his soul, he began to write his credo, the *Salvatores Dei*. But this was in Berlin, where he had moved the same year. He lived there until 1924, during a period when Germany was prostrate and starving, racked by post-war inflation. Kazantzakis became friendly with a group of Marxists. Here was the cause he could give himself to! He had long been influenced by Spengler's theory that cultures, like humans, grow old and die; and the war and its aftermath seemed to him the last gasp of western Christianity. He felt that twentieth-century man had been left in a void, had nothing to relate to, to hold on to—but that he had the potentiality of fashioning a new world and a new god for himself, if he would but seize the occasion. This was precisely what the Bolsheviks seemed to be doing, and Lenin became Kazantzakis' new god. Besides, he reflected, how could a Cretan nursed on revolution and reckless heroism become a Buddhist? Impossible!

He was consumed with the desire to act, to do something concrete—and this meant he must go again to Russia. His desire became reality in 1925, when he spent over three months in the Soviet Union, but by this time a new hero, Odysseus, had already begun to attract him, and he had set to work on his epic, the *Odyssey*. In 1927 he returned to Russia for the tenth anniversary of the Revolution, after having travelled through Palestine, Spain, Egypt, and Italy, where his sojourn in Assisi reflected an interest which flowered almost thirty years later in a magnificent novel on St. Francis. He returned from Moscow resolved to embark on a new life, and began at once by writing newspaper articles about his experiences and addressing a mass meeting in Athens.

In 1928 he made his fourth trip to Russia. The Soviet government had given him a railroad pass, and he planned to travel from one end of the vast country to the other in order to write about the new saviour. But he found that his thoughts, instead of dwelling on the glories of the Revolution, drifted constantly to the *Odyssey*, the first draft of which he had just completed. He began to realize that everything he saw and heard must find expression not in propaganda, but in art: his epic was to become a vast depository of all geography and all ideas. Kazantzakis now found his vocation—it was to create. Poetic creation was the Saviour! A basic distrust which he had always had for "big ideas" now applied itself to Marxism, which, despite his great enthusiasm, he had never considered able to satisfy the spiritual needs of men; and by the early thirties Kazantzakis' allegiance to the communists had come to an end. He continued to dream, however, of an ideal system, which he called *metacommunism*.

Thus, at the age of fifty, he threw all his energies into what he considered his sole duty—to forge, like Joyce, the uncreated conscience of his race; to become a priest of the imagination.

He brought to this task an intense religiosity compounded of Christianity, Buddhism, Bergson's vitalism and Nietzsche's superman; an intellectuality balanced by a distrust of pure ideas and an admiration for spontaneous action; a wealth of practical experience gained from his service in government, his travels, his business venture; and perhaps strongest of all, his love of the land and people of Greece, ancient and modern. He had incorporated into himself the thought of the sophisticated west, while still retaining the simplicity and the expressive emotions of the east. Most important for his ultimate aim, he was able to synthesize all this and find the ideal "correlative" in order to transubstantiate his experience into art. Odysseus was Greek, yet a man of the world; he was renowned for both wit and action; he was an exile, a tireless seeker after experience. He was also a superman, and Kazantzakis, in creating this gigantic epic, became a kind of superman in his own right. Living in near-solitude, he worked feverishly from dawn to dark, eating but one scanty meal a day. Over a period of thirteen years he rewrote the *Odyssey* seven times, each time broadening its scope, until it came to include all he had ever seen and heard and thought.

In 1932 Kazantzakis translated the *Divine Comedy* into Modern Greek. Dante's Odysseus, like Kazantzakis', leaves Ithaca a second time, because "neither fondness for my son, nor reverence for my aged father, nor the due love that should have cheered Penelope, could conquer in me the ardour that I had to gain experience of the world, and of human vice and worth" (Wicksteed translation). But Kazantzakis' relation to Dante goes much deeper than this. He saw in the Florentine a parallel to himself: a man with a burning desire for perfection, a man who sought to convert flesh into spirit by means of art; a man exiled and scorned by his people, forced to become a homeless wanderer. Lastly, Kazantzakis saw Dante as a champion of the language of the people as opposed to a traditional "literary" language.

Kazantzakis, like Yeats and Synge, felt that great literature must be national literature. He was convinced that the soul and life-blood of Greece was its peasantry, and that the great achievement and expression of the peasantry was the popular language, known as the "demotic". He knew that the Greek people had (and have) an imagination "fiery and magnificent and tender"; in the *Odyssey*, therefore, as in all his works, he championed the demotic as against the "puristic" language favoured by the Athenian intellectuals. In translation this element of his work is largely lost, and the

English or American reader of the *Last Temptation* is in a sense cheated out of the exhilaration of meeting with a type of speech totally foreign to his own. Happily, although the flexibility of syntax and richness of vocabulary of demotic Greek cannot be reproduced in English, the language's reliance on metaphor can often be conveyed. Demotic always prefers the concrete to the abstract: the sun does not "hang" in the sky, it "tolls the hours" (that is, it is suspended just as the bell is suspended in the campanile); a camel does not "get up," it "demolishes its foundations"; the time is not measured by hours, but by how many reeds the sun has advanced in the sky. If this love of metaphor is retained in English often at the price of awkwardness, this is but a small price to pay for some feeling, however slight, of the essential Greekness of this novel, which although set in the Holy Land, is peopled by Greeks in disguise. (Witness the use of Charon as personification of death; and the lyre in Chapter XXVII, played with a *bow* as it is to this day by the peasants of Crete.)

Since it is impossible to reproduce the actual words Kazantzakis used and since he looked upon the extraordinary love of words as the key to the peasant imagination, as well as its expression, it is important to say something further about the nature of the demotic vocabulary. Its richness and flexibility are due to the free borrowing of words over the centuries from Romans, Franks, Italians, Turks, Slavs and others; to the ease with which new words can be compounded from existing roots; to the continued existence of dialect areas; and the never-ending metamorphosing of words by villagers who are not yet sufficiently awed by grammarians (as the English have been since the seventeenth century) to abandon these extravagances.

Languages are said to mirror the character of the peoples who speak them, and if so, demotic Greek shows us a race to whom imagination and audacity come before precision and efficiency. To comprehend how completely different this language is from present-day English (English too once had many of the fluid characteristics of Modern Greek), the reader is invited to contemplate the noun *aspálathos*, the name of a shrub which, as one might expect in Greek, also has four or five completely different names. To add to this multiplicity, the base-word *aspálathos* undergoes seemingly unlimited metamorphoses in the various parts of Greece. The vowels, for example, are juggled in numerous ways, as can be seen in the forms *aspílathos, aspálithos, aspólat-thas* and *asphélachtos*; the endings are altered: *aspálathrous, aspálethres, aspálathras*; the accent is shifted: *aspalathrós, asphelechtós*; the original gender (masculine) is changed to feminine: *aspaláthra*, and neuter: *aspálatho*; the first syllable is discarded: *spálathos, sphelachtós*, etc.; consonants are added: *aspálarthas*, or altered: *asphálachtos*; and so on and so on, until we find such nearly-unrecognizable forms as *xelsphtós, aspádaros, aspálichtro* and *spólasso*.

Now see what else the peasant imagination can do with this word. In Crete, the suffix *eas* is added to form *aspalatheás*, which means "an area covered with aspalathos" (or more precisely in English, since aspalathos is the plant we know as "hairy broom" —"an area covered with hairy broom"). This noun is then turned into an adjective—and here we can see how the audacious metaphorical language of the peasants comes into being. The Cretan farmer, observing his dingy grey cat near an *aspalatheás*, notices that the cat and the area of aspalathos have the identical colour. He therefore begins to call his—and soon all similar cats—"area-covered-with-hairy-broom" cats, using the new adjective to mean "dingy grey".

It is obvious that in the hands of an imaginative artist the potentialities of a language with such flexibility, such love of words for their own sake, such metaphorical richness and syntactical and grammatical looseness—are unlimited. The nature of the demotic vocabulary, for instance, enabled Kazantzakis in the *Odyssey* to apply over two hundred distinct epithets to Odysseus. (They are catalogued by Kazantzakis' friend and biographer Mr. P. Prevelakis.)

But it is also obvious why the "purist" professors of Athens, whose experience with area-covered-with-hairy-broom cats is apt to be limited, should want to curb the extravagance and looseness of the demotic by purging foreign and dialect words and by stabilizing spelling, grammar and syntax more or less according to Atticistic Greek, the traditional literary language.

In championing the demotic, Kazantzakis felt he was defending the soul of the common people against the unimaginativeness of pedantic intellectuals, and even more important, against the ever-expanding forces of newspaper jargon and faulty composition courses in the schools. He was violently attacked not only by the purists, but by the advocates of demotic, who claimed he went out of his way to use obscure words. But he zealously defended his position, and the fact that his work does so well convey the spirit of the people is perhaps the best proof that he was right.

The *Odyssey* was published in 1938. Soon after came the Second World War, and after that the Greek Civil War, during which Kazantzakis served for a short period as Minister of National Education in a quixotic attempt to reconcile the opposing forces. He resigned in despair, now more than ever convinced of what he had known for many years: that because of the political and religious situation in Greece he must live in exile. He settled in France (eventually at the ancient Greek city of Antibes on the *Riviera*) and entered public life once more as Director of the UNESCO Bureau of Translations. But after eleven months of intense labour he decided that he was not accomplishing what he had hoped to and he resigned in order to devote all his energies to his own writing. This was in 1948, when he was sixty-five years old. Encouraged by friends and his wife, he decided to try his hand at a novel written in a fully traditional style. In two months he finished *Christ Recrucified*. This unbelievable spurt of creativity continued and enabled him to produce in the nine years that remained to him a total of eight books, including *Freedom and Death*, *The Last Temptation* and *The Poor Man of God (St. Francis)*. By the time he was seventy he found himself known all over Europe: his novels were translated into thirty languages and he was nominated repeatedly for the Nobel Prize, losing in 1952 by just one vote. But with all this success came increasing bitterness. *Christ Recrucified* raised a furore in Greece which brought him close to excommunication. Next, with the publication of *Freedom and Death*, the newspapers branded him a traitor to Crete and the Hellenes: Kazantzakis, who for all his admiration of the peasants never romanticized them, had shown both the good and bad sides of Greek heroism.

The Last Temptation fanned the inquisitional flames all the more, but by this time Kazantzakis—who had experienced thirty years of non-recognition and then, when recognition came, the complete misrepresentation of his aims—had learned the Nietzschean lesson that the struggle for freedom must be fought not only without fear, but without hope.

He saw Jesus, like Odysseus, as engaged in this struggle, and as a prototype of the free man. In *The Last Temptation* Christ is a superman, one who by force of will achieves a victory over matter, or, in other words, is able, because of his allegiance to the life force within him, to transmute matter into spirit. But this overall victory is really a succession of particular triumphs as he frees himself from various forms of bondage—family, bodily pleasures, the state, fear of death. Since, for Kazantzakis, freedom is not a reward for the struggle, but rather the very process of struggle itself, it is paramount that Jesus be constantly tempted by evil in such a way that he feel its attractiveness and even succumb to it, for only in this way can his ultimate rejection of temptation have meaning.

This is heresy. It is the same heresy that Milton, led by his scorn of cloistered virtue and his belief in the necessity of choice (ideas shared by Kazantzakis), slipped into on occasion—as when he declared that evil may enter the mind of God and, if unapproved, leave "no spot or blame behind".

The fact that Kazantzakis not only slipped into this heresy, but deliberately made it the keystone of his structure, should give us some clue to his deepest aims. He was not primarily interested in reinterpreting Christ or in disagreeing with, or reforming, the Church. He wanted rather to lift Christ out of the Church altogether, and—since in the twentieth century the old era was dead or dying—to rise to the occasion and exercise man's right (and duty) to fashion a new Saviour and thereby rescue himself from a moral and spiritual void. His own conflicts enabled him to depict with great penetration Jesus' agony in choosing between love and the axe, between household joys and the loneliness and exile of the martyr, between liberation of the body alone, and liberation of both body and soul. Kazantzakis tried to draw Christ in terms meaningful to himself and thus, since his own conflicts were those of every sensitive man faced with the chaos of our times, in terms which could be understood in the twentieth century: he wished to make Jesus a figure for a new age, while still retaining everything in the Christ-legend which speaks to the conditions of all men of all ages. The measure with which the reader of this book feels (perhaps for the first time) the full poignancy of the Passion, will be the measure of the author's succews.

Kazantzakis, like Odysseus, had an unconquerable ardour to gain experience of the world. In 1957, against the advice of his physicians (he had been suffering from leukemia since 1953) he accepted an invitation to visit China. On the return trip he fell mortally ill due to a smallpox vaccination which was inadvertently given him in Canton, and he was hospitalized in Germany. There his last days were cheered by a visit from Albert Schweitzer, who had been one of the first to recognize his greatness. His remains were flown from Germany to Athens, preparatory to interment in Crete. Though his European fame had by this time convinced the Greeks that they should welcome him as a national hero, their Archbishop firmly refused to allow his body to lie in state in a church in the normal manner. In Crete, however, he was granted a Christian burial, and a colossus, seemingly right out of one of his books, seized the coffin and lowered it singlehandedly into the grave.

RIPARIUS, N.Y.   P. A. BIEN

ACKNOWLEDGEMENTS

I should like to record my indebtedness to my wife Chrysanthi, for her great patience in explicating the nuances of Greek idioms; to Mrs. Helen Kazantzakis, the author's widow, for explaining many difficult words; to Mrs. Boule Prousalis and Mr. Manos Troulinos for aid in Cretan dialect; to Mr. George Yiannakos, agriculturalist, who put his intimate knowledge of peasant life and language at my disposal; to Mr. F. I. Venables and Mr. George C. Pappageotes for valuable suggestions; and to Mr. C. H. Gifford and my colleagues at Bristol for true hellenic enthusiasm.